Praise for The Faithful and the Fallen series

'Great characters and plot – it gets faster and more fascinating
by the page . . . A hell of a debut: highly recommended'
Conn Iggulden

'With all manner of battles, betrayals and revelations. I particularly
enjoyed the battle scenes and duels . . . If it sounds like
your thing, then it probably is'
Mark Lawrence

'A strong contender for the "if you like *Game of Thrones*,
why not try this?" award'
Independent

'John Gwynne hits all the right spots in his epic tale of
good vs evil . . . Gwynne is definitely one to watch'
SFX

'A breathtakingly perfect finale to a series that has grown
from strength to wonderful strength. Poignant, pulse-pounding
and phenomenally paced, *Wrath* is a satisfying – and
heart-breaking – climax that Tolkien himself
would be proud to have penned'
Fantasy-Faction.com

'With three-dimensional characters, a gripping plot, and a world
that became real to me, John Gwynne's *Malice* is a great debut.
In short, this is the kind of fantasy I love to read'
Fantasy Book Critic

'A masterpiece in modern fantasy and a breathtaking finale
to what is my all-time favourite fantasy series'
The Tattooed Book Geek

'It's not often these days that I find a book I entirely immerse
myself in. John Gwynne's first book *Malice* is one of these books'
Culturefly.co.uk

WRATH

JOHN GWYNNE studied and lectured at Brighton University. He's been in a rock 'n' roll band, playing the double bass, and has travelled the USA and lived in Canada for a time. He is married with four children and lives in Eastbourne, running a small family business rejuvenating vintage furniture. His first novel, *Malice*, won the David Gemmell Morningstar award for best debut fantasy. *Wrath* is the fourth and final novel in John Gwynne's epic fantasy series, following *Malice*, *Valour* and *Ruin*.

www.john-gwynne.com

By John Gwynne

The Faithful and the Fallen series

MALICE

VALOUR

RUIN

WRATH

JOHN GWYNNE

Wrath

Book Four of
The Faithful and the Fallen

PAN BOOKS

First published 2016 by Tor

This paperback edition published 2017 by Pan Books
an imprint of Pan Macmillan
The Smithson, 6 Briset Street, London EC1M 5NR
Associated companies throughout the world
www.panmacmillan.com

ISBN 978-1-4472-5970-1

9

A CIP catalogue record for this book is available from the British Library.

Typeset by Ellipsis Digital Limited, Glasgow
Printed and bound by CPI Group (UK) Ltd, Croydon, CR0 4YY

Visit www.panmacmillan.com to read more about all our books
and to buy them. You will also find features, author interviews and
news of any author events, and you can sign up for e-newsletters
so that you're always first to hear about our new releases..

For Edward,
who has walked the Banished Lands with me,
been at my side and shared in this journey
from beginning to end.
I love you, son.

And for Caroline,
my love,
the reason I rise each day.

ACKNOWLEDGEMENTS

So, this is the end.

I can't believe this is the fourth and final book of The Faithful and the Fallen. It has always seemed like a distant goal, hovering vaguely on the horizon. But now *Wrath* is finally here.

I hope that you enjoy it, and that it provides a satisfying and emotional end for you. For me it has been a long road travelled to reach this point. I have a vivid memory from early in 2002 of returning home after watching *The Two Towers* at the cinema with my family. We were sitting around the table and having dinner, and my remarkable wife said, not for the first time, 'You should try writing a book!'

I proceeded to tell her that was a ridiculous idea, and went into great detail as to why, but by then my children were caught up in the excitement of it all and so my resistance began to crumble, until eventually I thought, *Why not? It might be fun.*

And so, fourteen years later, here we are.

It's been a rollercoaster ride involving an ever-growing warband of heroes who have helped The Faithful and the Fallen to see the light of day. There are many people to thank:

First of all, I must express my heartfelt gratitude to my wife, Caroline, and my children, Harriett, James, Ed and Will, for their unending support and enthusiasm for all things Banished Lands. I can say without any shadow of a doubt that these books would not have been written without their support and encouragement, as well as the frequent re-enactment of key battle scenes. They have also found the grace to forgive me for the many absent hours that I have spent hunched over my laptop, as well as the distant 'off-in-the-Banished-Lands' look that I wore around the dinner table.

Thanks must also go to my agent, John Jarrold, for his belief in The

Faithful and the Fallen, and for his unerring guidance through the mystifying world of publishing. Not only is he a consummate professional, but a very fine fellow as well! Lunches in Rye at The Mermaid Inn are becoming a thing of legend.

My fabulous editor Julie Crisp, who has somehow manged to whip into shape the beast of a manuscript that was *Wrath*. Her passion for her work is unequalled, as evidenced by the fact that she was editing *Wrath* right up to the day she gave birth to her beautiful baby, and then continued with the edit a day or so later! She has also officially retained her title of 'most bloodthirsty person I know'.

All those at Tor UK who have worked feverishly behind the scenes to put this book into the wild – the wonderful Bella Pagan, James Long, Rob Cox and the rest of the fantastic team at Tor Towers. You have my deepest thanks and utmost respect for the work you put into making the magic of books happen.

My copy-editor, Jessica Cuthbert-Smith, who has worked on the series from the beginning. Her eye for detail is staggering. She has saved me from humiliation more times than I can count, and I have learned so much by working with her.

My editor across the pond, Will Hinton, and the whole team at Orbit US, for their labours undertaken on my behalf.

My small band of readers, who have given their time to read the first draft of *Wrath* – not a small book by any stretch of the imagination – when they could have been doing far better things, I'm sure.

My wife, Caroline, always honest, always seeing the heart of a character.

My boys Ed and Will, the truest shieldmen any man could find. Their knowledge of the Banished Lands is scary (far better than mine) and their passion for the story and characters has been a source of joy to a father who began writing this tale to read to his children.

Sadak Miah, my oldest and thoroughly cherished best friend. It has come as a great shock to me that you have actually read ALL of this one before it is published! I have to say, your thoughts were invaluable, and also made me smile, as I couldn't help but think back to the two of us as teenagers (a VERY long time ago) discussing Middle Earth, Druss, Snaga, Waylander, and so many other fantastical realms with earnest enthusiasm.

David Emrys, my 'weapons and combat expert'! One of the unexpected pleasures of this writing malarkey is making unexpected friends. I met David at a Goldsboro Books 'Fantasy in the Court' event, and we have been firm friends ever since. Much of the battle detail in *Wrath* is a result of his knowledge and experience. Don't ask!

Mark Roberson, who has provided much helpful feedback of both a fantastical and historical nature. His enthusiasm for The Faithful and the Fallen has been an encouragement throughout the writing of the series.

And last, though definitely not least, I would like to thank all of you who have read these books and taken Corban and his motley crew to your hearts. One of the greatest and most surprising rewards of this journey has been hearing from so many of you, taking the time to contact me and let me know you've enjoyed the journey so far. It's been a real pleasure to hear from you all.

Writing *Wrath* has been a bittersweet experience. It felt absolutely wonderful to be writing scenes that I've been imagining for such a very long time, but also tinged with sadness, to be saying goodbye to the characters that have become such a part of my life and almost real to me – even those of the four-legged and winged variety!

I hope that you enjoy this final instalment of The Faithful and the Fallen. Thank you for joining the warband and seeing it this far.

Truth and Courage.

John

Cast of Characters

Brenin – murdered King of Ardan, father of Edana.

Brina – healer of Dun Carreg, owner of a cantankerous crow, Craf. Escaped with Corban and Edana from the sack of Dun Carreg. After much tragedy and adventure, she journeys with Corban and his growing band of followers to Drassil, the fabled giant fortress hidden deep within Forn Forest. Now she is counsellor to Corban, having survived the fall of Drassil, escaping with a small band of Corban's friends.

Corban – warrior of Dun Carreg, son of Thannon and Gwenith, brother of Cywen. Escaped with Edana from the sack of Dun Carreg and fled to Domhain. From there he travelled to Murias, a giant fortress of the Benothi clan, in search of his sister, Cywen. It was there that he saw Kadoshim spirits possess Jehar warriors, and there that Calidus slew his mam, Gwenith. Corban resolved to fight Asroth and his servants, and led his warband to Drassil. Here he discovered that Meical, his Ben-Elim counsellor, had deceived him, that the prophecy was a strategic ruse, and that he was not in truth the Bright-Star. Corban went to the forest to think, only to be attacked and eventually captured by Jotun giants. He was dragged from his wolven Storm's side, leaving her mortally wounded.

Cywen – from Dun Carreg, daughter of Thannon and Gwenith, sister of Corban. Taken as both prisoner and bait by Calidus and Nathair. Rescued by Corban and his companions during the Battle of Murias. She travelled to Drassil with Corban, along the journey becoming Brina's apprentice, and learning something of the old ways of blood and bone.

Cast of Characters

Dath – fisherman of Dun Carreg, friend of Corban. Escaped with Edana from the sack of Dun Carreg. Accompanied Corban in the pursuit of Cywen to the fortress of Murias. He accompanied Corban to Drassil, and married Kulla, a Jehar warrior.

Edana – fugitive Queen of Ardan, daughter of Brenin. She escaped the fall of Domhain on a ship, accompanied by a handful of faithful shieldmen and Roisin. Back in Ardan she joined a small band of rebels hiding in the marshes of Dun Crin and slowly lit the fires of resistance. She won a great battle against Evnis, regent of Ardan.

Evnis – counsellor and murderer of King Brenin and father of Vonn. In league with Queen Rhin of Cambren. He became regent of Ardan, ruling as Queen Rhin's right hand, and led a warband into the marshes of Dun Crin to crush Edana's fledgling resistance. He lost in a crushing battle and was killed.

Farrell – warrior, son of Anwarth and friend of Corban. Escaped with Edana from the sack of Dun Carreg. Accompanied Corban north in search of Cywen and then on to Drassil. He became one of Corban's most trusted shieldmen.

Gar – stablemaster, secret guardian of Corban. A Jehar warrior and son of Tukul, lord of the Jehar. Escaped with Corban and Edana from the sack of Dun Carreg. Accompanied Corban north in search of Cywen. From here he travelled to Drassil with Corban, losing his father in battle at Gramm's hold. He became Lord of the Jehar whilst at Drassil.

Meg – orphaned child from a village on the outskirts of Dun Crin's marshes. A bond developed between her and Camlin.

Pendathran – battlechief of King Brenin, injured during the fall of Dun Carreg. Held prisoner and tortured by Evnis. He escaped with the help of Cywen and became a leader of the resistance based at Dun Crin.

Rafe – young warrior belonging to Evnis' hold. Childhood rival of Corban. Trained as a huntsman, and present during the escape of Edana from Domhain. He travelled as Braith's companion back to Ardan, tracking Halion in a bid to find Edana. He fought at the Battle of Dun Crin and, although on the losing side, he escaped and fled to safety. He drank from the starstone cup and passed into a coma.

Vonn – warrior, son of Evnis. Escaped with Edana from the sack of Dun Carreg and remained with her during the fall and flight from Domhain. He fought at the Battle of Dun Crin, and when his father

Evnis tries to lure him into betraying Edana he refused. Evnis attempted to kill Vonn, but Camlin shot Evnis, killing him and saving Vonn's life.

CAMBREN

Braith – warrior and huntsman. One-time leader of the Darkwood outlaws, revealed his true allegiance as huntsman of Queen Rhin. Slain by Camlin in the marshes of Dun Crin.

Geraint – warrior, battlechief of Queen Rhin.

Morcant – warrior, once first-sword of Queen Rhin, defeated and replaced by Conall. He became one of Rhin's battlechiefs, loaned to Evnis to assist in the suppression of resistance against Rhin in Ardan. Suffered a crushing defeat in the marshes of Dun Crin, but survived and escaped. He is now Regent of Ardan.

Rhin – once-Queen of Cambren, now Queen of the West, having conquered Narvon, Ardan and Domhain. Servant of Asroth, Demon-Lord of the Fallen. She is searching for Evnis, as she believes he has knowledge of the starstone necklace.

CARNUTAN

Gundul – King of Carnutan and ally of Nathair. Son of Mandros, who was thought to have murdered King Aquilus of Tenebral and was in turn slain by Veradis. He is building a road into Forn Forest in the hope of reaching the lost fortress of Drassil.

DOMHAIN

Baird – one-eyed warrior of the Degad, Rath's giantkillers. Now shieldman and protector of Edana.

Brogan – warrior of Domhain, also known as No-Neck. Shieldman of Lorcan, one of the survivors who fled with them and Edana.

Conall – warrior, bastard son of King Eremon. Brother of Halion and half-brother of Coralen. Sided with Evnis in the sack of Dun Carreg. Now the lord of Domhain, ruling in Queen Rhin's name.

Coralen – warrior, companion of Rath. Bastard daughter of King Eremon, half-sister of Halion and Conall. Accompanied Corban north and then to Drassil. She fought in the Battle of Drassil and escaped its fall.

Halion – warrior, first-sword of Edana of Ardan. Bastard son of King Eremon, brother of Conall and half-brother of Coralen. He was captured by Conall as he fought rearguard to enable Edana's escape, but was later released by Conall and made his way to Ardan, reuniting with Edana in the swamps of Dun Crin.

Lorcan – young fugitive King of Domhain, son of Eremon and Roisin. Escaped from Domhain by ship with Edana. He was forced by his mother's scheming to choose between her and Edana; he chose Edana and now is a stalwart warrior in Ardan's resistance.

Roisin – Queen of Domhain, widowed wife of Eremon and mother of Lorcan. Fled by ship with Edana. Having attempted to assassinate Edana during the Battle of Dun Crin, she was exiled by Edana.

HELVETH

Lothar – once battlechief of Helveth, now its king. Murderer of the previous king of Helveth, Braster. Ally to Nathair and Calidus. He is now building a road into Forn Forrest towards the ancient fortress of Drassil.

ISILTIR

Dag – huntsman in the service of King Jael of Isiltir. He survived the defeat at the walls of Drassil and has fled with Jael and a small band of survivors, whom he is attempting to guide through Forn Forest to safety.

Gramm – horse-trader and timber merchant, lord of a hold in the north of Isiltir. Father of Orgull and Wulf. Allied to Meical. He was slain during the Battle of Gramm's hold.

Haelan – fugitive child-King of Isiltir, fleeing Jael. Went into hiding at Gramm's hold, in the far north of Isiltir. Joined Corban's warband and travelled to Drassil, and now is 'chief carer' of Storm and Buddai's cubs.

Hild – woman of Gramm's hold. Wife of Wulf, son of Gramm. Mother of Swain and Sif.

Jael – self-proclaimed King of Isiltir. Allied to Nathair of Tenebral. At present he is stumbling through Forn Forest with a handful of shieldmen after suffering a great defeat at the walls of Drassil.

Maquin – warrior of Isiltir and the elite Gadrai who was taken captive during the fall of Dun Kellen by Lykos of the Vin Thalun. He was enslaved and thrown into the fighting-pits, where he fought his way almost to freedom. Escaped Lykos during rioting at Jerolin, capital of Tenebral, on Lykos' wedding day and became a fugitive on the run with Fidele of Tenebral, once-regent of Tenebral and recently wedded to Lykos. Through hardship and danger they make it to Ripa, a fortress in the south of Tenebral ruled by Lamar, a friend and hater of the Vin Thalun. During the course of their journey Maquin and Fidele fall in love. Maquin is wounded and hovers on the brink of death, only his love for Fidele and burning will to see vengeance served upon Jael and Lykos holding him to life. Later he is captured and tortured by Lykos, saved by Veradis and taken to Brikan in Forn Forest for trial before Nathair. Veradis sets him free.

Sif – child of Gramm's hold. Daughter of Wulf and Hild, sister of Swain.

Swain – child of Gramm's hold. Son of Wulf and Hild, brother of Sif.

Tahir – warrior of Isiltir and the elite Gadrai. Protector to Haelan, child-King of Isiltir and became a captain of Corban's warband, leading the men of Isiltir.

Trigg – orphaned child raised at Gramm's hold. She is a half-breed, part giant. She helped Haelan escape his enemies at the Battle of Gramm's hold, but later gives away the location of Drassil to Calidus, thus her allegiances are uncertain.

Wulf – warrior, son of Gramm and brother of Orgull. Wed to Hild and father of Sif and Swain. A captain of Corban's warband.

NARVON

Camlin – outlaw of the Darkwood. Now companion to Edana. Fled with her from Domhain, fought in the rearguard to protect Edana as she boarded a ship and fought Braith before escaping on the ship. He became Edana's guide in Ardan, his skills as a woodsman and brigand proving very useful. He fought and killed Braith in Dun Crin's marshes and slayed Evnis after the Battle of Dun Crin.

Drust – warrior, shieldman of Owain. Escaped the defeat of Owain and his warband, aided by Cywen. He has become one of the captains of Edana's growing resistance.

Cast of Characters

Owain – King of Narvon. Conqueror of Ardan, with the aid of Nathair, King of Tenebral. Executed after his warband was defeated on Queen Rhin's order.

Teca – woman from a northern village of Narvon, joins Corban's warband as she flees Nathair and the Kadoshim.

Uthan – Prince of Narvon, Owain's son. Murdered by Evnis on Rhin's orders.

TARBESH

Akar – captain of the Jehar holy warrior order travelling with Veradis. He joins Corban's warband. On Tukul's death he stood for leadership of the Jehar, but was defeated in combat by Gar. He has become a valued captain in Corban's warband.

Ilta – Jehar warrior, captured after the fall of Drassil as she attempted to assassinate Nathair. She was set free by Calidus to take a message to Corban.

Javed – slave and pit-fighter of the Vin Thalun, set free by Corban and now a captain in his warband, leader of the Freedmen.

Kulla – warrior of the Jehar, part of Akar's company that joined Corban. She has married Corban's friend Dath.

Sumur – lord of the Jehar holy warrior order.

Tukul – warrior of the Jehar holy order, leader of the Hundred and Gar's father. He was slain at the Battle of Gramm's hold by Ildaer, Warlord of the Jotun giants.

TENEBRAL

Agost – Captain of Fidele's shieldmen.

Alben – swordsmaster and healer of Ripa, at present in Forn Forest with Krelis and a warband of Ripa's warriors.

Arcus – warrior of Ripa who has travelled to Forn Forest and Drassil.

Atilius – warrior of Tenebral. Fought with Peritus against the Vin Thalun during the uprising. Captured, enslaved and put to work on a Vin Thalun oar-bench. He joined Corban's warband but fell in combat with Jotun giants.

Caesus – warrior of the eagle-guard, now high captain of Nathair's warband.

Ektor – son of Lamar of Ripa and brother of Krelis and Veradis. A scholar where his brothers are warriors. He was secretly in league with

Calidus and responsible for the death of Lamar, his father. He was
slain by his brother, Krelis.

Fidele – widow of Aquilus, mother of Nathair. For a time she was Queen
Regent of Tenebral. Lykos used dark magic to bewitch and control
her, eventually marrying her. Riots broke out in their wedding
celebrations, during which the spell controlling her was broken. She
stabbed Lykos and, with Maquin's help, fled in the confusion. During
their journey she fell in love with Maquin and over time became the
leader of a rebellion in Tenebral, fighting against the Vin Thalun. She
journeyed to Brikan to speak against Lykos and the Vin Thalun before
her son, Nathair, but was herself put on trial and imprisoned. Veradis
freed her and she escaped into Forn Forest with Maquin, Krelis,
Alben and a warband from Ripa.

Krelis – warrior, son of Lamar of Ripa and brother of Ektor and Veradis.
Became Lord of Ripa after the death of his father, Lamar, and
travelled to Brikan to speak against the Vin Thalun before Nathair.
He was imprisoned as a rebel but later set free by his brother, Veradis.
He escaped into Forn Forest with his warband.

Lamar – Baron of Ripa, father of Krelis, Ektor and Veradis. Slain during a
rowan-meet.

Marcellin – Baron of Ultas, appointed Regent of Tenebral.

Nathair – King of Tenebral, son of Aquilus and Fidele. In league with
Queen Rhin of Cambren. He once believed that he was the Bright
Star, the one prophesied to be the chosen champion of Elyon, but
then learned the truth, that he is the Black Sun of prophecy, chosen
champion of Asroth. He took the starstone cauldron and discovered
the whereabouts of Drassil, leading a surprise attack and routing
Corban's warband. He now holds the fortress of Drassil.

Pax – son of Atilius. A young warrior captured during the uprising in
Tenebral, who was made a slave and set to work on a Vin Thalun
galley, alongside his father. He helped Corban flee a band of Jotun
giants in the forest beyond Drassil, saw his father slain and has been
sent by Corban to find help.

Peritus – once battlechief of Tenebral, then leader of the resistance against
Lykos and his Vin Thalun. He was slain by Ector in the dungeons of
Brikan.

Spyr – Shieldman of Fidele.

Veradis – first-sword and friend to King Nathair. Son of Lamar of Ripa
and brother of Ektor and Krelis. He commanded a warband of

Tenebral instrumental in the defeats of Owain of Narvon and Eremon of Domhain. He was sent back to Tenebral to deal with the uprising against the Vin Thalun. During a rowan-meet his father, Lamar, fell upon Veradis' sword and died. Veradis took the leaders of the rebellion to Brikan in Forn Forest, to take their claims and arguments before High-King Nathair. Here the truth was finally revealed to him, that Nathair is not the Bright Star, but instead is serving Calidus, a Kadoshim, and is in league with Asroth, Lord of the Fallen. Veradis set his brother Krelis, Fidele and Maquin free from the dungeons beneath Brikan, then attempted to slay Calidus. He failed, but was saved by the giant, Alcyon.

THE THREE ISLANDS

Lykos – Lord of the Vin Thalun, the pirate nation that inhabits the Three Islands of Panos, Pelset and Nerin. Sworn to Asroth, ally and co-conspirator of Calidus. Appointed regent of Tenebral by Nathair. He used sorcery to control and marry Fidele, mother of Nathair. He travelled with the full might of the Vin Thalun to Forn Forest and was instrumental in the battle and taking of Drassil.

THE GIANT CLANS

The Benothi

Balur One-Eye – Benothi giant. Joined forces with Corban and his company during the Battle of Murias. He took the starstone axe from Alcyon. Now a captain of Corban's warband, he was grievously injured during the fall of Drassil.

Eisa – Benothi giantess, companion of Uthas.

Ethlinn – Benothi giantess, daughter of Balur One-Eye, also called the Dreamer. Companion of Corban's, she has travelled to Drassil.

Fachen – warrior of Benothi. Allied to Ethlinn and Balur.

Laith – female giantling, one of the survivors of the Battle of Murias who joins Corban and his companions. Became a friend and lover to Farrell.

Nemain – Queen of the Benothi giants. Betrayed and slain by Uthas.

Salach – Benothi giant, shieldman of Uthas.

Uthas – giant of the Benothi clan, secret ally and conspirator with Queen Rhin of Cambren. Slayer of Queen Nemain and now self-proclaimed

Lord of the Benothi. Dreams of reuniting the giant clans and being
their lord.

The Jotun

Eld – Lord of the Jotun. A cautious and cunning man.
Hala – giantess of the Jotun clan. Healer and high in the counsel of Eld.
Ildaer – warlord of the Jotun.
Mort – Captain of Ildaer's warband.
Sig – shieldmaiden of Eld, Lord of the Jotun.
Varan – warrior of Ildaer's warband.

The Kurgan

Alcyon – servant and guardian of Calidus.
Raina – giantess. Mother of Tain and long-lost wife of Alcyon.
Tain – giantling. Son of Raina and Alcyon.

The Ben-Elim

Adriel – warrior of the Ben-Elim.
Israfil – warrior of the Ben-Elim.
Meical – high captain of the Ben-Elim. Chosen as the one to leave the
    Otherworld, to be clothed in flesh and sent to the Banished Lands to
    prepare for the coming war.

The Kadoshim

Asroth – Demon-Lord of the Fallen.
Calidus – high captain of the Kadoshim, second only to Asroth. Chosen as
    the Kadoshim to be clothed in flesh and prepare the way for Asroth in
    the Banished Lands. Adversary and arch-rival of Meical, high captain
    of the Ben-Elim.
Legion – many Kadoshim spirits that swarmed into the body of a Jehar
    warrior as the gateway through the cauldron was closing during the
    Battle of Murias.

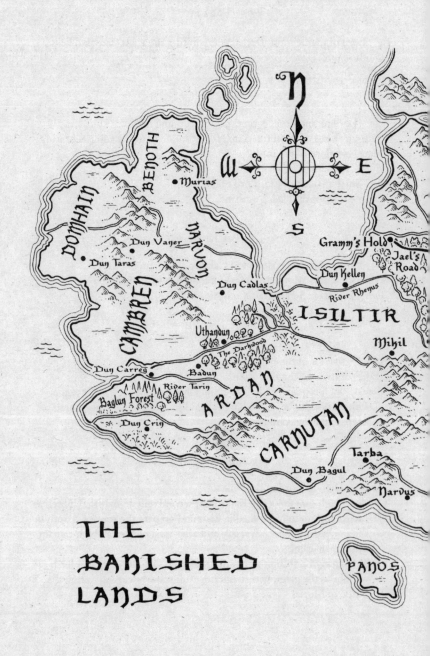

THE
BANISHED
LANDS

THE BONE FELLS

JOTUNHEIM

Kavala mountains

FORN FOREST

Drassil

Lothar's Road

Haldis

Brihan

Halstat

Bairg mountains

HELVETH

Taur

Ultas

Jerolin

Agullas Mountains

TENEBRAL

Balara

Ripa

NERIN

PELSET

ARCONA

Isle of Kletva

Tethys Sea

TARBESH

Telassar

'. . . wrath and vengeance poured.'

John Milton, *Paradise Lost*

Wrath

CHAPTER ONE

VERADIS

The Year 1144 of the Age of Exiles, Hound Moon

Veradis fell through the night air, weightless. He caught glimpses of the tower of Brikan, Calidus' still-smouldering outline at the window, then below, the river coming up to meet him.

He slammed into the water, the cold shocking the breath out of him. He panicked, disorientated, realizing he didn't know which way was up; all about him was darkness and ice. Then something grabbed his hair and he was surging upwards, breaking through the water in a burst of spray, and saw Alcyon's pale, broad face staring back at him.

'They will come hunting for us,' the giant shouted over the roar of the river as the current gripped them, sweeping them away from the thunder of warriors' feet crossing the bridge. 'Let the water take us far from them.'

Veradis saw the sense of that, though his hands and feet were already numbing from the cold. He put some effort into swimming, speeding his way from Brikan, from Calidus – *from the Kadoshim*. The thought still jolted him like a blow.

They turned a bend in the river and the fortress was gone, darkness enfolding them.

The soft, weak sheen of dawn's grey light filtered down through the lattice of branches above as Veradis met Alcyon's gaze, an unspoken agreement passing between them, as they both headed for the riverbank. It was harder going, swimming across the current, and Veradis realized how exhausted his body was, but eventually he felt silt beneath his feet, his hands grasping at reeds as he pulled himself out of the water and flopped onto his back, gasping, his limbs feeling lead-filled.

Turning, he saw Alcyon on the bank, thirty of forty paces upriver from him, staggering wearily towards him, before he slumped down beside him with a groan, water dripping from his drooping moustache.

'Thank you,' Alcyon said.

'For what?'

'Everything. Most of all for helping my family escape Brikan's dungeons.'

His wife and bairn. How long has he gone without seeing them? And what must he have suffered, knowing they were Calidus and Lykos' prisoners?

'And for destroying Calidus' effigy of me,' Alcyon continued. 'You have set me free.' He gave a shudder, followed by a smile. 'A shadow is gone from my soul. I feel reborn.'

'If you mean you feel weak as a newborn bairn,' Veradis muttered as he emptied his boot of water and tried to pull it back on, 'then I feel the same.'

'That is not what I mean,' the giant rumbled, regarding Veradis with serious eyes. 'You set Raina and Tain free; you set me free. I owe you a debt beyond all imagining.'

'You are in no debt to me,' Veradis said. 'I kicked the effigies into the fire on impulse, not really knowing what they were, or what power they held over you.'

'But you suspected?'

'Aye. Something that Fidele said . . .' He thought of Nathair's mother, hoped that she had made it to freedom, along with his brother Krelis, Maquin and Alben. 'And your wife and son – I set them free because it was the right thing to do. There was no other choice.'

'Ah, but there was, True-Heart. There always is.'

Veradis shrugged. 'There is no debt between us. You are my friend.'

One of my only friends, it has turned out. His thoughts swept bitterly to Nathair and the confession and revelations that had stunned Veradis. He remembered Calidus' confession: that Nathair had slain

Aquilus, his own father. Anger and shame twisted through him. There had been so many signs . . .

How can I have been deceived for so long? I am a fool.

'How long?' Veradis asked him. 'How long have you been Calidus' prisoner?'

Alcyon's smile withered. 'Sixteen years.'

'That is a long time.'

'It is.' Alcyon clenched his fists, knuckles cracking. 'I should have killed him.'

'To be fair, we both tried hard on that count. I put a knife in his belly, threw him in a fire and you shattered his chest with a warhammer.'

'Kadoshim are hard to kill.'

'I'd have to agree. *Can* he be killed?'

'Maybe taking his head. That is how the others are slain.'

'Others?'

'The Jehar – they are demon-possessed by Kadoshim. At Murias . . .' Alcyon said to the question in Veradis' eyes.

'The Jehar,' Veradis muttered, shaking his head. 'I have been so blind.'

'You trusted your King, and your friend.' Alcyon shrugged. 'There are worse failings to have.'

Are there? I have dedicated my life to a lie.

They both sat in silence, water dripping from clothes and hair.

'What now?' Veradis said to himself. 'It feels as if my whole life has been dedicated to Nathair and his cause. What do I do now?'

Alcyon regarded him gravely, then poked his chest with a thick finger. 'What does your heart tell you?'

'I would not trust it. Look where it has led me thus far,' Veradis said sourly.

'Your eyes are open now.'

Veradis sucked in a deep breath, felt exhaustion seeping through him. 'What would you do?' he asked the giant.

'Find my kin. My Raina and Tain.' He smiled as he said their names.

Kin. My father is slain, as is my brother Ektor. Only Krelis is left. Suddenly he was desperate to see his older brother.

'Find our kin,' he echoed. 'A good place to start.'

Something squawked: a handful of wood pigeons suddenly bursting from the trees and flapping noisily overhead.

'We should move.'

We need cover.

'Aye. To the trees,' Veradis said as he stood, suppressing a groan.

They were halfway across the clearing when Alcyon stopped abruptly, staring back along the riverbank.

Forms appeared around a distant bend on the track, shadows in the half-light that Forn's canopy created. Black shadows with curved swords sheathed across their backs.

'Kadoshim,' Alcyon growled.

Veradis counted at least seven of them, moving quickly, a loping, ground-eating pace, like a pack of wolven. They were spread in a half-circle between the riverbank and the treeline.

They are hunting us. Have been running all night long, following the river in search of our trail.

One of the figures paused, the others rippling to a halt about it. It lifted its head, as if tasting the air, then gave an ululating howl and leaped forwards, a new energy in its stride.

They've caught our scent.

Veradis felt a jolt of fear. He'd faced giants, draigs, warbands, but somehow knowing that the demons of the Otherworld were hunting him sent a cold shock of fear tingling through his veins.

Kadoshim. Calidus' kin. My enemy. Calidus filled his mind, an image of the man he had thought counsellor and ally emerging from the fire in Brikan's tower, flame-wreathed and snarling. *He has corrupted Nathair and has deceived me for so long. He is the author of this evil.*

Fear morphed into a cold rage and he reached for his sword, lips twisting.

'Move,' Alcyon grunted and broke into a run. Veradis resisted for a moment, inexplicably wanting to stand and fight these creatures, but Alcyon dragged him along and in a heartbeat they were only a few strides from the treeline. He realized the giant had no weapon – no war-hammer or battle-axe strapped across his back, no sword or dagger at his hip. They crashed through the first layer of undergrowth and were immediately enveloped by a twilight world of shadow and thorn. Alcyon forged ahead, grunting as branches snapped upon his rock-like torso, thorns whipping at Veradis, vines tangling about his boots. For what seemed a long time Veradis only heard his own heart thumping, the rasp of his breath, the thud of Alcyon's feet, then there were sounds behind him, faint at first, like the rustle of wind through foliage, but soon louder, keening cries were floating about him.

They splashed through a stream, something sinuous slithered beneath Veradis' feet, making him stumble.

'They are almost upon us,' he gasped to Alcyon.

Better to turn and fight, hold a sword in my fist, than die running.

'I know,' the giant said, turning, chest heaving.

Veradis drew his sword as they put their backs to a huge tree, the stream before them, and waited.

Forms flitted through the gloom, emerging from a curtain of shadows and thick foliage. One was a long way ahead of the others, clothed in the dark mail of the Jehar, pale-skinned, dark veins making a tapestry of its flesh. It saw them and leaped the stream, arms reaching for Veradis, not even bothering to draw its sword.

'Remember, you must take their heads,' Alcyon grunted as he pushed away from the tree, hurling himself into the oncoming Kadoshim with bone-crunching power. The two fell to the ground.

Veradis hurtled forwards, sword raised, hacking two-handed at the Kadoshim's arm, its hand spinning away, blood like oil pumping languidly from the stump, then the two forms were rolling together again. Alcyon growled in pain, then he was on his knees, arms wrapped about the Kadoshim's torso, pinning its arms at its side.

The creature's head writhed, veins bulging as it strained to break free, Alcyon's face turning purple with the effort, his locked fingers slowly pulling apart.

'What . . . are you . . . waiting for?' the giant rasped, and Veradis swung his sword, chopping into the creature's neck. Dark blood spurted from the half-severed neck, the Kadoshim screeching with fury; Alcyon roared with the strain of holding the creature. Veradis wrenched his sword free and swung again.

The Kadoshim's head flew through the air, landing with a splash in the stream. Its body slumped, legs drumming as Alcyon fell away and rolled clear. A black ichor-like mist flowed from the Kadoshim's neck, hissing and swirling, gathering above its body, forming a human shape with tattered wings of smoke spread about it and red eyes glowing like coals at its heart. Veradis stared, frozen. It screamed savagely, then it was melting away, torn and dispersed by a slight breeze.

'What the hell?' Veradis gasped.

'Down,' Alcyon yelled as he surged up from the ground, a fist slamming into the jaw of a leaping Kadoshim, hurling it spinning into the undergrowth. Almost as soon as it hit the ground it was back on its feet, twisting like a feral cat. Veradis hefted his sword, spread his legs to meet the impact and then something crunched into his side, sending him flying through the air, another Kadoshim's arms locked around his waist. He caught a glimpse of Alcyon standing, Kadoshim swarming upon him, then Veradis was slamming into the ground. Pain exploded in his shoulder and his sword skittered away. He rolled, punched at his attacker, for a moment staring into its black soulless eyes, then they were sliding into the stream, the Kadoshim beneath him, his hands fastening about its neck, squeezing, seeking to crush the life from the black-eyed abomination.

It bucked and kicked like a wild stallion, thrashing a tempest amidst the stream water, but Veradis would not let go. He felt its strength ebbing, some of its vitality fading, then hands gripped him from behind, dragging him backwards, his fingers slipping as he was hauled to the bank. Another Kadoshim stood over him, drawing its sword from its back as the one from the stream splashed into view. He rolled and saw a handful of Kadoshim circling Alcyon, who had fallen to one knee, the giant bleeding from a dozen wounds. Veradis tried to drag himself through the mud towards his friend. Another Kadoshim was held in Alcyon's arms, he had one hand gripping its jaw, the other wrapped about its chest. With a savage wrench, Alcyon heaved; Veradis heard the Kadoshim's neck break, then the sound of flesh tearing, Alcyon screaming his defiance as he ripped the Kadoshim's head from its shoulders. He flung the corpse to the ground as the black mist boiled from the dead creature's wound.

A searing pain lanced through Veradis' leg: a Kadoshim blade scoring along his thigh. He dropped to the ground, looked back at the two Kadoshim on the stream bank. They were following him. Toying with him. The one with the drawn sword slashed his blade across Veradis' upheld forearm, a new cut burning like fire.

'Think we'll bleed you awhile,' the Kadoshim said, leering with pale lips. 'Pay you back for the chase you've led us.'

It should not end like this. Frustration gave Veradis a last surge of strength and he rolled to his feet, pushed himself upright.

The Kadoshim before him grinned, then paused, cocking its head to one side.

Figures burst out of the gloom. Veradis' hopes rose and then fell as he saw the newcomers were dressed in black breastplates with silver eagles on their chests.

Eagle-guard – no doubt sent by Nathair to make sure that his monsters complete their task.

Ten, twelve, fifteen more men . . . one of them tall and wide. Veradis blinked, something familiar.

'Well met, little brother,' the big man bellowed, grinning wildly.

A moment's confusion, followed swiftly by elation.

Krelis!

Then Krelis and his men were attacking the Kadoshim, Krelis taking a head in one great swing of his longsword.

Another warrior swept into view, this one not dressed as a man of Tenebral, but gripping a knife in each hand. He joined Krelis, and together they attacked the Kadoshim before Veradis.

Maquin and Krelis.

CHAPTER TWO

NATHAIR

Nathair stood in the great hall of Drassil and stared at the giant's skeleton on its throne. The bones of the ribcage surrounded a thick-shafted spear, the wood dark and pale-veined, only a hint of black iron of the blade visible, the rest buried in the great tree of Drassil.

So that is Skald, High King of the giants, and that is the starstone spear. Skald, the last man to rule a united empire where giants and men lived together in peace. Will I be the next to unite this shattered world? The skeleton was mottled yellow and brown, ancient, the brow of the skull broad and thick, eye-sockets black holes that seemed to stare at Nathair, questioning him.

Are you worthy? Are you capable?

He sighed. *History shall be my judge – nothing and no one else.*

A hand touched his shoulder. Caesus was standing at the head of three score eagle-guard. The young warrior had been recently promoted to high captain of Nathair's warband, now that Veradis was gone.

Ah, Veradis. Are you dead or alive, old friend? It does not seem right that you are not beside me to share in this great victory. He had been informed of Veradis' betrayal, his attempt on Calidus' life, and he and Alcyon's escape.

Veradis, how could you abandon me, break your oath to me? He looked at the white scars on the palm of his hand, one of them made as a blood-oath of brotherhood to Veradis on a moonlit hillside in Tenebral. It felt like a lifetime ago, words and promises spoken by different people.

'My King,' Caesus said. 'It is Calidus. He asks for you.'

Nathair looked back at the skeleton one last time, then turned and strode through the huge chamber. The dead were still being cleared from the battle of the day before. Blood stained the stone floor; mounds of corpses lay in stinking piles. Hundreds of them – Kadoshim, Jehar, Vin Thalun, eagle-guard, Benothi giants, many others. The cost of taking Drassil had been high, higher than he would have imagined considering that the element of surprise had been on their side.

But victory is victory. The fortress is ours, the back of our enemy broken. Though many had escaped: reports were coming in of pitched battles still being fought beyond the walls of Drassil.

Nathair glanced to his right as he passed an open trapdoor as wide as the gates of Jerolin, and the dark stain of blood on the stone before it.

Meical's blood.

The Ben-Elim's head now adorned a spear set in the ground of the courtyard before the gates of Drassil. It was not alone.

But what of Corban, their Bright Star? Where is he? He glared mistrustfully into the yawning dark of the tunnel, knew that Meical had chosen to stand and fight there to gain time for many who escaped into the tunnel.

Was Corban one of them?

There had been no reports of Corban being seen during the battle. *Had he even been here?*

It had been a long night and Nathair felt a greater weariness settling upon him than he had ever known before. Caesus snapped an order behind him and eagle-guard spread to either side, forming a protective column.

'Drassil is not yet secure,' Caesus said in reply to Nathair's enquiring look.

The courtyard also bore the signs of yesterday's battle, bodies scattered all about, flies buzzing, the metallic aroma of blood everywhere. For an instant Nathair thought he saw a wolven cub tugging at the leg of a dead Kadoshim, but looking back realized it was a small white-furred dog.

They turned a corner in a street and Nathair glimpsed the towering outer walls of Drassil beyond the layers of stone buildings latticed with thick branches.

This is a truly remarkable place.

Branches soared above him as thick as towers, with buildings of stone and iron wrapped about them, bound tighter than leather armour.

It looks almost alive: the tree the bones, the fortress its flesh.

The rasp of a sword drawn from its scabbard drew his attention, and he glimpsed a black-clothed warrior hurtling from the shadows of a doorway. Abruptly Caesus was yelling as more dark figures emerged, iron glinting. The eagle-guard moved, shields thudding together around Nathair, obscuring his view.

Blood sprayed, spattering Nathair's face as an eagle-guard before him collapsed. A black-clothed Jehar slipped into the gap carved in the shield wall, surging towards Nathair.

Nathair drew his sword, fear and rage, his constant companions, igniting within him. The shouts and screams of battle faded, his world contracting to the Jehar warrior before him. A woman, her dark-skinned face all sharp bones, almost fragile-looking.

'Truth and courage,' she yelled, curved sword rising.

There was an explosion of sparks as their weapons met, the power of the Jehar's strike making the tendons of his wrist shriek, shuddering on into his arm and shoulder.

He pushed forwards, knowing to retreat was to die, tried to move within her guard, use his short sword where her longer blade would hinder her. They collided, limbs tangling as both crashed to the ground, wrestling, punching, kicking and biting at each other as they rolled back and forth across the stone street, with the battle raging all about them. The Jehar struck a glancing blow that made his vision blur. Then her knee crunched into his groin and he slumped, pain exploding, pulsing through him in savage waves, draining his strength. She pulled herself free and half rose as he coughed into the cold stone, tried to rise, knew if he didn't he was dead.

Fear and rage sparked inside him, sent new energy coursing through his veins.

I'll not die here.

The Jehar stood over him, sword raised, her eyes bright with victory.

Then a form crashed into her, throwing her to the ground. She started to rise and a boot slammed into her jaw, sent her crashing back down. The figure was blurred, a buzzing cloud swirling about it. Hands gripped him and pulled him upright, Caesus' concerned face appeared, blood sheeting from a long cut across his forehead. Nathair looked past him, saw his rescuer pull a sword from a scabbard upon its back and raise it over the unconscious Jehar.

A Kadoshim.

'No,' Nathair called; the figure's head turned to look at him, the buzzing cloud parting.

Flies, Nathair realized, recognizing the Kadoshim. 'No, Legion. I want her alive.'

The Kadoshim regarded him for a moment with its cold black eyes.

'Better dead,' it said.

'I want her alive,' Nathair snapped. 'Calidus may have questions.'

'Dead after, then,' the Kadoshim said, then sheathing its sword. 'Calidus wants you.' The flesh of its face and neck rippled, seemed to move of its own accord, as if something were locked within, trying to get out.

About them the battle seemed almost done.

Nathair scanned the street, counted nearly a score of his eagle-guard dead to five or six of their Jehar attackers.

'This part of Drassil is supposed to have been cleared,' he snarled. 'How did they get in here?' He looked down at the unconscious Jehar's form at Legion's feet.

'Bring her,' Nathair said as he marched away.

As Nathair entered the courtyard before Drassil's gates he heard a rumbling growl reverberate from one of the many stables that edged the courtyard. He looked fondly at the doors that contained his draig.

Calidus stood before the closed gates of Drassil, to either side of him were a host of spears driven into the ground, most of them adorned with a head. A handful of Vin Thalun warriors were planting new spears into the ground, while behind them Kadoshim prowled in the courtyard's shadows. Before Calidus knelt a ragged group of people, bound at wrist and ankle: over three hundred prisoners from yesterday's battle. Above them eagle-guard stood upon Drassil's walls.

My warriors.

They were easily the best-disciplined troops amongst those that had stormed Drassil – the Kadoshim and many of Lykos' Vin Thalun were involved in the pursuit of their scattered enemy out beyond Drassil's walls, but Nathair suspected that most by far were ranging throughout the fortress, looting and drinking.

The Kadoshim are doing other things, such as eating their victims . . .

Lykos was standing behind Calidus, a dozen Vin Thalun ranged about him – hard-looking men, bodies lean and muscular, skin weathered and scarred. Lykos lifted a water skin to his mouth and took a long drink.

I'd wager it's not water that he's drinking.

The Vin Thalun saw him approaching and nodded a greeting. Nathair hid his disgust.

Him, and my mother . . .

'Ah, Nathair,' Calidus said. He raised an eyebrow at the blood on Nathair's face, then saw Legion dragging the Jehar warrior across the courtyard by her ankle.

'Calidus,' Nathair said with a dip of his head. His old counsellor was not looking his best. Part of his face was burned charcoal black and peeling, silver hair was growing in tufts from patches on his head, elsewhere singed to stubble or burned clear.

'It would appear that the streets of Drassil are not yet cleared of our enemy,' Nathair said sourly as Legion dumped the Jehar warrior in front of Calidus. She groaned, pushing herself to her knees as Legion's hand clamped on her shoulder, holding her before Calidus.

'What is your name, child?' Calidus asked, regarding her with his cold eyes.

She spat blood at Calidus' feet and glowered up at him. 'Ilta,' the Jehar said. 'And I am no child.'

'Well, Ilta, I shall ask you the same question that I have just put to your comrades. Where is Corban?'

'You will see him soon enough,' a voice said from amongst the prisoners. 'He will come for you.'

'And when he does,' said Ilta as she turned her head to look from Calidus to Nathair and Lykos, 'he will kill you all.'

'He is a boy, a puppet. Your real master is already slain,' Calidus said angrily, sweeping a hand towards Meical's head.

'You are wrong,' Ilta said. 'Corban is our lord; he slew your best, Sumur, in single combat. We all saw it. He will do the same to you.'

'Sumur?' Calidus frowned. 'I saw his head decorating your gates . . .'

'Corban killed him,' the prisoner's voice called out again, one vaguely familiar to Nathair. A figure straightened amongst the captives, black hair hanging lank about her face. 'He took Sumur's head, and he will take *yours*, too.'

Ah, Cywen.

'I want nothing more than for him to come and try,' Calidus said with a sigh, his expression mocking, but Nathair glimpsed something else in his eyes. *Doubt?*

'But so far he does not seem inclined to do so,' Calidus continued. 'Perhaps a message will speed him to us.' He looked to the Kadoshim. 'Legion, choose one prisoner and impale them upon a spear,' he ordered.

Legion grabbed Cywen and pulled her, struggling, towards a spear.

'Not her,' Calidus said with a wave of his hand.

Legion grabbed another prisoner. He was a man of Isiltir by the look of him. The Kadoshim hoisted him effortlessly into the air and brought him down slowly upon the upright spear.

Then the screaming began.

When it was over the prisoner was skewered like a squirrel ready for the cook-fire. He was writhing upon the spear, blood pooling about his feet, screaming himself to oblivion. Nathair resisted the urge to cover his ears.

'On your feet,' Calidus said to Ilta. 'Go and tell Corban what is happening to his followers, what I am doing. Tell him I will not stop until he has faced me.'

Legion pushed her stumbling forwards as, with a rumble, the gates opened. She looked back once and then ran, the gates slamming behind her.

Calidus barked an order and the remaining captives were led away. Cywen caught Nathair's eye as she walked in line, hatred pouring from her.

'We must talk soon,' Calidus said to Nathair and Lykos. 'Highsun in the great hall.' Then he was striding away.

Lykos raised an eyebrow and offered Nathair his water skin. Without thinking, Nathair took it and drank, then coughed, almost choking on the contents.

'Is that . . . ?'

'Mead,' Lykos finished for him. 'Found a dozen wagons with barrels full of the stuff.'

Nathair handed it back to him and Lykos walked away, chuckling to himself, his Vin Thalun following him.

Nathair headed for the wide stairs that scaled Drassil's walls and he climbed to the top, stopping above the great gates, where he stared out at the world beyond. A wide plain circled the fortress, clear blue sky bathing the ground in sunshine before the great trees of Forn blotted it from view. He caught a glimpse of Ilta just before she disappeared into the treeline. Behind him he heard the footsteps of Caesus and his eagle-guard, stopping a respectful distance away.

The screams of the impaled in the courtyard were much fainter up here, fading to a pathetic mewling. He wished he would just die.

How have I allowed myself to come to this? It is for the greater good. For me to win the war Corban must die. To bring peace to the Banished Lands, Corban must die. He felt his resolve stir, but still the screams wormed their way into his head, reminding him of other battles, other deaths in the name of this great cause.

And now I follow the path of Kadoshim, of demons, of Asroth himself.

He remembered Calidus' words to him in Murias, so persuasive. It had all been so logical when Calidus explained it, made sense of the alliances, the lies – deception upon deception heaped in a great pile.

But the truth is simpler, a voice seemed to whisper inside his mind.

Deep down, he knew. It was more basic when all was stripped away: Calidus' persuasive arguments and philosophical debates on good and evil, right and wrong, the abstract meanings that were attached to names. Politics, power struggles, who deserved what. The honest answer was much simpler than any of those meandering debates, and one that had been clearly reinforced by his brief struggle with the Jehar warrior before him.

I don't want to lose.

CHAPTER THREE

CORALEN

Coralen sat with her back to a tree, staring into the dawn gloom of Forn, absently twirling a knife between her fingers. Behind her were the sleeping forms of three score or so of the survivors with whom she had fled Drassil. Amongst them was Brina, grey hair poking from beneath her cloak, beside her the bulks of Farrell and Laith curled close together. She glimpsed the Jehar, Akar, standing guard on the far side of their camp. Exhaustion hovered at the fringes of her consciousness, and in so many ways it would be wonderful to lose herself in the nothingness of sleep. But she couldn't. Her mind was reeling, a whirlwind of grief, fear and rage as fractured moments of the previous day played out in her mind's eye. Out of them all, though, everything kept returning to one thought, circling.

Where is Corban?

The fog of tiredness crept upon her again, a relentless assault, but she knew that sleep would not come; the shock and horror of yesterday's battle was still too present.

There was a soft footfall from behind and a figure came to stand beside her.

Gar.

The lord of the Jehar looked at her, lines of worry etched upon his usually unreadable face. He was clothed in a shirt of dark chainmail splattered with grime and blood, his curved sword sheathed across his back, a single-bladed throwing axe hanging at his belt. Even he was not free of injury: a bloodstained bandage was tied around his forehead.

'Storm is with him,' Gar said, as if he could read her thoughts.

They must be as plain to read upon my face as are his.

Storm.

That was a measure of comfort; Coralen knew that the wolven was a better guardian than a dozen shieldmen. But still . . .

'We *will* find him,' Gar said.

Coralen had seen the familiar scuff marks of Storm's claws in the tunnel, which was why they had exited at this spot. After a brief search she'd found more tracks, leading to the brow of the slope, but darkness had settled upon them and no matter how frustrating, it was pointless to stumble around in the dark.

But where can Corban be? He must have heard the din of battle from Drassil, even if he were this far away.

The thought rose unbidden in her mind, the one thought she had refused to acknowledge throughout the long dark of night.

What if he is slain? What else could have kept him from returning to Drassil? She felt a worm of fear wriggling through her belly but refused to consider it. *He lives. He must.*

She nodded and stood, sheathing her knife, a myriad of cuts, bruises and strains aching for attention. She ignored them all.

'We need to go,' she said.

'Aye,' Gar agreed. He continued to stare at the trapdoor. 'I had hoped that Meical would find us. That he escaped . . .'

Coralen remembered her last sight of the Ben-Elim, wielding his sword two-handed, feet planted before the entrance to the tunnel in Drassil's great hall as they had retreated into its shadows. Swathes of blood had surrounded him as he swung his sword in deadly arcs, holding back the enemy, protecting them, purchasing them time to escape.

'He would have come by now. If he could,' Coralen said.

Gar sighed and nodded.

Coralen cocked her head, listening, staring down the hill. Something was moving in the undergrowth, heading towards the trapdoor.

Gar saw it too, and without words the two of them separated, slipping into the shadows as they quietly surrounded the intruder.

Bushes rustled, a twig snapped and Coralen caught a glimpse of dark hair. She knew it wasn't Corban – *even he isn't that clumsy.*

A figure burst from the undergrowth, a young man clad in leather and wool, his dark hair tousled and a scabbing cut marking his forehead. He started at the sight of her, fumbled for a weapon at his belt, his eyes widening.

'I know you,' Coralen said, though she didn't remember his name. 'Your da is Atilius.' A competent, unassuming warrior, Atilius had been a slave oarsman on a Vin Thalun ship.

The lad nodded, his lip trembling.

'Pax, what are you doing here?' Gar said, stepping silently from the shadows, making the young warrior jump again.

'You must come, quickly,' Pax blurted. 'My da, Corban, giants—'

'Corban?' Coralen hissed.

'Aye; we must go.' Tears were spilling down Pax's cheeks now, tracing tracks through blood and grime. 'He's dead.'

Coralen froze, feeling as if a fist had just clamped around her heart.

'I ran,' Pax said. He began to shake, an involuntary twitching that quickly became more violent.

'Where is Corban?' Coralen asked, trying to control the panic leaking through her, reaching out to grab the now sobbing boy and shake the sense from him.

'Hold,' Gar said, putting a hand upon her arm. 'Pax, you must tell us, as clearly as you can. Where is Corban and your da? What happened?'

Others were coming down the hill now. Coralen glimpsed Dath and Kulla, a handful of Jehar, Laith looming behind them.

'We heard fighting, knew Corban was out there,' Pax began haltingly. 'We found him, facing giants, and bears.'

What? But there were no giants with Nathair at Drassil!

'Da, he threw a spear at a giant. Then we all ran. We thought we'd lost them . . . then . . .'

'Go on,' Gar said. The whole group was gathered around them now, listening in absolute silence.

'They came from nowhere. My da . . .' He rubbed his eyes, blew out a long breath. 'They killed my da. Corban told me to run, to fetch help.'

'When did this happen?' Gar asked, not able to keep the urgency from his voice.

'Yesterday. After highsun, before sunset.' Pax's face had grown paler as he spoke. Now he looked like a corpse. 'I ran. I fell, hit my head.' He raised a hand to the cut on his brow. 'When I came to, it was dark. I've been trying to find my way since then.'

'Take us, now,' Gar said.

'I will try.' Pax nodded. 'I became lost, for a while, but I know it was that direction.'

Gar barked orders and then they were moving, Coralen taking the lead with Pax, Gar jogging beside the lad, a steadying hand on his arm.

Corban and Storm facing giants, alone. Yesterday. She sent a silent prayer to Elyon, one of many that she had made over the last half-day.

Let them still live.

Coralen was the first to enter the glade. At its far end was a sudden ridge and beyond it the sound of a fast-flowing river. The smell hit her first, the metallic tang of blood and decay. Death. Flies were buzzing in great clouds about bodies heaped on the floor. She counted three giant corpses on the ground, and Atilius, pinned to a great oak by a giant's axe. She could not see Corban or Storm. She ran to the first giant, who was on his back, a hole in his belly, throat cleanly cut, his wrist bearing the tell-tale ripping wounds of the wolven. Coralen moved on, dimly aware of others spilling into the glade behind her, the sound of Pax's sobs as he dropped to his knees before his da, Gar's presence at her shoulder. The other two giants were close together, the ground trampled, rutted, dark and still sticky with blood. One's throat had been ripped out by Storm, the flesh mangled and torn.

He is not here, nor Storm. The relief was a physical thing, though she knew their absence did not mean that they were safe, or even alive, but it was clear they had fought here, and won. *They slew three giants.* She felt a flush of pride at that feat, knew that it would be a story told around the campfire this very night, adding to the tales that were growing up around Corban and his wolven companion.

The other giant lay upon his front. Gar and Coralen tried to turn him over together, flies buzzed angrily, the huge warrior's dead weight like a boulder. Farrell and Laith joined them and together they rolled the giant, the stench of corruption and decay wafting up to them as they disturbed the body.

'He is of the Jotun clan,' Laith spat as they stood and stared at the dead giant.

What are they doing here?

Coralen's eyes were drawn to the glint of leather and iron amidst the congealed blood. She bent and wrapped a fist around the hilt of a sword buried deep in the giant's thigh, angled upwards into its groin. It came free with a sucking sound, and she lifted it for them all to see: the pommel shaped like a howling wolven. The relief she'd felt fled, replaced by the crushing weight of fear.

'That's Ban's sword,' Dath said as he joined them, Kulla a pace behind him.

Coralen stared at them a moment, felt a wave of sympathy for them.

They've been wed less than two nights.

Gar took the sword from her and stared at it. 'I watched Ban's da give him this blade.'

'In the Rowan Field at Dun Carreg,' Farrell said. 'I remember it.'

'And I,' Dath muttered.

Coralen turned away, her eyes scanning the ground, searching for any sign.

He is not here. Storm is not here. They escaped, but they did not make their way back to Drassil. Why?

Brina was on her knees beside the giant. The old healer had a vial in one hand, a knife in the other that she was using to scrape blood from the trampled grass. One side of Brina's face was still an angry red, seared by the explosion she had generated that had rocked the chamber in Drassil yesterday.

Whatever benefit Brina thought the giant's blood would bring, she was welcome to it. As Coralen scanned the rest of the clearing, her eyes caught a patch of crushed grass spattered with blood. It was close to the edge of the glade, leading to a sheer drop to the river below.

As if something were dragged.

She followed the marks and dropped to a crouch, looking down to the river. Further down she spied a dark smear on a boulder.

Blood.

'They jumped into the river,' she called out. Gar was first to join her. His eyes found the same evidence and he gripped her wrist.

'After them,' he said.

Coralen led the way, running along the ridge that shadowed the river, twisting around thick-rooted trees and dense vegetation, her eyes flitting between the path she was navigating and the banks of the river.

Rounding a sharp bend in the path, she suddenly saw a shape lying on a grassy verge, fur matted and bloodstained. Her heart stopped.

Storm.

She skidded to a halt on the ridge above the wolven, a part of her mind noticing large boot-prints in the grass. In a spray of dirt she scrambled over the edge, clinging to root and vine as she made her way down to the riverbank.

Storm lay still as stone, and she was covered in blood; a huge wound was visible above her shoulder.

Coralen crouched, too scared to touch her, not wanting to confirm what her eyes were telling her.

Stifling tears, she remembered the first time she had seen Storm, when she had threatened to turn the wolven into a cloak. Even then she had seen the bond between Corban and his faithful and vigilant shadow. Since then she had developed her own bond with the wolven – more like a sword-brother to her than a mere animal.

As Gar joined her she tentatively reached out a hand and laid it upon Storm's body. She felt nothing.

No. Please, Elyon above.

She screwed her eyes shut tight, pressed harder, flattening her palm against Storm's deep chest, willing her hand to feel the movement of life, a drawn breath, the pumping of Storm's heart. With every moment her hopes faded, a bleakness taking hold inside, spreading through her like ink through water.

And then she felt it.

A flicker, a heartbeat deep within the cavern of Storm's broad chest. Coralen opened her eyes and saw Storm's amber gaze regarding her. The wolven whined, a weak, miserable sound, but one that gave Coralen a rush of joy. Storm's tail thumped feebly on the turf.

CHAPTER FOUR

CORBAN

Corban walked through a world of grey, dimly aware that he was staggering close to a wide and dark river. There was a splash and a wide ripple, the hint of something large and sinuous in its depths. Bloated dark clouds boiled above him, flickering with lightning, and black shapes winged through them with an occasional gleam of chainmail and iron.

This is the Otherworld.

His knee throbbed and a pain spasmed through his chest with every indrawn breath. He fixed his eyes on the ground before him, concentrating on each step. There had always been an element of the Otherworld that calmed him, a serenity that settled within him, that gave him a sense of strength and hope. But this time was different. There was something frayed about the peacefulness, it felt false. Something lurked at the fringes of his mind, trying, needing to be remembered.

When next he looked up, the river was flowing into a valley, cliffs rearing up either side of him, tall and forbidding. Ahead of him the river spilt into a lake. Vibrant colour was seeping into the landscape with every step into the valley; the grass grew greener, the river bluer, as if colour were seeping up from the rock below.

I know this place, have been here before.

The green valley and the lake of deep blue. Gentle waves lapped against the shore. A sound drew Corban's eye, towards the lake's heart: a splash and ripples, as if a stone had been thrown into water. His memory prodded at him and his eyes wandered back to the lake-shore, searching for something else and then he saw it – the red-leaved maple that he had once sat beneath. Without thinking, he made his way to it and sat down, his back to the trunk. Everything was still, no breeze to stir the grass or leaves, no hum of insects. The silence was oppressive. And then, high above, like a heartbeat, there was the beat of wings. He glanced up through the lattice of leaf and bark and saw a figure silhouetted against the clouds, human-like, a spear clutched in one hand, broad white-feathered wings powering it through the air.

The Ben-Elim. Meical.

Meical . . .

Then, like an avalanche, he remembered.

Meical, in the great hall of Drassil, telling Corban about the deception of the Ben-Elim, how the prophecy was nothing more than a strategy, a trick to force Asroth's hand, to lure Calidus and the Kadoshim to Drassil. That the Bright Star and Black Sun were an invention, fabricated to snare Asroth in a trap of his own making. A sound strategy, maybe, in the great war between Ben-Elim and Kadoshim, the Faithful and the Fallen, apart from the fact that it used people's lives like pawns on a throw-board.

My da's life. My mam's. So many others.

Rage swept through him, veined with betrayal at the memory of Meical's confession. He remembered resisting the urge to strike Meical, then leaving, knowing his rage was at the boundaries of his control, and had ended up sitting upon a hill in the forest. He had sat there a long time, contemplating Meical's words, trying to make some sense of what it would mean for the future.

And then the Jotun giants had come. Ildaer, their warlord, slayer of Tukul, Gar's da.

Images flickered through his mind: a bear roaring, spittle spraying from its red maw, running, foliage whipping his face, the thunder of the bear's pursuit, the wounds to his knee and chest, a spear piercing Storm, a river, ice-cold water. Storm howling as giants had dragged him away from her side.

Storm.

Pain shuddered through Corban's chest, as if someone were gripping his heart, squeezing and twisting it.

He couldn't breathe; his sorrow was a physical thing that crushed the air from his lungs. He staggered towards the lake, dropping to his knees at the water's edge. Even as he did so, more memories flooded his mind, an unstoppable wave – of Drassil, the frantic blowing of horns and sound of battle that had drifted up to him. Images of his loved ones swam before his eyes: Coralen, Gar, Cywen, Dath and Farrell, Brina, so many others.

Do they still live? Who was attacking Drassil?

Dimly he became aware of movement. Before him the water of the lake started to shift and foam, something rising from the depths. A shape appeared, water cascading and masking, for a moment, the creature within.

Then a man was striding from the lake, with water dripping from the dark cloak that trailed him like seaweed. He approached Corban, an interested, amicable smile upon his face. His skin was grey-mottled and veined like a dead thing, his hair was black and slick as oil. A black-scabbarded sword hung at his hip.

'Well,' the man said, 'it's not often that I get visitors.' His voice was liquid, flowing like a shallow stream over shingle. 'What brings you to my home?'

'I . . . I've been here before,' Corban said.

'I know; I've watched you.'

'This is the Otherworld,' Corban said.

'It is, and this lake, this tree, this valley,' the dark-haired man said with a wave of his hands, 'are mine.' He shrugged, water dripped from his hair.

'Are you Ben-Elim?' Corban asked.

The man laughed, a damp exhalation. 'Those pompous fools. No, though to my shame we are related.'

'Kadoshim?' Corban asked, fearful.

'Hardly.' The man snorted. 'Those fawning, debauched deviants? Do I look like one of them?'

'No,' Corban admitted.

'Well, then. I am just me. Viathun.' He lifted his hands, held one up to the sky, splayed his fingers. Corban saw that they were webbed, like a frog's feet.

'You are from the world of flesh, are you not?' the man said.

Corban nodded warily.

'And what is your name, creature of flesh?' Viathun asked him, leaning in uncomfortably close, his breath washing over Corban, moist and full of rot.

Corban did not want to tell him. 'I'm going to go, now,' he said, standing, wanting to be far away from this creature.

'I don't think so.' Viathun sighed. 'I think we should continue this conversation somewhere a little more *private*.'

Corban backed away, turning to leave. Something grabbed his ankle. Looking down, he saw that it was a tendril of Viathun's cloak, flexing like a grasping limb. It wrapped itself around his leg as Viathun walked back towards the lake, then with shocking strength the cloak pulled tight and started dragging Corban.

For a moment Corban was too shocked to resist, but then he scrambled back, yanking at his ankle, hand grasping for his sword.

'Come on, don't dally,' Viathun called over his shoulder as he reached the lake. He walked in, sinking rapidly.

The cloak seemed to split, to flow, forming a myriad of strands, reaching up to Corban, each one contracting around his ankles, wrists, and throat. Then he was being pulled down to the lakeshore, trussed like a fly in a spider's web, into the water. Panic filled him as his head sank beneath the surface and he struggled desperately, straining, veins bulging, muscles screaming. With a sinew-tearing effort he pulled one arm free and then he was bursting out of the water, hoisted into the air, dangling before the creature, held up by his dark cloak that looked now more like a squirming nest of snakes. Corban gasped for breath, ripping at the cloak strands enclosing him, to little effect. Viathun regarded him with a cold fascination.

'Tell me your name!' Viathun said, anger swelling in his voice, the crash of waves upon rocks.

'Let me go,' Corban grunted through his constricted chest.

'You have trespassed here, disturbed my rest,' Viathun said wetly as he pulled Corban closer. 'In return I will have some answers. And then, after . . . I may see how you taste.' A wave of foul breath engulfed Corban, making his stomach lurch.

'What are you?' Corban coughed.

'I am Viathun,' the creature said, his mouth opening wide, seeming to grow before Corban's eyes, wider and wider, revealing rows of razor-sharp teeth glistening and dripping with mucous. 'Eater of souls.'

There was a whistling sound and a spear slammed into Viathun's cloak, piercing it. Viathun screamed as Ben-Elim swept down from the sky. More spears flew, stabbing into Viathun's body. His yell deepened into a bellow of pain and rage, and Corban found himself thrown to the ground as the creature turned its attention to its attackers.

Then hands were grasping Corban and he was hoisted into the air again. There was a Ben-Elim either side of him, surging skywards, their wings beating hard.

Within heartbeats the conflict in the lake was below them, Viathun and his living cloak sinking into the water, one strand coiling around a Ben-Elim, dragging it beneath the surface. The Ben-Elim's scream cut short as the water closed over its head.

They flew higher, following the course of a winding valley, twisting and turning amongst peaks and sheer cliffs until Corban saw a fortress appear in the crags, a series of towers and battlements. Carved from bone-white stone, it seemed to glow, even under the dark clouds that pressed down from above. The silhouettes of Ben-Elim filled the air about its towers, some spiralling amidst the clouds, others hovering sentinels with long spears and glistening mail. He saw that many more patrolled the long winding walls, and the sounds of combat drifted up to him from the huge courtyards between the high towers.

They are sparring, as we were in Drassil. They are preparing for war . . .

His rescuers alighted upon the flat roof of a tower and half-dragged Corban through an archway, down a flight of stairs, marching him into a huge, high-ceilinged chamber. Within it thousands of Ben-Elim stood, all gleaming mail and white feathers, a dense crowd which parted before Corban and his guards in an elegant ripple of feather and mail, their pale, emotionless faces staring at him.

In front of him was a raised dais, wide steps leading up to it, and upon it a great white throne, pale as bone, a splayed back fashioned to look like feathered wings that rose and curled about the figure slumped within it. Its white-feathered wings were wrapped around the figure like a great cloak, feather-tips draping the floor. The figure's head was bowed, dark hair hanging, concealing its face. As Corban was marched closer the figure raised its head, its hair parting to reveal a familiar face that stared back at him.

Meical.

Emotions ignited within Corban, warring with one another. Relief at seeing the face of a comrade, a friend, in this strange place, but alongside that the still raw wound of Meical's betrayal. Corban felt his cheeks flush with anger even as Meical sat straighter, his face racked with grief and pain, an expression that was so out of place on the face of creatures normally marble-carved and expressionless.

What is wrong with him?

Meical drew in a shuddering breath.

'Thank Elyon,' Meical said. 'You still live in your world of flesh. If your spirit is here, then your body has survived.' Meical seemed to struggle with this speech, as if each word took an effort of pain and will. 'Otherwise your spirit would have crossed the bridge of swords.'

Corban blinked.

Meical reached out, beckoning Corban to come closer.

Corban flinched away.

'Don't touch me,' Corban snapped, remembering the great hall in Drassil.

The great lie.

Corban heard a hiss of outrage ripple through the room behind him. Meical held a hand up.

'Peace,' Meical said.

'But,' one of the Ben-Elim spluttered, 'this creature of *flesh*, he gives insult to you, our high captain, second only to the All-Father.'

'He has good cause,' Meical said, lowering his head. He leaned back in his chair and gestured for Corban to stand. Corban saw that Meical was paler than he had ever seen him. Around his neck was a red wound, raw and angry. It was leaking some clear, ichor-like substance.

'What happened to you?' Corban said.

'Sometimes, if the wound is bad in the world of flesh, we bring a shadow of it with us back to the Otherworld.'

Corban's hand went to his chest, the dull ache he felt with every breath, and understood that it was an echo of his broken ribs.

'So, what is that a shadow of?' Corban said, pointing to Meical's wound.

'I was beheaded, in Drassil,' Meical said.

'What!' *The horn blasts, the sounds of battle that I heard.* A seed of dread unfurled deep in Corban's gut.

'Calidus, Nathair. They attacked.'

'How?'

'The tunnels,' Meical said wearily.

'What of my friends and kin? My people . . . ?'

'Some escaped,' Meical breathed. 'Gar led a retreat down the north tunnel. I held the Kadoshim, as long as I could.' He shook his head. 'Drassil is taken.'

The fortress fallen, taken by Nathair and Calidus . . .

The implications hit Corban like a stone fist.

My warband defeated; those that followed me, trusted me – dead. My friends . . .

'See what your scheming has achieved,' he snarled and launched himself at Meical. His attack was so unexpected and so fast that he had his fingers clamped about Meical's throat before anyone could move. Then there was an explosion of activity behind him: shouting, hands grasping him, wings flexing, beating. Blows rained upon Corban but he shrugged them off, continued squeezing. Meical did not fight back, just sat within the great wings of his throne and stared into Corban's eyes as he cried tears of grief and rage.

'You've murdered my friends,' he yelled, a red rage swallowing him, replacing his despair. Something crunched into his head and the world disappeared for a moment in a white explosion. He felt his fingers slipping from Meical, tried to hold on, but then more hands were gripping him, dragging him back, pressing him onto his knees.

He looked up to see weapons raised over him and angry faces encircling him. A spear was speeding towards his heart.

'No,' Meical said, and the spear froze, a handspan from Corban's chest. Angry voices called out; Corban heard words like *punishment* and *sacrilege*.

'No,' Meical repeated, and the crowd parted before Corban to reveal Meical still sitting upon the throne. He regarded Corban with his emotionless face back in place, though Corban thought he saw cracks within it. 'He has cause to be angry with me.'

'Angry . . . ?' Corban shook his head. 'You *lied* to me, to all of us in Drassil, used us as bait, as pawns. All of you,' he added, glaring at the Ben-Elim gathered around him. Most of them were glaring back at him. 'And now it seems that your plan has worked a little too well. You certainly brought Calidus running to Drassil. Tell me, Meical, was it also part of your plan for Drassil to fall, for my friends, my kin, my people to be slaughtered . . . ?' He ground his teeth, swallowed. 'Or for you to be beheaded?'

'No, it was not,' Meical said with a slow sigh.

The war is lost before it even began. The Banished Lands conquered, all those whom I love slain or scattered. Despair rose up in him then, draining all energy from his limbs. He slumped in his captors' grip.

'It is not over,' Meical said. It took a few moments for his words to seep through the fog of misery and hopelessness that engulfed Corban.

'Of course it is,' Corban whispered.

'No. Not while you live. Not while Calidus still seeks the Seven Treasures. He needs them all to fulfil his plan, and until then Asroth is bound here, in the Otherworld.'

'There is no way back from this . . .'

'We don't know that,' Meical said. 'Gar led many from Drassil. They may still live. There are those who would still stand against Nathair and Calidus. There is still hope.'

Corban's head snapped up, locking eyes with Meical. 'Do not speak to me of hope, you who have fed me lies all my life. You are no better than Asroth and his Kadoshim; a liar, a deceiver, and I wish I'd never met you.'

Angry words rippled around the chamber.

Meical's gaze hardened. 'I have allowed you the courtesy of expressing your anger, but do not go too far. There is more at stake here than your hurt feelings. You are behaving like an angry child.' He paused, visibly sagged in his chair, passed a hand over his eyes. 'Your whole world lies in the balance. It is not over yet; there is still hope, a fighter's chance.'

'There is *no* chance – nothing that I can do. Back in the Banished Lands I am a captive of the Jotun, wounded, my bones broken. And Storm is dead . . .' His voice choked in his throat, a fresh wave of emotion swelling in his chest.

Meical lowered his head. 'Another grievous blow,' he muttered. 'Storm was a better guardian than a score of shieldmen.'

'She was more than my guardian,' Corban snarled. 'She was my companion. My *friend* . . .' He rubbed his eyes, angrily brushed away his tears. 'Your lies have caused the death of my kin – my da, my mam, my friends, and so many others. All of them dying for a hope that never existed. All of them dying for *me*. And because you underestimated Calidus, you have left us with no chance—'

'While there is breath in your body there is a chance!' Meical shouted, leaning forwards in his chair, hands gripping the armrests. For a moment his cold face melted away. 'And if there is no chance of victory, then what of vengeance? Do more than talk and whine: seek your vengeance for those fallen. Or would you rather wallow in self-pity than try to save your loved ones?' He sagged, the effort clearly draining him.

I will not be told what to do by him. I will be controlled and manipulated by him no longer. Nevertheless Meical's words affected him, images of Gar and Cywen, Coralen, Farrell and Dath, Brina, Edana, so many others that he had met during the long hard journey from his home in Dun Carreg to Drassil. And the thought of them without him, perhaps fighting, maybe dying . . .

For a moment all he wanted was to get back to them, to be at their side.

I will not abandon them to death or torment, let them face the end alone. I must go back. If there is a chance to help them.

He looked up at Meical, felt his fists clenching. 'I will go back, but not for you. Not for any of you. I am your puppet no longer. I go to help those that I love.'

Meical stared at him for long, silent moments, then nodded his head. 'I will help you all that I can, though I am bound to the Otherworld now. I cannot return to the Banished Lands—'

'I don't want your help,' Corban growled.

Meical finally nodded. 'Good,' he whispered. He approached Corban and placed a palm over his eyes, whispering words that Corban could not hear. He opened his mouth to say something, but then the world seemed to fade about him . . .

CHAPTER FIVE

RAFE

Rafe felt something wet and rough scratching across his cheek. He wanted to move but found he lacked the ability. Even opening his eyes was too much of an effort. So he just lay there, allowing his other senses to wash over him. He ached; his muscles, joints, his very bones seemed to throb, but even as he became aware of the sensation it began to fade, transforming into something else – a sense of relaxed exhaustion, like lying in a hot bath after a long hunt. He could hear birdsong, the ripple of river-water and the hulls of moored boats nudging into one another. Beyond that the drum of hooves, many feet. Voices.

He did not know how long he lay on the ground like that, but at some point the rough wet scratching on his face came back. A dog's tongue licking him. A smile cracked his lips and he opened his eyes. An explosion of light burst upon him, feeling as if rays of the sun had pierced his skull, lancing through his head. He screwed his eyes shut, the pain dimmed. He tried again, slowly this time. He saw a black nose snuffling, fur tickling his chin.

'Hello, Sniffer,' he croaked, his voice raw and cracked. Ignoring the pain, he pulled himself to his knees, then to his feet. He staggered and braced himself against the wide trunk of a tree.

What has happened to me?

He stretched, the stiffness in his body melting away. For a while he stood there, feeling his muscles uncoiling, enjoying the sense of energy. Of strength and vitality that flowed through him.

'I feel good,' he muttered, smiling and reaching to pat Sniffer's head. He saw Scratcher standing further away, eyeing him suspiciously.

'It's all right,' he said, beckoning the hound. 'Nothing to fear.' The hound came to him, ears still flattened, tail tucked low, and he laughed, ruffling the hound's fur.

I'm starving.

Memories filtered back. Of the battle in the swamp against Edana's warband, his desperate escape, of walking away from Morcant's tower after his interrogation by Rhin and her giant, Uthas. Then walking along the riverbank, finding a solitary spot beside a tree to drink a skin of wine and eat some cold lamb. He scratched at his chin, felt a thick layer of stubble, which felt strange.

How long have I been here?

He looked around, at the marshland trees and bushes, the birds nesting amongst them, blue and orange butterflies flitting, then up at the sky, which was a clear blue, the spring sun warm upon his face. Somehow everything felt sharper, brighter, and clearer.

I feel reborn.

He looked down and noticed the shoulder of lamb he'd brought with him from the camp. The hounds had stripped it clean and cracked the bones. Beside it were the broken shards of the box he'd found in the bog near Dun Taras. And next to that was a cup, dark metal, runes carved into its rim. A dribble of wine ran from it.

And he remembered, like a punch in the gut.

I drank from it.

His legs felt weak and he leaned against the tree as he felt for a moment an echo of the pleasure and pain that had racked his body after drinking from the cup. He felt scared.

What have I done? It is an enchanted cup, it has some kind of spell upon it. But I am not dead. If anything I feel more alive than ever before.

He took a tentative step away from the tree, reaching down to pick up the bag that contained his kit. For a few heartbeats he stood and stared at the cup, then quickly bent and grabbed it, stuffing it into his bag.

He picked his way along a twisting trail amongst the tall grass banks of reed, eventually coming across a stream that led him back to the river.

The river was full of moored boats, the strong smells of newly cut pine, sap and fresh-soaked pitch filled the air. Frames of scaffolding timbers that held half-constructed boats lined the riverbank, skeletal hulls like the bones of flesh-picked whales. Teams of men were working on them. Rafe walked past unnoticed, moving out onto the rolling meadows that spread beyond the marshlands and ended in the north at the fringes of the Baglun Forest. He stopped here, staring, surprised at the difference in what felt like only a half-day, but had clearly been longer. Immediately before him was Morcant's tower. Wains pulled by shaggy-coated auroch filed in and out of the tower gates. On the meadow about it the tents of Rhin's warband of black and gold had multiplied. To the west Rafe saw horsemen riding at straw targets, other men on foot sparring with practice swords and spears.

They are readying for another stab at Edana, then.

'Rafe.'

Morcant was striding towards him, looking striking in his black cuirass and sable cloak edged in gold trim, hair pulled back, warrior braid freshly bound with gold wire. Two guards walked at his back.

He looks far better than the last time I saw him – in Rhin's tent, fresh from the battle, covered in marsh slime and blood and stinking like a stagnant pool.

'Where have you been, boy?' Morcant snapped at him.

'I, uh, over there. Sleeping,' Rafe said, pointing vaguely at the river and marshes.

'Sleeping?' Morcant snorted. 'For a ten-night?'

A ten-night!

'I thought you'd deserted – didn't think you had the stomach for any more battle.'

'I have so,' Rafe said, bridling at Morcant's veiled insult.

'Watch yourself,' Morcant scowled. 'I'm Lord of Ardan now and can put your head on a spike with a snap of my fingers.'

Rafe felt a blossoming of anger, hotter and faster than he was used to. With an effort he suppressed it.

'I thought Evnis was Lord of Ardan.'

'Evnis has not returned, is believed dead,' Morcant said disdainfully. 'Rhin has appointed me to rule in his absence.'

Dead? In truth Rafe had lost sight of Evnis when the rebels' fire had started sinking their boats and Rafe had become too preoccupied with his own survival to worry about anyone else.

But he would grieve for Evnis if he was dead. He had been his lord for as long as he could remember; his da had served Evnis as huntsman for many years.

'So,' Morcant told him arrogantly. 'I am your lord now, and you shall remember it. Now, come with me; Queen Rhin wishes to speak with you.'

He followed Morcant around the rim of the hill, skirting the palisaded wall as they made their way through lines of tents to a central larger one. Towering like statues, two giants stood outside, alongside a handful of Rhin's shieldmen. Rafe gazed at them as he waited to be announced. The giant nearest to him was a female. She stood with folded arms, returning his stare, two knife hilts as long as short swords criss-crossing her back. Her brow furrowed as she regarded him.

'Queen Rhin will see you now,' a shieldman told them and Rafe stepped out of the sunshine into the cool shadow of the tent. Rhin was sat at a broad table, her silver hair braided with golden wire, a bearskin cloak pulled high about her neck. A huge parchment was unrolled on the table. Rafe glanced at it and saw it was a map of the marshlands, their position at Morcant's tower marked upon it. The marshes were largely a blank, with a circle roughly marking the position of Dun Crin.

Behind Rhin stood Uthas of the Benothi, gripping a thick-shafted spear, and about his neck hung a necklace made from long, curved fangs.

'Ah, the wanderer returns,' Rhin cried when she saw him. 'I thought you dead. Or captured,' she added, her eyes narrowing. 'Can I trust you, now? Where have you been?'

'Sleeping,' Morcant said before Rafe could reply.

'Who with?' Rhin asked.

'No one. Myself,' Rafe stuttered. 'My dogs . . .'

Rhin raised an eyebrow. 'No need to be shy – everyone needs some time to relax and indulge in their personal pleasures, else what is life for? But sleeping for a ten-night, a little extreme, don't you think? And a little unbelievable. Are you lying to me?'

'No, my Queen,' Rafe mumbled, 'I drank something . . .'

Morcant snorted laughter.

Rhin paused and stared at Rafe, head cocking to one side. 'Are you well? You seem . . . different.'

Rafe returned her gaze steadily, his eyes drawn to the details of her face: the wrinkles creased around her mouth, tracing a tapestry upwards across the arch of her cheeks to cluster around her eyes. Her skin appeared so fine, almost translucent. His gaze was drawn deeper, the pulse of myriad veins beneath her diaphanous skin a steady and hypnotic beat. His gaze drifted higher, to her eyes, which were a deep, dark blue, like still waters. They transfixed him.

'Answer your Queen,' Morcant snapped, raising his hand to cuff Rafe across the back of the head. Rafe saw it all as if in slow motion and, before he'd even realized what he was doing, his hand shot up, grabbing Morcant's wrist and stopping it dead in its tracks. There was a moment of shocked silence, everyone staring at Rafe as Morcant tugged on his arm, unable to break Rafe's grip.

'How dare you?' Morcant snarled, as he struggled to free himself, before reaching for the knife at his belt. 'I'll carve off your bloody fingers one by one.'

'Enough,' Rhin said.

Morcant froze and, with a conscious effort, Rafe suppressed the bubbling anger within him and released Morcant's wrist. Red marks were already purpling into bruises.

'I don't like being struck,' Rafe muttered.

'So we can see,' Rhin said with a calculating smile. Morcant scowled at him as Uthas leaned forwards, grey bushy eyebrows bunching together in a frown.

Morcant is Lord of Ardan, now. What have I done?

'I . . . I am, sorry,' he said, quietly, then rubbed his eyes. 'I do not know why I did that, or what is happening to me . . .'

Rhin exchanged a quick unfathomable look with Uthas before turning back. 'I have need of you, so I shall forgive you, this once.'

'Thank you, my lady.' Rafe had the sense to dip his head as he spoke, avoiding the urge to glance at Morcant and smirk. 'And I am sorry, my Queen,' he added for good measure.

Rhin waved a hand. 'Sorry is not good enough,' she said, a tone entering her voice that scared Rafe. 'I *am* your Queen. And you are my subject. Learn your place.'

'I will,' Rafe muttered.

'See that you do,' Rhin said. 'And also make sure that the next time I send for you, you come. Your life is mine.' She stared at him, no hint of expression on her face. 'I can make it a good life, or an unpleasantly short one.'

Rafe gulped.

'Do we understand one another?'

'Aye, my Queen,' Rafe nodded.

'Good. Now, come over here and help me with this map. I aim to have Edana's head on a platter within a ten-night.'

CHAPTER SIX

CAMLIN

Camlin padded along the stream's edge, his bow held loosely in one hand. He was returning to Dun Crin from a hunting trip.

Hunting men. It had been a ten-night since the Battle of Dun Crin, where Evnis and Morcant's warband had been largely scattered. He and a score of others had set about hunting down the stragglers.

The more we kill now, the fewer will come back to try and kill us later.

Camlin had split his hunting party into pairs, although he himself had ended up in a group of three.

He glanced down at Meg, the bairn who he'd rescued from a village on the outskirts of the marshlands.

Though she's more than paid me back, the times she's saved my hide, now. She was walking alongside him, wearing a warrior's leather jerkin, holding a spear in one hand, her other resting upon the pommel of a new dagger that was hanging at her belt, all of them spoils taken from the Battle of Dun Crin. Camlin had helped her cut down and restitch the jerkin, as well as chopping an arm's length off the spear to make it more manageable for her.

Part of him had been concerned about her accompanying them.

She's seen worse, though.

A memory of the mottled feet of a bairn swinging from gallows insinuated its way into his mind, beneath it bloated corpses littering a courtyard.

Much worse . . .

A shadow crossed his path and he looked up to see the third member of his party flying above him. Craf swooped down and squawked loudly.

'*Dark waters, tall towers.*'

'I know,' Camlin muttered. 'Don't need a bird to tell me when I'm close to home.' Nevertheless he raised a hand at Craf.

When I first met that bird I must confess I didn't like him much. Turns out he's right handy to have about, though.

Craf had led him straight to over a dozen enemy warriors lost in the marshes. Camlin had made sure they stayed lost, left them lying face-down in the mud.

He walked through a last bank of reeds and came out on the shore of a huge lake. The towers and walls of Dun Crin reared out of the lake's waters, damp and moss-covered like some frozen leviathan. Figures moved on the battlement walls, boats scudding between towers. All about him on the lakeshore there was motion. The wives and bairns of the warriors who had fought in the Battle of Dun Crin had finally returned from their hiding place deeper in the marshes, and all manner of rough shelters were being erected, mostly consisting of linen tents and panelled walls of woven willow.

Best not make themselves too comfortable.

Meg dashed off and merged into the crowds.

Camlin watched as a pair of children rummaged amongst the piles of war gear that had been stripped from the dead and heaped in mounds along the lakeshore: great stacks of swords and spears, shields, boots, belts, knives, quivers, shirts of mail, cuirasses of boiled leather and cloaks of black and gold.

Meg reappeared at his side, now with an iron helmet much too big for her head added to her outfit. Camlin tried not to laugh but wasn't wholly successful.

'What?' Meg scowled at him.

'Think that helmet might slow you down,' he said. 'Besides, your head's thick enough. Doubt if you'll need it.'

She punched him in the leg.

'When are we leaving?' she asked.

'Don't know.' He shrugged. 'Probably talk about it a while before we get around to doing it.'

He paused as the crowds opened up before him. Edana was walking calmly through their midst, stopping now and again to address someone directly, holding a hand here, cupping a cheek there, always seeming to be interested in what was being said to her. Baird, the one-eyed warrior of Domhain, and Vonn accompanied her. Camlin frowned as he watched the young warrior, his eyes shadowed with dark circles, grief carving new lines upon his face.

Though I'd guess I'm partly to blame for that. Me having killed his da might have something to do with his current mood. He'd tracked Vonn after the battle, found him leagues from anywhere, alone apart from his da, Evnis. Camlin had watched as they'd argued. It had ended with Vonn turning his back on Evnis and walking away. Evnis had followed, hand dipping inside his cloak and coming out with a knife in his fist.

Camlin had put two arrows through the man's chest.

His eyes flickered back to Edana.

She has grown, since that night in Dun Carreg when she saw her da murdered. Even fought Roisin of Domhain in the court of swords and won. Mind, exile was too good for a woman like that. She'll never stop her troublemaking.

He searched behind Edana, looking for his friend Halion. *He should be back by now.* Then he saw him, sitting beside a fire with Lorcan, Halion's half-brother, Roisin's son, heir to the throne of Domhain and unofficially betrothed to Edana, with his shieldman, Brogan No-Neck, as Meg affectionately referred to him.

'Good to see you,' Halion said, rising and gripping Camlin's forearm.

'You too,' Camlin said with a grin.

Camlin looked at their faces, saw they were all sombre; a tension in the air. Lorcan's dark eyes were red, looked as if he'd been weeping.

'Am I interrupting?' Camlin asked. 'Just tell me t'bugger off if I am.'

'No, Camlin,' Lorcan said, standing and surreptitiously wiping his eyes. 'I was just going.' He bade them farewell, Halion squeezing his shoulder, and left; Brogan followed faithfully in his wake.

'He all right?' Camlin asked.

'No,' Halion said honestly. 'But I think he will be. I know Conall hates him, just for being Roisin's son, but I like him. There's no malice in him.'

'Well that's a rare thing,' Camlin observed. 'And he did the right thing, with Roisin. Choosing Edana over his mam wasn't easy.'

'True,' Camlin said, 'sometimes the right thing can be a grim thing, too.'

'Aye, and it's weighing heavy on him.'

And you, by the look of it. Halion looked tired, a strained look about his eyes.

'Job done, then?' Camlin asked Halion.

'Aye,' Halion breathed. 'Got back yesterday.'

'Did it go . . . ?' He was going to say *well*, but that didn't seem like the right word.

Halion looked away, staring out into the marshland. 'Roisin didn't try to escape, if that's what you mean.'

'That's something,' Camlin said.

'Aye,' Halion shrugged. 'Not the easiest thing I've done,' he added as Camlin continued to stare at him.

'Thought you hated Roisin.'

'I do. She murdered my mam, wanted to kill me and Conall, was the reason we fled Domhain. And she would have murdered Edana, too. Exile is better than she deserves.'

'But?'

Halion shrugged, his sea-grey eyes hinting at the emotion he kept buried within. 'Walking away was hard.'

Execution is hard, you mean. We called it exile, but leaving her in the middle of the marsh, it was a death sentence.

Camlin patted Halion's shoulder.

'Good hunting?' Halion asked him.

'Aye. There're a few less warriors in black and gold to tell the way to this place. Am I the first back?'

'No. You're the last,' Halion said. 'We've all been waiting on you. Edana refused to hold the council until you were back, safe and sound.'

Camlin felt himself blush at that, a smile twitching his lips. It felt strange to be valued.

Camlin looked around the circle of familiar faces. They were gathered in a clearing, amidst the ruins of what looked to have once been Dun Crin's gatehouse. A collapsed tower rose above them, bird's nests poking from its crumbled ramparts. The old wall lay in ruins, granite boulders scattered in the grass. Beneath their feet ancient flagstones lay twisted and shattered by the encroaching roots of willow and alder.

A crumbling archway framed Edana, who sat upon a moss-covered boulder. She looked at home in a coat of mail and boiled-leather surcoat, a grey cloak about her shoulders and a sword at her hip.

Surrounding her were those she trusted most closely – Pendathran, her barrel-chested uncle, and Drust the red-haired warrior from Narvon, once shieldman to Owain, Narvon's fallen king. Lorcan, the young king-in-exile of Domhain, gazed solemnly at Edana.

The others that filled the area were mostly warriors, shieldmen to those present. Halion, Vonn and one-eyed Baird watching Edana. Close to them Brogan loomed protectively close to Lorcan.

Craf perched upon the broken archway above Edana like a carved statue.

And I've no doubt that Meg is eavesdropping somewhere close by.

Edana stood, and the quiet conversations that had whispered amongst the ruined walls hushed.

'We are leaving Dun Crin,' she said without any preamble.

Above her, Craf ruffled his feathers. '*Leaving,*' he cawed quietly.

'Our warriors' kin have only just returned,' Drust objected. 'Not even dried their feet. And this is a good defensible spot.'

There were rumbles of assent.

After our victory they don't want to leave. I've seen it before – victory makes them feel secure. But our enemy's no fool. Rhin's as canny as they come. We'll not defeat her here again. And he'd said as much to Edana.

'I agree,' Edana said. 'We won the *last* skirmish. Rhin and her battlechiefs underestimated us and did not scout well enough – but they will not repeat that mistake. And they *will* be back. We faced over five hundred swords, put more than three hundred in their cairns, but however many we slew, some escaped. They know where we are, and they will report back to Rhin. Next time they will be cautious, and Rhin rules four realms now; she has the numbers to keep throwing warriors at us until we are overwhelmed.'

Pendathran nodded dourly in agreement. 'But where else is there?'

'There are one or two other spots in these marshes,' Drust said. 'Not as good as here, but still . . .'

'We need to change our tactics. Only the families are staying in the marshes,' Edana interrupted. 'I'm leading the warband out into Ardan.'

'*Ardan?*' Craf muttered above Edana. He didn't look pleased, the feathers of his neck suddenly bristling.

'What?' Pendathran blurted. 'Now that is –' he paused, face turning redder as he made an obvious effort to master his tongue – 'unwise.'

'We cannot win the war hiding in these marshes. If Rhin is to be defeated and Ardan, Narvon and Domhain set free, then we must take the battle to her. We must become an enemy she fears.'

'Winning one battle does not decide the war,' Drust said. 'You've done well, but we could lead Rhin a merry dance around these marshes.'

'I know full-well that the war is not won,' Edana said, her voice abruptly cold. 'Do not patronize me. I am not a bairn, and I am no stranger to loss and hardship.' She looked around at them all. 'Each night I close my eyes, each day I awake, I see the same thing. My dead kin. My friends, cut down. My home, burning. My people. Who cares for them while we are here? Never forget what Rhin has taken from us. It is time we took something back. Time we took the battle to her.'

Drust snorted.

'We cannot face Rhin in open battle,' Pendathran growled.

'Of course not,' Edana said. 'We are too few in numbers – less than two hundred swords – but we can use that to our advantage. We can move quickly, strike fast. Disappear, strike elsewhere. Show Rhin, and the people of Ardan, that we have teeth.'

Pendathran nodded, obviously considering it. 'That'll only last so long,' he said.

'Indeed,' Edana said. 'Which is why the word needs to spread that Rhin has lost a great battle, that her regent Evnis is dead—' Her eyes flitted to Vonn and she took a deep breath. 'That the rightful Queen of Ardan has returned. The people need to know they've not been forgotten. I know them. They will join us if we offer them hope.'

Pendathran glanced at Drust. They shared a long silence, then Drust nodded grimly.

'When did the girlie I used to bounce upon my knee become this daring battlechief I see before me?' Pendathran said.

Edana just smiled, though her eyes flickered in acknowledgement to Camlin and Halion who had had long conversations with her, discussing the options.

Though to be fair much of this plan came from her.

There was a flapping of wings and Craf glided down to alight on the rock beside Edana.

'*Drassil?*' he croaked.

'I'm afraid we are not going to Drassil,' Edana said solemnly to the crow.

'*Wrong, wrong, wrong,*' Craf cawed, flapping his wings vehemently, muttering, '*God-War, Seven Treasures, Brina, Corban,*' over and over.

'We are needed here, Craf,' Edana said, reaching out a hand tentatively to touch the crow's ruffled feathers. He looked at her, then with a disgusted squawk flapped into the air and soared away.

Edana watched him for a few moments, a dark smudge that faded quickly.

Camlin followed Edana from the clearing. The sun was dipping behind the trees; the smell of cooking from the lakeshore wafting over made Camlin's belly grumble.

'What are you planning on doing with the plunder on the lakeshore?' he asked Edana as he drew up alongside her.

'Taking what we need, dumping the rest in the lake so that Rhin can't use it,' Edana replied.

'Make sure you keep the cloaks of black and gold,' Camlin said. 'Think they might come in handy.'

'I had thought exactly the same thing,' Edana said with a vicious smile.

'My lady,' a voice said behind them. It was Vonn, his expression pensive. They halted to let him catch up.

'Craf – the things he said—'

'I miss our friends as much as he does,' Edana sighed impatiently, interrupting. 'Corban, Brina, Dath, Gar, the others . . .' She fell silent, eyes distant. 'But, much as I long to see them all again, I cannot dash off on a fool's errand to Drassil. The journey alone would take half a year, and I have a duty to my people—'

'You misunderstand me,' Vonn said. 'It is the other things he said, about the God-War, about Drassil and . . .' He took a deep breath. 'I need to talk to you, about what my father told me, before he died.'

'About what?' Edana said.

'About the Seven Treasures,' Vonn said quietly. 'I think I know where one of them is.'

CHAPTER SEVEN

CORALEN

Coralen crouched beside Brina and watched the healer run her hands over Storm's torso. The wolven had closed her eyes again, her breathing so shallow that she appeared dead, but as Brina's fingers probed Storm's ribs there was a faint growl and the flash of teeth as Storm curled a lip.

'That hurts, then,' Brina murmured. 'Sorry, my darling,' she soothed, fingers lifting a lip to look at the colour of Storm's gums, opening an eyelid, lifting legs and bending them at the joints.

It must be bad – Brina never calls anyone 'my darling', even if they've lost body parts. Coralen looked up, hearing voices from beyond the ridge – Gar, organizing a search of the area. While desperate to go and help continue the search for Corban, worried that the others might miss something, she still couldn't bear to leave Storm's side.

'Can you help her?' Coralen whispered.

Brina ignored her. Eventually she paused, sat straight, her head bowed in thought. She blew out a long breath and nodded, then with a quick movement she pulled out the vial Coralen had seen her scrape giant's blood into. She scooped out some of the congealing blood and muttered as she lifted Storm's lip and ran her finger across Storm's lolling tongue.

'*Fuil namhaid, a thabhairt as shlainte agus neart.*' She repeated the phrase again and again, gently massaging Storm's throat to help her swallow. The air seemed to grow chill about them and Coralen shivered, feeling as if a spider had just crawled the length of her spine. Eventually Storm shuddered, a spasm that rippled through her whole body. Coralen was not sure if it was wishful thinking, but the wolven's breathing seemed to become stronger, steadier. Brina stopped and looked at Coralen.

'What have you done?' Coralen whispered.

'Not a word to anyone,' Brina hissed fiercely, eyes locking onto Coralen's. 'Without it she is dead. She is too far gone. Even now I cannot say . . .'

Gar dropped down beside them, his usually emotionless face twisted with concern.

'Well?' he said, looking between Brina and the wolven.

Brina held Coralen's eyes still, waiting. Coralen gave an imperceptible nod and then Brina sighed and shook her head. 'I don't know. She is battered, ribs broken, one lung punctured and collapsed. There is a hole through her shoulder and into her chest the size of my fist. If none of these things ends her, still the loss of blood might.' She shrugged. 'Her spirit's strong.'

'None stronger,' Gar said.

'Aye. That may give her a chance,' Brina said.

'Can she be moved?' Gar asked.

'No.'

'I'll set a guard. Coralen, I need your eyes in the search for Corban.'

Coralen nodded. She brushed her fingertips across Storm's muzzle, shared a lingering look with Brina and then she was hauling herself up the ridge.

Coralen stood staring at the corpse of the great bear, for a moment speechless. It was huge – twice the height of a horse and three times as wide.

The bear was a patchwork of wounds. A great flap of flesh hung loose above its shoulder, more a tear than a cut. Half the length of its side had been opened with what looked like a sword-cut, ribs shattered and flakes of white bone sprinkled amongst the red ruin.

'Corban,' Coralen said as she pointed to the sword-wound in the bear's side.

'That's not what killed it,' Farrell said, pointing away from the gaping slash in the bear's side. 'That is.' The bear's throat had been opened, the flesh lacerated and hanging. They'd all seen that type of wound before.

'Storm,' Gar said.

'This is where we found them,' Pax said, his voice raw with grief. 'Where da speared the giant.'

'Describe this giant,' Gar said.

'Fair-haired, the colour of fresh straw. A war-hammer. He looked . . . regal. In charge. And he was talking to Corban.'

'Could it be Ildaer?' Laith said.

Coralen felt a pulse of anger at the name, saw Gar stiffen. Ildaer was the Warlord of the Jotun. He had slain Tukul, Gar's father, at Gramm's hold and broken Gar's ribs when he had tried to avenge his da's death.

The ground showed the signs of more bears – at least another four, maybe more – as well as other giants on foot. Tracks led northwards into the forest, away from Drassil.

Ildaer and the Jotun had fought alongside Jael of Isiltir, who in turn was allied to Nathair, so the logical conclusion was that the Jotun would have taken Corban to Drassil, would have joined the battle. But their tracks headed north.

'Where are they going?' Coralen asked.

Dath moved first, breaking the spell the dead bear had put upon them. 'Don't know, but we won't find them or Ban by standing here,' he said.

'When did this happen?' Gar asked.

'Yesterday, after highsun,' Pax replied.

'We've seen no sign of a camp,' Coralen said. 'No cook-fires, nowhere slept upon – little spoor. My guess is they set off after capturing Corban, so there must have been enough light to make a good start. If we follow their trail, see how much ground they covered before making camp, we'll get a better idea of how far ahead of us they are.'

Gar grunted an agreement and together they moved up a steep slope, entering an area of dense vegetation.

The hill levelled out and opened up, sunshine breaking through the canopy above. It was past highsun, the day beginning its slow crawl towards night. To the south Coralen could see Drassil, pillars of smoke spiralling from it. She looked back to the hill she was standing on, at the bear and giant tracks that led down the hill, north, away from Drassil.

The sound of movement drew Coralen's attention, a rustling. Immediately her sword was in her fist and she was seeking cover, the others following suit, Dath with an arrow nocked. Laith pulled one of her throwing knives, as big as a sword, from the leather belt strapped across her chest. Gar signalled to the Jehar before and behind them, and then they waited.

Beyond the peak of the hill the forest was shrouded in shadow, hindering Coralen's vision, but the crunch of forest litter and approaching rustle amongst the foliage spoke of many feet. A figure appeared, crouched, moving carefully, dark shadows taking form behind it. Iron glinted. Then Gar was stepping from behind a tree, sheathing his sword and striding down the hill.

'Well met,' he said to Tahir, the shieldman of Haelan, boy-King of Isiltir. The warrior gave a lopsided grin of relief and took Gar's forearm in the warrior grip. He was not overly tall, but was broad and thick-muscled, his arms looking too long for his body. Dark hollows ringed his eyes, and there was a long tear across the shoulder of his chainmail shirt, blood caked around it.

'Been looking for you,' Tahir said.

'And you've found us,' Gar said. 'How did you know where to search?'

'One of my lads saw Meical defending the door to the northern tunnel. You don't defend a door for nothing. We retreated out of the main gate, made it to the forest and started circling this way.' More men appeared behind him: forty, fifty, others hidden in the forest gloom, most wearing the red cloaks of Isiltir. 'Taken us all night and half the day, forest was crawling with Kadoshim and Vin Thalun. Think we've taught them to fear the forest better, though.' A rumble of agreement spread through the warriors behind him.

'Where's Haelan?' Gar asked, and Tahir's face dropped.

'I don't know. I tried to find him.' Tahir's mouth twisted with something between pain and shame.

'He's a resourceful lad,' Gar said. 'I'd wager he's found a hole to hide in.'

'I hope so,' Tahir replied, a tremor in his voice.

'How many with you?' Gar asked him.

'Hundred and forty-six swords that can fight,' Tahir said, 'another dozen wounded.'

'You've done well, saving so many,' Gar said.

'Aye, well. Slow and steady wins the race, as my old mam used to say.' Tahir looked around. 'Where's Corban?'

'Taken, by the Jotun. We have just found his trail.'

Tahir scowled and spat. 'Giants,' he muttered, then looked back to Gar. 'So. What do we do now?'

Gar looked at him and blinked.

With Corban and Meical gone, Gar is our natural leader, now. And not just for us, but for all who fought at Drassil. He is Lord of the Jehar and Corban's first-sword. All Coralen wanted to do was find Corban, but with survivors scattered throughout the forest, Gar had more to consider.

'I am going after Corban,' Gar said and turned away to stare at the trail that led northwards.

Tahir gripped his arm. 'What about us?' he asked.

'You and your warriors will rest a while, drink, eat, tend to your wounds.'

'I don't just mean *us*,' Tahir said, waving a hand at his men. 'I mean the warband of Drassil. Many still live – can you not hear them still fighting? For Corban. You cannot just abandon them.'

Gar stared at him, face twitching.

Coralen crouched beside the burned-out fire and brushed the ash with her fingers. It was cold, not even the memory of heat lingering within it. She glanced up, saw Dath at the edge of shadow poking at a mound of bear dung.

It was sunset; the forest was slipping into layers of shadow. After talking with Tahir, Gar had sent out scouts to see if the survivors of Drassil could be brought together. Coralen had left with Dath and Kulla to find the giants' camp.

She sprang up and ran from the site, easily following the path the giants had left.

They are overly confident, are making no effort to hide their passage. They would not think that we were hunting them. If only I could reach them, it may be possible to steal Corban back in the darkness . . .

'It's too dark – we'll lose their trail,' Dath called after her but she ignored him, just ran on into the forest, following the tracks up a steep incline. She climbed it and stopped, kicking at a moss-covered stone, her heart sinking as she realized the implications of what she could see.

'The old giants' road,' she said to Dath and Kulla as they joined her. It had been rebuilt by Jael's warband. 'And they're moving fast.'

'Aye,' Kulla said. 'Wherever they're going, they want to get there quickly and are not worried about any pursuit.'

'Probably think we're all a bit busy with Nathair in Drassil,' Dath added. He looked at Coralen. 'How far ahead do you think they are?'

'A day,' Coralen grunted. 'If they stick to that ruined road, maybe ten, twelve leagues.'

'We'll not catch them this night, then.'

Coralen sucked in a long breath. 'No,' she growled.

'What do you want to do?' Dath asked her.

I want to keep running, keep moving until we find them. Find him. But there would be no quick rescue now. They would be fortunate to catch them in half a ten-night. *Probably longer, if their bears have an open run.*

'Back to Gar,' she said.

They had made it back to camp in good time, considering they were travelling almost blind, the moonlight little more than a shimmer above the forest canopy.

Warriors were everywhere, clustered around small fires that had been surrounded by wicker panels to hide their glow. Coralen saw Gar standing beside a larger fire with a group around him; Tahir was there, as well as others whom she was pleased to see: Wulf in his bear pelt, a notched axe resting across his shoulder, Javed the pit-fighter, small and wiry, a giant outlined behind them.

Gar saw her enter the glade and their eyes met. Coralen nodded, signalling that she'd found the giants' camp.

'We should strike, attack Drassil now,' Javed said. 'They'd not be expecting that. The Vin Thalun are in there.' There was a barely contained rage edging his voice. 'Lykos is there; the man who gave me this.' He twisted to show the scar burned into the back of his shoulder, a twisting spiral. 'He and his kind did this and worse to many of us,' Javed said, waving a hand at his warriors. Angry murmurs spread amongst them.

'Kick a stone in anger, you'll hurt your foot,' Tahir said.

Javed just stared at him. The giant behind them laughed, a low rumbling like drums.

'Just something my old mam used to say,' Tahir muttered.

'And what the hell does it mean?' Javed scowled.

'That acting from anger will get you killed,' Gar said. 'Anger is the enemy.' He turned to the group close to him. 'Fachen of the Benothi,' Gar continued. 'What would your clan advise?'

The giant stepped forwards into the firelight, a double-bladed axe silhouetted across his shoulder.

'Balur One-Eye is wounded, on the edge of life and death. Ethlinn will not leave him. We will not fight without her.'

Gar nodded thoughtfully. 'How many of your kin are with you?'

'A score. Perhaps more are scattered in Forn.' The giant shrugged.

'I will send Brina with you when you return to them.'

'Good. Ethlinn bade me ask for her.'

'We cannot just do nothing,' Javed snapped.

'I do not intend to do nothing,' Gar said.

Other voices joined in, each proposing a different way forward – attacks, ambushes, strategies.

This could go on all night.

Coralen slipped across the glade, moving beyond the small council to the side of the glade. A makeshift rope-ladder hung over the edge, another fire flickering below, by the river's bank. Coralen climbed nimbly down to find Brina with Storm. Farrell was there too, sitting with his back to the slope, eyes closed, a big hand resting upon Storm's shoulder.

'How is she?' Coralen asked.

Brina looked at her with sad eyes, tears glittering in the firelight.

'I fear she will not win this fight,' the healer said.

Coralen's heart lurched in her chest. *But she used magic, said a spell.* 'But, what you did . . . ?'

'It has helped,' Brina said, 'given her strength, but her wounds . . .' She looked at Farrell, then lowered her voice to little more than a whisper. 'And I used giant's blood. Another wolven or something closer to her own species would have more power.'

'There is a dead bear half a league from here,' Coralen said. 'One of those that the Jotun giants ride.'

Brina reached into her cloak and removed an empty vial. 'Fill this with its blood,' she said, taking Coralen's hand and closing her fingers about it. She glanced at Storm, at the wolven's shallow breathing. 'And be quick about it.'

Coralen was.

Most of the camp was sleeping when she returned from her grisly task. Gar and the other leaders were still in deep conversation.

Brina was alone with Storm, the small fire crackling, casting shadows across the healer and wolven. Without a word, Brina took the vial and massaged the fluid into Storm's gums and tongue.

'*Fuil namhaid, a thabhairt as shlainte agus neart,*' Brina muttered, over and over, her voice sounding like a stick scratching on slate. Coralen's flesh goose-bumped. The fire seemed to dim and then flare; a twig popped. The wolven stirred, lifting her head to regard Brina with her amber wolven eyes.

'Come back to us,' Brina whispered. 'Corban needs you.'

Storm's legs twitched and she gave a weak rumbling growl, then with a sigh she laid her head back on the turf.

'Thank you,' Brina said to Coralen, looking weary.

Dirt skittered about them and Dath, Kulla and Laith appeared out of the darkness, waking Farrell.

'How is she?' Dath asked.

'A little stronger,' Brina said.

'We'll take it in turns to watch over her,' Farrell said. 'Even you must need to sleep.'

'Well, for once you may be right,' Brina muttered. She curled down beside the fire, pulling her cloak over her head. 'Wake me if there is any change. And no going to sleep on watch.' A bony finger poked out of the cloak and wagged at them all.

Within moments Brina's breathing changed, became slower and deeper.

'So,' Dath whispered to Coralen once they were all sure that Brina was soundly asleep. 'When do we leave?'

'What do you mean?' Coralen asked.

'You'll be going after Corban. We're coming too.'

Coralen had decided to leave a little before first light, to slip away before the camp woke and started asking her questions. She needed to use every moment of daylight possible. Perhaps leave a message for Gar. It was clear that he was needed here, that his duties would force him to stay and oversee the fight against Nathair.

'You can't come,' Coralen said, 'Farrell and Laith'll be too noisy, too slow.'

Farrell leaned forwards. 'Ban's my friend. More than that. Closer than kin. I'm going after him, with you or without you.' He shrugged. 'I'd rather we travelled together. But I'll not be staying here.'

Coralen looked at them all, saw the resolve in their eyes.

'All right then,' she said. 'Before dawn.'

Morning came grey and damp, false dawn giving a half-light that helped Coralen to see beyond the fire-glow they'd kept crackling all night to give Storm a little warmth. Farrell, Dath, Kulla and Laith had all stayed, taking it in turns to watch over Storm. Now, silently they all stood, checked weapons and packs.

'I would come with you, if not for Storm,' Brina said as she stirred within her cloak.

'We know,' Coralen answered.

Brina checked on the sleeping wolven. 'Her heart beats stronger,' she said.

'That is good news,' Coralen grinned. She crouched beside the wolven and ran her fingers through the thick fur of her neck, then leaned forwards and kissed Storm's head.

'I'll be back, with Corban,' she whispered.

'Bring him back,' Brina said watching them leave.

I mean to, or die in the trying.

The camp in the glade above was still and silent. Coralen and the others picked their way through the sleeping figures. As they slipped amongst the trees a figure stepped out in front of them.

Gar.

He had a pack slung across his back, a grim look upon his face. He nodded as he looked fiercely at the small gathering.

'Good. Let's be after him, then.'

'We thought you were needed here, that you would have to stay,' Coralen said.

He gave her a withering look.

'Only death would stop me from going after Ban.'

CHAPTER EIGHT

CORBAN

Corban woke to pain. He opened his eyes, stared up at a dappled canopy of leaf and branch, grey light leaking through it. It was passing him by, like clouds scudding across the sky.

No, not the trees. It is I that am moving. And I am in Forn, he realized. *Still in Forn.* He felt relief at that. Being in Forn was not such a bad thing; he liked the forest, and it also meant that he was not a thousand leagues from Drassil and his friends, if any of them had survived. But the constant rocking, bumping motion *wasn't* such a good thing, making his chest spike with pain and exacerbating the deep, dull throb in his knee, pulsing out in time with his heartbeat. Also, there was a terrible stink in his nose, musky and stale, making him want to gag.

Time passed in something of a haze. His mind drifted and he thought of the Otherworld, of his meeting with Meical.

He used me, manipulated me. Lied to me. But his words had also rung true. He needed to find his friends, to be at their side.

How? That is the question. When I am broken and battered. A prisoner, travelling Elyon knows where.

He moved his head slowly, from side to side, saw that he was on a makeshift litter that was being dragged through the forest. Behind him a huge figure loomed, thick with fur, a black snout and muzzle, yellowed teeth edging its jaw.

A bear. One of the Jotun's bears.

A face reared over him, pale and blond-haired, a long braided moustache drooping down almost to Corban's face. Corban recognized him as one of the giants that had dragged him away from Storm. 'I'll kill you,' Corban hissed, instinctively reaching for his sword. When his fingers reached the empty scabbard he remembered that he'd left it in the body of a giant, back in the glade where he and Storm had fought and slain three of this giant's kin.

The giant's eyes watched Corban's gasping breathlessness and grunted.

'You'll not be killing any more of us Jotun today,' the giant said in stilted speech. 'But I like your spirit.' He chuckled. 'There's fire in this pup's belly, yet. Hala,' he called over his shoulder, 'seems you'll make a healer, after all.'

'I've been one for four hundred years, you idiot,' a voice called back.

The giant looked back at Corban and checked the binding of his leg splint, sending jolts of pain through Corban.

'Don't go dying on us,' the giant said. Another giant face appeared beside it, this one red-haired and glowering.

'He and his wolven killed Hronn, Rulf and Lut,' it rumbled, reaching round with a hand the size of a shovel and cuffing Corban across the head. Just the blow was painful enough, but the fire it ignited in Corban's chest was like a hammer strike and he screamed, the world fading to darkness. The last sound he heard was giant voices yelling at each other.

'Drink this,' a voice said.

Something was shoved into his hand – a bowl – and to his surprise he found that he was propped up against the trunk of a tree, a rope tying him to the wide bole.

Not that I can get up and run away.

Two giants were crouched before him, both of them cloaked in the twilight gloom of Forn. One of them was the blond giant he'd talked to earlier. Beyond them he heard the familiar sound of camp-making, shadowy figures moving at the edge of his sight.

'Drink,' the voice said, a huge hand wrapping around his and lifting the bowl to his lips. Corban sniffed it, wrinkling his nose at the familiar earthy smell.

'Brot,' he muttered.

'You know brot?' the voice said in surprise.

Corban looked into the gloom and saw that one of the dark figures before him was a woman, her face slabs of bone highlighted by the dim gleam of moonlight.

'Aye,' Corban mumbled. He sniffed suspiciously at the bowl.

'Go on,' the voice said. 'If we wanted to kill you, you'd be dead already.'

That's a fair point. Why haven't they killed me?

He took a sip, the brot closer to porridge in consistency than fluid. After swallowing, he felt an after-taste, something bitter.

'It's not the same,' Corban said.

'As what?'

'As what Balur gave me.'

There was a pause, the giants shared a look.

'Balur *One-Eye*?' the blond-haired male asked.

'Aye,' Corban said. 'There's something else in this. Goldenseal?'

Another silence.

'Aye,' the female giant said. She almost sounded pleased.

Goldenseal to fight infection, Brina always said. The worse it tastes, the better it is for you. I never quite believed that bit.

Another figure loomed out of the shadows.

'*Bogadh*,' the giant rumbled and his captors parted to let this one crouch down before Corban.

'*Eadrom*,' the new arrival said, and a moment later Corban heard flint being struck, sparks catching on a torch and light flared.

Corban blinked, looked away a moment.

'Look at me,' the new voice said, a grating rumble, stern and grim. A hand gripped Corban's face and lifted his chin. He was looking at another blond giant, a thick warrior braid in his hair, threaded with red-gold wire. This one had a wide bandage wrapped around his shoulder and chest, a dark stain at its centre.

'You are Ildaer, King of the Jotun,' Corban said.

'Warlord, not king,' Ildaer murmured. 'But who are you?'

'Why am I still breathing?' Corban asked. 'I slew your bear, three of your kin in the glade.' *With a lot of help from Storm.* 'Why would you keep me alive?'

'You do not question me,' Ildaer said, then with one thick finger prodded Corban in his ribs.

Corban suppressed a scream; it came out as a gurgled hiss.

Ildaer's hand brushed over Corban's torn surcoat, rested on the sigil of the Bright Star stitched upon his chest, felt his mail shirt, rolling links between his fingers. He grunted approvingly, then moved on to Corban's arm-ring, wrapped around his bicep. It had been gifted to him in Drassil, a spiral of dark iron veined with a silver thread, a snarling wolven head at each end. It was a thing of beauty, more so because it reminded Corban of the night back in Drassil when the whole of the warband had pledged their loyalty to him and he had sworn his oath to them in return. He felt a lump rise in his throat and blinked away tears.

'Who are you?' Ildaer asked him again.

'No one,' Corban grunted, feeling a surge of bitter despair at that admission. *Certainly not the Bright Star everyone believed I was. I even came to believe it. I am the greatest of fools; that is who I am.*

'There is giant skill in this,' Ildaer observed, fingers running over the spiral of the arm-ring. 'At Gramm's hold warriors stood about you. You commanded and others listened. And yesterday, men came to save you.' He moved closer, face almost touching Corban's, his small dark eyes staring. 'I do not think you are no one. Start with your name. Tell me that.'

Corban clamped his lips together.

'I could hurt you,' Ildaer said matter-of-factly, hand opening and resting lightly upon Corban's injured knee. Corban sucked in a breath but said nothing.

'Your name?' Ildaer said, flexing his fingers.

'Something for something,' Corban said, as calmly as he could manage.

Ildaer stared at him a long, sweat-filled moment. Then a smile cracked the slabs of the giant's face, his moustache twitching.

'You have stones, little man, I'll give you that. Bargaining with *me*, at a time like *this*? Very well – something for something. Now, what is your name?'

'I am Corban ben Thannon,' Corban said, lifting his chin high. *That is who I am. My father's son, no more, no less.* At that moment he had never missed his da more fiercely, nor felt so proud of his memory.

Ildaer nodded thoughtfully, as if he were turning the name over in his mind.

'All right, then,' the giant finally said. 'Ask your question.'

'Where are you taking me?' Corban asked.

'Away from Drassil and this cursed forest,' Ildaer said, looking up at the shifting shadows and impenetrable trees around them.

'Where?' Corban repeated.

'A place you know well enough. We are going to Gramm's hold.'

CHAPTER NINE

FIDELE

Fidele walked the lines of their camp, nodding to guards, offering a word of encouragement here and there. Trees loomed, towering colossi that transformed daylight into perpetual twilight. Within this shadowed world the warband of Ripa camped: close to a thousand men, five hundred leagues from home.

They must wonder why they are here, so far from home, caught up in a war they hardly understand. A war that I barely understand.

What she did know, though, was that her son was at the heart of it. *Nathair.*

At the thought of him a tide of emotions swept through her. Shock. *He is allied to the Kadoshim. My own son. How could he choose to be part of such a great evil?* Anger, that he had not chosen differently, that he had not stood for what was right. *He is naive, has trusted flattering words and deceptive tongues, and walked the wrong path.* Betrayal, that he had chosen Calidus over her, a point made so clear during her trial. Regret, that she had not seen the course he was treading earlier and done something to help him, while there had still been time. Sadness. No, something far deeper than that, more akin to grief. It almost felt as if he had died, that she had lost him forever.

Not forever. There is still hope for him. There must be . . .

Hatred. For Calidus, the catalyst and centre of her fury. A Kadoshim demon made flesh, his will set on corrupting Nathair and bending him to his purposes.

Threaded between and amongst all those emotions was one more. Love. A mother's love for her son, built upon the vulnerable child she had nursed at her breast, whom she had nurtured and protected, a fierce love that had always seen the best in him, that believed in his ability, his strength and intellect, believed in *him*. A love that still fuelled a hope that he would eventually see the wrong he had done, that he would turn back from the dark path he was being led down.

At the perimeter of their camp two guards with the eagle of Tenebral upon their breastplates saluted her. Men always stood together in this forest, never alone. The creatures of Forn were better defended against that way.

Fidele stood and stared out into the shadows of the forest.

'We must leave,' a voice said beside her, making her jump. Alben, the white-haired healer, had followed her, his footsteps little more than a whisper upon the forest floor. A bandage was wrapped around a wound between his shoulder and chest that the traitorous Ektor had given in the dungeons beneath Brikan. *Quiet, shy Ektor, brother to Krelis and Veradis. More accustomed to holding a scroll than a sword.* And yet he had betrayed them and slain one of her most trusted companions, Peritus.

It had been little more than a ten-night ago and her grief was still fresh, but Alben seemed to have recovered well.

He is a remarkable man. And a mysterious one. A warrior and a healer, both, but so much more than that. Friend to Meical, part of a secret group that has been waiting for these days, preparing . . .

'We must leave,' Alben repeated. 'Time is against us.'

'No,' she replied, an automatic response. She drew in a long breath, composing herself. 'This warband will not just march away from Krelis. They are men of Ripa.'

'They'll do what you order them to do,' Alben said quietly. 'You are their Queen.'

I don't want to be queen. So many years I have put duty first. She looked at Alben, saw him studying her face. *He knows why I do not wish to leave.*

'I'll not leave without Maquin.'

The warrior's face filled her mind, beaten and scarred. Proud. Fierce. She felt her spirits lift at the thought of him, remembered sitting at his side in the tower at Ripa, when he had opened his eyes after lying on the brink of death for so long. He had told her that he'd stood upon the bridge of swords, that one of the Ben-Elim had given him a choice.

To cross over or go back, he'd told her.

Why did you come back, then? she had asked him.

Three reasons. Three people. Jael. Lykos. You. He had paused and looked up into her eyes. *Two for vengeance. One for love.*

Her lips twitched in a smile at the memory of it.

Alben's eyes creased with worry, and perhaps compassion. 'You'll lose this war for one man?'

So many answers flashed through her mind, most of them convincing in their own right, but she knew they were not the truth.

'It will not come to that,' she snapped.

Alben frowned. 'You cannot choose one man over a nation,' he said. 'More than that, the whole of the Banished Lands. We are in the God-War. We cannot just walk away from this, it will consume the Banished Lands, and when it is done those who stand against Asroth will either be victorious or they will be dead. There is nothing in between. It is war. Sacrifices must be made.'

'I am familiar with sacrifice,' she said coldly, 'but I'll not be a pawn to an absent god. I'll fight for my freedom, for my people, and follow my conscience. Yes, I fear for Maquin and I long for his return, but more than that, this warband is stronger with him, and with Krelis. And Veradis, if they managed to find him. We must give them more time.'

'They may never return, my lady,' Alben said quietly, voicing her deepest fear.

Doubt and worry gnawed at her. She remembered standing on the riverbank beyond Brikan's tower as the warband escaped deeper into the forest, camouflaged, amongst Nathair's warriors. Maquin, Alben and Krelis had stood with her, looking back at the tower, thinking of Veradis and what he had vowed to do: to slay Calidus, one of the Kadoshim. They had all seen the explosion of fire light up the tower window and moments later seen the forms leap from it, hurtling into the river. It was Veradis, they were sure. Maquin and Krelis had made to rush after him then and there, but Alben had stayed them a while, calling out names and gathering a score of men to go with them. Maquin had crushed her in a tight embrace.

Stay, she had whispered in his ear.

Veradis is my friend, Maquin had replied. *And he freed us.* She'd held his gaze a long, heartfelt moment, and then he was gone, running into the night.

Was that our last moment together?

'My lady,' one of the guards close by said, pointing into the darkness of Forn Forest. 'Someone approaches.'

Fidele stared into the shadows, Alben tense beside her, a fist clamped around the hilt of his sword. One of the guards had raised a horn to his lips, ready to sound the call to arms.

Figures separated from the gloom, dark silhouettes. Six, seven, then one more, looming behind the others, dwarfing them.

A giant.

Swords were scraping from scabbards, then Fidele recognized the first figure as it passed through a beam of daylight. Alben reached a hand out to the guard with a horn to his lips and pulled the horn away.

One of the scouts whom Alben sent to watch the road. He was leading a group through the forest towards their camp.

She felt her pulse quicken as her eyes scanned the shapes behind him and then she was running, pushing past the guards, ferns and branches whipping at her face. Another figure was moving ahead of the scout, running towards her, a loping stride, all controlled strength and grace.

Maquin.

He opened his stride and ran ahead of the others, meeting Fidele between two great oaks. They fell into each other, Maquin's arms gripping her around the waist and crushing her against him. Her lips found his and the next few moments were lost to the scent and taste of him. Eventually she heard the others approaching and stepped back, hands still holding his, and looked at him. He was sweat-stained, hair pressed dark against his head. And he was smiling at her, softening the hard lines and scars upon his face. He reached out and brushed a strand of hair from her cheek.

'Now that's a greeting worth fighting demons from the Otherworld for,' he said, 'even if it is most un-queenly behaviour.' A glance acknowledged the eyes gathering upon them.

'I am more than just a queen,' Fidele said with a shrug. 'And besides, in these times death feels never more than a few steps behind us. While I still draw breath I'll live my life as I choose.'

Her eyes drifted to his bare arm, a jagged wound hastily stitched. It looked more like an animal bite than the product of a weapon; the edges were torn and bloodied. He saw her gaze upon the injury and shrugged wryly.

'Can you never come back to me without a fresh wound?'

'It's a bad habit, I must confess.' He smiled at her.

The others gathered about them now, and Fidele saw Krelis standing with Veradis, the bulk of Alcyon the giant behind them. They were both bloodstained and sweating, exhausted, but both of them were grinning at Alben as the old warrior hugged them both.

There was a crashing behind her and they all turned to see Raina the giantess and her bairn ploughing through the undergrowth towards them. Alcyon pushed past Krelis and Veradis, sending them flying, and met his family with an inhuman howl, their arms wrapping around one another, holding, squeezing as if they were becoming one. Slowly they sank to their knees, still entwined, a shuddering sound pulsating from them. Alcyon's sobs. He held their faces, smothered them both with kisses, wife and son, and their tears and smiles mingled with his.

In such dark times as these it was heartwarming to see such love. She gripped Maquin's hand more tightly in her own. If only such happiness could last . . .

'So, what now?' Krelis asked them.

The small gathering were sitting around the burned-out remains of a fire-pit in the centre of their camp.

'We must go to Drassil,' Alben said.

'Must we?' Krelis asked, looking around at them all. 'I'm not one to walk away from a fight, but I've just lost nineteen men to . . .' His voice trailed off.

'To demons of the Otherworld,' Veradis said. 'To the Kadoshim.'

'Still can't quite believe it,' Krelis muttered, wiping a hand across his eyes. 'I'm not one for faery tales,' he said. 'But I know what I saw. My blade in an enemy's heart, and the bloody creature just smiled at me. I had to take his head to stop him trying to rip my throat out. I saw winged *things* of mist and shadow forming above the headless corpses.' He shook his head. 'If we go to Drassil it sounds as if we'll face an army of these things. My men are warriors, bred for battle, brave and true-hearted. But they are only men of flesh and blood. So

I must ask this question.' His gaze returned to Alben. 'Is this our fight?'

Slowly Alben nodded. 'It is,' he said. 'This is the God-War, Krelis. Meical and the Bright Star are there, so Drassil must be where it will be decided.'

'The battle is most likely already over,' Krelis said. 'Nathair and his . . . *allies* . . . have at least a ten-night's march on us.'

'If we do not go, who else will?' Alben said. 'It is our duty to go.'

'My duty is to my men,' Krelis said, waving a hand at the warband about them, 'and to the people of Tenebral. We are less than a thousand swords. We cannot win. A strategic man would withdraw, live to fight another day, when the odds are more in our favour.'

'There will not be another day if we do not fight now,' Alben said. 'Calidus and Nathair will destroy our allies one by one. We must stand with those who oppose them now – before it is too late.'

'And what if there's none of these allies left alive at Drassil by the time we get there?'

'We won't know unless we go there,' Alben replied.

A silence lengthened, all looking between Krelis and Alben.

'Well, maybe you're right,' Krelis eventually said, nodding thoughtfully. 'I've always come to you when it's wisdom I've been looking for. But what if you're wrong? Marching deep into the heart of Forn, into unknown ground against a foe that outnumbers us greatly – that's not wisdom, not when we could retreat and choose our own ground. But still, this is a fight we must all agree to. I say to all of you, ask you all as my brothers-in-arms, are you for this fight, here, now? Are you for Drassil, or are you for home?'

Home, thought Fidele. *Part of me longs to find a place of peace with Maquin where this war cannot touch us. But is there a place far enough from this war to escape it? And even if there were, I would not abandon the people of Tenebral to death and torment. And then there is Nathair. Whatever he has done, he is still my son. I cannot just leave him.*

'Well?' Krelis said, dragging Fidele from her thoughts. 'We are friends here, equals. We have not been ordered by our lord or king. We are free to choose. Let us put it to the vote. As for me, I say we leave this forest behind us. Back to Tenebral to raise more swords and choose our battleground.'

'I am for Drassil,' Alben said.

Fidele looked around the fire-pit, saw all lost in their own deliberations. *I would go to Drassil*, she thought. *To save my son and for vengeance upon Lykos. But Krelis speaks wisdom.*

'What of you, little brother?' Krelis asked. 'Are you for the great tree, or for home on the bay?'

Veradis finally raised his head and regarded them all with his dark, serious eyes. 'I have been a fool, been deceived, and committed dark deeds in the name of good.' His face twisted with a bitter grimace as he looked at his open palms.

Much blood those hands have spilt, for Calidus.

'I would do what I can to put that right,' Veradis continued. 'But how?' he mused. 'My heart says Drassil, my head says home. Krelis is right, we do not know what awaits us at Drassil, though I do know this: Calidus has charged Jael of Isiltir, Gundul of Carnutan and Lothar of Helveth to build roads to Drassil, and with them they bring the full might of their realms. If we managed to make the long journey through Forn we would face impossible odds at the end of it.'

'Not if Meical and the Bright Star still stand,' Alben said.

'And if they have fallen?' Krelis said. 'You are advising us to do the opposite of all you have taught. "Know your enemy, choose your ground." That's what you've always told me.' Krelis shook his head.

'I know,' Alben admitted.

'What of you?' Krelis asked, shifting his gaze to Alcyon and the giants. Raina was cutting Alcyon's hair with her knife, leaving the top long and thick, the sides shaved to the skin.

What is she doing to him? He looks more fearsome now than ever before.

'We will travel with you, whichever way you go. If you will have us,' Alcyon said.

'And why would you wish to join us?' Krelis asked, eyes narrowing. 'Why not just leave now and go back to your clan?'

'Two reasons,' Alcyon said, his voice like gravel. 'A blood-debt –' he glanced at Veradis – 'and a blood-feud.' As he said the last his fists clenched, knuckles popping. 'Calidus made me a slave. Kept my family prisoner. I would even that score. Fight him now, fight him later.' Alcyon shrugged. 'As long as I fight him, I care not.'

'If you don't mind me asking,' Krelis added to Alcyon, 'why the new haircut?'

Alcyon rubbed the side of his head, stubble rasping on his palm, the hair on the top of his head a thick wedge.

'This is my clan's tradition. When Calidus caught me and bent me to his will I was Kurgan no longer. I did not deserve the mark of my clan. But now I am Kurgan again.' He smiled viciously.

'Neither course is clear,' Fidele said, 'though wisdom suggests we retreat. Are there any other options?'

'We could fight now,' Maquin said.

All eyes turned to him. The grizzled warrior looked at his hands, turning them over. Fidele beside him saw the calluses and scars.

'In the pit I have faced one foe, and I have faced many foes. It is always easier against one.'

I saw him fight four men, and slay them all.

'Against many I strike fast, before they have a chance to join against me, and I strike hard, to kill with one blow.'

'Aye, but this is no pit. This is Forn Forest, and our enemies are not lining up before us,' Krelis growled.

'They will be, if we allow them to. But one of them is close to us, cut off from the others. Gundul and the warband of Carnutan are out there, close, building a road, distracted, spread out, with their backs to us. We'll likely fight him one day, though next time we see him will probably be with half the realms of the Banished Lands at his back. Whether we go to Drassil or walk away, I say we have an opportunity here to even the odds a little. An opportunity we'd be fools to miss. And besides,' he added, 'there's nothing like a good fight to clear the mind.'

CHAPTER TEN

JAEL

Jael stumbled and almost fell, swearing under his breath as he reached out to grab a thick branch.

I hate this forest.

He steadied himself, pausing to wipe sweat from his brow and catch a few breaths. His huntsman Dag was somewhere up ahead, setting a gruelling pace as they marched through Forn Forest.

How many nights have we lived in this twilight nightmare? Twenty? Thirty? A hundred? Will it ever end?

A line of warriors were strung before and behind him: a few hundred men, the only survivors of his warband that had marched so proudly to the gates of Drassil.

Thousands strong, the might of Isiltir, now broken, slain or scattered. And a third of those who fled with me have fallen since then to the forest, and to its inhabitants. He shuddered at the memory of finding guards grey and lifeless, their blood drained like juice from a ripe fruit, nothing much more left of them than skin and bone.

How did it come to this? Victory was so close, Drassil almost mine. How did that boy defeat Sumur? He ground his teeth at the memory of Corban taking the Kadoshim's head in single combat. It had been a blow, he could not deny, and it had done little for the morale of Jael's warband. So Jael had ordered his finest warriors, his personal guard, to swarm Corban and slay him. Sure victory had seemed mere heartbeats away. But then the gates of Drassil had opened, that devil-wolven and the stallion galloping out ahead of a host of giants and sword-waving lunatics.

It had all gone downhill from there.

That had been when Jael had made the decision to retreat.

Retreat, not flee. A strategic withdrawal. Better to retreat and live to fight another day. And that is what I shall do here. Retreat to Isiltir, raise a fresh warband, fight to hold on to what I have achieved.

'My lord,' a voice said behind him. A sweat-soaked warrior was giving him a concerned frown.

'What?' Jael snapped irritably.

'The line, my King,' the warrior said, jerking his head forwards.

Jael realized the warriors he'd been following were still moving, disappearing into the foliage and shadows. Fear jolted him into movement, the thought of being stranded in the forest without Dag to guide him was a horror he had no wish to endure. He hastened on, limbs heavy and leaden, catching up with the men ahead, then he was settling back into the monotonous march, his eyes fixed on the heels of the man in front of him.

Whispering ahead caused Jael to look up from the ground. Dag was moving back down the line, patting a shoulder here, pausing to say a few words there.

Never thought of him as leader material. For some reason the thought irritated Jael. *Always seemed like a loner. And those scars on his face don't make him more pleasant to be around.*

The huntsman eventually reached Jael.

'You have news?' Jael asked, ashamed of the desperation and hope that he tried to keep from his voice.

'Aye,' Dag said. 'There's men up ahead.'

Jael peered through dense undergrowth, for a moment struggling to understand what he was seeing.

Only a dozen or so paces away, the undergrowth ended. A man-made clearing dotted with cut tree stumps led towards an embankment. Men, hundreds of them, were swarming over the embankment, which stretched as far as he could see in both directions. They were working, many wielding long-handled axes, and hammers were rising and falling, the rhythmic thud of their blows drumming through the forest.

They are building a road.

It must be Lothar or Gundul, still building to reach Drassil and win the race that I had already won.

Just looking at the industriousness of what could only be his allies, even if they were also rivals in Jael's mind, he began to feel something of his old confidence returning.

I am safe. Safe from the forest, safe from pursuit.

'With me,' he said to Dag as he pushed his way through the undergrowth. He paused a moment, stood straighter and adjusted his tattered cloak, allowing his men to gather behind him, then marched across the clearing towards the embankment. The alarm was sounded when he was spotted, and warriors rapidly appeared, clad in mail and brandishing swords and spears. Cuirasses and banners bore the emblem of a burning torch upon a pale field.

Gundul's warband, then. Excellent. He is far weaker than Lothar, and much easier to manipulate.

Jael strode to a warrior standing amidst what was rapidly becoming a bristling hedge of sharp iron, already imagining that they were *his* warriors. *His* warband.

'Take me to your King,' Jael demanded imperiously.

Jael paused for a moment on the road down which warriors of Carnutan were leading him. He'd walked a good half-league away from the forefront of this new road, built upon a fresh-piled embankment with the forest stripped back to either side. Wains were moving up and down the road, warriors lining it. Gundul's camp appeared: a sprawling mass to the south of the new road, at its centre a huge tent upon a low hill.

'How many?' he whispered to Dag, who strode a step behind him. The rest of his tattered warband had been left at the side of the road.

'Three, four thousand swords,' the huntsman said with a shrug. 'Hard to tell with all the other hangers-on.'

They weaved through the camp, a host of sounds and smells assailing Jael as he was guided through a maze of tents and cook-fires; cattle lowed from paddocks, the stink of human habitation wafting towards him. After being a refugee in this otherworldly and oppressive forest for so long, he felt almost overwhelmed by it. The tent Jael had spied from the road rose up before him, larger than it had at first appeared. His escort of a few score warriors led him purposefully towards it.

Gundul.

A circle of pale-skinned and black-eyed warriors stood guard about the tent, clothed in dark mail and leather, curved swords arching over their shoulders.

Nathair's Jehar. A score of them had marched with his own warband, with Sumur as their captain. He remembered Sumur's skill in battle, the fury of the others as they had charged into battle. And the winged *things* that poured from them like poison when they fell. His skin crawled.

Whatever they are, they are not men. But whatever they are, they still died, still failed me. So much for Nathair's great warriors. He felt an irrational anger about that, even as he felt fear and revulsion crawling across his skin. He regarded the Jehar before him suspiciously.

What are you?

Respect them, don't fear them, he reminded himself. *They die the same as the rest of us – Sumur fell to Corban, and the rest no doubt during the battle before the gates of Drassil.*

A pair of warriors parted before Jael. One opened the tent flap and Jael entered, Dag still a step behind.

The tent was luxuriously furnished, thick furs carpeting the ground and gold-trimmed tapestries draping the walls. Perfumed candles burned, their scent thick and heavy in the air.

Gundul was sitting on a wide-backed chair, one leg draped across the chair's arm, women clad in diaphanous silk feeding him from various platters. A handful of young men lounged about him, their hair and beards slick and shining with oil; all of them were immaculately dressed in velvets and soft skins.

Look at them, fawning sycophants gathered about the pot of gold. Not a single one of them looks like they've held a blade in battle.

Jael suppressed a sneer.

'Well met, Gundul,' he said as he strode forwards.

Gundul studied him, a blank expression replaced slowly with recognition. He shifted in his chair, but did not rise.

'Well, if it isn't Jael of Isiltir,' Gundul said, a flaccid smile spreading across his face.

King of Isiltir, Jael silently corrected as he returned a forced smile.

'I did not recognize you,' Gundul said, taking a long moment to look Jael up and down. Jael was abruptly aware of his appearance. When he rode to the gates of Drassil he had been dressed in his finest war gear: a coat of gleaming chainmail, sable cloak trimmed with fur, breeches and boots of doeskin. Now his cloak was mud-crusted and in tatters, his chainmail smeared and rusting, his face and arms grimy and scratched beyond counting.

'What a wonderful surprise,' Gundul said with a barely disguised smirk. 'I had heard that you were lost, presumed dead, after your defeat by the rabble at Drassil. I rejoice that you live.'

Then why do you look so disappointed? Already planning the annexation of my realm, I'd guess. Nothing made Jael angrier than the thought of someone else stealing the realm he had so recently stolen for himself. He suppressed the urge to wrap his fingers around Gundul's throat. *If he thinks he can take Isiltir from me I will make him eat his own intestines.*

'A sentiment I share, I can assure you,' Jael said, strapping his smile upon his face. 'The enemy at Drassil used fell magic against us. Alas, brave hearts and strong arms were not enough against the dark powers of Asroth's Black Sun.'

'Really?' Gundul said, a more genuine smile twitching his lips. He sat straighter in his chair. 'Nathair had little trouble against their *fell magic.*'

'What do you mean?' Jael asked.

'King Nathair took Drassil over a ten-night ago. The enemy are broken and scattered.'

'What? The war is over?'

'Well, from what I hear, there is some resistance still, but little more than the death throes of a foe that has not realized its already lost.'

The war over, and my own warband defeated? I had hoped for more time, to return to Isiltir and raise a new warband, fresh battles and win some glory, before the war was ended. But now . . .

'That is wonderful news,' Jael said, speaking through a fixed grin. 'I can see that your road-building is going well. If I could ask one favour . . . ?'

'What do you want?' Gundul asked, looking suddenly bored with the conversation.

He thinks me broken, a defeated rival of no consequence. Jael stopped his teeth from grinding.

'Horses, for myself and my men. An escort back to Isiltir.'

'Your men?' Gundul sniffed, looking disdainfully at Dag, who stood silently behind Jael. One of the young men gathered about Gundul sniggered.

Calm. Get what you need. Just remember the sycophant's face.

'Yes, King Gundul,' Jael said in his most comradely voice. 'My warband are currently resting after their exertions.'

'How many?' Gundul frowned.

'Around three hundred,' Jael said.

'I am not sure that counts as a warband,' Gundul smiled slyly and Jael's fingers twitched. 'But even so, three hundred horses – I doubt I can spare so many. All my resources are going into building this road, you understand. I *will* reach Drassil before Lothar.'

So the race is still on.

'Perhaps we can help each other, then,' Jael said.

'How could you possibly help me?' Gundul sneered, looking pointedly at Jael's tattered appearance.

Jael bit back a harsh response and stood straighter. 'I am still the King of Isiltir. I could bring fresh workers to build your road – two thousand at least, maybe more.'

Gundul's smile broadened and he sat straight in his chair, waving away the servants offering him platters of food. 'You shall have your horses,' he said.

Jael opened his mouth to speak but paused, the faint sound of shouting was filtering through the tent's opening. Gundul heard it too and held his hand up to a man who was trying to whisper in his ear.

The noises rapidly grew louder, shouts turning to screams, punctuated with the distinct sound of iron clashing. Jael glanced at Dag, who stood poised like an animal on the edge of flight, one hand upon the hilt of his dagger.

'We need to leave,' the huntsman hissed to Jael.

'What *is* that?' Gundul snapped, standing, fear and worry flickering across his features.

It is battle, something that I don't think you are fully acquainted with.

Gundul strode from the tent, his gaggle of followers tight behind him. Jael and Dag slipped out after them.

Outside, Gundul was stood on the slope of the hill, staring with a look of confused disbelief towards the northern fringe of his camp. Warriors were pouring onto the road from its far side, cutting into the milling guards and workers. Jael saw resistance sluggishly forming, warriors from Gundul's warband attempting to form a defensive line across the road, but before they could organize themselves they were locked in combat with their assailants. Within moments the attackers had burst through the hastily formed resistance and were streaming down the embankment into the camp.

Asroth's stones, what now?

The Jehar on the hillside were drawing close about Gundul, black eyes staring.

'We need to get out of here,' Dag repeated.

'What's going *on*?' Gundul cried, part temper, part hysteria.

'It would appear you were right,' Jael said, not able to keep the smirk from his face at the sound of terror in Gundul's voice, even though he felt the coils of fear squirming in his own belly. 'The enemy that you said did not know they were beaten; they appear to be attacking you.'

CHAPTER ELEVEN

MAQUIN

Maquin gazed through foliage at the sprawling camp, feeling his body tense and fingers twitch for his knife hilt as he watched Krelis' men appear on the road and engage Gundul's men. Crouched on the far south of the camp, he saw a few dozen enemy guards standing with their backs to him in an open space cleared between the camp and the treeline. They looked unsure of what to do. The man beside Maquin gripped his sword and took a step forwards.

'Wait,' Maquin whispered, seizing the warrior's arm. 'Not till Krelis hits the camp.'

Maquin had been given the command of a hundred men and they were spread loosely around him, hidden in the shadows and foliage. Only one thing had he said to them before they'd moved into position: 'When I go, keep with me.'

Their task was to attack from the south and sweep up through the camp, spreading as much mayhem and panic along the way as was possible. Maquin was unused to leading men. The Vin Thalun fighting-pits had honed his will to survive, teaching him that above all else you fight for yourself.

But that is what Lykos wanted. To break me, to strip away my loyalties, to make me less than human. I will not be that man again.

The main attack was to be led by Krelis, his first objective to clear the new road of all resistance; it was there that their scouts had reported most of Gundul's warband were to be found. Once the road was clear Krelis was to assault the camp, which was the signal for the others. Maquin and Alben were leading smaller groups hidden to the west and south of the camp; the plan was to meet Krelis and his force at the command tent situated on a hill close to the camp's centre.

At the thought of it Maquin's eyes drifted to the tent on the mound. Men were appearing from its entrance, standing and staring at the commotion that Krelis was causing.

Gundul – it must be.

Two other men emerged from the tent, hanging back from the rest. One of them seemed . . . familiar, in the way he walked, his posture, a confidence.

Then dark-clothed figures were appearing from around the hill, drawing tight about those who had emerged from the tent. Even from this distance there was something clearly different about them.

Kadoshim. Damn it. We're outnumbered as it is, without those hell-spawn to complicate things. He shrugged to himself, knew they were committed now and there was no turning back. *And this whole attack was my idea. So I'd best be getting to that tent and making sure we win this thing.*

He looked back to the road and saw Krelis' warriors pouring down the embankment and into the camp.

Good.

With a battle-cry he exploded into motion, bursting from the treeline, drawing a knife in each hand as he sped towards the guards spread between him and the camp. A few paces behind him his hundred followed. He heard a distant roar from the west, knew that Alben and his warriors were doing the same.

Maquin ducked a spear-thrust and crashed into the man holding it, one of his knives punching through leather into flesh, ripping it free as his momentum carried him on, leaving the man on his knees, hands clutching at his belly. In moments the guards along the camp's edge were either dead or fleeing, the sudden onslaught of Maquin and his warriors too much for them.

Maquin gathered his warriors and charged into the camp, kicking at fires, smashing gates open, freeing cattle, hacking and slashing at anyone who got in their way. In heartbeats flames were licking at tents and smoke was billowing; stampeding cattle knocked men flying, the whole world seemed to dissolve into chaos. Maquin turned a corner and almost ran into a dozen warriors, the ensuing combat savage and short, Maquin's knives finding throats and arteries as he slipped through them like a violent wind, the men following him crashing upon those still standing.

He sped through the camp, a knife dripping blood in each hand, leaving a trail of bodies in his wake. As he travelled deeper, any kind of resistance melted away: those he came across ran from him, and he was happy to let them go. For the most part they were not Gundul's warriors, but merchants, smiths, tanners, cobblers, drovers, whores and bairns. *I may be a killer, but I'll not slay the innocent.*

Soon the initial red mist of battle began to fade and he glanced behind, saw the black and silver of Ripa's warriors following him.

Not used to leading men these days, or being in a fight this big. Mustn't forget they're with me. Mustn't forget the plan.

Pausing, he gave his men a chance to gather behind him as he tried to get his bearings. Screams and the concussive clash of iron drifted down from the north.

Krelis sounds closer. Best get to that command tent. Gundul must die for this to succeed, and to do that we must carve a way through his Kadoshim. He reached up to his shoulder and felt the hilt of a short sword, one of a pair strapped across his back. Maquin preferred using his knives, but taking heads from Kadoshim was sword work.

He set off again. Close-packed tents suddenly gave way to an open space – cook-fires spread about it, tents forming a loose circle. Weapons racks were rowed along one edge; a mass of men were pulling spears from stands, strapping on helms, hefting shields. Maquin skidded to a halt, realizing what he had stumbled upon.

A barracks for the warriors of this warband.

With a snarl he ran at them.

He hit a knot of men before they had any time to react, his knives tracing a red ruin across their bodies. In moments he was through them and hurling himself at a new wall of men. Weapons thrust at him, but the battle-rage was upon him, the world seeming to slow and he twisted and flowed around every blow aimed at him, his knives licking out to slice throats, puncture groins, cut hamstrings. Dimly he heard the clash of arms behind him, knew his men were following. Faces appeared before him, grim, fearful, shocked; all fell to his twin blades.

His progress slowed. The men crammed together now, his ability to move and sway hindered by a crush of bodies. A quick glance showed his men behind him, fighting furiously, but they were out-numbered and the enemy was beginning to curl around their flanks. Surprise and savagery had taken them so far, but had not broken their foe.

Things are about to get messy. Maquin stepped to the right, deflected a thrust aimed at the ribs of one of his men, slashed across the face of the attacker, kicked another in the knee, saw him buckle and stepped close to cut his throat.

There was a great crash and a concussion that undulated through the hard-pressed warriors.

Someone else joining this party.

Maquin glimpsed a giant figure: Alcyon, wielding two woodsman's axes as Maquin was using his knives, carving a way through the enemy like a scythe at harvest time. Heads and limbs flew through the air in great gouts of blood.

Alben's crew. Maquin grinned and leaped at his enemy, new strength powering his muscles. Within moments Gundul's warriors were wavering, a ripple of doubt and fear spreading through them, and then they were fleeing. Maquin buried a knife in a back, ripped it free and stood over the collapsing figure, gore-covered and breathing heavily. He saw Alcyon decapitate one more fleeing warrior, his wife Raina and their son Tain either side of him, Alben's warriors spread about them.

'Well met,' a voice said and Maquin turned to see Alben striding towards him. The old man was pale and had blood seeping from the bandage around his shoulder.

I told him to stay at our camp. He'd have been better off there, and I'd have been happier knowing someone of his skill was guarding Fidele. He felt a wave of fear for her, as he did every time that he was parted from her, but this was war, they both knew that she could not be here, in the midst of this.

'Well met,' Maquin replied, sheathing a knife and gripping the old man's arm. He left bloodstained fingerprints. 'Think you might just have saved my skin.'

Alben looked around at the bodies piled about Maquin and throughout the barrack ground.

'I doubt that,' he said. He glanced up through the rolling smoke at the hill that loomed not far away.

'Gundul,' Maquin said.

'Aye. Let's go and find him.'

Both of their warbands were about them now.

'There's Kadoshim on that hill,' Maquin said loudly. 'They don't die easily; remember, you must take their heads.' Alben and others nodded grimly.

Maquin grinned at them, then ran for the hill.

Clouds of smoke billowed about him, parted for a moment, and he saw the hill, the huge and gaudy tent upon it strangely out of place in the sombre gloom of Forn.

Maquin ran faster, the camp a place of flame and shadow, the thud of his comrades' feet behind him, screams and battle-cries swirling on the eddying smoke, then the ground began to rise and he burst from the haze and tents, Alben, Alcyon and their men only a few paces behind him.

Men were still on the hill, but they were retreating, at least three score of the Kadoshim that encircled them were herding them north-east, towards the newest part of the road.

They're fleeing, running for Drassil. And further along the road there'll be more reinforcements. Can't let them reach that road.

Maquin sheathed his knives and drew the two short swords as he ran.

The space between them narrowed quickly. Maquin and those with him were silent, no battle-cries, only the drum of their feet and the jangle and creak of mail and leather. Abruptly Gundul and the Kadoshim were aware of them, Gundul yelling orders. A score of the Kadoshim peeled away from the group, curved swords being drawn from behind their backs. One fixed its black eyes on Maquin and ran at him, a dark grin splitting its pallid face. Maquin felt a fist of fear squirm in his belly, remembering their ferocity and other-worldliness when he'd encountered them previously. He growled in anger at his own fear and ran faster.

The first Kadoshim almost took his head, its sword whistling a finger's width above him as he threw himself into a roll, coming to his feet behind the creature, his own strike at its neck blocked with blinding speed, his second blade slicing through the back of its leg as it spun to face him. Maquin leaped away, the creature stumbling as it tried to follow, its hamstrings cut. Even so it was unnaturally fast, lurching after him.

It should be on the ground, not still trying to gut me.

All around him his warriors were locked in combat with the Kadoshim. Battle-cries and death screams rang out. He glimpsed Alben take a head, saw that terrible black vapour fill the air. His distraction nearly cost Maquin his life as his attacker launched a combination of two-handed blows at him. He parried two and slipped inside the third, instinctively punching a short sword into its belly. The Kadoshim's mouth gaped wide, foul breath washing over him as its teeth snapped, trying to fasten on his throat. He head-butted it, pushed away, leaving one sword in its belly, his other blade whistling around to crunch into its collarbone, blood and bone spraying as he wrenched it free and hacked again, this time cutting deep into the creature's neck. He darted in, swerving away from its curved sword, chopping at its neck to finish the job. Somehow the Kadoshim's hand snaked out and caught his blade in its fist. A finger flew through the air but still it held on, as it tried to bring its own sword round to bear. Maquin grabbed its sword wrist and for a few heartbeats they lurched together in an ungainly dance. Within seconds Maquin knew he could not win a contest of strength: the Kadoshim's grip was unnaturally strong. Then, in the blink of an eye, its head was spinning through the air and Alben's face appeared before him. The Kadoshim's body slumped, fist still gripped around Maquin's sword-blade, oily black smoke pouring from the open wound of its neck. A winged creature formed in the air above him and screamed wordless hatred at him, then the wind caught it and it was gone.

Maquin sagged, Alben's hand reaching out to steady him.

'There's no getting used to that,' Maquin breathed as he yanked his swords free of the creature's corpse.

He looked around, saw more of the demon forms appearing in the air above them and then evaporating. At a glance it seemed that most of those Kadoshim that had attacked them had fallen, though many of Maquin's and Alben's men were lying still and silent upon the ground. As Maquin watched, Alcyon, Raina and Tain dispatched the last Kadoshim.

'Gundul?' Maquin breathed.

'Down there,' Alben gestured.

Maquin saw the King of Carnutan disappearing amongst the tents, far more Kadoshim still about him than Maquin had hoped to see. Two men were moving with them. One of them paused as the others disappeared from view and looked back, for a moment Maquin's eyes locked with him. He staggered, felt as if he'd just been punched in the gut.

It cannot be.

Maquin's heart was suddenly pounding in his chest, a wave of shock spilling into fury.

Jael.

CHAPTER TWELVE

JAEL

Jael stood and stared at the warriors on the hill.

One man had emerged ahead of the others, blood-soaked and battle-grim, a short sword in each hand. He was staring back at Jael, and although they were a good hundred paces apart, Jael was certain he saw hatred twist the man's features.

There is something familiar about him . . .

'My lord,' Dag said, pulling at his sleeve. 'We must keep moving.'

They were following the Jehar that were shepherding Gundul and his retinue of lackeys to safety, hoping that the Jehar would guard Jael and Dag as well as the others as they passed through the camp. Jael had heard the sounds of battle from the hilltop and paused to watch the bloody work of the handful of Jehar warriors that had remained behind. They had fallen, but then it was a score against close to two hundred, and even so the Jehar had decimated their enemy.

As Jael stared he saw the man burst into motion, running hard towards him, screaming Jael's name.

He knows me!

Jael took an involuntary step back.

Doesn't seem to like me much, though.

Who?

Then he knew.

Maquin.

He had changed almost beyond all recognition: slimmer than Jael remembered him, his body chiselled, arms and legs a striated mass of muscle, face a place of ridges, scars and hate-filled eyes.

How is he here? He should be dead, or at least a thousand leagues from here, and in shackles.

Jael remembered the last time he had seen Maquin, on the bridge at Dun Kellen, chained and being dragged away by Lykos to a Vin Thalun slave-ship.

The fool had challenged me to the court of swords, insulted me in front of my men. From the look on Maquin's face, that court of swords was still high on his agenda.

Jael gulped. If Maquin's expression did not convince him that it was time to go, the warriors charging down the hill behind Maquin did. There were giants amongst them.

'This way,' Dag snapped at him as they entered a maze of tents, banks of thick smoke rolling through it, the shouts and screams of battle drifting and swirling all about them. Footsteps drummed on the turf of the hill somewhere behind him and the Jehar were nowhere to be seen. Panic clenched a fist in his gut.

'JAEL,' a voice screamed behind him.

Keep running.

Then he saw Dag, the huntsman moving fast, head dipped, scanning the ground. Jael followed him around a tent, ran down an empty isle of churned mud and barrels piled high, then turned again and saw the dark figures of the Jehar hurrying ahead of them. Relief swept him and he picked up his pace, he and Dag steadily catching up with Gundul and his protectors.

They were close to the Jehar now, only a score of paces separating them. A final burst of speed and Jael was at their heels. He tried to shoulder his way between two of them and enter their protective circle, but one turned and fixed him with its black, dead eyes.

'Let me through,' Jael gasped. 'I am Jael, King of Isiltir, you must protect me.'

The Jehar warrior cocked its head at him, then it pushed Jael back, sending him stumbling. Dag reached out and steadied him.

Shouldn't have left my men on the roadside.

'Need . . . my . . . men,' Jael breathed to Dag.

'Think this lot are going that way,' Dag said. 'Safer to travel with them.'

'Aye,' Jael muttered. He saw Dag surreptitiously glance down corridors made by rows of tents.

He looks as if he's thinking of slinking off. Would probably do the same if I was him.

'Gold,' Jael hacked out of his burning lungs. *I need this man.*

'What?'

'Gold, for you. When you get me to Mikil. More than you can carry, more than you've ever dreamed of.'

'I've dreamed of a lot of gold, in my time,' Dag said.

'You've earned it,' Jael breathed.

'Reckon I have,' Dag muttered. A greedy smile crept across his face. 'I'll get you to Mikil,' the huntsman said.

The sounds of battle suddenly grew louder. A knot of enemy warriors clothed in black and silver appeared ahead of them.

They look like Nathair's colours.

Jael drew his sword as a warrior lurched before him: one of Gundul's men, his sword wildly parrying a flurry of blows from a warrior in black and silver. Jael stabbed his sword into the attacker's side. Ripping his sword free, he pushed the dying man away and leaped over him, eyes searching for Dag, his heart pounding desperately when he could not see him.

'This way,' Dag called to him.

Something slammed into Jael's back.

He flew through the air, weightless for a moment, then hit the ground, air crushed from his lungs, and he was sliding in the mud, rolling. He came to a stop and rose to one knee, trying to ignore the pain in his chest and shoulder, hand grasping for his sword hilt, looking back to see a lunatic covered in blood rising from the ground.

Maquin.

Run! Jael's mind screamed at him, but he knew he would not make it. Maquin was too close for him to make a safe escape. Jael rose to his feet and hefted his sword.

I am the finest sword in Isiltir. I slew Kastell in single combat, and he was a great swordsman, in his prime, not old and half-mad like this man before me. He set his feet and raised his blade.

The world around him faded, the battle raging only a handful of strides away dimmed as a cold focus settled upon him, as it always did when he committed to the blade.

'Come,' he shouted, 'and I'll send you to meet Kastell.'

He'd thought to anger Maquin, unbalance him with rage, as

angry men make mistakes. By the look on Maquin's face his tactic worked. The man gripped his second blade and launched himself forwards, face twisted in a snarl.

He's moving too fast. A smile twitched at Jael's lips as he stepped forwards to meet Maquin, lunging as he did so, his sword-tip aimed straight at Maquin's heart.

His own speed will impale him, the idiot. He's a dead man.

But then Jael was stabbing into empty air, Maquin no longer where he was supposed to be. A blow slammed into Jael's side, crunching into his ribs, white pain exploding in his chest as he dropped to one knee. The sudden urge to vomit almost consumed him.

He's broken my ribs, he realized in shock, his hand probing at his side, all the chainmail links bent and broken.

Move or die.

Jael heaved himself to his feet, raised his sword and pivoted on his heel, but the expected blow never came at him. Instead Maquin was standing a few paces away, just staring at him.

'I've waited a long time for this,' Maquin said, his voice as cold and hard as frosted iron. 'Killing you quick's too good for you.'

A seed of fear blossomed in Jael's chest, the utter confidence in Maquin's eyes chilling him.

Don't be a fool, I've watched him train on the weapons court. I know his strengths, his weaknesses. He's old, slow. I know I can beat him.

'Kastell said something similar, just before I bled him like a sow,' Jael said, trying to keep the pain of his splintered ribs out of his voice.

Maquin came at him, slowly this time. Jael noticed knife hilts protruding from half a dozen places on Maquin – two on his belt, a shoulder strap, a hilt poking from a boot.

One of Maquin's short swords trailed a lazy circle as the battle-scarred warrior rolled a wrist, then, almost faster than Jael could follow, Maquin was striking at him. Jael staggered backwards, pain from his ribs exploding with every breath and step as he blocked Maquin's blows, each parry more ragged than the last.

He's as fast as the Jehar – it's impossible. What's happened to him? Panic threatened Jael now, as a line of white fire ignited along one thigh where Maquin cut him, moving too fast for him to defend against, another wound appearing on his forearm, a slash across his forehead sending him tumbling backwards as blood sheeted into his eyes.

Jael lay on his back, an arm wiping the blood from his eyes. Looking up, he saw grey sky veiled by the trees of Forn, and then Maquin appeared, looming over him. His face was latticed with scars, one ear mostly gone, just a lump of flesh remaining, his hair more grey than black.

Jael searched the ground for the hilt of his sword, felt its worn leather and snatched at it. Maquin's boot crunched into his ribs as the old warrior kicked him.

Jael screamed, rolled over, vomited bile into the mud.

'When you see Kastell, be sure and tell him I kept my oath,' Maquin said above him.

This can't be happening. He's OLD!

Jael rolled onto his back, arms raised, wanting to beg for mercy but he couldn't seem to get his lungs to work properly; only a blubbering wheeze came from his gaping mouth.

Maquin raised one of his swords.

Then there was a crunch and Maquin was gone.

He turned his head and saw Maquin borne to the ground, grappling with another figure, small and wiry.

Dag. I love that man!

Jael climbed to his knees, grabbed his sword and levered himself to his feet, a wave of dizziness and nausea threatening him as his broken ribs complained. All around him men were fighting, the Jehar seemingly reduced to a handful, and more men in black and silver joining the battle. Gundul and his protectors were nowhere to be seen.

I need to get out of here.

Maquin and Dag were still fighting, Maquin's short swords lying in the mud, a knife glinting in Dag's fist. Jael stumbled towards them, raised his sword, waiting for a clear thrust at Maquin.

A new battle-cry rose up, this one deep and alien. The giant he had seen in Maquin's company had appeared from out of the smoke and chaos, two more giants behind him, as well as a knot of warriors in black and silver. The first giant saw him and bellowed, then charged at him, all those behind him following. Jael felt the ground tremble. He glanced down at Dag and Maquin.

I need Maquin dead, and Dag alive. He is going to get me back to Isiltir.

Jael looked back up at the onrushing giant and the swarm of sharp iron behind it.

He turned and ran.

CHAPTER THIRTEEN

FIDELE

Fidele paced around the cold ash of the fire-pit. In the distance she could hear the screams of battle and the clash of iron.

They say I am queen, that I must do my duty and lead the men of Tenebral, yet they leave me here with a score of men, guarded like a prisoner. To keep me safe. How is this leading?

She muttered a string of curses under her breath; some of the shieldmen left to guard her glanced at her. A smile twitched the mouth of one.

I should not be here.

When Maquin had suggested the attack on Gundul's camp she had known instantly that it was the right thing to do, and the thought of *doing*, of attacking instead of running, had its own heady appeal. Fidele had seen the others warm to the idea quickly and had felt a jolt of pride in Maquin, seeing him listened to by the lords of Ripa. Not that it had surprised her. She'd recognized something rare in Maquin during their escape through Tenebral: intelligence and strength, and a lack of ego. He had the ability to look at a situation and know what had to be done. And then to do it, with absolute commitment, or die in the trying.

More screams echoed through the forest, the din of battle ebbing and flowing, and she ground her teeth in frustration.

I will not be a bystander, or a leader that does not lead.

She brushed the knife hilt at her belt and strode away from the cold fire-pit towards a rack of weapons, gripped a slim-shafted spear and hefted it, testing its weight. For a moment she was back in Tenebral, in the forest with Maquin, fighting her fear as she plunged a spear into the throat of a Vin Thalun warrior.

'My lady?' one of the warriors said questioningly.

'I am going to the battle,' Fidele said.

'What? Is that . . . wise?' The warrior blinked. 'My lady,' he added. He was not young, by the look of him he was a veteran of battle, a scar running through the red and silver of his beard.

But unused to talking to queens, it appears.

'What is your name?' she asked him.

'Agost, my lady,' he said.

'Well, Agost, I am going to see how the battle fares.'

'But, Alben—'

'Is not my lord, and does not command me,' Fidele finished for him. 'My people are out there, fighting; my place is with them. I have seen war and dark deeds,' she continued, louder, for all to hear. 'I am no stranger to blood, and right now the men of Tenebral are spilling theirs. I'll not stand hidden and await the outcome. Though we are few in number we could still be needed at some hard-pressed moment. Battles have turned on less.' She looked around at their faces, saw the eagerness in their eyes, knew they did not want to be standing guard over her when their shield-brothers were dying.

With that she gripped her spear like a staff and marched resolutely out of the camp.

The sound of battle grew steadily louder as they moved through the forest, Agost and a few others slipping in front of her, a protective hand.

Agost paused, held his hand up, and they stopped.

'What?' Fidele whispered.

'Someone's out there,' Agost said, pointing deeper into the forest, away from the sound of battle. He signalled and a handful of men followed him into the trees, disappearing into the shadows. For a hundred heartbeats Fidele heard nothing, then shouting, a clash of iron. Voices.

'My lady,' Agost's voice called and Fidele stepped through the trees, the remainder of her guard about her.

Agost and his warriors stood with three men, all clothed in leather and fur, beards braided and bound with leather. Axes hung at their belts, single-bladed and short-hafted. There was a hardness about these men that Fidele was used to seeing in veterans of battle.

'Tell her what you told me,' Agost said.

'We come from Drassil,' one said, 'sent south in search of allies.'
'Allies for whom?' Fidele asked. 'Who do you fight for?'
'We fight for Corban, the Bright Star,' the three men said together.

CHAPTER FOURTEEN

MAQUIN

Maquin rolled in the dirt, grunting as his attacker butted him in the mouth. He spat blood into the man's face, butted him back and felt the grip on his wrist loosen, then he was rolling free, pulling a knife from his boot.

The man facing him climbed to his feet. He was small, lean with wiry muscle, face a burn-scarred mess.

We have much in common.

'Whatever he promised you, Jael's not worth it,' Maquin growled.

'Gold's always worth it,' the man snarled back, pulling a knife of his own from a sheath at his back.

Maquin lunged in, their blades clashing, sparking, Maquin ducking a hooked punch, pivoting away, swaying back in close, knife stabbing for his enemy's throat. He was blocked, the man backing away. They parted and circled, Maquin crouched and circling like a stalking wolf.

A bellowing roar rang out. Maquin's eyes were drawn to the battle about them. Alcyon was there, hacking with his two woodsman's axes at a Kadoshim that was standing over another giant figure – *Alcyon's son?* The Kadoshim's head arced through the air, black mist hissing from the collapsing corpse.

A scuffing of earth drew Maquin back to his enemy. He swayed left, avoided a knife in the eye, kicked out, his foot connecting with a knee, heard cartilage crunch, then Maquin was in close, plunging his knife into his enemy's belly. He twisted the blade, ripped it free and shoved the slumping figure away.

'Can't take gold where you're going,' Maquin grunted at the dying man.

He didn't answer, eyes already glazing and vacant.

The battle around him was all but done, the Kadoshim that had fallen back from Gundul's honour guard all slain, though many men had fallen to their blades. A scattering of Gundul's other warriors were still fighting against the black and silver of Krelis' men, but they were all but broken. Maquin stared into the distance, searching for Jael.

But I know the direction he was running. His eyes lifted over the tents to look towards the road and embankment that cut into Forn Forest.

Fastest way out of here.

Alcyon and Raina were lifting their son from the ground. Maquin approached them, retrieving his short swords as he did so. The giant-ling was loose-limbed, a cut on his temple swelling, but other than that he looked well enough.

'He'll live,' Maquin said. Then, 'My thanks, for following me.'

The giant shrugged. 'Raina has spoken to me of you, of what you did for her and Tain.'

Maquin didn't know what to say about that. He looked beyond the giant, saw a scattering of the warriors who had been put under his command, realized that the sight of Jael had driven all else from his mind.

'Alben?' he asked.

'On the hill, waiting for Krelis,' the giant said.

'I'm here,' a voice called: Krelis, emerging from an aisle between tents. He was blood soaked and grinning. 'Remind me to listen to you next time you say you have a plan,' he said to Maquin.

'The plan's not done until Gundul's dead,' Maquin said.

'Aye. Where is that little snot-nosed arseling? Alben got him trussed up on the hill?'

'No,' Maquin grunted. 'He's fled, with a few score Kadoshim about him. That way.' He pointed.

'Well, what are we doing standing here flapping our jaws, then?'

'Just what I was thinking.'

Krelis tugged on his beard, eyes narrowing as he looked the way Gundul had fled. 'Best go and tell Alben to follow us,' Krelis said to Maquin. 'We'll need all the swords we can muster against those damn Kadoshim.'

'Send someone else,' Maquin said as he strode away. 'I'm going after Gundul.'

And Jael.

CHAPTER FIFTEEN

VERADIS

'Shield wall,' Veradis shouted, lifting his borrowed shield and expecting those either side of him to lock into place. There was a sporadic thudding as shields came up, lacking the controlled discipline that he was used to.

These men are not my Draig's Teeth, not veterans of a score of battles in the shield wall. He bit back a curse. *I am lucky they are here at all.*

When Veradis had spoken of using the shield wall to clear the road, Krelis had curled a lip in disgust. Veradis' brother had never liked the idea of men fighting in such a way; to him it lacked honour.

'It works, and it will save lives.' Even as Veradis had said the words he'd heard Nathair's voice echoing them in his mind.

'Your task is to keep the road clear and then to hold it,' Alben had said, stepping in between the two brothers. 'How you do it is your decision, Veradis. Only guard our backs and stop the reinforcements that will surely come from further along the road.'

Krelis had said no more, and so the plan had proceeded, Krelis attacking the road from the north, Alben and Maquin spearheading two smaller groups into the camp, Veradis and his reserve group holding the road as Krelis moved on to the main camp, and guarding against the counter-attack that would inevitably come.

So far it had all gone remarkably smoothly: the enemy breaking and scattering, surprise and ferocity shattering any resistance before it had a chance to form fully.

It's amazing what a small and focused force can do against a larger, unprepared one.

He took a deep breath, knew that battle was close, tried to calm the anger he felt bubbling away inside his chest. That was his overwhelming emotion, right now. Anger. He was angry with Calidus, for the web of lies and deception he had woven, and for what he had done to Nathair, but that was nothing beside the anger he felt for his old friend. *Nathair, how could you believe Calidus? Why did you not resist, or come to me sooner? We could have stood against Calidus together.* And most of all, he was angry with himself. *I am a fool. How did I not see it all happening about me? Veradis the loyal. Veradis the trust-worthy. Veradis the blind idiot, I say.*

Calm yourself. Focus, you have a battle to fight.

He had gathered his two hundred on the embankment to the north-east of the camp, at the point where the road left the camp behind and ploughed into the forest. From this vantage point Veradis had watched Krelis, Alben and Maquin flood through the camp with their small bands of men. Fires and great clouds of smoke marked their paths as they moved ever deeper, inexorably towards the hill with Gundul's command tent on it. He'd seen movement on the hill, what looked like combat, though it was hard to discern any details because of the distance. Now the flames and smoke were so dense that it was hard to see anything at all, but Veradis' attention was needed elsewhere, anyway. To his left, in the depths of Forn, men were approaching along the road. Veradis saw a knot of warriors in mail and leather at the front and centre of a much larger horde that spilt down the embankments to either side.

At least a thousand strong.

Finally the shields either side of Veradis locked into his. He felt the urge to order the march, knew that the shield wall moving towards a larger foe had always caused hesitation and sown seeds of fear in the enemy, but he was uncertain of the men about him. Just getting into formation on the road and forming the shield wall had seemed to tax them. He glanced at the warrior to his right – a young man, his beard a straggly thing.

Young! I know him; it is Balen. He is only a few years younger than I. We used to spar together. But Veradis felt older than his years, knew that his travels and experience in the shield wall set him apart from most of those about him.

I cannot expect too much from them, yet. They only know this much because Nathair ordered that all men of Tenebral were drilled in the shield wall.

It will have to do, Veradis thought. *Marching may be a step too far. We'll wait here for them. We fill the road and block the path to the camp, so they'll have to cut us down and march through us to get at Krelis' flank.*

Looking at the men around him, earnest, brave men a thousand leagues from home, he felt some of his anger drain, replaced with sympathy and a deep sense of responsibility for them.

'Balen, listen to me,' Veradis said to the warrior beside him. The man returned his gaze and Veradis saw fear in his eyes.

'Follow my orders and we'll come through this.'

The warrior nodded at him, then looked away.

Shouts and challenges grew louder as the enemy came closer.

'If they get past us, our kin and sword-brothers die!' Veradis yelled, feeling the blood begin to surge through his veins, fear and excitement merging into the exhilaration that he always felt before battle. 'Remember your oaths and fight for your sword-brother beside you.'

He felt Balen stand straighter alongside him.

They were inexperienced, but to the warband of Gundul that was approaching him the shield wall was like nothing they had ever seen before. Veradis saw the front ranks of the enemy slow, close enough now to see looks of confusion and worry upon their faces.

Warriors are a superstitious bunch, always wary of the unknown.

'Swords,' Veradis shouted, drawing the short blade at his hip. About and behind him he heard the hiss of iron leaving leather. He began to thump his hilt upon the wooden boards of his shield, the rhythmic pounding taken up first by those about him, then spreading, rippling through the deep wall of two hundred men. He saw its effect upon those approaching, warriors hesitating in their steps, uncertainty spreading like a mist. Then one warrior stepped from the crowd, a big man, clad in mail, a helm of iron, his sword raised high. He bellowed a wordless challenge and ran at Veradis' wall of shields. A trickle of men followed him, warriors from the centre, then others – warriors, woodsmen and labourers from the flanks, all screaming blood and murder.

'Ready!' Veradis roared, spreading his feet and leaning forwards into his shield. A thread of fear clenched in his belly as it always did in this moment, when battle was inevitable but not yet joined.

Then men were crashing into his shield, blows raining upon it, shuddering through his wrist and arm, into his shoulder, numbing muscle and sinew, and the fear was gone. A face appeared above his shield rim, snarling at him.

'NOW,' Veradis bellowed, stabbing his short sword through the thin gap between his shield and Balen's, to either side warriors doing the same. He felt his blade bite into flesh, drew it back red, stabbed again. The face above his shield rim disappeared, replaced by another. He stabbed again, felt his blade turn on mail, drew it back and stabbed lower, heard a scream, kept stabbing, not frantically as Balen was doing beside him, but steady, a rhythm to it.

'Easy,' Veradis barked at Balen, 'they're not going anywhere.'

Balen shot him a glance, eyes wide and white, but his blade work became less frantic.

Men fell, blood sluicing down Veradis' blade, soaking his hand, muscles burning, the unrelenting thud of blows against his shield pushing his straining body to its limits. Sinews screamed against the constant pressure as men piled against the shield wall, some throwing themselves, others crushed by the oncoming mass behind them, like the sea against a tidal wall.

Fingers grabbed at the rim of Veradis' shield, pulling it down, and Veradis saw a woodsman, caught a glimpse of the road and forest behind him. Veradis chopped; another scream as fingers flew through the air. The constant pressure was easing, still the thud of weapons as men hammered at the wall, but the unrelenting press of bodies was gone.

The end is coming, Veradis recognized, when the initial rush of that first battle fury was spent and men looked about at the carnage reaped by the shield wall. He had seen it before, knew that the ground would be piled with the dead, warrior spirits crushed by the shield wall's faceless brutality.

We must strike now and break them.

'Forwards,' Veradis cried. He punched Balen to his right to get his attention, yelled his command again and took a step forwards. For a moment he thought he was alone, stepping out of the wall into certain death, but then Balen followed him, a heartbeat later the man on his other side doing the same, and with a stutter the front row of the shield wall took one shambling step forwards. Veradis stumbled on a body underfoot but managed to stay upright, even though the ground was slick with blood and snared with limbs. He felt the line sway, thought that the wall would splinter, break and be scattered, but then it steadied. Veradis felt the strength and solidity return.

He set his feet and stabbed through the gap in the shields, felt his sword pierce flesh, heard more screams as others did the same.

It's working.

'Forwards,' Veradis yelled again and did not wait this time to take another step. The shield wall shuddered forwards. Swords snaked out, more men falling, dying.

'MARCH!' Veradis shouted, his voice hoarse and dry. Banging his sword against his shield to set time, he felt the whole shield wall move with him, some of the men behind him thudding their swords against shields in time with him, the front row still stabbing as they marched.

They were a ragged mass compared to the disciplined ranks that Veradis was accustomed to leading, but still he grinned with the joy of it as his enemy fell before him, felt as if they were unbeatable, unstoppable, and then the pressure before them was gone, the sound of feet drumming on the road as men turned and ran before them.

Veradis called a halt. The wall stumbled to a ragged stop, and Veradis lowered his shield.

Bodies lay strewn everywhere. Trees loomed before them, the camp ablaze behind. Dim figures could be seen fleeing along the road, some escaping into the gloom of the forest to either side of the road.

Not enough to challenge us again.

Relief flooded through him.

They are broken. We've won.

They had all known that the greatest threat would come from the warriors and workers who were away from the camp, spread along the road. They were the ones who would be alerted to the attack, would be able to gather their courage and attack, unlike all those within the camp, who would be caught by surprise.

He looked and saw Balen grinning, the recognition of survival, the joy of victory, saw the same expression spreading amongst those about him.

Then voices yelled a warning. Death screams rang out. Veradis spun around, searching for the new danger. It came from behind. Figures were emerging from the camp, a solid mass of warriors appearing, dressed in black mail, curved swords in their hands.

Kadoshim.

They were running up the embankment, carving into the flank and rear of Veradis' shield wall: twenty, forty, sixty of them, more appearing from amongst the tents, as well as a tight knot of others behind them.

Gundul and his honour guard. He cannot get away.

Veradis began moving towards the Kadoshim, even as his mouth opened to shout for the wall to reform he knew it would not defeat these demon spawn.

We have to take their heads, and the wall will not help us do that.

He saw men crunching shields together, falling back on the strategy that had just served them so well, but a handful of Kadoshim leaped at the hastily formed wall, ripped it apart with savage fury, swords rising and falling in deadly arcs.

My men are dying. The Kadoshim are slaughtering my men!

Veradis broke into a run and hurled himself at the Kadoshim.

CHAPTER SIXTEEN

JAEL

Jael ran through the camp, with every jarring step, every wheezing breath, trying to somehow lessen the pain of his broken ribs.

Though that doesn't seem to be working.

Blood was still leaking into his eyes from a wound on his forehead, and Maquin's sword cuts on his leg and forearm burned as if he'd been branded.

He took me by surprise, before I was ready.

He risked a look over his shoulder, relieved to see that there was no lunatic armed to the brim with knives chasing after him. In fact no one was in sight, before or behind. It felt as if he was alone in a world of white tents and narrow aisles, of smoke and fire and distant screams.

The last he'd seen of Maquin he'd been rolling in the dirt with Dag. *He looked like a man with a serious grudge, and I really could do without that right now.*

Could be that Dag has killed Maquin? Much as he wanted to believe it, he wasn't convinced. The ease with which Maquin had shattered his ribs had shocked Jael.

How did he move so fast? It must have been a lucky blow. He's old and broken!

He heard screaming off to his left and so veered right, taking a new path through abandoned tents and cook-fires.

No more battle if I can help it.

Ahead of him the trees of Forn loomed, overlooking the fringes of the camp like a tribe of dour ogres.

Nearly out of this hell-hole. Even if Maquin still breathes, he'll never find me now. I just have to find my men – three hundred swords waiting for me half a league along Gundul's cursed road.

The clamour of battle drifted down to Jael. He was travelling straight towards it. He didn't turn away this time, though, as it was exactly where he needed to go. *My men are out there somewhere, and if I'm going to get out of Forn alive I will need them about me.* So Jael gritted his teeth and ran on.

He emerged from the tents into a scene of carnage.

Warriors were massed upon the road, more of the enemy in the black and silver of Tenebral, but to Jael's pleasant surprise the Jehar were loose amongst them. The road was a heaving mass of battle, the path into the forest blocked for the moment, but the Jehar were doing all that they could about that. Even as Jael watched, he saw one of the Jehar lift a warrior into the air and hurl him down the embankment.

Might be able to sneak through in the chaos, he thought, and began to climb; then he saw Gundul. The young King of Carnutan was standing upon the road, separate from the battle, his sycophants huddled about him, though their numbers looked somewhat thinned. About them were a dozen or so Jehar warriors, the rest of Gundul's honour guard trying to carve a way through the wall of flesh and bone that barred the way to escape. From what Jael could see they were doing a good job of it.

Stick with Gundul, or try and sneak past?

A warrior in black and silver flew through the air a handspan from Jael, struck the ground and rolled bonelessly down the embankment, crashing into a tent and bringing it down around him.

Jael reached the road and tried to skirt the combat, which had broken down into a series of scattered and brutal skirmishes. The enemy looked to be rallying against the Jehar – one man leading a charge that sent two of those disturbing black mists jetting into the air.

'Break, damn you,' Jael muttered at the enemy. 'Don't rally.'

'Jael,' a voice called, and for a terrifying moment Jael thought it was Maquin. His head jerked around to see Gundul waving wildly to him from the midst of his protectors.

'Over here,' Gundul beckoned to him. For a moment Jael considered his options and quickly concluded that he was safer within a ring of Jehar warriors. He hobbled over to Gundul, a Jehar stepping out of the way to let him through.

'I'm glad you are still alive,' Gundul said. 'Three hundred men, you said. Where are they?'

For a moment Jael didn't understand what Gundul was talking about, then he realized he was referring to Jael's men, left waiting further along the road.

Not a complete idiot, then.

'That way,' Jael pointed over the combat before them into the dark tunnel of the road.

'Good. Drassil is that way, too, and a few hundred more swords around me would be a good thing.' He looked back at his camp, at the flames and the black clouds of smoke, at the dead scattered all around.

'Look what they've done,' Gundul wailed, face twisting in misery. 'They've destroyed my camp, crushed my warband!'

Best hope they don't do it to you, too, you whining little worm. And more importantly, not to me.

'We need to move,' Jael muttered, not liking the feeling of standing still. The knowledge that Maquin was out there somewhere, hunting him, hovered at the back of his mind like a black cloud.

'Yes. Onwards,' Gundul yelled.

A Jehar warrior turned its black eyes upon Gundul, then with a shrug began to lead their small group along the road. The other Jehar – a dozen left with Gundul at best – fanned out in a tight half-circle, pushing into the fringes of battle.

Then something crashed into their group from the left, sending men tumbling, Jehar reeling, turning to face this new attack. Jael staggered into one of Gundul's followers, shoving the man to the ground as he righted himself.

They'd been attacked by a knot of warriors in black and silver, charged and rammed by them, all with shields raised and interlocked. Even as he looked, short swords darted out from the small wall of shields. Two of Gundul's followers were caught in the attack and fell, pierced many times. Gundul was shrieking, waving his sword around ineffectually. Jael saw blades sink into the flesh of a Jehar, but it shrugged off the blows and grabbed a shield rim, dragging the warrior behind it forwards and chopping into his neck, sending him crashing to the ground in a spray of blood.

The small shield wall fractured, men breaking away and attacking Gundul's party the old way, man to man.

Not a wise choice against the Jehar.

Jael backed away, put a few of Gundul's followers between him and this new attack.

I'm scared of no man, but . . .

He put a hand to his throbbing ribs, glanced down at the blood crusting his thigh.

Another warrior came at the first Jehar, this man in a black and silver commander's cuirass, using sword and shield together to push the creature back a pace, sword darting out to stab at its thigh, shield-boss punching into the Jehar's face. There was something familiar about the warrior . . .

I know him.

The Jehar staggered back a few steps, black blood dripping from its broken nose. Its face twisted in a snarl as it launched itself forwards, shoulder ramming into the warrior, sending him stumbling backwards, tripping over a corpse and falling hard. The Jehar stood over him, curved sword rising, then another figure was there, plunging a spear into the Jehar's throat.

A woman! She was dressed in travelling fur and leather, richly made, dark hair pulled back tight. Then warriors were swarming either side of her, chopping at the wounded Jehar as she wrenched her spear free. The Jehar warrior went down in a hail of blows, its head hacked from its body, that black mist spilling from its neck. A figure formed in the air, black-winged and red-eyed, hissing its fury, then it was gone, only a few ragged wisps remaining.

I wish they'd stop doing that.

Gundul was screaming orders to attack, though nobody seemed to be paying much attention to him. Most of his hangers-on were running in different directions. Jael saw one of the Jehar grab Gundul by the scruff of his neck and start dragging him through the crowd, three or four Jehar carving a way for them through the melee. Gundul spluttered a protest but the Jehar just marched resolutely on. Jael lurched into motion, saw them as his best way of getting out of this and stumbled close behind them.

A huddle of warriors crashed into them, mostly enemy all striking at a Jehar in their midst. With a grimace Jael drew his sword and pulled a knife from his belt.

Pain over death, always the better option. He hacked at a warrior's head, bursts of agony pulsing from his damaged ribs. He dented the man's helm, then slashed at another with his knife, leaving a long red wound, this warrior lurching away, then they were past them, Jael adding his blades to the Jehar as they cut, hewed, punched and stabbed their way through the battling mass. Off to his left Jael saw the woman, still wielding her spear, a group of warriors tight about her. He had seen her before, at the great-council of Aquilus in Jerolin. He blinked as recognition dawned.

Fidele! Aquilus' wife – or widow, now. Nathair's mother. What is she doing here? And fighting, against Nathair's ally? He grunted as he ducked a sword blow aimed at his head, chopped at an ankle, then glanced back to Fidele.

She'd make a good hostage, either to buy me safe-passage out of here, or a good trophy to present to Nathair, something to win back some favour and prestige from the disastrous mess this campaign has become.

They were almost through the main press of battle now. Jael could see empty road beyond a few clumps of combat, the darkness of Forn beckoning, promising safety.

Battle-cries snapped his attention back. Beside him one of the Jehar fell to its knee. It struggled to rise but another warrior lunged in close and his sword swing took the Jehar's head; black vapour spewed from the wound.

The Jehar that had been dragging Gundul let go of him to join the fray, sword rising and falling, a warrior staggering away with a terrible gash from his forehead to his chin. Gundul slipped and fell to the ground beside Jael and grabbed at his boot.

'Help me,' Gundul cried, trying to climb up Jael's leg and pull himself back to his feet. Jael sneered down at him, remembering how Gundul had mocked him back in his tent.

I don't need you or your horses now.

He pulled his sword back and stabbed it into Gundul's screaming mouth, smashing teeth, on into the soft tissue of his throat, jerked it out red, left the King of Carnutan bleeding out his life in the dirt of Forn.

Looking up again he saw that the last few moments of frantic combat had swung them close to the woman he was sure was Fidele.

At last, fate smiles upon me once more.

He swerved around a mass of combat and strode straight towards her.

CHAPTER SEVENTEEN

MAQUIN

Maquin burst out from the rows of tents onto the embankment. The tangled snare of Forn Forest loomed close by. At the top of the embankment Gundul's new road carved a line into the trees. Figures fought upon it, the clamour and stench of combat drifting down to Maquin.

Where is he? Where's Jael?

As he had run through the fractured camp, memory upon memory had flooded Maquin's mind: of a lifetime served as Kastell's oath-sworn shieldman, of friendship, loyalty and love, and finally one memory overwhelming all of the others, of Jael plunging a sword into Kastell's belly, those few heartbeats replayed in his mind time and time again, until his whole world was a place of heartbreak and rage.

Where is he? He came this way, I know it. Maquin had lived in Forn with the Gadrai and learned the way of wood and forest. Not that Jael was hard to track. He'd left a trail of his own blood for Maquin to follow.

But where now? Which way did he go?

Maquin knelt in the grass, searching, fingertips running across the ground. They came away sticky.

Blood.

Another patch a pace up the embankment.

Something crossed Maquin's face, part snarl, part smile, and he bounded up the slope to the road. Battle was mostly finished here, the dead littering the ground, others lying and waiting for death's last touch, wounds gaping. Screams and weeping, ragged breaths, some men just sitting, staring at blood-crusted palms. Battle still raged further along the road, the trees of Forn a tunnel about them. Maquin glimpsed Kadoshim in their coats of dark mail scattered amongst the black and silver of Veradis' rearguard. A figure moved beyond the combat, drawing his eye, disappeared, reappeared: a man, dark-haired – just a glimpse, but Maquin knew him.

Jael.

He ran, leaping the fallen, a short sword hissing from the scabbard across his back, a knife gripped in his other hand, never taking his eyes from Jael.

Behind him Maquin heard the drum of many feet, over it a heavier thud, knew that Alcyon and the others had arrived. He ran on, skirting the combat, glimpsed Veradis with a handful of men bring a Kadoshim to bay, like hounds snapping at a bear or wolven. Maquin gave it all barely a glance, because he was close to Jael now, so close he could see his eyes, the cut across his scalp. He was heading diagonally across the combat, through it, and Maquin followed, a wraith that wound his way through the tumult, ducking, bending, swaying, always moving. Dimly behind him he heard voices raised in battle-cry, Alcyon's deep bass rumbling over it like an avalanche as he joined the fray. Maquin hardly noticed. He was so close, a dozen paces behind Jael when he lost sight of him for a moment, heard the harsh clang of iron, a grunt, the thud of a body hitting the ground, then a scream, higher pitched. A woman's scream.

No. Dear Elyon, no.

He knew that voice, would recognize it anywhere.

Fidele.

He shouldered one of Ripa's warriors out of the way and burst through the last knot of combat. A warrior lay dead at his feet, others standing, pointing swords and spears at a figure further along the road.

Jael.

He stood facing Maquin, one arm around Fidele's throat, resting his sword-blade against the pulse in her neck, his other hand holding a knife tight to her ribs.

'Follow me and she's dead,' Jael said calmly. He shuffled backwards, dragging Fidele with him. She saw Maquin appear from the crowd, their eyes touching. She did not appear scared, if anything, she looked angry.

An emotion I know well.

A warrior beside Maquin took a step forwards and Jael moved; a line of blood trickled from the blade at Fidele's throat. Maquin grabbed a fistful of the warrior's shirt and held him still.

'That's better,' Jael said, a smile twitching his lips. How Maquin hated that smile. 'I'm going to walk away. Have no fear, I'll not harm this lady. I know who she is; Fidele of Tenebral. She will be safe with me; but she *will* stay with me. And if any of you should follow . . .'

He prodded Fidele in the ribs with his knife, making her grimace. She was still staring at Maquin.

Trust me, Maquin mouthed, then stepped out from the crowd.

The muscles in Jael's sword arm tensed, then he recognized Maquin and paused.

'Not you again,' Jael sighed. 'Don't you ever give up?'

Maquin took a pace forwards.

'Do you wish to be responsible for the death of Fidele, Lady of Tenebral?' Jael snapped, resuming his slow shuffle back down the road.

'Kill her,' Maquin growled, taking another step forwards, focused on Jael's eyes.

'Stay back,' Jael said, his voice rising in pitch, 'or she dies.'

'Did you not hear me?' Maquin said, taking another step. 'Kill her. I care not. Either way, this is where you die. Nothing will change that now.' He took another pace forwards, and another, closing the gap between them. Jael stumbled backwards, dragging Fidele with him.

'Are you mad? She is the mother of Nathair, she is the First-Lady of Tenebral. Her *warband* is standing behind you. Harm her and they will gut you.'

Maquin shrugged. 'Once you're dead they can do what they like to me.'

'Stop!' Jael screeched, his knife hand pulling back.

Maquin stopped. 'I have an offer for you,' he said as he slowly bent his knees, laid his sword and knife on the ground.

'An offer?'

'Aye.' Maquin reached over his shoulder and drew his other sword, laid that on the ground too, unsheathed a knife from his belt, another from a shoulder strap, one from the back of his boot, laying them all upon the ground.

'Let her go. I'll fight you unarmed. Keep your sword, and your knife.' He stood straight and raised his hands, started walking forwards again.

'You're insane,' Jael snorted, eyes glancing from Maquin to the pile of weapons on the ground.

'Maybe,' Maquin shrugged. 'You murdered my ward, my friend. Kastell was as a son to me. I will see you dead, even if I have to do it with my bare hands.' He could see the indecision in Jael's eyes. The man was tempted – that was clear, and why not? He was a master with the sword, with any blade, and had both sword and knife in his hands, against an unarmed man.

'You've more knives hidden away.'

'No,' Maquin shook his head. 'You're just afraid to fight me.'

Jael snorted, but stopped his backward shuffling.

'You're afraid,' Maquin said, louder. 'You, Jael, murderer and usurper, a coward as well.'

A moment's pause, Jael's eyes narrowing, then he was lifting his sword arm to club Fidele across the back of the head. In that breath she stamped on his foot and drove an elbow into his ribs, spinning around and driving her knee into his groin. Jael staggered and rocked backwards and then Fidele was leaping away from him.

'Bitch,' Jael snarled, moving after her, but clumsily. In a heartbeat Maquin was standing in front of her.

'Go,' Maquin breathed as he squeezed Fidele's hand. Dimly he was aware of silence settling behind him. 'Go,' he said, firmer, and heard her footsteps pad a dozen or so paces away.

Jael paused, looking at Maquin's empty hands.

'You really don't have any more weapons?' he said. Another smirk. 'You actually are insane. I'm going to enjoy this.'

'Don't need my own blade,' Maquin said, 'I'll just take one of yours.'

He strode forwards, swayed away from Jael's diagonally chopping sword, pivoted past a stab of Jael's knife, stepped in close and punched Jael in the ribs, making him cry out; another punch, to the sword-cut on Jael's leg, elicited a grunt of pain.

'For Kastell,' Maquin said close to Jael's ear, then he was spinning away.

Jael cursed, visibly mastered his pain, set his stance and came at Maquin, carefully, sword held high, knife low.

Maquin stepped in to meet Jael, palm of his hand slapping the blade of Jael's sword away as he attempted a straight lunge, grabbed Jael's knife wrist and headbutted the man full on the bridge of his nose. Jael spluttered, blood gushing, Maquin shoving him back.

'For Kastell,' Maquin growled.

Jael spat, cuffed blood from his face, danced forwards, swinging his sword. Maquin ducked, air whistling over his head. He twisted, felt a hot pain lance along his ribs, heard shouting behind him, punched Jael on his injured leg again as he spun out of range, heard another cry of pain.

'For Kastell,' he breathed.

Jael looked at a red line that his knife had scored through the leather of Maquin's jerkin.

'Bleed like the rest of us, then.'

Maquin ignored him and darted forwards, weaved past a sword thrust, kicked out at Jael's ankle, connecting, hand chopping at Jael's throat, grabbing his knife hand and twisting. Jael squawked in pain, his knife clattering to the road, Maquin kicking it away and darting out of range.

'For Kastell,' he said as he spun away again.

'Stop saying that!' Jael yelled at him, spittle flying, then ran at him, more of a hobble. Maquin stooped to sweep up the fallen knife, twisting away from Jael's sword, slashed once with the knife. Jael cried out with pain as he stumbled on, almost falling. He regained his balance and backed away from Maquin, limping as blood ran down the back of his leg. Maquin strode at him, for the first time seeing fear in Jael's eyes.

'Do you remember, in the tomb beneath Haldis?' Maquin said, not breaking his stride.

'It was a fair fight,' Jael said, pleading, shuffling away, leaving a trail of blood from his wounded leg.

'He was your kin, and you betrayed him; you murdered him,' Maquin said, exploding into movement, leaping forwards, dancing to the side around Jael's sword, a slice at Jael's arm – a yell and the sword was falling. They crashed into each other, limbs tangled, fell to the ground, rolled, Jael finding new strength as he punched, kicked and bit at Maquin. Maquin grabbed one of Jael's arms, pinned it as they rolled together, inched his knife blade up, towards Jael's throat. Jael's efforts redoubled: his free fist punching at Maquin's head, his gut, anywhere, everywhere. Maquin grunted but did not let go. Jael was grabbing at Maquin's wrist, unable to stop it moving remorselessly upwards. They rolled to a halt, Maquin squeezed, twisted, and Jael's pinned arm cracked. Jael screamed, high and long as a stuck boar, the fight draining from him. Then Maquin's knife was at Jael's throat, tip pressing into the soft flesh at the base of the jaw.

'Please,' Jael sobbed.

'For Kastell,' Maquin whispered, then he shoved the blade up with all his strength.

Jael made a choking sound, gurgling on dark blood that welled from his mouth, dribbled down his chin. He struggled but Maquin pushed the blade deeper, on, into his skull, kept pushing until the knife's hilt was tight to Jael's flesh. Jael's eyes bulged, then he spasmed, legs kicking, slowed, became still.

Maquin rolled away, slowly stood and looked down upon Jael. He grimaced, part snarl, felt suddenly weak and dropped to his knees, then sat and stared at Jael's corpse.

You are avenged, Kastell; you who were like a son to me.

He felt his shoulders begin to shake, tears blur his vision, and then a hand was stroking his head, a warm body beside him pulling him into an embrace. He laid his head upon Fidele's breast and wept.

He didn't know how long he remained like that, but in time the world opened up from that small pinpoint of grief and he became aware of voices. He looked up and saw the warband of Ripa gathered in a half-circle about him: Veradis, Krelis, Alben, Alcyon and so many others, hundreds of them, all watching him.

'Well, that was a cracking fight and no denying,' Krelis said, nodding to Maquin, lifting a skin of mead to his lips and drinking deep. 'What now?'

Fidele answered.

'Now we march on Drassil.'

CHAPTER EIGHTEEN

CYWEN

Cywen stood in the great courtyard before the gates of Drassil alongside her fellow prisoners.

Calidus walked down the staircase that led to the battlements where he had announced his challenge to Corban, as he did each and every morning.

'Save the lives of your people. Stop their torture.'

As always, Corban did not come, and now Calidus began the second half of each day's ritual. Choosing a prisoner to be impaled within the courtyard.

Almost a moon had passed since Drassil had fallen so unimaginably quickly, a moon of heartache and pain.

Although she was a prisoner, Cywen had been allowed to take charge of the makeshift hospice that she and Brina had spent so long stocking and preparing, choosing a few staff to help her from amongst the more able-bodied prisoners. She was permitted to heal the captured only if she also looked after those of Nathair's army who had been wounded in the battle. Much as Cywen despised doing so, she knew it was the only way to help her own people.

Calidus stopped a dozen steps up from the courtyard and looked at the gathered prisoners.

'It seems that your Bright Star has better things to do than save your lives,' he said, voice laced with anger.

Cywen shivered involuntarily at the thought of what was to come, of the screams. She was no stranger to death now, but nothing could make her immune to the horror she witnessed each morning.

Corban, come and save us.

With each passing day it seemed more impossible. For the first few days she had been practically convinced that her brother would somehow return with a warband and win back Drassil, defeat their enemy. But with each scream-filled morning that hope had withered.

Calidus gave a curt nod and a Kadoshim stepped out from the shadows of the stable-blocks, moving amongst the prisoners, dragging one forwards. As always Cywen's heart seemed to freeze, feeling as if it swelled to fill her chest as a single Kadoshim walked down the line that she was standing in. It was the figure that was always surrounded by billowing clouds of flies.

It paused before her, one fist grabbing her chin and lifting it to stare into her eyes, though there was nothing there; its eyes were black, soulless wells. A lunatic grin twisted its mouth and a black tongue flickered out from its mouth, thick and swollen, and slowly licked her cheek. She retched from its foul breath, but the Kadoshim held her immovable while flies crawled over her face, up her nose.

'One day, soon,' it whispered in her ear. 'I will crush your skull and suck the jelly from your eyes.'

Then it released her, grabbing the man beside her, one of those who had been saved from the Vin Thalun oar-benches, and dragged him towards a stake. He began to plead, then wail. It did no good, and soon his horrific screams were ringing out, a cacophony of torment.

There was no hiding from it. The sound climbed, sweeping over the walls and on, out over the plains surrounding the fortress, into the silent trees of Forn.

Have Corban and the survivors fled, or retreated?

Calidus strode down from the battlement steps and with an irritable wave of his hand signalled for the surviving prisoners to be taken away. The warriors of Tenebral, in black and silver, herded Cywen and the others out of the courtyard. She wrinkled her nose as they passed the stables, the stench of Nathair's draig clawing up her nose. She'd smelt a lot of bad things in her time, but nothing like the smell of draig dung.

She heard a horse neigh as they moved past the stables.

Shield?

When Drassil had fallen to Calidus and Nathair's warband the stables had been full of horses, great warhorses that the Jehar rode, a whole herd that had been saved from the destruction of Gramm's hold. They were still there, and created another task that the prisoners were used for – stable duty, tending to the horses. Every time that Cywen was picked she had managed to get close to Shield, Corban's stallion.

As they left the courtyard and entered a wide street shouts rang out from the wall, then horns sounded. The great bars across the gates were drawn back and the gates opened with a juddering creak.

Figures filled the open gates, silhouettes with the sun behind them. They became clearer as they spilt into the courtyard: Vin Thalun, a score, two score, maybe more. Many of them were wounded.

So, something is out there, then, hidden within the trees of Forn. Something with teeth of iron.

As she was marched away from the courtyard Cywen felt a seed of hope glimmer, deep inside. It was faint and fragile, and it wasn't helped much by what she saw around her on her way back to the hospice. Kadoshim were prowling the streets, moving like shadows, their heads twitching at every sound. All around her she saw a host of eagle-guard in their black and silver, manning gates and walls, filling once-abandoned buildings, working at forge and barn, and the Vin Thalun were everywhere. Many of them were half-drunk and fighting, loitering on street corners, sitting in impromptu circles and throwing dice of bone. The numbers of her enemy seemed vast, far more than Corban's warband had ever been, even at full strength.

Could we ever have won?

The dead from the battle had mostly been cleared from the streets now, here and there a dark stain on a flagstone acting as a stark reminder. As Cywen turned a corner she saw a dog sniffing at a heaped rubbish pile. The dog was small and white; a ratter.

I know that dog! It was Haelan's. *What happened to him?* She looked at the dog as she was marched past it. It was skinny and half-starved, ribs visible. *Haelan must be dead. He loved that dog. Pots, he called him.*

Just like my poor Buddai. What happened to him? She had not seen him since before the battle. Perhaps he had been killed, or maybe fled, though deep in her heart she doubted that.

He was too loyal, would not have left me like that.

She drew level with the white dog and clicked her tongue, reached inside a pocket in her cloak and pulled out a chunk of bread. The dog lifted its head, sniffing, and after a moment's cautious indecision, darted over to her. She dropped the piece of bread and it caught it deftly, then it was gone. She watched it scamper away, turn a corner and disappear. For a moment she thought she saw something waiting for it, moving in the shadows.

Guards ushered her and the other prisoners into the hospice, less than three hundred of them now because of Calidus' morning ritual. The building was large enough to accommodate their numbers, with a lower floor made of two interlinking chambers. Part of it had been partitioned off for the care of the injured, the rest turned into a makeshift prison for the others. Only one guard came into the hospice, the rest sitting out in the courtyard. Cywen heard the sound of dice on a throw-board.

Automatically she went into the adjoining chamber and checked on the injured – not many of them left now. There had been a lot more after the battle, but many had died, Cywen being unable to do little more for them than ease their passing across the bridge of swords. Now only a score remained in here – although, from what she'd just seen, she expected that her skills would now be required for the injured Vin Thalun. Frankly, she'd rather poison them than heal them . . .

Do not give up, she told herself, remembering her time as a prisoner with Nathair and Calidus. *All had seemed hopeless, then*. That time, Corban had come out of nowhere and rescued her. *Although Mam died in the undertaking. I'll not let that happen again – people dying for my saving. I'll not wait around to be rescued. I will make my own fortune. Whatever the cost.*

Cywen opened her eyes.

After counting a hundred heartbeats and not hearing anything else but the usual snoring, she turned her head to check on their Vin Thalun guard. As expected, he was asleep. Beyond the doors she heard the muted sound of conversation, the occasional burst of laughter; the rest of their guards sitting in the courtyard, drinking and gambling.

At first their guards had been vigilant, and rightly so, because there had been a smattering of Jehar amongst the captives and they did not take well to being made prisoners. On the first night two had attempted escape, killing eight guards, maiming three more and setting fire to another. Eventually they had both been subdued and executed in the courtyard the next day. Since then no more escapes had been attempted, and over time the guards had become correspondingly less vigilant.

Cywen padded slowly from the room, making her way to a set of stairs leading up to a balcony that looked down upon the main hall, with a dozen rooms opening off it. Almost silently she passed into one of those rooms. There was one large window that let in a wide beam of moonlight, shockingly bright in the darkness.

Cywen traced a familiar path to a cupboard, opened the door, shifted a loose board inside and lifted out a package.

She shuffled over to the window, sat with her back to the wall, facing the dark silhouette of the open doorway. She opened the old linen she'd wrapped round it, to reveal a book, leather-bound and worn. She opened it towards the back and started reading the spidery script.

Rud eigin lomhara a garda. A guarding spell. *A caitheadh an seal. Boiling water, worm-root, flayed skin . . .*

She paused there, a shiver goose-bumping her flesh. *What did I expect from a book of giant spells?* She pulled a face, fear and revulsion. *It depends who the skin belonged to, I suppose. If it came from Calidus, or Nathair, or Lykos, Morcant, or Rhin . . .* The list grew in her mind of enemies she'd like to do terrible things to.

Brina said it is a tool, not an evil of itself. It is how I use it that's important.

She became aware of a sound, a soft snuffling, from out of the window. Leaves rustled.

Something in the herb beds.

Slowly, as quietly as she could manage, she peered up over the window's edge and looked out.

Something was moving through the herb garden, nose to the ground, moving steadily towards the hospice. It paused, its white form reflecting moonlight, and looked up at Cywen.

It's the dog from earlier – Haelan's ratter.

The dog turned in a circle and jumped on the spot. Cywen was scared that it would start barking. Then movement caught her eye, further back in a shadowed recess on the far side of the herb garden. A solid patch in the darkness. It whined, moved into the moonlight.

Cywen's breath caught in her chest.

Buddai?

Without thinking, she jumped from the window, dropping into the soft earth of the herb bed. Before she had righted herself, Buddai was bounding across the soft earth, hurling himself against her, rough tongue licking her face, whining.

'Shhh,' she whispered, tears blurring her eyes as she kissed his muzzle. He didn't listen to her, sloppily licking her face.

'Where have you been?' she whispered, scratching him behind one floppy ear, running her other hand along the thick muscle of his neck.

Been feeding all right, by the look of you.

Something was tied around him. Cywen lifted it and inspected the long strip of leather.

A leash?

Then another sound caught her attention, a rustling close by in the herb bed, amongst the thick leaves of the basil and peppermint. She squinted, narrowed her eyes, saw someone appear from between the greenery. A face, small and pale, dirt-stained.

It was Haelan.

CHAPTER NINETEEN

UTHAS

'Ravens and crows,' Uthas muttered as he trudged through the marshland, eyes looking skyward. He stumbled, his foot sinking with a splash into a patch of soft ground and he leaned on his spear to lever himself upright. Salach his shieldman reached out a steadying hand from behind him.

Marshland is not a good place for a giant to walk.

'What's that?' Rhin said. She was sitting in the stern of a large boat, surrounded by a score of warriors as well as half a dozen rowers. Uthas was picking a path alongside the banks of the waterway she was being rowed down, a line of Benothi giants spread out along the bank behind him.

'Ravens and crows,' Uthas repeated, stopping and pointing up at the sky, to where a black shape spiralled high above them.

'What about them?' Rhin asked. She was in an unusually good mood this morning, the first that Uthas had seen since she had learned of her warband's defeat in the marshes, and of the death of her huntsman, Braith.

'I don't like them,' Uthas grumbled, thinking of Fech, Nemain's treacherous raven.

Rhin stared up at the speck in the sky. 'I've always rather liked them,' she said. 'And I suppose this one suspects that we'll be providing its dinner.'

Uthas scowled up at the bird.

Aye. As long as it's not our eyeballs and innards that it is feasting upon. He looked around him. More boats filled the waterway, bursting with over a thousand warriors.

Not likely that we'll be losing this battle, he thought, looking at the grim faces of men in every boat, bristling with iron, and the fifty Benothi warriors behind him. *More than enough to put down this little uprising.* But since they had left the tower at the marshland's edge a dour mood had fallen across Uthas' shoulders like a heavy cloak, and he could not shake it.

We should be getting on with the important business of finding Evnis and the necklace. That is all that matters.

Because when they found Nemain's necklace, one of the Seven Treasures, then Uthas would be one huge step closer to achieving his dream.

King of the Giants. No more clans, no more divisions, just my kin behind me.

But first, I must find the necklace. Then it is to Domhain and Dun Taras, to find the cup. And then . . .

He saw Rafe appear up ahead, moving smoothly across the ground, his two hounds with him. He ran across the marshland towards them, hardly glancing at where he was putting his feet. Everything about the lad screamed *vitality*.

Uthas rubbed at the small of his back and frowned.

There is something about him, Uthas mused. *Different. He hides something.*

'Rafe comes,' Uthas said across the water to Rhin. She held up a hand. The rudder-man of her boat guided them towards the bank, the rowers slowing. All along their convoy men did the same, the boats rippling to a halt like a long, sinuous water-snake.

'Is he alone?' Rhin asked as Uthas took her hand and helped her step from the boat.

'Aye.'

Rafe had been given a score of woodsmen to help him scout out the ruins of Dun Crin, not that he seemed to need help.

'Be careful,' Uthas said. 'I don't trust him.'

'I don't trust *anyone*,' Rhin replied with a scathing look and fixed her eyes on Rafe as he approached them. His two hounds reached them first, prowling a circle around Uthas, which he didn't like. Rafe sprang across a stream and pulled to a halt, dipping his head to Rhin.

'My Queen,' he said.

'Well?' Rhin snapped.

'Dun Crin is ahead.'

A smile touched Rhin's mouth.

'It is abandoned.'

Well, he wasn't lying, Uthas thought as he stepped around a long-branched willow and saw the ancient fortress towering out of the lake. He heard Salach mutter a curse behind him. His shieldman had not seen Dun Crin before, and it was a tragic sight: the once-proud fortress laid low by time and circumstance. Dark walls and towers reared from the lake's water like the submerged boughs of a rotting tree, reed and slime hanging from the decaying battlements.

A great work brought down. When I am king I will restore the glory of my kin.

Ahead of him Rhin hissed in frustration.

'There's no one here,' Morcant said.

'Your powers of observation are staggering,' Rhin said, barely contained rage dripping from each word.

A strange sound rang out overhead, making Uthas jump. He looked up and saw a scruffy-looking crow sitting in the branches of a willow. It was making a clacking sound, almost like laughing. Uthas gave it a dark look. Still making the odd noise, the crow winged into the air, spiralled up and flew away.

Warriors were disembarking from boats to stand all along the lakeshore. Others had rowed out to the waterlogged fortress, men climbing up onto the ancient battlements.

Uthas tugged on one of the wyrm teeth set in his necklace as he stared at Dun Crin, eyes sweeping the lakeshore, the willows and alders that lined it. The signs of recent life were all about: abandoned shelters, woven willow fences, cold fire-pits, fishing-nets hanging. A pile of burned clothing – old boots and belts, some twisted war gear, nothing of much use.

'The far shore,' he said to Salach and Eisa beside him. *They have younger eyes than I.* 'Men could be hiding there.'

'Can't see anything,' Salach rumbled. He was disappointed, Uthas could tell. His shieldman had been looking forward to a fight. 'But, it's far . . .'

'No one there,' Rafe said from a dozen strides away, his back to them. He was standing staring at the far shore.

'Your eyes are good?' Uthas asked.

'I can see a heron standing in the shade of that willow,' Rafe said, pointing. Uthas squinted but could see nothing. Neither could Salach. Then there was a distant splash and a heron rose from deep shadows flapping into the air.

Rhin barked orders and warriors began to sweep around both arms of the lakeshore, searching for hidden men, wary of traps. Word of the last campaign against this fortress was in everyone's mind.

'Why have they left here?' Morcant asked no one in-particular.

'To avoid you, I would suspect,' Rhin said.

Morcant nodded at that, thinking it a perfectly reasonable answer. 'Well, we must chase them, then,' he said.

'A fine idea,' Rhin muttered. 'Or, maybe not. What do you think, Rafe?'

The young huntsman frowned at that, was silent a while. 'I can track them for you, my lady,' he eventually said, 'but I don't think it would be wise for your whole warband to give chase. We could be led straight into another trap like last time, or worse. Here we know the land, now, and your numbers would tell. Out there –' he gestured at the stinking marshland – 'who knows?'

Calls were drifting over from the fortress, men signalling that the ruins were empty. Other men started adding their voices from the lakeshore as they circled around.

'They are fled,' Salach rumbled.

'Yes,' Rhin agreed sourly. 'But the question is not why, but *where*. Where are they? While we are stuck in the heart of Dun Crin, where are *they*? And what are they doing?'

And where is Evnis? Uthas thought. *He is the real prize. The only man with knowledge of where Nemain's necklace is. All else is smoke on the wind.*

Voices shouted from further along the lakeshore, a different tone and cadence . . . Men appeared, with someone definitely unwarrior-like between them.

She was brought before Rhin, a woman of exceeding beauty, Uthas surmised, beneath the starvation and grime that coated her. She was dark-haired with green eyes. As she was held before Rhin

Uthas saw a host of emotions sweep this new woman's face. Pride, fear, hatred. Hope.

Rhin stared at her, then began to laugh.

CAMLIN

'Torch it,' Camlin said, lifting his bow. A flaming arrow leaped into the air, followed by twenty more, all rising high into the blue sky, then arcing and falling towards the wooden tower and surrounding walls.

'Again,' Camlin ordered as the first volley slammed into the wooden palisade, gates and buildings beyond. Meg dipped her torch into an iron brazier crackling with fire and ran along the line, igniting the arrows of Camlin and the twenty other archers.

They were standing on a shallow slope between the marshes and Morcant's tower, Edana's warband spread in a loose circle about it. On a plain to Camlin's right stood the remains of an abandoned camp: trampled grass, fire-pits, torn tents, the stench of midden.

A lot of men filled that space. Rhin's not underestimating us this time, though she'll be finding out soon that we're not playing by her rules.

Camlin held his arrow-tip in Meg's torch, the pitch and kindling catching with a hiss, and then he was aiming high and loosing, his arrow rising and falling amongst the others, disappearing beyond the wall of Morcant's tower. Already black smoke was billowing into the clear sky.

'They'll see that for a fair few leagues around,' Baird said behind him, grinning as if he was at a midsummer's fair. He was stood to one side of Edana, Halion and Vonn close by, as well as Lorcan and his shieldman, Brogan.

'That's the idea,' Edana said. She was sterner. 'Too long Rhin has had this war her own way.'

Aye, this is a message as much as anything else. Well, we'll not be dancing to Rhin's tune any longer.

Camlin held out another arrow for Meg to light.

The gate tower was a crackling torch, now, Morcant's tower beyond catching, bright flames licking one side. Figures were running along the wall, buckets of water were being thrown, but it seemed to be having little effect.

Too few of them, Camlin thought. *Can't be more'n thirty men in there. Rhin's taken everyone else into the marshes, looking for us.* A broad smile cracked his face as he thought of Rhin's expression when she heard about this.

'That should do it,' he said, slapping men on shoulders, and the row of archers lowered their bows.

'Now what?' Edana asked.

'Now we wait,' Camlin said. 'Shouldn't take long.'

He was right, it didn't. Soon enough the palisade and enclosure were burning like a forest fire. One desperate man leaped over the palisade, apprehended immediately by Pendathran and his men, followed shortly by others. Soon after the gates creaked open, black clouds of smoke billowing out, and a huddle of men appeared, stumbling and coughing out onto the slope. Some collapsed to the ground, others stood with their arms raised in surrender as Edana's warriors closed in. Pendathran herded the gathered prisoners down the slope.

Camlin glanced at Edana as she sighed then strode off towards the prisoners. Camlin and the others followed.

Thirty-six men were kneeling in the grass before Edana. They all wore the black and gold of Cambren, Rhin's realm. Edana stood and stared at them a long moment.

'How many of you are Ardan-born?' she asked.

Faces looked up at her, some nodding, others raising a hand.

Twenty-eight, Camlin counted.

'Narvon?' Edana asked, and Drust stepped out from the warriors at her back.

Five raised their hands. Drust narrowed his eyes and stared at them.

'Which three are from Cambren?' Edana asked. Two raised their hands, and Camlin saw one other who was staring fixedly at the grass at his knees.

'Bring them before me,' Edana said and Halion, Baird and Vonn moved into the crowd, dragging the two who had raised their hands out of the group.

'That one,' Camlin said, pointing at the other one, and he was dragged forwards, too, and thrown to the ground before Edana. 'You are from Cambren,' she said. 'You have come here, to Ardan, with Rhin. Invaded my country, killed my people.' There was a tremor of rage in her voice. 'You deserve death,' Edana said, 'and I sentence you to execution.'

Edana approached the other prisoners.

'You others. You are Ardan- and Narvon-born,' she said. Men nodded eagerly. She frowned at them. 'And yet you wear the colours of Rhin, Queen of Cambren. You have betrayed your countries, served your enemy.'

Camlin saw fear ripple through them like wind through long grass.

'I will offer you my forgiveness. Once.'

Think more'n one of them'll need to change their breeches.

'I will give you a choice. Fight for me, for your countries, or go home. Either way, you redeem yourselves.' She looked long and hard at their faces. 'If you go now, I shall not judge you. But if I see your faces again and you're standing against me, I'll see you die a death worthy of your betrayal. Make your choice,' Edana said, and without waiting to see their reactions, she turned and strode away. Only Camlin saw the tears fill her eyes.

Camlin sat with his back to a tree and watched Morcant's tower crumble in upon itself, a great cloud of smoke and ash billowing up into the air. He could see the bulk of Pendathran as he led fifty men away to the east, skirting the treeline of the woods. Another group of men were waiting down there for Drust.

Going our separate ways for a while.

The plan was to split into three groups, Pendathran, Drust, and Edana each leading a band of warriors, the overall goal of each to make life in Ardan hard for Rhin.

With a loud crash, the final section of Morcant's tower collapsed. Camlin grinned, wishing he could see Morcant's face when he marched out of the marshes to see it.

'A pretty sight, that tower coming down,' he commented as he leaned forwards and took a skewer of squirrel meat off the fire, tossing it to Meg.

She took the meat, blowing on her fingers and biting, grease dripping down her chin.

Will have to talk to her, soon. He was surprised to find he felt sad about that. *Strange as it seems, she's not the worst company.*

The drumbeat of hooves drew his eyes and Camlin watched a dozen riders cantering away in different directions, each with a large bag of silver taken from Morcant's chest, each one tasked with travelling through as many villages and holds as possible, spreading the word of Edana's victory at Dun Crin, that she was alive and well in Ardan, and that she was fighting. And of course distributing a little silver to show that there was a bit of profit to be had if you rode with Edana.

We're moving forwards. Closer to the end, whether that be victory or death.

'We'll be leaving the marshes behind us, soon,' he said conversationally.

'I know that,' Meg said, as if he were stupid.

'Might be best for you if you and I made a trip to the next village along the marshes' edge, and I found a family to take you in . . .'

Her head snapped round and she glared at him. 'No.'

'This is your home, Meg,' he said with a jerk of his chin. 'The marshlands, these people. We'll be leaving here, going back to wood and forest.' *That's where my kind of fighting works best.* 'We're going to war,' he said, 'and that's no place for you. You're eight summers old.'

'War's here too,' she said, looking at her feet. 'What d'you call what happened to my village, my mam . . .' There was a tremor in her voice now.

He reached out and squeezed her hand.

She sucked in a deep breath, stuck her lip out.

'I've thought about it already,' she said. 'Bad things happen everywhere. My village didn't go marching off to war, but war still came and found them. You can leave me here, but who's to say Morcant . . .' She paused at his name, her sharp-featured face twisting with hatred. 'Who's to say the same thing won't happen again? Warband's out there.' She waved angrily at the marshes, staring at him defiantly. 'And you'd just leave me here and walk away?'

Well, didn't expect that.

'Asroth's toes, but that's the most words you've put together since I met you,' Camlin said, blowing out a long breath.

'I like it here,' she added, suddenly vulnerable, a child again. 'And besides, try and leave me here, or anywhere, I'll just give 'em the slip and follow you. Done it before.' She grinned mischievously.

Camlin sighed. 'Looks like you've thought it all through.'

She nodded.

'Well, seems that's settled, then.'

She gave him a long look, suspicious at first, which slowly changed to something resembling pleased, and she went back to eating her squirrel.

He looked back to the tower, saw a black smudge swirl around the cloud of smoke and come flapping up the hill towards them.

Is that Craf? He felt a little jolt of relief, hadn't realized he'd been worried about the old crow.

The crow saw him and spiralled down, started cawing as it drew close and alighted upon a branch over his head.

'*Craf hungry,*' it squawked, beady eyes staring at the pile of skin, bone and offal that had been a squirrel a short while ago.

'Help yourself,' Camlin said with a wave of his hand. 'Didn't think you usually asked,' he added.

When the crow had done it hopped closer to Camlin.

'Well?' Camlin asked, eager to hear the bird's news.

'*Edana,*' Craf squawked.

'Aye, you're right,' Camlin said, groaning at his stiff back as he stood. 'Best off saying your news once. She's over there.'

Camlin strode through wide-spaced woodland towards Edana. She had fewer about her now – just Halion, Vonn and Baird. Nothing of her earlier emotion showed on her face.

She just looks tired, Camlin thought.

'Craf's back,' Camlin announced and the crow fluttered down onto the log Edana was sitting on.

'You all right?' Camlin asked Edana. 'My Queen,' he added. 'After earlier – the prisoners.'

She passed a hand over her eyes and sighed. 'So much death,' she said. 'Will there ever be an end to it?'

'Gotta believe there will be,' Camlin shrugged. 'Called *hope*, I've been told.' He gave a lopsided grin. 'Long as it doesn't end with ours. Death, that is.'

She smiled at that, a little snort of laughter.

'How many stayed?' he asked, referring to the prisoners.

'Twenty-eight,' Halion said.

Camlin nodded. 'Trust them?'

'Not really,' Edana admitted. 'But if I'm going to raise a warband, more than half the men of Ardan are probably wearing Rhin's colours right now. I have to believe that it's against their will, that they'd rather fight for me.'

'Think that's most likely true enough. Always some rotten apples in the barrel, though.'

'I know,' Edana said. 'But how do we root them out?'

'New recruits, put 'em at the front of the first battle, and the second: let 'em prove themselves, risk dying for you. The bad 'uns will most likely run first chance they get.'

Baird grunted approvingly and Edana nodded thoughtfully at that.

'I'll do that,' she said. 'Now, Craf, what news have you for us?'

'*Rhin at Dun Crin*,' Craf said. He paused and looked at them all. '*Very angry.*'

Baird laughed at that.

'How many?' Halion asked.

'*Lots*,' Craf muttered. '*Thousand? Ten thousand? And giants from Murias.*'

Camlin raised his eyebrows.

That explains the strange tracks in the meadow near Morcant's tower.

'*God-War*,' Craf muttered, ruffling feathers with his beak.

That again.

Vonn tensed at Craf's words.

'It must be taken seriously,' Vonn said.

Vonn had already spoken to Edana and Camlin about this God-War, told them about how he had stolen the giant's book from his father, Evnis, which had in turn been taken from him by Brina during their flight to Domhain. Camlin and Edana had witnessed this. But Vonn also told them of a necklace hidden in Evnis' tower at Dun Carreg. A necklace with a black stone as a pendant.

Ask Craf what the Seven Treasures are, Vonn had said.

I don't need to ask Craf, Edana had replied, *I know the old tales as well as any. Cauldron and cup, spear, axe and dagger, torc and necklace.*

Aye, necklace, Vonn had said. *It makes sense – Dun Carreg, fortress of the Benothi. Nemain their queen.*

So what if you're right? Camlin had asked.

If one of the Seven Treasures is in Dun Carreg, then we must do something about it. Craf keeps squawking about the God-War, a prophecy, about Corban and the Bright Star and Black Sun. About the Seven Treasures.

It all sounds right strange to me, Camlin had said.

Aye, me too, Vonn had agreed, *but you are not understanding. If Craf is right, if this God-War is happening, then what is happening here, in Ardan, is just a pebble in the ocean. If this is true, then we must help.*

How would we help? Edana had asked.

We must go and get the necklace, and take it to Corban in Drassil.

Edana had just stared at Vonn, Camlin hadn't been sure if she thought he was mad.

I'll think on it, was all that she had said, and then left.

'I *am* taking it seriously,' Edana said to Vonn.

'Then what will be done about it, the God-War, the necklace?' Vonn pressed.

'I am going to retake Ardan,' Edana said slowly, 'or die in the trying. If by some stroke of good fortune I am victorious and Rhin is slain or sent back to Cambren, then I will gladly tear Evnis' tower down stone by stone until this necklace is found, and I will personally take it to Corban in Drassil. But until then, I must concentrate on what is in front of me. Ardan and Rhin first.'

'*Wrong*,' Craf said.

'I like that bird,' Baird chuckled. 'He's got stones. Speaks his mind.'

'Well, a good counsellor does, I suppose,' Edana said. 'But they also know when to stop, and not labour a point,' she added with one eyebrow raised. 'I have listened, weighed the choices, and I have made my decision.'

'But—' Vonn began.

'No,' Edana said, her voice rising. 'Enough, Vonn.'

Vonn scowled at her a long moment, jaw working as he struggled with the words itching to get out of his mouth, then he clamped his jaw shut and nodded.

CHAPTER TWENTY-ONE

HAELAN

Haelan stared at Cywen as moonlight silvered her face. He was terrified, being out, as he had grown so accustomed to hiding, but Buddai had been uncontrollable after he'd got a sniff of Pots, snapping his leash and heading off into the darkness, and Pots had run with him. For one elongated moment Haelan had watched them go, then he'd been scrambling after them, cursing them both the entire time it had taken him to catch up with Buddai and wrap the remains of the torn leash about his arm.

Buddai had calmed for a while when they reached this courtyard; maybe the sounds of guardsmen and the crackling fire reminded him that death lurked around every corner in this place. That was until the figure had appeared at the window. Buddai had taken a few deep sniffs through his broad muzzle, whined and then he was off again, Haelan standing no chance of even slowing him, let alone stopping him.

'Haelan, what are you doing here?' Cywen whispered.

'Chasing the dogs,' he whispered back, eyes flitting between Cywen and the firelight flickering at the building's corner.

Cywen smiled, ruffling Buddai's fur.

'I mean, how are you still alive? Where are you hiding? Are you alone? How do you have Buddai with you?' She took a breath, clearly framing more questions.

'It's not safe here,' Haelan said. 'Come with me.' He went to move away but Cywen gripped his wrist.

'I'll tell you everything, I promise,' he said. He looked up, the open sky, moon and stars feeling like it went on for ever. He shuddered.

Cywen stared at him, then nodded.

'Follow me,' he whispered and ran.

They passed through wide streets, always keeping to the edges, to the shadows. Soon they were entering a courtyard with an old oak at its centre, its trunk wide and thick, roots churning up the flagstoned floor. Haelan headed to a deeper shadow in its midst, and then he was scrambling into it, climbing into the hole that led to his den – his sense of safety grew palpably with each step deeper into his underground hiding place.

'This way,' Haelan whispered as they slithered down a slope about the length of a man and reached the spot where you could turn left or right. The familiar stench from the left drifted up to him, but by now Haelan hardly noticed. Cywen clearly did, though, wrinkling her nose and then putting a hand over her mouth.

'That's disgusting,' she whispered.

Haelan grunted and turned right. They shuffled along a dark narrowing space, forced onto hands and knees as the tunnel they were in followed a twisting root, then Haelan heard a welcoming whine and saw a flicker of light. He smiled.

A space opened up before him, wide enough for about six men to stand abreast, and about a dozen paces long. Beyond that the tunnel narrowed again, twisting off about the root it followed. The small chamber was lit by a bowl of oil on a knot in the thick root, flame dancing upon its surface.

Two faces greeted him, Swain and Sif – Wulf's son and daughter – and six bundles of fur, Buddai's and Storm's cubs bouncing and leaping in their excitement at his return. Seeing them like this, he realized how they'd grown. They were only five or six moons old, but already they were all taller than Pots, their necks and broad chests thickening with muscle.

Like Buddai. They'll not grow as big as Storm, but big enough, and they'll be wide and strong, I don't doubt.

'Calm down,' Sif scolded the cubs as they bounced into her. She was on her hands and knees, playing with her bag of stones and nuts, rolling them into each other. Some of them Sif had chalked white.

I still don't understand that game, but it's kept Sif quiet for over a moon.

Buddai and Pots burst into the chamber, making the cubs even more excited. One of them froze, black-faced and brindle-coated, and stared at the darkness of the tunnel. It growled, revealing a row of razor-sharp puppy teeth.

'Shadow,' Haelan said, reaching out a hand to the cub, but she didn't stop growling.

The other cubs stopped their frolicking and stared too, cocking heads, and then they were all growling as Cywen emerged from the darkness.

Shadow, the black-faced cub, took a snarling step forwards, legs bunching, about to leap, the others moving tight about her, all growling, hackles up. Haelan felt a real moment of panic, snapping a command at them that was completely ignored. Then Buddai was standing between the cubs and Cywen, baring his teeth, daring them. The cubs stopped, tails dropping, submitting. Shadow gave a last little growl of protest, and then she too was quiet.

Thank Elyon.

'I thought they were going to attack me,' Cywen said, looking relieved as she stroked Buddai's broad head. Then she threw her head back and laughed, long and sounding slightly mad.

'I can't believe you are all here,' Cywen said, sitting down and cuddling Buddai. Pots put his forelegs on Cywen's shoulder and licked one of her ears; the cubs tentatively approached her, sniffing. Cywen held her arms out and beckoned to Sif, who walked over and hesitantly allowed Cywen to hug her. After about a count of ten Sif was sitting in Cywen's lap, hugging her tightly in return.

'How has this happened?' Cywen asked.

'The battle,' Swain started, 'when it happened, we were here, with the cubs—'

'Because Corban had asked us to look after them,' Sif said with big, serious eyes.

'He did, I remember,' Cywen agreed.

'We didn't know what to do,' Swain continued.

I was terrified, Haelan thought, remembering the distant din of battle, the screams and battle-cries, flames, smoke. He'd been in the courtyard above, playing tug with Shadow. She'd heard it first, stopping and staring, ears going flat to her head.

'Buddai was here, with the cubs,' Swain continued, 'but he ran off when the fighting started, and then all the cubs were off as well, following him. We chased them, and then, a man appeared in front of us—'

'He had rings in his beard,' Sif said.

'Aye,' Swain said, eyes distant, remembering. 'He was going to kill us, tried to, but Buddai killed him.'

'Ripped his throat out,' Sif added matter-of-factly.

'We picked up all the cubs between us and tricked Buddai into following us back here.'

'How did you manage that?' Cywen asked.

They were silent a few moments.

'I pinched one of the cubs – twisted her ear and made her cry,' Haelan said. He still felt guilty about that. 'Buddai followed us back here, and then we tied him up.'

'We were scared he'd get killed,' Sif said.

'You were right to do it,' Cywen said, stroking Sif's hair. 'Buddai *would* have been killed. I think you saved his life.'

Sif smiled at that, nodding. By now all six cubs were rubbing up against Cywen, sniffing, nibbling her clothing; one was tugging at her hair and she absently pushed it off.

'And since then,' Swain went on, 'we've just . . . stayed hidden. Every now and then me or Haelan sneak out for food and water. Pots is good at foraging for the cubs – he's always disappearing and coming back with something for them.'

Sif screwed her face up at that, and Haelan remembered some of the things Pots had returned with – an arm once.

The cubs hadn't complained.

'What's happening, up there?' Swain asked Cywen.

'I'm a prisoner,' Cywen said. 'I tend to the sick – wounded from the battle. Most have recovered, or died, but there are still a few to tend to.'

'I meant Corban,' Swain said. 'And Da?'

'Wulf? I think he escaped,' Cywen said, and Swain and Sif physically drooped with relief.

Tahir? What of my shieldman? And my friend. Tahir had driven Haelan mad, with his strict rules about where Haelan could and couldn't go, what he could and couldn't do.

And his mam's old sayings. I wish I could see him and hear one of those sayings now.

'Tahir?' he asked.

'Your shieldman? I don't know,' Cywen shrugged. 'There was a lot of confusion. Many escaped,' she said hopefully, 'and they're in Forn, still fighting.'

'How do you know, if you're a prisoner?' Haelan asked suspiciously. He wanted good news, but he didn't want to be lied to, treated like a child.

'A patrol of Vin Thalun came back this morning. I saw them. There were more dead and wounded than the living amongst them.'

'Ha,' Swain barked a laugh. 'My da's work, for sure.'

'No doubt,' Cywen said.

'So, what now?' Haelan asked.

'You could stay with us,' Sif said.

'I wish I could,' Cywen replied, 'but I can't. I tend the sick and cannot abandon them. Besides, if Calidus found me gone, he'd tear Drassil apart looking for me. He might find you . . .'

'Why would he do that?' Sif asked.

'Because I am Corban's kin, and he thinks Corban will come for me. I am bait in a trap.'

'Will Corban come?' Haelan, Swain and Sif asked together.

'I don't know.' Cywen shook her head. 'He did the last time, when I was Calidus' prisoner.'

'But if it's a trap . . .' Haelan said.

Then Corban cannot come. He is our hope. Haelan loved Corban, admired him as the greatest warrior and leader the world had ever seen.

'Then you have to escape, get out of here, before Corban comes for you.'

A smile twitched Cywen's mouth, not light-hearted, but serious and determined. 'My thoughts exactly,' she said. 'It's just the how that I'm struggling with. And now that I know you're here.' She smiled. 'You'll have to come with me, else Calidus may find you in his search for me.'

That thought both excited and scared Haelan.

To be away from this danger, the daily fear of being discovered and caught. But being away from our den, which has kept us safe and hidden a whole moon.

'And, talking of being discovered, I should go back to the hospice, else the sun will be rising.'

Sif squeezed her harder and Cywen squeezed her in return.

'I cannot tell you how happy I am to know that you are alive and here,' Cywen said. 'And my Buddai . . .' She hugged the hound's neck, kissing him.

'I'll return soon,' she said, then made her goodbyes, ruffling the cubs' heads and hugging Sif again. She gave Buddai a stern order to stay and then backed into the darkness of the tunnel. Buddai whined but he did not follow her. Haelan did, though, and soon they were at the slope that led up to the courtyard. Moonlight showed them the way.

'That smell,' Cywen said, wrinkling her nose as they stood in the darkness at the base of the slope. She was staring into the darkness of the tunnel where the smell was drifting from. 'I recognize it,' she said quietly, her expression changing. She looked scared. 'Is that another tunnel?' she asked him.

'It is,' he said, remembering the first time he'd found this place, how he'd crawled that way first, eventually stopping and coming back. 'It gets too narrow.' Strangely, the cubs never went that way.

'Good,' Cywen said, her expression relaxing.

'Why?'

'Because I know that smell, and I think there are draigs down there.'

CHAPTER TWENTY-TWO

CORBAN

Corban sat upon a giant bear, hands gripping the high pommel of a saddle as it shambled along a fresh-built road that cut like a spear through the trees and undergrowth of Forn.

Jael's road, which he built almost from the boundaries of Gramm's hold to see him and his warband to the walls of Drassil.

The bear's pace was surprisingly fast, eating up the leagues at a relentless pace throughout each day's travel. His legs were aching; the girth of a bear was unsuitable for his human legs.

I miss Shield, he thought, not for the first time.

The trees were thinning, now, the terrain changing and more sunlight breaking through the canopy above. There was less vine and thorn on the ground, more grass and wildflowers. And then Corban saw the stumps of trees, a whole vale harvested of timber.

We are close to Gramm's hold.

With every league that he had travelled, every day that had passed, he had felt his spirits sink. After Meical's revelation about the prophecy, Corban had been in the deepest depths of despair, but focusing on the hope of being reunited with Cywen and his friends had given him the strength to endure. It had been something to live for. To fight for. Now he knew that, with every breath that he drew, he was being taken further away from them, if they still lived, and despondency had morphed into anger. Hated faces appeared in his mind.

Calidus. Nathair. Ildaer. Rhin. Meical.

He had thought about escape, but the simple truth was that, even if he could somehow break his bonds and slip away from his giant captors, he would not have been able to walk half a league because of his injuries.

Even now, over a moon from when he'd been captured, they were still not fully recovered.

Soon, though, perhaps.

His ribs now were little more than a dull ache, occasionally a twinge of pain if he over-stretched or twisted suddenly. His leg, though, was taking longer to heal. He could put weight on it, now, and walk if he favoured it, but it was still a considerable way from normal.

Surrounding him was a loose line of giants, a score of them, riding their huge bears, Ildaer at their centre. After his first interrogation by Ildaer, Corban had spoken little to the Jotun Warlord. The only people that Corban conversed with were Hala, the giantess healer, and Varan, the blond-haired giant who seemed in some way apprenticed to her.

'Do you recognize this place?' Varan rumbled in his ear. The giant's bulk was in the saddle behind him, his travelling companion and gaoler in one.

Corban didn't answer.

Will I ever see my kin and friends again?

The sun was sinking as the hill of Gramm's hold appeared. Ildaer paused to let the bears drink from a stream, Corban staring at the familiar outline of the hill, silhouetted by the red sun. It was hard to see details, but the memory of the place settled upon Corban like a shroud.

Tukul's death. Gar's grief and duel with Ildaer, his subsequent defeat by the giant, rage had made Gar reckless.

'Anger is the enemy,' Corban murmured, a mantra that Gar had drummed into him a thousand times as they had trained and sparred together.

Please, Elyon above, let Gar be alive, he prayed. He'd not considered other scenarios, the thought of Gar being gone, *slain*, was almost too much to bear.

He lives still. He must *live still.*

Ildaer called out a command and with a jolt Varan's bear lumbered into motion. Corban noted with some satisfaction the lack of pain in his chest and knee.

Hala's brot has worked wonders; I'll have to remember to tell Brina about adding goldenseal to it.

They covered the ground quickly, and soon Corban was passing the paddocks and meadows that Gramm's herds of horses had roamed in, empty now, the fences broken and grass long and swaying in a cold wind from the north. Steadily they climbed the gentle hill that led to the hold. New gates had been built, taller and wider, two squat towers with an arch of stone framing them. Corban passed through into what had been the courtyard.

A wall of sound greeted them as they rode through the broad gates, giants calling out Ildaer's name, stamping their feet and banging weapons on wood and stone. Ildaer lifted a fist in the air, like a champion, his face set in proud lines.

Corban blinked at the number of giants. There were more than he had seen in one place since he had entered the halls of Murias. Two hundred at least, probably more, moving on the hill and amongst the buildings. Of greater impact on him was the sight of Gramm's hall. Or the lack of it. The hall was gone, completely. Burned to the ground or torn down, Corban did not know. Jotun giants were gathered around the foundations of the old hall, laying new groundworks for a much larger building. Corban could see the top of a huge foundation stone sunk into the ground, and behind it a timber framework marking out the dimensions of the new hall, stretching back up the hill like the skeleton of some huge long-dead behemoth. Elsewhere, the same was happening: the myriad of smaller human-built wooden buildings – stables and barns and boathouses and dwelling places – all gone, slowly being replaced by larger stone buildings.

'What are you doing here?' Corban said to Varan as the giant slipped from the saddle behind him and dropped to the ground with a hefty thump.

Varan grinned at him as he helped Corban dismount.

'Moving in,' the giant said.

The next morning Corban awoke in a stone room. A dream lingered, of Coralen. She had been kissing him – or was he kissing her? *No, she was definitely kissing me.* He closed his eyes, trying to hold onto the memory of her, of her lips against his. For a moment he fancied that he could even smell her, the scent of apples on her breath.

I should have spoken to her, after she kissed me that day in Drassil. Not been such a bumbling idiot. What I would give to see her again, to talk to her . . .

The dream was gone, no point moping, as Brina would have said, so he swung out of bed. He had slept in a stone cot with a mattress stuffed with straw, and yet he felt stiff and cold – worse than he'd felt sleeping on tree roots in Forn. He sat on the side of his bed, fingers probing at his ribs, pleased with the results, and then he tested his injured leg upon the ground.

Not so bad, he thought, slowly allowing it to bear more weight. It was stiff, a dull throb, but no spikes of pain.

So. Good, then. If I am ever to get back to my kin and friends, and fight again, then I will need my leg back. He felt a glimmer of hope flicker in the darkness that his world had become.

Gingerly he walked to the doorway, opened the big oak door and peered out.

The hold was as busy as the night before, giants going about the business of rebuilding the settlement. The timber wall was being taken down, section by section: a new wall was going up, made of great stone blocks. At the moment it was only a man high, but even as Corban watched, more rocks were being drawn up in a huge wain, rolled from the back with a deep thud, clouds of dust roiling up about them.

They mean to be here a long time. This is no raiding party or foray. They are settling, building a new home.

A shadow fell across him. Varan appeared, Hala at her side.

'How is your leg?' Hala grunted at him as she shooed him back inside.

'Better, again,' he said, 'though I don't think I'm ready to start running around the paddock, yet.'

'Hold your arms wide, shoulder high,' Hala ordered, and when he did, she made him twist slowly either way. Again, he was pleasantly surprised at the lack of pain.

'Sit,' she said, and set about examining his knee. While she was about her work, the door opened and Ildaer entered; a red-haired giant followed him, with an axe-blade jutting over his back.

'*Is ga dom a labhairt leis an priosunach,*' Ildaer said.

'*Fan do sheal,*' Hala muttered.

Ildaer scowled and folded his arms, standing waiting and glowering at Corban. The red-haired giant stared at Corban with barely concealed hatred.

'It's doing well,' Hala said to him. 'I agree; no running. More brot, though.'

Corban pulled a face but nodded.

Hala grunted and left, Varan went with her.

'It is time for us to talk again,' Ildaer said to Corban, who was still sitting on his bed. Ildaer dragged over a stool and sat on it. He unslung the war-hammer from across his back and rested it upon his lap.

Varan came back in to stand leaning against a wall near the doorway.

'You are my prisoner,' Ildaer began, 'but also my guest. I will not keep you chained to a wall or throw you in a hole. You will live amongst us, and you may go where you please within the boundaries of this hold.'

Corban must have shown the shock he felt, because Ildaer paused and raised an eyebrow.

'What?' the giant asked.

'I am just surprised,' Corban said.

'We are not savages.' Ildaer shrugged. 'And besides, you are a worthy enemy. You slew men of repute amongst us, fine warriors. You have earned our respect.'

Giants are often not what they seem. More complicated.

'Thank you,' Corban said.

'Huh,' Ildaer grunted. 'Do not think that I will not break both your legs if you try to escape. And either Mort or Varan will stay with you, wherever you go.'

The red-haired giant gave Corban a stony stare.

Not such good news.

'Now, we will continue with the questions I began back in Forn.'

'Still something for something?' Corban asked.

'You can ask your questions. I'll answer if I see fit. I came to

Drassil expecting to see Jael's banner assaulting the walls, or raised in victory from the towers, but instead I saw a silver eagle upon a black field.'

'Aye,' Corban sighed, feeling sick that he had not been there to help. To fight. To stand with his kin and friends. 'The silver eagle. That is the banner of Nathair, King of Tenebral,' Corban said flatly.

'And Jael. What of him?'

'His warband was defeated a ten-night earlier. He fled into Forn with a few shieldmen. He is most likely dead.'

Ildaer sat back at that, frowning.

'My question?'

Ildaer waved a hand, inviting.

'Balur One-Eye. You saw him here, at the battle for Gramm's hold. You exchanged words. You knew him?'

Ildaer's eyes narrowed, and for a long moment Corban thought he wasn't going to answer.

'Aye. I know Balur One-Eye; or did. I was young and he was already old, I was a giantling to him.' Ildaer's eyes narrowed and he leaned forwards in his chair. 'Balur is no friend to men. How was he in your company?'

Corban thought of his first meeting with Balur, in the depths of Murias, of their long journey to Drassil, of sparring with the huge warrior in the weapons court, of his rumbling laughter. Of how Balur had charged from the gates of Drassil to come to Corban's rescue against Jael's host. And of the last time he had seen Balur, the two of them talking, alone before Skald's skeleton in the throne of Drassil. Balur had told of how he had been first-sword of the giant High King Skald, and had confessed that he had slain Skald rather than follow his order and strangle Queen Nemain. She had been pregnant with Balur's child, Ethlinn.

'I met Balur in Murias, in the far north of Benoth. We had a common enemy, and so became allies, and companions,' Corban said.

'Balur slew many of your kind,' Ildaer said. 'The tales of his deeds during what you call the Giant Wars, when the Benothi were driven from their fortresses, forced to flee into the north, they show he hates the race of men.'

'I can only tell you what I saw,' Corban replied. 'And life's not so simple, is it? One man is not the same as another, and I have come to see that the same is true of you giants. We are all capable of good and evil, kindness and cruelty.' He shrugged. 'Balur One-Eye *is* my friend.'

'Balur One-Eye is an oathbreaker. He slew Skald, the High King, murdered him when he was supposed to protect him. I spit on Balur One-Eye.'

Mort grunted an agreement.

'When you saw him here, you did not spit on him,' Corban said. 'You *ran* from him.'

Ildaer snarled and lifted a hand, fist bunching.

'*Coinnigh*,' Varan said, '*Hala ni bheadh a chadu*.' Ildaer froze.

'You know little of giants,' Ildaer growled at Corban, 'if you think you know us so well.'

'I don't claim to know you,' Corban said, 'but I do know Balur and some of his kin. Ethlinn . . .' The name had an effect: all three of the giants stared at him as if he'd said he'd broken his fast with Elyon the Maker.

'She lives, then?' Ildaer said.

'Aye, she lives. And she, too, is my friend.'

Ildaer sat and considered Corban a while, and silence settled upon them. Eventually he shifted in his chair.

'Tell me of this Nathair. Is he your friend, too?'

Corban felt his face twitch at Nathair's name.

'No,' he said through gritted teeth, 'he is not. He is the ally of Calidus, who is a Kadoshim made flesh. They are both my enemies.'

'Yet they sit in Drassil. Did you *run*?' Ildaer sneered.

'Why am I here?' Corban asked. 'Why am I still alive?'

'Because my heart tells me that you are someone of worth. Someone with friends, and with enemies,' Ildaer shrugged. 'Perhaps I will offer you to this Nathair, see what that may bring me. He would be in my debt, maybe?'

'Why did you not do it, then? We were at Drassil, Nathair before us.' Corban felt a spike of fear at the thought of being handed over to Nathair and Calidus like a trussed bird. And anger, the image of their faces . . .

'I was injured.' Ildaer touched his shoulder, where Atilius' spear had pierced him. 'You do not show any weakness to men such as Jael or Nathair,' he said, an admonishment. 'And I do not know this Nathair. I knew Jael, had bargained with him. We had an agreement, and I knew his measure. But Jael is dead, you say. And this Nathair . . . I do not trust strangers so easily.'

So he is cautious and mistrustful. Good.

'You cannot deal with Nathair, or Calidus. They have no honour; they are liars who will smile and stab you as they do.'

'So speaks their enemy,' Ildaer snorted.

'You cannot ally yourself to Nathair and Calidus. Cannot join their side.'

'We Jotun are not on any side, except our own.'

Corban shook his head. 'This is the God-War; it does not work like that. All choose a side,' he said. 'If you choose not to fight against Asroth, then you have already chosen him. Doing nothing does not absolve you of choice. Doing nothing puts you firmly on Asroth's side and makes you a coward, as well, for not having the stones to admit it.'

Ildaer stood abruptly, his chair falling over behind him. He gripped his hammer and loomed over Corban.

'Ach, little man,' he snarled, 'it would be so easy to kill you, just for the joy of it, and any advantage you may bring to me be damned.'

'Do it, then,' Corban said, glaring up at Ildaer.

Ildaer glowered back, his moustache twitching in anger, then he slung his war-hammer over his shoulder. 'Perhaps later,' he said. 'So you have chosen Elyon, then.'

'The enemy of my enemy,' Corban shrugged, remembering Balur had said those same words to him in Murias.

'That's no answer,' Ildaer rumbled. 'What do you fight for, if not Elyon?'

'For my kin and loved ones. So that we will not be enslaved or murdered. I've seen the Kadoshim, seen only a brief glimpse of what they would do, and it is terrible. I fight against that. I fight for my freedom.' He felt some of his anger drain. Even though he despised Ildaer, could not remove the memory of him striking down Tukul, he also saw in him a leader trying to steer his people through murky danger-filled waters.

He's scared. Scared of making the wrong choice and thus damning his people; instead he makes no choice and so damns them all the same.

'I tried running from it,' Corban said. 'From Nathair, from Calidus, but it *is* the God-War. It caught up with me, forced me to fight. It will do the same with you. The whole of the Banished Lands is the battleground.'

'I am not running; I am preparing,' Ildaer said. 'We will talk again.' Then he was striding from the room. Varan just stood and stared at Corban a long moment, the angles of his face alien and unreadable, then he followed Ildaer from the room. Mort picked up the chair and sat with his long legs out straight, eyes fixed on Corban.

Corban stood up and walked to the door.

'What are you doing?' Mort asked him in rusty common tongue, each word sounding as if he was tasting something disgusting.

'Going for a walk,' Corban said and opened the door.

Bright sunlight greeted him, the sounds of hammering, harsh voices raised in instruction. Corban stood there, then stepped out into the sunlight.

He walked around the courtyard first, taking it slowly, testing his leg with each step, careful not to over-extend, always mindful of the ground he was walking on. From the top of the hill he had a wide view. He walked on, thoughts slipping back to his conversation with Ildaer, the shadow of Mort following along behind him.

So, I am a bargaining tool, he thought. *Will likely be handed to Nathair and Calidus on a platter. I have no choice. I must escape.*

Noises pulled his attention back, and he looked up. He saw giants shouting, pointing and waving across the river to where a host was gathered on the far side of the river, a great dust cloud above it. In time he could make out individual shapes: bears, *hundreds* of them, each with a rider on its back, sunlight glinting on spear-heads and mail, and behind the bears a sprawling mass of wagons and giants on foot.

'Who are they?' Corban breathed.

'The Jotun,' Mort replied, pride and something else in his voice. *Excitement?*

'With our King at their head.'

CHAPTER TWENTY-THREE

MAQUIN

Maquin stepped out of the tunnel and blinked, half-blinded for a moment, even though he had only emerged into the quiet gloom of Forn Forest. After the tunnel's darkness it felt like the brightest of days.

After the defeat of Gundul's warband, they had gathered wains full of provisions from Gundul's camp. With the help of the men Fidele had found from Drassil and Alben's scouts, they located the old giant tunnel that led to Drassil. It had been a long, dank journey, over a moon of living in near-total darkness until they emerged from a side tunnel – not wanting to emerge too close to Drassil.

Behind him more figures surfaced – the warband of Ripa.

Veradis appeared with the warriors who had stood with him upon the road, as well as Alcyon, Raina and Tain. Maquin had heard how the shield wall had stood against at least three times as many and broken them, and then of how Veradis had rallied his men against the Kadoshim when they were close to being torn apart.

That was some feat. Gundul's warband numbered in the thousands, and we only lost a hundred men. Gundul is slain, the warband of Carnutan broken.

And Jael is dead.

Every time Maquin thought of that moment, and thought of his oath to Kastell fulfilled, he felt a lightness in his chest, like a child awaking on his nameday.

I have fulfilled my oath. He felt himself grinning, though he still felt the distant ache of losing Kastell.

I miss you, my friend.

Alben emerged from the tunnel, in conversation with the men they had found in the forest.

Glad to have them – they can help us find this warband of the Bright Star. Maquin fell in behind the old warrior, along with a score of other men, and together they scouted the land, setting a perimeter around the emerging warband.

It would not be a good time to be attacked.

It took a while for the warband to set up camp: clearing the ground, digging fire-pits and stacking weapons.

Fidele saw him standing on the fringes of their camp and approached, a handful of her new shieldmen at her shoulder. He felt his breath catch in his chest at the sight of her, and enjoyed watching her walk towards him. She saw the look he gave her and smiled shyly back at him.

How has this come to be? Me and Fidele! He barked a laugh at the treetops.

In the heart of Forn Forest, an enemy in league with the Kadoshim ahead of us. Outnumbered and heading into more pain and death, and yet I am the happiest I can ever remember being.

When she reached him he took her hand and kissed it. She smiled and stroked his cheek, pulling him into an embrace, and from the corner of his eye Maquin saw Fidele's new shieldmen look uncomfortable.

They can go spit, Maquin thought. *If Fidele doesn't care, then I sure as hell don't.*

'So, my lady,' he said when they parted, 'it seems the sun still shines.'

'Good riddance to that tunnel,' she said with a shudder.

'Aye. And now on to Drassil.'

'Yes,' she said, her expression turning pensive. He saw the pain and worry in her eyes.

'And Nathair is at Drassil,' he voiced her thoughts.

'He is,' she agreed. A pause. 'As is Lykos.' She couldn't keep the loathing from her voice.

Nor should she. He felt a hot wave of anger at the thought of the Vin Thalun Lord, anger at the little that Fidele had told him of her experience with Lykos, a flash of his own memories, of torture, of flame, of the branding-iron and the knife's edge. His hand reached up to touch the brand Lykos had seared into Maquin's shoulder.

Lykos. Another bastard I mean to kill before this war is done.

Maquin peered through a gap in the undergrowth and felt the air hiss from his lungs.

'So that's Drassil,' he muttered.

For so many years he had heard it only mentioned as a faery tale, a story told on cold nights beside a roaring fire, with a skin of mead being passed around. But to see it, somehow it was more than the tales ever led him to expect.

A wide plain rolled out before him, cleared of trees and undergrowth.

A killing ground, and purpose built.

And beyond the plain a huge fortress stood. Its walls were high, its oak gate wide and thick. Towers rose from within the walls, but behind and above it, overwhelming all else, the enormous trunk of a giant tree soared. Its bulk was so vast that Maquin did not realize at first what it was, its trunk broader than any great hall Maquin had seen, its branches arching above and over the fortress like some ancient giant protector.

Drassil, and the great tree. Well, that's a sight, and no denying.

Maquin looked at those lined beside him: Alben, their scouts and the giant Alcyon, who had joined them. All looked awestruck, even Alcyon. The only ones who were not were the warriors that they had found in the forest.

They've seen it before. Lived in it.

They had led Maquin and the others to Drassil, telling them that their own warband moved camp regularly, so the best way to find them was to go to Drassil and then hunt for scouting parties.

Maquin looked back to the fortress, saw a banner ripple above the gate tower, a silver eagle upon a black field.

So it is as we feared. Nathair has taken the fortress. Is there even anyone left here for us to fight alongside? If not, then we've walked a damn long way for nothing.

As he watched, the gates of Drassil opened, a slow, ponderous movement, the creak of oak and iron rumbling across the open plain. Figures appeared, marching onto the plain. There were a hundred men at least, heading off to the south, towards the forest. As the distance between them narrowed Maquin saw they were a combination of men, some clothed in the black and silver of Tenebral, long shields on their arms, intermingled with a more disorganized mass, men in leather and iron, bucklers instead of shields, short swords at their hips.

The Vin Thalun, Maquin realized, feeling his lip curl in a snarl. *What if Lykos leads them?*

Before he even knew it, he was slipping into the undergrowth and padding silently through the trees, shadowing the men on the plain. The sound of footsteps behind him told that some, at least, were following him.

The enemy patrol entered the forest to the south, moving along a well-worn path, winding through the maze of thick-boled trees.

'What are you doing?' Alben whispered in his ear as Maquin shadowed the patrol, careful to stay hidden. Alcyon was a few steps behind them. 'They are too many for us.'

'I know, but what are they doing?' Maquin whispered. 'Why are they out here?'

'Good question,' Alben muttered.

They followed them for a while, saw that more paths were being cut through the forest; areas cleared, stripped of foliage, and every now and then the patrol would stop, the men of Tenebral would set up a perimeter with their shields, while the Vin Thalun laboured within to clear a new stretch of ground.

'Perhaps they are attempting to make a new road from Drassil, like Gundul's?' Alben whispered as they lay on a bank behind the patrol and watched.

Maquin grunted. He was staring hard at the Vin Thalun, trying to pick out details. So far he had not seen Lykos amongst their ranks. Still though his fingers twitched for his knife. How he hated the Vin Thalun.

'I think it is time to leave,' Alben said with a pat on Maquin's shoulder.

'Wait,' Alcyon said beside them, a low rumble. 'Something's out there.'

Abruptly there was a tension in the air, a silence, then a whistling sound, the wet *thunk* of flesh being cleaved. Screams from Vin

Thalun and eagle-guard. Maquin stared harder and saw the hilt of a single-bladed axe protruding from a Vin Thalun skull. Then axe-wielding men were swarming from the undergrowth: warriors wrapped in fur and leather, long hair and beards braided, their appearance similar to those whom Fidele had found. From the far side different warriors attacked: some clad in mail and red cloaks hefting spears, others clothed more lightly, just leather and sharp iron. There was something familiar about them.

Then a great bellow rang out, war-cries, and out from the gloom of the forest larger shapes appeared, man-like, but bigger, wielding war-hammers and battle-axes.

Giants! What is going on here? Maquin counted at least ten of them charging at the enemy patrol like an avalanche.

The attackers struck into the patrol from three sides, breaking into their ranks even as the eagle-guard were lifting their shields and desperately trying to form their wall.

Don't let them, Maquin willed, knowing how deadly the wall of shields was. He had seen it first-hand in Haldis, when Veradis had used the shield wall to break through the might of the Hunen giants. Even as he watched he saw some of the black-painted shields snapping together, a dozen men forming up, others fighting through to join them, making a small square. Swords stabbed from behind the shield wall; the attackers were pierced, falling.

'Not going to just sit and watch this,' Maquin grunted, scrambling to his feet and breaking into a loping run. He knew that Alben and the rest would follow.

He reached over his shoulders, gripped the hilts of his two short swords and drew them as he ran. Behind him he heard Alcyon bellow his war-cry, 'KURGAN, KURGAN,' and in front of them the battle seemed to still for a moment, many pausing to look their way.

Got their attention now.

Maquin grinned, a feral thing, and then he was amongst them.

He veered around the flank of eagle-guard in their shield wall, swung at an ankle beneath a shield rim, felt his sword scrape along iron-banded greaves, saw a sword jabbing out at him and swerved away. Then he was amongst the Vin Thalun. In half a dozen strokes of his sword four men were dead or bleeding out on the floor.

Maquin screamed wordless joy as the battle-rage took him and he strode through them like death itself, parrying, chopping, stabbing. He left one of his swords stuck in an enemy's spine, drew a knife and fought on.

Behind him he glimpsed Alcyon hacking at the shield wall with the two long axes he'd taken from Gundul's woodsmen. He was standing back, not getting close enough for their short swords to reach him. He hooked an axe over the rim of a shield and dragged the warrior holding it stumbling forwards, his other axe chopping into the man, between neck and shoulder. He dropped with a gurgling scream, blood spraying as Alcyon wrenched the blade free, but before he could take advantage of the crack in the shield wall another man had filled the gap.

Four snarling Vin Thalun came at him. Maquin hesitated a moment, then he was running, spinning close amongst them. His knife opened a throat with his first strike, his sword hacking through a forearm with his second, leaving both arm and buckler on the ground. He blocked an overhead blow from the third Vin Thalun, lunging in, swayed away from a sword thrust, hooked his ankle and sent his opponent crashing to the ground. A sharp thrust of his sword finished the man, and Maquin was stepping over the dead warrior to get at the last man.

They circled one another, Maquin crouched low, sword and knife bloody, hands and arms slick with gore. He grinned at the young Vin Thalun warrior, who was staring hard at Maquin; as recognition dawned, he staggered back a step.

'It's the Old Wolf,' the Vin Thalun stammered, then louder. 'It's the OLD WOLF!' he cried, then turned and ran.

Maquin looked around for someone else to fight, saw that most of the battle was done, only a small knot of Vin Thalun still standing.

A glance over his shoulder showed Alben, Alcyon and their scouts still harrying the shield wall, which was marching steadily northwards, trying to break for Drassil.

Alcyon hammered another axe-blow into a shield, sending a shudder rippling through the wall, but doing no other damage. Suddenly the other giants were there and instead of attacking the shield wall, turned their attention to Alcyon, circling him, war-hammers and axes waving threateningly at him. One of the giants took a swing at Alcyon with a war-hammer. Alcyon deflected it with a blow from one axe. The warriors from Drassil who had travelled with them were shouting, 'Peace, they are allies,' at the giants, but to no avail.

In the distance Maquin glimpsed the eagle-guard shield wall disappearing into the forest. Furious at their escape, Maquin turned his attention back to the giants and ran straight at Alcyon's attacker. He threw himself into the back of the giant's knees, dropping him to the ground, rolled over the giant's torso and knelt upon his chest, sword-tip resting against the giant's throat.

'This isn't exactly the thanks we were expecting,' Maquin growled.

Then a young man was stepping out from the midst of the giants, in mail shirt and red cloak, thick-necked and long-armed. He was staring as if he couldn't believe his eyes.

'Maquin?' he whispered.

Maquin lifted his blade, climbing off of the giant, and gave a snort of laughter.

'Tahir?'

The man in front of him was grinning now, arms opening wide and then they were hugging each other tight, slapping backs, laughing.

'I thought you fell,' Tahir said, 'with Orgull. The two of you were holding the door beneath Dun Kellen . . .' Tears were streaming from his eyes, and Maquin realized he was crying, too, and laughing. Tahir, his last living sword-brother from the Gadrai. A friend from another lifetime.

'We were taken, made slaves by the Vin Thalun,' Maquin murmured.

'Orgull?' Tahir asked.

Maquin shook his head. 'He fell. Haelan?' he asked.

Tahir lowered his head. 'He survived; we made it to Orgull's kin. But in the battle of Drassil we were separated. I hope that he lives still . . .'

Another man stepped from the crowd, one of the axe-throwers. He was tall and muscled, a knotted braid in his thick beard.

'You knew my brother?' he said.

'This is Wulf,' Tahir introduced. 'Orgull's brother.'

Maquin could see the resemblance now.

'Aye,' Maquin said. 'A better man I never knew.'

Wulf nodded grimly.

'But how are you here?' Tahir blurted.

'It's a long story,' Maquin smiled.

'What's all the fuss about? It's not like he's the only pit-fighter to make it this far north,' another voice said, a small, wiry man stepping forwards with a sharp grin. He was dressed similarly to Maquin, favouring a leather jerkin and breeches over heavy mail. He was shaven-haired, his skin burned dark by the sun.

'Javed?' Maquin said. 'Have I died and crossed the bridge of swords?'

'Not yet,' Javed said, coming closer and punching Maquin in the gut, doubling him over.

'That's for leaving me behind in a Vin Thalun arena,' Javed said, 'while you ran off with a pretty lady!' Then Javed was laughing, slapping Maquin on the shoulder and helping him straighten; Maquin was coughing, still searching for breath. 'Damn, but it's good to see you, Old Wolf,' Javed grinned.

'It's good to see you, too,' Maquin said when he had his voice under control. 'Looks like mine isn't the only story to tell.'

'There is much to say,' Alben said from behind them, 'but perhaps after we have stopped a new giant feud.'

The giant whom Maquin had knocked to the ground had risen and was still glowering at Alcyon, who was frowning back.

'Fachen,' Tahir called up to the giant. 'These are our allies, come to help us.'

'He is *Kurgan*,' Fachen said, as if the two things were incompatible, and Alcyon gave a half-smile, half-snarl.

'Aye, and I am Tahir of the Gadrai, giant-slayer. But that was my old life; in this new one we're sword-brothers, and if he's come to fight alongside us, then so is he.'

Fachen and the other Benothi shared a look.

'You will put the old grievance aside?' Fachen rumbled.

'Aye,' Alcyon answered, lowering his twin axes.

'All right then, as will I,' Fachen said. 'Welcome to Drassil.'

CHAPTER TWENTY-FOUR

VERADIS

Veradis marched through Forn Forest, Krelis beside him, Fidele, Maquin and Alben just ahead. Alcyon, Raina and Tain were visible in front of them, walking with a handful of the new giants, as well as some of the others that Alben and Maquin had encountered in the forest.

The Benothi giant clan, so Alben said. It was a Benothi giant I met in Domhain, allied to Queen Rhin. Uthas . . .

Their warband marched behind them, a thick, winding column that disappeared amongst the trees. Twilight was a thick fog about them, limiting Veradis' vision. Alben had filled them in on the situation at Drassil: Nathair was holding the fortress, the warband of Corban had been broken and scattered, but the survivors were now reunited and fighting on, waging a war of stealth and attrition on their enemy. They were walking now to join these survivors.

'Been walking a long time,' Krelis said to Veradis.

'Aye,' Veradis agreed. He looked up at Krelis, tall and broad, not much difference between him and one of the giants who were leading them through Forn. 'Sore feet, big brother?' he said to Krelis.

Krelis looked down at him. 'I've had worse.'

'I'm glad to be at your side,' Veradis said. There had been years of tension between them, never actually coming to blows, but near enough on occasion. It had been caused by Veradis' conflict with their father.

And because of Father's treatment of Nathair. Perhaps he never trusted Nathair.

Seems he was right.

But surely there is still good in Nathair. It is Calidus who has misled him, lured him down a path that he now feels he cannot turn from.

'Aye,' Krelis grunted. 'Me too.'

It felt good to be on the same side again.

Those ahead of them stopped; shadowy figures emerged from the gloom around them. Veradis had a moment of panic, reaching for his sword and shrugging the shield from his back. The people appearing out of the forest were Kadoshim.

No, he realized, *they are Jehar warriors, untainted by the Kadoshim.*

Others appeared from the trees; Veradis recognized the men introduced to him as Tahir and Wulf.

Soon they were climbing a gentle hill, at its crown a plateau upon which a warband was camped, woven branches and hides making screens and tents, fire-pits were even crackling, well covered from view.

'Welcome to our camp,' Tahir said as he approached Veradis, a broad smile upon his face. He was young, a strong jaw, his face open and honest. Veradis liked him straight away.

Veradis looked around, gauging numbers by the tents and beds, by cook-fires and weapons racks. *We number seven hundred swords. There are perhaps another four hundred, maybe a little more here. Not the largest warband the Banished Lands have ever seen.*

As the men of Ripa settled in, digging more fire-pits, racking weapons, many approached them and began to help, whether they were Jehar, Benothi giants or men of Isiltir. Veradis noticed the relaxed camaraderie amongst them, regardless of race or gender.

When they were done, and Veradis had ensured that all of his men were settled with food in their bellies and drinks in their hands, Tahir and Wulf called for a meeting.

'Where are we going?' Veradis asked as they walked down the hill and were led into the forest where the trees grew thick and tall above them.

'To meet with our leaders,' Tahir replied over his shoulder.

So, finally the time that I will meet Corban. For so long I thought him my enemy, thought him the Black Sun of prophecy. And now he is to be my ally. The Bright Star. He shook his head. *These are strange days. Nathair, what have you done?*

They marched on, winding along a path that had been trampled through dense vegetation. Veradis heard the sound of running water and they spilt into a flat, open glade, on its far side a sheer drop leading to what sounded like a river. For a moment he thought he heard another sound – *growling?* But the noise of the river was loud, drowning all else out. Standing at the far edge of the glade above where the river must be was a grey-haired, thin, old woman. Her head snapped around at their entrance, a sharp intelligence in her gaze.

Many others were there: Jehar warriors patrolling the perimeter – the sight of them still made Veradis feel uncomfortable – and there were giants, two of them sitting near the fire-pit. One white-haired with age, his muscles thick and knotted as an ancient tree, a scar-latticed hole where one of his eyes had been. His good eye fixed razor-sharp upon Alcyon. Kneeling beside him was a giantess, long-limbed and muscled, though appearing slender beside the other. Her hair was sleek and dark, and she gripped a spear in her hand, watching as Veradis and the others entered the glade.

A Jehar warrior came to greet them, each movement graceful and economical. Veradis recognized him. Akar had been one of Sumur's captains. He had helped Cywen by removing an arrow from her stallion.

And Cywen. Where is she? No doubt I will hear an 'I told you so' *from her.* He smiled at the thought of it.

'Akar?' he said.

The Jehar paused in his stride, eyes narrowing. His eyes flickered from Veradis to his companions, pausing on Alcyon, then finally back to Veradis.

'You are the Black Sun's first-sword,' he said calmly. 'Are you here as a challenge, or a treachery?'

'Neither,' Veradis said. 'My eyes have been opened. I am Nathair's first-sword no longer.'

Akar stood in front of Veradis, just staring at him.

'And you,' the white-haired giant rumbled as he stood. Veradis noted he favoured his right side, his huge-knuckled hand moving to his ribs.

A wound, not yet fully healed.

'I fought you at Murias.' The white-haired giant strode towards Alycon. 'You held the starstone axe.'

'Well met, Balur One-Eye,' Alcyon said.

'Is it?' the giant said, stopping a stride from Alcyon. 'You served the Black Sun and his *aingeal dubh.*' He paused, spat. 'His black angel.'

'I was under an enchantment, controlled. A slave. I am bewitched no more. I would fight against that same Dark Angel, now.'

'So,' Akar said, 'a servant of Nathair, and a servant of Calidus. And we are just to accept you as allies?'

'They speak the truth,' Fidele said, stepping forwards. 'I am Fidele, widow of Aquilus, High King of Tenebral.'

'I know you,' Akar said. 'I saw you stand beside Nathair.'

'He is my son,' Fidele said, 'but I do not stand with him now.' She returned Akar's gaze, proud and defiant. 'And I saw you in Jerolin,' she said. 'A captain of Sumur, who followed Nathair.'

Akar nodded, Fidele's point made.

'Our enemy has already won,' Alben said, 'if those that would stand against him will not trust one another.'

'And you are?' Akar asked.

'Alben, swordsmaster of Ripa. I am a friend to Meical, have belonged to his cause for many years, now. Where is he?'

Akar looked grim.

'Meical is slain. He sacrificed his life in Drassil, so that many of us could escape.'

'What? Dead! That cannot be!'

'His head is on a spear in the courtyard of Drassil,' Akar said. 'It is a great blow to the cause.'

Alben put a hand to his eyes, shaking his head.

Maquin spoke up. He'd been standing silent.

'These are good people, and they have come here to offer their help.' He looked at them all. 'And I speak for us all when I say we are here to fight against Asroth and his servants. We have all been done wrong by them, suffered great loss because of them. Just to get here we have fought many a battle, destroyed the warband of Gundul, King of Carnutan, and slain Jael, King of Isiltir.' He paused there, with something flashing across his face. 'Near enough four thousand men who were cutting a way through this forest to come and fight you. They are slain or scattered now, because of us. And we bring with us a great stock of supplies, plundered from Gundul's camp. Food, water, fuel, war gear.' Maquin shrugged. 'If you do not trust us, do not want our help, then say the word and we will leave, go back to Tenebral, or somewhere else, perhaps, and Nathair can pick us all off, divided and weak.'

A silence filled the glade.

'At last,' a sharp voice said from the fire, 'someone who speaks some sense.'

It was the grey-haired old woman.

'Now stop this bickering,' she added, giving Akar a fierce look.

'I have been deceived once. I would not see it happen again. And Gar left me as lord of this warband, while he is gone,' Akar said defensively.

'True enough,' the old woman said. 'There is a place for caution. But these people are genuine. Or so I judge them to be. They are telling the truth. And as for Gar – yes, he did leave you in charge, and I'm sure he made the right choice. You're very good when it comes to chopping heads from Kadoshim. But there is more to winning than that. Allies, for example. Men, and women,' she nodded to Fidele, 'who have travelled far and endured many a hardship to reach us and offer their help. Besides, if that isn't good enough for you and you want to pull rank, then I can play that, too. I am Brina, counsellor to Corban, your Bright Star, remember. So what I say should be heeded.' She poked a bony finger in Akar's chest, and he flinched.

Akar finally nodded, convinced or just giving in, Veradis could not tell. *Probably a little of both. This Brina inspires fear.*

The giant Balur nodded, too. He walked around Alcyon, staring hard. 'You are Kurgan. There is no love between our clans.'

'Aye. That is a truth,' Alcyon answered.

'That was another age,' a new voice said, the giantess, moving to stand beside Balur. 'A broken age. I am Ethlinn, daughter of Nemain, and I say it is time now to build a new one. Instead of the five giant clans there need only be two: those that fight for Asroth, and those that fight against him.'

'Ethlinn?' Alcyon hissed. Something crossed his face: shock, hope? He dropped to his knees in the grass before Ethlinn.

'Aye,' Alcyon grunted, looking up at her. 'A new age. A new clan. I am for that.'

She smiled at him.

'Well then,' Balur said, looking between the two. He nodded to himself and held his hand out.

Alcyon grabbed his arm in the warrior grip and pulled himself upright.

'Well met, Alcyon of the Kurgan.'

'Well, I'm glad to see we're all getting along,' Krelis said. 'But there's one thing I'd like to ask.'

They all looked at him.

'Where's this Corban I've heard so much about?'

Another silence. Brina bowed her head. She sucked in a deep breath and straightened.

'He has been captured, taken prisoner.'

'Nathair has him?' Veradis gasped.

'No, not Nathair,' Akar said.

'The Jotun giants,' Balur rumbled.

'Some have gone after him,' Brina added.

Abruptly there was a savage snarling from beyond the glade, the distinct sound of wood crunching, splintering, followed closely by a loud crack, as of metal breaking, then a scrabbling sound and a dark shape was surging up from the darkness at the glade's edge.

Suddenly everyone was scattering and Veradis and his companions were drawing weapons, spreading into a line, Alcyon leaping to his feet. Maquin stepped in front of Fidele, sword and knife in his hands.

A huge wolven stood in the gloom, muzzle and head emerging from the darkness first, the rest of it a dense shadow behind it.

Veradis took an involuntary step backwards.

The wolven padded into the glade, a slavering, solid mass of muscle and fur. Huge fangs dripped saliva, lips drawn back in a snarl, its bone-white fur streaked with scars. A collar of iron links hung from about its neck, with the splintered remains of a thick wooden stake hanging from it.

Veradis felt his courage waver, just for a moment. He gripped his sword tighter, wishing he'd brought his shield.

And a shield wall, for that matter. That's no ordinary wolven. She's too big, too broad.

Then Brina was stepping between them, moving towards the fearsome beast.

She's insane, a dead woman.

'There, there, my darling,' Brina said as she strode over to the wolven, reaching a hand up to it.

The wolven padded to her and pressed its head into the palm of her hand, then rubbed its muzzle against her chest, making Brina stagger back a step.

I must be dreaming!

'Meet Storm,' Brina said, with something like deep affection in her voice, as she turned to see the shocked faces of Veradis and his companions.

Veradis blinked, finally breathing.

'Storm. Corban's wolven?'

'I wouldn't say she's *his*, exactly,' Brina said. 'More that they belong to each other.'

'Pack,' Tahir said. 'They are pack.'

'But it's got a big iron chain and stake about its neck,' Krelis pointed out.

'*She*,' Brina corrected, scratching the wolven under the chin. Storm seemed to like it. 'And she's been unwell. War-wounded.' Brina's hand went up to a scar at the top of Storm's shoulder, furless now. 'When Corban was taken, Storm fell defending him. She nearly died, hovered at death's doorway a long time. But she is better now. Better than she's ever been.'

'Then why was she chained and staked?' Maquin asked.

'Because from the moment she could stand she's been trying to go after Corban. I couldn't let her do that, it would have been too much for her.' Brina unhooked the chain about the wolven's neck, slipping it from her.

'Is she all right now, though?' Krelis asked.

'She's just broken a wooden stake as thick as your leg,' Brina said. 'Balur pounded it into the ground himself. And she's bitten through an iron chain. I'd say she's well enough.'

Storm looked about at them all, took a few deep sniffs of the air, then lifted her head and howled.

The sound echoed through the glade, long and mournful. Storm's muscles bunched and then she was leaping away; there was the crash of undergrowth as she ploughed through it and then she was gone, only her howl lingering in the air.

'Where's she gone?' Krelis asked.

'I think that's clear enough,' Brina said. 'She gone after Corban.'

CHAPTER TWENTY-FIVE

LYKOS

Lykos leaned back in his chair and drank deeply from his cup, spilling mead into his beard. He belched and looked around.

He was sitting in a stone-built hall with Vin Thalun all about him eating and drinking, rolling dice on throw-boards, fighting, without using anything sharp, of course, except perhaps their teeth.

To one side of him lay a pile of silver and gold, cups and plates, torcs and brooches, necklaces, fine-made swords and scabbards – a mountain of plunder taken from the dead and pillaged from this ancient, long-empty fortress. His men looked to him with respect, called him gift-giver and gold-friend. In short he was lord of all he saw, had strong men about him. Had achieved his dreams.

Then why am I so bored?

He puffed his cheeks out and belched again.

The gates to his hall opened and an eagle-guard entered, looked about, then wound his way through the revelry to stand at Lykos' feet.

'What?' Lykos asked.

'King Nathair and the Lord Calidus wish to see you, my lord,' the warrior said. He was a young man, dressed in gleaming mail shirt and a polished cuirass of black leather.

Lykos sighed.

'Now, I suppose,' he said as he rose from his chair, taking it slowly, but swaying nevertheless.

'Aye, my lord. They asked you to hurry.'

'Why? More prisoners to execute? Surely that can wait until the morning.'

'No, my lord. There is a patrol returning. They have been seen crossing the plain.'

'Ah, better,' Lykos grunted, grabbing his sword-belt from where it was hanging over the back of his chair and slinging it over his shoulder. He marched quickly through the hall after the eagle-guardsman and out into the night, with ten of his sworn men following him. Drassil was theirs, but it never hurt to be too careful, and Lykos had heard strange tales of men found dead, or going missing.

That won't be me.

So, the day's patrol is returning. Some good news, then.

It was unusual for a patrol to return at night; all were ordered to be back within the walls of Drassil by sunset. But when the patrol sent out that day had not returned at all, they had been assumed dead.

Sixty of my men. Lykos had been angry, for this was not the first time he had lost men on these patrols. He marched on; the eagle-guard ahead of him was setting quite a pace. He was happy to match it, pleased that there was something to do.

Who would have thought that I would be here, in fabled Drassil, having won a great victory, on the brink of achieving my wildest dreams, and yet I am bored. He looked about, up at the stone towers and twisting branches of the great tree and pulled a sour face.

I hate this place. I am a seafarer, a man of salt and sail, I should not be confined here in this . . . walled prison!

They turned a corner and entered the wide street that led to the gates. As Lykos entered the courtyard he was assaulted by the stench.

Draig dung and rotting flesh. Torches flickered from iron sconces set high in the courtyard walls, turning the rows of severed heads adorning the spikes into grisly creatures with maniacal grins. On the battlement he saw Calidus and Nathair standing together, looking out over the plain.

'Glad you could join us,' Calidus muttered in the firelight as Lykos joined them.

Calidus had ordered the building of fire-pits around the walls of Drassil, a few hundred paces out from the wall. A ring of them, so that it appeared that Drassil was guarded by a circle of fire. The intention was to put a stop to night-time raids that had been occurring randomly: Jehar warriors sneaking close to the walls, scaling a wall with a grapple-hook and then running amok amongst the wall guards, cutting down as many as they could before word spread or they came face to face with a few Kadoshim. So far the fire-pits seemed to have worked, and by the flickering light Lykos instantly saw a huddle of men moving across the plain, flames glinting on mail. He saw a lot of shields, marking the eagle-guard.

And not so many Vin Thalun.

'They do not look so many as when they went out,' Lykos observed.

'Thank you for pointing out the obvious,' Calidus snapped.

He doesn't seem so happy here, either. Certainly not as happy as he should be, considering he's close to conquering the world.

The men on the plain drew near to the gates. Calidus shouted for the gates to be opened, then he turned and swept down the stairs, his cloak a trailing shadow behind him.

Lykos shared a look with Nathair.

'Some people are never happy,' he said to the King of Tenebral, offering him a wry smile when Nathair only gave him a stony stare in response.

No one has a sense of humour in this forest.

When Lykos reached the courtyard, the gates were already closing. He saw a few of his men, collapsed on the flagstones, exhausted, leaning against one another. Calidus was talking to a captain of the eagle-guard.

'Ambushed,' the young warrior was saying. 'There were giants, axe-throwers, some others.' He looked exhausted. 'We only escaped because of the shield wall.'

'And left my Vin Thalun behind,' Lykos said, not able to help himself. Nathair gave him a foul look.

'We tried, my lord,' the eagle-guard said. 'Tried to pull them into our square, but the enemy were upon us so quickly, there was no time. Many of my eagle-guard fell, too.'

As if that's a compensation.

'So you saw no sign of Gundul or Lothar's scouts?' Calidus asked.

'None, my lord, but we left markers. The next patrol will be able to move deeper—'

'Not my men,' Lykos growled and walked away before Calidus

had a chance to respond. He strode to his handful of warriors, just six Vin Thalun left from the sixty who had marched through the gates that morning.

I have lost almost as many men on patrol as I did during the battle for this stinking dung-hole.

'Well?' he said wearily.

'I saw the Old Wolf,' one of the Vin Thalun said, looking up at him.

'What?'

'The Old Wolf, he was out there, with his knives, covered in blood. It was like being in the arena against him.' The Vin Thalun shivered.

The words sent a jolt of fear through Lykos.

'You are mistaken,' he said. 'If it was the Old Wolf, you would not be here.'

'Four of us attacked him,' the warrior said. 'He cut them down as if they were nothing. I only escaped by holding him off a while, then the giants started fighting and he was distracted . . .'

Lykos grabbed the young warrior by his leather vest and jerked him up onto his feet. 'Don't lie to me; tell me true. If I find out you're lying . . .'

'It was him, I swear on all I hold dear,' the warrior assured him. 'I saw him fight on Panos, put coin on him, and in Jerolin. It was him.'

'I saw him, too,' one of the others said. 'I wasn't so close, but I saw him. It was the Old Wolf.'

Lykos turned away, his mind reeling.

He was at the tower of Brikan, on the edge of Forn, and escaped from there. So it is possible that Maquin is out there. And if he is out there, then maybe so is Fidele . . .

And now he no longer felt bored. He felt scared, and excited. *Alive.*

Lykos frowned at the screams. He was back in the great courtyard, listening to a man as he was slowly impaled upon a spear.

Movement drew his eye and he saw Nathair striding from the courtyard, a few of his eagle-guard about him.

Doesn't have the stomach for this kind of thing. Some men are just not equipped to rule. I wonder what Calidus promised him to convince him to stay.

Calidus was still there, though, standing by the stable-blocks, staring at the remaining prisoners as they were led from the courtyard, still over two hundred of them left.

Lykos saw Cywen amidst all of the prisoners, dark-haired, face pinched and eyes grey with the horror of it all.

It can't be a pleasant way to start your day, watching a comrade skewered, and listening to them beg and wail and plead. Not a lot of dignity in that death.

Cywen walked past Lykos, her head bowed, and then Calidus was stepping out towards her, grabbing the scruff of her shirt and dragging her across the courtyard. Lykos hurried after them, intrigued by this display of emotion.

A chance at some entertainment, at least.

He caught up with them in the shadows of a stable door.

'Where is your brother?' Calidus was hissing in Cywen's face, bending her backwards with his grip on the back of her neck.

'Where is he? Why does he not come for you? For them?' He waved a hand in the general direction of the screams. 'He is supposed to be the Bright Star! Saviour of the world, defender of the innocent!' He was spluttering now, voice rising.

Cywen just stared at him with hate-filled eyes.

Calidus seemed to run out of energy and released Cywen with a disdainful flick of his wrist, sending her stumbling. She righted herself and began to walk after the other prisoners. After a couple of steps she stopped.

'You should be glad Corban has waited so long,' she said. 'It means you've had a few extra days of life.'

'Huh, please,' snorted Calidus.

'Be sure of this: when he does come, it is *you* he will seek out. You slew our mam. He won't forget that.'

'I am counting on it,' Calidus said. He reached inside his cloak and pulled something out, an old flower, purple and prickly.

A thistle?

Calidus twirled it slowly between finger and thumb, something of his old mocking smile returning.

Cywen looked at the flower, confused and frowning, then her

expression changed. To fury. She launched herself at Calidus, but he lashed out with a hand, connected with her cheek, sending her to the floor. As she tried to scramble to her feet Calidus nodded at a Kadoshim in the shadows, who sprang agilely forwards and dragged Cywen from the courtyard. She was spitting and snarling like an alley-cat as she disappeared around a corner.

Lykos walked out of the sunshine into the cool of Drassil's great hall.

The steps were wide, arched in a gentle half-circle around the hall, so big they were more like tiered seats that led down to the sunken floor of the chamber. Above him was a curving stone wall, with staircases spiralling upwards around it to disappear into cunningly fashioned towers. The floor of the chamber was sunken into the earth, wide and flat, periodically dotted with fire-pits.

At the chamber's centre was the trunk of the great tree, mottled and dark, wider than Jerolin's feast-hall. Huge knots studded the trunk, bark peeling, trails of leaking sap dried hard. Here and there were black holes, indentations bored into the tree by bird or creature, squirrel or owl. Even as Lykos looked, he saw a brightly coloured chaffinch swoop down from the chamber and alight on a hole's rim, pause for a moment, its beak full with straw and moss, and then hop into the darkness.

At the trunk's base, growing out of it, or so it seemed, was a carven chair, filled with the skeleton of a giant, held there still by the spear that had struck the death blow.

Skald, the giant High King. Skewered like a slaughtered pig. How the mighty can fall.

Either side of the chair, skeleton and the spear, two new objects had been placed. On one side the starstone axe was now hanging from a hook that had been hammered into the trunk, a heavy chain wrapped around it. And on the other side was the cauldron, huge and black, taller and broader than a giant, squatting like some great bloated toad.

Before the gathered Treasures there was a table, long and wide. A meeting table, and standing leaning against it was Calidus.

Lykos walked down the stairs and across the flagstoned floor.

Calidus ignored him and Lykos poured himself a drink from a jug on the table, dark red wine. He took a sip, slurping loudly and then smacking his lips. Calidus looked at him as if he were an annoying insect.

Which I probably am to him, with his great plans.

Lykos took another drink, smacked his lips louder.

Calidus tutted. 'You should stop doing that,' he said. 'It may get you killed one day.'

'Stop what? Drinking wine. That's a little harsh, I have few pleasures in life and—'

'Not drinking wine.' Calidus looked at him; the intensity of his attention made Lykos uncomfortable. His face was scarred from the burning Veradis and Alcyon had treated him to, half his face blackened and melted like wax, his silver hair reduced mostly to stubble now. He was no longer handsome, as he once had been.

'I speak of your tendency towards deliberate provocation and goading,' Calidus continued. 'It is a bad habit of yours.'

Lykos raised an eyebrow at that, then shrugged.

He's probably right.

'I'll drink quieter,' he said with a smile, then drained his cup. 'What are you looking at?'

'Skald, the starstone spear, the axe and cauldron, the great tree. So much history, and yet this same war is being fought.'

'Aye. A little closer to being over now, though, eh?'

Calidus ground his teeth. 'Closer, but still so much to do.'

'That's not what I wanted to hear,' Lykos said sullenly. 'I don't like this place. My men don't like this place. They are dying, whether out on your patrols, or gutting each other over a game of throwboard.'

Without Lykos really seeing Calidus move, the Kadoshim was nose to nose with him, a hand about Lykos' throat, and Lykos was stumbling back into the table.

'You think I care what you *want to hear*?' Calidus hissed. 'What you or your men *like*?' The grip around Lykos' throat tightened. 'I don't *want* to be here, either, amongst you *vermin*, consumed by your petty desires. Better for me if you and all your kind were slaughtered and hanging on hooks, ready for the feast.'

He needs me. He will not kill me.

With an act of will Lykos stayed motionless, forced himself not to struggle or retaliate.

Then Calidus was no longer there, the vice-like grip on his throat gone. Lykos slumped forwards, coughing.

'I did not mean to offend you,' Lykos wheezed when he had enough breath in his body.

'I overreacted,' Calidus said, not looking at him, but gazing back at the skeleton of Skald and the Treasures again.

The closest I'll get to an apology.

Calidus looked up at the sound of footsteps; Lykos followed his gaze. Nathair was walking through the open doorway and down the steps towards them, his usual honour guard behind him, Legion at his side. Somehow the Kadoshim always looked bigger than the others – something about the way he walked, a barely contained power exuding from him.

Perhaps because there are so many Kadoshim spirits crammed inside the one body.

The cloud of ever-present flies buzzed around the creature.

'Good, we can begin, then,' Calidus said, waving for Lykos to sit, as if the violence he had threatened a few moments ago had not happened.

Lykos did sit, pouring himself another cup of wine and leaning back in his chair, resting one boot upon the wooden table.

So, let's see what revelations and delights this meeting will bring us. And you, Calidus, I will add your name to those I am looking forward to killing.

CHAPTER TWENTY-SIX

NATHAIR

'Wait for me here,' Nathair ordered Caesus as he strode down the steps of the great hall, Legion beside him. His captain and the eagle-guard with him stopped on the stairs.

So, Lykos is here already. That makes a change. He's usually the last, and staggering.

Nathair reached the table and sat. He saw that a cup of wine had already been poured for him. Lykos gave him a grin and raised his cup. Nathair had to control himself so close to Lykos, resisting the urge to pull out his sword and gut him.

He wed my mother. Just the sight of him makes me feel sick to my stomach.

Calidus had explained that it had been a political move, a way of strengthening the bonds between Vin Thalun and Tenebral.

But Lykos and my mother! And I saw the way he looked at her during the trial in Brikan.

'It's good wine, my friend,' Lykos said to him, drinking from his own cup and spilling some wine into his beard. Nathair stopped his lip from curling.

A small sip of wine. He did not want his wits clouded when he was around Calidus.

Nathair considered his allies. *A drunken pirate. A demon-possessed attraction to flies and a half-burned Kadoshim. How have I sunk so low?*

It was not the first time he'd asked himself this question; the feelings of shame and self-loathing bubbling up within him were old and familiar.

How I long for the days when Veradis and I were leading our warband on a great adventure, and Calidus was a mere counsellor. He felt a hot rage at the way he had been manipulated, manoeuvred.

No. Stop. You must focus on the details, he told himself. *You have made your choice, walked your path. Now focus on how you will win. Then, when this war is done . . .*

'Welcome,' Calidus said. 'I have some news.'

'I hope it is about how we are going to destroy our enemy, camped out in the forest and doing considerable harm to my men every time they venture out of the gates of Drassil,' Nathair said.

'And mine,' Lykos murmured.

Calidus frowned. 'The survivors of our enemy are proving difficult to root out, and becoming a distraction to our patrols, it is true.'

'Distraction?' Lykos said, quietly, under his breath. 'If you class *death* as a distraction, maybe.'

Calidus gave Lykos a lingering look, laced with malice.

'Whatever word you use to describe our enemy, they are a problem that must be dealt with,' Nathair said. 'We need more men; that is the answer. The only answer.'

'Which is why we need our allies to arrive,' Calidus said.

'You could send out the Kadoshim,' Lykos said. 'I'm sure they would relish the opportunity of more battle. Is that not so, Legion?' Lykos asked the Kadoshim.

'I would delight in the death of my enemies,' Legion said, his voice deep and grating, a hint of many voices, a choir of the damned. 'In their destruction, the rending of their flesh and the breaking of their bones—'

'Yes, yes, yes,' Calidus interrupted. 'We understand your enthusiasm, Legion. But the answer is no. I will not send out the Kadoshim on this mission. There is more important work for them to do.'

More like their numbers are dwindling and you would not risk them, especially when you have warbands thousands strong full of Vin Thalun and my valiant men of Tenebral.

'But I would squeeze the eyeballs from their heads, suck the marrow from my enemies' shattered bones,' Legion grumbled.

Calidus held up a flat palm and he stopped.

'Lothar and Gundul have been building roads for almost half a year, now,' Nathair said. 'Why do they even persist, when we have the tunnels?'

'Because most of the tunnels are blocked,' Calidus said, 'and not just by rubble. There are creatures living beneath Forn that it would take a warband to destroy. Besides,' he continued with a wave of his hand, 'the tunnels were built in a different time. We need Lothar's road: it will connect us to the south, a straight road to Helveth and thus Tenebral. And Gundul's to the south-west, speeding us access to the great plains of Carnutan, with their herds of auroch for supply runs. We have Jael's road to the west almost complete. Once Lothar's and Gundul's roads reach us the Banished Lands will open up to Drassil. The roads are essential.'

Nathair nodded. 'How much longer will it take them to reach us?'

'That is the news that I spoke of,' Calidus said. 'A messenger arrived from Lothar soon after dawn. He has informed me that Lothar is thirty leagues south, making good progress, and with him he has a warband of approximately three thousand swords.'

Now this is better news.

'And what of Gundul?' Nathair asked.

'There is no word from Gundul,' Calidus said. 'I have sent messengers in search of him.' He shrugged. 'He should be closer than Lothar.'

'I have some news, too,' Lykos said, still slouched in his chair. 'Maquin was involved in the strike against our patrol yesterday.'

'Maquin?' Calidus frowned.

'A prisoner escaped from Tenebral in the company of Veradis and the warband of Tenebral.'

Maquin, beyond these walls. Then that means . . .

Mother. And perhaps even Veradis.

Nathair felt his guts twist, gripped the table's edge, thought for a moment he was going to vomit. He took deep breaths.

They cannot be fighting against me.

He had been pleased when he'd heard of his mother's escape, had not liked at all the thought of her in Calidus' power.

Calidus was staring at him.

'Maquin, you say?' Nathair managed to stutter, trying to act normally, to control his feelings.

'Aye. The Old Wolf, as my men are fond of calling him.'

'If that is true,' Calidus said, 'then the warband of Ripa is most likely with him.'

'Then we should do all that we can to speed Lothar and his war-band to us,' Nathair said.

'Perhaps,' Calidus said. 'I can see the benefit of him and his men being here, but let us not forget what our goal is.'

'To find the Seven Treasures, Calidus. That is the endgame, is it not? Bringing Asroth into this world of flesh.'

Besides him Legion shifted in his chair, growling enthusiasm for Nathair's statement.

'That's correct,' Calidus said fiercely. 'That is why we are here. Thus far we have three of the Treasures: cauldron, axe and spear.'

'Three of seven,' Nathair snorted. 'What of the others?'

Calidus gave him a cold, heavy-lidded stare.

'I have reason to believe that the cup and necklace will be ours soon. Or in my agents' hands, at least.'

That's better than I thought.

'And the final two – torc and dagger?'

Calidus scowled at that.

'That is the other reason that I have summoned you to this meeting.' He was silent again, hesitating. Eventually he spoke. 'I have been searching for a room within Drassil. I believe it will contain clues as to the whereabouts of the last two Treasures.'

'What room?' Lykos asked.

'It is the smithy where the Seven Treasures were forged,' Calidus sighed tiredly.

'Then we will help you search for it,' Nathair said. 'The more eyes and hands searching, the sooner it will be found.'

Calidus frowned. 'Just so,' he said.

'And what of the new arrivals beyond our walls,' Lykos said. 'I suspect they will not just sit around doing nothing.'

'What can they do?' Calidus asked. He looked hard at Lykos, then sighed again, seemingly bored of talking over such mundane matters. 'All right, as I can see you will not let this issue go, I shall take steps to deal with our unwanted woodland guests.' He cupped a hand to his mouth. 'Trigg,' he called, 'come down here.'

Trigg appeared on the staircase, tall and gangly, the half-breed who had shown them the secret tunnel to Drassil. Nathair had not seen her since they'd arrived, but obviously she had stayed around.

She approached them, her face broad and angular, her limbs long and already knotted with sinuous muscle.

'Aye,' she said hesitantly to Calidus.

'Trigg,' Calidus replied. 'I seem to recall that you are very good at sneaking around in the forest, spying on people and not being seen.'

Trigg shrugged, an admission.

'We have some unwanted guests camping on our doorstep. Out in the forest, and we would like very much for you to find them for us, so that we can go and kill them.'

CHAPTER TWENTY-SEVEN

CORBAN

Corban stepped into the courtyard of Gramm's hold.

I suppose it shouldn't be called that any more. Instead it is the first settlement of the Jotun clan this side of the river since the Scourging. Or so Mort told me.

Four nights had passed since Corban had watched the host of the Jotun crossing the stone bridge, leaving the Desolation behind them. The red-haired giant was standing behind him now, scowling at Corban as if he was a rat in his grain barrel. Mort did not talk much, not as much as Varan, anyway.

Corban found that very frustrating.

I need to find Varan, see if he's more forthcoming. First of all, though . . .

He looked around the courtyard and settlement, eventually seeing a stack of iron rods that would suit his purposes. Corban hefted one. It was heavy, the balance all wrong, but it was the closest he was going to find to what he needed.

What are they forging with all this iron? I doubt it's ploughs for farming the land.

'What do you want with that?' Mort asked him suspiciously.

'Well, I'm not going to try and bludgeon my way out of here with it, if that's what you're thinking,' Corban said. 'Come, I'll show you.'

He walked up the hill, alongside the new hall that was being built. When he reached the peak he stopped and took in a deep lungful of air. It was early, the sun a fiery globe balanced upon the rim of the world. Mist curled lazily from the river below him. He closed his eyes, pushed a hundred clamouring thoughts and worries out of his mind, and stepped into the first position of the sword dance, raising the iron bar two-handed over his head.

Stooping falcon.

The iron bar was far from ideal, but as he moved through the dance, holding each stance until muscles burned and complained, he felt the world slipping away. He finished with the boar-snout, stabbing upwards two-handed, ripping his imaginary blade high, free, controlling it down, rolling his wrists, finished in mid-guard, feet planted wide, iron bar diagonal, across his body. Muscles ached, wrists and shoulders throbbing, his recovering leg pulsing with the effort. He closed his eyes and without pausing began again, this time flowing from first stance to the next, and then the next, and the next, finding the speed and rhythm that allowed him to control the movement, willing himself to master the dull iron in his hands, and not to be mastered by it. He moved through the dance that Gar had drilled into him so many times, over so many years, adding the forms that Halion had taught him and tested him with on the day of his warrior trial, and more, including all he had learned since leaving Dun Carreg: ankle-hooks and headbutts, elbows, knee to the groin, the shrugging off of a heavier blade, the minutest rolling shift of wrists, shoulders, feet, that would knock an opponent off balance, all taught to him by a host of trainers, Gar, Halion, Conall, Coralen, Tukul, Tahir, Balur One-Eye, linking them all together with hardly a pause, just one long, fluid dance, as if he were ringed and beset by a host of foes.

When he stopped there was silence, just the rasp of breath in his throat, the thumping of his heart in his chest, distantly the murmur of the river. He wiped a forearm across his eyes and looked about, slowly coming back to the real world.

Giants were staring at him, scores of them, all paused in their work, some mid-hammer stroke, arms still poised. Mort was frowning at him, arms folded across his massive chest.

Corban shuffled his feet, abruptly self-conscious, and took the iron bar back to the pile where he had found it. Mort was following him, if anything looking angrier and less happy about being Corban's guard than he had before.

'Do you not train or spar?' Corban asked the giant.

He just received a stony look.

Corban walked around the settlement, seeing signs of the greater number of giants now that the new arrivals had settled in. Smoke rose from smoke-holes in new buildings that had been empty, gangly-limbed giantlings were running around, chasing dogs, laughing, others beating wet clothes hung on racks, or sitting on chairs in front of doorways, sharpening axes, gutting fish, stitching linen and leather.

They are not so different to us.

The sound of hammering and a flush of heat rippling from an open gateway drew Corban's attention. He approached the building, the smell of hot iron calling him. Memories of his da flooded his mind, of so many days working in the forge, holding glowing iron with tongs for his da to hammer, dousing iron, changing the oil, banking the furnace, then being taught the art by his da: how to draw out impurities, with fire and oil and sweat. His da's big hand over his, teaching him grip, how to keep his wrist loose, laughing when the furnace spat fire at them, singeing the hairs on both their arms. So many memories came all at once, they threatened to overwhelm him for a moment. When he looked up he saw a giant wearing a thick leather apron and holding a hammer in his hand. It took him a moment to realize it was Varan.

He has more than one job in this warband, then. Not just a healer's apprentice. I know the feeling.

He was tapping at something on the anvil, a smaller section of something huge, his movements controlled, almost delicate, then Corban realized what it was the giant was working upon.

A coat of mail. It's an odd shape, though.

Varan glanced up, saw Corban, his eyes almost instantly going back to his job. He was attaching wide leather straps to the coat of mail, fixing and clamping the iron rings that held it in place, riveting the leather.

'What is that?' Corban said over the sound of hammer-blows and the constant crackle of the forge fire.

'A mail coat for a bear,' Varan said, not taking his eyes from his handiwork.

A bear!

'Come, I'll show you,' Varan said, hanging his tools up meticulously. He shook the mail coat out and slung it over one shoulder. As he made to walk out of the forge Mort stepped in front of him, saying something in giantish. Varan answered. For a moment they stood facing one another in silence then, with an all too familiar scowl, Mort moved out of the way. Soon the three of them were in a long building, its vaulted ceiling held high by timber beams thick as trunks.

Bear pens.

Each pen was huge, three or four times the size of the stables at Dun Carreg. Varan walked along them, Corban following, peering in to see some empty, others housing bears.

Varan stopped at a gate and gave the coat of mail to Corban. He reached down into a tall barrel, pulling out a whole salmon, then slid the bolt across and opened the stable door wide.

'*Dia duit mo fiacail fada stór,*' Varan said. The bear inside was huge, its fur a dark brown flecked with black. One long canine poked from beneath its upper lip, the opposite canine was broken about halfway down. Corban recognized it as Varan's bear, the one he had ridden on for most of the long journey from Drassil. Varan tossed the salmon in the air and the bear lunged forwards, startlingly fast, snatching the salmon into its wide mouth. With a crunch the salmon was gone, then the bear was nuzzling Varan with its broad head. Varan was smiling, rubbing its ears, the bear's lip curling to reveal more sharp yellowed teeth.

That doesn't look right, Corban thought, eyeing the bear suspiciously, *but then I suppose people said the same thing about me and Storm.*

At the thought of Storm Corban felt a twinge of pain in his belly, like a sliver-thin knife being twisted. He'd tried hard not to think of her – the pain of her loss was too hard to face.

Varan shook out a blanket of fur and placed it over the bear's back, then beckoned for Corban to hand him the mail coat, which Varan slung over the bear, reaching under its belly. He indicated for Corban to help, and together they buckled and tightened the girth, then worked around the legs, threading buckles, with Varan finishing at the bear's neck, where the mail coat was riveted to a thick leather collar. When it was done Corban stood back and took a long look.

The bear had looked formidable before; now it looked like a weapon, fashioned from tooth and claw, fur and iron.

'It's not too heavy? Won't shift with movement?' Corban asked.

Varan slapped the bear's muscled shoulder and chest.

'Long Tooth could carry three of me,' Varan said, rubbing the bear's neck affectionately. 'The mail *is* heavy, but not as heavy as me. He'll get used to it quickly enough. And no, if it's fitted and buckled right, it won't slip.'

'I wish that I'd had one of those for Storm.' Corban felt a lump in his throat at the memory of her. He blinked away tears, saw Varan regarding him with serious eyes.

'Life is loss,' the giant said.

'Aye, that it is,' Corban said. 'But I'd wager some of us have lost more than others.'

'In the end, it's all the same,' Varan said. 'We all face death alone.'

Corban nodded. 'To my thinking, though, it's what happens before death that's important. All of us die. How many really *live*?'

Varan cocked his head, eyes fixed intently on Corban.

'I find you . . . interesting,' Varan said. 'Not what I expected.'

'Well, we judge things we've never seen. I judged giants, believed them wicked monsters that lived in the shadows. Now that I've met some of your kind –' he shrugged – 'I see you're just like us. Uthas slew Nemain, is a murderer; yet Balur and Ethlinn – I'd trust either one of them with my life. And even here, I've seen differences amongst you. Take you, for example. You're a lot more talkative than Mort,' Corban said, gesturing to the red-haired giant behind him.

'I see no harm in talking to you,' Varan said, 'I do not think you could escape.'

We'll see about that.

'But as for Mort, well, you did kill his brother, in Drassil.'

That would explain a lot.

'*Agus beidh mé tú a mharú,*' Mort said from the shadows.

In my defence, his brother tried to kill me first,' Corban said. 'And Mort is supposed to be my guard here. Is that wise?'

'Mort is Ildaer's captain. He is being prepared for leadership. Guarding you teaches him self-control.'

Corban looked at Mort, who was glowering at him.

'I don't think it's working.'

'You still live,' Varan pointed out.

Good point. But for how long?

'I saw you earlier, on the hill,' Varan said, changing the subject. 'With a rod of iron.'

'Oh aye. It helps,' Corban said, tapping his head and heart. 'Being a captive here, knowing my kin and friends may be fighting for their lives.'

'You were quite the sight,' Varan continued with a sidelong glance, almost a smile. 'And are all your enemies dead, now?'

'Only in my head,' Corban grunted. 'I've amassed more than my fair share, you see. So there are still a few to go.'

'What you said, to Ildaer,' Varan rumbled, 'about choosing a side.'

'Aye.'

'It's made me think.'

Good.

'Ildaer seems cautious,' Corban said.

'The Jotun are cautious,' Varan replied. 'For a Jotun, Ildaer is *not* cautious.'

'Ildaer is the best of us,' Mort said fiercely, studying them both with narrowed eyes.

'Ildaer has led us well, is a brave battle-leader. He has gained much for the Jotun,' Varan agreed.

'And your king?' Corban prompted.

'Eld, our king, has lived a long life. He *is* cautious,' Varan said.

Mort snorted in the shadows.

Eld, so that is his name.

'Eld witnessed the Scourging, saw the destruction it caused the giant clans,' Varan explained. 'At that moment he withdrew from the fight, and instead he led the Jotun north, to safety. That is where my clan has dwelt, for nearly two thousand years. Caution has kept the clan alive, and helped it to grow. I doubt the other clans have prospered so well.'

'How many of you are there?' Corban asked, thinking of the host he had seen crossing the river. *A thousand? Fifteen hundred?*

'Enough,' Varan said. 'More than any other clan can boast. Because our king has led us well.'

'So why has he come south now? When the God-War is upon us again?' Corban asked.

'There are, I do not know how to say it in your tongue – *grúpaí, faicsin?* We do not all think the same within the clan, especially the young, born after the Scourging. There are different opinions. Some long for honour and glory, for battle-fame, others still counsel caution, the safest path. Ildaer rose up amongst us, strong, proud. He wanted to come south and take back the land we had lost. The Desolation is not a fertile land, you understand. Life is hard there.'

'So Ildaer led a rebellion? An uprising that Eld crushed and banished south?'

'Ach, no,' Varan said, 'Eld clings to the old ways, the ways of tradition and honour, of blood-feud and guest-right, and he has ingrained those values upon all of us Jotun. That is why Ildaer treats you with respect, not as a prisoner. He remembers the guest-right that Eld taught him. Eld believes the old ways have kept the Jotun alive. And because many rallied to Ildaer's call, instead of treating Ildaer like a rival or an upstart, Eld named him Warlord of the Jotun and allowed him to take a warband south. No one thought he would achieve so much, and the cynical amongst us may whisper that Eld thought Ildaer would get himself killed, perhaps even hoped for that . . .' He gave Corban a smile. 'But now Ildaer has *land*.' Varan said the word like it was the greatest of Treasures. 'Ildaer has earned much honour amongst the Jotun, his name often upon everyone's lips, and so now people are saying, maybe Eld is too old, too cautious, it is a new time, a new age, time for the Jotun to rise up, to take back what they have lost. That is why Eld has come.'

'And what do you say?' Corban asked.

'Me? I came south with Ildaer, I was one of the young voices clamouring for battle-fame and glory. But I was apprenticed to Hala, and she is Eld's eyes and ears within Ildaer's warband. She is very wise, but also cautious. Sometimes caution *is* wisdom, but sometimes it is fear, and fear is not wise. Perhaps she has rubbed off on me a little.' He shrugged and smiled. 'Truth be told, I do not know what I say, what I think. I believe the Jotun will fade in the north, and besides, there is no life in the Desolation. As you say, all will die, but not all live.'

'So, a cautious warrior, and yet you forge battle-mail for your bear.'

'I do,' Varan smiled. 'You see much.' Again he shrugged. 'As you say, it is the God-War. Some battles find you, no matter how cautious you are.'

I fled across all the realms of the west, and the God-War still found me.

'Yes,' Corban agreed. 'That has been my experience. And Eld, will he join the war? Fight against Asroth?' He said it with a trace of hope, looking along the bear pens filled with the great beasts.

A lot of bears, and giants who ride on them. A warband like this could turn a battle, could win a war . . .

'That is for him to say.'

'I must speak to him,' Corban said.

'You'll get that wish soon enough. Ildaer is with him now, and no doubt he will want you brought before Eld.'

'Why?'

'To decide your fate.' He gave Corban a flat stare. 'Eld's word is law.'

CHAPTER TWENTY-EIGHT

CORALEN

Coralen ran between the trees, her feet a whisper across the forest litter. Unlike some of those behind her.

Farrell and Laith are like two lumbering auroch!

She gritted her teeth and looked back at them. They were on Jael's road, a score or so paces behind her. Coralen didn't like running on the road, it felt too exposed, but she admitted that it was the quickest, most direct route out of Forn.

Thank you for that, Jael, though I doubt you built it as an aid to us.

Farrell and Laith didn't share her misgivings about using the road. Farrell was first, red-faced, his hair dark and slick with sweat. His war-hammer jutted over the slabbed muscle of his back. He nodded at her, the most he could manage. Behind him Laith loomed, looking in slightly better condition than Farrell, but only just. She just stared at the ground in front of her, resolute. They were crushing anything in their path – logs and branches snapped, vine was torn from the ground, undergrowth barged through. Coralen resisted the urge to hiss some abuse at them.

No point, I've tried that, and it hasn't worked. To be fair, we've run all the way from Drassil to the edge of Forn Forest, and they've kept up.

Coralen had set a fast pace, every day rising before dawn, following the bear tracks through the forest until the last trace of light faded and they were forced to stop. Over a moon of it, mostly running, and still they had steadily slipped behind.

Those bears are too damn fast.

The forest had been thinning about them for a while now, the river widening to their north as it flowed into more open plains.

Keep on like this and we'll be seeing Gramm's hold in a day or so.

Even as Coralen considered that, she moved into an open space where tree trunks had been harvested like grain, only their stumps remaining. To her left she saw a flicker of movement; Gar appeared from the treeline, to her right Dath and Kulla were stepping into view.

Now those three I don't need to worry about. They could probably sneak up on Storm. Her heart jumped at the thought of the wolven; she'd last seen her at the edge of death. Coralen whispered a prayer for her; not that she was normally the praying kind, but if anything would help . . .

Her thoughts returned to Corban: how she'd felt so angry with him before the battle at Drassil.

I kissed him, and what did he do! Nothing! Well, he did kiss me back, at the time, which was nice enough. But afterwards . . . Well, time enough to talk to him about that once we've pulled him out of his latest troubles.

She crested a slope and saw meadowland opening up before her. In the distance was a hill, to its north the river glistening darkly in the sunlight. She waved a signal and the others veered in towards her, all of them meeting a little below the slope's crest. Farrell spent a while puffing, chest heaving as he caught his breath.

'Gramm's hold has some new tenants,' Coralen observed, looking at the pillars of smoke rising from the hill. She looked sidelong at Gar, remembering the last time they had seen this place. She felt Tukul's loss anew.

His father was a rare man, and no mistake.

Gar's face was stony, betraying nothing of what was going on within.

'Onwards,' he said. 'Standing around here isn't going to get Corban back.'

Farrell wheezed, and then they were off again, following the bear tracks that were clear for any to see, moving down the slope and across the meadows, heading unerringly towards the hill that had been Gramm's hold.

'He's in there,' Coralen said to Gar.

They had made camp about two leagues from the hill, in a small copse, a suitable place to remain unseen while they planned.

The six of them stood staring at Gramm's hold as the sun sank into the west, making a black silhouette of the settlement on the hill. Figures small as ants occasionally went up the hill, and every now and then the deep rumbling bellow of a bear would drift down to them on a cold wind.

'You're certain?' Gar asked.

Coralen, Dath and Kulla had spent a day scouting the hill.

'Aye. Unless they've taken him across the river into the Desolation,' Coralen said.

'But there are so many giants here, I can't believe there are any left north of the river,' Dath said. 'So why would they want to take Ban north, when it looks like they've all come south?'

'That's strange,' Laith said thoughtfully. 'The Jotun do not normally leave the safety of their homeland.'

'Tell me of the Jotun,' Gar asked.

'I am young,' Laith said, 'but our lore always spoke of the Jotun as fleeing into the Desolation after the Scourging, hiding themselves away. Their king – Eld, I think – preferred to run instead of face conflict.'

'Perhaps he was just prudent,' Gar murmured.

'He also had a reputation for adhering to the old ways: tradition, honour, our lore.'

Gar rubbed his chin, looking thoughtful.

'How many of them at Gramm's?' Farrell asked. He'd got his wind back from all the running now and looked much more fearsome for it.

'There's at least a thousand giants living on that hill,' Dath said. 'Probably more.'

'So killing them all's out of the question, then,' Farrell grunted. 'That's the end of the first plan.'

'What was the second plan?' Dath asked.

'I have an idea,' Gar said.

Coralen rose before dawn, standing and stretching, then making her way to the copse's border where Gar was staring into the darkness. Coralen came and stood silently beside him, both of them watching as the sun appeared on the edge of the world, washing Gramm's hold with rosy fire.

'All my life, it feels, that boy has been my sun. The centre of my world.'

'He's not a boy any more,' Coralen said gently.

'To me he always will be,' Gar replied quietly, little more than a whisper. 'More than that. He's *my* boy. The son I never had.'

'We'll see him, today. Have him back with us,' Coralen said, feeling tears mist her eyes.

Gar had explained his plan to them last night. It was insane. They didn't stand a chance. But it was all they had.

'Aye,' Gar grunted. 'And heaven help the man, woman or giant that tries to stop us.' He smiled down at her, a sight that Coralen had rarely seen, then reached out and squeezed her hand.

The others were up now, Farrell examining the head of his war-hammer, Laith oiling her throwing knives. Dath was checking arrows, running his fingertips over fletchings.

Gar took a step out of the copse and then paused, looking back at them all.

'Let's go and get Corban,' he said.

Or die trying.

CHAPTER TWENTY-NINE

RAFE

'What have they done to my *tower*!' Morcant screamed.

It had taken them a ten-night to extricate themselves from the marshes, half of Rhin's warband was disembarking just now and marching up onto the meadowland that circled Morcant's tower, or what was left of it.

Which isn't much.

The tower was a skeleton of charred timber, the palisade mostly collapsed; what was left of it looked like the blackened and rotting teeth of a hag.

Behind him he heard a female voice standing out from the murmur of men, a rare thing in this warband. Part of him noted that not so long ago he wouldn't have heard such a subtle sound.

I am changed, since I drank from that cup. Never felt more alive. I am stronger, faster, and I can hear things, smell things better than I could before.

The voice belonged to Roisin, the only living person they had found at the ruins of Dun Crin. She stepped out from a boat onto a wooden jetty, warriors lining up to help her.

For a prisoner, she's mighty popular, Rafe thought, though he could understand why, as he stood and stared at her, enjoying the arch of her ankle, the curve of her hips, skin pale as cream, black hair somehow still lustrous, even after a journey through the marshes.

Not that I think Rhin's very impressed with the attention Roisin's getting. She's lucky Rhin thinks her useful, else she'd most likely be face-down in a marsh stream by now.

*

'They've split up,' Rafe reported. 'Three warbands went in different directions. East, west and north.'

'What's the little bitch playing at?' Rhin spat. She was reclining in her chair, skin sweating and flushed, silver hair bedraggled.

Uthas the giant shifted behind her, made a sound in his throat.

'What?' Rhin snapped. 'If you've something to say, come out and say it, instead of lurking behind me, sighing and swaying like a stuttering tree!'

Definitely not at her most patient, then.

'Evnis,' Uthas said. Rafe detected a hint of something new in the giant's voice.

Anger? Scorn?

'You may have forgotten, but we have just spent most of a moon wandering around that stinking swamp trying to find my missing regent. He is either slain or fled; whichever one, he is gone.'

It was I who went wandering to find him, Rafe thought. *You just sat on a boat, giving out your orders.*

Rafe had spent a good long while going over a wide stretch of land that surrounded the northern half of Dun Crin's lake. There was one set of tracks that ended at the side of a stream; it looked as if they had been joined by another. Rafe could not be sure, but he suspected that something large had been rolled into the stream. He'd poked around in it with his spear, even jumped in, but had found nothing.

Not that the eels and snakes and Asroth knows what else lurking in those marshes would have left much by then, anyway.

He'd had no evidence, no proof, but something in his gut told him that it was the place where Evnis had met his end.

'I think he died in the swamp, my Queen.'

'Yes, I've heard your opinion on it – *opinion*, not fact.'

Rafe held his silence.

'You are a gifted huntsman,' Uthas the giant said, startling Rafe. The giant rarely deigned to speak to him. 'The first of Queen Rhin's scouts to return.'

I knew I would be. I am the best amongst them.

'The way you led us to Dun Crin,' Uthas continued. 'The way you saw that heron, on the far shore of the lake. The way you found the sets of tracks at Dun Crin, when all of the other huntsmen struggled.'

'What's this got to do with Evnis?' Rhin asked.

'Dead or not, Evnis might not have kept . . .' Rafe didn't like the assessing way the giant was looking at him '. . . *it*, upon him,' Uthas finished.

'I know that, but where else?' Rhin asked. She looked at Rafe now. 'You grew up in Evnis' hold, did you not? If Evnis had something of value, something that he treasured, where would he keep it?'

'Like a fine stallion, or a good hound?' Rafe asked.

'No, nothing like that,' Rhin snapped. 'Why do you woodsmen always have to think of something that's living?'

'Oh, like a sword, then? Or silver, or gold?'

'Yes, more like it,' Rhin said.

'His tower at Dun Carreg, I suppose,' Rafe said. 'He spent a lot of time up there, in his chamber right at the top. Didn't like to be disturbed.'

Rhin and Uthas shared a long look; a smile returned to Rhin's face. *Haven't seen one of those from her in a while.*

'To Evnis' tower, then,' Uthas said.

'But what about Edana?' Rhin said. 'I can't have her just wandering around the countryside, stirring up Asroth knows what trouble.'

'Send Morcant after her,' Uthas said. 'Let us be on with the important task.'

'But they've gone three ways!' Rhin said.

'So split this warband,' Uthas said. 'It's big enough.'

He's right. There are over a thousand men out there.

'If you're going back to Dun Carreg,' Rafe said, 'one of the trails goes that way. Take enough with you to deal with them, and leave enough to let Morcant look after the other two.'

Rhin looked at him, thoughtful.

'For a huntsman, you do have the occasional idea of worth,' she said. 'Why have I never noticed you before? You're starting to remind me of Braith.'

Rafe noticed Uthas leaning forwards and staring at him, bushy brows knotting together.

Rhin looked Rafe up and down, slowly. 'I wonder if the similarities stop there.'

CHAPTER THIRTY

CORBAN

Corban woke early and rose, pacing his stone room. He tested his injured leg, stretched and loosened his limbs. His leg was better again than yesterday, almost felt normal.

He felt tense, his conversation with Varan from the previous day heavy upon his mind. He'd hoped that Ildaer and Eld would have sent for him last night, but that hadn't happened.

Today. It will happen today. Or so he tried to convince himself. *Five nights, now, since Eld arrived. He's certainly not one for rushing things.* He sighed in exasperation.

If I could only convince him to side with us. To fight against Asroth.

Corban opened his door and strode through the courtyard, heading straight to the pile of iron rods, the silent bulk of Mort shadowing him. Taking one of the rods, he marched to the top of the hill, where Mort assumed his customary position, leaning against a pile of building materials, a sneer fixed upon his face. A handful of giants with the swagger of young warriors joined him, exchanging greetings.

From Ildaer's warband, then.

He breathed deeply and stepped into stooping falcon.

Begin, Gar's voice said in his mind.

When he was done he stood on the brow of the hill, sweating, aching, chest heaving, the peace that the sword dance brought him seeping through him, though unfortunately it felt as if it began leaking out of him almost immediately, drop by drop as the frustrations of the real world crowded their way back in.

He felt useless and at the same time infuriated. He looked around at all the giants: so many of them going about their daily routines, others building, labouring hard.

Can they not see how meaningless this is? If Asroth becomes flesh no one will escape his wrath; all this will be dust and ruin. I must get out of here. I must find Cywen, Gar, Coralen, Farrell, Dath.

His gaze fell upon Mort.

'Would you spar with me?' Corban asked the red-haired giant, who was standing a dozen paces away, leaning against a pile of timber.

The giant looked surprised, glanced at those gathered about him, all warriors with hammers and axes slung across their backs.

'Spar? No, little man. When I fight you, it will not be pretend.' He reached up and patted his war-axe. The giants around him murmured their approval.

Shame. I need to hit someone.

'Any of you, then?' Corban asked the others.

The thud of footsteps drew his attention. Ildaer was marching towards him, Varan at his shoulder.

'Follow me,' Ildaer said to Corban. 'It is time for you to meet our king.'

The new hall was vast, built over the old one, but wider, deeper, taller. Stone columns rose high, twisting spirals etched with runes. The roof was still unfinished, a skeleton of timber struts framing a pale blue sky.

Eld sat at the far end of the hall on a raised dais, tall as all giants, but as Corban drew nearer he thought that there was something vulnerable about him. His skin was pale, dotted with dark spots and looking paper thin; his hair was pale and tenuous, fine as old cobwebs, his moustache wisps that draped down to his chest. He was richly dressed in wool, polished leather and a cloak of white fur, with rings of gold upon his fingers. Corban saw that he bore no weapons, except for a dagger on his belt. The hilt was wrapped in sweat-stained leather, pommel and guard a dark iron that struck Corban as unusual. Eld studied Corban with small black eyes as he was marched along the length of the hall. Standing either side of the King were two giants. One was Hala the healer, dressed simply in wool and leather. The other was a female warrior, her fair hair bound in a single thick warrior braid that curled across one shoulder like a pale serpent, the hilt of a longsword jutting over her other shoulder. A tattoo of vine and thorn curled up from her wrist and disappeared into the sleeve of her mail shirt. She watched Corban with flat indifference.

'So, this is your man-prize,' Eld said, his voice old and cracked, a hiss like the wind upon shingle.

'It is, Great King,' Ildaer said, bowing his head.

Corban stood before Eld, King of the Jotun, staring like a bairn at the spring fair. Eld looked so *old*, as if his skin would float away like wisps of smoke if he moved too quickly.

Ildaer whispered something to Mort and the red-haired giant cuffed Corban across the back of the head, sending him staggering forwards onto one knee.

'Kneel before the Great King,' he growled.

Corban had been on the edge of doing just that, or at least bowing, but the anger that recently seemed a constant presence within him overflowed. He rose to his feet, glared first at Mort, and then stared at the giant king.

'Well met, Eld, King of the Jotun,' he said, looking the giant in the eye.

Mort lifted his arm for another blow.

'Hold; he is our *guest*,' Eld said, meeting Corban's gaze. 'Things will be done right, now that I am here.' He gave a disapproving look to Ildaer, held Mort's gaze a long moment, then finally looked at Corban. 'So, Ildaer tells me that you slew three of our kin.'

'I had some help,' Corban answered.

'Aye. I have heard tell of the wolven. Dead now.' He chewed at a lip. 'Even so,' he continued, 'three of our kin, and two of the death wounds were by blade, not tooth or claw.'

'It was a hard fight,' Corban said with a shrug, thinking of his broken ribs and shattered knee.

The shield-maiden snorted a laugh. Respect or derision, Corban wasn't quite sure.

'And Ildaer tells me that you are someone of note in the war that is happening.' Eld's eyes fixed pointedly upon Corban's arm-ring. 'Tell me, who are you exactly, and what part do you play in this war?'

Time to play my hand, though whether it will save or condemn me, I know not.

'I am Corban ben Thannon. Some have called me the Bright Star, champion of Elyon. I lead the force that stands against Asroth, against his Kadoshim and all those that follow him.'

There was a heavy silence as everyone stared at him. Hala leaned in close to Eld, whispering. Ildaer muttered something behind him.

Eld's face creased into a thing of fury, glaring at Ildaer. He gripped the hilt of his dagger, knuckles whitening, half-drew it; the iron of the blade was dull, almost black.

'It seems, Ildaer, you have snared more than you set out to trap. Did you stop to consider the danger you were putting your own neck into? And dragging the Jotun along with you?'

He doesn't sound so frail, all of a sudden. He sounds angry.

'The greater the prize, the greater the reward,' Ildaer said, jutting out his chin, though there was an edge of doubt in his voice.

'And the greater the *risk*,' Eld said. 'What if Calidus or his champion come looking for the Bright Star? What if they find him here? With the Jotun? Ach . . .' Eld shook his head, lips twisting with scorn. 'You will bring misfortune upon us.'

'It is as I said; as I planned,' Ildaer said. 'We could make a gift of him to Asroth, to Calidus. It would win us great favour, a place in Asroth's new world order. And it would keep the clan safe.'

Ildaer seeks to play Eld's own fears against him.

'Calidus. Aye,' Eld muttered. 'He is a thinker, that one. Perhaps, if we move quickly, we might put right your blunder and keep the clan safe . . .' He looked down, seemed to realize that he'd half-drawn his dagger. With a rasp he sheathed it again.

'You *cannot* give me to Calidus,' Corban said.

Eld turned his attention back upon Corban.

'You are not the one to tell me what I can and cannot do,' Eld said. 'It is *I* who shall decide *your* fate.' He shrugged, staring hard at Corban. 'The Bright Star,' he murmured. 'How the days have passed.' He sighed to himself. 'I must consider the fate of my clan, you understand. Must do what is best for their survival. But while you are with us you will be treated well, with respect. We are a people of honour and will do things the right way. And know this: whatever fate I decide for you, it will be for the Jotun's good. It is nothing personal.'

Well, that's a great comfort.

'You cannot side with Asroth,' Corban said. 'You saw the Scourging, you know more of Asroth than any of us. He *cannot* be trusted.'

'I saw Asroth set giant against giant, 'tis true,' Eld said in a whisper. His hand went back to stroking the hilt of his long dagger. 'But I also saw the Ben-Elim fill the skies like a murder of crows, blotting out the sun, and where they flew, death flew with them. They had no mercy, no compassion, no forgiveness.'

Corban shook his head. 'We can stop it from reaching that point. Together. You have the power to do something, to ensure that history does not repeat itself, or worse.'

Eld looked at him, considering.

He's listening.

'If you do not stand against Asroth he will enter this world, become flesh, and then we are all dead. I have seen only a glimpse of what the Kadoshim will do, and it is terrible. There will be no hiding, no safe place, no living in peace. You will all be slaughtered. Join me, and together we can halt this tide of darkness.'

He gazed about the room, saw them all staring at him, conflicting emotions warring upon each giant's face. He focused on Eld, sitting in his chair.

'And where is Meical in all of this?'

'Meical is dead,' Corban said without thinking. He saw Eld's mouth open in a gasp of shock.

'Dead!' Eld echoed, a trace of fear in his voice. 'Then this war is already over.'

I should not have said that.

'No, it's not,' Corban growled. 'While there is breath in my body, there is hope. There is more to this war than Meical.' He felt his anger at his old counsellor course through him. 'There are the Jehar, the men of Isiltir, the survivors of this hold, the Benothi giants, so many others from throughout the realms of the Banished Lands.'

'The Jehar!' Hala said. 'I thought that ancient order had disappeared an age ago.'

'They rode out to make a stand against Asroth,' Corban said.

'The Benothi?' It was the shield-maiden who spoke this time.

'Balur One-Eye, his daughter Ethlinn, the other survivors of Murias.'

'Balur,' sneered Eld.

'Ethlinn,' whispered the shield-maiden.

'It is too late for any of that, Sig,' Eld snapped at the giantess. 'We live in the now, not the what-might-have-been.' She frowned.

'We should gift Corban to this Calidus,' Ildaer urged. 'It will buy us favour with the winning side.'

'Aye, mayhaps it would,' Eld mused, 'but it will also bring the Jotun much closer to this God-War than I like. I have spent a thousand years protecting my clan from this war, and yet now . . .'

Eld sucked in deep, muttering under his breath.

'This is my judgement,' he said, leaning back in his chair. 'Ildaer; you will take this Corban into the Desolation and there you will kill him and cast his body into some pit. He was never here.'

Corban felt a jolt of fear shiver through him.

'Why not kill him here?' Mort frowned.

'The fewer eyes that see, the fewer tongues to wag,' Eld snapped, 'and sooner or later Calidus will be searching for him.'

Mort nodded.

Eld looked around, at the newly crafted building. 'And we must leave this place.'

'What?' Ildaer barked.

'We are too close to this war. We must be far from here when it happens. We must head back into the Desolation, travel further north, back to the Bonefells or even beyond.'

'No,' Mort cried. 'We cannot. We have achieved too much—'

'Silence,' Eld snarled, spittle spraying from his lips. 'Ildaer, keep your whelp under control, else Sig will reason with him.'

'This is my judgement,' Eld said, harsh as a winter wind. 'Corban is taken from here and executed, and he goes *now*. The sooner he is away from my clan, the better. Ildaer, I was soon to name you my heir, as reward for the good you have sought for the Jotun, but you have been rash, foolhardy, and I have been unwise to bring the clan south. I will think more on you, and the freedom I have permitted you.' He shook his head, a parent scolding a wayward child.

Beside Corban, Mort tensed, and he saw Ildaer's knuckles bunch white.

As he spoke, Eld's hand gripped the dagger again, fingertips tracing the hilt, across the dark iron of the cross-guard.

Corban frowned.

'Your dagger,' Corban said, 'the metal it is fashioned from . . .'

Then he knew.

'It is the starstone dagger,' he whispered.

'Take him from here, Ildaer,' Eld snapped, flicking his wrist towards the hall's entrance. 'Now. Carry him into the Desolation, as fast as your bear will carry you.'

Ildaer grabbed Corban by his collar, started pulling him backwards. Corban fought in his grip.

'It must be destroyed!' Corban shouted, struggling in Ildaer's grip.

Eld shook his head, snarling. 'The dagger is *mine*.'

'You cannot escape, cannot hide – nowhere will be far enough,' Corban yelled. 'Calidus will come for you, hunt you to the ends of the earth for that dagger.'

'Be gone,' Eld snarled, a wave of his pale flaking hand. 'The sooner he is dead the better.'

'The first command that I do not dislike,' Mort whispered to Ildaer, and then Corban was being dragged through the hall, fighting and shouting. Mort punched him in the gut; Corban retched bile. He gasped and spluttered, saw Mort grinning at him, Varan frowning as he followed behind. A last glimpse before he was dragged from the hall showed Eld sitting in his chair, staring at Corban.

Mort pulled Corban into the sunlight and across the courtyard. Corban managed to get his feet under him as he recovered from Mort's blow. Ildaer was a few strides ahead. Mort was talking in whispered hisses to giants gathering close about him, and then they were moving off in different directions. Corban saw giant faces staring at him as he was dragged towards the bear pens; he felt the heat rolling out from the doorway of the forge.

They're going to kill me!

'Hold him,' Ildaer said and disappeared inside the bear pens.

Mort threw Corban onto his face, giving him a mouthful of mud.

'I'll not lie,' Mort said, standing over him and flipping him with the toe of his boot. 'I'm going to enjoy this.'

He reached down and grabbed Corban's tunic, hoisting him up from the ground.

As he did, Corban kicked out, his boot crunching into Mort's groin. The giant crumpled, Corban rolling free.

Corban looked frantically about, saw giants everywhere; Mort was grimacing, rising unsteadily back to his feet.

No way out of here. Corban saw the pile of iron rods that he'd been using in his sword dance and snatched one up.

'Good,' the giant said, gripping the axe from his back. 'Now I can defend myself. If you die . . .' He shrugged.

Ildaer's bulk filled the bear pen doors. A glare as he took it all in. Corban shuffled away from them both, trying to keep them in front of him. He glimpsed other giants moving in.

They're going to kill me anyway – better to make a fight of it.

Panic had been racing through him, but with that last thought he felt a calmness descend.

I'd rather have been standing with my loved ones, but if this is where I die . . . He looked around, everything suddenly felt sharper, brighter.

Then so be it. And let's see who I can take with me.

He set his feet and lifted the iron rod into stooping falcon.

Begin, he heard Gar's voice in his ear.

'Come on then, and I'll send you to meet your brother,' he said to Mort.

The giant didn't seem to like that. He strode in at Corban, whirling his axe above his head, face twisted in rage.

Anger is the enemy, Gar's voice whispered.

Corban remained utterly still, remembering sparring with Balur on the weapons court at Drassil. The axe came out of its spin, began its descent, the intention of the blow to carve Corban in two from skull to groin. Still Corban did not move.

Then he was sidestepping, just half a foot, at the same time swinging his iron bar, nudging Mort's axe-blade away, not meeting it full-on – that was the quickest way to shattered wrists – the blade careened wide and hacked into the ground with an explosion of dirt. Corban swung the bar and crunched it into Mort's knee. The giant howled in agony and dropped to the ground.

Corban saw Varan on his right and pointed his iron bar at him. Varan lifted his hands and retreated. Other giants were closing.

They're going to rush me.

One giant lunged in and Corban swung the iron bar, connected with a wrist, heard bones crunch, the giant falling away, another stepping in, grabbing Corban's arm, but the bar glanced off its head, the giant collapsing. A spear shaft darted in at Corban and he knocked it away, connected with another jaw, the giant spiralling to the ground. Corban edged towards the gates, giants circling him. Suddenly Ildaer was there. Corban waited for him, a circle of fallen giants about him. Ildaer lunged, Corban's bar connecting with his shoulder, sending the giant stumbling, but other hands were gripping Corban, pulling the iron bar from his hands. He punched, twisted, bit, but within moments he was caught tight. Panic had him then and he bucked and kicked like a wild thing, for a moment felt the grip upon him loosening, something crunched into his head and there was an explosion of stars, his vision blurring, the world lurching out of focus as he fell.

Then, voices, shouting, from somewhere beyond.

Giant voices, raised in command, in question. And another voice, somehow familiar.

'What the . . .' Ildaer growled, and then Corban was being hoisted onto his feet.

The strangest sight greeted him.

A man was walking through the gates, dressed in black chainmail and breeches, a scabbarded sword held high over his head. Giants were standing around him, weapons aimed at him, but they were letting him through, almost appeared to be escorting him.

The man was shouting, the same phrase over and over again, but at first the words were incoherent to Corban, he was too busy staring at the man in black, a torrent of emotion sweeping him.

Shock, joy, fear, love.

Because it was Gar.

CHAPTER THIRTY-ONE

CORALEN

Coralen paused behind an old fence post and looked up at the settlement on the hill. Ahead of her she saw Gar enter the new-built gates, giants surrounding him. To her immense surprise he wasn't dead.

Yet.

So far so good.

To her left, Coralen caught a flicker of movement: Dath and Kulla, doing the same as her, creeping through the long grass. Farrell and Laith had taken a different path, using the vegetation along the riverbank as cover. If their timing was right they should be near the settlement.

'No changing it now,' Coralen muttered to herself. As she scanned the walls of the settlement the giants patrolling it disappeared from view.

Getting a closer view of Gar's entertainment, no doubt. Unless they've decided just to execute him, that is.

She sucked in a deep breath and ran, breaking out of the long grass and sprinting for the wall. She glimpsed Dath and Kulla breaking from cover on the far side of the gate and doing the same. Kulla was faster than Dath, hitting the wall before even Coralen. Then they had disappeared from view around the curve of the wall. She crunched into stone, looked up and froze as she waited for a giant's face to appear. None did. She dragged in a few deep breaths, unhooked a rope from her belt, looped and knotted the end, then cast it. It caught first time, hooking around a stone piling. She leaned on it, testing how well it had caught, then started to climb, feet against the rock.

A dozen heartbeats and she was at the top. Gar's voice was ringing out, giants shouting, clamouring.

Let's do this, then.

She pulled herself over the top, rolling over, dropping to the roof of a building below, half-expecting to crash right into a giant. She didn't; her feet thumped onto thatch and then she was crouching low and slipping onto her belly. A quick glance showed the wall was empty, a few giants halfway down a stairwell that led to the courtyard. Off to her left she saw Dath appear on the wall, dropping quickly down, crouching in the shadows and drawing an arrow from his belt-quiver. Kulla landed lightly on her feet beside him. Coralen crawled to the edge of the building she was on and looked over.

A new half-built hall towered at the peak of the hill, a wide courtyard before it, full with hundreds of giants, all gathered about Gar, who was standing with his scabbarded sword held high over his head and shouting out his challenge, time and time again.

Where the hell is Ban in all of this?

Her eyes swept the enclosure, and then she saw him, her heart feeling like it had just leaped into her mouth. A rush of fierce joy.

He's still alive. For now.

CHAPTER THIRTY-TWO

CORBAN

Corban stared, not quite believing his eyes.

It's Gar. He's here, standing fifty paces away from me.

He wanted to run to his friend, to embrace him, to yell at him to flee. Nothing good could come of him being here. Then he felt a rush of guilt.

He's come here for me, and he's going to get himself killed.

'I am Garisan ben Tukul, Lord of the Jehar,' Gar was yelling, 'and I challenge Ildaer, Warlord of the Jotun, by right of blood-feud.' He was repeating that sentence over and over, walking through the throng of giants. For some reason they hadn't killed him yet, were in fact parting for him, letting him through.

Ildaer was straightening, a deep frown etched on his face as he turned away from Corban.

'I know you,' Ildaer said, marching towards Gar.

'Aye, you do,' Gar said; the two of them were close now, Ildaer halting a dozen paces from Gar.

The crowd of giants parted and Sig appeared, behind her Eld and Hala.

'What is this new madness you bring upon us?' Eld said to Ildaer.

'I am Garisan ben Tukul, Lord of the Jehar, and I challenge Ildaer, Warlord of the Jotun by right of blood-feud,' Gar said.

'Yes, I think we've all heard you by now,' Eld snapped. 'Explain why you are here.'

'Ildaer slew my father.'

'Ahh.' Eld's head turned to Ildaer. 'Is this so?'

'It is,' Ildaer shrugged. 'I also fought this weakling, and defeated him. I would have finished the task, but that one –' he pointed back at Corban – 'stood over him, summoned his warband.'

'You ran from Balur One-Eye,' Corban yelled.

'None of that is important,' Gar said. 'All that matters is that you fight me. You *must* fight me. It is a blood-feud, and the Jotun hold to the honour of the old days.'

Ildaer's eyes flickered to Eld and Hala, then returned to Gar.

'I am Ildaer, Warlord of the Jotun; I have taken this land for my clan. You are a maggot, and will be squashed like one. Mort, take him from my sight and teach him the meaning of pain.'

'Hold,' Eld said, looking between Gar and Ildaer. 'We are the Jotun. All other clans may have turned from the old ways, but we have not; he claims the right of blood-feud.'

'You are not serious,' Ildaer sneered. 'He should be exterminated like the vermin he is.'

'He speaks true,' Hala said. 'You have confessed to killing his father. He has the right to claim trial by combat.'

'This is madness, a waste of my time,' Ildaer rumbled, glowering at Eld.

'You are Warlord of the Jotun,' Eld said, 'do not lose your honour over him.' Eld gestured at Gar.

Ildaer stood there a long moment. His eyes flickered to Mort, who was in the crowd close to him. Ildaer nodded.

'Very well,' Ildaer said, hefting his war-hammer. 'Come, then, you that are eager for death.'

'And if I win, I walk away from here?' Gar looked to Eld and Hala as he said it.

'Of course,' Eld snapped. 'We are not murderers.'

'And he comes with me,' Gar said, pointing now to Corban.

For the first time Gar looked straight at Corban. Their eyes locked – so much communicated in a few heartbeats.

'I think not,' Eld said. 'You go too far. You have claimed your right, under the old way of blood-feud, but there is nothing in the lore that says you have a claim to him, or any other prize.'

Gar shrugged and looked at Ildaer. He unsheathed his curved sword and tossed the scabbard away.

Ildaer rolled his huge shoulders and set his feet in a wide stance, towering over Gar.

Gar lifted his sword two-handed above his head, set his feet, waited.

'Ha, I've seen that before,' Ildaer laughed. 'Him, over there.' He gestured at Corban. 'Your father did the same, though it did him little good. You all fight the same. No doubt you'll die the same.'

'Begin,' Eld said.

Gar and Ildaer swung at each other, Gar's blade ringing out as it struck a glancing blow on the iron bands of Ildaer's hammer-shaft, knocking it wide. Gar quickly stepped inside the giant's guard, following up with two short chopping strikes, and Ildaer was staggering backwards, blood dripping from cuts on his face and forearm. Gar pursued, striking high and low, his sword a blur, Ildaer's war-hammer blocking wildly as he gripped the shaft with both hands, using it more as a staff to defend himself. Slowly Ildaer got his feet under him, using both ends of his war-hammer, the spiked butt stabbing out, the hammer-head blocking, punching at Gar's head, his chest, feinting, testing. Gar swung and ducked, sidestepped, spun around blows; nothing landed on him. Ildaer retreated slowly, uphill towards Corban, sweat and blood dripping from his face.

Gar's speed seemed to increase, each attack flowing seamlessly into the next one, sparks exploding from Ildaer's hammer-haft. More wounds appeared on Ildaer, on the back of his hand, across his thigh, his shoulder, Gar was still untouched. He circled Ildaer; the giant was breathing heavily.

'Do you think of your da?' Ildaer said.

'Every day,' Gar said and attacked again, another blistering attack forcing Ildaer backwards.

'Was he in pain, at the end?' Ildaer grunted as he fended off a strike to his throat, sidestepped and swung his hammer two-handed at Gar's midriff, the blow missing by a finger's width as Gar leaped away.

Corban saw muscles twitch on Gar's face, the grip on his sword tighten.

Anger is the enemy; control it. Anger is what defeated you last time, and Ildaer remembers.

Gar surged forwards, feinted high to the left, chopped low, but Ildaer caught Gar's sword on his hammer-head, turned it, lashed out and struck Gar across the head with the spike. Gar stumbled

backwards, legs unsteady, blood sheeting into one eye. Instinctively
Corban tried to leap forwards, but the giants held him fast, Corban
and his captors were alone on the slope as the crowd followed Ildaer
and Gar back down the hill and across the courtyard. For a moment
Corban could not see Gar – the crowd was blocking his view – a
silent scream filled his head at the prospect of Gar dying only a handful of paces away, and him powerless to do anything.

There was a thud close by, a grunt, and then, suddenly, the grip
upon Corban's wrists was gone. He held his hands up and stared at
them, as if to check. The giant that had been holding them was
crumpled on the ground, blood staining a patch on his leather jerkin.

CHAPTER THIRTY-THREE

CORALEN

Coralen saw Corban look in surprise at the giant's corpse, even as she was leaping on the second one's back and cutting his throat. Blood sprayed and he collapsed to his knees, toppling forwards onto his face.

'Cora?' She heard Corban's voice, looked back at him. He had a purpling bruise on his temple, an angry-looking cut on his opposite cheek, deep hollows about his eyes, and in general looked as if he'd been to the Otherworld and back, but the smile spreading across his face became her world, just for a heartbeat or two.

'How?' he said.

'No time for that,' Coralen said, grabbing his wrist and pulling him back towards the buildings behind them, into their shadow.

'What—'

'No time for that, either. Come on, got to get out of here before Gar's show is over.'

'Leave? Not without Gar.'

Still stubborn and difficult, then.

'It's *his* plan,' Coralen grunted. 'We're just doing what we're told. Come *on*!'

She cupped her hands to give him a boost up to the forge roof; the plan was to go from there to the wall and then over to the meadows beyond. After that running like hell was the general idea.

'Corban,' a voice called out.

A blond-haired giant was striding towards them. He saw the two dead giants, paused, eyes narrowing, then came straight at them. Coralen moved without thinking, leaping forwards with her sword rising, rolling under his arm as he tried to grab her, sliding on the dirt, one leg hooking behind his ankles, the other kicking his shins. He teetered for a moment, Coralen rolling and slamming her shoulder into his legs to make sure he went down.

He did, with a thud and a cloud of dust exploding, then she was kneeling on his chest, sword-tip stabbing at the giant's throat.

Suddenly she was yanked off him.

'Not him,' Corban said. He looked from Coralen to the giant, then offered his hand to the giant.

'You are not what I expected at all,' the giant rumbled.

He makes friends in the strangest of places.

Corban looked at Coralen.

'Damn, but it's good to see you,' he said, and grinned.

This is not the time or place for grinning. I think he must have had a blow to the head.

'The feeling's mutual,' she grunted. 'Maybe better if we talk as we run, though.'

'I can't leave Gar here,' Corban said.

'I've just told you; this is Gar's plan. We've come a long way to get you, so don't go spoiling the plan. You'll upset Gar.'

'You should go,' Varan said.

'Is *nobody* listening to me,' Corban said, 'I'm not leaving without Gar.'

'If he defeats Ildaer, Eld will allow him to walk away. It is his right,' Varan said. 'If Ildaer wins, well, you won't be leaving with him then, anyway, because he'll be dead. You should go, now.'

'You'd let me?' Corban asked.

'You just saved my life,' the giant said. 'I owe you. And you, little woman, are very fast. And stronger than you look.'

This is the strangest rescue I've ever been involved in.

'Can we?' Coralen said, pointing at the wall.

The giant grabbed them both by the waist and lifted them up to the forge roof, Coralen and Corban pulling themselves up. Coralen had just leaped and grabbed the top of the wall when a huge roar from the crowd behind them rang out.

CHAPTER THIRTY-FOUR

CORBAN

Corban turned and stared.

Gar was down, on one knee, one hand on the ground, Ildaer striding towards him. Corban felt as if every joint in his body was suddenly frozen. Coralen had been scrambling up onto the wall but now she thudded down beside him. They both stood there, on the forge roof, staring at Gar.

Ildaer raised his hammer and swung overhead, like a man striking at a tent peg with all his might, the intention to crush Gar to a pulp. Gar seemed dazed, slow. At the last moment he rolled to the side as the hammer crashed into the ground he had just occupied, dirt spraying. On unsteady legs Gar rose to his feet and shuffled backwards. Ildaer rushed at him, war-hammer moving faster than a heavy lump of iron had a right to, Ildaer's strength and speed phenomenal. Gar blocked, ducked and swayed, always retreating; Ildaer finally slowed a fraction, then Gar's sword was striking at the giant, a combination of loops and thrusts, each one flowing into the other. All were blocked, except for Gar's last strike, which slashed low, the tip slicing through the leather of the giant's boot, droplets of blood sprinkling the ground in the wake of Gar's blade.

Ildaer paused then, the two warriors facing each other. Both of them wounded, breathing hard.

'I'll admit, you're better at this than your da,' Ildaer said. 'But you're still going to die.'

With his free hand Gar reached behind his back and pulled at something strapped to the back of his belt, revealing a short-handled axe.

'This was my da's,' Gar said, 'gifted to him by Wulf ben Gramm.

He used it when he fought you here, left it in the skull of one of your bears.' Gar rolled his wrist, the axe-blade tracing a circle in the air. Then Gar was closing in, sword and axe blurring, Ildaer blocking frantically, the clang of iron ringing out. The entire courtyard was quiet before the savagery and skill unleashed before them. Gar leaped out of range, danced back a few steps, then he was launching himself forwards, running at Ildaer. The giant snarled and swung his hammer, low and horizontal, aimed to connect with Gar's hip and sweep him away. Gar dived to the ground head-first, rolled beneath the hammer-swing, came out of the roll behind Ildaer, and the giant was bellowing in pain as Gar's axe was buried deep in the back of his leg, between knee and buttock. Ildaer stumbled on a step, then dropped to one knee.

Gar rose, walked a wide circle around the wounded giant as a shocked silence filled the courtyard. Ildaer gripped the axe-shaft in his leg and ripped it free, roaring like a wounded bear, flung the axe at Gar. The Jehar's sword flashed, the axe was knocked aside. Ildaer tried to rise but his leg would not take his weight and he crashed back to the ground again. Gar stood before him, gripped his sword two-handed and raised it high. Ildaer swung wildly with his war-hammer, missing Gar and almost dragging himself over. Gar slashed with his sword and the war-hammer fell to the ground, Ildaer's severed hand still gripping it. Blood jetted from Ildaer's wrist, the giant howling in shock and horror. Gar stepped forwards, sword slashing again, and Ildaer's cry was cut short, his head spinning through the air and thumping into the dirt. It rolled, coming to a stop at Eld's feet.

Gar stood there, bloody and battle-grim, his chest heaving, nostrils flaring. He bowed his head, closed his eyes.

He is thinking of his da.

Corban blinked away tears, let out a hiss of suppressed emotion. His hand ached and he looked down to see Coralen's hand in his. He had no idea whether he had gripped her or she him.

Eld's voice rang out across the courtyard.

'Your blood-feud is done, Garisan ben Tukul. Leave us now; only remember that the Jotun dealt with you fairly, and with honour.'

Gar looked up, eyes opening as if coming out of a deep sleep.

'NO,' a voice cried out, ringing from the walls: Mort. He was close to Gar, staring at Ildaer's decapitated head with horror and rage. In a burst of speed, Mort clubbed Gar across the shoulders with his axe-haft, sending the warrior crumpling to the ground.

'Ildaer was our Warlord, our leader; he returned pride to the Jotun, washed away the shame of ages, amassed by Eld the coward,' Mort yelled out. Angry murmurs rippled through the giants.

'Mort, enough,' Sig said.

'And after all Ildaer has achieved, battle-fame and even winning us *land* beyond the Desolation, Eld is happy to watch Ildaer cut down, allow his killer to leave, and march us all back across the river into that desolate place again, never to return.'

'I said, enough.' Sig pushed through the crowd to reach Mort.

Eld just stared at him.

'Well, I for one will not go back to the Desolation. I have fought alongside Ildaer for our clan, spilt my blood, saw my brother slain. Under Ildaer's leadership we won renown and land, a new home, pride in ourselves, but now you say it is for *naught*!' Mort held up a fist and clenched it at Eld.

'I say *NO*,' Mort yelled. 'No to our cowardly King. Your time is done.'

He spat towards Eld, eyes bulging, then launched himself at the ancient giant, his axe swinging. It connected with a warrior-giant standing before Eld, one of the King's guards; the giant was hurled through the air in a spray of blood.

There was a moment's shocked silence, then the courtyard erupted into madness, giant fighting giant, hammers and axes swinging. Corban recognized many of Ildaer's warband attacking Eld's guards or warriors loyal to the King. Even as he watched, Hala went down in a mass of limbs, Eld staggering backwards, Sig's longsword flashing free of its scabbard and cutting giants down as she attempted to carve a way to Mort.

Corban and Coralen looked at one another, then leaped back down into the courtyard.

Without thinking, he grabbed his iron bar and ran into the fray, Coralen on his left, both of them heading for Gar.

Corban ran down the slope, heard roars and rumbles from the open gateway to the bear pens on his left.

If all of those bears have a bond with their riders, as Long Tooth did with Varan . . .

He veered into the stable-block and ran along the line of pens, releasing bolts and swinging doors wide. Together the bears burst out of the stables into the sunlight, a storm of angry fur, teeth and claws, turning the place into a seething mass of murder, crushing flesh and bone as they searched out their riders.

The courtyard was awash with violence, giants locked in combat with one another; some found their bears and mounted, to deal death out from their backs. Corban kept running, the need to reach Gar driving him; Coralen swung her sword at anything that threatened to slow them.

Corban hurdled a pair of giants that were grappling on the ground, then something crunched into his side, sent him crashing to the dirt. His iron bar went skittering from his hand. He tried to rise but a giant's boot shoved him back down, a dark-haired giantess loomed over him. Corban recognized her as one of Mort's young companions, a blood-crusted axe in her hands.

Move, roll, get up, or you're dead.

Then the giantess was stumbling backwards, a dagger hilt protruding from her chest. She looked at the weapon, confused, staggered another step. There was a *whirring* sound and an arrow-point exploded from her throat. She plucked at the tip even as another dagger slammed into her shoulder, sending her staggering back another few paces before she toppled like a felled tree.

Corban scanned the wall beyond the courtyard, saw a small dark figure kneeling, bow in hand, another figure standing at its shoulder.

Dath and Kulla.

It didn't last long, though; another giant was coming at him.

'Duck,' a voice shouted behind him, and instinctively he did. Something whistled over his head; there was a crunch and the giant in front of him was spinning and crashing to the ground.

Corban turned to see Farrell and Laith standing behind him. Then Farrell was hugging him, crushing him in a fierce embrace.

'I've run across half the world for you, Corban ben Thannon,' Farrell said. 'Cursed your name most of the way, but seeing you, by Asroth's teeth, I have to say it was worth it.'

'Not half the world, just half of Forn Forest,' Laith corrected as she collected her daggers back from giant corpses. 'He exaggerates.' She shrugged.

'Touching as this is, how about we save the reunion until we're somewhere with less chance of *dying*,' Coralen said as she joined them, yelling over the din of battle.

'Before you go running off, thought you might like this,' Farrell said, nodding and gesturing enthusiastically to Laith. She shrugged something from her back, long and wrapped and tied in leather. She ripped the thong off and unwrapped it, revealing . . .

My sword. The sword my da made for me.

Almost reverently, Corban gripped the hilt, a hand and a half of sweat-stained leather; he stroked the wolven-head pommel. He lifted the cross-guard high and kissed it.

'You left it in a giant,' Farrell said.

'True friends.' Corban looked up and saw them all smiling at him. 'The best of friends.' He looked about at the battle and gritted his teeth. 'Let's find Gar and get out of here.'

'First sensible thing you've said,' Coralen grinned.

They threaded their way through the melee, only engaging when they had to, heading ever closer to the steps that led up to the new hall, before which Gar had slain Ildaer. Right in front of Corban two bears slammed together, giants on their backs, the bears clawing, biting, raking each other with teeth and claws, the giants bellowing and swinging hammer and axe at each other.

Corban looked about frantically; the fighting on the steps was fierce. He sighted Sig near the top step, wielding her longsword two-handed, swinging it in great bloody arcs. A handful of warriors were ranged behind her, standing in a loose curling line.

Eld's honour guard? Does the Jotun King even live still?

Giants were hurling themselves up the steps at Sig – younger warriors, fierce and reckless in their rage.

'Gar? Where is Gar?' Corban shouted to the others, all of them searching for their friend.

Varan stepped into the clearing, carrying Gar in his arms, approaching Corban and holding Gar out. He was unconscious, battered and bruised, looked as if half the Jotun clan had trampled over him, but his chest rose and fell, for which Corban breathed out a silent prayer of thanks. Laith stepped forwards and took Gar from Varan; the Jotun giant's eyebrow rose at the sight of her.

'Thank you,' Corban said simply.

Varan nodded, then he was wading into the battle, swinging his war-hammer in a bid to reach the stairs and Sig.

Corban shared a look with his friends, and then they were running for the gate. A giant loomed before them, hammer rising, but an arrow sprouted from his eye and he crashed to the ground. Corban ran on, circled two bears that slammed into each other like two avalanches, and then he was at the gates.

They were open and clear, meadow grass rippling in the wind beyond.

CHAPTER THIRTY-FIVE

CORALEN

Coralen ran through the long grass, her heart thumping with exertion. Laith set their pace as she was carrying Gar, but even so they were running fast, probably faster than at any time during the chase through Forn Forest.

It's amazing what knowing there's a warband of angry giants and bears at your back will do.

Gramm's hold was now a silhouette behind them, their shadows running ahead of them, elongated dark streaks in the bloody glow of sunset.

Gar groaned over Laith's shoulder, his eyelids fluttering.

We must stop soon. She glanced at Corban, saw he was favouring one leg, though he was keeping up well enough. *Can't have an injury now, though. We may need to outrun bears in the not-too-distant future.* Looking at him, she felt a rush of emotion; his dark hair was sweat-stuck to his neck, the gash on his face red. The thrill of victory and success filled her, making her feel that she could run all night.

We did it. Found him, got him out, and no one dead. Relief was sinking in; only now did Coralen realize that she'd been living under the shadow of dread for over a moon. She risked another sidelong glance at Corban, their eyes touching for a moment, and then she looked away.

She grinned at the high clouds, glowing pink with the sinking sun, and enjoyed the feeling and sensation coursing through her. Whatever it was, it stopped her thinking about the burning in her lungs and the soreness of her feet.

*

It was almost full dark when they reached the outermost fringes of the forest. They stopped beside an ice-cold stream, drinking thirstily and resting briefly beneath a stand of hawthorn, its branches full of sweet-smelling white flowers. Gar propped himself up on one elbow and winced.

'Feel like I've been trampled by a herd of auroch,' he grunted.

That's close enough to the truth.

The Jehar made to stand, hissing with pain, and Coralen hurried over to him.

'Let me check you over, first. Things may be broken.'

'Ban, where is Ban?' Gar said, ignoring her and rising to his feet. She put an arm around his waist and helped him stand.

'I'm here,' Corban said, emerging from the darkness. They stared at each other a long moment, then Gar's arms were rising and Corban was stepping forwards, the two men embracing one another, hugging, both of them crying, laughing.

Coralen felt that she should look away, that she was intruding on something deeply personal.

'Don't ever do that to me again,' Gar said. 'You've led us a merry chase.'

'I'll do my best,' Corban laughed through his tears.

'You're back where you belong, now,' Gar said, cupping Corban's cheek.

'I am. Are you hurt badly?'

'I don't think so,' Gar said, testing limbs and joints, flexing, twisting slowly. He grimaced, fingers probing his ribs and one of his hips. 'Well, it hurts, but doesn't feel like there's anything broken.'

'Ildaer,' Corban said. 'Your da is avenged.'

'Aye.' A grim smile creased Gar's face. 'He is.'

The others were gathering round now, water skins filled.

'It was a fight, and no mistake,' Dath said to Gar, 'you and Ildaer, I mean. A dozen times I nearly shot that big tree – every time I thought he was going to kill you.'

'My thanks for holding back,' Gar said. 'I would not have appreciated that.'

'I guessed that,' Dath said. 'In fact, I said to Kulla, if I shoot that giant, Gar'll most likely stab me. Though you did drag it out a bit. I thought it'd be over quicker.'

Coralen shook her head. *That's Dath, always speaking before he thinks on it.*

Gar was staring at him.

'Sorry,' Dath muttered.

'No, you're right,' Gar said. 'I felt I had him, in the first rush, was almost ready for the killing blow, but then I remembered I needed to buy you time, to get Corban out. It struck me that a duel of ten blows or less wouldn't buy that much time.'

'Good point,' Dath commented.

'So I decided to prolong it a little. I thought I had his measure, could finish him when I was ready.' He gave a sheepish smile. 'I made a mistake. I forgot about the endurance of giants.'

'One of our strong points,' Laith said.

'Aye, something I should have remembered,' Gar said. 'So as my strength began to fade, Ildaer's didn't. It made things a little harder.' He reached over his shoulder for his sword hilt, only then realizing that it wasn't there.

'My sword?'

'There were a thousand giants trying to kill each other,' Farrell said, 'your sword was hard to find.'

Gar frowned.

'I'll tell you about the Jotun while I see to your wounds,' Corban said, tearing a strip of linen from his shirt hem and soaking it in the stream, then ordering Coralen to sit beside Gar.

'I'm fine,' she said.

'You've just run a hundred leagues to rescue me, the least I can do is wash a wound or two. And Brina has taught me a little. I won't poison you.'

Coralen acquiesced and Corban began to wash their wounds. Coralen unlaced her leather vest to reveal a puncture wound from a giant's hammer-spike. It hadn't gone deep, but it had bled a lot. Corban dabbed the dried blood away and washed it clean, Kulla bringing over her pack and handing him honey for the wound and a roll of linen bandage. Coralen watched Corban work with interest, feeling his hand upon her wound, his expression completely focused. She liked the sensation, it made her feel safe.

For a ham-fisted blacksmith's son he's remarkably good at this.

Corban finished with her and moved on to the cut on Gar's forehead. As he did so he told them all that had happened at the hold, filling them in on the Jotun, their hierarchy and something of their background. Dath and Farrell kept asking more questions, so Corban went back almost to the beginning, telling of his battle in the glade, the injuries he and Storm had taken.

No wonder he favours one leg.

Corban paused, reliving memories of that dark day, no doubt. After a few moments he continued, telling of being dragged from Storm and his journey through Forn.

I wish I could tell him that Storm lives, but she was on the brink of death when I left her. Better to say nothing now than give him false hope.

She listened in silence until he came to the part where the giants had tried to kill him.

'I saw something that Eld did not want me to speak of,' Corban said. 'He has one of the Seven Treasures. The starstone dagger.'

They all fell silent at that; talk of the Seven Treasures took them back to the attack on Drassil. Corban wanted to know what had happened.

Gar spoke mostly, telling the tale in his matter-of-fact way, of the surprise attack, Nathair's draig smashing through the trapdoor in Drassil's great hall, of the legions of Kadoshim and Vin Thalun and eagle-guard, of the desperate fight and then retreat, and the deaths.

'Cywen?' Corban asked when Gar had finished.

'We don't know,' Dath said, reaching out and putting a hand on Corban's shoulder. 'Brina said Cywen was with her in the great hall, but there was some kind of explosion, fire and smoke. They were separated, Brina escaped down the tunnel. We waited, but Cywen never came.'

'There were prisoners,' Gar said. 'Within Drassil, we heard. Before we left after you. She could be one – she is brave, smart and resilient. If she survived the battle Calidus would likely keep her alive, use her as bait.'

Corban grunted, head bowed, face in darkness.

'And Meical may be a prisoner, too,' Dath added.

'No. Meical is dead,' Corban said with grim certainty.

'How do you know?' Gar asked him.

'I saw him, in the Otherworld. After I was taken by the Jotun. He told me of the battle at Drassil, of how he stood at the trapdoor and defended your escape. Calidus took him captive, had him executed.' He looked up from the shadows, moonlight bathing his face. 'They took his head.'

'The Otherworld, huh?' Dath said, nudging Farrell and sounding a little awestruck. 'One of the advantages of being the Bright Star, I suppose.'

Corban stared at Dath, something battling within him.

'I am not the Bright Star,' Corban said.

Coralen looked around the small group, at their faces, disbelieving, confused. Corban stern and sombre.

'It's true. There is no Bright Star,' he repeated. 'Brina and Cywen came to see me, after your celebration,' he said with a weak smile at Dath and Kulla. 'Brina had found something in the giant book. It was confusing, contradicted things that Meical had told us.' He sat back, sighing deeply. 'I found Meical in the great hall, before Skald and the spear. I challenged him about it, and he told me . . . told me the prophecy is a ruse, a strategy devised by the Ben-Elim to force Asroth's hand, and to guide Asroth along a path where the Ben-Elim could defeat him.'

'They're not doing a very good job, then,' Farrell muttered.

'That's what I said,' Corban agreed.

Gar was staring at him. 'Tell us again; *everything* that Meical said to you.'

So Corban did. Coralen saw the muscles in his jaw bunching as he recounted parts of it, reliving his shock and anger, his devastation. He explained how Meical had asked for Corban's forgiveness, that the Ben-Elim viewed the race of men and giants as collectives, not individuals, and that the end goal was to defeat Asroth, once and for all. If a few hundred or few thousand men and giants died along the way, then so be it.

'I wish he were still alive so that I could kill him again,' Farrell said through gritted teeth, his knuckles popping as he clenched his fists.

'But, Storm and Shield,' Dath said, frowning. 'How could Meical know about them?'

'He didn't,' Corban answered. 'I asked him the same question. He just shrugged and said maybe Elyon was stirring . . .' He was silent, as if remembering. 'Meical said he didn't write all of the prophecy, only the core of it, and even *that* he whispered into Halvor's ear. He said over the generations it has grown and changed, become more.' He shrugged. 'But he wrote it, set the whole thing in motion.'

'It cannot be true,' Gar said, rubbing a hand across his face. 'Some mistake . . .'

'It is no mistake,' Corban said. 'I felt as you do now. Betrayed. Angry. I almost drew my sword on him. That is why I walked away, left Drassil for a time. To be alone, to think, to calm down.'

Coralen looked at Corban. His face was twisted with so many emotions.

'I am sorry,' he said. 'Sorry to you all, and to all those at Drassil in the warband, those who fought, died.' He looked away, his mouth a bitter line. 'All those who followed me, believing me to be some-thing that I am not. You've pursued me here, risked life and limb to save me. To save the Bright Star.'

Coralen could hardly take in what she was hearing. She wanted to believe that Corban had made a mistake, misunderstood, or that Meical had some madness upon him.

But no. I believe Corban. He's no idiot, much as I might tell him that he is. And look at him. It has broken his heart, more for us than for his own self.

She felt the sudden urge to reach out to him, to hold him and comfort him. It took an act of will to remain where she was.

'I believe you,' she said, her voice quiet.

Corban nodded at her, a thanks.

'And we came after you because you're our *friend*, Ban,' Farrell said. 'Bright Star's got nothing to do with it.'

'So, what do we do now?' Dath said. 'If it's true, if it's all been a lie! What do we do now?' There was an edge of panic in his voice.

Corban put his head in his hands, rubbed his face hard, then looked up.

'We could leave,' he said. 'Most of the people in this world that I still hold dear are here, before me. We could leave, walk away from war and death. Find somewhere quiet. Build a new life for ourselves.'

They all just stared at him, each thinking over his words, imagin-ing. Coralen found herself thinking of a cottage by a stream, Corban working a plough in a field, her out hunting deer in green-dappled woodland.

'You don't mean that,' Gar said.

'I did think on it,' Corban said. 'Part of me would love nothing more than to walk away, to start a new life, maybe build a hold somewhere together.' Coralen saw Farrell and Laith look at each other, Dath nodding to himself.

'But I know that there is no hiding from Calidus, from Asroth,' Corban continued. 'They would find us. They mean to destroy all life in these Banished Lands. That includes us, no matter how far or fast we run. And there's Cywen. I could never just walk away not knowing if she were alive or dead.'

'So what does that leave?' Gar asked. He looked as if he already knew the answer, but wanted to hear Corban say it.

'We fight,' Corban said with a shrug. 'The prophecy may be a ruse, but Calidus and his Kadoshim are real enough, and they are murdering their way through our lands, our kin. I may not be the Bright Star, but I can still hold a blade. I fought Sumur and took his head. I don't say that as boast, but as fact. One man, or woman –' he nodded to Coralen, Kulla and Laith – 'can make a difference. Can do something. It may not change anything, but we won't know unless we try.'

He sighed. 'It's taken me a long time to come to this conclusion. I've thought long and hard on it, come through the darkness of Meical's deceit, and now I can see it for what it is, and what it isn't. But you've only had a few moments. Think about it, sleep on it, we can talk again on the morrow.'

'No need for that,' Farrell said. 'Least, not for me. You're my friend, Ban. I'll go where you go. It's as simple as that.'

'Me too,' Dath said. 'You were my friend before all this seven disgraces business came along. My only friend. You're good, Ban, in here.' Dath put two fingers over his heart, tapped his chest. 'And I'll follow you wherever you choose to go. You're my friend, and I trust you, Bright Star or no. And I'm still your shieldman, unto death.'

'Aye,' Farrell rumbled his agreement.

Corban was looking at their faces, ranged in a half-circle before him. His eyes rested upon Gar, who was looking back at him, unreadable as always.

'Good advice. We'll talk more in the morning,' Gar nodded. 'Decide which way we'll be running.'

Farrell groaned. 'Always the running!' he muttered.

'I'll take first watch,' Coralen said, and walked away, jumping across the stream and standing beneath a tree. She looked east and west, deciding whether Gramm's hold or Forn Forest was the greatest danger, then faced west, towards Gramm's hold.

Giants and bears, and some of them tried to kill us today.

What a day. A duel, a battle, an escape. And a revelation.

Her head was spinning with it, but sitting alone in the darkness helped her think it through.

In truth Corban not being the Bright Star didn't matter to her. She'd met him and known his worth before she'd heard any mention of prophecies. And he was right, there was a war that still needed fighting, an enemy that still needed killing, regardless of the names and titles you gave the combatants. She knew what her choice would be come sunrise. Had known all along.

She heard the murmur of conversation amongst her companions, even that slowly dying out, the rasp of a whetstone, Corban lovingly tending to his reunited blade, then silence. Finally, Laith's snoring. And a while later, a soft footfall, the crackle of leaves underfoot. From the corner of her eye she saw Corban approaching through the hawthorns.

A smile twitched her lips, her heart suddenly beating faster.

CHAPTER THIRTY-SIX

CORBAN

There she is.

'Ban, you're as loud as a lumbering bear,' Coralen said, not even turning her head.

I thought I was being my most skilfully quiet!

'I couldn't sleep,' he said, his eyes picking out the shape of her in the darkness. Her shadow merged with the tree, a curve gilded by the moon. She looked at him, red hair dark in the starlight, face pale and dappled with freckles, her eyes deep shadows. His heart was beating hard in his chest, as fast as it had been during the battle and long run all the way here from Gramm's hold.

'I . . . It's good to see you,' he mumbled, 'all of you.' He waved a hand behind him. 'I'm grateful, to you all, for . . .'

What is wrong with me? I can fight Sumur, a Kadoshim demon from the Otherworld, yet now I've lost the ability to speak!

She stepped close to him, so close that he could smell the hint of apples on her breath.

Like in my dreams.

'Unless you've come here to *finally* return my kiss,' she said, 'then you'd better turn around and walk away. I've been angry with you a long while and may not be responsible for what I do to you.'

He leaned forwards, hesitantly brushed his lips against hers, his heart pounding louder than a Benothi war-drum, then harder and, suddenly, his arms were around her, pulling her close, and he felt as if he was drowning, spinning.

Their lips parted; a jolt passed through him, like thinking there was an extra step as you walked down a stairwell.

'Well, better late than never,' Coralen murmured with satisfaction, and Corban realized she was smiling, saw the glint of teeth through her parted lips.

'Apples,' he said.

'What?'

'I dreamed of kissing you, and in my dream you tasted of apples.'

'You dream about me?' Coralen asked. She didn't sound so angry now. She grabbed his shirt and pulled his lips onto hers.

Why have we not done this sooner. It's wonderful.

His thoughts disintegrated. Time passed – how long, Corban could not tell.

Abruptly Coralen pushed him away, her head turning, cocked to one side.

What have I done now?

Then he heard it. A rumble, like distant thunder, but rhythmic, growing louder.

Not louder. Closer.

I recognize that sound.

'Bears,' he said.

They exploded into movement, running back through the trees, leaping the stream.

'Ware the Jotun,' Corban cried, snatching up his sword from where he'd left it beside his cloak.

All were jumping to their feet, Coralen standing and calmly buckling her wolven claws onto her left fist. Corban went and helped her.

'Wish I still had mine,' he said as he buckled the last strap for her.

'We'll have to go get it back for you, then,' she grunted and drew her sword, staring back into the darkness. Dath sprinted away a score of paces, turned, started stabbing arrows into the earth around him, stringing his bow, Kulla at his shoulder as always.

Gar limped close to Corban; Laith drew one of her many daggers, flipping it and tossing it to Gar, then another one.

'That's better,' Gar said, running the blades of the two daggers together. They were like short swords for him.

Farrell hefted his hammer.

Corban set his feet, shifted his weight from left to right, testing his knee. It was throbbing, a dull pulse, but felt good enough.

It'll be all right. It'll have to be.

Then trees were splintering, cracking, and a bear was bursting out from the midnight dark in an explosion of leaves, a giant on its back.

Mort.

The giant saw Corban and bellowed a victory cry, raising his battle-axe over his head. Others were behind him, shadows huge as boulders – four, six, seven, Corban could not tell. Then the bears were amongst them.

Corban jumped to his left, a bear leaping at him; he felt Mort's axe hiss by his ear. Corban gripped his sword two-handed and hacked with all his might, his blade-tip slicing into the bear's back leg as it hurtled past him. It bellowed. Corban pivoted and swung his sword over his head, moving into the dragonfly stance. Mort was yelling commands at the bear, trying to get it to turn as it slammed broadside into a tree, leaves erupting from above.

Corban glimpsed Farrell swinging his hammer, deflecting an axe-blow, a shower of sparks cascading about him while Laith was hurling her daggers at a giant atop a bear. Then Mort and his bear were charging at him again.

He held his stance as the bear pounded towards him. At the last possible moment Corban spun away, his sword slashing at the animal's neck, ducking as Mort's axe swung at his head. Then Mort and the bear were beyond range.

Corban heard a rage-filled scream from Kulla and saw Dath swiped by a bear-paw slashing at his back, sending him flying, smashing face-first into a tree. Kulla half severed the still-raised paw, her sword rising and falling in a frenzy, hacking, chopping, the bear dropping, rolling onto its side and pinning its giant rider. Kulla ran up the bear's broad chest, beheading the trapped giant, then stabbed two-handed down into the bear, her sword slipping through ribs and on, deeper and deeper, piercing its heart.

A giant on foot came at Corban, looming out of the shadows, wielding a war-hammer. He feinted right with the hammer-head, struck with the end, the iron-shod butt catching Corban on the shoulder, sending him stumbling off balance. The giant followed, swinging his hammer, Corban ducking, slipping within the giant's guard, stabbing up into the giant's belly, through leather and fur, angling up, under the ribs.

As he ripped his sword free the giant crashed to its knees. Two more bear-riding giants burst through the hawthorns and leaped across the stream.

How many more? We will be crushed, have no chance.

The first bear had a coat of mail buckled about it, a thick leather collar around its neck, and on its back rode a familiar blond-haired giant.

Varan. Has he come to kill me? Or to bring me back, on Eld's command?

Corban watched as Varan leaned low in his saddle, whispering something to his mount, Long Tooth, who leaped forwards, Varan's war-hammer whirring above his head, crunching into a giant that was attacking Gar.

He's helping us!

At the same time Corban saw the rider behind Varan send her bear into the fray, striking at another giant. It was Sig.

There was a bellowing behind Corban, another bear was towering up, one of Laith's daggers sunk to the hilt in its eye. It reared high on its two hind legs, then it was toppling, thundering to the ground, trees shattering in its ruin.

Its rider rose from the wreckage, searching the glade. She was a shield-maiden, who fixed her eyes on Laith and went striding for her. Farrell saw and intercepted, their hammers ringing out, a dozen heavy blows traded as Laith circled, looking for a dagger-opening. Then Farrell was hurled from his feet, crashing to the ground, Laith ducking as the giant switched her focus. She was too slow: the giant's hammer clubbed her to the ground before Farrell's prostrate form. Corban heard a bear roaring and crashing in the trees – Mort bearing down upon him again. The giant maiden was raising her war-hammer high over Laith and Farrell.

Too far, I'm too far away, Corban screamed internally as he ran towards them.

Then Coralen was there. She barrelled into the giant, her sword and wolven claws slashing, sending sparks from the giant's mail shirt, staggering her foe. Coralen punched her wolven claws deep into a thigh, the giant roaring in pain. She dropped to one knee, hammer falling from her grip, but Coralen's claws were stuck in the giant's leg. A fist crashed into Coralen's face, hurling her through the air, crashing to the ground. She tried to rise, dazed, as the giant staggered to her feet, kicking Coralen in the ribs, lifting her from the ground. The giant raised an iron-shod boot over Coralen's head.

Corban was screaming, and then he was there, sword swinging from on high, hacking down diagonally across the giant's chest, a spray of blood and bone, his face twisted in a snarl, striking again and again as the giant tumbled backwards, dead before she hit the ground.

Corban stood over her a moment, blood-spattered and nostrils flaring, then he spun on his heel and ran to Coralen.

She was dazed, grunted with pain when Corban put an arm about her, but she was alive.

Few broken ribs, maybe. I know how that feels. Corban lifted her in his arms, carried her to a tree and placed her against it, then turned and stood before her.

Their small campsite had become a place of carnage, the stench of death filling the air, moonlight glimmering on iron and blood. Farrell and Laith lay still upon the ground – Corban had no idea if they were dead or alive – while Kulla was standing guard over Dath with her feet set and sword raised high, another giant dead at her feet. Gar was still standing, fighting against a riderless bear; Varan and Sig were battling two Jotun on bears.

A bear lumbered in front of Corban, its rider glowering down at him.

Mort.

Corban took a dozen paces forwards and raised his sword high.

Mort snarled and kicked his heels into the bear. The animal jumped forwards.

I'll not be leaping out of its way this time, it'll have a clear run at Coralen. Need to draw it away from her.

Corban lunged at the bear's head, his blade crunching into its skull, glancing off. The blow shivered up through Corban's wrists and arms, numbing his elbows and shoulders but left only a shallow gash upon the bear.

That's why Gramm and Wulf learned how to throw an axe.

He retreated a pace, deflected a blow from Mort's axe as the giant tried to take his head. He backed up another step, stabbing at the bear's eye and missing and grazing its cheek, only seeming to enrage the beast further. A quick glance showed him that Coralen was a few steps behind him leaning against a tree and looking in no condition to fight.

Corban hacked at Mort's leg, felt his blade bite and pulled back to stab into the bear's neck. Then its paw hit him. It must have been a backhanded blow or its claws would have eviscerated him, but it was still powerful enough to hurl him through the air. He hit the ground with bone-jarring force, the bear shambling after him, Mort's pale face grinning.

Then from out of the trees came a monstrous howl, starting deep, finishing high and keening. The sound of undergrowth being torn up, crashed through, then, much closer, a terrifyingly deep snarling growl that set Corban's blood running cold.

The bear paused, looking beyond Corban to the edge of the clearing. Corban rolled on his back to see what new horror was entering the battle.

A creature burst from a wall of undergrowth, huge fangs, snapping jaws, knotted muscle and pale fur.

What monster from Forn is this?

It slammed into the bear, smaller in bulk, but the power and ferocity of its assault was enough to hurl the bear backwards, sending it crashing to the ground. Mort flew through the air and hit a tree – *the crack* of his spine breaking audible even above the battle. The bear and this new creature locked together: a maelstrom of snapping teeth, bone-rattling snarls, tearing at each other.

They rolled to a halt, the bear underneath, scrabbling to rise, the new creature a lump of bulging muscle and fur atop it. Huge jaws bit down, a tearing sound, the bear's roaring rose in pitch, and then abruptly cut short as its throat was torn out. The creature stood upon its victim, shoulders bunched with power, pale fur and dark stripes upon its torso. It carried on frenziedly ripping at the bear's throat for a few moments, then looked up, teeth bared in a snarl as it looked around the campsite.

Long fangs dripped red, its muzzle and head broad, fur matted with blood and scarred from old battles. Amber eyes regarded him, and suddenly Corban knew.

'But, you're dead,' he whispered, rolling to one knee, standing.

Storm.

In a bound she was in front of him. She took a deep sniff, then lifted her head to the heavens and howled, a victory howl, of a hunt ended. She gave his face a long, rasping lick with her rough tongue, nuzzling him, pushing her body against his, curling around him protectively, jumping away and back again, licking at his mouth, whining.

Corban just stood there for a few shocked moments, buffeted and battered by her greeting, grinning all the time like a fool, tears streaming down his cheeks.

It's really her. He felt as if his heart would burst. All that pain and heartbreak that threatened to overwhelm him every time he thought of Storm howling as he was carried away by giants, of when she had stopped howling – it was just gone, transformed suddenly and completely into a deep and overwhelming joy.

And then he threw his arms around her neck and buried his face in her fur, weeping and laughing.

CHAPTER THIRTY-SEVEN

CORALEN

Coralen watched Storm turn into a scampering cub at her reunion with Corban and couldn't help but smile. She hobbled over to the pair; Storm, for a moment, raised a lip and bared her fangs at Coralen before she recognized her scent, then she was nuzzling her as well.

Corban looked at her and smiled, tears streaking lines through the dirt and dried blood-spatter on his face.

'I thought she was dead,' he said.

'I found her, on a riverbank,' Coralen said smiling. Somehow it was important to her that Corban knew that. 'I thought she was dead, she had the faintest heartbeat. Brina was looking after her when we left to find you, though she said there was little hope.'

'Well, whatever she did, it worked,' Corban grinned, ruffling the thick fur around Storm's neck and tugging on one of her ears. She licked his face with a rough tongue, then licked Coralen for good measure, making her stagger. Coralen grunted in pain.

'I need to look at your wounds,' Corban said.

'I think I may have to wait my turn,' Coralen said. 'There're others in more need than me.'

Farrell and Laith were still unmoving, Laith lay prone across Farrell. It was he who was groaning.

Laith swore when they tried to lift her. Coralen breathed a sigh of relief at hearing her; she'd feared the giantling was dead.

'Concussion,' Corban said, looking in Laith's eyes. 'No broken bones.'

Gar came to help them and the three of them rolled Laith off of Farrell, as gently as they could. The two giants that had joined them – Varan and Sig, as Corban introduced them to Coralen – helped.

Sig had a vicious-looking cut along the length of one arm, but still she lifted Laith as if she were as light as a bairn.

'You saved us,' Corban said to the two Jotun giants. 'We are in your debt.'

'We'll talk later,' Varan said. 'But now, take this and tend to your wounded.' He offered Corban a bag. Corban opened it and sniffed.

'Comfrey, yarrow, peppermint,' Varan said. 'Being apprenticed to a healer has its benefits.'

'Hala,' Corban said. 'How is she?'

'Unconscious,' Varan replied.

'Mort struck her,' Sig snarled.

'She may never wake,' Varan added.

'I am sorry for that.' Corban shook his head.

Sig grunted.

'And take this,' Varan said, offering a drinking skin to Corban.

'Brot?'

'Aye,' Varan smiled.

Corban nodded and bent down beside Farrell.

'My thanks,' Farrell breathed, 'much as I'm fond of her, Laith's not a light lass. I feel half-crushed to death.'

'Might have something to do with the hammer-blow you took to your sternum,' Corban said, pressing on Farrell's midriff. He yelped in pain.

'Aye, you might be right,' Farrell said. 'I'm guessing, as we're still alive, we won.' He blinked. 'Is that Storm?'

'Aye,' Corban and Coralen said together.

'She looks meaner,' Farrell commented. 'Wilder.'

I thought that.

'Where's Dath?' Farrell asked.

A muffled sob drew all of their eyes. Kulla. She was still standing over Dath, who was lying face-down in the grass, a vicious set of claw-marks raked across his back. Gently Corban lifted his friend and turned him over. He made no sound, head flopping back in Corban's arms.

'Please, no,' Farrell whispered when he reached them. Coralen just stood and stared, hoping. Corban had his ear to Dath's chest, searching for a pulse.

'Thank Elyon,' he said with a long exhalation, 'he's alive.'

'He's alive?' Kulla asked.

'Aye. For now, though that wound on his back needs cleaning, probably stitching.'

Kulla dropped to her knees, lifted Dath onto her lap and stroked his face, tears rolling down her cheeks. 'When you wake up, we're going to have a serious talk,' Kulla said quietly, 'getting yourself injured like that.'

Coralen helped Corban and Gar tend to the others. Dath's wounds were the most serious, each claw-wound needing washing out then scraping clean with a knife, making them bleed again. When Corban was eventually happy that the wounds were dirt-free, he slathered them with honey and stitched them closed. While they were doing that, Varan and Sig gathered the giant corpses and laid them together, eight giants in all. The dead bears they left where they fell, Storm feasting on one of them.

Coralen had her own collection of cuts and bruises, her jaw was tender and throbbing where the giant had punched her.

Lucky I don't have a broken jaw.

She cleaned and washed her cuts down by the stream, but her worst injury was to her ribs, where the giant had kicked her. Already a purple bruise the size of her head was blooming across her ribs. Eventually Coralen consented to Corban checking her over. He touched her ribs, fingers gentle, but still she winced.

He strapped her ribs and gave her a bowl of something he'd heated over a pot, telling her to wash it down with the brot Varan had given him. She did so without complaint.

It was late by the time all was done, the moon fading in the sky.

Corban sat beside Coralen as she lay on the grass, trying not to groan with the pain in her rib.

'Quite a day,' he said quietly.

'And night,' Coralen said. She felt a warm glow spreading through her, the relief that she always experienced after a battle survived. None of their crew had fallen. Battered to the shadow of death's doorway, maybe, but they were all still breathing. She knew the odds they'd faced this day and night had been overwhelming. It was verging upon a miracle that they had all survived.

She looked up at Corban and saw that he was watching and smiling at her.

'Come down here and get some sleep,' she said to him.

He did, lying down beside her, then turning over to put an arm across her. He kissed her cheek.

'Good night,' he whispered in her ear, and within about thirty heartbeats he was snoring softly. She lay there and smiled.

Just before sleep took her she realized they'd not set a guard. Then she heard Storm shift, get up and pad over to them, curling down behind Corban, the smell of her fur wafting over them.

Don't need to set a guard tonight. Storm's back, and she's pack.

CHAPTER THIRTY-EIGHT

LYKOS

Lykos wandered the wide stone streets of Drassil, a score of Vin Thalun at his back, more of his men emerging from shadowed doorways, all of them shaking their heads.

Nothing.

Where the hell is this blacksmith's chamber where the starstone Treasures were fashioned?

At first Lykos had thought that searching for this mysterious room might be an interesting distraction from the boredom of being stuck in Drassil. Discovering that Maquin and probably Fidele were out in Forn not too far from him had perked him up for a while, but after giving a lot of thought to imagining how he would capture and kill Maquin, and capture and enjoy Fidele, he'd started to try and work out how he was actually going to make that happen. So far he'd not come up with anything. Marching his warband into Forn didn't seem to be the most sensible option, not least because Calidus would probably stick Lykos on one of the spears before the great gates for even suggesting such a wasteful use of manpower.

He seems very highly strung these days. He needs to learn to relax and enjoy the moment.

Lykos unstoppered a fresh skin of mead with his teeth and took a long swallow. Then he belched.

Like me.

He grinned to himself.

Calidus had given Lykos and Nathair different sections of the fortress to search. They were in the last street of Lykos' allocated area, now, opening up into yet another abandoned courtyard, a gnarled old tree at its centre, and still nothing.

We have searched every building. Every room, every tower, every barn and basement. And yet, nothing. I wonder if Nathair has had more luck?

He sat under the shade of the ancient oak, waiting for his men to finish their search. While he waited he drank some more from his skin of mead.

What's that smell?

He looked about. The most terrible stench was drifting up his nose. He stood and looked around, saw only the empty courtyard, his men, the tree, its thick roots lifting flagstones.

Is that a hole in the ground amidst the roots, in the shadows of the tree?

Footsteps slapped on stone and a voice called his name. One of his runners, a young lad who he set to watch the gates and bring him news, if there ever was any. He was red-faced and sweating.

'Someone has arrived,' the lad said. 'A Kadoshim.'

Lykos raised an eyebrow. Calidus was very protective of his Kadoshim these days, rarely let them pass through the gates of Drassil.

'And he looks like he's scrapped his way through all the pits in the Three Islands to get here,' the lad added.

'Where did he go?'

'The great hall, looking for Wax-Face.'

Wax-Face. Ha.

Lykos hastened through the gates of Drassil's great hall and saw Calidus sitting at the long table before Skald's throne, in deep conversation with Nathair. A dozen eagle-guard stood straight-backed close by, and Legion was lurking in the shadows.

The Kadoshim is not here yet. Good.

'What?' Calidus said as Lykos approached.

His manners are failing him. When he was pretending to be nothing more than a counsellor he was so much more polite.

Lykos nodded a greeting at Nathair, who looked away. Sometimes, the way Nathair looked at him, or *didn't* look at him, made Lykos convinced that the young King of Tenebral intended him genuine harm.

He needs to mask his feelings better. Like me.

'I have finished searching the section of this fortress that you set me. No old secret forge.' He opened his hands wide, pulling a sad face.

Calidus opened his mouth to say something, but then his eyes focused over Lykos' shoulder.

Our Kadoshim has arrived, then.

'Mavet, why are you here? Has Gundul arrived?' Calidus called out.

Ah, so he was one of the hundred Kadoshim gifted to Gundul.

Lykos turned to watch the Kadoshim. He was flanked by two more of his kind; seeing them together highlighted how shockingly different this Mavet appeared.

First of all, he was missing a hand. He limped down the stairs, clothes and mail shirt torn and rent, his pale-veined flesh gashed and battered. One eye was gone from his head.

I don't think he's bringing good news.

When Mavet reached them he dropped into a chair at the table, scratching absently at the empty socket where his eye had been.

'Sustenance,' the creature said, its voice a croak.

Calidus poured him wine and the Kadoshim drank deeply, head arching back as it drained the cup.

'Well?' Calidus said through thin-clenched lips.

'Gundul is dead,' the Kadoshim said as a board of meat, bread and cheese was brought for him. He began stuffing food into his mouth. 'And his warband slain or scattered.'

'How?' Calidus said, voice cold and hard as iron.

'Men clothed like them,' the Kadoshim said, pointing at Nathair's eagle-guard.

Veradis and the warband of Ripa.

Lykos looked to Nathair, who appeared stunned by the news.

'But, there were fewer than a thousand men in the warband from Ripa,' Nathair said. 'Gundul's warband numbered in the thousands – three, four thousand strong.'

'And a hundred Kadoshim,' Lykos pointed out.

'It's Veradis and his damned shield wall,' Nathair whispered.

'Yes, there was a wall of shields,' Mavet rasped, 'and many skilled fighters. They knew to take Kadoshim heads. There was a giant.'

'Alcyon,' hissed Calidus.

'I wish I had been there,' Legion muttered. 'I would have smashed their bodies and crushed their skulls, I would have broken their bones and fed from their flesh and danced on their dead and sucked out their souls and—'

'Shut up, Legion,' Calidus snapped.

'And now Veradis and the same warband are camped somewhere out there, beyond our gates.' Nathair shook his head. 'We're going to need a bigger warband.'

There was a long silence, then Calidus surged to his feet, hands beneath the table, grabbing it, hurling it into the air. Snarling and gnashing his teeth like a wild beast, Calidus stormed up the stairs, to the cauldron, and gripped its sides.

'Asroth,' he yelled. 'The years I have worked and toiled and laboured to bring you here, and now we are so close. So close. How much longer before we see your glory? Until you are flesh before us?' He grabbed the starstone spear and with a great wrench pulled it from where it was embedded deep in the great tree and the skeleton of Skald, hurling it at the table he'd just overthrown. It skewered the wood, the shaft vibrating. There was an almighty crash as the bones of the long-dead giant king fell to the floor. And there was another sound, a loud *hissing*, and a *crack*. Lykos looked on in disbelief, because there was now a door swinging open from the trunk of the great tree, high and wide as two giants abreast.

Calidus laughed hysterically and hurried into the darkness, reaching up to take a flickering torch from a sconce set into the tree; Nathair went after him, accompanied by Legion. Lykos made sure to retrieve the skin of mead from the floor where it had fallen in Calidus' outburst before following them.

Mustn't forget our priorities.

Firelight from the torch revealed a stairwell carved into the tree spiralling down, the walls slick and sticky with resin. The steps opened out into a wide room, its edge filled with iron racks, weapons rowed within them – war-hammer, battle-axe and sword, as well as all manner of tools, tongs, pincers, chisels and working hammers. In the room's centre stood a huge anvil, and behind it loomed a massive bellows and forge, still banked with eons-old charcoal and cinder.

Lykos walked deeper into the room, hesitantly, reverently; the room felt thick with antiquity, almost sacred.

It was here that the Seven Treasures were forged. Axe and spear, cauldron, cup and dagger, necklace and torc. Here that the great war began.

He took a swig from his skin of mead.

Calidus touched his torch to bowls full of oil set upon stands. They ignited with a sibilant hiss, blue-flickering light and shadow illuminating the room. Calidus grinned, for upon the wall were carved giantish runes and skilled engravings. At first Lykos could not understand what it was – almost the entirety of the wall that circled them was filled with the scribing. Then it fell into place in his mind.

It is a map!

A huge map, rising high, filling the whole wall, encompassing the room.

'Halvor did this,' Calidus whispered. 'The Voice of Skald, survivor of the Scourging. The last giant to dwell here, in this fortress.'

That was a very long time ago.

Drassil was clear upon it, at the centre of Forn Forest, which spread like a dark stain on the wall. The likeness of a spear was etched alongside Drassil.

The starstone spear.

Lykos looked closer, saw another marker within Forn, to the south of the forest.

'That is Haldis,' Calidus said, 'burial ground of the Hunen, where we fought them, broke them. Where we found the starstone axe.'

'And here is Mikil, Jael's seat of power in Isiltir,' Nathair said, 'and it has an axe engraved besides it.'

'But you say the axe was found at Haldis,' Lykos said, 'not Mikil. Is this map wrong, then?'

'No, I would think it is a depiction of the Banished Lands when Halvor scribed this. Mikil was built by the Hunen giant clan,' Calidus said. 'Dagda was their king, Mikil his seat of power and so it was at Mikil that the starstone axe was kept.'

'How did it end up in Haldis, then?' Lykos asked.

'We know that the starstone axe was still at Mikil until about five years ago, a great relic that King Romar of Isiltir exploited to great financial reward. Then it was stolen by mercenaries and in turn taken from them by the Hunen as they raided out of Forn. It was the Hunen that took the axe to Haldis, the last fortress of theirs not conquered by men.'

So this is the Banished Lands as Halvor knew it then, ruled by the five giant clans. And the whereabouts of each starstone Treasure, at that time. Lykos blew out a long breath, turning in a circle, the enormity of the map staggering him.

That was a long time ago, though. Many things have changed since then.

'Look, here is Murias in the west,' Calidus said, pointing to a carved mountain. Beside it the likeness of a cauldron, a cup, and a necklace, and above them, a word scribed in runes.

'Nemain. Queen of the Benothi,' Calidus said. 'It is saying that she had control of the cauldron, cup and necklace.'

'So three of the Treasures were at Murias, not just the cauldron?' Nathair asked.

'No, not at Murias. See, it suggests that they were in Nemain's care, but not necessarily at Murias. The Benothi ruled all of the west – Dun Carreg, Dun Taras, Dun Crin, Dun Vaner, all were their strongholds.' He was silent a moment, poring over the map. 'Uthas most likely spoke true,' he muttered, 'the cup at Dun Taras and the necklace at Dun Carreg.'

'So what does this say, then?' Lykos asked, pointing up high at a peninsula to the north-west of Forn Forest. There was a word scribed there, and a dagger etched beside it.

'That is the Desolation,' Calidus said, 'and it says, *Eld.*' He tugged at the peeling flesh on his chin, where his silver beard had once been.

'Eld was King of the Jotun giants when the Scourging took place,' Calidus mused.

'I remember the Scourging,' Legion said wistfully. 'Death and destruction, battle with the Ben-Elim.'

'I remember it, too,' Calidus said sourly. 'We lost.'

'Not this time, though,' Legion said, a malicious grin creeping across his face.

'Eld, King of the Jotun?' Nathair prompted.

'Yes. He was King of the Jotun, back at the time of the Scourging, and apparently he has, or at least *had*, the starstone dagger. He took his clan out of the war, marched them into the Desolation, never to be heard of again.' Absently he rolled and flicked his dead flesh away.

'He is surely dead, now?' Nathair asked.

'That would depend, on whether he drank from the starstone cup; it prolongs life. Substantially. But even so, he may still have died, perhaps slain by someone's hand since, or just a fool accident. But even if he is dead, we must think it likely that the dagger remains with the Jotun.'

'Jael of Isiltir had dealings with them,' Nathair said. 'He told me of a warlord of the Jotun.' He pinched his nose, trying to remember. 'Ildaer was his name. And what about this?' Nathair pointed to one last place on the map. To the east of Forn. It was hard to tell, but it looked like a lake, or an inland sea, and within it, an island. And about that island was a broken circle. No, something else.

A torc.

The starstone torc.

Calidus smiled at Nathair and Lykos, looking more like his old self than he had since they had arrived at Drassil.

Nothing like finding the whereabouts of a starstone Treasure to brighten up your day.

'Nathair, you will take a sizeable force of your eagle-guard, up to two thousand swords – large enough to comfortably defeat Veradis and his rabble, while leaving a thousand or so here to guard the cauldron, axe and spear – and you will march out with Mavet to find Lothar. You will warn him of our enemy lurking in the forest, protect him from attack and guide him here with all possible speed. If you hear from our half-breed spy, then you shall act on her information. If you can destroy the rabble in the woods, then by all means do so.'

'Aye, that sounds like a good plan to me,' Nathair said. 'And what of you and your few hundred Kadoshim?'

'I would like to seek out the dagger, in the north, but I am not happy to leave the cauldron, spear and axe with so few to guard them.'

He stood with head bowed, leaning on the huge anvil at the centre of the room, fingers drumming, long nails click-clacking on the age-old iron.

'So,' he said, looking up. 'I shall contact Rhin and tell her to muster the warband of the west and march with it to Drassil. Once she has arrived and the Treasures here are beyond all assault, then I shall go in search of Eld and the starstone dagger.'

He is good at this. It's no wonder we're winning.

'And you, Lykos, I think it is time for you to leave Drassil for a time.'

I couldn't agree more.

'You are going to Arcona and the isle of Kletva to get the starstone torc. Take as many men as you see fit. And Legion will go with you.'

'Yes,' Legion muttered. 'Enemies to kill, bones to shatter, blood to spill and brains to splatter. Flesh to pound and hearts to tear from chests and—'

'I do not care if you murder half the Banished Lands,' Calidus snarled. 'Just bring me back the starstone torc.'

CHAPTER THIRTY-NINE

CORBAN

Corban woke to the smell of Storm's dew-damp fur and Coralen's hair tickling his face. He didn't mind either sensation. In fact, they both made him smile, because they reminded him of the good things that had happened yesterday.

Coralen. How is it that one kiss can have such a lasting effect? And Storm – when I'd thought her dead. I feel . . . happy. Should that even be possible under these circumstances, in these dark days? He didn't know what the answer should be to that, and in truth didn't really care.

Dawn washed the land in a clean glow, pale and crisp, the sky above sheer and blue, the land below dew-sparkled and still. Birds sang from their vantage in the hawthorn ring, though there were new additions to the usual chorus of blackbird and wren, of warblers and robin and thrush. A gathering of crows weighed down the branches, hunched and dour in their black-feathered cloaks, all eyeing the feast of corpses beneath them, once-proud giant and fierce bear, now just mounds of skin, meat and bone, a feast for crows.

I wish Craf were one of them. Strange to say, but I miss that scruffy old crow. Dath, the others – I need to check on them.

Storm shifted behind him, a deep breath and a rumble in her chest as she woke and climbed to her feet.

Corban did the same, his body complaining as he did so, joints stiff, bruises aching and making themselves known.

Storm followed him, rubbing her head against him, pushing into his chest.

You've grown! You're taller. He looked at her broad chest. *And wider.*

He scratched her muzzle, picked blood from a tooth, tugged on the fur of her cheeks, then saw the scar where she had been stabbed with a giant's spear: a pink patch of skin just above her right shoulder, about the size of Corban's fist. As he looked closer he saw that her body was a patchwork of scars, a blend of claw and iron, dealt by both man and beast.

You poor thing. What have I dragged you into? What have I dragged all of us into?

He stretched and gazed down at Coralen.

I kissed her.

He blew out a long breath and felt a lightness flutter in his chest. She opened her eyes and saw him, a smile of her own creeping across her face. It made him want to lie back down beside her, and maybe reacquaint himself with her lips.

'What're you gawping at?' Coralen asked him, though she was still smiling.

'You,' he said.

Someone groaned behind him and he shook his head, feeling as if it was filling with a warm and pleasant mist.

There are wounded who need tending.

'Help me up,' Coralen said as she tried to rise, a grimace replacing her smile.

He did, and after taking a look at her bruised ribs and giving her some more brot they both set about checking on the others.

Gar was already up. He'd lit a fire and had a pot boiling over it, Kulla and Varan were sitting with him. Sig was checking over the giants' bodies, rummaging through packs, cloaks and belt pouches.

'I thought it was safe,' Gar said, pointing at the small fire and curl of smoke. 'Don't think we've any more enemies left alive. Within eyesight, at least.'

Corban looked nervously at his oldest companion, who had said little to him since the previous night's revelations. Of everyone, he knew that it would hit Gar the hardest. He had devoted his whole life to the prophecy, to the belief that Corban was the Bright Star.

But now Gar knows I'm not the Bright Star. Has it changed what he thinks of me? Changed us? That thought scared Corban, made him feel that the ground was shifting beneath his feet. It made him angry at Meical all over again.

'I've checked Dath,' Gar said as Corban strode over to his friend.

'His wounds look all right, not infected, anyway. I've left the others to sleep.'

'I'm not asleep,' Farrell's voice drifted up to them. 'Just in too much pain to move.'

Corban helped the groaning Farrell to his feet and over to the fire, then went back for Laith, who groaned a lot less, but still seemed unsteady on her feet, her eyes not always focused.

'I'm fine,' she said, brushing him off and slurping some hot tea from a bowl that Gar gave her.

Coralen was sitting on a log close to the fire, a row of weapons arrayed before her – sword, wolven claws and three knives. She was methodically cleaning them, scouring blood and dirt away, rasping nicks out, then oiling and scouring again. Corban liked the sound of it, there was something comforting about it.

Sig strode over to them, sitting down beside Varan, her face flat and cold. She gave Varan a curt shake of her head. Corban offered his arm to Varan.

'We'd have been dead without you,' Corban said. 'We owe you our lives.'

'I'm not so sure about that,' Varan said, eyeing Storm. 'Not with friends like that. I'll still take your arm, though, and be happy to call you friend.' He took Corban's forearm in the warrior grip, his fist wrapping around Corban's. 'Though I'm not the first giant to call you friend, I think.' He looked at Laith.

'You're not,' Laith confirmed. 'Corban's a popular man.'

'I'm understanding that,' Varan said. 'In truth, we did not come just to save your skin, though I'm glad that we did.'

'We came for Mort,' Sig said, glowering into the pot over their fire.

'He slew Eld,' Varan said. 'And many more of the Jotun.'

'Well, we thank you all the same,' Gar said, refilling Varan and Sig's bowls of tea from the pot.

'I have something for you,' Varan said, reaching into a pack at his feet and pulling out a bundle wrapped in deerskin. He unrolled it to reveal Gar's sword, back in its scabbard, and his throwing axe. 'You look to be people who value their blades.'

Gar gave a rare grin at the sight of his sword and axe. He took them gratefully, turning them over in his hands, examining them.

'I am most thankful, and in your debt,' he said.

'You slew Ildaer with them. That is thanks enough,' Sig said grimly.

'It seems Ildaer was planning a coup,' Varan said. 'He'd been plotting to assassinate Eld soon, but when Eld ordered the Jotun back into the Desolation – well, it brought his plans forward.'

'I thought you were part of his warband,' Corban said.

'I was, but as I said to you, I think Hala rubbed off on me a little. Ildaer certainly did not trust me enough to speak to me of his plan. And he was right not to. I came south to win battle-fame and honour for the Jotun. Assassinating our King is not how I'd think to achieve that.'

Sig muttered something under her breath, more ways she'd like to re-kill Mort, no doubt.

'So,' said Varan, 'what would you do, now? I would offer the Jotun's hospitality to you, if you want it. You are welcome to come with us; you would find shelter and healing at our hold.'

'Do you speak for all of the Jotun?' Laith asked Varan.

'*I* do,' Sig said.

Be the guests of the Jotun? Of all the options, I did not think about that one.

A rest is tempting, especially to heal. Look at us all. But in the end it would be no different to leaving, to building a hold somewhere far away and trying to find some peace and happiness.

He glanced at Coralen. *Which is very appealing. But in the end there is only Asroth, Calidus and the Kadoshim. We will have to fight them eventually, or kneel to them, and most likely be killed anyway.*

'We spoke of this, last night,' Corban said. 'I told you all my feelings on it, what I would do. But as for you all . . .'

He did not want to speak for them, or put words in their mouths. Or persuade them to do something they didn't want to do.

Gar was staring at him, his face unreadable, as usual.

'Surely you know,' Gar said. 'I'll not speak for the others, but as for me, prophecy or no, I go where you go. You are my life, Corban, my breath, the reason I wake and rise. When my da died . . .' He paused then, looked away, a muscle clenching in his jaw. 'When my da died, the world became a dark place. It was only you that caused me to rise from my cot each day.'

'But, now that you know . . .' Corban said.

'Ach, that makes no difference to me,' Gar said with a wave of his hand. 'No difference.' He was silent a few moments, thoughtful. 'Once, yes, it was about the prophecy, but that was a long time ago. So long ago. Now, I believe in *you*.' He poked Corban's chest with his finger. 'I'll follow you wherever you go. To hell and back.'

'Haven't we just done that?' a weak voice said – Dath, finally awake. Kulla ran over to him. 'Feels like it, at least,' the bowman mumbled.

'Always so dramatic,' Farrell muttered.

'I was hit by a *bear*,' Dath pointed out. 'A *giant* bear.'

'He's feeling much better,' Kulla pronounced.

Corban shook his head, smiling.

These people, my friends. I love them, would die for them, as they would for me, it seems.

'So,' Varan said, 'what are you all going to do?'

Gar looked at them all and gave a vicious, cold grin.

'We're going to fight,' he said. 'It's what we do best. Asroth, Calidus and Nathair will all come for us soon, when they're stronger. Best fighting them now. Win or lose, it's the best chance we have. And besides, I think they deserve some pain.'

'Aye,' Farrell agreed. 'Fair's fair, after all.'

Sig looked at Varan.

'I like these people,' she said.

By highsun they were packed and as prepared as they could be. Varan had given them one of the saddles from a dead bear, and with some reworking it had been adjusted to fit Storm. She hadn't been very impressed, in fact had growled with enough malice to convince Corban she'd bite anyone except him who tried to fit it to her, and even then she'd flattened her ears and attempted to make a dignified retreat. He'd had to scold her to make her stand still, which he was aware must have looked ludicrous.

She killed a giant bear last night. Today she's scolded by me, and takes it.

Now Dath was sitting in that saddle, looking as unhappy as Storm about the situation. 'Stop pulling faces,' Kulla said. 'It's the only way.'

'You could always walk,' Coralen pointed out.

He scowled.

All the others were ready. Gar checked his kit bag for the hundredth time, it seemed. Coralen strolled up to Corban and kissed him on the lips, hard. He was breathless when she pulled away.

'What was that for?' Corban asked her.

'Just because,' Coralen said, then turned her back on him and walked away.

'Finally,' Kulla said, and Corban saw Farrell and Dath staring at him. He felt himself blushing and shrugged, decided he needed something to do and so he went looking for the Jotun giants; Sig was by their bears. She was tying a bag to her saddle, dried blood crusted the bag's bottom.

'It's Mort's head,' Varan said. 'Proof to the clan that we caught up with him, and that he's received Jotun justice. Even if it was dispensed by a freakishly huge wolven. Is she the one you wanted a chainmail coat for?'

'Aye,' Corban said. 'I thought she was dead.'

'So did I,' Varan said. 'It was I that pulled you away from her, that day by the river. She has a strong spirit, that one, to survive. Something she wanted to live for.' He looked between Corban and Storm. 'Walk with me,' he said and strode away, towards his bear, passing around to its far side. Corban followed, and suddenly he and Varan were alone, hidden from all others by the bulk of Varan's bear.

'Hello, Long Tooth,' Corban said, patting the bear's flank. Varan had stripped it of its chainmail coat, which was now rolled and tied in a big pack that hung from buckles on the saddle.

Varan looked at him a moment, then reached inside his pack and pulled out a package rolled in fur. He held it out to Corban, holding one big finger to his lips.

Corban took it, unrolled the fur a little, then nearly dropped it.

It was the starstone dagger.

'What! Why?' Corban hissed, Varan signalling for quiet.

'Mort had it,' Varan whispered. 'Sig is searching for it, but I found it last night, fallen to the ground during the fight.'

'Why are you giving it to me?' Corban asked.

'That is a very good question,' Varan said, but didn't answer immediately. Eventually he shrugged. 'Because you saved my life, even though it put yours at risk. Because you stayed for your friend, when you could have run. Because these people here ran through the length of Forn to find you, fought the Jotun, fought bears, risked death, all for you. That speaks a thousand words. Because there is something about you, Corban ben Thannon.' He looked about him, at the dead giants and bears. 'As you said, conflict and war seem to be overtaking us.'

'You could come with us,' Corban said.

'No. My clan is in chaos, our King dead. I cannot abandon them.' He turned, put one huge foot into a stirrup and hoisted himself onto Long Tooth's back.

'Farewell, Corban ben Thannon,' he said from what seemed a very long way up. 'I wish you well, and may your enemies feel the strength of your arm and the edge of your sword.'

Corban covered the dagger and slipped it inside his cloak, just as Sig appeared upon her bear. She looked none too happy.

'Farewell, Varan of the Jotun,' Corban said. 'And farewell to you, Sig the first-sword.'

'I am first-sword no longer,' Sig said, leaning in her saddle. 'My King is dead.'

'Somehow I think you will always be a first-sword,' Corban said.

She smiled bitterly, and then the two giants were spurring their bears away, towards Gramm's hold.

Corban walked slowly back to his friends and they began a slow, limping gait into Forn – back to Drassil.

But we are together. Battered, but not beaten. And Calidus, Nathair – we are coming for you.

CHAPTER FORTY

RAFE

Rafe ran ahead of the warband on a sun-dappled woodland path, the sounds and scents a constant barrage on his senses. In the world beyond the trees the sun was setting, sending eerie shadows dancing and flickering through the forested paths.

To either side of him ran Sniffer and Scratcher. They slipped through the undergrowth like grey wraiths, but to Rafe they sounded like a herd of auroch pounding through the woods.

They'd been travelling almost a ten-night, the journey back to Dun Carreg made quicker as they took the old giantsway that carved through the heart of the Baglun, the old woods that spread across the heart of Ardan like a blanket of russet and green. Not quickly enough for Rafe's liking, but considering they had a warband of five hundred swords and enough wains of provisions to feed a campaign into winter, it was never going to be a gallop all the way to the fortress by the sea.

Rafe was aching to see the walls of dark stone, rising high above the bay.

Dun Carreg. Home.

Darkness settled about him as he padded on. Then a horn blast was ringing out through the trees.

That'd be Rhin, with the call to make camp.

He found them spread along the giantsway: Rhin, the giant Uthas and his followers, fifty Benothi giants stomping along the road, loud enough to wake the dead. Next came a long line of wains, pulled by lowing, shaggy-haired auroch, and behind them rode around five hundred warriors. A dozen fire-pits had been raised along the road, with pots of water boiling or meat turning on spits. A perimeter of sentries spread into the trees, though none feared any real attack, not against five hundred swords and fifty giants.

Rafe saw Rhin in conversation with Uthas; she looked up when she saw him. Behind them stood Uthas' two guards, the male one with his axe, the female with two long knives, hilts jutting over her shoulder.

'Rafe,' Rhin said, beckoning to him. He walked over, the hairs on his arm prickling.

Uthas nodded to the female giant, who drew one of her blades – it was as long as a short sword – then hurled the knife directly at Rafe.

Acting on instinct, he spun to one side, reached out and caught the knife by its hilt. He stood frozen a moment, staring at the leather-wrapped hilt in his hand, the blade of dark-mottled iron. Then looked up at Rhin.

'You see,' Uthas said to her. She was staring at him as if she were seeing him for the first time.

'Where's the cup?' Rhin asked coldly.

He took a step backwards.

Rhin sighed.

'Bring him here,' she said and the two giants behind Uthas leaped for him. Rafe stumbled backwards, turned and ran.

He wasn't sure why he was running; he had reacted without thinking.

I just don't want to give her the cup, he decided as he slithered down the embankment of the giantsway, heading towards the tree-line, then there was a *whirring* sound as something smacked him in the back of the legs, tangling with his ankles, sending him flying. He rolled over, saw that Uthas had hurled his spear sideways at him, like a stick. The female giant was bearing down on him, one arm reaching out for his throat.

Then two bundles of grey fur and snapping teeth slammed into her chest, toppling her back to the ground.

Scratcher and Sniffer!

In a heartbeat Rafe was back on his feet and running.

There was growling and snapping behind him, then a high-pitched whine, more growling. Rafe skidded to a halt and looked back to see Scratcher standing over Sniffer's prone form; the other giant had arrived now and was raising his axe over them both.

'NO,' Rafe screamed, arms reaching.

'Stop running,' Uthas said, reaching the bottom of the embankment and retrieving his spear, 'and come here, or the hounds will feel Salach's axe-blade.'

Rafe stood, paused between flight and surrender, looked at Scratcher and Sniffer.

Don't have many friends. Don't have any, really, and definitely not ones that'd take on a giant or two for me.

He blew out a long breath and walked back to the giants.

Rhin appeared at the top of the embankment as Rafe was marched back to the camp, Sniffer limping along beside him.

'You should never, *ever*, run from me,' she said calmly as he stood before her. 'No matter how special you are.' She ran a long-nailed finger down his cheek, along the line of his jaw, scratching at stubble.

'Now, where is the *cup*?'

'I'll show you,' he sighed.

He led them along the giantsway, then down the embankment, and before long was standing before an old oak. He jumped up to grab the first branch, swung himself up and reached into the knotted bole for his pack.

Again he was taken by an overwhelming urge not to hand over the cup, the thought of sharing it, of giving it up, filling him with a sense of dread.

I could run again.

He looked down, saw Rhin and the giants gazing up at him with their small, suspicious eyes. Scratcher and Sniffer were standing with them, watching him too.

He sighed and fished the pack out of a natural bowl in the trunk.

Salach grabbed the pack from him and emptied out the contents onto the ground – a whole bundle of things he deemed useful falling out: rope, flint and tinder, a hemp bag of herbs, his eating knife, a spare wool tunic. And then the cup.

It fell to the mossy ground with a dull thump, as if heavier than it looked. It was crow-black and smooth, pale veins of silver running through the darkness, like lightning on a storm-ridden night. Around its rim old runes curled in a scrawling script. For long moments they all stood around it and stared. Scratcher took a sniff of it and whined. Uthas moved first, his hand twitching down for it, almost of its own accord, but then Rhin was snatching it up greedily.

'It's heavy,' she gasped, 'and cool to the touch.'

The female giant lifted her hand towards it and Rhin pulled the cup away.

'Don't touch it,' she hissed.

'It is the starstone cup,' the other giant said, 'kept by the Benothi for two thousand years. I have more right than most to touch it.'

'Eisa,' Uthas breathed, a warning in his voice.

The starstone cup! One of the Seven Treasures! No wonder it's made me feel . . . different.

'You lost it over a thousand years ago,' Rhin snarled. She looked about at the three giants glowering down at her. 'But that is the past. We have it now, and will share in its gifts soon enough.'

'But first?' Uthas said.

'First we must tell Calidus.'

Rafe had been in Rhin's tent a number of times now, but it felt different this time. Torches of dried rushes crackled and smoked, the tent a place of vapour and fume, of flickering torchlight and baleful shadows, making Rafe feel sick and uneasy. He'd tried to slink off once they were back within the perimeter of the camp, but Rhin was having none of that.

'You are set apart, now, belonging to an elite group,' she said to him as they entered her tent. 'You shall stay close to me, from now on.'

He'd looked at her blankly, and she laughed.

'You really have no idea what you've done, do you?'

He just shrugged at that, too embarrassed to answer with the truth.

'Drinking from the cup. It prolongs life, and I am told it enhances everything: strength, vision, hearing, stamina . . .' She gave him another lingering look that sent the sensation of spiders running across his skin.

'Long life?' Rafe said uneasily.

'Uthas drank from that cup, over two thousand years ago,' Rhin said, smiling. 'Close enough to immortal, wouldn't you say.' She searched through a bunch of keys, old iron rattling, then opened a shadowed chest in the recesses of her tent.

Immortal!

'I don't feel immortal, now,' Uthas rumbled. 'My bones creak and my body aches, my vision fails and my grip is weak.'

'Yes, that is why you wish to drink from the cup again,' Rhin said, pulling things from the chest she'd opened, setting them upon a table. A wooden frame, velvet cloth, a small box, an iron bowl.

'Tell me how it feels,' Rhin asked.

'And how you found it,' Uthas said. 'I lost it in Domhain, a long time ago.'

'That's where I found it,' Rafe began. He recounted how Sniffer had fallen into a bog beyond the walls of Dun Taras and how he'd gone in after the hound, ended up climbing out of the bog with a wooden chest under his arm. And he told of drinking from the cup, the wondrous sensation spreading through him, then the agony, and then . . . nothing. A ten-night he had slept while the cup had worked its magic upon him, and then he had woken. Transformed.

Rhin and the giants were staring at him with eyes glistening.

'How did you know?' Rafe asked them.

'I suspected,' Uthas said. 'Your speed, your vision, other things. And when you caught Eisa's knife . . .'

'It could have killed me,' Rafe grumbled. He looked at Rhin, saw that she had put the iron bowl upon her table and set a small fire within it, had placed the wooden frame before it and was unfolding the velvet cloth and lifting something carefully from it. It looked like old parchment, thick and creased. Rhin was attaching it to each corner of the frame by small suspended hooks, stretching the parchment out. Rafe's eyes narrowed as he looked at it. There were holes in it, and as he stared, the sense of dread he'd experienced earlier returned.

'Is that . . .' he began.

'A face, yes,' Rhin said. 'Flayed from an enemy,' she added, as if she were talking about making some hot tea.

She opened the small casket, drew out a vial full of dark liquid, unstoppering it and sprinkling a few droplets on the fire, making it spit and hiss. Rhin's voice rang out, a whisper that filled the tent.

'*Thoghairm mé leat anois, Calidus, aingeal dubh, tríd an flesh agus fola ar mo namhaid,*' she said, time and time again. The torches set about the tent blazed and went out, darkness closing in about Rafe like dark wings, only the iron bowl on the table aglow, the flayed skin stretched before it illuminated with an orange fire.

Then it moved, a ripple through the skin, like a sail filling with wind, and the flayed face of a long-dead man was inhabited, the dead lips were moving, fire-glow through the eyes looking like something else entirely now.

'Rhin . . .' the lips whispered, dry as the tomb, 'what providence, I wished to speak with you.'

'Welcome, Calidus,' Rhin said. 'I have excellent news.' For the first time Rafe saw something vulnerable in her, even submissive. 'I have the starstone cup.'

The face's lips moved, a stuttering hiss escaping from them. Rafe was slow to realize that it was laughter. 'A good day,' the voice said. 'You must bring it to me.'

'We are searching for the necklace, too. We are close, will have it soon.'

'Find it. Muster your warbands and then march to Drassil.'

Rhin took a step back, blinking, glanced at Uthas.

'The day is almost upon us,' the lips hissed, a crackle of winter leaves, 'now is the time to fulfil your oath.'

'I, of course . . .' Rhin said. 'This is unexpected – sooner than I thought.'

'We have prepared for this hour, spilt rivers of blood to ensure it arrives. Now you must act, send out your messengers, call upon all sworn to you. You know what to do.'

'It will be done,' Rhin said.

'Make sure that it is,' the face of skin snarled, lips rippled and wrinkling. 'You do not want to fail me in this.'

The skin stretched and moved, the firelight flicker in the eyes seemed to darken, become red, and for a moment they appeared to look around the room, fixing upon Rafe. He felt transfixed, wanted to run, to scream, to squeeze his eyes shut, but instead he just stared back, mesmerized, gazing into a fiery well of malice and despair and dark power. He felt his bladder loosen, warm liquid soaking into his breeches. The eyes released him and fastened back upon Rhin.

'Come to me,' the voice hissed and then the skin was slack and empty, drooping like melted wax.

One of the dogs began to bark outside the tent and Rafe turned and stumbled away, fumbled through the opening, past Rhin's guards. He heard laughter behind him.

Torches were burning along the roadside, making Rafe blink as his eyes adjusted. A movement drew his attention, in the treeline beyond the embankment. Something glinted.

Iron? It shone in firelight, glimmered in a way that any warrior worth his salt would recognize.

Scratcher and Sniffer's barking grew louder, but they were not barking at something in the trees, they were jumping, looking *up* at something, on Rhin's tent.

'What are you doing, idiot dogs?' Rafe muttered. He felt ashamed of himself as the wet stain in his breeches began to cool, but fragments of his terror still lingered. Looking up, he saw a darker shadow upon the tent pole. He squinted, and then the shadow moved. A huge black crow, wings unfurling. On instinct Rafe jumped and grabbed at it, one hand closing about a taloned claw, and with much squawking and protesting he dragged the crow down, with his other hand pinned its beating wings. *I hate crows*, he thought, fingers closing about its neck, still staring into its malignant, intelligent little eyes.

He heard something from beyond the treeline, the creak of wood. *What was that?*

'*Get off, bad man*,' the crow squawked at him.

CHAPTER FORTY-ONE

CAMLIN

'Quick!' Meg hissed beside Camlin. 'He's going to kill Craf!'

I know him. Rafe. He was with Braith, in the marshes, and Vonn knew him, too. Talked me into letting him live.

Even as Camlin released his arrow he saw Rafe jerk in shock as Craf pecked furiously at his hand, then Camlin's arrow was slamming into his shoulder. Craf was thrown free in a burst of feathers, he swooped in at Rafe's face, talons raking, before he winged higher into the air, squawking insults as he went.

There were guardsmen around Rafe, and before Camlin could move the alarm was sounded.

So much for surprise, Camlin thought as he pulled an arrow from the turf in front of him and loosely nocked it.

'Now, Meg,' he snapped, and light flared as she sparked her torch soaked in pitch.

He lit his arrow, drew and released, the hiss of flame an incandescent arc through the darkness. He'd aimed for Rafe, but somehow he twisted away, at the same time gripping the arrow in his shoulder and ripping it free.

Did he see my second arrow coming for him? No, can't have.

The flaming arrow thudded into a pole, caught in the tent fabric, and fire crackled into hungry life. All along the treeline arrows flashed from the shadows, screams rang out from the giantsway, and to Camlin's satisfaction the sound of grain sacks igniting. Within heartbeats a handful of wains were roaring infernos.

'Another,' Meg said, jabbing him in the ribs.

He ignited another arrow, aimed, saw figures emerging from the main tent – giants, and then behind them, Rhin.

Well, if I could put an arrow through that old bitch's heart I'd make Edana's day.

He sighted and released, his arrow flying true, and he knew before it hit that it was heading straight at Rhin's chest, but just as it struck there was a flash of iron and his arrow was spinning away. In its place Rafe stood there, sword in hand, glaring straight at him.

Did he just cut my arrow out of the air? Camlin felt some anger at that, and a small jolt of fear. He'd seen that kind of thing done, but not in a night fight, chaos and flames and death all about. His pack of raiders – archers every one of them – were raining fiery hell down upon the extended camp on the giantsway. Camlin nocked and drew, not bothering to ignite this one, but Rhin was already moving as he loosed, his arrow punching into the meat of a giant's arm instead.

Better 'n nothing.

There was the sound of dirt and gravel sliding, and he saw Rafe charging at him, two huge hounds with slavering jaws either side, giants and warriors in black and gold behind him.

'Time to go,' Meg said and dashed into the darkness.

'You're not wrong, lassie, but I think I'll stay for one more,' he muttered, drew his bow, sighted and released; a warrior in black and gold stumbled and crashed down the embankment. He didn't get back up.

'Now it's time to go,' Camlin said, snatched a handful of arrows, turned and sprinted into the undergrowth.

The plan had been to destroy as much of the baggage train as possible as well as killing as many men in black and gold as they could. Many of the wains were burning so as far as Camlin was concerned the job was done. He knew his crew could look after themselves, all twenty of them were woodsmen.

There was crashing and snarling behind him, closer than he'd hoped.

He sped through the dark woodland, heard the odd crackle of forest litter ahead of him as he caught up with Meg. They were following fox and hare trails that he'd found days earlier, walking them day and night to settle them into their heads. He'd been planning this ambush for a while now, and, truth be told, he'd hoped to do more damage, hadn't expected to be running quite so soon.

It's Rafe's fault. He must have seen the fire as I lit my arrows to know where to run. That and his hounds. He swore under his breath. *I'm going to wring Vonn's neck for making me let that bastard go.*

He ran on, heard the faint sound of the river ahead of him, knew that once he reached it he could shake off the hounds and he'd be safe.

Nearly there.

Horn blasts rang out behind him, distant, haunting.

Rhin's warband. A recall to those chasing through the woods? He hoped so.

He burst into an open glade that ran alongside the river, saw Meg standing on a fallen tree, beckoning to him. He skidded to a halt and sucked in a deep breath, muscles bunched to leap. Moonlight bathed the glade and river in pale light, glistened like scattered silver dust on the river-foam.

Then something slammed into his back and he was spinning and rolling, his bow and arrows cast into the air, grass, moss, forest litter in his face. He came to a halt spluttering, searching for his weapon, saw a hound rolling a dozen paces away, scrabbling to get its feet under it.

He saw his bow, arrows scattered about it. He lunged, grabbed wood, rolled and drew as he heard the thud of the hound's paws, turned to see it leap.

Others were bursting into the glade as he loosed: Rafe, another hound, a giant. His arrow punched into the leaping hound's chest. It yelped, crashing to the floor, floppy-limbed. Then Rafe was screaming, charging at him with bloody murder scrawled across his face.

Camlin struggled to his feet, drew his sword, and turned swinging at Rafe, the lad swaying and ducking impossibly fast. Camlin flailed his bow at him and lucky timing knocked Rafe off balance, sending him sprawling face-first.

Camlin glanced frantically about the glade. Meg was gone, nowhere to be seen. Rafe was on the ground, dazed. A giant, weapons in her hands, strode towards him, and another hound was sniffing and whining at the one he'd put an arrow into.

A giant, a hound and Rafe, who's become someone to worry about. Not the kind of odds I like in a fight! He had his sword in one hand, his bow in another, though no arrows. They lay spread around the glade.

He heard the whistle of air, threw himself to the ground as one of the giant's knives slashed where his head had been. He came out of his roll with his sword connecting with the giant's boot, with a crack that he hoped was bone breaking.

Something hit him in the head and he was spinning, the ground rushing up to thud into his face.

No time for lying around, he told himself as he saw the giantess hobbling after him.

He went to heft his sword, then realized it was no longer in his hand.

Damn it!

Then the giant had caught up with him and put her good foot on his chest, sending air rushing from his lungs.

'Stay still, you little ferret,' the giant growled, raising one of her blades over him.

There was a crunch and she staggered back a step, blood leaking down her forehead.

What?

Meg was back on her log, throwing stones at the giant. Another one smacked into the giant's face, sending her crashing to one knee, swaying, bellowing in pain.

'Come on,' Meg yelled at Camlin.

Good advice.

Camlin clambered to his feet, head spinning, staggering across the glade, then a dark figure grabbed him, slamming him into a tree: Rafe.

With no weapons Camlin fought dirty: a knee to the groin, head-butting Rafe in the nose but still the boy didn't let him go, his hands fastening around Camlin's throat and squeezing with more strength in them than Camlin would have expected.

'You. Killed. My. Hound,' Rafe grunted as he squeezed, Camlin flailing, gouging his thumb into the boy's arrow wound, grabbing fingers, trying to prise them loose, break them, but nothing seemed to affect Rafe.

How is he doing this? He's . . . not . . . right.

Camlin's vision started to blur and then there was a squawking and flapping of wings, talons and beak slashing at Rafe's face, clawing at his eyes. Abruptly the grip around Camlin's throat was gone and he was sliding down the tree, coughing and spluttering. Rafe staggered away, clutching his hands to his face.

Craf, I could kiss you.

Camlin pushed himself up, away from the tree, and staggered to the glade's edge. The giant saw him and stumbled after, one arm reaching out and grabbing his jerkin.

I'm getting away from this, not even a giant's going to stop me.

Camlin hurled himself towards the glade's edge, the unsteady giant was dragged off balance and together they crashed into the dead tree, careened over it and fell, spinning head over heels into the river.

CHAPTER FORTY-TWO

VERADIS

Veradis walked along the line of his men, straightening a shield here, testing a grip there, pushing to ensure that the warrior was balanced, feet set right, shoulder into his shield. They stood before him, a hundred and forty men, twenty men wide, seven rows deep, shields raised, interlocked.

Better. This is better. The shields were solid, overlapped correctly, the flanks protected, and the manoeuvre had been carried out in a matter of seconds. Moving in formation was getting better, or at least the wall was not falling apart once the men began to march. And the best part of all was that they now *believed*. Before the battle against Gundul's warband those under Veradis' authority had been unsure of the shield wall's capabilities, and worse, considered it unworthy of a warrior.

Staying alive while your enemy dies is a great convincer.

They had seen first-hand the value and power of the shield wall, seen Gundul's ranks throw themselves against it and die.

But they are not my Draig's Teeth. Veterans of scores of battles, drilled in marching, rotating, protecting flank and rear, the array of horn blasts that I'd developed to maintain communication on the battlefield. How can these men take them on?

Looking at them ranged in front of him, the answer was obvious. *If they do, they'll die.*

If he were honest with himself, the thought of lining up on a battlefield against the Draig's Teeth made him feel sick to his stomach. How could he fight, kill, men he had trained, led, respected and fought alongside.

Save that for another day. One day at a time. Train. Prepare.

He yelled out an order, the wall breaking up, men setting down shields and pairing up for individual sparring.

'You work your men hard,' a voice called out to him and he turned to see Javed, the leader of the Freedmen, as they'd become known, who had been liberated from Lykos' slave galleys, walking towards him.

'No more than others,' Veradis said to Javed, nodding to the Jehar warriors, whom he could see gathered under the trees, going through the forms of their sword dance. Elsewhere giants were sparring with the men of Isiltir, most of them warriors in cloaks of red and wielding sword and spear, but also others wrapped in thick furs and brandishing single-bladed axes. Veradis had learned that these were the survivors of a hold in the north, led by a warrior named Wulf. A serious man; Veradis liked him.

'Looks like a lot of heavy lifting to me,' Javed said, still grinning.

'Not for you, then?' Veradis asked.

'I've done a lifetime of training in the pits,' Javed said.

'Some of your kind still train,' Veradis said, pointing to Maquin, who had just returned from a dawn run and was now sparring against half a dozen of the men whom he had been given authority over in Ripa's warband.

'The Old Wolf,' Javed said, 'he's a kind unto his own.'

'Doesn't look like it's doing him any harm. For me, training keeps me sharp,' Veradis said, 'not just my body, but my mind.'

'I believe in training,' Javed said, 'but I'd rather do it against a foe that bleeds and dies. That's why I volunteer to join whatever team is raiding against our enemy. Every single day.' His grin was gone now, fierce hatred burning in his eyes.

'Of one thing I am sure, and one thing alone,' Veradis said. 'Battle is coming, and we will either be ready, or we will be dead.'

'You're a very serious fellow, are you not,' Javed said, his smile returning as he wandered away. 'But don't worry about me, it won't be me that's doing the dying.'

Veradis found a trio of men to train with. Afterwards, sweating and weary, he made his way to a stream and washed down. For a moment he just sat resting against a tree.

He looked about and saw the bustle of normal camp life: foraging, collecting firewood, food and water, organizing meals, repairing garments and weapons. He saw Brina hurrying past, snapping orders to a dozen men, a giant following her. Elsewhere a row of figures were loosing arrows, a percussion of thuds as they hit their targets; a woman walked along their line checking them. Teca, her name was, a villager from the north of Narvon.

Woodsmen, hunters, brigands, warriors, giants – what a disparate band!

He blew out a long breath.

But do we actually have any hope of winning? We are outnumbered, out-positioned and not as experienced in battle. Calidus has played us all well. Prepared well for this war.

We cannot win.

We need more men. More women. More giants. More fighters.

I hope this Corban comes back to us at the head of a vast warband. That would be something.

He sighed.

'Am I intruding?' a voice said. Fidele was standing a dozen paces away.

'Of course not, my lady,' he said, making to rise.

'No, please don't,' she said, stepping over and sitting beside him. A handful of her guards stood back, alert and watching.

She was dressed like a woodsman, in woollen breeches and shirt, a stout leather vest. And she had knives on her belt. Two that Veradis could see, and a hilt poking out from her boot.

She saw his gaze and laughed, genuine and warm.

'You pick up the strangest habits when fleeing the Vin Thalun,' she said with a shrug. 'And I've had a good teacher.' She glanced through the trees at Maquin, smiling at the sight of him. 'Strange times we live in,' she added.

'I'm no one to judge, my lady. And if I may say, you seem happy.'

'You may,' she said with a dip of her head, 'and I am.' She looked back to Maquin, watching him sway and duck, moving around his sparring assailants like forest mist, never being touched.

'And what the future holds, who knows?' she said quietly, then looked back at Veradis. 'We know only that we are alive, now.'

'Indeed,' Veradis agreed. She had changed so much since he had first met her. A king's wife. The mother of his Prince, she had seemed born for that role, that high position beside Aquilus. Yet, now in the wilds of Forn Forest, she seemed more comfortable, more at ease than he had ever seen her before.

'I want to see my son,' Fidele said into the silence.

I want that, too. To speak to him, just to talk, me and him, as we used to. Without Calidus, or the Kadoshim hovering nearby.

'Why?'

'Because he is not evil.'

'He is not,' Veradis agreed.

'And because he has been fooled—'

Veradis shook his head regretfully. 'Maybe once, but he is fooled no longer. He knew exactly what was happening when I spoke to him in Brikan. You must trust me on this; I have been over it a thousand times in my head.'

'He has been manipulated, then: forced onto a path that he now feels he cannot escape from. He is proud, would find it difficult to admit to such a mistake, but he can still choose . . .'

'He has chosen,' Veradis said angrily, the betrayal by his friend still a raw wound. 'He asked me to make the same choice and made it sound so logical, so natural.' Veradis sighed angrily, remembering Nathair's argument to him in the tower room at Brikan, how history was written by the victors, that it was all a lie. That Elyon and Asroth, Kadoshim and Ben-Elim were just sides, warring realms or factions, like Ardan and Cambren. He had made it sound so reasonable.

I've thought many times on what Fidele is saying. I want it to be true. To believe that Nathair would return to the right path, if only he had the right opportunity.

But would he?

'It is all just talk, anyway,' Veradis said. 'Nathair is in Drassil with five thousand swords about him. Not just eagle-guard, but Vin Thalun and Kadoshim. And Calidus. It is impossible—'

'Perhaps,' Fidele said.

'Why are you telling me this, my lady?'

'Because only you can understand how I feel. He is like a brother to you. I know what you say is truth and sense, but if a way did present itself, for me to speak with Nathair.' She stopped then, looked him in the eyes, and he saw a well of pain looking back at him. She reached out and squeezed his wrist.

'Would you help me? If . . .'

He just stared, not knowing what to say.

Nathair slew his own father. Would she still believe in him, knowing that? And yet, there was good in him, once, I know it.

'I—'

Footsteps sounded and Maquin appeared from amongst the trees, sweating and smiling.

'Found you,' he said, reaching out and trailing his fingers across Fidele's shoulder as he made his way to the stream, discarded his clothes and jumped in. The water that splashed Veradis and Fidele was icy-cold, making them both gasp.

'Think on it,' she said, giving his wrist one last squeeze.

'So that's Drassil,' Veradis said.

He'd joined a scouting party led by Tahir, along with Maquin, Alcyon and Tain. They were all in a row, lying on their bellies, peering out from the undergrowth at the open plain ringing the fortress, the walls and gates rising tall and forbidding, beyond them towers and the tree mingling in a twisted snarl.

It's like nothing I've ever seen before.

It was still early in the day, the sun beyond the trees had a long way to climb before highsun.

'Did you help build that?' Tain whispered to Alcyon.

'No, my son,' Alcyon chuckled, 'I was not born until a thousand years after those walls were raised.'

They fell silent as figures appeared on the wall, above Drassil's wide gates. A voice rang out across the plain, challenging Corban to come and save his people.

Veradis felt the blood freeze in his veins, then melt, become a molten torrent of rage.

'Calidus,' he said. Beside him he felt Alcyon tense, and saw his son Tain look away.

Piercing screams suddenly drifted across the plain.

'What is going on?' Veradis asked.

'Prisoner being sacrificed,' Tahir said grimly. 'It is the same, each day. Calidus challenges Corban. When he does not come, someone dies. Corban would fight him, if he were here.'

'Calidus is hard to kill,' Veradis said, and Alcyon grunted.

'So was Sumur, and yet Corban took his head, out there, in front of two warbands. It was quite the sight.'

Veradis felt his respect for Corban grow by a considerable leap.

The screams grew harder to bear, rising in pitch, a terror and agony contained within them that made Veradis wish it would stop. He thought of Cywen, his hope that she'd somehow survived Nathair's attack on Drassil. Now he was filled with concern that her voice was the one that was screaming.

How can Nathair bear this? Stand by and do nothing?

'Calidus has prisoners, then. Survivors from the battle.'

'Aye. He executes one each day,' Tahir told him.

'He must have a considerable supply.'

'He does. On the first day after the battle he set one free, a Jehar named Ilta. She said there were hundreds captive.'

Hundreds.

'We must get them out,' Veradis said.

'I'd love to,' Tahir muttered, 'it's the *how* that I've had a problem with.'

'Well, let's think on it. Two heads are better than one.'

'That's what my old mam used to say.'

They began to crawl back from the treeline when the gates of Drassil creaked and opened. Out from their shadowed arch lumbered a monstrous shape, wide and squat, bowed legs and claws like curved daggers, a head broad and reptilian. Upon its back sat a man, tall and proud, black hair, a polished cuirass of black leather, upon it a white eagle, his sable cloak fluttering in a breeze.

'Nathair,' Veradis whispered, all of them frozen in the act of retreating back into the forest.

His draig walked out onto the plain, head casting from side to side, long tail in constant motion, and behind it marched a warband; line upon line of long shields and silver helms. They turned south with immaculate precision, following Nathair and his draig.

Nathair's Draig's Teeth. My men.

'They all look like you,' Tahir commented to Veradis, looking at his cuirass emblazoned with a white eagle. The warband of Ripa were clothed in the silver and black of Tenebral, but they wore the tower of Ripa on their chest, not the eagle.

'Not so long ago I led them. They were my men,' Veradis said.

'Sure you know what side you're on?' Tahir asked.

He's an honest one. Speaks his mind.

'Oh aye,' said Veradis bleakly. 'They fight for Asroth, even if many of them do not realize it. I'll never walk that path, not for oath, love nor *friendship*.'

CHAPTER FORTY-THREE

CAMLIN

Camlin spluttered river-water, spinning in its grasp, the giant that was bobbing along beside him grabbed his head and shoved him beneath the surface.

He struggled, lungs burning, breathing in a mouthful of water and panicking. He struck out wildly, tearing free from her grasp momentarily, his head bursting through the surface and desperately sucking in a lungful of air.

Current's taking me the right way, at least, back towards Edana and the warband. Might make it back alive, after all.

'Got you,' a voice said in his ear, a huge hand clamping down on his shoulder.

He tried to kick her underwater, but his legs weren't as long as her reach, and even if he'd connected he doubted she'd have felt it, the river leaching any power from his blow.

The river swept them into a clearing, the moonlight abruptly bright. Camlin looked into dark eyes staring with murderous intent at him.

Then she crunched into the branch of a fallen tree, hitting it so hard that the branch snapped off with a loud crack. Her grip on Camlin's shoulder was suddenly gone as she swirled away.

Is she dead?

Camlin grabbed the broken branch, instantly easing the strain of staying afloat. The giant came back into view, the current swirling her towards Camlin, a dark gash on her forehead, eyes dazed and vacant, a groan escaping her lips. As Camlin watched, she began to sink. For no reason that he could think of, he swam towards her and grabbed her, trying to lift her vast bulk above the surface. Using the broken branch, he managed to raise her a little higher, enough to keep her alive a while longer.

Something dark blotted the moonlight for a moment, a whisper of air above him, and he looked up to see the outline of Craf above him, wings spread.

I owe that bird.

Then he heard splashing, a rhythm to it. Meg appeared behind, paddling hard in the little canoe they'd made together over the last few days, too small to take any more weight than hers.

'What you doing?' she asked him as she paddled alongside him.

'Trying not t'drown,' he grunted.

'Why're you carrying a giant, then?' she asked.

Fair question.

'Seemed like a good idea at the time.'

Meg raised an eyebrow. 'And now?' she asked.

'She's getting heavy,' he admitted.

'Let go, then.'

Don't want to do that, really. This giant walked out of Rhin's tent, reckon she might know a thing or two.

'Paddle ahead, tell Halion I've caught me a big fish,' he grunted, catching a mouthful of water.

'Think I see me a river rat,' a voice called out.

Baird. Thank Elyon, I've had enough of this river.

Camlin paddled hard with his free arm and then felt a hook snag his jerkin and he was being dragged unceremoniously towards the riverbank.

'Welcome back,' Halion said, pulling Camlin onto dry land.

'You look more like a river rat than our Meg,' Baird said from behind Halion. 'What've you brought us, then?'

'When Meg said you were carrying a giant,' Halion said, 'I didn't think that you were actually carrying a giant.'

'Might need some help, here,' Camlin said, trying to drag the unconscious giant onto the bank.

Figures splashed into the water to help – Halion and Baird, as well as Lorcan and his shieldman, Brogan.

Baird was checking her for weapons, pulling knives from her belt, as well as one more, as long as a sword, that was sheathed on her back. The other scabbard was empty.

Left it in the glade.

'Best bind her quick,' Camlin said, 'she's a strong 'un.'

'Quite the gift you've brought us,' Baird said.

'She's here to answer questions for Edana,' Camlin told him firmly knowing of Baird's hatred for the race.

'Fair enough,' Baird said. 'She's your fish, you can have the pleasure of filleting her. Doubt you'll get anything out of her except lies, though.' He hawked and spat in the river, then, none too gently, set about wrapping thick rope around the giant's wrists.

'She's heavier than my mam with a barrel of mead in her belly,' Brogan No-Neck grunted as they dragged the giant ashore, with a lot of splashing and swearing.

As they were tying her securely to a tree the giant started to wake, jerking in shock, throwing herself feebly about, clearly still suffering from the blow to her head.

'It's all right, lass,' Brogan said. 'Stay still now, or you'll hurt yourself.'

'Lass!' Baird said. 'She'd as soon eat your still-beating-heart as speak to you. She's a monster.'

'Looks more like a woman to me,' Brogan said. 'On the big side, sure enough, but so's my Aunt Berit.'

Baird shook his head, a disgusted look on his face.

The sun was rising when Camlin met with Edana. He felt a little better, dried and dressed in a new set of clothes, though he was bruised and aching after his fight in the glade and dip in the river, trying not to limp as he walked. To make matters worse he was dismally aware that his scabbard was empty and that he'd lost his bow.

What kind of leader am I? Organize an ambush, get myself beat up by a giant and a snot-nosed apprentice huntsman, and lose all my weapons.

The good news was that every single man on his crew had returned to their camp, and Rhin's warband had been hit hard, most of her wains turned to fiery bonfires, tents ablaze, horses scattered and a fair few dead soldiers into the bargain.

He found Edana sitting on a log, scooping some hot porridge into a bowl. Vonn was squatting by the fire, digging at the ash and embers. He nodded a greeting to Camlin.

'Sit,' Edana said, blowing on her porridge, 'and eat something. You look like you're about to collapse.'

Camlin's belly rumbled and he happily helped himself to a bowl of porridge, sitting down on the log beside Edana, though his throat hurt with each mouthful, a reminder of Rafe's fingers around his neck.

'Well done,' Edana said. 'A successful mission, by all accounts, and most importantly, everyone's back and still breathing. Including you.' She looked pointedly at him and smiled.

Sometimes we just get lucky.

'Where's your bow?' she asked him.

'Lost it,' he said glumly.

'You don't look right without it.'

Don't feel right, either.

'And you've brought me a prisoner?'

'Aye.' Between mouthfuls Camlin told Edana of the ambush. 'I saw Rhin, got a shot off at her, but hit a giant instead.'

'Shame,' Vonn said.

'Aye, it was.' Camlin carried on. As he was coming to an end there was a fluttering up above, then Craf was there.

'*Look what Craf found,*' the crow squawked.

Camlin's bow fell into his lap. It was scratched, the gut string ruined, but after giving it a quick check-over, Camlin was sure the bow would be fine. He grinned at Craf, who was hopping about looking pleased with himself.

'Craf, I'm coming to realize that you are a fine bird indeed,' Camlin said, grinning.

'*Camlin save Craf from the bad man,*' the crow muttered.

'Rafe,' Camlin told Edana. 'He tried to twist Craf's neck.'

'*Bastard,*' muttered Craf.

'Rafe?' Edana said. 'He just keeps coming back.'

Like a curse.

'Aye. Shame he's still breathing, is my thought on it,' Camlin said, eyeing Vonn, who was making a good effort at looking the other way.

'He nearly put an end to me,' Camlin added, rubbing his neck. 'He's . . . changed, somehow.'

'*Drank from starstone cup,*' Craf said.

They all looked at the crow.

'*Craf heard them,*' Craf said. '*Rafe found cup, drank from it. Rhin, giants, all want some now. Make you strong. Fast. Live long.*'

They were still staring, speechless.

'*Rhin told Calidus. Bad man. Very bad man.*' The crow shivered from his talons to his beak, feathers ruffling.

'Calidus? Who's he?' Edana asked.

'*He is Kadoshim. He with Nathair. Kill Corban's mam.*'

'He killed Gwenith?' Edana asked.

'*Craf told you, BAD MAN. Calidus told Rhin find necklace, come to Drassil,*' Craf squawked, jumping up and down.

'*Craf keep telling you, God-War, Seven Treasures, DANGER!*'

'See,' Vonn hissed. 'We are lurking in the woods while the world is ending! This war is much bigger than Ardan.'

'*Craf keep telling you,*' the bird said. '*Nobody listen to Craf. Ask Camlin's giant. She was there.*'

'That's not a bad idea,' Edana said.

Baird threw a bucket of water into the giant's face, making her head snap up, eyes open.

'Think we've got her attention,' Baird said to Edana.

The giant's face was a mass of wounds, a large gash across her forehead, blood dried and crusted in a trail down her face, as well as cuts and bruises. She squinted up at them with her small black eyes, focusing finally upon Edana.

'I am Edana ap Brenin, Queen of Ardan,' Edana said. 'Who are you?'

'*Téigh go dtí ifreann,*' the giant said. She sat up straighter against the tree she was bound to, jutted her jaw out defiantly.

Craf fluttered down to land on a branch above Edana's head.

'*Don't be rude,*' he squawked.

So Craf understands giantish.

The giant looked up at the crow, face creasing, eyes squinting.

'*Fech?*' she said, her expression changing from defiance to dismay.

Fech! I remember that bird – the raven that Edana nursed in Domhain. She sent it north to Corban with a message. Craf said Fech reached them, but was later killed.

'Yes, this is Fech,' Edana said. Craf hopped off of the branch and fluttered down to perch on Edana's arm.

'*Yes, me Fech,*' Craf said. '*Talk nicely,*' he added.

The giant peered at him, blinked blood from one eye. '*Ní féidir liom a thuiscint,*' she whispered.

'*In common tongue,*' Craf said.

'I don't understand,' the giant said. She looked scared, all of a sudden.

Perhaps Fech had an influence on the Benothi giants. He was a messenger of Nemain, their queen.

'*You betrayed Nemain,*' Craf said.

The giant recoiled at that, as if struck.

Think he's got the same idea. That twisted a nerve.

'I, Nemain chose wrong—'

Craf flapped his wings, cawing and screeching. '*Nemain was good, Nemain was murdered.*'

'No, she fell. Uthas said she fell.'

'*She was pushed,*' Craf spat.

He's really embraced Fech. Glad he can remember all this.

'No,' the giant said. 'Who . . . ?' She paused. 'Uthas.'

'*Uthas, Uthas, Uthas,*' Craf cawed. '*Bad giant.*'

'I . . . Fech?' The giant looked at Craf, something pleading in her expression.

'*Uthas, murderer,*' Craf muttered.

'Rhin's tent, last night,' Edana said. 'What did you do?'

The giant looked away, lips clamping tight.

'*Tell her, tell her,*' Craf squawked. '*About the cup, tell her all.*'

'Why would I do that?' the giant said, quietly, to the ground.

'*Make right your wrong,*' Craf said. '*For Nemain.*'

The giant stared at Craf, back and shoulders rigid and straight, jaw jutting, emotions flickering across the flat planes of her face: pride, loyalty, betrayal, despair. Slowly she slumped.

'Rhin contacted Calidus in Drassil, by the old way of blood and bone, told him we'd found the starstone cup,' she said, a whisper.

'*More,*' Craf squawked. '*Tell all.*'

The giant sighed.

'Calidus ordered Rhin to muster her warbands, to find the necklace at Dun Carreg, and to march for Drassil.'

A silence settled upon them all, leaving only the ripple of the river and the sighing of wind in branches.

'Told you,' whispered Vonn.

CHAPTER FORTY-FOUR

UTHAS

Uthas strode across the stone bridge that spanned the precipice between Dun Carreg and the mainland, the breeze tearing at his cloak. He looked back, saw Rhin mounted on a warhorse, Salach striding beside her, and behind them what was left of Rhin's beleaguered warband. Most of their baggage wains had been destroyed, which at least meant that they travelled faster. The might of the Benothi – *what is left of us* – strode behind the warband, fifty giants, clad in mail and leather.

To the north-west the sea sparkled and glittered beneath the setting sun, and to the north-east, Uthas could see the dust cloud that marked Rhin's messengers as they galloped along the giantsway, taking word to her battlechief Geraint to muster the warband of the west.

The time is upon us. The God-War is reaching its end, moving towards its last great battle, which will decide the fate of this land, and all who dwell within it.

And we have the cup. And perhaps the necklace.

He could not stop the smile that spread across his face.

He turned and strode through the arch of Stonegate, into the courtyard of Dun Carreg. Ahead of him he saw Rafe and his lone hound, the huntsman's head bowed and sullen. Even from here Uthas could see the long scratches on Rafe's face, scabbed and red where he had been clawed. A bandage was wrapped around one shoulder, a red stain on it.

An arrow wound, deep into the muscle of his shoulder, yet it seems to be causing him little bother – another sign that he has drunk from the cup.

Uthas lengthened his stride to catch up with Rafe. Behind him hooves rang on stone, Rhin cantering up beside him.

'Take us to Evnis' tower,' she said to Rafe, who gave a surly nod and marched ahead.

He sulks because he lost a hound last night. I lost Eisa.

Uthas, Rhin and Salach marched through the streets of Dun Carreg, Rhin's honour guard of twenty warriors following behind. No people lined the streets to greet Rhin, though Uthas noticed that there were many warriors stationed throughout the fortress.

Then Rafe was at a set of gates that creaked on rusted hinges as he pushed them open. They all passed through into a small courtyard, beyond it an abandoned squat tower, wide-based, no more than six or seven storeys high. Uthas saw a row of kennels along one side of the tower, Rafe's hound running over to sniff in them, but they were as empty as the tower. Further on, the outer wall rose above Evnis' tower, dwarfing it. Uthas spied a stairwell climbing to the wall's battlements, the sound of sea and surf rising up from the sheer cliffs beyond.

'Here we are,' Rafe said, gesturing to the steps that led up to the tower's wide doors.

'Evnis' chamber,' Rhin said, dismounting.

Cobwebs grew thick across the doorway, stretching and tearing as Rafe shouldered through them. They entered a wide entrance hall, ahead of them a spiral stairwell that Rafe led them up, leaving footprints in the dust-covered steps. At the top there was a landing, a single door into a shadowed chamber, sparsely furnished: a bed, a table, one chair, some tapestries hanging across one wall.

'This is, *was*, Evnis' chamber,' Rafe said with a shrug.

'Find *it*,' Rhin told them.

Uthas and Salach began to search the room, Salach dragging the furniture away from the walls, Uthas running his fingertips across cold stone. He found the hidden door behind the tapestry, a depression and crack that looked like a fault in the stone. Uthas pushed into it, and then there was a breath of stale air and a click, the outline of a door appearing. Rhin clapped and laughed as Uthas pulled the door open. Inside was a small room, another table and chair, a wall sconce. On the table was a casket, big enough to hold a large book. Uthas opened it, feeling the throbbing pulse of power that emanated from it before he'd peered inside.

There was no book.

But there was a necklace.

Uthas sat at a table in a chamber of the great-keep. Rhin was with him, and Salach, and Rafe, who stood at an unshuttered window, staring out into the night.

Beside a jug of wine and drinking cups Rhin's dread devices were set on the table. The iron bowl crackled with fire, the wooden frame had the flayed skin already hung and stretched upon it.

And there were two other items upon the table, side by side. Uthas' eyes were drawn to them. The necklace: a dark stone the size of an egg wrapped in silver wire, bound and set within a silver chain. And a cup, larger than the other two on the table, carved from black stone, dull, unremarkable.

The starstone cup.

Uthas stared at it covetously, his eyes only drawn away by a sudden movement from Rhin as she opened a vial and sprinkled droplets of blood upon the flames, a hiss as they flared bright, and then Rhin's voice, harsh and brittle.

'*Thoghairm mé leat anois, Conall, slayer agus bhfeallaire ghaoil, tríd an flesh agus fola ar mo namhaid,*' she said, repeating the phrase countless times until it filled Uthas' mind, the skin and flames all he could see, the dark words all that he could hear.

Dark words indeed, slayer and betrayer of kin, slayer and betrayer of kin.

The skin on the frame rippled and stretched, features forming, an animated parody of life. A spluttering wheeze escaped the desiccated lips, sounding like the crackle of flames, the flicking of dusty parchment.

'By Asroth's teeth, Rhin, but I'm not liking this,' a voice said, fear-laced.

'You don't need to like it, Conall,' Rhin replied, haggard in the firelight, the deep lines on her face filled with shadow.

'Aye, well, it feels . . . strange. Like there's a cold-fingered hand clutching my face.'

'Listen to me,' Rhin said, commanding. 'Muster your warband.

Not just an honour guard, or a few hundred swords. I mean the whole strength of Domhain, and I want you to lead it to Dun Carreg.'

'What! But—'

'Do it,' Rhin hissed, 'and do it quickly, or there will be a new regent in Domhain.'

'Ach, no need for temper,' Conall said. 'Of course I'll do it, I'll not forget who put me here. But it's no easy task, is all I'm saying.'

'If it was easy, anyone could do it,' Rhin replied. 'I need you here in one moon.'

'I'll be there,' Conall said.

I do not think that is what he was going to say.

'Good. I knew I could count on you. Then I shall see you in one moon's time. And, Conall,' Rhin said.

'Aye?'

'Sharpen your sword.'

Rhin sat back, breaking the connection, and lifted a cup, drinking deeply, her hand unsteady.

When she was calmed she took a sheaf of parchment, weighted its ends, dipped a quill in ink and began to scribe. Eventually she sat back, pinched some ground powder from a pot and sprinkled it over the ink and parchment. Then she beckoned to Rafe.

'This is to go to Morcant,' Rhin said. 'I want him back here, not gallivanting around Ardan. Edana is of small matter in the lie of things, now. An inconvenience. You will take this to him, and bring him back to me.'

'Aye,' Rafe grunted.

Rhin shifted in her seat and scowled at him.

'My Queen,' Rafe added.

Rhin smiled coldly, running a finger down his face, a long nail tracing the arc of his wound where a talon had scored him from temple to chin.

'You have a lot of potential, my young huntsman,' she said. 'Great things lie ahead of you, and I shall help you achieve them, as you shall help me.'

'Aye, my Queen,' he gulped.

'Off with you, then,' she said and Rafe hurried from the room.

Rhin put her sorcerous paraphernalia into her travelling chest, then the starstone necklace. She snapped the lock shut and turned the key. There was only the starstone cup left on the table, now, a jug beside it.

'Well, we have finally reached the moment,' Rhin said, looking at Uthas. 'The one we have both longed for. Time to drink.'

'It is,' Uthas agreed, surprised at the tremor in his voice.

She poured wine into the cup, then took Uthas' hand and led him to a door in the chamber, opened it to reveal a wide bed.

'We shall be incapacitated a while,' Rhin said, 'so we shall remain here, under guard of your shieldman and mine. And when we awake . . .' She smiled languorously at Uthas as she led him into the bed-chamber and shut the door.

She sat on the bed, lifted the cup to her lips and drank a long, deep draught. She smiled and passed him the cup; even as he lifted it to his mouth her eyes were widening, a gasp of pleasure escaping her parted lips, the wine upon them black as heart's blood.

He remembered what it was like the first time, pleasure and pain, and steeled himself for what was to come.

He drank greedily, emptying the cup, felt the wine hit his belly, a warm glow radiating outwards, creeping into his veins, spreading, an expanding wave of pleasure magnified. Rhin sank back onto the bed, writhing, a beatific smile upon her face, her hands gripping the woollen bed sheets, twisting them. His body felt like liquid gold, warm, melting, and he was unable to keep himself upright, felt himself sinking onto the bed, groaned with pleasure, laughed for the joy of it.

Then Rhin began to scream.

CHAPTER FORTY-FIVE

HAELAN

Haelan slipped along the street, clinging to the deeper shadows, despite it being full dark. Pots ran in front, and he heard Cywen and Buddai behind.

Cywen had news for them all, so they were making their way back to Haelan's den together. He'd accompanied Pots on more midnight missions in search of food and provisions since that first reunion with Cywen.

I've changed since Buddai broke loose and took me to Cywen, he thought. *I don't feel quite as afraid all the time.*

It was good to have a proper grown-up around, someone who could make the decisions and take responsibility. He had been so scared for so long, and even though Swain was older than him and a lot more capable, Haelan had somehow felt that the final decisions on their life in the den had fallen on him. Once he would have loved that, especially when Tahir was ordering him around, but now that he'd had a good taste of it, he'd decided he didn't like it so much.

Not all it's rumoured to be.

'Haelan, stop,' Cywen hissed behind him.

He slipped into a deep-shadowed doorway and Cywen paused, catching her breath. Buddai stared at her, big tongue lolling from his jaws.

'What?' Haelan asked.

'I thought I heard something,' she breathed. 'Behind us.'

Haelan stared back down the coal-black street, no light except that of a cloud-swept moon and stars pale and distant as home. A dozen heartbeats passed, fifty, a hundred.

'There's nothi—' he started, then Pots growled, Buddai joining him shortly after.

Not a good sign.

Haelan shared a look with Cywen; she looked as terrified as he felt, and they both bolted, running hard down the street, Pots and Buddai following them.

Who is it back there? Have we been followed, or is it a random patrol? A drunken Vin Thalun who's stumbled the wrong way and got lost?

Whoever it was, Haelan knew he and Cywen could not afford to be seen. He ran as fast as he could, heart thumping in his mouth, twisting and skidding to turn down side streets that led deeper into the fortress.

And then they were in the courtyard, sprinting across the uneven flagstones, Pots leaping into the dark hole beneath the oak as if it was a race that he was set on winning, Haelan tumbling after him into the darkness. Cywen fell on top of him, both of them scrambling out of the way as Buddai's bulk jumped in.

Haelan started heading down the winding tunnel to his den, but Cywen's grip on his arm stopped him.

'Wait,' she hissed. 'We have to know.'

He understood. Quietly they positioned themselves below the entrance, Buddai with Cywen, Pots with Haelan. They settled into the darkness and waited.

Time passed, marked by the beating of Haelan's heart, the panting of Pots. His eyes adjusted to the gloom. The smell from the other tunnel crawled up his nose, grew to the point of being unbearable. Then he heard something, from up beyond the entrance, which was just a grey patch against the darkness of the tunnel. A figure passed in front of it, blocking the moonlight, crouching, sniffing, a head moving in. Cywen leaped, grabbing whoever it was, then they were both falling back into the hole. Buddai snarled and jumped, his growl deepening and teeth snapping; there was a muffled curse of pain.

'No, stop. Haelan, help me,' a panicked voice shouted. Not Cywen's.

I know that voice.

They all froze, the newcomer's face becoming recognizable as a patch of moonlight filtered through the hole.

Trigg.

Haelan laughed and threw his arms around her neck.

'Welcome to our home,' Haelan said, standing in his den with the cubs surrounding him, Swain and Sif behind him.

Haelan was overjoyed to see the half-breed girl. Back at Gramm's hold he had started a fragile friendship with Trigg, and she had helped him escape the hold when Jael's warband had come for him. To his great shame he had not thought of her since, but now he felt happy to see her familiar face, one that he linked to a happier time.

'Look who it is,' Haelan said to Swain and Sif as Trigg fell into the small chamber, a tangle of limbs on the ground. As she unravelled herself, Swain's expression changed from confusion to horror, then anger.

'It's the half-breed *traitor*,' he snarled, reaching for a knife at his belt as Haelan jumped to stop him.

'What's this all about?' Cywen said. 'What's going on?'

'Back at Gramm's hold, that filthy half-breed betrayed you, Haelan,' Swain said, 'gave you up to Jael's man. Told him you were hidden in the basement.'

'But that doesn't make sense,' Haelan said. 'It was Trigg who got me out of the basement, she helped me escape the hold.'

Trigg was sitting in a corner, knees pulled up to her chest, looking just about as miserable as it was possible to be.

'Then why did you betray Haelan and show Jael's lot where he was hidden?' Swain said, frowning at Trigg.

'To stop them torturing your da, and Gramm,' Trigg said, shrugging her massive shoulders. 'I knew Haelan wasn't down there, because I'd already pulled him out.'

'Then after, why did you run?' Swain asked, some of the anger missing from his voice now.

'Because Wulf was going to gut me,' Trigg said venomously. 'He wouldn't believe me; I tried to tell him. And of course no one thought to defend me, *the filthy half-breed*.' She looked down at the floor, a tremor in her voice, tears in her eyes. 'Wulf's men chased me, tried to kill me. I ran until my feet bled.' She shook her head, lip curling in a snarl. 'Wulf, all of you, believed I would betray you like that. No doubt in your mind.' She cuffed snot from her nose.

'Gramm took me in, gave me a home.' She was almost shouting now, 'I would never have betrayed him.'

'Shh,' Cywen said, 'or you'll bring the Kadoshim down upon us.'

'Why didn't you come and find me?' Haelan said, guilt creeping through him now, and making him react as it often did; defensively. 'Just showed yourself to us. I would have spoken for you, explained to Wulf.'

I never gave her a second thought, after I was safe.

'I tried,' Trigg said, quieter now. 'I followed you all into Forn, tried to get close enough, but there were scouts all the time – good ones, a girl with red hair—'

'Coralen,' Cywen said.

'And Wulf's men. I knew if I revealed myself they would strike me down before I got close to you.' Trigg looked at Haelan, a hidden accusation in her eyes.

'Well, you've found me now,' Haelan said, trying to make his voice sound lighter than he felt. 'When we are back with Corban and the others, I will explain to them – to Corban, to Wulf. Everything will be all right.'

'Corban, the Bright Star?'

'That's right,' Haelan said.

'He's my brother,' Cywen added, eyes narrowing as she studied Trigg. 'How did you get into Drassil?' she asked Trigg.

'I followed you.'

'We've been here over half a year,' Cywen said. 'You've been living amongst us all that time? Hiding?'

'No,' Trigg grunted. 'In Forn, waiting, hoping to see Haelan.' She was talking to her knees now. 'I never did,' she added.

'That must have been hard, through the winter, with the creatures of the forest,' Haelan said. Trigg nodded dejectedly and Haelan shuffled forwards and took her hand, though she pulled away at first.

'I am so sorry, Trigg. Truth be told I forgot about you, and I am ashamed. I was so scared when Gramm's hold was attacked, terrified. And you helped me, pulled me from the cellar. I would have died without you. And then it was safe, Corban came to our rescue—'

He looked at Trigg, feeling a great wave of sympathy. 'But I won't forget you again.'

Trigg squeezed his hand, returned his gaze a moment, then looked away.

'You think much of this Corban?' she said.

'I do,' Haelan replied. 'He is our leader. Brave. I trust him, would follow him . . . anywhere.' He shrugged.

Trigg eyed him thoughtfully.

'How have you not been caught in Drassil?' Cywen asked her.

'I am careful,' Trigg said with a shifting of her shoulders.

'Well, you can stay with us now,' Haelan said, 'you need not fear being caught. No one will ever find us down here.'

Trigg looked at him through her heavy-lidded eyes.

'My thanks,' she said.

CHAPTER FORTY-SIX

VERADIS

Veradis sat beside the fire-pit, methodically tending to his war gear with whetstone, oil and cloth.

Nathair, two thousand eagle-guard, Lothar, his road from Helveth to Drassil, a warband thousands strong. Maquin was right to suggest we attack Gundul before he reached Drassil, and we should do the same with Lothar. But how? We need more swords. The prisoners in Drassil, how can we get them out?

It was late, the flicker of firelight amongst the trees drawing moths and other things that lurked or hovered just beyond the touch of illumination in the forest. Alcyon and Tain were sitting with a handful of the Benothi, Balur and Brina amongst them. Abruptly, Veradis jumped up and marched over to them, calling to a dozen of his own men as he went.

'I've an idea,' he said to Alcyon, looking around, grabbing branches and shaking them. 'Here, Alcyon, cut this branch down for me,' he asked, holding a branch about as thick as his wrist.

Alcyon raised a questioning eyebrow but stood to do it, swinging his axe and shearing the branch with one blow. Veradis drew a knife, stripped the off-shoots and trimmed it.

'Can I borrow one of your axes, please?' he asked Alcyon, at the same time cutting a strip from his cloak then binding the axe-haft to the sapling branch, making something that looked like an axe on a spear shaft.

'Shield wall,' he said, without looking at his own men gathered behind him, and was excessively pleased when he heard the thud of linden; just by the sound of it he knew that the shields had come together well and in fluid time.

'You,' Veradis said, pointing to a seated giant. 'What is your name?'

'Fachen,' the giant said.

'Well, Fachen, I have an idea, but to test it I need a demonstration. Would you do me the honour of helping me?'

The giant's brows knitted. 'All right.' He stood, as Veradis stepped behind the shield wall and took up a shield and a practice sword. He looked over the rim, saw that the giant Fachen had a war-hammer slung across his back.

'Attack me,' Veradis said to him. 'Break this shield wall apart, if you can.'

Fachen looked at the others, eyes gravitating to Balur, who was looking on with interest, leaning with his back to a tree, arms folded.

Fachen swung his war-hammer two-handed, stepping in and using his weight to add power to his blow, slamming the weapon into Veradis' shield. It was a mighty strike, rocking Veradis back a step, the shock of it shuddering up his arm, numbing it, but most of the force was dispersed through the interlocked shields.

Fachen's momentum pushed him on and his body crashed into the shields, rocking them again, but still the line held. Veradis' harmless practice sword darted out, punching into Fachen's waist, the giant grunting in pain.

'You're dead, or dying,' Veradis said, lowering his shield.

'Are you mocking me?' Fachen asked, taking a step back and hefting his hammer.

'No,' Veradis replied. 'I'm demonstrating how dangerous the shield wall is, even to giants.'

'I was not taking it seriously,' Fachen shrugged.

Brina snorted and Alcyon smiled.

Veradis looked at his shield, saw the wood dented and grooved.

'Looks serious enough,' he said. He noticed others gathering around now, Wulf and Tahir, Krelis and Alben, Maquin, Fidele, a few of her shieldmen. 'We must treat the shield wall with respect,' he continued. 'It is a widow-maker, a death-dealer, no one is safe before it – man or woman, the skill of the Jehar will not save them, nor the strength of a giant. Nathair marched out with two thousand men, many of them veterans of the shield wall. They have fought many battles, and never lost.'

'They have not fought against the Benothi,' Fachen said.

'True enough,' Veradis replied, 'though I think some of your kin clashed with them during the battle of Drassil. But Nathair's men did stand against the Shekam and their draigs in Tarbesh, and they stood against the Hunen at Haldis. Both clans were broken on the wall of shields.'

'You lie,' Fachen said.

'He does not lie,' Alcyon said.

'How do you know this?' Balur One-Eye rumbled.

'I know, because I was there,' Veradis said. 'I led the shield wall, stood in the front row, weathered the storm of iron, bore the brunt of their hammers and axes.'

'The Hunen?' Balur asked.

'Aye. Calidus pulled those strings. He was after the starstone axe.'

'And the Shekam?' Ethlinn said, standing and walking over to look at the damage done to Veradis' shield.

'Calidus, again,' Alcyon said. 'He had his reasons for wanting the Shekam gone.'

'But they are the draig-riders,' Balur said, as if that made them invincible.

'Admittedly, the draigs were a bit of a problem,' Veradis conceded. 'But the Shekam were still destroyed, only a handful escaping the battlefield. Nathair is a strategist, an excellent general with an eye for the straight path to victory. The shield wall is his creation.'

'It was the shield wall that felled Balur in the battle at Drassil,' Ethlinn mused.

'Aye, that's so,' Balur said. 'I smashed a dozen men down, but more kept filling the hole I hacked.' He put a hand to his side, up to his shoulder. 'They gave me many wounds.'

'How do we beat that?' asked Tahir. 'I led men against it in the great hall of Drassil.' He shook his head. 'Many fell.'

'It is not invincible,' Maquin said.

'No, it is like any weapon, any tool,' Veradis said. 'It has strengths and weaknesses.'

'The Kadoshim did a good job of ripping it open,' Maquin said.

'They did,' Veradis agreed. 'Because they are happy to take a sword-wound in the belly, or anywhere else for that matter, and fight on regardless. Most of us would not. The Kadoshim's strengths are not our strengths. That is not how we will crack the shield wall open.'

'How, then?' Maquin asked.

'If we fought them on a hill and we were at the top we could roll wains or trees down at them,' Tahir said. He looked around. 'Not so many hills in Forn, though.'

'Terrain is correct,' Veradis said. 'The shield wall works best on open spaces, flat ground. So if we could choose our battlefield, that would help.'

'And what if we cannot?' Maquin asked.

'There may be other ways,' Veradis said. 'But we would need a forge, and blacksmiths skilled at weapon-making.'

'We could dig a forge,' Balur said. 'I have seen it done. And Fachen is a weapons-smith.'

'I can work a bellows and shape some iron,' Wulf grunted, 'but what of tools and materials?'

'We have a good supply of iron,' Alben said. 'There were wains full of charcoal, iron rods and tools that we found amongst Gundul's supplies.'

'And what would you do with this forge?' Brina asked Veradis. 'What would you make?'

Veradis lifted the axe and branch that he had bound together.

'I'll show you. Wall,' he commanded. His men gathered tight and brought their shields up. Veradis advanced on them.

CHAPTER FORTY-SEVEN

CAMLIN

Camlin led his small band along a narrow trail, forty of the best woodsmen, hunters and archers that he had found in Edana's rag-tag warband. They wound single-file, so as to not give away their numbers if they were tracked, which Camlin thought all but impossible. Those who might have had half a mind to follow them they'd left dying on the giantsway.

Another supply train ruined, some grain burned, the rest stolen, and two score fewer of Rhin's warriors left to fight us. All in all, a good day. Besides, Craf will let me know if there's any trouble on my tail.

Only a ten-night had passed since Camlin had been fished out of the river with the giant, Eisa.

He'd not liked the discussions of God-Wars and the Seven Treasures, and Craf hadn't helped matters since. Every time Camlin had sat still the damn bird had come and perched on his shoulder and started muttering about Kadoshim, death and the end of the world. He shivered.

And then there was Rafe. Camlin had thought about him a lot over the last few days, how he'd been transformed, become stronger and faster. That had added weight to Eisa and Craf's words, and Camlin didn't like that.

Gods. Angels and demons. What next? I prefer something I can face and kill. Not myths and stories.

He shivered at the thought of it, the concept that everything they were doing was a small part in a much grander scheme. He didn't like the idea, not one little bit.

Best not to think of it at all, so keeping busy is a much better idea.

And busy seemed to be working. Half a dozen raids by his crew alone on baggage trains, on warbands and warriors, even a merchant barge travelling up the river Tarin to Dun Carreg, all taking coin and food from the enemy.

Camlin passed the first checkpoint of their camp, saw a shadowed face and a drawn bow. He raised a hand in greeting, knew he was recognized, and that Meg had gone ahead, announcing his imminent return.

Nice to see the guards are working.

Soon afterwards he was emerging into their camp. It had grown. Word was spreading throughout Ardan of Edana's return, and for a while now new recruits had been trickling into the Baglun.

Camlin was struggling to trust them, and the thought that just one could be a spy or an assassin was not helping him to sleep at night, but Edana was right. She was never going to raise a warband capable of overthrowing Rhin without Ardan's people.

He found Edana in her tent, which was a crude thing stitched from sails, but it did the job. Inside Edana was sitting with Baird and Halion. Camlin told them of his successful raid. The central tent pole creaked and Camlin looked up, saw the outline of a dark shape through the tent.

Craf. That bird is a compulsive spy.

'More food for us, and less for them,' Camlin said with a smile. 'Grain's on the way, left some of the lads to bring it in.'

'Rhin's holed up at Dun Carreg,' he continued. 'Got eyes on the place. She went in, and definitely hasn't come out. Warriors are trickling in, though. It's early days, but looks like that giant might've been telling the truth. Over the last four days over two hundred swords have ridden through Stonegate. Looks like she's gathering some strong arms about her.'

'Mustering a warband to ride with her to Drassil,' Edana mused.

'*God-War,*' a voice croaked from above their heads, beyond the tent fabric.

Damn that bird.

Vonn and Lorcan, returning from a meeting with Pendathran, entered the tent, the bulk of Brogan following Lorcan.

'Good news, my bride-to-be,' Lorcan said enthusiastically.

Edana winced. Camlin knew that the long-ago agreed betrothal between them was something that Edana had no intention of continuing with. It was just that no one had told Lorcan that yet.

Someone needs to tell the lad.

'Pendathran has swept through much of Ardan's east,' Lorcan said, 'and he says the people are with you. Many have joined his warband – they were two hundred strong when we left him, all warriors.'

When he marched away from the banks of Dun Crin's swamp Pendathran had fifty men with him.

'That is excellent news,' Edana said. 'And Drust? Is there news from him?'

'Messengers from Drust arrived while we were there,' Vonn said, frowning at Lorcan and stepping shoulder to shoulder with him. 'Drust is camped in the Darkwood, has spread word of your return all through the west and is now doing the same in the north. And he has sent men into Narvon, declaring your return. He, too, has raised men. There are over a hundred with him now.'

'We spoke to many travellers while upon the road,' Lorcan said quickly, taking another step forwards. 'All had heard of your return, and many seemed . . .' He searched for the right words. 'Cautiously pleased.'

'It is going as we planned, then,' Edana said, her eyes touching Camlin's.

Better than that.

Edana asked more questions of Lorcan and Vonn, eventually finishing and telling them to go and eat and rest. She called Vonn back. Lorcan hovered in the tent entrance, then left with Brogan, his constant shadow.

Edana looked at them, Camlin, Halion, Baird and Vonn. She sighed and stood, as if coming to a decision.

'Come with me,' she said to them all.

Edana walked out of the tent and led them down towards the river. Camlin heard the tell-tale swish of wings above him, and the creeping of footfalls close by.

Craf and Meg, more alike than they realize.

Soon they were standing before Eisa, the Benothi giant. She was chained to a tree, legs hobbled, guards a dozen paces away.

'I will not keep you a prisoner,' Edana said. 'It is not practical – we must move camp or be discovered, and I cannot be wasting man-power on escorting you from one place to another. And besides that, it does not sit well with me. Better a clean death than captivity, eh? So . . .'

Edana nodded at the guards and warriors she'd brought with her, and before Eisa had a chance to move they were all leaping forwards, grabbing her arms, pinning her. Baird stepped behind the giant, one hand in Eisa's hair, the other holding a knife to her throat.

'Not an execution,' Edana said, and turned the key in the chain's lock, releasing Eisa.

'You cannot know how much this pains me,' Baird said as he tied a cloth tight around Eisa's eyes.

'You are free to go,' Edana said. 'My men will take you into the forest, far from here, and from there you will be on your own. Baird, give her back her knife when you take the blindfold off.'

'Aye,' Baird grunted, though he looked none too pleased about it. With a hard tug on the bonds around Eisa's wrist, he led her along the riverbank, the score of guardsmen wrapped around her.

'Well, I wasn't expecting that,' Camlin said, blowing his cheeks out. 'But she's still likely to die wandering around in the Baglun.'

'*Craf show giant way out of forest,*' the crow muttered from his perch in the branches.

'Thank you, Craf,' Edana said.

'*Welcome.*'

'There's something I want to talk to you all about,' Edana said to Camlin, Halion and Vonn. 'I've been thinking about what the giant said, what Craf has said. And, yes, what you have said, Vonn.'

She looked long and hard at them.

'I think we need to do something about these Treasures that I'm told are at Dun Carreg.'

'Aye,' Halion grunted, tugging on his short beard. 'What, exactly?'

'I think someone needs to go and steal this cup and necklace.'

Above them a branch creaked and swayed.

'*YES,*' squawked Craf.

CHAPTER FORTY-EIGHT

RAFE

Rafe cantered across green meadows; to his right the river Tarin, wide and sluggish as it neared the sea, to his left the Baglun Forest, a sea of leaf and bark undulating into the horizon. Ahead of him in the distance he could just make out the grey-topped pinnacle that was Dun Carreg, behind it the shimmer of the sea, and he smiled.

Home.

Besides him Scratcher ran, Rafe was still not used to seeing her without Sniffer. He'd raised a cairn over the hound in the Baglun, in the glade by the river where Camlin had killed him.

I'll kill that bastard. Nearly did then, if not for that cursed crow. I'll kill him 'n' all, if I see him again.

He craned in his saddle to look back at the warband behind him. Five hundred men, Morcant at their head in his fine war gear, helm and chainmail gleaming, cloak of black and gold billowing behind him, looking like a hero out of the old tales.

How I hate him. Bloody fop, even if he can wield a sword.

Rafe had found Morcant burning a village to the east of the Baglun, obviously taking out his frustration at his failure to prevent Edana's attacks.

She's only got a few hundred men, and what can they do? They may cause some trouble, but in the end won't do much worse than a boil on the arse. A pain, and annoying, but won't kill you.

'How long until we see Dun Carreg?' Morcant asked him as he drew alongside Rafe.

'I can see it already,' Rafe said, pointing.

Morcant squinted. 'You must have good eyes,' he muttered. Then, 'Roisin – what has Rhin done with her?'

'In the dungeon beneath the keep, last I heard,' Rafe said.

'Dungeons! That's no place for a lady, especially one as fine-looking as Roisin,' Morcant said.

A movement drew Rafe's eye: within the murk of the Baglun, a figure was forming out of the shadows, tall and long-limbed.

A giant.

She stumbled out from the undergrowth and shadows, favouring one leg, head bowed.

'Eisa,' he called, touching his reins and kicking his horse towards her, glad to be getting away from Morcant.

She was battered and bruised, her lower leg swollen, lumps and cuts on her face, a long scabbed gash upon her forehead, only one of the scabbards criss-crossing her back containing a blade. She raised a hand in greeting to him.

Hooves clattered on stone as they crossed the bridge into Dun Carreg. It was strange to see giants standing on the wall above Stonegate.

He looked at Eisa stumbling beside him. She'd proudly refused any litter they'd offered to carry her in.

'Uthas ordered the forest searched, but we could not find you,' Rafe said, feeling a stab of guilt as he remembered he'd refused to join the search, choosing to bury Sniffer instead, and then to sit upon the cairn and grieve.

'I hit my head on a branch in the river,' Eisa said, touching the long cut on her forehead. 'Woke up on the riverbank.'

'Taken you a long time to find your way here,' Rafe said.

'It's a big forest,' Eisa shrugged.

'Aye, it is,' Rafe acknowledged.

'You can follow me to the keep,' Morcant said to Eisa. 'You, huntsman, go and find Roisin. Have her released from the dungeons on my order and brought to me.'

Rafe bit back an angry retort and only nodded.

He found Roisin in a cold dungeon, a bucket in the corner for her bodily requirements.

'You're to come with me,' Rafe said to her. She was lying upon her cot, black hair spread about her shoulders. She held out her hand to him.

'I feel a little weak,' she said in her warm accented voice, and Rafe found himself taking her hand without even thinking about it. Her skin was smooth and warm.

'This way, my lady,' he said, and led her up through the keep's stairwells and corridors.

'Where are you taking me?' Roisin asked.

'You'll see soon enough,' he grunted.

Soon they were in a deserted part of the keep, their footsteps echoing down a long corridor. Turning a corner, Rafe saw a dozen of Rhin's elite shieldmen in their black and gold, as well as a handful of giants, lurking in the shadowed alcoves, as still as cobwebbed-statues. They were nearing the complex of rooms where Rafe had last seen Rhin. He came to the first door and knocked.

'Enter,' Morcant's voice called out. He was sitting at a table, sipping from a cup of mead. When he saw Roisin he stood and took her hand, kissing it.

'I cannot believe that you have been kept in a dungeon, my lady,' Morcant said. 'It has been some dreadful mistake, and one that I mean to make amends for.'

'I do not think I am high in Queen Rhin's favour,' Roisin said, eyes dipping demurely.

'Well, you are her prisoner, granted,' Morcant said. 'But a royal one. I can assure you that Rhin would not treat you like this, and once the culprit that chose to lock you in Dun Carreg's dungeons is discovered, I will have him flayed. As soon as I heard, I sent my servant to release you.' Morcant glanced at Rafe.

Servant! He felt his face twist in anger.

'And if it was on Queen Rhin's orders?' Roisin asked.

'Well, then I shall intercede with her on your behalf,' Morcant said. 'Though for now, I am told that Rhin is not here and will not be for at least a ten-night.' He gave Roisin a conspiratorial smile. 'I have ordered clothes for you, and a girl will be along shortly to attend to you. You may be a prisoner of war, but we are not animals, and you are noble and so you shall be treated as such. I will ensure it myself.'

'My thanks,' Roisin said, lifting her eyes. 'I cannot tell you how grateful I am.' She held his gaze then, a silence settling over the room.

'You can go,' Morcant said to Rafe with a dismissive flick of his hand.

Hope Rhin catches you and turns you into a toad, Rafe thought as he closed the door behind him.

CHAPTER FORTY-NINE

NATHAIR

Nathair sat on the back of his draig, absently patting its back and feeling an answering rumble from deep within its chest as it crushed a path through Forn. Behind him the tramp of two thousand booted feet and ahead strode the messenger who had arrived from Lothar, a man named Helred. They'd left Drassil half a ten-night gone, now, every day and night the same, surrounded by the endless ocean of oak and ash, the forest bearing down upon them, oppressive and dour.

Despite his surroundings, Nathair felt his spirits were lighter. It was being away from Drassil, he was sure, away from Calidus and the Kadoshim, from Lykos and the Vin Thalun, where he was forever reminded of the hand that had engineered his unwitting path.

Out here I can think and plan, without feeling that my every step is monitored, my every thought read.

My only regret is that I am going the wrong way – south instead of north-west. Sent to watch over Lothar when I could have been travelling to reclaim the starstone dagger.

He felt his better mood melting away at that thought.

Does Calidus not trust me? Or does he think me incapable of completing the task?

His mind filled with scenarios, battles, confrontations, each one taking him down a different path.

But we do need more men, if the cauldron, axe and spear are to be kept safe at Drassil. Now that Veradis is with my enemy. Look what he did to Gundul's warband. We must not underestimate him.

He glanced left and right, scanning the deep shadows of Forn.

Veradis could be out there right now. Watching me.

But would he really attack me?

'Helred, how much longer?' Nathair called out to the messenger before him.

'A few more nights, at least,' Helred replied, an older man, more grey than black in his hair. He was dressed in a huntsman's garb, hardwearing boots and breeches, a woollen tunic, leather vest and cloak. He walked with a spear in his hand, only a knife at his hip.

He knows his craft, though, the only one of ten men sent by Lothar to get through to Drassil.

His draig raised its head, its long tongue flickering out to taste the air, thick-muscled neck casting its head from side to side. It slowed.

Helred noticed and dropped back.

'Something wrong?' the huntsman asked.

By now everyone had heard of the destruction of Gundul's warband, and added to that were the raids and ambushes that had befallen every party that had ventured forth from Drassil and had dared the forest.

Nathair raised a hand and horn blasts echoed out, bouncing off of the trees, the warband rippling to a well-trained halt.

'What is it?' Nathair whispered, looking around. The forest was calm and still, a crow cawing angrily somewhere high above, the rustle of branches caressed by a breeze. Nowhere could Nathair see or hear any movement of men amongst the trees, the glint of pale light on iron, the creak of a bent bow or the rasp of a drawn sword. Nothing that suggested an ambush.

He flicked the reins to give his draig its head. Its tongue flitted out again, and then it was lumbering on, to the right, away from their path, into a patch of dense undergrowth thick with thorn and vine. The draig trampled through it, burst into a clearing, then stopped, staring down at a carcass on the floor. Not even that, no skin, flesh or sinew left, not even cartilage, just a collection of bones. The draig was leaning close, tongue fluttering over the bones. It opened its jaws to clamp on one but Nathair barked a sharp order, the draig's jaws snapping shut as it turned and gave him a doleful stare.

It was a wolven, a big one, its skeleton intact, from muzzle to tail, the skull broad and thick-boned, long curved canines in its jaw.

'There's more here,' Helred said, joining them, circling the huge skeleton. 'Another skeleton here. Much smaller. The big one's cub, maybe. It broke its leg – look,' Helred said, pointing at where the foreleg of the smaller skeleton was stuck down a hole of some sort.

Rabbit hole, maybe.

Whatever it was, it looked as if the cub had fallen, broken its leg, been unable to move and the adult wolven had stood over its offspring in an attempt to defend it.

That didn't work out too well.

Nathair crouched beside the skeletons and prodded at a rib with the tip of his sword. The bone was immaculately clean, as if it had been dipped at a tanner's yard. Usually, no matter how fed-upon a carcass had been, there would be small strips of skin and flesh, some gristle, matted fur. Here there was nothing.

'What did this?' Nathair asked.

'This is Forn,' Helred said with a shrug. 'Maybe one beast slew them, a host of others stripping it after. Best not to linger,' he added, looking at their surroundings suspiciously, eyes drifting upwards to the distant cawing of crows, a macabre choir.

'Aye,' Nathair muttered. 'Feast,' he said to his draig and the beast snapped at the wolven's bones, jaws clamping around the back leg of the adult, followed by splintering sounds.

They retreated, Nathair staring at the remains, the warband lurching into motion behind Nathair.

It is only another death within Forn, one of many. And soon there shall be a glut.

CHAPTER FIFTY

CYWEN

Cywen lifted Shield's foreleg.

'Easy, boy,' she murmured, feeling his breath on her head. 'Good lad, good lad,' she repeated as she saw to her task, using a small blunted knife to clean out his hooves, then trying to trim them back a little, as they were growing long from inactivity.

You need a run, some exercise. But at least you are still here, and in one piece.

She stood straight, ran a hand over his muscled flank, and he nudged her with his head, gave a whinny.

'I miss him, too,' she said quietly. 'Corban will be back soon, you'll see.'

At her brother's name the stallion's ears pricked forwards and he whickered gently, arching his neck and dipping his head to rub it against her.

She patted him hard enough to stir dust from his coat, gazing along the length of the stable-block.

So many empty pens. We came here with a herd of close to three hundred horses. Now there can't be more than seventy left. All gone into hungry bellies.

'At least it smells better in here,' she muttered, looking along the line of pens to the stable that had housed Nathair's draig. It was empty now; Nathair had been gone over a ten-night.

And good riddance to both of them.

Every time Cywen saw the draig pen, though, and smelt it, even if it was only a shadow of the stench it had once been, it reminded her of Haelan and his den.

The stench of draigs is down there. And it must come from somewhere. Somewhere beneath Drassil.

She gave Shield a distracted kiss on the muzzle, lifted her one-wheeled cart, piled high with straw and dung, and pushed it along the stable-block out into daylight.

A Kadoshim was leaning against the stable wall, arms folded across its chest, eyes fixed on Cywen's every movement. It was guard to Cywen and the other able-bodied prisoners on stable duty. It followed Cywen as she merged with the others, all pushing their carts of dung. They filed outside into the courtyard and Cywen averted her gaze from the mass of stakes and corpses that hung from the gates like grisly ornaments.

Ahead of her she saw Hild, one of the prisoners, only recently recovered from her battle injuries. She was Wulf's wife, Swain and Sif's mam, and every time Cywen saw her she felt a stab of guilt that she hadn't told her of her children. That they lived, that they were safe, and so very close. But the risk was too great.

Would she give us all away, the thought of seeing her bairns overwhelming her sense? As it is, it's amazing that they have stayed hidden in the middle of this vipers' den, and raised Storm and Buddai's cubs as well. And we have a new addition. Trigg.

Over a ten-night since she joined us, she seems to have some bond with Haelan, even though Haelan abandoned her. She hangs on his every word, wants to please him.

It was strange and made Cywen feel uncomfortable.

There is more to her that I do not understand, though. There is something brittle about her. Not broken, quite, but close.

They turned another corner, moving behind the stable-block into a hidden courtyard, where Cywen was surprised to see a set of scaffolding had been erected, five boats sitting suspended within it. They looked all but complete, men slapping caulking onto the hulls and spreading it along the timber strakes. As Cywen walked past them the smell of pitch-tar and pine oil filled her nostrils.

Why are they building boats in the middle of Forn Forest, hundreds of leagues from the nearest sea?

She frowned as she thought on that while waiting in line to empty her cart on the dung heap. Upon finishing, she found the Kadoshim standing in her way.

'Knife,' the Kadoshim said to her, holding her hand out, swirls of dirt staining the creases in her skin like some intricate tattoo.

Cywen thought about denial, but she had seen what happened to those who lied to the Kadoshim. She bent down and pulled the knife from her boot, where she'd stuffed it after finishing Shield's hooves.

'It's blunt, anyway,' Cywen muttered.

'A blunt knife can still do much damage . . . to your kind, at least,' the Kadoshim said with a smile, making Cywen shudder.

She heard voices, a rush of hatred flooding through her veins as one stood out. Calidus. She glanced around the Kadoshim's bulk and saw Calidus examining the boats, Lykos with him. After a few exchanged words, Lykos began waving his arms in the air, remonstrating the workers. Other figures walked with them, a little behind. One was shrouded by a swirl of flies.

That Kadoshim. I hate him.

The Kadoshim remained close to the other figure, almost like a guard. It was cloaked and hooded, standing in the shadows of the scaffolding, but Cywen recognized her anyway. The knife in her hand dropped to the ground, her fingers forgetting they held it.

The figure she'd seen was Trigg.

CHAPTER FIFTY-ONE

LYKOS

Lykos ran a hand along the strakes of one of his new-built boats, eyes closed, savouring the lines, the smell of pitch. He swore he could almost hear the crying of gulls. Then an image of Fidele swam into his mind.

Ach, why can't I get that bitch out of my head? It's because I know she's so close. It'll be good to get away and feel the roll and sway of water beneath my feet, even if it will only be river-water, and not the swell and the salt spray of the ocean. I'll forget about her then.

He opened his eyes to see Calidus staring at him, mouth a thin line.

'I said, when will they be ready?'

Lykos inspected the boats more closely, saw the oar locks were being fitted by Alazon, his best shipwright.

Not that these are ships. Just rowing-boats, but they are best equipped for a long journey upriver.

Short masts, rigging, sails woven from wool, and sets of oars were all close by.

'As long as it takes for the pitch to dry. We could leave on the morrow. Or tonight?'

'Good. Ensure that all is ready. You've chosen your men?'

'Aye,' Lykos grunted.

A harder, nastier bunch of cut-throats you're not likely to see. Legion'll fit right in.

'And all else is ready?'

'Aye. A bit of last-minute packing,' Lykos shrugged.

I need to find enough mead to last me to Arcona.

'Leave tonight, then. If you can get away from Drassil without being seen, then all the better. We don't want any interference from those brigands in the forest.'

Unless Fidele wants to come and try stabbing me again. No doubt she'd bring her faithful Old Wolf with her. He lifted a hand to his cheek, felt the uneven puckered scar where Maquin had bitten a chunk of flesh from his face. For a moment he was lost in his imagining of that encounter. Always Maquin died first. Screaming.

Calidus tutted.

'I hope I can rely on you to complete this task,' Calidus said.

'Of course,' Lykos grunted.

'Your lack of focus is unsettling. Need I remind you what hangs upon this mission?'

'You can trust me. I'll return with the starstone torc, of that you need not doubt. And yes, leaving under cover of dark is a good idea. Not so many eyes. Our enemies in the forest are likely to be watching our walls.'

'Aye, they are. And, talking of those blackguards in the forest, Trigg, come here.'

The half-breed took a hesitant step forwards, out from the shadows.

'Have you found them?'

There was a silence, too long for Lykos' liking.

'Yes,' Trigg said, head bowed, hood up.

'Well?' Calidus said into the silence. 'Where are they?'

'They move regularly, so as not to be caught. I will need to go back out there.'

'I see,' Calidus said, stroking the stubbly whiskers on his chin – they were finally growing back. 'But it would be possible to track their movements from the camp you discovered?'

Another long silence.

'Most likely,' Trigg said.

'And where is this camp? The one that you found, before they moved?'

'North-west,' Trigg said with a jerk of her chin, sounding sullen, reluctant.

She knows more than she's telling.

'Is there a problem?' Calidus asked, stepping closer to Trigg, staring into her eyes. Legion moved up behind her, flies buzzing irritably.

'No,' Trigg answered. 'Forn is dangerous. I prefer it here.'

'Aye, well, you can stay here as long as you like once those irritants in the forest are dealt with. You will be rewarded well.'

'My thanks,' Trigg grunted.

'Well, things are starting to work out rather well,' Calidus said. 'I will prepare a force for you to guide into the forest. On the morrow. Don't wander too far. If I cannot find you when I need you, I shall be vexed. You won't like me when I'm vexed.'

The master of understatement.

'I'll stay close,' Trigg said.

'Good,' Calidus clapped his hands together. 'Everyone away, then, and do what you need to do. Lykos, be here at midnight with your men and your mead.'

Lykos snorted and then they were all marching away, Legion accompanying Calidus, Trigg striding ahead and veering right at the first opportunity, away from the Kadoshim. Lykos watched them all go, his eyes finally fixing upon Trigg.

I've a lot to do, but something about her is not right.

He followed her.

At first she seemed to wander randomly through the wide streets, Lykos keeping well back, clinging to alcoves and shadows, but eventually he saw a pattern to it.

She's doing a wide loop, ever tighter. She's going to the great hall.

Soon they were there. The gates were wide open, with eagle-guard before them. The guards watched Trigg suspiciously as she walked into the huge chamber, and stood straighter when Lykos appeared.

Inside the chamber the Treasures and doorway to the ancient forge were roped off, the boundary patrolled by a score of Kadoshim. Between them, along the perimeter, a unit of eagle-guard were stationed. Trigg stopped on the stairs and stared down at the cauldron. Lykos sidled off to one side and stood in the shadows of one of the many stairwells that wound up to towers and chambers above.

What the hell is she up to? If she's come here to steal the Treasures she's not doing a very good job of it.

Abruptly Trigg moved, climbing a stairwell up into the cavernous heights of the chamber, then disappeared. Lykos followed, moving as quietly as he could manage.

He reached an archway that opened onto a corridor, the stairwell continuing to spiral upwards. Trigg was there, at the far end, standing before another doorway, staring at it. She reached out and lifted the latch, then stepped inside.

Lykos frowned.

What is she doing here?

This corridor was not used by them. Most of the troops had been barracked in buildings spread in a loose half-circle between the great tree and Drassil's gates. Only Calidus actually slept within the tree's chambers to stay close to the Treasures. Moving as quietly as was possible, Lykos crept down the corridor, finally stopping just before the open doorway.

He peered inside.

It was a chamber that had been lived in. The cot had a rumpled blanket on it, the mattress of straw was slashed and scattered, the room in disarray. After the main part of the battle for Drassil had ended, many of Calidus' forces had run amok throughout the fortress. From the looks of it, it was the Kadoshim that had torn through here. There were too many things remaining that the Vin Thalun would have found of worth. Lykos saw the shine of a chainmail shirt, a fine-made shield, iron-rimmed, with battle-scars testifying to sword strokes across it. A well-made pair of boots, iron greaves stitched into them.

Someone high up, with war gear like that. A captain, a leader.

Trigg was walking slowly around the room, examining. She saw the chainmail shirt, lifted it, shook it out, and then rolled it up, stuffing it inside her cloak. Moving on, she bent and picked up an empty bowl, what looked like mildewed porridge dripping from it in lumps. She dropped it and walked on.

What is she doing?

She carried on, then stopped again, bent and picked something up from the floor. Iron glinted amongst the leather. At first Lykos thought it was a belt of knives, but then Trigg slipped the leather over her fist, up her forearm, and Lykos saw it was a leather gauntlet with three curved iron claws extending from the knuckles. Trigg tugged on the leather thongs that tightened it, then gave an experimental swipe.

That could do a lot of damage. Wouldn't like to be on the receiving end of those.

She took it off, rolled it up and secreted it away within the folds of her cloak.

Enough's enough.

'What are you doing?' He asked as he stepped into the room, casually drawing his short sword.

Trigg took a step back, startled.

'Nothing,' she blinked.

'Doesn't look like nothing,' Lykos said, picking his way through the debris. 'Looks like you're collecting. Question is, why?'

The half-breed shrugged, Lykos noticing the breadth of her shoulders, the length of her arms.

Don't underestimate this one. She's strong, and fast.

He twitched the tip of his sword, pointing at her now.

'You've pocketed some fine keepsakes – not sure the chainmail shirt'll fit you. Looked a bit short for you.' He shrugged. 'Wonder what Calidus will think of it?'

A twitch of her jaw, small eyes widening.

She doesn't like the thought of that.

'Don't tell him,' Trigg hissed.

'Why not?'

'He wouldn't understand,' Trigg said, 'he suspects betrayals, conspiracies where there are none. I just liked the shirt. It's . . . shiny.' Her eyes flickered between Lykos and the door, judging.

She's thinking about taking me on, he realized with a jolt. *I want information, not her blood.*

'Where's the enemy camp?' he asked. 'You've seen it. I want to know exactly where it is.'

'I told you, they move, regularly.'

'When did you see it?' he asked.

'Day before yesterday,' she muttered.

'Tell me where it is,' he hissed, taking a step towards her, sword rising.

'North-west,' she said.

'You already told us that. It's a forest, I need something more specific.'

She looked at him a long moment.

'From the first trapdoor on the north-western tunnel, travel north, to the river, then west. Over Jael's road, and half a league further there's a hill, at its base the corpse of a great bear. Another half-league west.' She shrugged. 'That's where it was.'

'My thanks,' Lykos said, half-bowing.

'There are scouts, it's well protected. And they've probably moved.'

'No matter,' he said, backing to the door.

'Why do you want to know where their camp is?' Trigg called after him as he reached the doorway and backed through.

'Got an old friend who's been on my mind of late,' he said, and slipped away down the corridor.

CHAPTER FIFTY-TWO

CYWEN

'Where's Trigg?' Cywen blurted as she burst into the den. Pots, Buddai and the cubs bounded all over her as behind them Sif muttered a curse, collecting her spilt stones and nuts.

It was dark outside, the best part of a day had gone since Cywen had seen Trigg in the company of Calidus and Lykos, but this was the first chance she'd had to get away.

'Out,' Haelan said. 'She may be big, but she's good at foraging and not getting caught, and she always comes back with something.' He grinned.

'Don't know how she does it,' Swain grunted.

'She's a *traitor*, that's how,' Cywen said. 'I saw her today, with Calidus.'

'The filthy half-breed,' Swain hissed.

'That doesn't make sense,' Haelan said. 'Why hasn't she led Calidus here, then? Why let us stay free?'

'I don't understand that part myself,' Cywen said, brow furrowing. 'But I know what I saw. Trigg, with Calidus and Lykos.'

'Maybe they're watching us, think we can be useful to them,' Swain said. He was gripped by rage. 'Maybe they're spying on our den right now, hidden around the courtyard.'

'No, Pots and Buddai would have sniffed them out,' Haelan said, shaking his head.

'You sure?' Sif asked. She sidled closer to Swain, a hand reaching out to grip the hem of his shirt.

A sound drifted down the tunnel that led to the den.

They all froze, listening. Heard the pad of footsteps, then Trigg calling out a greeting.

'I'll kill her,' Swain snarled, rummaging inside a sack and pulling out a knife and the snapped shaft of an axe or spear.

'Questions first,' Cywen hissed, as Swain threw the knife to her.

She pushed herself tight against the back wall, where the tunnel opened into the den, and blew out the torch closest to her.

'Act normally, see what you can learn,' Cywen hissed.

Moments later Trigg squeezed herself through the opening that led from the tunnel to the den, dropping onto the ground with a thud and picking herself up. She was smiling.

'Why're you so happy?' Swain asked her, not able to hide the rage that made his voice tremor.

Trigg frowned at him.

'Where've you been?' Sif asked.

Not so subtle at questioning, those two.

'Out, foraging,' Trigg said.

'You hungry?' Haelan asked.

Better.

'Aye,' Trigg grunted. 'You admire this Corban?' she added, almost shyly.

'Aye, of course,' Haelan said, pretending to be taken up with ripping a loaf of bread into five equal parts. 'He is our leader, he saved us.'

'Do you think he would be happy to see this?' she said, pulling a bundle wrapped in cloth from her cloak.

'What is it?' Sif asked.

Trigg unfurled the cloth. In one hand she held up a chainmail shirt, the other revealed a leather gauntlet, three iron daggers affixed to it, curved like claws.

'Corban's wolven claws!' Haelan said.

And his mail shirt.

'How did you get them?' Swain asked venomously.

Trigg's head snapped around.

'I'm good at sneaking,' she said.

'Don't know how you can walk around the fortress in broad daylight. You're half-giant, how can you be good at not being seen?'

I've heard enough.

Cywen sprang out from the shadows, kicking Trigg in the back of the knees, sending her crashing to the ground. Even as she hit the floor Trigg was twisting, dragging Cywen off balance, a fist crunching into her jaw. Stars exploded, her vision blurred and she fell, her cheek slamming onto cold earth. Then Swain and Trigg were rolling together, the cubs were a mass of fur swirling around the struggling pair like the detritus of a whirlwind. Haelan and Sif stood back, looking unsure how to help.

Buddai leaped at Trigg, his teeth clamping around her arm, while Shadow slammed into the half-giant's chest, knocking her back.

Cywen threw herself at Trigg, grabbing Corban's wolven claws, and a heartbeat later had them pressed to Trigg's throat, the iron tips making indentations in her flesh.

'Stop,' Cywen snarled.

Buddai had Trigg's arm clamped in his jaws, growling menacingly. The other cubs were snapping and snarling at Trigg's legs, blood spattering the ground. Shadow bounded onto Trigg's chest and growled in her face, saliva dripping from her canines.

'Call them off,' Trigg whispered.

'Hold,' Cywen said to Buddai. Haelan clicked his tongue, Shadow looked at him, then reluctantly retreated to stand by his side. Sif ran to Swain, who was groggily sitting up.

'Why?' Trigg asked.

'I saw you,' Cywen said. 'With Calidus.'

Any fight left in Trigg drained then, she literally deflated, going limp.

'You're a traitor,' Swain hissed at Trigg, standing unsteadily, his fists bunching.

'I've said nothing about you, about this place,' Trigg said.

'You were with Calidus?' Haelan said with hurt in his voice. 'I don't understand. I thought you were my friend.'

'I *am* your friend,' Trigg said pleadingly, 'even if you abandoned me, forgot I existed, left me to die.'

'Explain,' Cywen said.

Trigg looked at her defiantly, then her face creased with barely controlled emotion.

'I have done a terrible thing,' Trigg said. 'But I didn't know it at the time; I was so angry. Cold, starving. Thought I was going to die, and it was your fault – you Haelan, and Wulf. But now I'm so sorry, wish I could turn back time, or make amends, somehow. By helping you, finding Corban's belongings . . .'

'What terrible thing?' Haelan asked.

The half-giant looked at them all, a tremble in her lip, tears slipping down her cheeks.

'I showed Calidus the way into Drassil.'

Showed Calidus the secret tunnel. So many dead because of that one thing. Meical beheaded, the warband scattered.

Cywen's clawed hand dug deeper into Trigg's throat; the urge to kill the traitorous wretch was overwhelming, a host of faces spinning through her mind – the dead, framed by the screams of those executed each day.

'I have information,' Trigg blurted, 'valuable information.'

'What information?' Haelan asked, stalling Cywen's thoughts of retribution.

'About the Seven Treasures, about Calidus' plans.'

'Speak,' Haelan said.

So Trigg did, telling them all she knew, of the ancient forge in the heart of Drassil's tree, of the whereabouts of the starstone dagger and torc, of Lykos' mission, of Nathair and Lothar, and of the resistance that was lurking in Forn Forest.

'You've *seen* them?' Swain gasped.

'Corban?' Cywen asked.

'He is not there,' Trigg said. Cywen's heart felt as if it stopped.

'But he is still alive. Or was. I heard him being discussed. He was taken by the Jotun. Some of your friends have gone after him.'

Thank Elyon he lives. And that explains why he has not responded to Calidus' challenge.

'Mam and Da? Were they there?' Sif asked, tears in her eyes.

'I saw Wulf,' Trigg said, her lip curling. 'Not Hild.'

'Hild is with me, at the hospice,' Cywen said, looking at the anguish in the children's eyes and unable to keep it from them any longer.

'Why did you not tell us?' Swain gasped.

'Fear,' Cywen said. 'I'll explain and apologize properly later.' She was staring at Trigg, still trying to process all that she'd heard.

How can I trust her? She's betrayed us once. I do not understand her.

'Why are you doing this?' Cywen asked her. 'You have made your deal with Calidus, you'll be rewarded by him. Why are you even here, trying to be our friend, bringing Corban's claws and mail, trying to win his favour?'

Trigg shifted, sat up against the wall. Buddai growled. 'Because this is not who I *am*,' she eventually said. 'One act of darkness, of treachery. But also many of loyalty, too. Judge me by the sum of my deeds, not just the one mistake.'

Tears leaked from her eyes, her expression as miserable as anything Cywen had ever seen.

Trigg looked around at them all, settling upon Haelan.

'And, I do not want to be alone. I thought Haelan was my friend.'

They stood there in silence a while, each of them going over Trigg's revelations.

Eventually Cywen took a deep breath.

'They have to know,' she said. 'The warband out there. About all of it – the Treasures, the Jotun, Lykos.' She looked at Haelan, Swain and Sif, their faces so serious, so scared.

'We're getting out of here, tonight.'

CHAPTER FIFTY-THREE

CAMLIN

Camlin stood on the riverbank adjusting his chainmail shirt. Beneath it he was wearing a linen shirt and wool undershirt, and yet still the chainmail chaffed his shoulders.

'Don't like this,' he muttered, tying an iron helm to his belt.

'Stop complaining, you look quite fetching,' Edana said, 'even if the colours are all wrong.'

Camlin pulled a face, shrugging the black and gold cloak over his shoulder.

He was standing alongside Vonn, who was dressed similarly in the black and gold worn by Rhin's men.

'Reckon we'll pass for men out of Rhin's warband,' Camlin grunted. 'Glad we kept and carried all that war gear around, now.'

'I'm not happy it's just the two of you,' Halion said, standing at Edana's shoulder, a frown on his face.

'Three,' a voice piped up; Meg was standing by their boat.

'You're only coming so far,' Camlin said, waving a stern finger at her. 'And this time you do what you're told, else you'll not be invited next time.'

'Have to tie me up,' Meg muttered.

'That can be arranged,' Camlin said firmly. 'And Halion, we've talked it through. Numbers won't make any difference, unless we march a thousand swords into Dun Carreg. The fewer we are, the easier to sneak in, snatch what we want and get out again. Vonn's got to be there, because only he knows where his da's secret room is. And me, the perfect choice when sneaking and stealing are called for.'

'Aye, well. I'd be happier if you had a couple of solid lads with you,' said Halion.

'Then you'll be glad I'm here,' a voice said behind them.

They all turned to see Lorcan stepping out of the forest gloom, Brogan with him, a long spear in his hand. Both were clad in Rhin's black and gold, a poor-fitting helm on Brogan's big head.

Thought this was a secret mission.

'No,' Edana told him. 'You're heir to the throne of Domhain. You can't just go wandering into your enemy's stronghold.'

'You're not my lord, Edana. We are equals, you and I,' Lorcan said, his jaw set in a stubborn line, 'and I will not be told to stay here, not by you or by anyone else.'

He stood there, a silence settling between them, Edana looking as if she had just swallowed a wasp.

'It's your mission,' Edana finally said, looking at Camlin. 'What do you think?'

He is handy with a blade; I've seen him sparring. And No-Neck is always good to have around.

'You'll obey my every order, no questions?' Camlin asked Lorcan.

'Every one, meticulously,' Lorcan said, sensing victory.

Camlin looked at Vonn, who shrugged.

'All right. Time's wasting, let's away,' he said, and with that they were clambering into a rowing-boat that Camlin had stolen while on a foraging and reconnaissance run beyond the forest. Camlin lay his unstrung bow down, wrapped in deerskin and tied tight.

Halion pulled Lorcan into an embrace. 'Look after yourself, little brother,' he said, and Lorcan's eyes shone.

Soon Vonn and Brogan were rowing them downstream, Edana and Halion standing on the riverbank, hands raised in farewell. They left the Baglun behind them as twilight settled, climbed out and carried the boat over a shallow ford, then clambered back in, rowing a little further before their tributary joined the river Tarin. A shadow flitting across Camlin and a squawk from above told him that Craf was with them.

'Darol's hold,' Vonn murmured, and Camlin saw the young warrior gazing up at a shallow hill to the north that rose between them and Dun Carreg. With a jolt Camlin remembered it, a sick sensation unfurling in his gut. It was the hold he had raided while working for

Braith, under the guidance of Evnis. A raid that had gone badly wrong, women and bairns dying . . .

I've done bad things, sure enough, or been party to them. But things are different now. I'm different now. Got a cause to fight for. Friends. People I believe in. Can't change the past, but I can be a better man now.

The river widened, carving through the coastline, a cove of granite cliffs rearing above them. As the current met with the tide and rowing became harder, Camlin and Lorcan lifted oars, and Meg in the prow searched for mudbanks and rocks as waves slapped against the hull.

They grated on something, stuck for a few heartbeats, and then a swell lifted them free.

'It's not a good stretch of coast for night rowing,' Vonn said over the roar of the sea.

Now he tells me.

The dark maw of a cave loomed before them. Camlin looked up at a sheer cliff face composed of varying shades of darkness and shadow, the moon appearing from behind scudding clouds to turn the foam-flecked sea silver-tipped for a few heartbeats.

They'd made it to the bay at Dun Carreg, somehow avoiding being dashed on the cliffs and treacherously submerged rocks, and now Meg was holding the boat steady on the gentle swell, as Camlin stood with Vonn, Lorcan and Brogan before the huge cave that bored into the base of the precipice that Dun Carreg sat upon.

'Must confess, this doesn't bring back good memories,' Camlin muttered, staring at the great hole they were about to enter.

Once they turned the first bend in the tunnel Camlin reached into his pack, pulling out a torch of dried rushes, and lit it to show the path they were walking on, slick with water and seaweed, beside them the swell and roar of an ever-narrowing channel. Then they were at the cave's end, or so it appeared. Camlin walked into the wall, felt a pressure build around him, a resistance, like walking through water, then with a popping in his ears he was through, standing in a wide chamber, at its far end steps leading upwards into a dark corridor.

Behind him Vonn, Lorcan and Brogan pushed through the glamour of the wall.

'Didn't much like that,' Brogan muttered, then stood open-mouthed as he pointed at a huge skeleton that lay upon the ground before them. 'What's that?'

'Oh, that's a white wyrm we killed last time we passed this way,' Vonn said lightly.

'Think there's any more of these beasties slithering around down here?' Brogan asked, scanning the shadows.

'Guess we'll soon find out,' Camlin said, and began the long climb to Dun Carreg.

'There it is,' Vonn said, pointing to a blacker shadow in the wall ahead of them. They'd been climbing endless winding stairwells for what felt like days.

'There what is?' asked Lorcan, who despite the darkness and potential for sudden death seemed remarkably cheerful.

'The entrance to my father's tower,' Vonn replied and led them to what turned out to be a hole in the granite, partly bricked and boarded up, that led into a basement.

There were no signs or sounds of life.

'It's empty,' Vonn said. 'I thought as much. This is the place where my mother lived. And died . . .' He trailed off a moment, lost in some memory.

Camlin patted him awkwardly on the back.

'This way,' Vonn said, leading them up a stairwell that opened up into a reception hall. At the far end of the hall were two great doors, one of them ajar, letting in a beam of silver moonlight. Vonn continued up the stairs, pausing to hold his torch closer to the steps, frowning. Camlin saw it too. Footprints in the dust.

Vonn hurried up the remaining steps, across a landing and into a single chamber, sparsely furnished. An open window let moonlight in; shutters had been ripped from their hinges and cast upon the floor. On the far wall a tapestry hung, half-torn, an open door visible behind it.

Vonn swore as he strode to the door and peered through it.

'They got here before us,' he said, stepping out and punching the wall.

'There must be something we can do,' Lorcan said, ever the optimist.

'What, like sneak into the keep and steal it from under Rhin's nose?' Vonn said bitterly. 'Camlin might be a good thief, but he's not that good.'

'*I am,*' a voice croaked from the open window.

CHAPTER FIFTY-FOUR

RAFE

Rafe paced down the corridor, walking past Roisin's new chambers. He heard laughter echoing from within and ground his teeth as he turned a corner.

Morcant is a puffed-up fool, taken in by a woman's smile and charms. Don't think Rhin'll be too pleased.

He grinned viciously at that thought.

Days had passed since Rafe and Morcant had returned, in which Rafe had discovered that Rhin and Uthas had drunk from the star-stone cup and as yet had not awakened. Rafe had used the free time to reacquaint himself with the fortress. He looked around Evnis' tower, the kennels he used to tend, and wandered the halls of Dun Carreg, reliving memories, with Scratcher a constant shadow at his side. Today had left him in a black mood, though, because all memories led to that hateful night when he'd fought Corban in the court of swords, and lost. The night when Corban and his wolven had slain Rafe's da. Now he was heading for Rhin, hoping that she'd awoken.

I want to get on with this war. Rhin said we're going to Drassil, and that's where Corban is supposed to be. Maybe I'll get to challenge him to another court of swords. Now that is something I'd look forward to.

He spent some time imagining how that would turn out – each version ending with Corban defeated and begging for his life. Rafe was smiling by the time he reached Rhin's chambers.

Rhin's guards greeted him with a curt nod, one of them opening a door for him. He walked in, shivering as he remembered the last time he had been in here, when Rhin contacted Conall through her frame of wood and flayed skin.

The table was empty of all of that now, just one thing sat on it: an old casket, a black velvet cushion within it, and upon that a necklace of silver and jet.

Not jet – the stone is carved from a fallen star. The starstone necklace.

The necklace was of twisted silver, thin wire knotted around a black stone, like silver veins threading through a black heart. As Rafe stared, it seemed to pulse, and for a moment he thought he heard whispered voices, a host of them swirling around him.

He shook his head, staggered a little, as if dizzy.

'You all right?' Salach asked him, one eyebrow raised. He was standing with Eisa by the open window, the sound of the sea and the smell of salt spray drifting in from the darkness. Eisa looked much better now than when Rafe had found her staggering out from the Baglun.

'Aye,' Rafe grunted. 'Rhin?'

'No change,' Salach said, nodding to a closed door. 'With Uthas. The cup does its work upon them.'

Rafe knew what that was like, remembered the ecstasy and the agony. And the waking up, too, a tidal wave of new sensations crashing upon his senses.

'How long before you woke?' Eisa asked him.

Rafe shrugged. 'Morcant said it was a ten-night.'

'It's been sixteen nights, now,' Salach grunted.

Rafe pulled up a chair and sat before the necklace, staring at it.

'I had strange dreams last night,' Eisa said to Salach. 'In them I saw Nemain.' The giant was staring at Salach, watching him intently. 'She spoke to me. She called me a traitor.'

'Traitor, hero, all depends on your perspective,' Salach muttered.

'How did she die?' Eisa asked.

'I have told you. She attacked our allies at the gates of Murias. Uthas challenged her and they argued, struggled. She slipped and fell from her tower window, a tragic accident.'

'I remember now,' Eisa said, nodding to herself. Rafe saw her eyes flicker briefly to the twin blades of Salach's axe, curving over his back like iron wings.

The door suddenly creaked open. Rhin was standing there, silver hair dishevelled, yet she looked radiant, younger, a glow to her skin, a sparkle and vitality in her eyes. She threw her head back and laughed, the sound warm and resonant. Behind her Uthas stirred on a bed, sitting, rubbing his head.

'Food and drink,' Rhin clapped as she strode into the room, swaying a little, her legs unsteady, like a newborn colt taking its first steps around the paddock. She grabbed Rafe's hand, staring disconcertingly into his eyes, and licked her lips.

'I seem to have quite an appetite.'

Uthas filled the doorframe behind Rhin, staggering like a drunkard, but nevertheless appearing more youthful, his skin having lost its grey pallor.

Then Salach and Eisa were talking at once, Uthas laughing a deep, booming laugh, Rhin still holding Rafe's hand and staring into his eyes, far too intently for Rafe's liking.

A blast of cold air and a flapping sound filtered through the noise. Rafe turned to see something black come hurtling through the window. A bird, flapping and landing on the table, skidding to a halt and grasping the chain of the starstone necklace in an oil-black beak. For one moment it stood on the table, beady eyes darting about, locking with Rafe's, silence settling upon the room as men, giants and a queen all stared in dumbfounded shock at the crow. Then it was airborne, flapping away, back out of the window.

CHAPTER FIFTY-FIVE

CAMLIN

Camlin watched the crow swoop out of the window.

'Got it!' Lorcan declared with satisfaction as he caught and dangled a necklace from his hand.

'*Hurry*,' the crow squawked.

Not yet, thought Camlin, his arm starting to tremble from maintaining the draw on his bow. The outline of a head appeared at the window high above. Camlin released his arrow, the head leaped back. He heard the crack of an arrow-point skittering off stone, a yell from within the room.

'Lead on,' Camlin grunted, turning and following Vonn as they ran through a dark and deserted street. Behind them, from the room in the keep, shouts rang out, closely followed by horn blasts.

Camlin and the others sprinted through a maze of streets, all about them lights appeared at windows, doors opening, warriors emerging, pulling on boots or buckling on sword-belts, the fortress coming to life in the wake of their passing.

They were heading back to Evnis' tower, Vonn leading the way. He was the first one through the gates, Lorcan and Brogan close behind, Camlin acting as rearguard. They pounded across the courtyard towards the stone steps and open doorway beyond that led to the tunnels and escape. Camlin skidded to a halt, shouted a warning.

When we left, the doors were closed.

A figure burst from the shadows of Evnis' tower, crashing into Vonn, sending them both tumbling down the steps. A giant's figure filled the doorway, at the same time as Camlin spun to see the gates filling with more men and giants behind them.

No going back through the gates, and there'll be no getting into the tower and to the tunnels. He looked around frantically, past kennels to a stairwell set in the outer wall. Hardly slowing, he grabbed Lorcan's cloak and shoved him that way, Brogan following, at the same time drawing and nocking, sending an arrow into the mass of men coming through the gateway. He heard a scream, didn't wait around to see who his arrow had hit; instead he tracked the man locked in combat with Vonn, but they were too entwined. They rolled to a stop and then Vonn's voice grunted.

'Rafe?'

The other figure froze for a heartbeat, and Camlin drew, blocking out the sound of onrushing feet from the gateway, and released.

Somehow Rafe knew, whether by some instinct or he heard the creak and twang of the bow, Camlin did not know, but Rafe hurled himself away from Vonn, the arrow aimed for his throat sinking into the meat of his thigh instead.

A giant surged out of the doorway towards them, Rafe bellowed, a mixture of pain and rage, and then Camlin was running, Vonn tight on his heels, both of them sprinting along past the wooden kennels and up the stairwell, taking them two at a time.

They climbed, higher, Vonn's laboured breathing right behind him, the bulk of Brogan above him, waiting.

What do we do when we get to the top of the wall?

A hurled spear hissed past his ear and cracked into the stairs ahead of him, falling away.

'Duck!' Brogan yelled, as he hurled his own spear over their heads. It struck a warrior a stride behind Vonn hard as a hammer, piercing chainmail, sinking deep into his chest, sending the man flying back into those behind him.

Then Camlin was at the top, a cold wind whipping across the battlements. Vonn hurried behind him, Brogan was moving forwards to cut down the first man he met with a diagonal slash carving through cheek and jaw. A two-handed swing sent the next one slipping and tumbling off the steps.

Camlin loosed an arrow hissing into the mass of men crushed on the steps, heard a scream, nocked again, loosed, saw another man fall.

I could do this all night, he thought, *or as long as my bag of arrows lasts.* Without taking his eyes from the enemies on the stairwell, he brushed a hand over the quiver at his belt, counted ten or twelve more feathers.

Shouting drew his attention along the wall, where a knot of warriors were heading their way. They'd soon be surrounded.

Really need t'think of something, quick.

'Any ideas?' he yelled.

'Hoping you'd be the man for that,' Vonn grunted back to him, deflecting a spear aimed at Brogan.

Then a giant was on the steps before Brogan, a double-bladed axe in his hands, and Brogan was stepping back, defending raggedly, the power in the giant's blows too much for him.

Camlin aimed at the giant's heart, loosed, saw his arrow chopped from the air, splintered; Rafe was standing half a step behind the giant, eyes fixed on Camlin.

I put an arrow through his thigh. He shouldn't be here. I really need t'put that lad in the ground.

Brogan stumbled back another step, one more and he was back on the battlements.

'Hold,' a voice cried from the stairwell.

The giant paused, looked back.

A figure in gleaming mail and black leather climbed the stairs, slipping past the giant.

'Morcant,' Camlin muttered with hatred. He knew him from way back.

'You've got nowhere to go,' Morcant said, raising a hand to the warriors closing on Camlin and his companions. They formed up a score of paces away, swords and spears bristling. Behind Morcant half-shadowed warriors gathered, iron threatening, and another hulking giant. Camlin blinked, recognizing Eisa.

'You can fight to the death, brave men that you are,' Morcant shrugged. 'Or you can give us the necklace, and him.' He pointed at Lorcan. 'Oh, aye, I know who you are, Lorcan ben Eremon. So, the stone and Lorcan, and the rest of you walk out of here alive.'

'You're a whore-born liar,' Camlin said calmly, and sniffed. 'No point making deals with the likes of you.'

'On my honour,' Morcant said.

'That counts for nothing,' Camlin laughed.

Morcant's eyes narrowed. 'I remember you,' he said. 'Braith's snivelling arseling in the Darkwood. You've been a thorn in my flesh a long time. I think I'm going to kill you soon.'

'He's mine!' Rafe shouted from a few steps back.

Camlin glanced at the others: Vonn frowning, Brogan's face set, ready. Lorcan was chewing his lip.

He's a good lad, and still with a head full of nobility and glory. He'd like t'save us.

'Morcant's a snake,' Camlin said, 'you can't trust him.'

'I do understand your reasoning,' Morcant said. 'But if you can't trust me, perhaps you can trust . . .' He beckoned and a cloaked figure appeared, obviously a woman, the warriors on the stairs parting for her. She walked a step higher than Morcant and stopped, pulling the hood from her head.

Lorcan hissed.

'Mam,' he whispered.

'Oh, Lorcan, my boy,' Roisin said, a tremor in her voice.

She's supposed t'be dead in Dun Crin's swamps!

'I forgive you, my darling,' Roisin said to Lorcan. 'I understand. You were infatuated with Edana. But come, join me now. Make everything right again.'

'You made me choose. And what you wanted to do – it was wrong. And what of Rhin?' Lorcan said. 'You said she will kill us. You always said that.'

'Things have changed,' Roisin replied. 'Rhin has bigger enemies than us to deal with now. I have been talking with Morcant, and he is regent of Ardan, high in her favour. Rhin is unhappy with Conall's rule in Domhain, and she searches for someone who will rule Domhain in her name. That could be us. You. Morcant says if you bend the knee to her, swear fealty, Rhin will be merciful.'

'Serve *her*?' Lorcan snapped. 'She killed my da.'

'Aye,' Roisin admitted, 'a terrible deed, and a mistake. But this is war, bad things happen, and we must look to the future. Sometimes we need to forgive and move on. For all our sakes, and for the sake of our people in Domhain.'

'And my companions?' Lorcan said.

He's wavering. Sure enough, she might have made some bargain t'save her and Lorcan's skins, but I don't reckon Morcant's about t'let me and the others walk out of here with our heads on our shoulders.

'Morcant's a liar,' Camlin said to the boy.

'Enough,' Roisin said. 'Lorcan, come to me.' She held her hand out. 'Please.'

'I have your oath, Mam? They'll live?'

'Of course, my darling,' she said.

'On my life?' Lorcan said.

'Yes, and mine, too.'

'Don't do it,' Camlin hissed at Lorcan.

'It's our only chance,' he said quietly. 'She'll not harm me, she's my mam, and I've seen the effect she has on men. Once she has them they'll do anything for her. Look at the way Morcant's looking at her.' He shrugged. 'I'll be a prisoner, but who knows, maybe you'll come and rescue me. But only if you get out of here alive.'

And then, before Camlin had a chance to grab him, Lorcan strode down the steps, towards Roisin.

'You *and* the necklace,' Roisin said. 'I've begged and pleaded for your life, and the bargain only stands if you have the necklace.'

'It's here,' Lorcan said, putting his hand inside his shirt of mail. He'd placed it around his neck while he fought. He sheathed his sword and lifted the necklace free, clutching it tight in his fist, and walked down the stairwell. He took Roisin's out-held hand.

'Set them free,' Lorcan said to Morcant.

'Of course,' the regent of Ardan said. Then he stepped forwards and punched a knife into Lorcan's throat.

Roisin screamed as Lorcan began to crumple. With one last great surge of strength Lorcan heaved his arm upwards, launching the starstone necklace high into the air. Morcant stared at it, reaching out. There was the whisper of wings, a dark shape swooping down to pluck the necklace from the air, just before Morcant's fist snapped shut, and then Craf was swooping upwards, a shadow in the night.

Roisin wailed, wrapping her arms about Lorcan, falling to her knees as his body collapsed, one hand on his throat, trying to stem the pulsing blood.

Another cloak-wrapped figure strode up the stairwell. Rhin. She grabbed the wailing woman and effortlessly dragged her to her feet.

'Did you think that my Morcant was under your spell?' Rhin snarled. 'That he was yours to use?' She stabbed Roisin in the belly with a knife, twisted it and pulled it free. Roisin gasped, hands clutching at her wound. Her legs buckled and she fell to the steps.

'Foolish woman,' Morcant smiled, kicking Roisin's body down the steps, limbs flopping.

Brogan gave out a great bellow as he bunched his huge shoulders and charged down the stairwell like an enraged bull.

'No-Neck!' Camlin yelled after Brogan, but the warrior was battle-mad and full of vengeance for Lorcan, deaf to words. He threw himself into the cluster of figures on the stairwell, all of them crashing to the ground, even the giants, figures unbalanced, tumbling down steps, some falling with a wail over the edge, Brogan rolling amongst them, still bellowing his fury.

Camlin looked at Vonn, both of them knowing there was no getting Brogan back.

'Let's jump,' Camlin shouted at Vonn.

'We'll die,' Vonn said.

'Probably,' Camlin shrugged, 'but some chance is better'n no chance in my book.' He leaped onto the battlement, Vonn hesitating a moment, then climbing up beside him.

'I'll see you after,' Camlin shouted, wind snatching his words as he jumped into the darkness.

CHAPTER FIFTY-SIX

LYKOS

Lykos hoisted his pack onto his back, pacing in front of his gathered men.

My ship-breakers.

His best men, the ones he used to storm a ship in a sea battle. Many of them were men who had been with him from the beginning, when he had united the Three Islands, and that meant wading through a sea of blood and iron to crush his rivals and take the islands for his own. Eighty killing machines, each one proven a hundred times over, with the scars to give testimony.

Hard men, one and all.

He glanced up at the sky; the full moon was painting the world in shades of blue-black, gossamer clouds shimmering as if they were gilt-edged.

The drum of footsteps, and Calidus was walking into the courtyard, Legion looming behind him, more Kadoshim following.

'All is ready?' Calidus asked him.

'Aye.'

'Many years we have laboured together, you and I, and now we are so close. I have been faithful, made you Lord of the Vin Thalun, the Three Islands united behind you. You remember, your heart's desire?'

'I do,' Lykos whispered, his mind abruptly cast back to a windswept starry night on a hilltop, surrounded by the glistening velvet of the sea. A fire, a pot, knife and blood.

And Asroth. He felt the scar across his palm.

'There will be more, so much more, if we win this war,' Calidus said. 'Riches and rewards beyond your wildest dreams.'

My dreams can be very wild, but I like the sound of that. Though when Calidus talked of dreams only one thing hovered in Lykos' mind. *Fidele.*

She could be my reward.

But what of Nathair? He would take a very dim view of how I would wish things to turn out.

Lykos licked his lips.

'We need the starstone torc. Bring it back to me, make the end of this war that much closer.' Calidus' grip upon Lykos' shoulder tightened, became painful, but Lykos did not shrink away.

'I will,' Lykos said, 'or die in the trying.'

'Good,' Calidus smiled, teeth glinting in the moonlight. He released Lykos' shoulder.

'Onwards, then.'

And with that they were moving out, his men shouldering their five boats, the great gates opening. Calidus stopped at the gateway and Lykos passed beneath the deep stone archway, leading the way out onto the dark plain, Legion beside him, the other ten Kadoshim split between vanguard and rearguard.

Ninety-two of us, all told. Hardly the hugest warband the world has seen, but this is all I will need. Speed and stealth is the key, and good men at my back if it comes to a scrap.

They crossed the plain quickly enough, soon reaching the treeline, where they took advantage of Jael's road for a short while. They left it when the road curled north-west, and carved their way north into the forest. It was not long before Lykos heard the sound of running water.

The river was wide, sparkling with foam, the current strong.

It'll be hard going, rowing a hundred leagues up this beast, but it's better than walking through Forn.

Lykos oversaw the boats being set into the river, mooring them to trees, steering rudders set into their fixings, oars threaded through oarlocks, masts and sails tied tight, not enough wind to make them useful.

'Lads, when you're done, have a breather,' Lykos said. 'I'll be back soon. Hesp, Damas, with me.' He turned and paced along the riverbank, heading west, the two Vin Thalun setting off after their lord.

'Where are you going?' a voice said behind him; Legion was joining them. The familiar buzzing of flies surrounded his voice.

'Going to see an old friend,' Lykos said.

'The mission,' Legion growled.

'Will be fine,' Lykos grunted, 'I'll not go far.'

Legion fell in beside him, the four of them passing through dense undergrowth, climbing over fallen trees, skirting around thickets with as little noise as possible, always keeping the river within hearing distance. They came across Jael's road, clambering up the embankment and down the other side, and then travelled on a while longer.

Did that half-breed bitch lie to me? Lykos thought, the sense that he should stop and turn back growing and building inside him.

You're being a fool, risking everything, and for what? Calidus would have my skin peeled if he knew. He glanced at Legion.

Just a few more paces, then I'll turn back.

Yet still he walked on, his obsession drawing him like a lodestone.

Eventually Legion put a hand out and grabbed Lykos' wrist. It wasn't a pleasant sensation, the Kadoshim's flesh cold and clammy, flies crawling over Lykos' arm.

'We must be away before dawn,' the Kadoshim said. 'No further.'

Lykos felt a rush of anger. He didn't take too well to Calidus telling him what to do, and he was damned if another Kadoshim was going to suffer with delusions of grandeur and start pushing him around.

Legion's head snapped around, cocked to one side, listening, sniffing.

'What?' Lykos whispered, hand on the hilt of his short sword.

'Something ahead,' Legion said. He sniffed again, a long indrawn breath. 'Something dead.'

'Show me,' Lykos said, excitement dancing in his belly.

Legion padded ahead of him, Lykos following, the Kadoshim stopping before a dense shadow, big as a boulder. The whiff of rot hit Lykos' nose. He reached out, touched the boulder-like shadow before Legion, felt fur, a ridge of bone. Looking down, he saw a huge head, flesh from the muzzle gnawed away, revealing a set of long sharp teeth.

'What is it?' Legion muttered.

'A giant bear,' Lykos said. He was grinning and started to walk on. 'Just a little further,' he whispered into the darkness.

CHAPTER FIFTY-SEVEN

FIDELE

'How will you get in?' Fidele asked Veradis.

'I haven't quite figured that out, yet,' Veradis said, frowning. 'We'll need a diversion so we won't be scrutinized too closely.'

Fidele was standing with the leaders of the resistance, all of them looking at Veradis and his hundred or so men, the warriors clothed in the black and silver of Tenebral. Veradis' cuirass was polished to a high shine, the white eagle bright upon his chest. The men behind them had blacked out the sigil on their breastplates, the tower of Ripa.

Fidele held a torch high and peered closer at the first row.

'It won't bear up to any kind of close inspection,' she said, not for the first time.

'That's why I need to do it at night, and why some kind of diversion needs to be happening,' Veradis shrugged.

'We could fake an attack on Drassil's walls, make some noise . . .' Balur said.

'Are you sure this is wise?' Fidele asked Veradis.

Veradis tugged at his short beard. 'No,' he said eventually, 'but there are prisoners being tortured to death in there, every day. Our people.'

He is a good man. In many ways the man I wish my son had grown into. Fidele felt a twist of pain at that thought, a pinch upon her heart.

'If we can get through the gates I can take you to the hospice where they are all kept,' Ilta the Jehar said. She was standing in the ranks of Veradis' men, wearing one of their cuirasses, her long black hair bound up and pinned within an iron helm.

'Won't you be recognized?' Krelis asked Veradis. 'Aside from the

Draig's Teeth, which you hope have gone with Nathair, there are likely to be others who recognize you. Like Calidus. There are close to another two thousand eagle-guard wandering around inside those walls.'

'I know,' Veradis muttered. 'I thought to boil up some tree bark and dye my hair.' He shrugged and smiled sheepishly. 'And it will be dark,' he added.

'I could do it,' Krelis said.

He fears for his brother, but would never say it, so he seeks to find another way.

'Don't be a fool, you're as tall as a giant,' Brina said snorting her contempt. 'The idea is to be inconspicuous.'

'We should wait, think on it some more,' Alben said.

'Why?' Veradis said. 'Every day more will die. This plan is as good as it's going to get. I would go tonight.' His eyes flicked between Fidele and Brina, who out of this disparate council of captains seemed to have gravitated to the position of leaders.

Fidele looked at Veradis; the man was earnest, brave.

I admire him for wanting to do this, but it could end in disaster.

'It would be a bold strike,' Javed said, smiling. 'One that we'd sing songs about. I'd like to come.'

'And trust you to keep your knives sheathed amongst all those Vin Thalun?' Wulf said.

'No,' Veradis said. 'Only me and my men. Discipline and a knowledge of the shield wall's formations are essential. Your strengths are best used elsewhere,' he added to Javed.

'So?' Veradis asked, looking again to Brina and Fidele.

Brina gave a short nod.

'Go with our blessing,' Fidele said, 'and come back to us alive.'

'I'll do my best,' Veradis grinned.

There he is, Fidele thought, standing and watching the day's scouts returning. Maquin was amongst those coming back. She enjoyed the sense of relief that flowed through her body, the same as she always felt upon his safe return.

This is Forn; it is not just Kadoshim, Vin Thalun and eagle-guard that are our enemy out there.

She smiled, relishing the sight of him, all lean muscle and gracefulness, an economy in every step, nothing wasted or overdone. He saw her and returned her smile, his stern face of sharp lines, scars and shadows transformed for a few moments.

'What's going on? Looks like someone's kicked an ants' nest,' he asked as he reached her, sweeping her into a bone-crushing embrace, their lips meeting. She loved that he did that, no regard for status or standing, just the two of them, as if the world around them did not exist.

'Veradis is leading a rescue attempt on the prisoners inside Drassil,' she said.

'What? I knew he'd been thinking about something, but tonight? I'd best go see where he wants to use me,' Maquin said, taking a step away.

'I'll tell you the plan,' she said, gripping his hand and pulling him away. 'After.'

'After what?'

She smiled and led him away.

'What's the occasion?' Maquin asked as Fidele gestured to the ground. A small patch of grass and wildflowers alongside a narrow stream, furs of bear and deer laid out upon it, with two cups and a skin of something, as well as fresh-cooked meat and vegetables.

'I wanted to talk with you,' Fidele said. 'It is rare, living as we are, to have any privacy.'

'It is,' Maquin agreed.

'So,' she said, gesturing at the furs.

Maquin reclined on them and Fidele poured him a cup of mead, some of the last from the supplies they'd taken from Gundul's camp. She watched him drink, Maquin's eyes never leaving Fidele's.

They ate in silence, slowly, enjoying each other's company, the fact that they didn't have to speak.

Fidele poured Maquin some more mead.

When they had finished eating, Fidele sat straighter. 'I want to talk to you about . . . after,' she said.

Maquin blinked at her.

Not what he was expecting, then. Even the champion of the pits can be taken by surprise sometimes.

'You're a queen; me –' he paused, brows furrowing – 'I'm not sure what I am any more. Was a shieldman, then one of the Gadrai, next a slave, then a pit-fighter. Now, I don't know what you'd call me. Except happy.' He smiled at her, a shy, tentative shifting of his lips, almost out of place on the face of this death-dealer before her. 'But, whatever you feel you need to say, I understand. You've the responsibility of a realm upon your shoulders, I—'

'Quiet,' Fidele ordered.

Maquin looked as if he was going to argue for a moment, but then he shrugged, lay back on one elbow and waited for her to speak.

'I am a woman who sees things as they are, and I think this war will most likely be the end of us,' she said. 'Not just you and me, but all of us. We are outnumbered, and our enemy are terrible. Kadoshim, a nation of Vin Thalun.' She shook her head. 'My own son and his warband, most of the strength of Tenebral. But we fight on, because it is what we should do. But the chances of us surviving this . . .'

'Are slim,' Maquin finished for her.

'Aye. But if we manage those rarest of things, both to win and to survive, then I would have you know that to me at least, this, *us*, is for always. Not just now, or while this war lasts, but for as long as I draw breath.' She had held his gaze throughout every word. 'You are precious to me,' she finished, her courage fading at the last, her eyes dropping away.

A silence settled on them. The chattering of the stream, the sounds of Veradis' warband making ready for their expedition, all faded around her.

Maquin moved, suddenly close to her, a handspan between them, and her heart was racing. He leaned closer and kissed her lips, a soft caress.

'I came back from death for you,' he said, his voice a whispered tremor. 'For me it was always forever, however long that may be. And those words you just spoke, they are the greatest gift I've ever been given. They are written upon my heart and soul.'

'Then let me give you another gift,' she said, smiling, her heart soaring, grabbing his leather jerkin and pulling him onto her.

*

Maquin's gentle snoring tickled Fidele's ear. She'd been lying beside him, running a finger along the contour of his jaw, down his neck and across his chest, most of it criss-crossed by an abundance of scars. The two of them lay wrapped in fur, bodies entwined. Slowly, carefully, Fidele extricated herself, stood and dressed. When she was ready, she bent and kissed his cheek.

'Forgive me,' she whispered, then stood and slipped to where Agost and her shieldmen were a few dozen paces away, waiting for her.

'All is ready,' Agost said, handing Fidele her spear.

'Who is staying with Maquin?' Fidele asked.

'Spyr,' Agost said, and a warrior stepped forwards, a younger man, dark-haired.

'Give him this when he wakes,' Fidele said, handing Spyr a rolled parchment scroll. 'It will likely not be before highsun.'

Brina's sleeping potion is powerful.

Fidele had asked Brina for it a few days ago, saying she had trouble sleeping and it had been simple enough to slip it into the skin of mead that Maquin had drunk from.

Maquin would have tried to stop me, fearing for my safety. But I know what I am doing is right. It must be done.

'Come, then,' Fidele said, and strode through the camp, her half-dozen shieldmen wrapping around her, Agost at their head. Veradis and his men were moving out, marching into the forest, torchlight and darkness revealing giants moving like shadowy trees. Fidele and her men attached themselves to the rearguard, marching with them out of the camp and into the forest. She stayed with them for a while, then Agost signalled to her and they dropped back a little, stopped beside the trunk of a huge tree and waited for Veradis' men to disappear into the darkness.

'This way, my lady,' Agost said, and they turned away from the warband's path, heading east for a while.

The plan was to find Jael's road and take it south-east to the plain of Drassil. From there they would skirt the forest's edge and follow the path that Nathair's draig and warband had trampled through Forn.

I will find my son and speak to him. I will bring him back to us, if I can. And if not . . .

Her hand rested fleetingly upon the knife hilt at her belt.

She felt a pang of regret at not telling Maquin, at not confiding in him. And worse, drugging him so that he would not stop her.

A fly buzzed around her head. She swiped at it, only for more to appear, loud in the darkness. In front of her Agost slowed and stopped, staring into the darkness.

'Ware!' Agost yelled, sword hissing from his scabbard.

One of Fidele's guards fell into her, blood spurting from his throat as he toppled to the ground.

Fidele gripped her spear two-handed, spread her feet, spear-tip pointing at the darkness. Iron clashed behind her and she spun around, saw her guards fighting furiously against a black-clad figure, curved sword in his hand.

Fear clutched a fist around her heart.

Kadoshim. What are they doing out here? My men! What have I done?

She heard Agost's grunts, and she turned back to him, saw him trading blows with a bearded man in leather vest and breeches, a short sword in his hand, flesh pale in the moonlight.

A man. Better.

She gritted her teeth and stabbed her spear into his thigh. His face stared at her, shocked, as Agost finished him, hacking him down. She saw the glint of iron rings in his braided beard.

Vin Thalun.

Fidele turned, saw another of her men falling, an arc of black droplets.

A hand grabbed her wrist and she swung her spear like a staff, stopped when she saw it was Agost.

'This way,' he snarled. There was blood on his face.

Fidele looked at her men locked in combat.

'Leave them; they fight for you to survive. They will come if they can,' Agost grunted, dragging her a dozen paces, until a black shadow of a figure rose up in front of them, curved sword held high. Her vision was blurred; flies everywhere were drowning out other sound. She stabbed out half-blind, felt her blade bite into flesh.

The Kadoshim hacked at her spear shaft, splintering it.

Agost was there, his sword stabbing into the Kadoshim's throat, but it grabbed the blade and ripped it from Agost's grip, hurling it away into the undergrowth. Fidele drew her knife and threw herself at the Kadoshim, hacking at its neck, determined to saw its head from its body. The Kadoshim ignored her, chopped down at Agost as he tried to rise, the curved sword denting Agost's helm, sending him crashing back to the ground.

A fist snared in Fidele's hair, yanking her off the Kadoshim as she saw the creature grabbing Agost and lifting him up.

There was a wet ripping sound, Agost screaming sharp and loud, gurgling, the shieldman's arms flailing at the Kadoshim tearing at him. Then Agost was limp, silent, only the sounds of an animal feasting.

Fidele fought the urge to vomit, tried to spin in her attacker's grip; her knife still in her fist, she stabbed it at her assailant's waist, but a fist slammed into her jaw and she saw an explosion of stars, strength draining from her like water from a holed bucket and she slumped, only the fist still entwined in her hair keeping her upright.

'Hello Fidele,' Lykos said.

CHAPTER FIFTY-EIGHT

CYWEN

Cywen lay in her cot, staring at the Vin Thalun guard by the door. It was dark, probably the other side of midnight by now, and still the guard sitting in the hospice was awake.

You're usually snoring by now.

She heard a creak behind her, someone shifting in their bed.

Hild. Maybe she senses something. Cywen had been desperate to tell her of the plans. She wanted to tell everyone, to run through the hospice and warn them that tonight was the night. Over two hundred prisoners were in the hospice, none really unwell or needing treatment, now. Two were without limbs – one on a crutch, the other missing an arm to the elbow – but all were in their right minds, capable of making a decision, capable of leaving.

I have thought of this moment for so long, and now that it is here I am terrified. Only two options.

Escape or death. She gulped, because she knew failure and capture did not just mean death, it meant impalement.

Do not think on it. She knew that would lead to fear and indecision, and then it would be sunrise, and the time would be gone.

She pulled her blanket high, up to her neck, and beneath it she very carefully and slowly took Corban's wolven claws out from her cloak and buckled them onto her wrist.

She waited, watching through half-closed lids. The Vin Thalun guard shifted, eyes drooping, then a hoot of laughter from beyond the doors jolted him fully awake.

Now or never, Cywen thought and slipped from her cot.

The guard scowled at her and she pointed at the bucket in the room's corner, what passed for a latrine for them.

He gave her a surly nod and she walked across the room, out of his line of sight. She kicked the latrine bucket over, gripped her stomach, groaning, doubled over.

'What is it?' the Vin Thalun asked irritably as he strode over to Cywen, putting a hand on her back. She punched the wolven claws up, into his throat, pushing him stumbling backwards into the wall. He tried to scream, only a gurgling hiss escaping from his lips, then he was sliding down the wall, a bloody smear upon it, eyes rolling up into his head.

Cywen stood there, frozen, listening to her heart thumping in her skull, eyes fixed on the doors, expecting them to burst open and Vin Thalun to pour in.

'What are you doing?' a voice hissed: Hild, rising from her bed. Others were sitting up, blinking, men and women from Gramm's hold, warriors who had been part of Jael's warband.

'Put these clothes on, quickly,' Cywen hissed as she stripped the dead Vin Thalun of his leather vest and belt. She took the knife for herself, scowled as she felt its weight – all wrong for throwing – passing the rest to Yalric, a warrior from Gramm's hold. His beard grown long while he'd been unwell, he was the closest amongst them to a Vin Thalun. The grin on his face as he buckled a sword-belt around his waist said he was ready for this.

'Help me,' Cywen grunted, dragging the dead Vin Thalun into the shadows. Hild hefted his ankles and they carried him into a corner, dropping him into darkness. Others were gathering around them, faces shocked, confused, blinking sleep away.

'What's going on?' one asked.

'We are getting out of here, now,' Cywen whispered.

'No – the stakes,' someone said, too loudly for Cywen's liking.

'There's just as much chance of that tomorrow and every other day while we stay here just waiting to be picked off,' hissed Cywen. 'I'm going, and I'll take as many as want to come with me.' She looked at Hild.

The stern woman returned her gaze, then gave a stiff nod.

'How?' Hild said.

'Out of the back window, across the herb gardens. There is a tunnel—'

'How do you know this?' Yalric asked her.

'I've seen it. No time to explain. We must go now.'

There was a moment's silence, then they were all moving, quietly waking any who were still asleep, whispering instructions, moving on. Cywen went to Brina's cupboard, selecting vials and pouches that she knew would come in useful. Soon they were all gathered at the foot of the wide stairwell that led to the balcony.

A shout of victory and a burst of laughter drifted through the doors, someone obviously winning on the throw-board in the court-yard beyond.

'We could just rush the guards,' Hild told her. 'We outnumber them.'

'No,' Cywen said, 'the noise. Others would come. We must get out, fast, silent, and be gone from here before any of them know about it.'

Cywen looked to Yalric, who was sitting in the guard's chair, dragged back a little from the fire so that he was more in shadow than light, a cloak pulled up around him. It would fool a cursory glance, nothing more. He held her gaze, nodded to her. He knew what would happen if any Vin Thalun walked through the door.

I'll get them all out.

With that she turned and sped up the stairs, twisted into her room, where bright moonlight was shining through the unshuttered window, ran to her cupboard, lifted the loose board and grabbed Brina's book, secreting it into a pocket in her cloak. By then others had followed her and Cywen started helping them climb through the window. Each one scurried into the herb garden and hid amongst the leaves, waiting in the shadows.

Ten out.

Hild went next, Cywen's heart thudding like a drum, and for an instant she smiled, thinking of Hild's reunion with Swain and Sif.

A noise rippled through the fortress like distant thunder, con-stant, repetitive, like hammer-blows upon a wall. Then horn blasts were echoing from the stone and bark, men's voices shouting, yell-ing. The slap of feet on stone.

What in the Otherworld's going on?

Everyone froze, inside the room, on the balcony, out in the herb garden, the same thought filling all their minds.

They know.

But then Cywen realized it all seemed a long way off. Yes, men were rallying from the streets around them, but they were heading *away* from the hospice, not towards it.

'Keep going,' she said, pulling on the next person.

Then the doors to the hospice were opening, an order barked. Shouting, the rasp of iron hissing from scabbards.

Cywen sprinted back to the balcony, saw Vin Thalun crowding through the doorway, Yalric on his feet, sword swinging, blood spraying. The first Vin Thalun fell back with his throat open, a dark jet. Yalric strode after the falling body, stabbing at the men crowding behind him, but in heartbeats too many men were surging through the door; Yalric was forced to step back. Another Vin Thalun fell, howling as he clutched his belly, then Yalric was spinning, stumbling back, swords chopping and stabbing at him. He tripped and disappeared as the guards closed about him.

Other Vin Thalun swarmed through the door, eyes searching the shadowed room, many of them running to the stairwell. Someone was frantically blowing a horn.

We have no weapons. It will be a slaughter.

'Move,' Cywen yelled, running back into the escape room. The window was crowded, too many trying to cram themselves through at the same time.

No, it cannot end here.

Some panicked, bolting from the room back onto the inner balcony of the hospice, Vin Thalun yelling and giving chase. Cywen took a step back, flexed the wolven claws on her fist, her other hand disappearing into her cloak, searching, grasping.

'Escape or death,' she muttered to herself, repeating it like a mantra.

Vin Thalun loomed in the doorway and she slashed at the first, sending him reeling with three red stripes across his face.

Others pushed past him, grabbing for her. She severed fingers with one swipe of the claws, raked across a thigh, stabbed into a throat, each time retreating a few steps, then she turned and ran, diving straight at the open window, even though there were still a handful of figures climbing through it. She slammed into them, sent them all hurtling through the opening, falling.

Cywen crashed into leaf and stem, moist earth exploding into her face, up her nose. She clambered to her feet, grunting with pain, saw Vin Thalun staring out of the window after her, some already clambering through.

The herb garden was chaos, her fellow prisoners, well over a hundred of them, milling and unsure what to do. Vin Thalun were appearing around the side of the building, coming from the main courtyard, the drum of many more feet behind them.

Cywen saw Hild and grabbed her hand.

'This way!' she yelled, everyone following her across the herb garden. 'Stay with me.'

Vin Thalun warriors blocked her path and Cywen skidded to a halt.

'Come quietly,' one of them said, 'and we won't kill you.'

Cywen reached inside her cloak, found what she'd been searching for, an oddly shaped vial. She hurled it at the man who had spoken and it smashed against his chest, liquid soaking into his jerkin, spraying those about him.

'What are you trying to do, soak me to death?' He grinned, his companions laughing.

Cywen threw another vial, this one dark, smashing and splattering.

'That's enough, now,' the Vin Thalun said, stepping forwards. 'I won't kill you. Might hurt you a little, though,' he added with a leer.

'*Fuil agus tine, salann agus lasair*,' Cywen hissed. A spark rippled across the Vin Thalun's chest, blue flame igniting, engulfing him in heartbeats. He spun, arms windmilling, crashing into those behind him, and the flame eagerly leaped between them, the stench of charring flesh suddenly thick in the air.

On Cywen ran, Hild behind her, the slap of other feet, then another Vin Thalun was leaping at her from the shadows, barrelling her to the ground.

Cywen bucked and slashed at him, but he punched her in the face with the buckler strapped to his forearm.

'Saw what you did, you witch,' he snarled, hatred and fear in his voice as he dragged Cywen to her feet. 'You set my lads on fire.'

He heaved her back towards the courtyard at the front of the hospice, where the Vin Thalun guards had been playing knuckle-bones around a fire, but were now rounding up the escaped prisoners. A glimpse over Cywen's shoulder showed Hild and a handful of others hovering in the shadows, watching her. Cywen tried to signal for them to go.

Go where? They don't know where I was taking them.

Cywen's captor threw her to the ground before the main doors to the hospice and, snatching up a spear, rammed it into the ground between two flagstones.

They're going to impale me, here and now.

She found some strength, then, throwing herself between her captors, hissing and spitting, kicking, biting, but they held her tightly, clubbed her across the head, sending her dropping to her knees, vision swirling.

She was hauled back to her feet and they bound her to the spear, smashing up stools and scattering the shattered wood around her.

'Set fire to us, will you? Well, you'll see what kind of a death that is,' her captor muttered as he stuck a wooden brand into the fire.

CHAPTER FIFTY-NINE

VERADIS

'Open the gates!' Veradis yelled as he ran towards the gates of Drassil, his hundred men in loose formation behind him, their shields up in a ragged wall. The sounds of a great tumult swept down from the northern edge of the fortress. As he glanced that way, Veradis saw a flaming branch spin high up over the battlements and fall inside the wall. Screams erupted.

When Alcyon said they'd make a distraction, I did not expect this.

He looked at the gates as he approached them. They loomed before him, still closed. Shadows framed by torchlight peered over the battlements above them.

Behind him battle-cries echoed from the forest and figures burst from the treeline: Balur and a dozen Benothi, all charging at him, brandishing hammer and axe, bellowing blood-curdling threats.

Remember – they must seem to be our enemies and we're scared of them.

Instinctively he picked up his pace, yelling again for the gates to open, praying that they would.

Closer, two hundred paces, still the gates remained closed.

Open, damn you, open! Veradis yelled in his head.

With a creak, a sliver of light appeared down the centre of the gates and they opened, just in time for Veradis and his disguised men to pour through them, maintaining their formation, the gates slamming shut behind them. A dozen heartbeats later and there was a series of concussive thuds as Balur and his kin reached the gates.

The courtyard was lit by fires and braziers, heaving with warriors, eagle-guard, Vin Thalun, and Veradis thought he glimpsed a few Kadoshim prowling amongst them. Horses whinnied and screamed from stables lined around the courtyard. Smoke billowed through the courtyard, a sign of the chaos caused by Alcyon at the north wall.

They think it's a full-on assault. Have we kicked the hornets' nest too hard? Will we ever get out of this pandemonium?

Amidst the smoke he saw something else, a mass of figures, standing in formation, he thought, then the smoke cleared a little and he realized what he was seeing. Men and women staked upon spears, looks of absolute terror and agony fixed in rigid lines upon their faces. The stench of decomposition wafted over Veradis, blending with the smoke.

He fought his first urge, which was to vomit, and his second, which was to draw his sword and start stabbing his enemy, those all around him who had committed or at the very least allowed this atrocity.

Faces appeared in front of him and he sucked in a deep breath, with difficulty subduing the urge for indiscriminate slaughter that was bubbling up within him. He had his helm tied tight, hair blackened with bark juice and grime smeared across his face, but still his heart was pounding in his throat as he saw dozens of faces that he recognized, men from the eagle-guard, though thankfully none of them was from his Draig's Teeth.

'I bring word for Calidus from King Nathair,' Veradis gasped to the first man who approached him. 'Where is he?'

'The north wall, I think,' the warrior said, a young man, all nervous energy, glancing beyond Veradis to the way the gates were shaking as Balur hurled things against them.

Veradis glanced at Ilta the Jehar, dressed in the silver and black of Tenebral, long black hair bound and hidden beneath an iron helm. She stepped out of formation and strode ahead of him, Veradis and his hundred following.

'This has to be quick,' Veradis said to Ilta as he caught up with her, 'else we're never getting out of here.'

She nodded, leading them through empty stone streets, towers and walls rearing high about them, the shifting movement of branches far above sending shadow and light dancing in ever-changing patterns.

I marvelled at Jerolin, the first time I saw it. Built by giants, but this . . .

The sound of shouting, raised voices, reached Veradis.

'Almost there,' Ilta said, falling back to him. 'There's a courtyard at the end of this street, the building at its far end is the hospice.'

'Marching formation,' he called. His men straightened their lines, Ilta merging with them, all of them slowing, looking more like eagle-guard. The darkness helped.

They swept into the courtyard, the building looming tall at its far end, before it a host of people. Veradis saw mostly Vin Thalun, fifty, sixty of them – it was hard to tell in the flickering light. They surrounded a huddle of people crushed close together, all on their knees. And before them, tied to a post, a fire licking at her feet, catching in her cloak, a young woman he recognized, screaming, her head lashing wildly.

Cywen.

'Stop this!' he yelled, striding forwards, drawing his short sword and banging it against his shield, his men behind him following suit. Heads turned, Vin Thalun and captives alike.

'Stop,' he shouted, pushing through the first row of Vin Thalun. He made it so far, then a warrior stood before him, feet spread, barring his way.

'Cut her free,' Veradis ordered, trying to push around the man.

'The witch burns,' the Vin Thalun snarled.

'I said, cut her free. Calidus wants all the prisoners, now,' Veradis barked, trying to get around the Vin Thalun, but the man moved to block him again.

'You can take the others, but she stays till she's cooked,' the Vin Thalun growled.

The plan had been to tell any guards present that Calidus had sent for the prisoners, and Veradis was going to initiate a violence-free hand-over, escorting the prisoners out of the courtyard and on to freedom. No fuss, no fighting, no noise. The thought occurred to him that if he backed down now, he could take every other prisoner out of here without a drop of spilt blood. All he had to do was sacrifice Cywen.

He punched the Vin Thalun in the face with the boss of his shield, saw him stumble backwards, nose smashed, spitting teeth. Veradis followed him and hit him again, sent him crashing to the ground.

Another Vin Thalun came at him but Ilta charged forwards, her sword rising and falling, slipping past the Vin Thalun's fumbled block to slice into his skull. He collapsed and she ripped her blade free, stood there glaring at her enemy, challenging them.

'TRUTH AND COURAGE!' she bellowed.

A frozen moment of shock, and then the Vin Thalun were leaping at them, howling. Veradis' shield and sword sung, trailing bloody arcs as he carved a way through to Cywen, where he saw prisoners struggling to free her. Behind him he was aware that the prisoners were joining the fray, leaping at their Vin Thalun guards. The flames flared, sent him reeling, and another Vin Thalun was swinging a sword at him. Veradis kicked the man in the chest, sent him hurtling into the flames. They flared brighter as the warrior screamed, Veradis leaping at the stake in the fire's heart. Lifting his shield high, he crashed into it, his momentum carrying him on, out the other side of the flames, rolling. He came to a halt on the flagstones, looked down.

At a burned and blackened spear shaft.

Where is she? Has she collapsed in the flames? Did I miss her?

He jumped to his feet, scanned the fire, could see no shape within it but prepared himself to leap back in.

'Well met, Veradis,' he heard a familiar voice say behind him.

Cywen.

CHAPTER SIXTY

HAELAN

The sounds of battle and alarm echoed across the fortress as Haelan ran through the streets, Buddai and Pots either side of him.

What's happening? Did Cywen's plan go wrong?

He'd left Swain and Sif guarding Trigg, the half-giant bound wrist and ankle as they didn't know what else to do with her. Cywen had gone earlier, saying she would be back with the rest of the prisoners, and that they should make ready to leave. That had felt like a very long time ago, and when the sounds of uproar echoed down to them and there was no sign of Cywen, Haelan decided he'd had enough of waiting.

He skirted the street that led to the herb garden and hospice, then slowed, smelling smoke and fire, hearing the sounds of battle, but the dogs ran on and so after a moment's hesitation he followed and burst into a scene of madness.

The first thing he saw was dead bodies littering the ground, burned and blackened, some still smoking, then a fire blazing in the courtyard, all about it people locked in battle. One of them was Cywen, rolling on the ground with a Vin Thalun warrior. Buddai leaped towards them but the Vin Thalun was dead before he reached them.

Cywen staggered to her feet, looked down at the dead man as Haelan ran to her.

'You're late,' he said. 'I was worried.'

Hild saw him and gasped.

'Swain and Sif will be glad to see you,' he said to her.

'What?' she hissed.

'I didn't want to tell you, for a host of reasons. Stab me later if you think I was wrong,' Cywen said to Hild as the older woman's expression transformed between shock, joy and hope.

'What's going on?' Haelan blurted, staring around. He saw prisoners fighting Vin Thalun, which he could understand, but there were also eagle-guard in the black and silver of Tenebral amongst the combatants, and they were also fighting Vin Thalun. Only a handful of paces away, one eagle-guard was in hand-to-hand combat with two Vin Thalun, though being outnumbered didn't seem to be an issue for him. Even as Haelan watched, one Vin Thalun collapsed with blood spurting from his groin, the other falling as a shield rim smashed him in the mouth, teeth spraying. A quick downwards stab and then the eagle-guard was looking around, eyes fixing upon Cywen. He strode over.

'We have to go,' the eagle-guard said. 'Balur's diversion will be over soon, and we need to get to the gates before then.'

He's on our side, then. What's going on?

'How are you planning on getting us out of here, Veradis?' Cywen asked.

Veradis slipped a pack off of his bag, shook out a black cuirass and cloak, an iron helm, a scabbarded short sword and belt.

'Brought you all a change of clothes,' he said with a brief smile. 'We'll be walking out the front door.'

'Swain and Sif,' Hild said to them all, 'where are they?'

'Back at the den,' Cywen said. 'We were attempting an escape tonight, but not through the front gates,' she told Veradis.

'We have to get them,' Hild said. 'I'm going nowhere without my bairns. Tell me where this den is, I'll go get them.'

'Too difficult. I'll show you,' Cywen said. 'Veradis, we'll meet you at the gates.'

He didn't look very happy with that, but was distracted as more Vin Thalun men poured into the courtyard. They yelled and charged.

'Shield wall!' Veradis shouted, and beyond the fire Haelan saw warriors crunching shields together before the onrushing Vin Thalun.

'Come on,' Cywen said, ruffling Buddai's head. 'Let's get out of here.'

And with that they were running east, Veradis gesturing for three of his men to follow Cywen and the others. Haelan heard the fresh sounds of battle erupting behind him.

Then Haelan was pounding through the streets, for the first time giving no heed to hiding or hugging the shadows. Somehow they avoided being seen, warriors passing by on other streets as great swirling masses of shadows and flame, torches trailing incandescence. He turned into another street, sprinted hard, Pots yapping at his feet as if it was the greatest game in the world, and then they were spilling into the abandoned courtyard, the old oak at its centre.

Cywen accelerated past him and skidded into the hole.

'Wait here,' she called over her shoulder, and Haelan came to a halt by one of the huge roots. Hild and the three warriors joined him, Hild gasping for breath, hands on her knees.

'Where . . . are . . . they . . . ?' she gasped.

'In there,' Haelan pointed. Hild peered into the hole, then took a step towards it.

A face appeared, small and pale, dirt-stained. Sif.

She climbed out almost fearfully. Haelan realized that this was the first time she'd been out of the den in over three moons. A large pack on her back made her look twice her real size. She saw Hild and then with a strangled sob the two of them were in each other's arms, hugging and squeezing, Hild lifting Sif into the air, kissing her cheeks.

'Mam?' a voice said behind them; Swain was appearing from the hole, a few of Storm and Buddai's cubs about his legs, they were tall now, Haelan saw, standing almost as high as Swain's thighs.

Swain was enveloped by Hild and Sif, the three of them crying, laughing, hugging.

He felt tears blur his vision and blinked them away.

More cubs emerged from the hole, then another face, broad, flat and angular, hoisted up and rolling out awkwardly, hands still tied at the wrist.

Trigg.

She climbed to her knees and stood, eyes taking in Haelan, Hild, the eagle-guard. Cywen emerged behind her, the last of the cubs too. Shadow appeared, padding up to Haelan.

'We need to go,' Cywen said.

'What about her?' Swain said, looking at Trigg.

'Take me with you,' Trigg said.

'How can we trust you?' Cywen asked.

Trigg just looked at her, eyes pleading.

'She could have betrayed us, but hasn't,' Haelan said. 'We can't just ignore what she's done, but I don't think she means us harm. Let Corban be her judge. He's our lord.'

A shout went up from the edge of the courtyard, a score of eagle-guard appearing from a darkened street.

'Ho there,' a voice called. 'What goes here?'

Haelan looked to Cywen, waiting on her word.

Run? Talk our way out? Can't fight, there's too many.

Cywen whispered frantically to one of the warriors who had accompanied them. After a few moments he turned and faced the new arrivals, raising an arm.

'Found some escaped prisoners,' he said, walking towards the approaching eagle-guard.

The newcomer peered at Haelan and his companions, pausing on Trigg, moving on, then noticing some of the cubs.

His eyes narrowed.

Buddai growled.

He looked back to the warrior in front of him, stared at his plain black cuirass.

'Where's your eagle?' he asked, hand moving to rest upon his sword hilt.

The friendly eagle-guard stabbed him in the throat, ripped his sword free and launched himself at the warriors behind, his companions' blades hissing into their hands as they took a protective stance before Cywen and the others.

Three against twenty. Don't like those odds.

There's no getting out of this, too many of them. Even if we run and get past them, they'll chase us, either catch us or follow us to the gates? What do we do?

'The tunnel,' Cywen shouted, 'it's our only chance. Go.'

The tunnel! That had been the escape route they'd planned on taking, even though they'd all been uneasy and fearful about it.

What's down there? Does it even lead out of this fortress?

Indecision dissolved as Haelan saw warriors charging at him. He turned and ran, pulling Shadow with him, straight back to the hole.

He heard the clash of iron, knew Cywen and the others were locked in combat now, heard a terrible plurality of snarls and screaming, glanced over to see one of the enemy eagle-guard on the ground, most of the cubs swarming over him, biting and ripping, blood pooling.

Sif yelled at the cubs, Swain adding his voice as they both pulled Hild with them back towards the hole beneath the tree roots, diving in without a thought. Hild following a little more cautiously, cubs jumping in after them. Trigg was standing close to the den entrance, hands still tied behind her back, looking straight at Haelan, shouting.

A hand grabbed the back of Haelan's cloak, yanking him backwards, off of his feet. He squawked, his cloak tight about his neck as he caught a flash of a surly face beneath an iron helm, then he was on his back, heard growling, saw Pots snapping at the shins of the warrior who had grabbed him, from the other side Shadow snarled and leaped. The warrior grunted in pain, shaking Pots free and raising his sword over Shadow, crunching the pommel onto her head. She fell, yelping, back to Haelan and crouched over him, still defiantly baring her teeth. The warrior cursed and strode at them both, sword rising.

'No!' Haelan screamed, thinking that Corban would be so disappointed with him if any harm came to Storm's cubs.

Then a figure was jumping over him: Trigg, charging at the eagle-guard. Even as she ran, she yanked her arms apart, breaking her bonds easily. Trigg ducked a sword swing, grabbed the warrior's wrist and gave it a savage twist. If the loud crack didn't tell Haelan that bones had broken, the following scream definitely did. Trigg punched him in the face, the man's nose exploded and he dropped to his knees. She grabbed his head with both hands, gave a savage twist and there was another louder crack, the warrior falling bonelessly to the ground. Trigg stood over him, legs splayed, chest heaving, face distorted in a snarl.

Haelan staggered to his feet, heard the clash of iron somewhere to his right, saw more eagle-guard running at them. Trigg saw it too and burst into motion, grabbing Haelan under her arms, lifting him and throwing him with more strength than Haelan had ever known she possessed. For a few heartbeats he was weightless, then he was crunching into the ground, grunting, rolling, darkness closing about him, the dank smell of earth and root and he realized he was back in the hole that led to his den.

A cub's tongue licked his face. He stood and looked out through the hole onto the courtyard, just in time to see Pots and Shadow racing after him, skidding and sliding into the hole. Beyond them Haelan saw Trigg fighting with half a dozen eagle-guard, swinging her long arms, keeping them at bay. Cywen was standing close to the remaining warrior that fought with them, many eagle-guard closing about them, Buddai a dark blur leaping at his foe.

'CYWEN!' Haelan screamed and he saw her head turn, her wolven claws dripping red, one hand reaching inside her cloak.

Then she was running, a burst of speed as she broke away from her attackers, yelling to the warrior fighting alongside her. He followed her as she leaped for the hole. Haelan jumped to one side as she fell in amongst them, the warrior was tumbling after, Buddai's bulk crashing through on top of them.

'Move,' Cywen told them all, pointing into the darkness of the tunnel, down the fork that travelled away from the den, towards who knew where.

'And you,' Cywen said to Haelan, who had pushed back to the hole, looking out at the courtyard. 'We've got to go,' she said.

'But Trigg,' Haelan said, leaning out of the hole and yelling the half-giant's name. Through the legs of the onrushing eagle-guard Haelan saw her look up and see him. She smiled fiercely at him and then she threw herself into the melee. Her bulk scattered a few of the eagle-guard, but others were there, moving in, their swords stabbing. He saw the enemy closing on Trigg, heard her cry out, saw her fall.

'NO!' Haelan screamed and began to scramble out of the hole as Cywen grabbed and shoved him stumbling after Swain and the others. He looked back, saw an eagle-guard's face appear at the hole, peer in, Cywen's wolven claws slashing at him. A scream and he fell back, but more crowded around him.

Cywen threw a small vial and yelled something, sounding *strange*, making Haelen stumble and shiver. Suddenly there was a *whoosh* of wind rushing past Haelan and then fire ignited as if from nowhere, fierce and hungry, curling out of the tunnel's entrance, men screaming, throwing themselves backwards as the flames engulfed them.

Cywen hurled herself backwards, slamming into Haelan's back. Behind her flames raged, the smell of wood and sap mingling with burning flesh, screaming, a cracking as one of the roots gave way, and then the hole was disappearing, earth crumbling down.

'GO!' Cywen shouted, shoving Haelan hard, sending him staggering on into the others.

On into the darkness.

CHAPTER SIXTY-ONE

VERADIS

Veradis stamped his boot onto the Vin Thalun's chest, pinning him to the ground, and stabbed down, his attacker gasping, choking, dying. Looking up, he saw the shield wall his men had formed was still standing strong, a tide of dead Vin Thalun about it.

It appears that there are no more Vin Thalun left to fight.

He wiped his sword clean and sheathed it, listening to the crashing, thuds and screams that still echoed from the fortress' walls, a sign that Balur, Alcyon and their kin were still causing chaos.

Can't last much longer.

'We are here to get you out of Drassil,' Veradis yelled, striding to the cuirass, cloak, helm and sword that he'd emptied earlier from his pack, lifting the disguise up for all to see.

'Every prisoner, find one of my men, they'll have one of these for you, and more.' He looked around at the faces, shadowed and bloody. 'Quickly,' he shouted, and the courtyard burst into motion. While he waited, his heartbeat counting time, he looked eastward, in the direction that Cywen had disappeared.

Come on, girl, he willed.

'We're ready to go,' Ilta told him.

Only five of Veradis' men had fallen in the melee, and there were one hundred and eighty-eight prisoners now standing with them.

One hundred and eighty-eight who will not die screaming on stakes. One hundred and eighty-eight who will fight alongside us in Forn.

If we can get out of here.

Veradis marched in front of them.

'You'll be leaving here as eagle-guard. We are going through the gates to sally forth and fight off the enemy attacking Drassil's walls,'

Veradis said with a fierce grin. 'Keep your heads down and wits about you, and you'll soon be sitting around a fire with your kin and comrades.' There was a ragged cheer and then they were moving, forming a rough square, the prisoners enclosed at its heart, in the hope of hiding the fact that they didn't know how to march in formation.

The streets were less crowded than they had been on the journey to the hospice, Veradis seeing small bands of warriors, mostly Vin Thalun. He strode past them as if he had more right to be there than they did, all the while his heart in his mouth.

Where are you, Cywen? he thought, scanning the shadows of the buildings ahead of him, checking back over his shoulder, but there was no sign of her.

There were more warriors on the road now, a score of eagle-guard passing them, the crack of their shoes on stone a familiar, almost nostalgic sound to Veradis. Windows in buildings were lit, the fire of forges, a host of barracks, then the whinny of horses and the huge courtyard inside the gates of Drassil opened before them.

Veradis held his fist up, barking an order, the warriors behind him stumbling to a halt. He paused there, on the edge of the courtyard, searching the shadows for Cywen and her companions.

Where is she? How can I leave without her?

'We can't just stand here,' Ilta hissed at him. 'We are like a goose putting its head on the chopping block.'

Veradis sucked in a deep breath, tugged on the chin-strap of his helm, then marched straight through the courtyard's heart, ordering any too slow to get out of his way.

A man strode towards Veradis, one of the officers he'd seen earlier.

'Open the gates,' Veradis said as they drew near to one another.

'For what purpose?' the warrior asked, surprised.

'A sally against the enemy, to push them back from the walls.'

'I've had no orders,' the young captain frowned.

'I'm giving them to you, now,' Veradis said, the habit of command rising up to help him along with his fear.

The captain hesitated, looking from Veradis to his men. 'This is unusual,' he said. 'Orders to open the gates are always delivered by the Jehar.'

You mean Kadoshim. You are as unwitting as I was. I wonder, if you knew the truth, what would you do?

'These are not usual circumstances,' Veradis snapped, 'and if I don't get out there soon the enemy may well be breaching our walls.'

'You have only just returned to Drassil,' the captain said, still frowning. 'Why would you be leading this sortie?'

'I volunteered,' Veradis said. He tapped his pack. 'And I have fresh orders for King Nathair. Darkness offers good cover, as the fortress is watched closely.'

Veradis' words were having an effect: he could see the captain teetering, but still he hesitated.

'I do not have time for this,' Veradis snapped. 'Send a runner for Calidus, let him explain to you the workings of his plans.' He looked pointedly at the skewered corpses that lined the courtyard.

One last long stare and then the captain was turning on his heel, shouting for the gates to be opened.

'Onwards,' Veradis yelled, stepping into the archway beneath the thick wall of Drassil. Half of his warband was through the gates now, Veradis standing in the archway's shadow, looking back into the courtyard, hoping to see Cywen appear.

But she did not come.

The last lines were passing him by now, and still he did not move.

A thought struck him.

The gates are open. I have warriors about me, giants out there in the darkness. Will we ever have an opportunity like this again?

Could we win?

A thousand against three, maybe four thousand?

Kadoshim appeared out of the half-lit darkness of a wide street and at their head strode Calidus, a dark cloak billowing behind him like smoke.

He was much changed, his long silver hair and short beard gone, his ageless skin and smile now cracked and ruined, the skin charred and peeling, hair burned away, only tufts here and there.

You may be hard to kill, but at the very least you can be hurt, you bastard.

As if he heard his thoughts, Calidus' eyes fell upon Veradis. Recognition and hatred suddenly flared.

Calidus snarled.

'Run,' Veradis whispered. Then, louder. 'RUN.'

Behind him the Kadoshim bounded forwards on Calidus' orders, sprinting faster than Veradis thought possible, smashing people out of their way, leaping over them.

Veradis' feet thudded, echoing in the archway of Drassil's walls, out onto the plain, urging his men on. Shouts were rising up from the courtyard, screeches from the Kadoshim, yells from the battlements of Drassil, and spears began to hiss down from above. Some of Veradis' people fell, skewered, but most ran on, the darkness enveloping them. Veradis looked back over his shoulder, saw the first line of the Kadoshim come hurtling through the gates. They sprinted across the open ground, dark blurs, curved swords glinting in moonlight as some drew their blades.

They're going to catch us. No point running. Maybe some of us can hold them, let the others get to the trees.

Veradis yelled an order and turned, drawing his sword and hefting his shield, a dozen others turning with him. Ilta was one of them.

The Kadoshim were almost upon them, five well ahead of the rest of the pack. Veradis could see the dark glint of their teeth as they smiled gleeful, grisly smiles.

'You have to take their heads,' he yelled.

Then shadows were rising from the grass around him, taking shape: giants and men wielding war-hammers and battle-axes. Veradis recognized one of the figures.

Krelis.

'Didn't think I'd let you win all this glory for yourself,' Krelis called to him with a wide grin, and then they all fell howling upon the Kadoshim.

He saw Balur One-Eye swing an axe and take a Kadoshim head with his first blow, a hiss of vapour forming an inky shadow in the air, punctuated by two red coals for eyes. It shrieked its fury at them, the sound torn and frayed by the breeze a lingering moment, then it was gone. One giant fell as two Kadoshim leaped upon her, but they were soon dispatched by Alcyon and his son, swinging their axes as if they were felling trees.

Horn blasts echoed and a voice rang out across the plain; Calidus, calling his demons home.

The first wave of the Kadoshim were down, but those that followed were surprisingly disciplined, wheeling and fleeing back towards the walls of Drassil like a colony of bats. Veradis punched his sword in the air and gave a fierce victory howl, grinning fiercely.

We did it.

HAELAN

Haelan stumbled along the rough tunnel, old roots sticking out, poking and tripping him. He was the last of their motley group, Cywen leading the way, Shadow and Buddai padding almost silently beside him. Haelan didn't fear pursuit, at least not straight away; the tunnel entrance had collapsed after the mysterious fire had occurred.

Did Cywen . . . make that fire?

The smell of burning flesh was still thick in his nostrils, the screaming of men echoing in his mind. And Trigg, poor Trigg.

Tears filled his vision, blurring the torch light ahead.

Every time he closed his eyes he could see her face, eyes locked on him, choosing to sacrifice herself to save them.

Abruptly the torchlight ahead disappeared as if Cywen had just turned a corner. When Haelan reached it he realized it was a corner of sorts, only that it went down, not sideways. Cywen climbed down it, hanging onto the root that the tunnel followed. She reached what looked like a dead end and stopped, stamped one foot on the ground, then crouched to inspect the earth around the root.

The smell that had drifted up from this tunnel was stronger now, an acidic burn that clung to the back of your throat and felt like it was singeing the hairs inside your nostrils.

Cywen dug the end of her torch into the earth, then she stood and climbed back to them, using the tree root to pull herself up.

'There's another tunnel down there. We just have to dig through to it,' she said.

'What's that smell?' Hild said, pulling a face.

'Good question,' Cywen said. 'It smells like draig dung to me.'

'Draig dung!' the warrior from Tenebral, who had introduced himself as Arcus, said.

'Aye, draigs. It makes sense,' Cywen said. 'Coralen told me she'd come across a draig den on one of her scouting trips north-east of Drassil. A great mound, dung hills about it, tunnels boring into it.'

Coralen also said that a draig attacked her and tried to eat her.

'This could well be part of the same draig nest,' Cywen said. 'Perhaps it bores under the forest for leagues.'

'Only one way to find out,' Arcus said, jumping down past Cywen to land heavily on the hard-packed soil, which promptly collapsed under his weight. He fell with it, grabbing on to the tree root to break his fall. He climbed down the root, disappearing into the darkness.

Cywen followed after him, taking her torch with her, one hand grasping the root. Buddai landed with a thud on the earth behind her.

'Pass the cubs down to me,' she said, dropping her torch to Arcus.

The cubs weren't happy about being passed into the hole, muzzles wrinkled, growling.

They've never met a draig, but they must know it doesn't smell like anything good.

Sif went next, then Swain and Hild. Haelan followed, gripping the old root with one hand and being helped to the ground by Arcus. Pots jumped down after him and Shadow sniffed and whined, wrapping herself tight around Haelan's legs.

Haelan looked about, as the torch shed some light on the place they were now standing. It was a tunnel, much wider and higher than the one they'd just been stumbling through. All of them would be able to walk abreast here if they'd wanted to. It was roughly circular in shape, the floor and sides showing long raking claw-marks, as if they had been gouged out. The earth was dry and hard, the air musty and stale.

What if this tunnel goes nowhere, except to hungry draigs? Haelan thought. He eyed the root and hole above him.

We could probably all climb up to the passage above, but it wouldn't be easy getting Buddai and the cubs back up there, and less so with a draig chasing us.

He shivered, trying not to think about that.

'What now?' Swain asked.

'Now we walk, and find a way out of here,' Cywen said.

'You said your friend found this draig den north-east of Drassil?' Arcus asked.

'Aye.'

'So,' Arcus said. 'This tunnel goes two ways.' He gestured with his torch, showing a wall of darkness that seemed to swallow his torchlight. He pointed ahead of them. 'That way's close to north, from what I can make, so I suppose that's the way we are going.'

They all stood and stared into the darkness beyond the torch's reach, black as pitch, the silence was almost a physical thing, heavy and stifling.

'What if there's no way out?' Sif asked, a tremor in her voice. 'No matter what way we go.'

I was wondering that, but wasn't going to say that out loud.

Hild pulled her close, hugged her. 'We'll find a way, even if I have to dig a new tunnel.'

Arcus took a new torch from Haelan's pack and lit it with the one already burning, then held it up high. It flickered a moment, weakly, its flames ruffled as if by a dying breath.

'Well,' Arcus said, something close to a smile flitting across his face.

'Good,' Cywen said, a hint of victory in her voice. 'A breeze down here tells us there's an entrance it came in by. I told you these tunnels would be our route to freedom.'

A route to freedom. That's wonderful. Now all we have to do is wander these tunnels until we find it and hope that we don't stumble into a hungry draig while we're looking for the way out.

He didn't think sharing that thought would be appreciated, though, so he stroked Shadow's head.

'Right then, best be doing this,' Arcus muttered as he lifted his torch high and drew his sword, looking suspiciously into the darkness. They set off in a line after him, Cywen and Buddai, Swain, Sif and Haelan in the middle, Pots at his ankles, Hild behind them with a torch of her own. For once the cubs were remarkably subdued, the six of them staying huddled near the centre of their small company, tails tucked between their legs and ears twitching.

Not very comforting, Haelan thought as he looked at them. *They're not usually scared of anything.*

They marched through the dank tunnel that twisted and turned, and in no time at all Haelan had lost absolutely all sense of what direction they were travelling in. Occasionally they would reach a fork in the passage, with another huge tunnel leading off who knew where. They would stand at these junctures a while, listening, holding the torches high to see if a breeze flowed from either way. Sometimes they waited for what felt like a long time until eventually something tugged at the torch-flame. They were repeating this ritual for the fifth or sixth time when Haelan felt a hard piece of earth underfoot. He crouched down and rubbed at it, brushing it away to reveal a long, curving talon. He tugged and scraped and it came free. Holding it up to the torchlight, he could see it was pale, like bone, wide at one end, curved and tapering to a point.

'It's a draig claw,' Cywen said behind him.

'It's too big, surely?' Haelan said.

'I've seen Nathair's draig, been closer than most. That's definitely a draig claw.'

They all stood in silence, looking at the huge talon, letting the implications of Haelan's find sink in.

'This way,' Arcus said, staring at his torch, and they set off again, walking along another wide passage. Haelan looked at the claw one last time and then slipped it inside his pack.

The ground was softer now, and the walls. Haelan stumbled and steadied himself with a hand against the wall, his palm slipping on mud, something squirming beneath it. He regained his balance very quickly.

As they walked Haelan listened, straining to hear beyond the tramp of their feet and their breathing, which sounded disproportionately loud in the stifling tunnel.

How long have we been walking? We must be leagues beyond Drassil by now.

They reached another junction, Arcus stopping and raising his torch into the face of one passage and then the other. Haelan looked at the ground, wondering if he might come across any other claws. Close to one foot, the ground looked different, as if the soil had been turned recently. He bent closer, frowned, then realized.

'We've been here already,' he said.

'What?' Cywen and Hild said, the others stooping over him.

'Look,' Haelan said as he pulled his draig claw from his pack and slotted it into the groove in the ground. It fit perfectly.

Arcus cursed.

We'll never get out of here, even if there are no draigs, Haelan thought, feeling as if he was close to weeping. *How can we guard against this, down here in the choking darkness?* Then he had an idea.

'Sif, did you bring your pack of stones?'

'Of course,' Sif said.

'Can I have them?'

'Why?' she said suspiciously.

'Please, Sif. I want to test something.'

Grudgingly she rooted in her pack and pulled out her makeshift bag of stones.

'Here,' she said.

Haelan rummaged around inside and pulled a stone out, one that had been chalked white on one side. Carefully he placed it on the ground, pushed it in a little.

'What're you doing?' Sif asked.

'Everyone back,' Haelan said, ushering them back the way they'd just come, until the stone was taken by the darkness.

'Now, as we walk forwards, look at the ground,' Haelan said.

They did, and when Arcus' torchlight washed over the stone it glittered like a prize jewel.

'Good lad,' Arcus said, and Cywen patted him on the back.

'Can I have my stones back now,' Sif asked.

'No,' everyone said at the same time.

Haelan walked at the head of their group, beside Arcus, the warrior seemingly calm, focused on the path his torchlight was revealing. Behind them the company walked in silence.

They'd walked a long way since he had come up with the idea of using Sif's stones as markers. It had served them well already – twice now the passages they'd taken had led back to where they'd placed one of the stones. Haelan had added a second stone beside each one they saw again.

A sound rumbled in the distance, like faint thunder, almost too low to hear. Buddai, Pots and the cubs heard it clearly enough, though, stopping with their heads cocked, ears pricked. Shadow curled a lip and growled. They all froze, listening as the distant sound rolled on, rising and falling, until it faded away to nothing.

He felt a twinge of fear.

Is that what draigs sound like?

Cywen shared a look with Arcus and Hild.

They walked on in silence.

The smell's getting worse, Haelan realized. With each step it grew stronger, Haelan breathing through his mouth to try and lessen the stench, but that just made his throat burn.

And then they stepped into a chamber, dug wider for about fifty paces, like the fat belly of a snake that had just consumed its prey. Mounds were scattered about, as wide as the base of a large shield, rising as high as Haelan's head. Cywen bent close to inspect one, Haelan reaching out to touch it with his finger. It had a hard crust, like baked clay, or bread left in the oven too long, except that it was rough. Haelan poked a little harder, the crust cracking, a hiss of gas leaking from it, then something thick and slimy oozed out, like pus from a picked scab. The stench almost put Haelan on the ground and made Cywen gag, sending her reeling back a few steps.

'It's draig dung,' she said when she could breathe properly. 'These draigs seem to be animals of habit, which use the same spot for their waste. I don't think this chamber has been used for a very long time. This dung's old. The stuff I've shovelled from Nathair's stable did not have a crust like this – not even after it had been on the midden for a moon.'

'Perhaps they've dug out a new one,' Haelan suggested.

'I think you might be right,' Cywen said, trying to summon a reassuring smile. She wasn't wholly successful.

Just so long as we don't walk into that one as well.

Another rumble reverberated through the hall, echoing on and on, a rhythm to it, eventually fading. It was much louder than the previous one.

Sif sniffed.

'We'll be out of here soon,' Swain said.

A shared look amongst them all and they set off again.

No point going backwards, can only go forwards.

They trudged on, a sense of foreboding growing in Haelan's gut, hovering on the edge of all-out fear. He knew if they were caught by a draig down here there was very little to do except die.

Horribly.

The thought of ending up in a draig's belly was not appealing.

It's different, being slain in combat, even if it means your enemy wins. At least then you die fighting for a cause that means something; not just dying to satisfy an animal's hunger.

They stepped into another chamber, this one so much larger than the last one. Swain lit more torches and handed them out.

It was a circular room with a number of dark tunnels leading from it – six, eight.

Haelan saw a mound of something at the centre of the room. Not like the dung hills: this one was much lower, and wider. It looked like it was made up of separate objects, all piled together, like pumpkins on Midwinter's Day. Without realizing, he found that he was walking towards it. He stumbled over something on the ground, looked down and saw that objects were scattered all over. Then he recognized what they were.

Bones.

A ribcage here, a spine there, a long skull, large canines protruding from a jaw.

A wolven?

He carried on, picking his way more carefully. Then he stepped over a bone with fingers at the end of it, close to a human skull with a great hole in it.

That's beyond worrying.

Something tickled Haelan's face, tugged at his hair. It took him a moment to understand what it was.

A breeze.

He paused and saw Arcus' torch flicker and crackle as the warrior stepped in front of one of the many exit tunnels. Haelan looked around at his companions, saw that they had all felt it, hope lighting up all their faces within a few heartbeats.

He crossed the last few strides to the mound, stood for a moment with his torch held high, just staring.

It was a shallow circular pit, like one of the fire-pits they'd built while travelling through the forest.

Except this one's got things in it.

Twenty, thirty, each one about as big as his head, roughly oval in shape, colours rippling across their surfaces, hues swirling, like paint spilled in water as the light of the torch caught them.

'Haelan, what are they?' Cywen hissed at him.

He gulped. 'I don't know, it looks like . . . eggs?'

'Oh no,' he heard Cywen whisper.

Somewhere behind Haelan, Buddai, Pots and the cubs all started to growl.

CHAPTER SIXTY-THREE

CYWEN

Cywen rested a hand upon Buddai's shoulder, dread trickling down her spine, watching in horror as with a sinuous movement a shadow rose up from the ground and lumbered ponderously into the room. Taller than a horse and twice as wide, a long body set upon four bowed, powerful legs. Its head was broad and flat-muzzled, somehow reptilian with curved teeth as big as daggers protruding from its powerful jaws. For a moment it stood still as stone, only its tongue flickering, tasting the air. Then it raised its head on its long-muscled neck and roared.

The sound was deafening, the blast of it almost snuffing out Haelan's torch. Cywen clasped her hands over her ears, feeling the ground tremble beneath her feet, a cloud of dust rising up about the draig.

Then Arcus was yelling, pointing down the tunnel from where the strong breeze had emanated, and they were all running. Cywen was the last through, looking back to see the draig powering across the chamber towards her, the sound of other draigs roaring ringing from other tunnels.

She was too scared to think coherently, just ran.

It's in the tunnel, right behind me.

Somehow her legs pumped faster. She *felt* the draig closing in on them, heard a *crunching* just behind her head as jaws snapped at her.

They turned a long bend in the tunnel, bursting into another chamber-like room. Arcus sprinted straight through it, disappearing into the only tunnel at the far end, Hild and Swain half a step behind him. Haelan stumbled ahead of Cywen with the cubs and Pots.

Cywen and Buddai were last through, the sound of the draig thundering up behind her filling her with terror.

Then she saw light ahead.

It was pale and weak, a pinprick in the distance, her companions black silhouettes before it. She felt hope lurch in her chest and moved faster, at the same time realizing that she wasn't going to make it. The draig behind her was so close she could feel its breath. She reached inside her cloak, tried to remember which pockets she'd put which vials in, grasped one, two, hoped they were the right combination, yanked them free, hurled them behind her, down at the ground, heard the glass smash.

'*Fola agus lasair, comhlacht agus tine,*' she yelled.

There was a sucking sound behind her, as if the tunnel took an indrawn breath, and then a *whump* as fire ignited, the force of it hurling her on. The draig roared, pain and rage blended. Cywen risked a glance back, saw a wall of fire filling the passage, glimpsed sharp teeth and leathery skin through the flames.

Cywen ran on, stumbling, one hand reaching out to the wall, only then noticing she still had Corban's wolven gauntlet strapped on her arm. With each step the light ahead grew brighter and bigger, and then Cywen was flying out of the tunnel, her companions spilling onto a slope that rose up before them.

Cywen looked behind her, back into the tunnel, saw her flames still burning, though even as she watched a draig burst through them, snuffing them out.

'It's coming!' Cywen yelled, scrambling up the slope, almost on all-fours. She burst over a lip and saw the forest spread out before her. It was day; after the darkness of the tunnels the usual half-light of Forn was unbearably bright, trees rearing above her, and there were more dung hills, scattered in a loose arc around the rim, stretching back into the trees like a field.

Behind Cywen the ground trembled, the draig surging up after them. She caught up with Haelan, reached out and grabbed his hand, pulling him on. The draig was closing the gap at a terrifying speed, crashing through the undergrowth, jaws opening.

Cywen leaped, dragging Haelan with her, sending both of them smashing into a mound of dung, faeces exploding around them.

The draig skidded past them, great talons raking the ground, sending earth and forest litter spraying through the air. Cywen came to her hands and knees, clawed dung from her eyes and nose and mouth, retched. Haelan fought in Cywen's arms, spluttering and choking, the stench of dung thick as sea fog about them both.

Then the draig was before them, head bent low, tongue flicking, so close that Cywen could see the saliva dripping from one long, curved tooth. She froze, absolute and utter terror stealing everything from her, and she found herself unable even to scream. Judging from Haelan's frozen expression he felt something very similar.

The draig's head swayed on its powerful neck, its bulk filling her entire world. It seemed confused, searching for something it couldn't find; it shifted its weight, one of its clawed talons scouring the earth a handspan from Cywen's foot.

It can't smell us, Cywen understood, *because of the dung. But why can't it see us? Is it because we're not moving? Just make no noise, no noise.*

There was shouting, in the distance, Hild was stepping out from behind a tree, Arcus and the others with her, waving their arms in the air, crying out.

Trying to save us, Cywen realized.

The draig gave an angry rumbling growl and thundered into motion, away from Cywen and Haelan, after their companions.

'Run,' Cywen hissed, dragging Haelan to his feet by the scruff of his neck and chasing after the draig.

They followed the draig's trail of destruction, speeding through the forest. Undergrowth was being torn and scattered, the rhythmic pound and scrape of the draig's claws ripping through all in its way. Cywen caught a glimpse of the draig's whipping tail, beyond that the silhouettes of her friends fleeing, saw the flash of fur, the cubs darting through the undergrowth.

The draig didn't see me or Haelan when we were covered in dung and motionless. Smell must be its primary sense, which makes sense, living in those tunnels. And what about sight? It definitely sees us when we are moving. What if we all just stood still?

No, it would still smell the others.

Screams echoed through the forest. Fear spread its wings in Cywen's chest. She ran faster.

The draig was poised over Hild and Sif, Arcus standing over them, sword red to the hilt.

Cywen yelled wordlessly and reached inside her cloak.

The draig's tail slammed into her as it twisted to look and she was flying through the air, weightless, spinning, then crunching onto the ground, rolling, snared in clinging vine. She came to a stop, her back and chest on fire, gasping for breath. She rolled over, saw the draig looming over her, jaws open wide.

Then Buddai was crashing into it, his teeth snapping at the draig's neck, scoring red gashes but unable to penetrate deep into the beast's flesh. He fell to the ground, leaped away from a slashing claw that would have eviscerated him.

Cywen dragged herself to her knees, staggered upright, hand reaching into her cloak.

Then Arcus was running at the creature, stabbing at its belly. Blood gushed as his sword sank deep, the draig bellowing in pain, jerking away, ripping the sword free of Arcus' grip, tail whipping around and smashing the warrior full in the chest. He flew, crashed into a tree and slid to the undergrowth, the draig following, front paw landing on Arcus' torso, pinning him to the ground. Its head dipped, jaws fastening upon Arcus' head. A twist of its neck and blood was jetting from Arcus' shoulders, his head in the draig's jaws. It crunched through bone and swallowed.

Sif screamed, hands clasped over her mouth, again and again. The draig saw her. Hild ran for her daughter, who was standing frozen, shrieking hysterically. Cywen staggered after the draig as it pounded towards Sif. Movement flashed from different directions, converging upon the draig – the cubs, Shadow leading, the others close behind, all of them leaping at the beast, snapping, tearing at its thick scaly hide, Buddai hurling himself at the draig again, this time sinking his teeth into one of its back legs, dark blood welling, splattering upon the ground. Pots appeared and jumped on one taloned foot, biting and snarling.

The draig ignored them all, as Cywen would ignore flies. Its jaws opened above Sif, then another figure was flying at it: Swain, jumping and hanging from a long tooth in its lower jaw, legs wrapping around its neck, as he'd cling to a branch. He had his knife in his hand, stabbed it into the soft tissue of the draig's mouth, fast and furious, again and again; blood and saliva mixed, the draig rearing up onto its back legs, shaking its head. Hild reached Sif, swept her up into her arms and kept on running.

The draig crashed back to the ground, making the earth tremble. It opened its mouth and roared, filling the world with its rage.

Swain had somehow kept his grip on the draig's tooth, though his legs had left the ground, and he was swinging beneath the creature's lower jaw. He stabbed again with his knife, this time into its neck. The draig gave a massive shake of its body, like a hound after a swim in the sea, Swain, Buddai, the cubs and Pots were all sent flying in all directions.

Cywen skirted the rear end of the draig, ducked as a cub flew past her, gripped two vials she'd pulled from her cloak and raised her arm. She hesitated, seeing how thick the creature's hide was, waiting to get a shot at its head, where its vulnerable parts seemed to be – eyes and the soft tissue of its mouth.

The draig clawed its way towards Swain, who was scrambling to his feet and running after his mam and sister. The draig's head snaked out and the jaws snapped, clamping upon Swain's leg, dragging him back, lifting him into the air.

Swain screamed, high and piercing. Hild skidded to a stop.

Cywen gave up trying to get a clear shot at the draig's head and threw the vials, muttering her words of power as glass smashed upon the draig's scaly back, the two liquids mixing, combining, igniting in a flash of incandescent light, flames spreading over the beast's body.

It bellowed its pain, dropping Swain. Haelan and a handful of the cubs appeared from the undergrowth, running to Swain, dragging him away. Swain cried out, blood pulsing from his torn leg, and the draig, mad with agony as the flames licked its back, lashed out wildly with a taloned foot. Haelan hurled himself flat to the ground, the cubs leaping away, but the draig's claws caught one, sliced it to bloody ruin in a heartbeat.

Haelan screamed horror and rage, then he was back on his feet, pulling his hatchet from his belt, leaping at the draig, latching on to its foreleg, one arm rising and falling in furious motion, chopping maniacally at the creature's knee-joint.

Cywen ran at it, punched her wolven claws into its tail, ripped them out, scored a long line as the tail whipped furiously, the draig turning on Cywen, with Haelan still clinging to its foreleg. Cywen leaped away from a slash of the draig's talons, Buddai bounded in again, worrying at its belly, his jaw coming away blooded, more cubs returning to the attack, a white streak as Pots jumped at the leg Haelan was attached to.

The draig was mad with fury and pain. The last of Cywen's flames was flickering across its back, leaving the skin there blackened, and the beast swung its head, caught Cywen in the shoulder, teeth slicing across her. A line of burning pain sent her spinning, falling, the draig lumbering after her. Buddai flew at its head, jaws clamping onto the draig's cheek and the bone of its heavy brow, but a furious jerk of the draig's neck sent Buddai spinning up into the air, crunching to the ground a dozen paces from Cywen. She heard bones break and half crawled, half dragged herself to her beloved hound's side, saw the draig rearing over both of them, open jaws bearing down upon them.

We're all going to die.

She wrapped an arm around Buddai, the hound whining as he tried to move, settling for licking Cywen's face.

There was a whirring sound, a *thunk*, like a slap, and a white-feathered arrow was suddenly sprouting from the draig's neck.

And then another.

Then there was a louder whistling sound and a dagger hilt was protruding from the draig's side. The draig bellowed its challenge and frustration as a crashing, splintering onrush of power tore out of the forest.

Storm, hurtling from the shadows, a thunderbolt of muscle, teeth and fur, leaping and slamming into the draig, huge jaws clamping about the muscled neck, canines sinking deep, the two creatures rolling, forest litter and earth exploding in great gouts as the draig thrashed, talons and tail wreaking devastation.

Then, a war-cry.

'TRUTH AND COURAGE!' and Corban was charging out of the undergrowth, his sword held high, Gar one side of him, Coralen the other, and behind them the bulk of Farrell, long-shafted war-hammer in his hand, Laith beside him, bristling with daggers, the smaller figure of Kulla, adding her voice to Corban's. They struck the draig in two waves, Corban, Gar and Coralen first, swords carving through the beast's thick hide, leaving long bloody gashes in their wake, then spinning away, after them Kulla and Farrell, sword and war-hammer swinging, Laith standing back and hurling dagger after dagger at the great beast.

It reared up, clawing at Storm upon its back, tail whipping at its new assailants. Corban leaped over the tail, surged forwards and buried his sword two-handed into the draig's softer belly, pushing deeper, leaning into the blow, then twisting his grip, shifting his weight and ripping his blade free, an eruption of near-black blood and the draig was roaring, collapsing, slamming to the ground, an explosion of leaves and dirt, its neck and head flopping and then, with a shiver, it died.

Corban stood over Cywen and held his hand out to her, Storm snuffling and nuzzling at Buddai, the hound's tail wagging, thumping the ground.

Cywen gripped Corban's wrist and he pulled her upright.

'Still getting yourself into trouble, then,' he said, a grin splitting his face as he pulled her into an embrace.

CHAPTER SIXTY-FOUR

MAQUIN

Maquin awoke to bright light and pain in his head. He rolled over, expecting to see Fidele lying beside him, but he was alone, the wool and furs on her side of their bed cold to the touch. It was a little past dawn, a chill in the air, mist curling up from the stream close by.

He sat up slowly, memory returning of last night, a smile spreading across his face as he remembered her words to him.

This, us, is for always. His grin widened. He saw the empty skin of mead close by and rubbed his temples.

I must be getting old, he thought, his head feeling full of fog. *A few cups of mead and I sleep the night away.*

With some effort he knelt before the stream, dunked his head up to his shoulders and came up gasping, the water ice cold and invigorating. Sounds of celebration drifted down to him, and he frowned, remembering Fidele telling him of Veradis' impending rescue attempt.

I was going to volunteer for that. By the sound of the cheering I wasn't missed, though I may have missed out on a fight worth a song.

He pulled on his boots, a wool tunic and his leather vest, slung his sword-belt over his shoulder and headed towards camp.

He saw Veradis first, walking alongside Krelis. They were leading a long column: Balur, Alcyon and what looked like the full strength of the Benothi clan striding with them. Amongst them were a mix of warriors, mostly men of Ripa, clothed in the black and silver of Tenebral. Many of them were discarding cloaks and helms, being greeted by warriors of Isiltir, Wulf's men, Javed's Freedmen – all were out to welcome this warband home. People were embracing, laughing, crying.

He did it, then, Maquin thought, looking at Veradis. *I imagine that was quite the tale, and I look forward to hearing it.*

First things first, though. Where's Fidele?

A young warrior, dark-haired, a man of Ripa approached him. Maquin recognized him as one of those who had become part of Fidele's unofficial honour guard.

'This is for you, my lord,' the warrior said, holding a rolled parchment out. He didn't meet Maquin's eyes.

'I'm no one's lord,' Maquin muttered as he took the scroll, saw the wax was sealed with Fidele's ring. Something shifted inside him, like a chill wind on a summer's day.

I have gone to seek Nathair, the parchment began. *I gave you a sleeping draught last night, knowing that you would seek to dissuade me, or failing that, you would accompany me. I must speak with Nathair alone. I know there is goodness in him yet, but I need an opportunity to draw it into the light.*

All of last night is true. What we did, what I said to you, meant with all that I am. But I must do this alone.

He is my son.

Please forgive me.

And then her signature.

Maquin bowed his head, crumpling the letter to his chest.

A whirlpool of emotions – he was hurt that she didn't trust him with this, that she'd deceived him. He was angry that he'd been tricked, fooled. But most of all he felt scared, a worm of fear squirming in his belly.

Forn is dangerous. The journey alone . . .

'When did she leave, and how many went with her?' Maquin asked the young warrior.

'I was told to bid you wait, my lord,' the warrior said.

'Might as well ask the sun not to rise,' Maquin growled, stepping close to the warrior. He returned Maquin's stare.

Brave lad, but I don't have time for this.

Anger swelled, fuelled with fear for Fidele. His fingers twitched. 'What's your name?'

'Spyr, my lo—' the warrior answered.

'Stop calling me that,' Maquin snarled. 'I commend your loyalty, Spyr,' he said, 'but that won't stop me emptying your guts all over your boots.' He didn't move or touch a weapon, but the warrior took a step back.

'She's chasing after Nathair, you fool,' Maquin said to him, quietly. 'A ten-night's travel through Forn, and then she'll walk into our enemy's camp. Do you think Nathair will let her just walk back out again? The man who has betrayed his kin, his realm, the whole Banished Lands?'

He held Spyr's gaze.

'Now, I'll ask you one more time. When did she leave, and how many went with her?'

'Six,' Spyr said, looking at the ground.

'When?'

'Last night. They left when Veradis led his warband to Drassil.'

Clever. Cover to mask her leaving.

He thought a moment, then spun on his heel and strode back to the stream, filled a couple of fresh water skins, stuffed dried biscuit into his pack, checked his kit-box was there, slung it over his back. Checked his knives. Then he was striding through the camp, skirting the celebrations. On his way he saw Teca and changed his direction, approaching her.

'I need your help,' he said to her. He knew she was the best tracker in their warband. 'Fidele has run off on a fool's errand, and I need to catch up with her before she gets herself, and this warband, into a lot of trouble.'

Teca took a long look at Maquin's face.

'All right. Let's be after her, then.'

They left immediately. Maquin heard footfalls behind and he glanced back to see Spyr following him, shamefaced.

Lad was only following orders, he thought. He nodded as Spyr joined them, and the three of them made their way through the forest, following the path that Veradis, his hundred and more than a score of giants had trampled last night. It wasn't long before Teca stopped, looking at the broken leaves of a red fern, then crouched, studying the soft forest litter. Abruptly she rose and headed into the undergrowth, away from the wide trampled trail of destruction that Veradis' lot had left.

They passed through the forest in silence, dark thoughts spiralling in Maquin's mind like crows before a battle.

Wolven, draigs, bears, bats, all manner of unpleasant ways to be eaten. Forn is a predator. And if Fidele makes it to Nathair, what will he do with her?

He fought the urge to run through the forest, calmed himself a fraction by telling himself he needed to allow Teca to work.

And then she stopped, staring at the ground in front of her.

Maquin, tense as a drawn bowstring, stepped around her.

First, he saw the flies, clouds of them, buzzing in dense swarms, like smoke over fire. Then the smell: blood, faeces, thick in the air, cloying. Bodies were strewn about a small area of the forest. Behind him Spyr cursed and rushed forwards, crouching beside the first figure.

'Clem,' he whispered, looking back up at Maquin with guilty eyes.

Maquin stalked amongst the dead, a quick glance showing him four, five dead men of Ripa in their black and silver. Then another figure, clothed in leather vest and breeches. Maquin's blood turned to ice as he bent, saw the iron rings in the man's beard.

'Vin Thalun,' he hissed.

Maquin stood and moved on, saw another body lying face-down in the undergrowth. Spyr turned him as Teca hissed in horror. The man's face had been half-eaten – the upper lip and cheek chewed down to the bone, one eyeball hanging out of its socket – though it was still recognizable as Agost.

'Over here,' Teca said, beckoning him. 'They left this way.' She pointed into the forest. East.

This time Maquin did run, the tracks easy to follow.

Not going to Drassil. Even in his state of focused fury he found that strange.

Where else would they go? And why?

They came to Jael's road, the tracks leading them to the river, and eventually to a muddy bank. Into the water.

'Boats, more than one,' Teca said, fingertips tracing the deep grooves in the mud.

Fidele is a prisoner of the Vin Thalun, and they've put her in a boat and rowed away. Lykos must be behind this.

He fell to his knees in the mud, face a rictus of rage, snarling and spitting like a trap-caught beast.

'We should go back. We need more eyes,' Teca said.

'You go,' Maquin said, knowing the sense of it, but unable to walk away from here, the thought of moving further away from Fidele a physical pain in his chest. 'I'll stay, begin the search along the bank.'

'I'll stay, too,' Spyr said, 'and help . . .' he trailed off. Guilt gnawed at him – that was clear.

And grief. He's lost sword-brothers today. Men he was close to.

Teca stood still a moment, looking at him.

Most likely gauging if I can be trusted. If I'm in my right mind.

He forced himself to turn away from the river, to look Teca in the eye.

'Fidele is all that matters. Me being maddened beyond all thought will not help her, so I will control that beast,' he said, his voice as cold as winter rain. 'And I swear, by Elyon above and Asroth below, I will find her. And if she is hurt . . .' He ground his teeth, made a sound in his throat beyond words, fingers closing around a knife hilt, pulling it out and cutting across his palm. He held it out, a white-knuckled fist, blood dripping into the river.

'There will be blood.'

CHAPTER SIXTY-FIVE

CAMLIN

Camlin coughed, pain ripping through his chest, and he opened his eyes to a bright, glaring light, like staring into the sun.

I'm dead.

He coughed again, felt his lungs burning, throat raw. He tasted salt. Pain in his back, and his shoulder.

No, not dead. There's pain. Don't think you feel this kind of pain when you're dead. Don't suppose you feel anything at all.

A freckled face with red hair and a too-large helmet filled his vision, blotting out the glare.

Meg.

'He's waking up.'

Meg bent down and hugged him.

He opened his mouth to talk but only a dry rasp came out, his throat feeling as if it'd been scraped out with a tanner's knife. So he tried to sit up instead. That was more painful; the movement waking up a host of injuries that he tried to ignore, a groan slipping out of his throat.

He was in their rowing-boat, waves slapping against the hull. Craf was perched upon the prow like a scruffy figurehead, while Vonn and Brogan sat at a bench, pulling on oars as if their lives depended on it.

'You're dead,' Camlin managed to croak at Brogan.

The bull-necked warrior was soaked to the skin, a huge mottled bruise spreading from the arch of his eyebrow down across one side of his face, all the way to his jawline.

'That's what I said,' Vonn grunted.

'Should be,' Brogan agreed, the muscles of his prodigious back bunching and straining.

'You all should be,' said Meg with a frown. 'I was waiting where we agreed. Then there were two great explosions of water either side of the boat. Thought some monstrous leviathan had come to eat me for supper. But it was just you and Vonn, falling out of the sky. Craf helped me find you both. Vonn was easier, as he was splashing about and choking. You were bobbing face-down. Thought you were dead. Vonn hauled you in and pounded on your chest a bit, then you started breathing, threw up, coughed yourself half to death, threw up again and passed out.' She shrugged.

'Then No-Neck fell out of the sky. Lucky he didn't capsize us with the wave he caused.'

'Huh,' grunted Brogan.

'Wasn't easy getting him in the boat,' she said.

'Can say that again,' Vonn managed to get out between oar-strokes.

'Why aren't you dead?' Camlin asked Brogan.

'Well, I was on the stairs, knocked everyone flying. I was the first back on my feet, trying to get a sword in my fist, then that giant appeared.'

'The one you fought, with the axe?' Camlin breathed.

'No. The one that was our prisoner. The woman. She gave me this,' Brogan said, shaking the side of his face that was one huge bruise at Camlin. 'Punched me in the head, knocked me off my feet, back up onto the wall. Then she chased after me, picked me up . . .'

'Can't have been easy,' Meg commented.

'And then she threw me over the wall.'

Camlin nodded.

Was that to kill him or save him?

Then Camlin remembered why Brogan had thrown himself at the enemy on the stairwell.

'I'm sorry, lads,' Camlin said. 'I've made a right mess of things. Lorcan . . .'

'Not your fault,' Brogan said sadly. 'There was no stopping Lorcan. You'd have had to tie him up.'

I should have. Might have hurt his pride, but least he'd still be alive.

'*Poor Lorcan,*' Craf croaked from the prow. '*Morcant bad man.*'

He is, thought Camlin. *One that needs killing.*

'I hope I meet him again,' Brogan snarled, his knuckles abruptly white on his oar.

'Careful of him,' Vonn said, 'for all his mouth, he's deadly with a blade.'

'We'll see,' Brogan said.

'And we're going back without the necklace, as well.' Camlin shook his head.

'What's this, then?' Meg said, pulling a length of silver and black stone from a pocket inside her cloak.

'*Craf catch it*,' the bird squawked. '*Craf clever.*'

'Damn it but you are, Craf my lad,' Camlin said.

Hope that wipes the smile off of Rhin's face.

Camlin checked himself over. He was soaked to the skin, but by some miracle his new sword was still in its scabbard, and a few arrows left in his belt-quiver.

'My bow?' he asked them.

Meg shook her head. 'Burial at sea.'

The Baglun was growing closer and larger. Camlin's skin started to prickle as he realized how exposed they were.

Need to get under some cover.

They reached the ford that crossed the river and climbed out of the boat, starting to carry it across the shallow stretch of water, boots crunching on shingle, Craf launching into the air in an upwards spiral. Within moments he was squawking, circling back down to them.

They all stopped in the middle of the ford, looking north to where Dun Carreg rose like an iron spike in the distance.

'*No, THERE!*' squawked Craf, swooping northwards, drawing their eyes beyond Dun Carreg. Camlin blinked, squinted, rubbed his eyes.

'Asroth's teeth,' he whispered.

The giantsway to the north of Dun Carreg, and all the land about it was filled with a crawling tide of men. Thousands of men, the iron of helms, mail, weapons sparkling in the rising sun, an ocean of flame. Rhin's warband had come in all its strength.

CHAPTER SIXTY-SIX

CORBAN

Corban walked beside his sister. She was injured, walking with a limp, battered and bruised, though no broken bones, and besides her Buddai hobbled along, too, though he'd still managed a little frolic and caper with Storm.

'Ah, but it's good to see you, Cy,' he said, wrapping an arm around her shoulder and pulling her close, kissing her head. 'Now tell me how you escaped from Drassil.'

He listened as she told him, puffing his cheeks out and shaking his head.

My sister's a hero out of the old tales. He told her so and she elbowed him in the ribs.

'You're the one that slew the draig!' she said.

'Aye, well, I had a lot of help there. And I think you softened it up for us.' He looked at the wolven claws strapped to Cywen's wrist, the crusted blood on the blades.

'These are yours,' she said.

They were walking through Forn, Coralen taking them back to the glade where they'd last seen the camp. Coralen hoped that the new one would be close by, and that they'd be spotted by camp guards or a scouting party.

Corban felt exhilarated to be back finally, at the same time a tension and anxiety was growing within him. The journey back from Gramm's hold had been . . . pleasant, a time when he had been with his closest friends, every day. They had laughed a lot, talked constantly, or Dath had, and he had been with Coralen, of course.

And that's been very good. More than good. The best thing. His eyes drifted to her, a rare beam of sunlight was touching her red hair, making it look like a burning flame. He realized he was smiling, just from looking at her.

But now they were back, and with that would come the revelation about Meical and the prophecy. He wasn't looking forward to that.

Corban and Cywen had caught up with what had happened to each other after their separation but Cywen paused when it came to describing what had happened to her fellow prisoners.

'Calidus had a daily ritual,' she said after a long pause. 'He challenged you, called you out, thinking you were with the resistance in Forn. When you did not answer he killed a prisoner. He impaled them upon spears. I didn't want to tell you, but once you're back at the camp you'll find out soon enough. Better to hear it now, from me.'

Corban felt a mixture of rage and shame at that.

More death, because of me. He felt muscles twitching in his jaw and cheek as he thought on it, and saw Cywen looking at him.

'There's a lot more to tell,' Cywen said. 'I have news, about Calidus. About the Seven Treasures, and about his plans.'

Footsteps pattered behind them, Haelan running up. His white ratter was with him, as well as one of Storm's cubs. Corban could not believe how they had grown, this one the size of an adult hound already, a dark brindle coat and face black as night giving her a formidable appearance, her amber eyes unsettling.

'I wanted to say I'm sorry,' Haelan said, looking up at Corban. There were tears on his cheeks.

'You've done no wrong,' Corban said. 'I wanted to thank you for looking after Storm and Buddai's cubs so well. They're a fine-looking lot.' They all looked over at Storm, who was beset by her cubs speeding around her, nipping at her, rolling around, bouncing about like spring-born lambs. Storm was swaying between noble indifference and puppy-like playfulness, throwing herself on her side, slapping them with her paws, putting their heads inside her prodigious jaws, then jumping back to her feet and proceeding as if they were not there.

'You're wrong,' Haelan said. 'I have done something wrong. Storm had six cubs. There's only five now.'

'What happened to the sixth one?'

'The draig . . .' Haelan said, then dipped his head, shoulders shaking. 'The draig killed Fierce. He was standing over Swain, trying to protect him, the fool cub.' Haelan sobbed a little, then turned away and looked behind them. Corban followed his gaze, saw the injured Swain in Laith's arms, his leg bound as best they could. Hild and Farrell were striding beside her, Sif upon Farrell's shoulders.

'Sometimes courage is foolishness,' Corban said, 'but I'll never scold someone for it. It wasn't your fault, Haelan. You can't stop something or someone being what they are. These cubs are Storm's and Buddai's; they've got courage and loyalty flowing through their veins. They'd die for you, kill for you, because they love you.' Corban looked at Storm, a tear in his own eye. 'She's stood over me enough times, and I know I wouldn't be here now if she hadn't. And I'd do the same for her.' He ruffled Haelan's hair. 'You've done a grand job with them, but this is a dark, cruel world, and terrible things beyond our control happen every day.' He looked at the cub padding along beside Haelan, tall as the lad's waist already. 'This one seems to be your shadow.'

'That's her name!' Haelan said, a smile stretching across his face. 'I named her for her colour – she looks like a shadow when she moves in the dark.'

'Well, in her case the name definitely fits,' Corban said.

'There's something else, as well,' Haelan said. He reached into the pack strapped across his back, and with a grunt pulled out a shirt of mail.

'It's yours,' Haelan said.

'So it is,' Corban said. 'How did you get that? It was in my chamber, with my claws . . .' He looked at Cywen.

'A friend managed to bring them out,' Haelan said, sniffing.

'Well, I'm grateful for that, I can tell you,' Corban said, taking the coat of mail and holding it up. 'Farrell and Laith forged this for me, and I think I'll be having great need of it, soon enough.' He squeezed Haelan's shoulder. 'My thanks.'

Ahead of them Gar and Coralen stopped, Coralen holding up a fist.

'Here they come,' Coralen said.

Then the undergrowth around them was shaking, coming to life. Dark-clothed warriors with curved swords were emerging all around them. Corban recognized Akar, Gar's one-time rival and now friend. The two Jehar embraced.

Akar saw Corban and dropped to one knee, the other Jehar with him following suit.

Corban sighed.

I'd forgotten about that.

Corban walked into the camp, straight and resolute. Word of his return had spread, and cheers were ringing through the forest. Many faces he recognized, smiling and greeting them, holding hands thrust at him, squeezing shoulders, sharing a few words. He met Wulf like that, who grinned to see him, but then was running past him, falling on his knees before his wife and bairns, scooping them into a weeping embrace. And Tahir, the young captain of Isiltir, who, upon seeing Haelan, fell to one knee and wept as Haelan threw himself into his arms. There were also a host of faces that Corban didn't know, many men clothed in the black and silver of Tenebral. Despite Cywen warning him of their presence, his hand reached for his sword hilt when he saw them. There were also giant faces that he didn't recognize, one with striking black hair, a spiked strip of it running down the centre of his head, the sides shaved to skin.

Much has happened here in my absence.

And then he saw Brina.

She was standing upon a shallow rise, a small figure, pale-faced and worn. Corban broke into a run, and then he was sweeping her up into his arms, spinning around with her, squeezing her tight, tears running down his face.

'All right, you oaf,' Brina grunted, 'enough. You're going to crack my ribs.'

Corban put her down, held her shoulders and looked her up and down. She was grinning, too, tears glistening upon her own cheeks. She looked older, the lines in her face deeper, a grey pallor to her skin that he did not like.

He pulled her close again and kissed her cheek. Usually she would have swatted him away, but this time she let him, even kissed him back.

'I see she found you, then,' Brina said, nodding her head at Storm. 'I thought she might.'

'Coralen told me you healed her,' Corban said, 'that she was on the brink of death.'

'Aye, well, she's a tough girl,' Brina said, affectionately scratching Storm's chin as she padded over and nuzzled the old healer, almost knocking her over.

'Thank you,' Corban said.

'You can make it up to me by helping me organize this rabble, kick that demonic horde out of Drassil and teach Calidus and Nathair what happens to people who make me angry,' she said.

'All right,' he grinned.

The others were joining them now, Gar and Coralen, Dath and Kulla first.

'You've managed to keep Dath alive a little longer, then,' Brina said to Kulla.

'Yes,' Kulla replied seriously. 'Though he has done his best to test me on that.' She shot Dath a dark look.

'A bear hit me, Brina. It wasn't my fault.'

'I'm sure it was,' Brina said, though she couldn't quite remove the smile from her face.

Hulking figures loomed behind Brina: Balur One-Eye and Ethlinn, with the giant with the fearsome hair standing behind her.

'Ach, but you're a sight for sore eyes,' Balur said to Corban and they embraced, looking more like father and child.

'It's good to see you,' Corban said, 'and you too, Ethlinn, Queen of the Clans.'

Ethlinn raised an eyebrow at that, but smiled at him.

'I've been talking to the Jotun about you,' Corban said.

'To Eld?' Ethlinn asked.

'Aye. Before he was slain.'

'Slain!'

'Aye. I'll tell you of it after. And who are you?' Corban asked of the dark-haired giant with them. He looked at him more closely. 'You are familiar to me.'

'I am Alcyon, of the Kurgan,' the giant said. 'I have heard much of you, Bright Star. Your sister did nothing but talk about you on our long journey from Dun Carreg to Murias. *My brother will kill you*, she said, more than once, though to be fair she aimed that mostly at Calidus rather than me.'

Corban frowned.

'Alcyon!' Cywen cried, running up the hill. 'How are you here?' She looked at him, suspiciously at first, then shook her head. 'I never thought that you were like them. There was something else in you. Kindness.'

Alcyon dipped his head to her, a thank you. 'I am glad that you still live,' he said, 'and I am sorry for my part in your troubles.'

'But Calidus?' Cywen said. 'How did you escape him?'

'I am under his spell no more,' Alcyon said. 'Thanks to Veradis.'

Cywen smiled. 'He is here? Made it out of Drassil?'

'Aye. He is there,' Alcyon said, pointing down the hill at three men who were striding up to them.

'Let me introduce our new recruits,' Brina said to Corban. She looked behind the three men, as if searching for someone.

'Strange,' Brina said. 'Where is Fidele?'

'Fidele?' Corban asked.

'She is Nathair's mother, and deeply opposed to him. A good woman, a good leader, respected and loved by her people. I like her.'

Corban frowned, staring intently at the healer. 'Brina, are you sober?'

'What?'

'You don't usually appear to like anyone, is all.'

'I like Storm,' Brina said and poked him with a bony finger. 'Make the most of it,' she added, 'I doubt it'll last.'

The three men approached. One of them, little short of giant proportions, stepped forwards and Corban offered his arm.

'I'm Krelis ben Lamar,' the man said, taking Corban's forearm in the warrior grip. 'Lord of Ripa. Heard a lot about you.' He looked Corban up and down. 'I thought you'd be bigger.'

Corban shrugged. 'Well met,' he said. He returned Krelis' look. 'To be honest, I've never heard of you, or Ripa. But I'm glad you're here, and I hear you've brought men with you, for which I'm even more grateful.'

Krelis stared down at him, eyebrows knotting, then he laughed. He elbowed a stern-faced man besides him, staggering him. 'I like him,' he said.

'This is my baby brother, Veradis ben Lamar,' Krelis said.

'Have we met?' Corban asked, frowning.

'Aye. Briefly.' Veradis regarded Corban with serious eyes. 'It was dark, though, and you had a wolven pelt over your head, and claws on your fist.'

Corban's eyes narrowed. 'Domhain?'

'Aye. You challenged Nathair to fight you. I answered, because I was Nathair's first-sword, but the men of my shield wall pulled me back.'

'I remember now. Why did they do that?'

'Because they thought that *he* would kill me.' Veradis nodded over Corban's shoulder and he looked to see Gar standing behind him, face blank and his eyes fixed on Veradis.

'You killed my friend,' Veradis said to Gar, taking a step forwards, away from Krelis. 'At Dun Carreg.'

Abruptly there was a tension in the air. Corban had been at Gar's side in Dun Carreg, when Gar had slain men in black and silver. Nathair's eagle-guard.

The men who murdered my da.

And now Corban was fighting the urge to draw his sword, feeling an irrational anger at the man before him. He mastered the emotion and compulsion. Just.

'If he was dressed as you, then it is likely that I did,' Gar said. 'I killed a few of your kind that night.'

Corban saw a flicker of movement in the fingertips of Veradis' sword hand.

'The only eagle-guard that Gar slew at Dun Carreg were in the feast-hall,' Corban said, his voice measured and cold. It was the only way he could keep it from breaking. 'I was there too, and saw him do it. He was taking vengeance upon them. For they had just slain my da.'

'Your da?' Veradis said, eyes still fixed on Gar.

Corban opened his mouth to speak, but nothing came out, emotion like a great wave drowning his words.

'Nathair put a sword through Thannon's heart,' Gar said. 'After your eagle-guard had attacked him. One man against many. Thannon was as a brother to me,' Gar said. 'The finest man I've known, besides my own da, and Corban.'

'Twelve of your eagle-guard stood against my da,' Corban continued, monotone, reciting it like a lay. 'And he fought them because

386

they were attacking our King Brenin, murdered him, under the eye of Nathair. Your King.'

Veradis ripped his eyes from Gar to look at Corban.

The moment stretched.

'I did not know,' Veradis said, eyes finally dropping. 'He was a good man, my friend Rauca. He was not evil, had no malice in him. He was serving his King. He was obedient and loyal. He was deceived, as I was.'

Gar stared at him, stony faced.

'Then I am sorry for his death,' Gar said eventually. 'He is as much a victim of treachery and deceit as Thannon was. His death should be avenged.'

'Aye. That was always my opinion,' Veradis said. 'But now I see that the guilty man is not the one I thought. Nathair is the one responsible.' His hand dropped away from his sword hilt and he sighed, a long exhalation.

There was a hush around them. Corban realized that the whole warband was silent, watching. His heartbeat loud and fast.

'Well, I for one am glad that's over,' Krelis said. 'I nearly wet my breeches.' He nudged his brother. 'Don't go doing that again,' he whispered, though all heard.

Veradis stepped forwards and held his arm out to Corban.

Corban hesitated a moment, and then took it.

'Well met, Corban,' Veradis said. 'I am sorry for the grief that Nathair has brought upon you, and for any part that I have played in it. And I swear to you, here and now, before more than a thousand witnesses: I will do all that I can to right those wrongs, or else avenge them.'

Corban held Veradis' gaze, saw only honesty in his eyes, a genuine remorse and conviction. Despite the fact that they had just been heartbeats away from trying to kill one another, Corban decided that he liked the man.

'Can't say fairer than that,' he said, and Veradis nodded.

Then the third of the group, a silver-haired man, stepped forwards.

'My name is Alben, and I have the dubious honour of having been swordsmaster to these two reprobates.' He gave Veradis and Krelis a hard stare. 'I have been waiting for this day for many years. I am a follower of Meical, as your King Brenin was, and am ready to give my life for you, the Bright Star.'

Corban just stared at him a moment, felt a wave of sympathy for the man.

Someone else who has been deceived, used. Given his life to a manipulation.

Corban drew in a deep breath.

Best get this over with.

He turned and strode to the crown of the hill he was standing on.

'It is good to be back,' Corban called out, and a roar rose up from the crowd.

'I'm happy to see so many of my sword-brothers and -sisters again. And to meet new ones. Many of you must wonder why I was not at the battle of Drassil, how it came about that I was taken prisoner by Jotun giants.'

He looked around the hill, saw many heads nodding.

'I was not in Drassil because I had argued with Meical, my Ben-Elim counsellor, and had gone into the forest to think. I had discovered that the prophecy that he had spoken of, used to steer me, was but a ruse, a strategy of war, manufactured by him and his Ben-Elim kin to lure Asroth and the Kadoshim into moving too soon.'

He paused, allowing time for his words to sink in.

Some faces were shocked, some appalled – like Alben, who had just spoken to him, and many of the Jehar. Others became angry, some confused.

'So what does this mean? What are you saying to us?' a voice called out: Wulf.

'I am saying that many of you followed me thinking I am the Bright Star of prophecy. I believe it is right that you know the truth. Truth and courage, remember, is the code I strive to live by, that my da taught me. So if you do not wish to follow me any longer, that is your right, and your choice.'

'Meical lied to you?' Akar said, many Jehar gathered behind him.

'Aye,' Corban said. 'The Ben-Elim wish to win their war against Asroth and his Kadoshim. The prophecy was designed to lure Asroth from his fortress in the Otherworld, to manoeuvre him into a position of vulnerability. You, me, all of us, we are but pawns in that plan.'

'The Ben-Elim have betrayed us,' Akar said, shaking his head. 'Our whole lives we have believed a lie.'

'They have used us,' Corban said.

'Asroth is no lie,' Gar called out, stepping forwards. 'Calidus, Nathair, the Vin Thalun. Our enemies. They are no lie. The Ben-Elim have used and deceived us, but our enemy remains the same. The fight remains the same. And prophecy or no, I follow Corban, unto death.'

Corban looked at Gar, words failing him.

'You *are* the Bright Star,' a voice cried out, higher pitched than the others. It sounded angry. Corban suspected it was Haelan.

'Aye. You slew Sumur, when no man could have,' Akar said, lifting his head. 'You are our Bright Star.'

'The Bright Star,' Dath called out, grinning at Corban.

'The Bright Star,' Ethlinn boomed.

'The Bright Star,' another yelled, and another, until it was being chanted by hundreds. Corban shook his head.

'But, the prophecy is a lie,' Corban said when they quietened.

'So what?' a voice shouted – a voice and face that Corban recognized. Javed of the Freedmen. 'I for one do not care. I never followed you because of a prophecy. I followed because you saved me, and because my enemies are here, and if I don't face them, they will kill me, or worse, make me a slave again. I still want to kill them. The prophecy changes nothing.'

'For once, Javed, I agree with you,' Corban shouted, and laughter rippled around the hill.

'Death to our enemies,' Javed yelled, repeating it.

'Death to our enemies,' Wulf joined him.

'Death to our enemies,' the cry was taken up by them all, a wave of sound, a recognition of injustices endured, of kin murdered, homes burned, friends and loved ones slain.

Corban looked around at them all, more than a thousand men and women raising their voices, and he thought of the long list of crimes committed by his enemy, the deaths of his mam and da, his

King, so many throughout Ardan and Domhain, the slaughter at Gramm's hold.

'DEATH TO OUR ENEMIES,' Corban cried out, joining his voice to theirs.

CHAPTER SIXTY-SEVEN

CYWEN

'DEATH TO OUR ENEMIES,' Cywen yelled, her mind and heart full of memories: of Ronan in the Darkwood, his blood running through her fingers, of her mam, dying in her arms, of the dead and wounded at Gramm's hold, of the daily screams of the impaled in Drassil.

It must come to an end, and the only way is death. Death to Calidus, death to the Kadoshim, death to Lykos and Nathair.

Slowly the cries died down, the crowd falling quiet, a hush settling over the forest. Cywen looked up at Corban, saw the emotion running though him.

She felt an arm wrap around her shoulders and saw Brina's wizened face looking at her.

'Welcome back, my apprentice,' Brina said, gazing at her with concerned eyes. 'I'm glad you're here, because I've had so much to do; I could do with some help, someone to do my bidding.'

Cywen laughed at that, though there was a cracked, manic edge to it. 'I never thought I'd be glad of the day I got to do chores for you,' she said.

'Well, then, all I can say is that you're going to be very glad, indeed,' Brina said with a twitch of lips. 'First, though, I think you could do with a cup of tea and some honey.'

A commotion rose up from the edge of camp, someone was running through the trees and tents, up the hill. A woman, dressed in leather and furs, holding a bow in one hand. Cywen recognized her as one of the first that had joined them in Narvon, fleeing villages that were being devastated by the Kadoshim as they marched south from Murias.

Teca. Her name is Teca.

Teca ran up the hill, pushing her way through the crowd, then saw Corban, her troubled expression giving way to shock, and then to a flash of joy.

'You're back,' she said, a smile upon her face now.

'Aye. Well met, Teca,' Corban called down to her. 'What's wrong?'

'Fidele,' Teca said, her smile vanishing, 'she's been taken.'

Uproar broke out then, hundreds of voices calling out at once.

'QUIET,' Balur boomed, and a new silence fell.

'What can you tell us, Teca?' Brina asked grimly.

'Fidele left in the night, with Veradis' rescue party. From what I understand, her intention was to go to Nathair, hoping to reason with him, to turn him from his dark path.'

Grunts and murmurs rippled around the camp.

'But not far from here she was set upon, her shieldmen slain, and she was taken. Vin Thalun were amongst the dead. The strangest thing, though, is that their tracks led to the river, not back to Drassil. Maquin is searching along the riverbank now, but we need more hands and eyes.'

A hammer-blow of realization struck in Cywen's head.

Lykos!

Alben was coming forwards now, calling out orders, organizing a group to go with Teca and widen the search.

'I know where she is,' Cywen called out, striding forwards, repeating herself over the clamouring. Alben saw her.

'Where?' he asked her.

'Lykos has her, and he is bound for Arcona.'

Alben stared at her, horror-struck.

'Lykos,' he whispered. Then, to Teca, 'Take a score of men. Fetch Maquin back here.'

Brina stepped forwards. 'A meeting of captains, I think,' she said, clapping her hands together. 'Follow me.'

Soon Cywen was in a small clearing, sitting upon a tree stump with those whom Brina deemed should be in attendance. Storm was pacing the shadows. She seemed . . . bigger; more ferocious.

Not a bad thing, in days such as these.

Cywen looked about the circle, at this gathering of captains: Jehar, giants, warriors and ex-slaves.

What a strange and diverse group we are.

Brina passed Cywen a small bowl of tea.

'Tell us what you know,' Alben asked her.

'Wait,' Brina said, holding a hand up to Alben. 'Wait for Maquin. He will be here soon, and Cywen will only have to repeat herself.'

'Maquin?' Corban asked.

'Fidele's shieldman, and her lover,' Brina said. Cywen raised an eyebrow at that, and Krelis coughed into his hand. Veradis blushed.

Brina will always say the truth as it is. Or as she sees it.

'He's one of the few men in this rabble I like,' Brina said. 'Straight-talking. Single-minded. Some might call him rude.'

A male version of you, then, Brina.

'And he is a killer. Not a man that can kill, like the rest of you. Look in his eyes.'

'She's not wrong,' Javed muttered. 'He is the greatest pit-fighter that ever lived. And that means he's better than me.' He wiggled a hand in the air and grinned. 'On his best day.'

'Fidele is his life,' Brina said. 'So I suspect that you will not see him at his best.'

There was the sound of tramping feet, then Teca led a number of men into the circle. Amongst them stalked a man whom Cywen recognized from Brina's description. There was a stark elegance to his movements, his eyes scanning constantly for threats. He was not overly tall or muscular, but still he radiated strength, a power controlled in his every move. He was not young, his hair was iron-grey with streaks of black in, his face a lattice of scars, most of one ear missing.

No doubt that's Maquin, then. He looks like one of those granite crags that poke from the sea, off of Dun Carreg's cliffs, weathered and battered, but unbroken.

'Why am I here,' he said to Alben, his words clipped short, as if he were having trouble breathing.

'Cywen thinks she has information about Fidele's capture,' Alben said. 'She is Corban's sister, who has returned to us.' He gestured to Corban, and Maquin gave him an absent nod.

'Tell me,' Maquin said, turning his wolf gaze upon Cywen.

'Lykos has set out on a mission for Calidus,' she said. 'Calidus is seeking to gather the Seven Treasures to himself. He needs them all to perform a ritual that will release Asroth and his Kadoshim, allow them to enter the Banished Lands and become flesh.'

'We know this,' Brina said.

'Well, he has discovered their whereabouts, or at the least, clues to their likely whereabouts.'

'How?' Javed interrupted.

'He found a hidden room, a forge, carved within the heart of the great tree in Drassil's great hall. It is the room that the Treasures were forged in, and upon its walls is scribed a map by Halvor, the counsellor of Skald. On the map are the likely locations of the Treasures, or at least, where Halvor thought they were at the time of his scribing.'

Balur One-Eye shared a look with Ethlinn. 'I heard rumours of such a place,' he said, 'but I never knew.'

'The map placed the cauldron, necklace and cup in Benoth with Nemain,' Cywen recited them as Trigg had told her. 'The spear at Drassil. The dagger with the Jotun in the Desolation and the torc in Arcona. We know about the axe.'

Alcyon hissed. 'I dwelt in Arcona before Calidus took me as his prisoner,' the giant said, 'and I never heard even a whisper of the Treasures.'

'Well, the map says it is on some island, called Kletfar? Something like that. It is in the centre of a great lake.'

'Kletva,' Alcyon whispered. 'A place of shadow and death. None go there.'

'That's it,' Cywen said. 'Anyway, that is where Lykos is going. To get the starstone torc,' she finished.

'Why the river?' Maquin asked.

'It flows from Arcona,' Alcyon growled. 'It is like a road carving through Forn for them.'

'How many swords went with him?' Maquin asked Cywen.

'I did not see them leave,' Cywen said, 'but they had five boats – rowing-boats they built for the task.'

'How many oars did their boats have?' Javed asked.

Cywen considered. 'Three on one side, three on the other. So six.'

Javed nodded. 'Six-oared rowing-boats. Five of them. A hundred men and they'd be overloaded, so probably less. Eighty to ninety men is my guess.'

'Not a great warband, then,' Corban said.

'No. A raiding crew, designed to move fast and strike hard. Lykos' ship-breakers, no doubt.' Javed glanced at Maquin, who nodded a curt agreement.

'My thanks,' Maquin said and turned to leave.

Alben grabbed his arm.

'You cannot go alone,' he said to Maquin. 'You will fail.'

Corban stood up. 'We need that torc,' he said. 'Fidele must be rescued and Lykos stopped. So someone must go, and you're right, Alben. They cannot go alone.' He strode to Maquin. 'Maquin, are you fit to lead?' Corban asked him. 'Brina said you speak the truth, even if it is harsh. Would you turn that truth upon yourself?'

Maquin regarded Corban, as if seeing him for the first time. 'I am fit to lead,' he said grimly.

'You will have two tasks: rescue Fidele, and bring the starstone torc back to us.'

'Fidele will come before the torc, always,' Maquin said. He thought about it a few moments. 'Fidele said we are all dead, in the end, if we do not defeat Calidus and the Kadoshim. So if the torc is vital to that, then, yes. I will bring the torc back, if it is in my power.'

'Then choose who you will take with you,' Corban said.

'I need hard men, men of endurance to hunt him down; men who can keep up with me,' Maquin said, looking around the ring of captains. 'The Vin Thalun called me the Old Wolf,' he growled. 'Now they will find out how true they spoke. We shall all be wolves, and Lykos will be our prey.'

'I'll come with you, Old Wolf,' Javed said. 'And I'd think a fair few of my Freedmen will be like-minded. A chance to kill Lykos and Vin Thalun – sounds like fun.'

'How many?' Maquin asked him.

'Fifty of us, if they all want to come.'

'Good. But not enough.'

Alcyon, Teca and Alben all stepped forwards.

Maquin nodded but looked at Alben.

'It'll be a long run,' Maquin muttered, 'and you're recently injured.'

'I'm well enough, and if I can't keep up, then just leave me behind,' Alben said. 'I'll pick some men from Ripa. Fidele is in their hearts and many will wish to come.'

'Good, then,' Corban said. 'Without boats it'll be a long, hard journey. You'd best make ready.'

Maquin didn't need telling twice, he marched off.

'How are you feeling?' Brina asked Cywen.

'Better,' Cywen said.

Corban began to pace about the circle, looking at his remaining captains. 'We need to work out how we're going to win this war,' he said. 'But I've been away too long. So first, tell me, where do we stand now?'

They gave Corban a run-down of the warband's numbers and the new arrivals. They spoke of their tactics, orders left by Gar, to harass and disrupt wherever they could, but to avoid open engagement.

'At first there were daily patrols that ventured forth from Drassil,' Akar said. 'Vin Thalun, eagle-guard, even Kadoshim. They thought us beaten and routed and wanted to keep us running. That strategy didn't work so well for them.'

Cywen remembered seeing the gates of Drassil opening, a ragged band of wounded Vin Thalun limping through it.

'So now they patrol no longer,' Akar said.

'Nothing?' Corban asked. 'Not even scouting parties? No reconnaissance at all?'

'Nothing,' Akar said, a touch of pride in his voice. 'Since Nathair left to join Lothar, the gates of Drassil have remained closed. Apart from when Veradis tricked his way inside. See! Another victory through guile.'

'Much to be said for guile,' Wulf said.

'I'm fond of a good ambush, myself,' Coralen said beside Corban, her hand brushing his just for a moment, a gentle caress.

Looks as if those two have sorted themselves out at last!

Krelis informed Corban of how they had eradicated the threat of Gundul's warband from Isiltir, and told him of Lothar's warband cutting its way closer to Drassil, building a road with the protection of Nathair and two thousand eagle-guard.

'We should try and stop them reaching Drassil,' Corban said. 'As with Gundul, they will be weaker apart than together.'

'Aye,' Veradis said.

'So we must find a way for fifteen hundred to destroy six thousand, without losing many swords along the way.'

'That won't be easy,' Veradis said. 'Gundul was unprepared, taken totally by surprise. Also, Lothar is a different beast. I knew him when he was Braster's battlechief. What I saw of him was capable and efficient. He fought well at the battle of Haldis. Not innovative, though. A traditional man.'

'What does that mean?' Krelis said.

'It means he's like you,' Veradis said. 'He doesn't like change.'

'That's true,' Krelis nodded. 'I don't.'

'But he has Nathair and two thousand eagle-guard,' Veradis said. 'Their shield wall will be very hard to beat.'

'But beat them we must,' Corban said.

'We are working on some ideas,' Veradis said with a small smile.

'What about the earth power?' Corban asked. He looked from Brina to Ethlinn. 'You giants are versed in it, are you not?'

'Things are not as they were,' Ethlinn said. 'When the clans split, all were powerful in the earth power, but as the years passed, faith dwindled. I do not know what you understand of the power, but faith is . . . important.'

Cywen felt the weight of the book still inside her cloak.

There are different forms of the earth power, she thought. *The way of faith, more powerful, but less reliable, or the other way – the way of blood and bone. But that has a price, and it is difficult, awkward.* She glanced at Brina, saw that the healer was watching her like a hawk.

'Some remained scattered throughout the clans who were versed in the power,' Ethlinn continued. 'Nemain and Uthas were two such in our clan. But for the most part the power withered amongst us and died out.'

'Each road feels as if it is blocked before it is even begun,' Corban said. 'And what of Calidus and his Kadoshim? What is he up to now?'

'He has not ventured from Drassil since the day they took it,' Akar said.

'Nor will he,' Cywen said. 'His every thought is of the Treasures – to protect the ones he has, and to gather the others to him.'

'So we are back to the Treasures again,' Corban observed.

'I've a feeling the Starstone Treasures will decide this war, one way or another,' Brina said to them all. 'I have the beginnings of an idea, but it would be fraught with danger, the risks high. And it would only be possible if the Treasures were all together.'

Which is a danger in itself, if Calidus were involved.

'Three are accounted for in Drassil,' said Ethlinn. 'And we have heard tonight about the others. The torc is in Arcona. The dagger with the Jotun in the Desolation. That still leaves the cup and neck-lace in Benoth.'

'Rhin has them,' Cywen said. 'Or says she will have them, before too long.'

All in the circle looked at her.

'Rhin and Calidus communicate, somehow. By dark magic, I think.' She glanced at Brina. 'Calidus has summoned Rhin here, ordered her to muster her warband and ride to Drassil with the other Treasures.'

'So Drassil is the heart of the web,' Veradis muttered.

'It is,' Ethlinn agreed.

'Only one Treasure would be left unaccounted for, if Cywen's information is right,' Brina said, tapping a long finger on her chin. 'The starstone dagger.'

'It is not unaccounted for,' Corban said, standing and reaching beneath his cloak. He pulled a scabbard around that was hooked to his belt, hidden on his back. He grasped the hilt of what looked like a short sword, similar to the one that Veradis wore at his hip. Corban drew it, held it up, and Cywen saw that its blade was coal-black.

'The starstone dagger,' Corban said.

CHAPTER SIXTY-EIGHT

RAFE

Rafe rose from his cot and stretched tentatively, testing his wounded leg.

Better, he thought, putting some weight on it. The wound was healing well, scabbed up and itching. It had been a hell of a job to cut the arrowhead out of his leg, taking two giants to hold him down as someone dug around inside his leg with a knife.

That Camlin's got a lot to answer for.

He'd seen wounds like his before, a cut deep into the muscle of his thigh, and he'd known they could take well over a moon to heal, if ever, so he should be pleased, really. *Who'd have thought drinking from an old stone cup would help me heal twice as fast as another man? Faster.*

Only a ten-night had passed since Camlin had put an arrow into him and run off with the starstone necklace.

Horns sounded, coming from the direction of Stonegate.

Visitors?

The fortress and village were already full to bursting. Geraint had brought four thousand to Dun Carreg over a ten-night ago, which had made Rhin's mood only slightly better after the loss of the star-stone necklace.

Scratcher got up, stretched, and came over, licking Rafe's hand. Rafe pulled on his breeches, his new boots and a linen shirt and buckled his sword-belt, draped with silver, then set off in search of whatever had set off the horns.

He was staying in his old chambers in Evnis' tower, had swept out the room and brought in fresh linen for the bed, an armful of rushes for the dog to sleep on. Rafe was happier here, slept better.

When he reached the courtyard of Stonegate a crowd was already gathering. He climbed the wide stairwell by the gate tower, the exercise helping to reduce the ache in his leg. Once on the wall he looked out over the rolling meadows to the north-east of the village, which were awash with tents, men and temporary paddocks. Beyond them the giantsway cut a dark swathe through the land, and as Rafe looked at the ancient road he saw a new warband upon it, well over a thousand strong.

The heavy thud of giants' boots drummed behind him: Uthas and his shieldman, Salach, striding into the courtyard, Eisa behind them. Rhin followed, walking with her battlechief Geraint and a score of shieldmen. The crowd parted for her and she climbed the stairwell, saw Rafe and joined him.

'Good morning, precious,' she said, smiling at him and running one finger down the length of his spine, ending with a squeeze of his buttocks.

'My Queen,' he dipped his head and blushed.

Rhin had come to visit him in his tower room twice now since she had woken from the starstone cup's sleep. Both times she had stayed all night, leaving him exhausted and unnerved when she padded from his chamber as the sun rose. It was all a bit of a shock, becoming a queen's lover, and it had happened so quickly.

Not that it hasn't got its advantages, he thought, his hand resting upon the hilt of his fine new sword. On both occasions Rhin had brought him gifts, a silver torc one night, and this sword the other, complete with fine-tooled belt and scabbard.

'It's Conall,' Rhin said beside him. 'And only twenty-six nights have passed since I summoned him.'

'He must have been riding through the night, my Queen,' Rafe said.

'Indeed. He must *really* want to keep his position as my regent in Domhain.' She smiled at Rafe. It wasn't a pleasant smile. Rafe remembered sitting with Rhin in a chamber in Dun Taras, Domhain's seat of power, watching through Rhin's sorcerous means as Conall had set his brother Halion free from her dungeons and helped him escape.

Rhin's not one to forget, or to forgive.

Rafe recognized Conall; he was leading a small band up to the fortress, sitting tall and proud on a roan stallion. He looked up to the battlements and saw Rhin as he clattered across the wide bridge, through the arch of Stonegate and into the courtyard, where he turned his stallion in a tight circle, slipping from its back and landing lightly on his feet.

He met Rhin by the gate tower, dropping to one knee before her, taking her hand and kissing her ring.

'Up,' Rhin said, and Conall rose with a wide grin on his face. He was dressed in travel gear but it still looked regal – wool and leather of the finest quality, a new gold torc about his neck, his warrior braid threaded with gold wire, his cloak the green and blue of Domhain. Rafe noticed more than one knife sheathed upon his sword-belt, both the belt, sword scabbard and knife sheaths finely wrought and studded with silver.

Looks as if Conall's enjoying the life of a ruler, but I see that old habits die hard. I'd wager he has half a dozen more knives secreted about his body.

'Well, but I never thought I'd be riding through these gates again,' he said, looking up at the brooding bulk of Stonegate. He turned back to Rhin.

'I must say, you're looking fine,' he said.

Rhin smiled. 'I think this sea air agrees with me.'

'That it does,' he said, looking Rhin up and down. She seemed to like the attention.

'You are not dressed for war,' Rhin observed.

'I'm dressed for fast travel, my Queen,' Conall said. 'Brought my war gear with me, though, never fear.' He flashed a smile. 'Thought there might be a fight at the end of the road.'

'You're right,' Rhin said, 'there will be. Though there's still a long road left to travel, and we'll be leaving on the morrow. Rest your men and your mounts today, Conall.'

'And where will this road be taking us, if you don't mind me asking?' Conall enquired.

'Drassil.'

Rafe entered Rhin's chambers and saw that he was not the first to arrive. Conall was sitting with his boots up on a table. He greeted Rafe with a warm smile.

'Good to see you, lad,' Conall said, sounding as if he meant it. He was like that, all warmth, like your oldest friend, or hard as frost-bitten nails. There was no in-between or subtlety with Conall; he wore his emotions openly.

'You too,' Rafe said. He actually liked Conall.

'So you're not coming to Drassil with us, then,' Conall said. 'More's the pity. It'll be a rare sight, I'm thinking, and a good fight at the end of it.'

'Rafe will join us there, won't you?' Rhin said as she stepped out from her bedchamber, gold wire wrapped through her silver hair. She was dressed in riding gear: woollen breeches and long boots, a leather fur-trimmed jerkin. She looked as healthy and fit as a much younger woman, her skin all but glowing with vitality, her eyes sparkling.

'I will,' Rafe said. 'Once I've completed a task.' He shared a look with Rhin.

Others were entering the chamber now, Uthas and Salach, last of all Geraint.

They all sat around the table in Rhin's antechamber, apart from Salach, who assumed his customary place behind Uthas.

'Quite a day,' Rhin said. 'At first light on the morrow we begin a long journey, taking the might of the west to fabled Drassil.'

'And what awaits us at Drassil, my Queen?' Geraint asked.

'Battle and blood,' Rhin said. 'Victory and glory.'

Conall slapped the table, grinning.

'Our allies are there,' Rhin continued, 'Nathair and the lords of his alliance. He needs us. His enemies close on him, and so we must go.'

'Over four thousand men are gathered on the meadows, not counting Conall's warband, and more will be travelling down the giantsway over the next ten-night,' Geraint told her. 'It will be a long journey, though, and some of it through winter, I would guess.'

'Aye,' Rhin said, 'you are correct, Geraint, and practical as ever. We must travel fast. Spare horses for every man, and no wains. All our provisions must be carried by pack-horse. This will be no ponderous crawl through the Banished Lands. No, this will be a sprint to the finish line. A race to the greatest battle of our time. We must not fail.'

'Sounds like my kind of war,' Conall said. 'I hate all that waiting around for battle. This is much better. Run at them. Hah!' He slapped the table enthusiastically again.

'We will be travelling through our allies' lands,' Rhin continued, 'and I have been assured that we will be welcomed at their fortresses along the way, and reprovisioned. As for winter, if we move fast, we will be at the outskirts of Forn Forest by winter's first kiss. Seasons are different within Forn, I am reliably informed. Stripped of their extremes. We must make good time, and then all will be well.'

'When do we leave?' Conall asked.

'First light on the morrow,' Rhin said. 'Morcant, you will remain, as regent of Ardan.'

'What about Edana?' Morcant asked.

'That spoilt bitch not still causing you trouble?' Conall asked.

'A little,' Rhin said, watching Conall closely.

Does he know that his brother Halion is here, fighting for her? Surely he must.

'That is why you will stay, Morcant. I will leave you fifteen hundred men, more than enough to see her and her fledgling warband rooted out of their hole and put into a cairn. And when you are finished with her you shall lead those men to join me.'

'It shall be done,' Morcant said.

'Good, then all that is left is for us to make ready and go,' Rhin said, clapping her hands. She stood, her chair rasping on stone, then paused and looked at them all. 'These Banished Lands will be a different place when we are done.'

Rafe stood with Morcant above Stonegate, watching Rhin and her monstrous warband ride away, close to five thousand warriors riding out, the late summer sun turning them into a glittering wave sweeping eastwards.

'That is quite the sight,' Rafe said.

'It is,' Morcant agreed. 'And if you do your job well we shall soon be joining them.'

'Don't need t'worry about that,' Rafe muttered.

Morcant sneered at him and walked down from the battlements, leaving Rafe to watch Rhin's warband fade into the east.

Wish I were with them now. Looks like something the songs'll tell of for many a cold night.

'I will go,' he murmured to himself. 'I will see Corban again.'

As soon as I have the starstone necklace in my keeping.

Rhin had come to him last night and made it clear that he must bring her the starstone necklace before she reached Drassil, or he would lose his head. One or the other. And he knew she'd do it, because she was scared – no, *terrified* – of arriving in Drassil and not having the necklace to present to Calidus.

I have to get that necklace back. It is life or death to me.

And one other thing Rhin had said to him: 'This Camlin that I am hearing so much about. He killed my Braith, thwarted Morcant and Evnis in the swamps of Dun Crin, sneaked into my own fortress and stole from me. I want him dead.'

It'll be my pleasure.

CHAPTER SIXTY-NINE

FIDELE

Fidele groaned as she awoke.

Better to be asleep. Better not to know where I am. I cannot stand another day of hearing his voice, of seeing his face.

Not for the first time, she thought of throwing herself over the side and into the river, of ending it all. But something kept her from that final act. Perhaps it was because she still dreamed of seeing Maquin again, and of seeing Lykos' death.

'Did you sleep well, my lady-wife?' Lykos said from behind her.

When Fidele didn't answer, he turned on his bench and looked down at her.

'Ah,' he muttered, bending down amicably to wrap his arms around her and lift her onto the bench beside him. He pulled the cloth from her mouth. On the first day he'd removed the cloth first, and then lifted her, but she'd bitten a chunk out of his ear, and now he left her mouth bound until he was sitting a little further away from her.

She looked about her. Five boats rowing up the river, the one she was in leading the way, the others spread behind, like the blade of a spear. It was early, mist curling on the river, hiding the dark depths, and she regarded it suspiciously. On the first day of rowing one of the boats had grated on a submerged boulder and the collision had thrown a man into the water. He was being hauled back on board when something had grabbed him from beneath the surface. Fidele had only had a glimpse of it: long and sinuous, a mouth full of razored teeth.

Men were grunting, sweating as they pulled oars against the

current, but the river was wide and sluggish here, and it felt as if they were making good time, water hissing against hulls.

Five nights we've been travelling. But where? The trees of Forn grew thick about them, the canopy above thin and frayed as branches stretched over the river, letting sunlight through in greater abundance than Fidele had seen for some time.

'Where are we going?' Fidele asked.

'We're on a quest, my wife,' Lykos said good-naturedly. He looked as if he'd just finished pulling at an oar, his hair sweat-soaked, his leather jerkin loose. Fidele glimpsed the rippled flesh of his chest where Maquin had burned him.

'A quest where? For what?' she asked.

'We are going to Arcona, searching for one of the Seven Treasures,' Lykos said.

Arcona! The grass plains to the east of Forn Forest.

'Which Treasure?' Fidele asked, hoping against hope that she would somehow become free and be able to share this information with her people.

Lykos gave her a long, measuring look. 'No harm telling you,' he said, smiling at her. 'Not like you'll ever leave my side again.'

That made her shudder, and she refused to dwell on it. When she had been captured she had been certain that her life would be measured in moments, Lykos dragging her through the darkness of the forest, bound, gagged and stumbling for what felt like a ten-night. She'd thought she was being hauled back to Drassil to be presented as a prize to Calidus, but instead she had soon heard the rush of the river and seen five boats sitting in the water, full it seemed with grim-looking men and a handful of black-eyed Kadoshim. Ninety-two bodies in total, it turned out, including her. Enough that three shifts of rowers could split the day, so even though the boats were heavy-laden and they were rowing upstream it seemed to Fidele that they moved incredibly fast. Lykos was skilled on the water, whatever else she thought of him.

'The starstone torc,' Lykos said. 'I am reliably informed that it is to be found in Arcona.'

'And Calidus needs the Treasures to fulfil his plan,' Fidele said. She looked at the Vin Thalun sitting in the boat, some rowing, a man at the back manning a steering oar, others resting. Two of the

Kadoshim were also in the boat, their black eyes fixed on the path ahead. Thankfully the one surrounded by a swarm of flies was on another boat.

I wonder if Lykos' men know what Calidus would do with the Seven Treasures. Would they be so eager to aid him if they did?

Fidele had spent much time in conversation with Brina, a woman she had come to respect, and she had told her what had come to light regarding Calidus and his schemes.

'To open a portal between the Banished Lands and the Otherworld,' Fidele said loudly, 'so that Asroth and his Kadoshim may cross over and become flesh.'

A few heads twitched to look at her.

'Exactly!' Lykos said, beaming at her. 'A woman of intellect,' he said. 'I admire that, and find it attractive. Far more than just a fine shape to you.'

She shuddered.

So far Lykos had not touched her in that way. It was something that she had been both immeasurably grateful for and also the thing of which she lived in perpetual fear.

But it will happen, if I remain in his power. I see the way he looks at me. Hungry.

She willed herself to think about something else.

The starstone torc. If it is important to the enemy, then it is important to us. If by some miraculous twist of fate I escape Lykos and get back to my people, this knowledge could be valuable.

And Lykos says it is in Arcona. What do I know of that land? The whole realm is mostly grass land; vast, rolling plains, and it lies to the east of this great forest. No doubt at the end of this river. The Sirak dwell there, I remember them from Aquilus' council. Strange-looking men, shaven-haired, scar-latticed. Small, fierce and war-like. They were not unified. A realm of many clans and kings, or whatever they call them, forever in some conflict or dispute with one another. And they rode shaggy-haired ponies, rather than warhorses. Even their kings.

Fidele racked her mind for any other shred of memory, but could think of nothing else.

If I don't get away from this boat I will see the plains of Arcona soon enough.

She sat and stared behind them, eyes scouring the riverbank, wishing, willing, that she saw movement. Wishing that she saw Maquin.

Rain dappled the river, darkness a cloak over them as Fidele's boat moved slowly through the night.

Torches had been lit, fore and aft, and the two Kadoshim bent their backs relentlessly to rowing, a Vin Thalun leaning over the prow, scanning for rocks or anything else that could give them a nasty surprise.

'We'll not stop,' Lykos' voice said behind Fidele, a bodiless whisper on the night. 'Day and night we'll row, because I mean to be back in Drassil before Midwinter's Day. A fitting time to renew our wedding vows, don't you think?'

'That will never happen,' Fidele said, her voice cold and hate-wreathed. 'I will die, first.'

'Oh aye, no doubt that would be true, if I tried to take you now.' Lykos twisted his fingers into her hair, jerked her hard so that he could whisper into her ear, his breath foul. 'I imagine you'd throw yourself into the river, let the things of tooth and slime have your flesh, rather than me.'

'That's right.'

'But Calidus is back in Drassil. It's amazing what he can do with only a lock of hair.'

Revulsion goose-bumped her flesh, a thousand spider-legs skittering across her skin. She remembered a clay effigy with a lock of her hair set within it, remembered the control it had given Lykos over her. Made her a slave-puppet to his every wish and whim. But inside, she had been screaming.

'So I shall wait,' Lykos said, 'and you can dream of escape, and I shall dream of Drassil, and we shall see whose dream comes true.' He licked her ear and she jerked away.

He moved away, chuckling softly, and Fidele lay on the boat's floor, her mind filled with horror. Slowly she controlled it, thought of better things.

She thought of Maquin, of her last night with him, their bodies intertwined. Thought of stroking his face before she'd left, watching him sleep. Tears bloomed and she blinked them away.

I will see you again.

CHAPTER SEVENTY

RAFE

Rafe kicked at his mare, urging more from her gallop along the giantsway. Wind snatched at his hair, pulling it out wild as a mane behind him as he bent over her arched neck, sweat staining her coat, Scratcher pounding along on the meadow parallel to them.

'Almost there,' he yelled as he pulled on the reins, sending her skidding down the giantsway's embankment and onto a hard-packed road, galloping like the north wind through the outskirts of Havan village and then pounding up the track that led to Dun Carreg.

Rafe had to rein in hard once in the courtyard, as it was crowded with warriors, all with mounts, clad in Rhin's black and gold. A quick glance showed mud-stained boots and cloaks, dust-caked horses.

Probably more latecomers answering Geraint's muster. Other warriors had passed through Dun Carreg's gates for the same reason, and Morcant had sent them on their way after Rhin's warband, over a ten-night gone already.

Rafe rode on to the courtyard before Dun Carreg's keep, leaped from his horse's back and sprinted up wide steps into the feast-hall.

It was dark, a low fire crackling in the fire-pit, Morcant sitting at a table upon a dais; a warrior in black and gold stood before him.

'. . . food, rest, provisions for your journey from our kitchens,' Morcant was saying to the warrior, the captain of those in the courtyard, Rafe guessed. He was broad-shouldered, with red hair streaked with silver, a scar dissecting his braided beard.

'How many of you?' Morcant asked.

'Two hundred and fifty swords, my lord,' the warrior replied.

'I've found them,' Rafe blurted, skidding to a halt before Morcant.

'What?' Morcant said, turning a bored expression upon Rafe.

'Edana and the rebels, in the Baglun,' Rafe all but yelled. 'I've found them!'

Morcant stared at him a few moments, then slowly stood.

'Sound the call to arms,' he said to a guard standing close by. 'Prepare my war gear.'

The guard hurried to the feast-hall doors, put his horn to his lips and blew.

'Sounds as if it's about to get busy round here,' the red-haired warrior said to Morcant. 'If we can just restock our provisions, we'll be on our way.'

'To hell with that,' Morcant said. 'You're Rhin's warriors, you can ride with my warband and fight her enemies. You can damn well earn your food.'

Rafe sat impatiently upon his horse as Morcant rode into the courtyard, followed by a score more mounted warriors, all in gleaming mail and iron helms, clutching spears, shields slung across backs or strapped to saddles.

Morcant pulled his black stallion in a tight circle.

'Time to clear this land of some vermin,' he yelled. 'They've been raiding and burning, striking and running away, the cowards. But now we know where they are.' Men rattled spears on shields. 'Time to show them how real warriors behave. We'll return to these walls when our enemy lie dead at our feet.'

Louder cheering, and then Morcant was kicking at his horse's ribs and cantering out through the arch of Stonegate, Rafe falling in beside him. Together they rode across the bridge and down the hill, an endless double column of riders flowing from the fortress, seven hundred men. At the base of the hill more men gathered, a larger force, falling in as Morcant rode past them, surging up to the giantsway and heading south, towards the Baglun.

Rafe had found Edana's camp in the trees close to the Oathstone glade and the giantsway. They'd even cut trees down from the glade, making it more habitable. Rafe had caught a glimpse of Edana, thought about trying to sneak in and put a knife through her eye, but thought it more risky than storming the camp with fifteen hundred swords.

Over seventeen hundred now. He smiled, glancing back at the mass of warriors behind him.

'Let me take a hundred men east,' Rafe said, 'and flank them. I'll flush them out into the open glade, and then . . .' He grinned.

'Vengeance,' said Morcant. 'For my silver, my tower, the humiliation at Dun Crin. And the score of arrows that Camlin has put into you.' He looked at Rafe and smiled back.

'Time for Camlin to die,' Rafe agreed.

CHAPTER SEVENTY-ONE

CAMLIN

Camlin sat on a stolen horse, trotting down the giantsway, sun dappling the flagstoned road.

Regardless of the sun and blue sky, there was a crisp chill to the air, and about them the leaves were shifting from green to russet and gold.

Autumn's coming, and winter won't be far behind. Not a good time to be living rough in the forest.

Behind him fifteen more men and women rode, Baird one of them, humming a tune as he itched absently at his eyeless socket. Baird had insisted on coming along because he was bored; he was the only one of Camlin's crew with a shield slung over his back. The rest of them were mostly woodsmen and hunters, happier with bow and spear than sword and shield.

The trees of the Baglun thinned and Camlin heard the chatter of water over shingle as they neared the ford across the river Tarin, then the trees were gone and they were in open ground, the river before them, meadows rolling towards Dun Carreg.

A dark shadow came plummeting down from the sky, screeching and squawking.

'*WARE THE ENEMY,*' Craf was crying, over and over again.

Then Camlin heard them – a rumble that grew quickly, setting stones rattling and dirt sliding down the giantsway's embankment. Mounted warriors appeared from behind the curve of a gentle hill. A great wave of Rhin's black and gold, no end to them.

'By Elyon above and Asroth below,' Baird breathed.

For timeless moments Camlin and his raiders just sat on their horses and stared, open-mouthed.

From the head of the warband a rider drew his sword, pointed it at Camlin and his crew and shouted some battle-cry. A wordless roar rose up from the warband as they spurred their horses on.

As if a spell had broken, Camlin lurched into motion, tugging at his reins, kicking, swearing at his mount, everyone doing the same, back towards the Baglun.

Camlin felt panic spreading as he struggled to get his horse moving in the right direction, others jostling into him, then he was away, reaching a gallop as he passed under the eaves of the Baglun's first trees.

And then everything was sound and motion. The thunder of hooves about and behind him as a storm crashed across the old river ford, Camlin clinging to his horse, Baird in front of him, whooping like it was a Midsummer's Day race.

Camlin's crew clustered about him, faces set in hard, frightened lines, all knowing that death resided in heartbeats, the road speeding by beneath pounding hooves, branches above growing thicker, all the while the thunderous avalanche of horseflesh and screaming warriors behind them growing ever closer.

I'm a dead man.

And then they were bursting into a glade of bright sunlight, the Oathstone standing dark and tall to Camlin's left. He reined in hard, others about him doing the same, a few galloping on, ducking low in their saddles so that heads and bodies lay tight against their mounts' necks.

Camlin scrambled from his saddle, slapping his mount's rump, and the mare was flying off down the giantsway again. He heard Baird yelling for him to hurry as he slithered down the embankment, broke into a run, heart pounding in his mouth, legs pumping as he sprinted with a dozen others towards the treeline, leaping into its shadows as their pursuers hurtled into the glade.

Shadowed figures appeared around Camlin, a short one thrusting his new-made bow of elm into his hand, waving a quiver of arrows at him. Then he was turning, crouching behind a bush and gasping in gulps of air.

'Well, that worked a treat, eh?' Baird said to him, grinning wildly.

'Bit too well,' Camlin said. 'Think I've soiled my breeches.'

That made Baird laugh like a madman.

CHAPTER SEVENTY-TWO

RAFE

Rafe squinted at the sudden brightness of the sun as they burst into the Oathstone glade, dazzlingly bright after their gallop through the twilight of the Baglun.

Horses galloped ahead, their enemy disappearing into shadow as they sped through the glade and back into the Baglun's gloom.

Camlin's leading them.

Seeing him had incensed Rafe, and the plan of sneaking and flushing the enemy out of hiding was suddenly so much wasted breath.

No matter. We have Camlin now, he cannot escape from this, and we are too many for Edana's rabble, whether we take them by surprise or not.

The Oathstone reared dark and rune-written to Rafe's left, the glade around them wide and sunlit.

Different from how I remember it. Wider. Not a glade now, more a meadow. Then Rafe saw the stumps of fresh-cut trees.

'MORCANT,' Rafe yelled over the din of their charge, 'STOP!'

Morcant glanced at him as Rafe leaned back in his saddle and dragged on his reins.

Morcant followed suit, sawed on his reins, his horse tossing its head, hooves skidding. Riders about them sped on through the glade and into the shadows as the forest closed above them. A heartbeat later those same warriors were thrown from their saddles, as if some invisible god had just flicked them hard in the chest, sending them hurtling through the air. The horses galloped on. In moments a dozen men were down, rolling on the giantsway and trampled by those behind, more men falling with every heartbeat.

Then Rafe saw it, a glint in the dappled light.

Ropes.

'They've strung ropes across the giantsway,' he bellowed to Morcant.

Morcant and Rafe were yelling, waving arms at the riders behind, horses skidding on the flagstones, down either side of the embankment, spilling onto the meadow grass as the bulk of the warband came galloping into the glade. More men fell to the ropes across the road, but the rest were slowing now and milling on the giantsway, spreading deeper into the glade. A great groaning creak rose up behind them and Rafe twisted in his saddle to see a tree toppling across the giantsway, a great booming crash as it slammed into the road.

It's a trap.

Fear raced down Rafe's spine.

A moment's silence, dust settling. A bee buzzed industriously about a cluster of purple foxglove, oblivious of the warband it was sharing the glade with.

Then figures were stepping out of the shadows: men and women, all with long bows in their hands. Thirty, forty of them. They formed a ragged line, pulled arrows from quivers, nocked and drew their bows.

Loosed.

Blood in the sunlight, men and horses toppling, screaming, death throes churning the turf. Another flight of arrows thumping into flesh, muscle, mail, Rafe swinging out of his saddle, running behind his horse, using it as cover, heading down the embankment. Morcant yelling orders, mostly ignored. Then battle-cries from the far side of the giantsway, hidden from Rafe's view. The clash of iron rising up from that direction, more screams. Rafe saw horsemen spur their mounts at the archers – forty, fifty riders together, maybe more, led by a quick-thinking captain – a wall of flesh and hooves and iron, spraying grass and earth as they leaped into motion.

The archers didn't move, just kept on drawing, loosing, a handful of riders toppling back in their saddles, a horse's front legs collapsing, ploughing into the ground, but the rest continued their charge. Fifty paces from the archers, and still they didn't move. Another volley of arrows saw more men thrown from their saddles, but the wave of horsemen held their line, only twenty paces from the archers now.

Rafe grinned.

They're dead. They'll never get out of the way in time.

And then the wall of riders disappeared, as if swallowed by the earth itself.

CHAPTER SEVENTY-THREE

CAMLIN

Men and horses screamed.

Camlin drew and loosed, again and again and again, firing down into the trench that had taken back-breaking days to dig, then been covered and hidden with a lattice framework of willow branches overlaid with a layer of turf and scattered with autumn leaves. Now the trench was full of men and horses, some screaming with broken bones or pierced with arrows, others desperately scrambling to get out. Two warriors right in front of Camlin were close to climbing out, forsaking their mounts and using sword and spear as spikes to pierce the earth and pull themselves up the steep slope. Baird lunged forwards with his sword and one warrior fell back, gurgling blood. The other one collapsed twitching with one of Camlin's arrows through his eye.

'Like mice in a grain barrel,' Baird said as he stabbed a warrior, then kicked another in the head.

Those who had charged them were mostly dead, a pile of butchered meat in a ready-made grave. Camlin looked up, saw more of Morcant's warband coming their way, further back a mass of horsemen clustered around the tree that had blocked any retreat down the giantsway. From the far side of the giantsway the din of battle echoed, where Pendathran and his men fought.

The gruff battlechief had arrived two days ago, bringing three hundred and forty men with him.

The time for us to roll our knuckle-bones is here, Edana had said. *It's do or die.*

That it is, Camlin thought, looking from the ditch before him, full

417

of blood and guts and slime, then up to the giantsway, clogged with raucous battle. And so far the plan had worked well.

Almost too well. That race before Morcant's warband was too close for comfort.

Camlin had seen Rafe enter the Baglun two days gone, had been waiting for him, and had left a trail for him to follow. Not too obvious; he'd been trained by Braith, and so Camlin knew Rafe would be good. No, just enough to ensure that Rafe would get a glimpse of Edana's camp. Once Camlin saw Rafe slinking away he knew he'd be back with Morcant and a warband. All that was left to do was lure them into Camlin's killing ground.

Other riders were gathering on the meadow and giantsway, orders flying, organizing, swords and spears pointing at Camlin and his crew.

'Ready, lads and lasses?' Camlin shouted, drawing, nocking, choosing his target. His arrow took a man through the throat, sent him tumbling sideways from his saddle, one foot stuck in his stirrup, his horse running off. Others fell as Camlin's archers released their deadly hail.

Then the riders were moving, not bounding into a gallop, but a more controlled canter that ate up the distance between them and Camlin's crew.

'Ready!' Camlin yelled again, another arrow nocked and loosed. He saw it skitter away, a glancing blow across an iron helm.

'Back,' he shouted as the riders swept around the edges of the long pit, bearing down on Camlin's forty from their flanks, but Camlin and his crew were stepping back into the treeline, melting into the shadows, the horses crashing into the undergrowth after them, men ducking beneath low branches, weapons snaring.

And then new figures were appearing: a host of warriors rising up from the undergrowth and roaring out of the shadows, led by a blonde-haired woman, clothed in chainmail shirt and leather surcoat, hair knotted in a thick warrior braid that curled beneath her iron cap.

Edana, spear in her hands, Halion at her side.

They carved into the riders with a deafening roar.

A crashing of hooves to his left, and Camlin was spinning, a horse bearing down on him, iron glinting as a sword rushed towards his head.

Sometimes you can be too busy watching someone else's back to take care of your own.

Camlin threw himself backwards, tripped and fell as a sword hissed through the air where his neck had been. He rolled to the side, as hooves sought to trample him.

Another figure appeared, moving in close to the rider, iron clashing, then the figure was jumping away, the rider's saddle girth cut and he was slipping, crashing to the ground.

'He's all yours,' Baird grinned at him and swept off amongst the trees.

Camlin rushed forwards and kicked the rising warrior in the face, stabbed down into his mouth, sprayed teeth as he ripped his blade free. The man's boots drummed on the turf, then were still.

Camlin stood over him, breathing heavily, then he wiped his sword clean on the dead man's cloak and retrieved his bow. The enemy within the trees were dead or retreating, Edana leading her warriors out onto the meadow. They ran after the retreating horsemen and charged at the milling crowds upon the meadow. Pendathran and his warriors were spread amongst them, visible upon the giants-way. Camlin gathered his archers about him, seeking a spot from where they could wreak the most ruin.

'Good fight,' Baird grunted at Camlin as he pulled his sword from a dead man's ribs.

'Aye,' Camlin said, pausing to survey the field. They were still vastly outnumbered, but the enemy were fighting in milling confusion. Edana's and Pendathran's men on foot were slipping amongst the too-close horsemen, swords and spears slashing at thighs and horses' bellies.

We may be outnumbered still, but the odds are a damn sight more even than when I came galloping into this glade.

Baird ran at a rider, leaped, one hand grabbing the back of the saddle and heaving himself up, sword raking across the warrior's throat, then Baird was jumping away, the dying warrior spraying blood between fingers.

Camlin saw Morcant; his sword was red to the hilt. Warriors were gathering behind him, hundreds, more rallying to him, forming up into a wedge and pushing into Edana's men. Morcant chopped savagely to either side, face twisted in a snarl, men falling before him, his followers widening the gap that he was making. He was heading straight towards Edana.

'Meg,' Camlin shouted, 'you up there?'

'Course I am,' a squeaky voice drifted down.

'Think you'd better blow that horn.'

Morcant was closer to Edana, dead warriors left in a bloody wake behind him. Camlin pulled an arrow from his quiver, nocked it and drew, aiming at Morcant's chest. A knot of riders passed in front of him, obscuring him momentarily from view.

Come on. Got you now.

CHAPTER SEVENTY-FOUR

RAFE

Got you now, Rafe thought as he crept up on Camlin.

He saw him pull an arrow from his quiver and aim into the battle. At Morcant.

Rafe drew his knife and gathered his legs under him.

Then a horn blew out, long and loud. It startled Rafe because it came from almost directly above. He craned his neck, saw a small figure standing on a branch, a horn to its lips.

Then something happened in the battle.

The warriors at the far end of the giantsway – at least two hundred men, all mounted and clustered by the fallen tree – were tearing off their cloaks of black and gold and charging into their comrades. Men were screaming, horses rearing, hooves lashing, swords rising and falling.

What! Who? Then Rafe realized. *The warriors who had just arrived at Dun Carreg this morning.* He spied their red-haired captain, stabbing and hacking his way along the road.

Betrayed. Rafe felt a rush of fear, for the first time truly considered the possibility of losing this battle.

And I'd wager you've played your part in it all, you sneaky bastard, Rafe thought, glaring at Camlin's back. There was a tremor in the archer's arm as he waited for a clear shot at Morcant.

With a snarl Rafe leaped at Camlin.

The collision sent Camlin's arrow skittering high, his bow flying from his grip, Rafe stabbing at Camlin's back. The blade scraped off mail, the coat hidden under a jerkin and tunic. They rolled on the ground together, Rafe with one arm tightening around Camlin's throat. Then stars exploded in Rafe's vision and he tasted blood, was rolling, felt grass on his face. The world lurched back into focus and he was on his hands and knees, knife still in his grip, blood gushing from his nose.

Camlin had butted Rafe in the face with the back of his head. The ageing huntsman was climbing to his feet now, sword in his hand.

'I was hoping I'd run into you,' Camlin said.

Rafe jumped to his feet and hurled himself at Camlin, consumed with the urge to smash, stab and beat the life from him.

Camlin swung away, but too slowly, Rafe clipping Camlin's hip with his shoulder, sending the older man spinning, Rafe slashing with his knife but only cutting through air. Camlin's sword hissed over his head but Rafe was skidding, turning and leaping at Camlin again.

Just get close, let my knife do the rest.

They crashed together, tumbling to the turf, Rafe's knife pinned between Camlin and the ground. Pain exploded in Rafe's head as Camlin pounded him with the hilt of his sword. He bit Camlin's shoulder, swung his head up, connected with Camlin's chin, felt him go limp for a moment and put his free hand over Camlin's face, started grinding it into the ground, fingers searching for his eyes, nose, anything to rip or gouge. He felt panic in the old man as Rafe's fingers inched closer to Camlin's eyes.

Then another explosion in his head, the world spinning, and he was flat on his back, looking up at branches and blue sky. He rolled, felt his stomach lurch.

A girl was standing over Camlin. Her arm drew back and she threw something; fresh pain erupted in his shoulder.

'Little bitch,' he snarled, stumbling towards her and Camlin, backhanding her, sending her flying through the air, rolling to a stop. She didn't move.

He stood over Camlin, who was on his hands and knees now, hand searching for his sword hilt. Rafe kicked him in the ribs, lifted Camlin from the ground, sent him tumbling towards the ditch full of dead riders and horses.

'Best stop that,' a voice said behind him, 'that's my friend you're kicking.'

Rafe turned to see an ageing warrior, small and slim, his sword red to the hilt, only one eye in his head, the other socket a scar-latticed hole.

Rafe switched his knife to his left hand and drew his sword.

CHAPTER SEVENTY-FIVE

CAMLIN

Camlin spat blood.

He heard a voice, *Baird?* then the clash and grunt of blows. He rose unsteadily, a sharp pain in his ribs.

Pain's good, he told himself. *Tells me I'm not dead.*

Rafe . . .

He was a dozen paces away, trading blows with Baird, who was retreating before a savage onslaught, Rafe's attack not so much skilful, but relentless and adder-fast. Camlin took a step towards them, then he saw a small, crumpled shape in the grass.

'Meg?'

He stumbled to her side, fear spiralling within him, dropped to one knee and lifted her head.

She groaned, which helped him to breathe. Her jaw was broken, bruised and slack.

Rafe.

Camlin lay Meg down gently and advanced on Rafe and Baird.

They were both breathing hard, both bleeding, Baird along the length of one forearm, Rafe a gash across his cheek.

Boots drummed; Brogan joined them.

'This the one you told me about?' he asked Camlin, eyeing Rafe. 'The one you keep putting arrows into that won't die?'

'Aye, that's him,' Camlin said.

The two of them circled Rafe, who was edging back towards the treeline, Baird making feints and lunges. Camlin's knuckles whitened as he gripped his sword, awaited an opening. Brogan was on Rafe's far side now. He raised his sword.

Then Rafe was throwing his weapons down, dropping to his knees, arms raised behind his head.

'Mercy,' he cried, 'mercy.'

Camlin blinked, stared at Baird and Brogan, both of them looking as shocked as Camlin felt.

Baird laughed.

Camlin took a limping pace closer, sword-point hovering over Rafe's chest.

Just kill him, put your sword through his heart. He's trouble. Put an end to it, put an end to him.

Camlin's blade hovered, trembling. Rafe was weeping, snot running from his nose.

'Mercy,' he begged.

Camlin lowered his sword.

Then a horn was blowing, ringing through the clearing.

It was Vonn. He'd climbed the Oathstone and was sending blast after blast reverberating around the great glade. Camlin felt the battle ebb, men pausing to stare at Vonn.

'Edana is merciful,' Vonn cried as the last horn blast still hung in the air. 'Men of Ardan, if you fight for Rhin, lay down your arms. Edana is merciful, so lay down your arms and live.'

'Never,' a voice cried out – Morcant. He was on foot before the Oathstone, still a score or so of his men about him, Edana and her shieldmen close. 'Edana leads this rabble and nothing else, Rhin is Queen of the West.'

'Morcant is Rhin's whore,' Vonn cried out, 'a puppet of Cambren. If there are men of Ardan or Narvon amongst you, lay down your arms and save yourselves. The battle is lost for you, but Edana is merciful.'

And slowly, from only a few men at first, Camlin heard the clatter of weapons dropping to the ground, the sound growing, rippling about the field.

Morcant screeched with rage and hurled himself towards Edana, a handful of warriors following him, the sounds of battle ringing out again, but only there. Elsewhere about the field men were falling to their knees and raising their hands in surrender. Morcant cut a man down, almost within reach of Edana. Camlin saw his bow and retrieved it, took a few paces towards the battle.

Behind Camlin there was a thud, a grunt, the sounds of a scuffle. He turned and blinked, confused at first.

Baird was standing, swaying, his hands pressed tight to his stomach, looking down at Brogan and Rafe as they rolled on the grass. Even as Camlin took a step towards them he heard a crunch, saw Rafe club Brogan's skull with the pommel of his dagger, once, twice, Brogan slumping. A third time. Rafe wriggled out from beneath the bulk of the big warrior and jumped to his feet.

Camlin drew an arrow, aimed it at Rafe's heart.

Baird took a staggering step, lifted his hands from his stomach, blood-drenched. He sighed and dropped to the ground.

Camlin's arm wavered and Rafe ran, ducking, twisting, towards the treeline. Camlin loosed, his arrow thumping into a trunk, Rafe spinning away, a shadow amongst the trees. With a snarl, Camlin ran to Baird, dropped and cradled him, saw the warrior's one eye staring lifelessly back at him.

Mercy, Rafe said, shed a few tears, and I lowered my sword. And now Baird's dead. I've gone soft. Braith would have exiled me from the Darkwood for such foolishness. He shook his head, mouth a thin line.

He moved to Brogan. Blood was matting the big man's hair. A pulse beat faintly at his neck.

Camlin stared into the forest, searching for Rafe, but there was no sign of him. He stood and took a pace towards the trees.

'Camlin,' a voice whispered. It was Meg, groaning as she moved. Camlin limped over to her, carried her to a tree and laid her against it. He stroked hair from her eyes.

'My thaw urts,' she mumbled.

'I know, lass,' Camlin whispered. 'It's going t'hurt for a while longer.'

He stared after Rafe for long moments – no sign of him within the forest gloom – then looked towards the sound of battle where Morcant fought on.

Another time, Rafe, Camlin vowed. *I will hunt you down.*

'You rest here, now, girlie, where you're safe, and I'll be back soon enough,' Camlin said to Meg, then he stood and hurried towards Edana, threading his way through a field of slaughter.

Only Morcant was still fighting. Even as Camlin watched, he cut his way through two more men in a last attempt to reach Edana. But a ring of warriors stood before her. Pendathran was bellowing orders on the giantsway, organizing the rounding-up of those who had surrendered, and Drust came cantering towards Morcant and Edana with a score of riders at his back.

We've done it. I can't believe we've actually done it. All the planning, the tricks and traps and deceptions, I never dared think we'd actually win. Not when I saw Morcant galloping down the giantsway, over a thousand men at his back.

Morcant threw himself at the wall of men gathered before Edana, near enough bounced from their shields, chopped with his sword, splinters spraying, screamed in his fury, spittle flying. Then the wall parted and Halion stepped through it, dark hair tied back into his warrior braid, mail shirt red with gore, Edana behind him. She was blood-spattered, a sword in her hand now, spear gone. The blade was red. She walked tall, face fierce and exultant.

'It's over, Morcant,' Edana said.

'You foolish girl!' Morcant snarled. 'This means nothing. Rhin will return, and when she does . . .' He looked at the warriors gathered silently about him. 'Rhin will decorate this land with your innards. You'll all be food for crows.'

'If Rhin comes back, I'll have a fine reception awaiting her,' Edana said, voice proud and clear, 'but that's for another day. This day, we will be celebrating the freedom of Ardan.'

A cheer rose up, louder than the horn blasts.

A large ring had formed around Morcant, men stepping aside to let Camlin through, nodding at him, patting him on the back.

'And now for you,' Edana said, 'Morcant, puppet of Rhin, slayer of women and bairns.'

A hand slipped into Camlin's and he looked down to see Meg standing there, glaring at Morcant with a ferocious look upon her face.

Morcant just stared at Edana, proud and haughty.

'This glade stirs memories within me,' Edana continued, 'of a glade in the Darkwood, where I was riding with my mother, Queen Alona. You led that ambush. My mam . . .' She looked around at the glade. 'Ironic, that your end should happen here, in this way. Tricked, taken by surprise in a forest glade. My mother died soon after, you know.'

'I remember,' Morcant said. 'I remember hearing that news, and I was glad.'

'And I shall be glad to watch you die, now,' she replied.

Morcant spat on the floor, then lunged at her, fast as anything Camlin had ever seen. Morcant had been a half-dozen strides from Edana, but he covered them in a heartbeat, sword whipping out as fast as a snake, aiming straight at her heart. Camlin tried to move, reached for an arrow, but it was as if he were moving through water compared to Morcant's speed.

Then Halion was knocking Morcant's sword aside, punching Morcant on the jaw, sending him sprawling, stepping into the space between Morcant and Edana.

'Get up,' Halion said.

Morcant didn't need telling twice; he leaped up, circled to Halion's left, sword extended, hovering low.

'You're not even from Ardan,' Morcant said to him.

'That is of no ma—' Halion began, then Morcant was lunging at him, sword-point darting high. Halion knocked it away, parried a sideways slash from Morcant. A roll of Morcant's wrist and he stabbed at Halion's throat. Again the blow was slapped away, Halion's gaze fixed on Morcant's eyes. Then Halion took a shuffling step forwards, feinted low and struck high, stepped back with blood on his sword-tip, a thin line trickling down Morcant's cheek.

'I've seen you fight,' Halion shrugged, then he was walking forwards slowly, Morcant darting blows at him, lunges, short savage chops, looping two-handed strokes, but Halion seemed to walk through them, parrying, counter-striking, Morcant retreating, circling left and right, probing for weaknesses in Halion's defence. His blows came faster, fluid combinations that rained down upon Halion from all angles and his advance stopped, Halion setting his feet and weathering Morcant's barrage. Slowly Halion began to counter, first a single blow here, a parry turned into a strike there, then striking again and again, until they were trading back and forth at each other, blow for blow, the speed a blinding blur. Camlin watched, entranced by their skill.

Then Morcant took a step back, breaking the hypnotic power of their contest.

Halion watched him, still fixed on Morcant's eyes.

Morcant was breathing heavily now, sucking in deep breaths, one hand on his knee, sword-point dug in the earth. Morcant leaned on his weapon as if it was a walking stick.

'You don't fight, like your brother,' Morcant breathed.

'I could have told you that,' Halion said.

'Rhin knows, you know. About your brother,' Morcant said.

'Knows what?'

'That Conall set you free, from Dun Taras' dungeon.'

Halion's eyes narrowed.

'She'll kill him for it, when she's ready. Use him first, of course. But then . . .'

'You're lying,' Halion snarled.

'Really? Then how did I know who set you free?'

Halion frowned.

Morcant jerked his wrist, flicking earth from his sword-point at Halion's face. Halion swayed away, but Morcant was attacking. His sword, stabbing at Halion's throat, grated off Halion's torc, left a red line. He pressed on, chopped down at Halion's thigh, Halion blocking frantically, Morcant relentlessly pressing Halion back, towards Edana. Their blades clashed, grated, clashed again, then Morcant was in close, slipping his foot behind Halion's and shoving him hard in the chest. Halion spun gracefully away.

'See you've been learning from Conall,' Halion said. 'Unlikely to work on me, though.'

'Depends what result you're after,' Morcant smiled. Watching, Camlin realized that as Halion and Morcant had fought, Halion had remained between Morcant and Edana, but now, to avoid Morcant's trip, Halion had spun away from the young Queen and Morcant was standing only two paces away from her, nothing between them but air.

Morcant grinned, moving in a blur, his sword snaking out, slicing towards Edana's throat.

An arrow punched into Morcant's side, staggering him half a dozen paces.

Camlin stepped into the circle, another arrow already nocked and drawn. He loosed as Morcant gathered himself and took an unsteady step towards Edana, the arrow slamming into Morcant's belly, piercing leather and mail, sinking deep. Morcant grunted, sank to one knee, his sword dropping from his fist. He looked up at Camlin.

'Should have killed you, back in the Darkwood,' Morcant whispered. He swayed and coughed blood, speckling his chin.

'Aye,' grunted Camlin, striding closer, another arrow on his bow, nocked and aimed at Morcant's heart. 'But you didn't. Instead it's me killing you.'

He stopped a pace or two away from Morcant and looked to Edana. She gave him a curt nod.

Camlin's arrow flew from his bow, plunging into Morcant's chest, half the shaft disappearing, the force of it slamming Morcant onto his back. He looked up at Camlin, whispered something and then his eyes glazed, sightless.

A silence settled over the glade.

'Hang his body from a tree,' Edana snarled. 'Let Craf have what's left of him.'

'*Thank you*,' a voice cawed from the branches.

Camlin walked through the streets of Dun Carreg. It was sunset, with long shadows. The sun was warm upon his back but a chill was filling the world.

Despite the day's victory, Camlin's mood was melancholy. Despite how easy it had been to walk into Dun Carreg, the people overwhelming the handful of guards manning the gates before Edana's warband had even crossed the bridge to Stonegate, despite the celebrations that had welcomed them into the streets, and despite the feast that was even now going on in the feast-hall.

It was Baird's death more than anything that had stayed with him. A good man. A brave man. One whom Camlin had trusted.

A friend.

Not so many of them about. And one less, now.

His feet took him to the courtyard before Stonegate, the doors closed and barred now. A few men milled by the gatehouse. Camlin angled away from them, raising a hand to their cheerful greetings, and climbed the stairwell.

Guardsmen stood on the wall, spears in one hand, skins of mead in the other.

And why not? It's a night to celebrate, if ever there was one. I remember the night this fortress fell, the night we ran, fled, across a sea, two realms. And here I am back again.

A solitary figure stood apart on the battlements, gazing out over the land. A big man, neck muscled like a bull. Camlin stood beside him. Beyond the steep drop of the wall the world spread before him, the sinking sun painting the meadows and coves, woodland and pastures in hues of amber and pink.

'I'm surprised you're not dead, No-Neck,' Camlin said. 'Glad you're not, is what I mean.'

'Got a hard head,' Brogan grunted, a bandage wrapped around his skull.

'For sure.'

They stood in companionable silence for several minutes, watching the grey of dusk seep into the world.

'I'm going after Rafe, on the morrow,' Camlin said. 'Leaving at first light.'

Brogan glanced at him. 'Thought you'd be staying here a while,' he said.

'Job's done here,' Camlin muttered. 'And we have the necklace. It's not much use here, and I'm thinking Corban and the others could do with it.'

'That the only reason you're going?' Brogan asked.

'No. Thought Baird deserved better'n that, today. Doesn't sit well with me, celebrating, when Rafe's out there, and my guess is he's headed after Rhin. Least I can do is send him after Baird.'

Brogan grunted and looked back out over the landscape. 'I'll come,' he said after a while.

The shadows deepened and torches were lit. Camlin thought he saw movement beyond the bridge, a denser shape in the shadows. He stared hard, but saw no more sign of movement. Then he heard footsteps entering the courtyard. He looked back and saw Edana there, changed from her blooded war gear, but still in breeches, shirt and leather jerkin, a sword hanging at her hip. Her cloak was a little finer, dyed the grey of Ardan, edged in ermine. Halion and Vonn were with her.

There was a whisper of wings in the darkness, the scrape of talons on stone.

'Here you are, then,' Edana said, climbing the steps. 'I've been looking everywhere for you.'

'Why's that, my Queen,' Camlin said, giving her a bow. He had to admit, it did feel good to see her home, after years of running, living on the road. He smiled at her.

'What?' she asked.

'The cloak suits you.'

'Thank you,' she said, smiling in return.

'Now, my lady, what is it that I can do for you on this night of nights, when you should be feasting and basking in the glory of your victory.'

'I just wanted to tell you not to drink too much tonight,' Edana said, 'because we've an early start on the morrow and a long journey ahead of us.'

Camlin frowned. 'What journey?'

'I'm going to take the starstone necklace to Corban, and I'm taking as many men as Pendathran can spare me,' she said. 'No doubt Rhin will have every intention of coming back and trying to take my realm away from me, so I thought, I might as well kill the old bitch now, and do us and the world a favour.'

'*FINALLY*,' Craf squawked triumphantly, hopping into the torch-light.

Vonn blinked at Edana's language, a smile twitching Halion's lips.

'I think you've been spending too much time with a Darkwood brigand,' Camlin said. 'You're starting to think and talk like one.'

CHAPTER SEVENTY-SIX

CORALEN

Coralen was positioned on a ridge, her strung bow propped against a tree beside her as she stared through a gap in thick foliage at the western perimeter of Lothar's warband. She listened to the wet slap of axes meeting wood, rhythmic and constant as teams of wood-cutters felled trees, orders shouted to a myriad of workers, the creak of wains as they rolled heavily laden along fresh-laid wooden tracks, the whinny and neigh of horses and rattle of chains as they dragged logs. And in the distance, behind them all, the slow creep of Lothar's warriors.

For half a moon now Coralen had commanded the attack on Nathair and Lothar's warbands, a war of attrition that was proving frustratingly slow. Her network of scouts tracking and mapping the progress of the warband as it edged remorselessly towards Drassil estimated that it, and its road, would be at Drassil within two moons.

How are we going to stop them?

It was proving to be extremely difficult to disrupt or obstruct the road-building in any significant way, and Elyon knew that Coralen had tried, because those had been Corban's last words to her.

Until I arrive, just slow that warband down, he'd said. *Harass them, unnerve, demoralize them. And kill as many as you can.*

Coralen had planned and led more than a score of raids now. She had over a hundred hand-picked men, women and giants in her crew, and they had struck at workers, paddocks, latrines, grain stores in the camp itself, and while they had always come away with few casualties and a handful of kills between them, the strikes were never as successful as Coralen had envisaged they would be. The most effective of the raids had been on the supply train that wound the long road behind the warband, stretching all the way to Helveth in the south, but even that had not seemed to have much of an effect on the constant roll of the warband towards Drassil.

It's because of those damn eagle-guard and their wall of shields.

No matter what her tactics, the eagle-guard were incredibly disciplined, and whether the raids took place in night or day, at dawn or dusk, within heartbeats Coralen would hear that now-hated sound of shields thudding together as Nathair's eagle-guard formed protective walls about whoever was being attacked.

It was beyond frustrating.

Corban will be here soon with more swords. We need to sow fear. To whittle down numbers, make them miserable and scared before they meet us in battle.

She shifted, felt the damp of the earth she was lying upon seeping into her breeches. Behind her she heard the pad of Storm, quiet yet heavy, and the scuffle of smaller paws as three of her cubs followed her. Storm's muzzle sniffed Coralen's cheek, then licked her.

'Yuk,' Coralen muttered absently. Movement caught her eye, a few hundred paces to her right, and she saw Dath, just for a heartbeat, as he settled into his position. There were more of her people out there, she knew. Over a score of them spread around this section of the camp.

Then she heard the creak of a wain as the guard-line parted and more eagle-guard appeared, stepping out of the protection of the camp and into the twilight of Forn.

Here they come.

Six men walking in a tight line, shields overlapping, behind them a shaggy-coated auroch pulling a wain, then another. Eagle-guard marched in column either side of the wains, and another six brought up the rear. A handful of men walked behind each wain, shovels over their shoulders, eyeing the forest.

Twenty-four eagle-guard, ten labourers.

The wains were piled full of night-soil, taking it to be dumped in the forest away from the camp – a sensible measure to reduce the chances of sickness and infection.

Coralen rose into a crouch and followed them, Storm and her cubs slipping into the shadows.

The small convoy wound its way into the forest, picking a way between high-branched trees. It stopped no more than six or seven hundred paces from the camp. Coralen crouched behind a thorn bush, drew an arrow from the quiver at her belt, nocked it, and waited.

The eagle-guard formed a loose ring as the labourers began emptying the wains.

Coralen counted fifty heartbeats, then drew her bow and aimed, finding a guard with his shield held too low.

Her arrow took him in the throat. He dropped, choking on his own blood.

Then arrows were flitting from the forest, a buzz of angry wasps. Two more guardsmen and four labourers fell before the shields were up and horns were sounded. Answering horns rang out from the camp. A huge spear slammed into a shield, piercing it, throwing the eagle-guard to the ground.

They have too few men, only enough for one row of men around the wains. They cannot reinforce any gaps – if a man falls they will become impossibly stretched.

Another spear hissed out of the forest, one of the auroch was bellowing.

Only heartbeats left before reinforcements from the camp come running. It's now or never.

Coralen burst from her cover, running at the wall of shields.

'Storm,' she called, even as she saw others of her crew closing in around the wains, a shuffle of shields as the eagle-guard saw Coralen coming, and other forms emerging from the forest, mostly archers, men and women, three giants with hammer and axe.

Coralen stopped a dozen paces from the shield wall, respecting their blades, an arrow drawn and aimed. Dath stood beside her.

Eagle-guard stood staring at Coralen, quietly confident that they could withstand any hail of arrows or blows for the small amount of time it would take for their sword-brothers to arrive.

Then Storm was leaping past Coralen, high, over the eagle-guard with their shields, landing behind them with a roaring snarl beside a wain, a swipe of her claws disembowelling one of the labourers, then she was spinning, throwing herself at the eagle-guard from behind.

Screams rang out, blood spurting in fountains, and Coralen and Dath were loosing arrows into the gaps appearing as men in the wall turned, died. A giant skewered a man with a spear and lifted him bodily into the air, hurling him into the forest.

The shield wall disintegrated; men were running in all directions, Coralen's crew slaughtering them as they ran, even as more eagle-guard from the camp appeared a few hundred paces behind them.

You are too late, Coralen grinned fiercely as she loosed one more arrow, saw an eagle-guard stumble and fall, feathers sprouting from his back, then she was running too, chasing two fleeing guardsmen as they ran the wrong way in their panic to get away from Storm, charging deeper into Forn, away from the camp.

For a while they crashed heedlessly through the forest, unaware of Coralen behind them, moving steadily away from the camp, one of them dropping his shield as they twisted around obstructions. Eventually they stopped. The one without his shield was a young warrior with straggly wisps for a beard, the other an older man, grey sprinkling his black hair. They looked around, bewildered.

Coralen nocked an arrow.

'Which way's the camp?' the younger one asked.

The older one just turned a circle.

'This way,' he said, marching off in the wrong direction.

There was a wet slap as Coralen's arrow slammed into his shoulder, sending him staggering into a tree, shield falling from his grip. He grunted, the other man spinning wildly, holding his sword two-handed.

There was a rustle of undergrowth as Storm leaped and crunched into the older warrior, both of them crashing to the ground. The younger warrior took a look at Storm and sped off. Coralen saw Storm on top of the man she'd attacked, her jaws clamped about his forearm, sending his sword spinning through the air, disappearing into the undergrowth.

Then she stepped off him.

What's she doing? Usually has their throat out by now.

And then the cubs were emerging from the shadows. The one with the black face first, that Haelan called Shadow, and then two others.

Storm yipped at her cubs and Shadow padded forwards, hackles up, growling at the old warrior.

He turned and ran. The cubs burst into a loping run after the fleeing man.

She's teaching her cubs to hunt.

Coralen left them to it, setting off after the other warrior, whose sounds of flight were fading but still audible. She caught up with him in less than fifty paces, just as a chilling scream rang out through the forest.

Storm's first lesson.

The forest changed around them, subtly, until something struck Coralen as being wrong. There was no birdsong. Then the warrior in front of her ran into a glade, his footsteps crunching, making him slow and stop. All about the clearing were mounds of earth and forest litter, at least ten of them, maybe more. They were as wide at their base as one of the wains Coralen had just ambushed, rising in a conical shape to the height of two men. Coralen paused on the glade's edge, her skin prickling. Something under her feet crackled and she looked down to see tiny bones underfoot. Birds, rats, shrews, larger bones of foxes, badger, deer. She blinked, realized the whole glade was covered in them.

She took a faltering step away.

The warrior in the glade stared at her, holding his sword up, retreating towards the mounds.

'Stay back,' he snarled at her.

Don't have to tell me twice.

The mound closest to him began to move.

Coralen thought it was her eyes, but the surface of the mound seethed, a dark shadow spilling from its base, spreading towards the young warrior, covering the ground in heartbeats, reaching his heels, pooling around his feet, a black stain that climbed up his ankles, higher, to his knees.

He began to scream.

He swatted at his legs, his hand coming away black, covered in something that squirmed and writhed about his fingers and palm, began swirling up his wrist. Droplets of blood fell from his fingertips, spattering the ground.

He lurched into motion, stumbling towards Coralen, still screaming, dropped his sword and ripped at the stain as it reached his groin, climbed higher, ever up, like ink soaking into parchment. A dozen paces from Coralen he fell to his knees, fingers clawing at his face as the darkness crawled into his mouth, up his nose, into his eyes. He toppled forwards onto his face, feet drumming on the earth.

Coralen recoiled, understanding what it was that she saw.

Ants.

Thousands of them, tens of thousands, each one as big as one of her fingers, razored mandibles snapping and tearing at his flesh, swarming over the fallen warrior.

Even as Coralen watched, the ants began to move towards her, a great dark mass of them, like water overflowing a bowl, unstoppable. She stamped on the forerunners, felt something nip at her calf, then she was spinning around and running, heart in her throat, faster than she had ever run before.

CHAPTER SEVENTY-SEVEN

CYWEN

Cywen found Brina sitting on a tree stump with the giant book open upon her lap. She looked up as Cywen approached and smiled, her face drawn with deep lines.

'This book,' Brina said, tapping the ancient pages, 'may have the answer.'

'Answer?' said Cywen. She had given the book to Brina upon her return to the camp, and Brina had shown a rare display of excitement at having it back. Since then, though, Brina had become more and more irritable. Until now.

'Yes. To the war. It hints at something. A spell . . .' She closed the book with a snap. 'Where's Corban?'

'He's just returned to camp, back from a raid on Nathair and Lothar.'

'Come on,' Brina said, jumping to her feet, and marching off through the camp, which was full of activity, a band of a hundred or so leaving to begin a fresh raid on Nathair and Lothar's warbands. Coralen had split the camp so that there was always some kind of assault on the enemy, giving them no respite. Even so, Cywen had heard that the road was still moving steadily towards Drassil.

They found Corban pulling on his breeches after washing in a stream. He was bare-chested, bruises mottling his ribs, a long gash down one forearm. Gar and Farrell were with him, tending to their own collection of wounds.

'I'll look at that,' Cywen said, moving to inspect Corban's arm.

'Can we destroy the starstone dagger?' Brina asked as she marched up.

'No,' he said.

439

'How do you know?'

'Well,' Corban blinked, brow furrowing. 'Meical told me.'

Brina gave him a long hard stare and waited for that response to sink in. Corban reached to his belt and pulled the dagger from its sheath, turning it in his grip. They all bent close to stare at it, the blade dull and black.

'We need someone big and strong to hit it,' Cywen said.

'Balur,' Corban called out.

The giant didn't answer or appear.

'I'll have a go,' Farrell said, sliding his war-hammer from his back. 'Put it on that rock.'

Corban did, and Farrell swung his hammer high, bringing it down with all of his prodigious strength. There was a concussive *boom* and Farrell's war-hammer bucked high into the air, dragging Farrell staggering backwards. The starstone dagger remained upon the rock, completely unmarked.

'Maybe you didn't hit it hard enough,' Cywen said.

Farrell scowled at her. 'Tell that to my wrists.'

'A forge?' Gar suggested. 'Perhaps we could melt it.'

Footsteps sounded and Balur One-Eye emerged through the trees, Veradis with him. Balur looked from Farrell to the starstone dagger.

'You can't destroy the Treasures while they are apart,' he said.

'How do you know?' Brina asked him.

'We tried hard enough with the cauldron in Murias,' Balur answered. 'I spent a long time pounding it with my war-hammer. No. The Treasures must be together, and even then Nemain told me that only words of power would unmake them.'

'Unmaking,' Brina whispered.

'Aye, that is what Nemain called it,' Balur replied.

'Looks like Meical told you the truth, then,' Brina said to Corban.

'This time,' Corban agreed, a hint of bitterness edging his voice.

Meical's betrayal cut you deep, my brother, Cywen thought.

'Well, my thanks,' Brina said, picking up the dagger and passing it back to Corban. 'This has been most helpful. One more question, Ban.'

'Aye.'

'Your visits to the Otherworld. How do you get there?'

Corban shrugged. 'Meical has called me, somehow. Like a summons, I think. And sometimes I just . . .' He frowned. 'I don't know. There have definitely been times when I have been there without Meical's call. But how? The last time I was there, Meical told me that I am drawn to the Otherworld.'

'Could you go there, at will?' Brina asked.

Corban shrugged.

'Think, because that could prove very helpful,' Brina said.

'I will think on it,' Corban murmured, looking as if he already was.

Brina walked away, calling Cywen after her. She followed, then heard Veradis say something to Corban and hesitated.

'I would speak to you, of Nathair,' Veradis said.

'Aye,' Corban answered slowly. 'Go on, then.'

'Fidele left to try and reason with him. She believed he *could* be reasoned with.'

'Didn't you already try that?' Corban asked coldly.

'I did, but I was too shocked, and Calidus was close. He is the true villain here, the deceiver and manipulator. And Nathair is far from him, now, away from his influence.'

'Calidus is the head of the snake,' Gar said, 'and it was Calidus who slew Gwenith.'

'I know that well,' Corban growled. 'Calidus is the true enemy here, but every king has his battlechief, and that is what Nathair is to him.'

'Nathair has been deceived and manipulated,' Veradis repeated.

'As were you,' Corban said. 'But now you and Nathair both know the truth, and yet you are here, and Nathair is not.'

Veradis hung his head, Cywen seeing the pain in the warrior's eyes.

'Nathair knows the truth, and has made his choice,' Corban continued.

'And if Nathair chose to renounce the path he's on? Chose to stand here, before you, and ask your forgiveness?' Veradis whispered.

Corban stared at Veradis in silence.

'Would you forgive him?'

'He slew my da.'

'He did. As I have slain many while I was deceived. Deaths that I deeply regret. You speak of truth and courage. Forgiveness can be the greatest act of courage.'

The silence lengthened.

'Cywen!' Brina called, making Cywen jump and sending her running after the healer. She caught up with her in the shadow of a great oak, a fire-pit dug before it, a pot hanging suspended over the flames. Brina was prodding at the embers, the giant book open on the ground. As Cywen skidded to a stop, Brina stood and drew a knife from her belt, a look on her face Cywen had never seen before: dread and determination mingled.

Brina put the knife to her thumb and cut a red line, blood dripping into the pot.

'What are you doing?' Cywen whispered, something about the scene sending ice down her spine.

'Learning,' Brina said. 'Starting small, with just the pricking of my thumb. But if we are going to do this, we will need a lot more blood.'

'Do what?' Cywen asked.

Brina gave her a long, sad look.

'Master the spell of Unmaking,' she said.

CHAPTER SEVENTY-EIGHT

MAQUIN

Maquin ran alongside the river, and about him, as always, it seemed, Forn Forest reared, the world an ocean of oak and linden and ash. He was sweat-soaked, salt stinging a hundred scratches from thorn and branch, each breath and heartbeat a drumbeat that marked time.

Time until he caught them. Time until he saw her.

Fidele.

A thousand thousand times he had been over the last night they had had together, replayed every moment, sifting through it for clues, signs that he could have read, *should* have read, that might have alerted him to her plan.

And avoided this.

Avoided her being taken by Lykos.

Behind him he heard the tell-tale splintering of undergrowth that marked the passage of Alcyon and his son, Tain. They had kept up with him, through rain and sun, day and night, without complaint. As had the others, even Alben.

From across the river Maquin glimpsed a shadow, knew it was Teca, a dozen strides behind her Javed and his crew of Freedmen strung along the riverbank. His small band of hunters had split into two groups, one on each side of the river, in case Lykos and his men had decided to leave the river for some reason and travel on foot. A moon into their journey and there had been no signs that they had left the river. Every once in a while they'd come across a footprint and evidence of an emptied bowel, but even that was rare.

Lykos is in a hurry, and I fear they are rowing faster than we are running. Every day he is with her, every night, and I am not. What he did to her before . . .

He forced himself to stop.

Just keep running. This river has an end. I will find them. And when I do, I will kill Lykos.

Maquin broke up a hard biscuit and chewed on it. He was sitting beside the river – no fire, only a little clouded moonlight edging the darkness. He was going through his nightly ritual, checking his two short swords and his multitude of knives, sharpening, greasing. It took a long time. Alben, Alcyon and Tain sat with him.

Alcyon passed his son a water skin, his two woodsman's axes that he had taken from Gundul's camp jutting over his back. His son had one, and a spear as well. It was thick-shafted, with a heavy wide blade and an iron spike on its butt end.

'A good spear, that,' Maquin commented.

'Balur One-Eye gifted it to me,' Tain said proudly. 'I will blood it on our enemy soon.'

Alcyon grunted approvingly.

'You are of the Kurgan, and they dwelt in Arcona, yes?' Maquin asked Alcyon.

'Aye,' Alcyon grunted.

'Tell me of Arcona,' Maquin asked the giant.

'It is flat,' Alcyon said. 'A realm of long grass, gentle hills and great plains.'

'Do you know where they are going? For the treasure.'

'Cywen said the island of Kletva, set within a lake. I know of this place. This river runs from the same lake. I saw it once, when I was little older than Tain.' He ruffled his boy's hair, Tain pulling a face at the gesture.

They are not so different to us. A youth, wishing to be treated like a man.

'You saw it once?' Maquin prompted.

'Aye. The isle of Kletva. No one went there. I was told it was cursed, that a great evil dwelt there and that any that ventured there never came back.' He shrugged. 'It was a place of death. I saw dead fish floating in the lake, down the rivers. Dead horses – there are great herds of them in Arcona, small, shaggy-haired beasts that your people rode.'

'So none of your clan tried to go there?' Alben asked. 'That sounds like a challenge to the young.'

'Aye,' Alcyon said. He chuckled. 'Some did try. I tried. Went with two of my kin, all of us young, and full of pride. Delg and Cota were their names.' He nodded to himself, moustache twitching in a smile. 'We reached the island, swam through the dead fish, but something leaped upon us from rocks. I hit my head. When I awoke I was back on shore, my friends were gone, and there was blood and guts everywhere. I am ashamed to say I ran. All the way home, about thirty leagues.' He shrugged.

'I never knew that!' Tain exclaimed.

'Don't tell your mam I told you,' Alcyon said. 'After that, no one went. When younglings are born to you so rarely, and then many of them sneak off on a quest that they never return from, well . . .' He shrugged. 'You take better care of the ones you have left. Over the years that island took many of the clan. Fifty of us, at least.'

'How long, until we reach Arcona?'

'Another twelve, fifteen nights to the borderlands, if we can keep to this pace.' Alcyon pulled a face. 'Maybe. It has been a long time.'

We must be faster.

'What of your clan?' Alben asked him. 'Where are they now in Arcona? Perhaps they would wish to join our fight, if you tell them of Ethlinn.'

'They would, if any of them still drew breath,' Alcyon growled. He stared into nothing.

'Calidus,' Tain whispered when Alcyon did not speak. 'He fell upon our camp one night, a horde of the Vin Thalun at his back. The clan fought valiantly, but there were too many.'

'How did you survive?' Alben asked.

'He wanted a giant,' Alcyon shrugged. 'As his servant. To aid him in his great quest.'

'Why did he choose you?' Maquin asked.

'My father was clan chief,' Tain said with pride, 'and Calidus took me and my mother as surety, if ever his sorcerous manipulation of my father failed.'

'My son. My wife. The last of my clan,' Alcyon murmured.

'Calidus has much to answer for,' Maquin said.

'And Lykos, too,' Alcyon replied. 'He was there. Had just become

Lord of the Vin Thalun. He led them as they fell upon my people in the dead of night. It was a massacre.'

This war has been decades in the making. But it will end soon.

It was daylight, and Maquin was running again. A ten-night had passed since Alcyon had told them of his past, the tale of it sitting heavy upon Maquin. Once he had thought of giants as the enemy, as savage and cruel. Inhuman. He thought differently now.

Perhaps, when this is all over, the old hatreds will be gone. The giant clans might become one and live in peace with men.

It was a good thought, but one he had little room in his head for right now.

Fidele first. And Lykos.

The river showed flecks of foam, which had set a fire beneath Maquin's feet.

Still deep enough for rowing on, but it would be slower going. Which means we might be gaining, at long last.

Highsun came, and Maquin realized it was brighter in the forest, the trees were thinner, more sunlight breaking through from above.

We are on the outskirts of the forest.

He ran faster.

Soon after, he broke from the trees into open ground. There were patches of woodland around him, but open meadow as well. The sky was blue and clear of cloud, a pale, cold sun looking down on Maquin. And ahead of him the land rose into a steep hill, the river foaming and tumbling down slick-black rocks, not quite a waterfall. They all stopped, looking at the hill and cascading river.

'They won't have rowed up that,' Teca called out from the far bank, hands cupped to her mouth.

'Not likely,' Maquin grunted.

Soon they found tracks. The scrape of hulls on mud. Boot-prints. Maquin found a set that were much smaller, and his heart raced.

Fidele's prints. They must be.

The tracks led up the hill, following a rock-strewn winding path that twisted its way alongside the fast-flowing river.

New energy fired Maquin, the idea of being closer driving him, fear and rage swirling in his gut at the thought of what he might find when he finally caught up with Lykos.

He was the first to reach the top, just as the sun was setting over Forn behind him. He climbed onto a granite boulder beside the river and stared into the realm of Arcona as the others puffed their way onto flat ground.

An ocean of grass opened out before him, undulating and sighing into the horizon, a cold wind rolling off it. The river cut a dark line through the ocean of green, and as Maquin tracked it he saw a lake unfold in the distance, a dark stain upon the land. An island of tree and rock stood at its centre.

And on a stretch of the river, just before the lake, were five darker dots, moving slowly, spilling into the lake.

Lykos – I'm coming for you.

CHAPTER SEVENTY-NINE

CORBAN

Corban stood on a mountain ledge, oil-black clouds boiling above him, wreathing the peak. He whispered a word.

Meical.

Wind streamed around him, tugging at his hair, his cloak. Below him a vast land stretched, colour leached from it, valleys and plains, rivers and lakes painted in shades of grey. In the distance a great mountain reared, in the air about it a host of dark shapes swirled, like crows or bats. The air was thick with them, a black halo.

But it is too far away; those shapes cannot be birds.

Kadoshim.

There was a rushing of air behind him, a gentle impact.

'That is the host of the Kadoshim,' a voice said.

Meical.

Two more Ben-Elim were with him, white-feathered and gleaming in their mail shirts and silver greaves.

'You look better than the last time I saw you,' Corban said, and Meical did. He looked strong again, and the red weal around his neck was healed, only a thin silver scar remained. Meical was dressed in scaled mail, a long spear in his hand, sword at his hip, jet hair bound and tied with silver wire. He looked like a god. A memory of lies and tears flashed through Corban's mind.

'I heard you call me,' Meical said, his expression troubled. 'Why are you here?'

'To observe my enemies.'

'I am glad you have come. I've long wished to speak with you again.'

Corban looked at him, felt a stirring of his anger, but it faded, replaced by something else.

'I hated you,' he said sadly.

Meical regarded him with his purple-tinged eyes. 'And do you still?'

Corban shrugged. 'No. Now when I think of you I mostly feel . . . grief.'

'I am sorry,' Meical whispered, and the Ben-Elim behind him stiffened.

'I know you are,' Corban said. 'What did you wish to speak of with me?'

'You found your friends?'

'Some. The ones that still live.'

'And you fight on. Against Calidus. How goes it?'

'Why would I tell you?' Corban frowned.

Again, the two Ben-Elim behind Meical bridled at that, one of them hissing.

'Because, regardless of how things stand between us, we share a common enemy. We both want the same thing.'

'Do we?' Corban asked. 'I do not think we do, entirely.'

'Elyon's creation protected. Asroth destroyed,' Meical said, staring at the demon-wreathed peak in the distance.

'I want my loved ones safe. Alive. I want my mam and da avenged. I want to protect the people of the Banished Lands,' Corban said. 'Asroth does not have to be destroyed for that. Calidus and Nathair – now they are another question . . .'

Meical gave him a quizzical look. 'Asroth is the author of every evil that has befallen you,' he said.

'Not every evil,' Corban said. 'But I take your point. Many of them, and yes, he is our common enemy.'

'We could still fight him together.'

'That would be hard, when I no longer trust you,' Corban said. He was not speaking from rage or malice, but the truth as he felt it. It was strange, because he saw that his words hurt Meical far more than anything he could have said in the grip of spiteful rage.

'I give you my oath, I will not deceive you again.'

Corban nodded at that. 'Trust must be built.'

'Yes,' Meical said. 'That is all I ask.'

'Why do you not just attack him, here?'

'We are . . . taking steps,' Meical said. 'You glimpsed the Ben-Elim preparing for war, the last time you were here.'

Corban remembered the sounds of combat in that high mountain fortress, the sight of winged warriors sparring, thousands of them. He nodded.

'But Asroth is protected here. Has spent many an age building his defences about the peaks of Ufernol.'

'Nothing's ever simple,' Corban remarked.

'Hah, that is a truth,' Meical barked, a smile ghosting his lips. 'I have missed you, Corban, and the company of your kind. I did not realize how attached I had become to you all.' He looked intently at Corban. 'Does Calidus have all of the Treasures?'

Corban looked at Meical, was silent a while.

'No, not yet,' he finally said.

'They are vital to your cause,' Meical said.

'We have come to the same conclusion,' Corban agreed.

'You should let me help you. At the very least, I can give you good counsel.'

Corban frowned at that. 'Brina is my counsellor, and we already have a plan,' he said.

'Asroth means to become flesh,' Meical said, his tone shifting, more forceful. 'Let me help you.'

'Calidus needs all of the Treasures for that to happen.'

'You cannot hide the Treasures from Calidus,' Meical said. 'He will find them, eventually. It may take him years, but in the end he will have them all. He is inexorable. I could help you find the Treasures . . .'

'I think they are all found,' Corban said. 'Rhin has the cup and necklace. There is a race for the torc. And the dagger . . .' He stopped talking, felt that he'd said too much.

'The dagger?' Meical asked him. 'Do you have it?'

'I told you,' Corban said. 'We have a plan.'

'You do not mean to destroy the Treasures?' Meical said, a look of horror sweeping his face.

Corban stared at the distant mountain. He shifted his gaze to Meical. 'You told me they cannot be destroyed.'

'They cannot, unless they are gathered together . . .' Meical's eyes narrowed. 'You must tell me your plan.'

'As you have told me yours?' Corban said.

With a growl, one of the Ben-Elim strode forwards and grabbed Corban by his shirt and jerkin. 'Who are you to question the Ben-Elim, you foolish mortal,' he hissed, lifting Corban from his feet, holding him over the ledge, dangling thousands of feet above the valley floor. 'We are the Sons of the Mighty, the Firstborn, Guardians and Watchers. Immortal. And you . . .' The Ben-Elim snarled, grabbing Corban's chin and pointing him at the swirl of Kadoshim in the distance. 'You see them? They would storm your world. They would feast on your flesh, gnaw on your bones, turn your rivers and oceans to blood. We saw it once, and it was but a glimmer of their full intent, yet even so it was terrible. Elyon was there to stop it, then. He will not be there this time.'

'Take your hands off me,' Corban said, meeting the Ben-Elim's baleful glare and returning it a thousandfold.

The Ben-Elim hissed.

Meical grabbed the Ben-Elim's wrist. 'Release him, Adriel,' he commanded.

Adriel held Corban's gaze a moment longer, then hurled him onto the ledge, Corban rolling and slamming against solid rock. He stood slowly, Adriel advancing on him, and Corban reached for his sword.

'You must do as Meical tells you,' the Ben-Elim growled, eyes blazing. 'Only then will we have any hope—'

'ENOUGH!' Meical yelled, the sound of his voice buffeting Corban like the north wind.

'Go back to your world of flesh, Corban, we will speak again,' Meical said, then began whispering and Corban's vision was blurring, the world around him fading. He heard Meical's and Adriel's voices, harsh, arguing, then nothing.

Corban awoke, dizzy, his mind full of the Otherworld, a memory of his feet dangling above endless cliffs. He groaned and sat up, Meical's words ringing in his ears.

I need to tell Brina.

He stretched, slung his sword-belt over his shoulder, two scabbards on it, and made his way through their camp to a stream.

People were stirring, fetching wood, boiling water, a thousand tasks happening methodically around him. He splashed water on his face, his skin goose-bumped.

It's getting cold, sure enough, he thought, looking up at branches naked and stark, grey sky visible beyond the canopy.

Hunter's Moon already. A moon away from winter. He stamped on the ground to warm his feet, leaves crunching underfoot, and heard footsteps behind him.

'I know we're friends,' Corban said, 'but you don't have to shadow my *every* move.'

'Think I do,' Farrell said. 'I'm your shieldman, remember, and I take that seriously. I can't risk you wandering off and being abducted by giants again. I could never stand all that running.' He shivered. 'And besides, with Dath not here, I'd get all the blame. He'd never let me hear the end of it.'

Corban flicked water in his face. 'All right, then. Come on.'

The camp was heaving with activity now. Corban could smell food cooking, behind it the sound and smell of the forge as bellows were pumped and the hammer began its work. Jehar were gathering for the sword dance, Gar beckoning to Corban to join in. Elsewhere he could hear the thud and crack of shields as Veradis drilled his men in the shield wall, orders bellowed, the wall rippling into different formations, extra shields on the flanks, raised above, marching.

'It does look impressive,' Corban said, and Farrell gave a grudging grunt.

In another part of the camp Wulf had his men from Gramm's hold hurling their vicious throwing axes at targets – a succession of thuds as they all sank into wood. Laith was with them, throwing her daggers. She grinned at Farrell.

'You and Laith?' Corban said, raising an eyebrow.

'Aye, me and Laith,' Farrell grinned. 'Who'd have thought, eh?'

Corban just patted his back.

'You know what,' Farrell said, eyes taking in the camp, 'I think we might just be a force to be reckoned with.'

'You're not wrong,' Corban said.

Though we are too few. Just too few.

Gar beckoned insistently to Corban.

'Do I ever get a day off?' Corban muttered, not that he really minded; he loved the sword dance. A day would not feel complete without it. As he was approaching Gar he heard the familiar sound of Storm's padding gait, the drum of her cubs about her. She loped up to him, pushing her head against his chest as he leaned into her, tugged an ear.

'What have you got for me, girl?' Corban said, checking the leather thong around her neck; a scroll of parchment was tied to it. He unfurled it and read Coralen's spidery script.

When he looked up he saw Veradis had joined him, as well as Gar, Brina, Balur and Ethlinn.

'Two ten-nights before Nathair and Lothar's warbands are at the gates of Drassil,' Corban said, blowing his cheeks out. 'We must make our move soon.' He looked at Veradis.

'They will be ready soon,' Veradis said. 'And then a few more days for some training.'

'Training will not take long,' Ethlinn said. 'I suspect Balur and the others will take to it speedily.'

There was a commotion at the northern end of the camp and Akar emerged from the trees, a handful of Jehar with him, more of the camp guards appearing beside him.

Why so many?

Behind them there was the sound of branches snapping, and then a great bear was emerging from the foliage, a giant sitting calmly upon its back. Akar and his guards were warily escorting them into camp as the bear's great head swayed from side to side, its lip curled in a contemptuous snarl.

The giant rider gazed at them with a similar expression, her blonde hair bound in a thick warrior braid, tattooed thorns swirling up one arm, the hilt of a longsword jutting over one shoulder.

'My scouts found her close to Jael's road,' Akar said as he drew near. 'She claims to know you, Corban.'

'Aye. She saved my life,' Corban said. 'Well met, Sig,' he continued as her bear stopped before him. He shifted his sword-belt, sliding the starstone dagger round to the small of his back. Storm padded to stand beside Corban, looking up at the bear, a silent growl vibrating in her chest. Beside her, the cubs growled and snapped. The bear ignored them.

Sig looked about at all those gathered around her, eyes hovering on the giants, especially Balur and Ethlinn, finally resting upon Corban.

'This is Sig of the Jotun, first-sword of Eld,' Corban said loudly.

'Well met,' Balur said to her. She looked down at him.

'I know who you are, Balur One-Eye. Balur, slayer of Skald. And I guess that you are Ethlinn, seed of Balur and Nemain.'

'I am,' Ethlinn said, raising her chin. 'And I am glad this day has come, the day I meet one of the mighty Jotun. You are welcome here.'

Sig gave her a stony stare, then shifted her gaze back to Corban.

'I have something for you, Corban Bear-Slayer,' she said, and unbuckled the fur-wrapped bundle strapped to the side of her saddle. It fell to the ground with a heavy thud; Corban knelt to unwrap it. It was a collection of chainmail, leather straps and iron buckles.

'A gift from Varan, for your wolven,' Sig said.

Corban ran his hands over the iron links and tooled leather etched with runes and whorls.

'This is a fine gift,' Corban marvelled, looking up at Sig.

'I'll tell him you're grateful, then,' Sig said, and with a whispered word and a light touch to her reins the bear was turning.

'Wait,' Corban called after her. 'Stay, be welcome, eat with us.'

Sig ignored him, her bear lumbering through the camp and disappearing into the trees.

Corban looked at his friends and captains, then at the mail, finally at Storm.

'Storm, lass, you are going to look fine when you go to war.'

CHAPTER EIGHTY

UTHAS

Uthas ran through the meadow in a loping gait, one he could maintain for days without end, feeling a cold wind blowing out of the north. He would have struggled to do this not so long ago, but not now.

I have drunk from the starstone cup, he exulted, basking in the strength and energy that coursed through his veins, the scents and sounds that clamoured for his attention, the knowledge that he would live another thousand years and more.

As long as I avoid an iron-tipped death.

Alongside him ran Salach, and behind was Eisa and the rest of the Benothi, fifty giants. They ran with a warband as big as any Uthas had seen from the Giant Wars. Over five thousand men, all a-horse, riding across the rolling meadows of Isiltir, the sound of their passage like constant thunder.

Behind them Dun Kellen had long since disappeared. They had stopped there to re-provision. Now they were headed north-east, the cold wind against Uthas' face a bitter fist greeting them from out of the Desolation, and to the east the brooding green of Forn Forest grew larger with every league travelled. They could have been in Forn already, close to Drassil, but Calidus had commanded that they take a different route. He wanted them to pass the Desolation, to visit a place named Gramm's hold, and see if there was sign of the Jotun.

In the distance a hill appeared, upon its brown the dull gleam of stone walls.

'This is giant-built,' Salach said to Uthas as they strode through the stone-arched gateway into a courtyard of hard-packed earth at

Gramm's hold, a half-built keep of stone and wood looming over them.

'And it is empty,' Eisa called out as she appeared from one end of the courtyard, other scouts filtering through the hold echoing her call.

'It will do for tonight,' Rhin said as she rode through the gates behind Uthas, her warband spread across the great meadows about the hill and deserted hold like a rippled cloak of leather and iron, flesh and blood.

Uthas strode around the deserted hold. Everywhere were signs that this place had been inhabited once, and recently. Salach called him into a long building, a stable-block, separated into many pens and scattered with straw and hay. Uthas wrinkled his nose.

'It was not horses that were kept here,' Salach said, sifting through the straw with his axe-shaft, uncovering a pile of dung. 'The creatures penned here were meat-eaters.'

'Bears,' Uthas murmured, and shared a look with Salach.

'The Jotun,' they said together.

Uthas called the clan about him and set them to searching the hold and surrounding area for any indication of where the Jotun were now. He marched with Salach and Eisa over the peak of the hill and saw a wide river curling across the land, a stone bridge arching across it, a road running from the bridge into a barren wasteland of rock and ash.

'The Desolation,' he whispered, twisting one of the wyrm teeth set in his necklace. Salach and Eisa just stared.

They marched down to the bridge, saw the signs of a great migration, rutted tracks in the road before and after the bridge, boot-prints and huge paw-prints leading into the Desolation. They crossed over the bridge, walked only a little further.

'They left this way, it is clear,' Salach said.

'Aye. What happened, that brought them here, and then sent them back again?'

Other scouts were returning as they marched back towards the feast-hall on the hill. Uthas conferred with them briefly.

He found Rhin in chambers beyond the feast-hall of the new keep, black and gold-cloaked warriors parting for him. She was in a shadowed chamber, the roof a skeleton of dark-timbered bones, and she was bent before her sorcerous frame of flayed skin, fire crackling in the iron bowl, sending shadows dancing, the skin rippling with a twisted parody of life. At his entrance both Rhin and the flayed face stared at him, a red-eyed spark of intelligence flickering in its eyes.

Calidus.

'What news?' the flayed face hissed.

'The Jotun were here,' Uthas said. 'My guess is that they built this –' he waved one arm in a wide circle – 'but then they left. There are tracks crossing the bridge and travelling back into the Desolation. What made them leave . . .' He shrugged, a rippling of his slab-like shoulders.

The flayed face cursed.

'What would you have me do?' Rhin asked.

'Send scouts after the Jotun, track them, find them, but nothing else. You must come to me now, bring me the necklace and cup. They must be made safe in Drassil, protected. And I suspect our enemy are preparing for battle, the fools. I need your swords about me. After, I will go to the Jotun myself. But for now, come to me. There is a great road built by Jael that carves into Forn. Travel east and you will find it. Once in Forn I will send some of my Kadoshim kin to guide you.'

'How long, before we are with you?' Rhin asked.

'A moon, if you ride hard. The road is good.'

Then the skin sagged in its frame, the distortion of life gone.

Rhin stared at the flames in the iron bowl.

'A moon,' she whispered.

Uthas knew what she was thinking. One moon until she was face to face with Calidus. One moon until he discovered that she had lost the starstone necklace.

Uthas and his Benothi were ready to march at dawn, but Rhin's warband were not. It was a task, it seemed, for five thousand men to break fast and camp. The hill and meadows were awash with the rattle, creak and jingle of leather and iron, horses stamping hooves, neighing, men shouting orders and insults. Uthas stood upon the brow of the hold's hill and stared at Forn. The world felt new to him, this morn, scoured clean by a harsh wind. The sky above was heavy with rain-bloated cloud. He felt the weight of destiny upon him, as if he stood upon the brink of a precipice. One half-step and he would be over, could not return.

He felt scared.

This is what I wanted. I have fulfilled my promise to Asroth, found the cup and necklace, no matter what Rhin has done with them since. My part of the bargain is complete. And in return I shall be made lord of the giants. King of them.

The thought filled him with joy.

He turned his gaze southwards, wishing Rhin's warband more speed.

I would be on my way.

In the distance, beyond the warband, he saw a lone rider on the southern horizon.

Rhin was mounted on her grey mare, sable furs about her shoulders when the rider drew near to them, galloping along a road of hard-packed earth that led to the massing warband.

A hound ran at the horse's side, and Rhin guessed what Uthas had already seen.

It was Rafe.

Rhin rode out to meet him, Uthas striding one side of her, Geraint and Conall the other. They met upon the meadows beyond the hill.

'Why are you here?' Rhin asked, her voice tense, a tremor to it.

No lover's greeting here, then.

'I bring news,' Rafe said, his horse blowing great bouts of air, its sweat-soaked ribs and flanks heaving, 'news both great and dire.'

'What news?' Rhin snapped.

Rafe slipped from his saddle and dropped to his knees in the dirt before Rhin, head bowed.

Not a good sign.

'Morcant is slain; Ardan fallen. Taken by Edana.'

Rhin's lips twitched, the colour draining from her face.

'And what of the starstone necklace?' Rhin asked, voice heavy with venom and tinged with fear.

'Edana still has it, my Queen.'

'Then why are you here?' Rhin snarled. 'Answer well, if you would keep your head upon your shoulders.'

'Edana is riding to Drassil, and she is bringing the necklace with her.'

'How do you know this?'

'I heard her say it, my Queen, upon the walls of Dun Carreg.' Rafe looked away, licked his lips. 'I thought of fleeing,' he whispered, 'of running away, as far from you as my legs would carry me, but when it came to it, I could not do it. I have failed the task you set me, but I would serve you still, if you would have me.' He looked up at her then. 'And that is why I sneaked back to Dun Carreg, how I managed to overhear Edana talking of her plans.'

Rhin stared down at him, her face a cold mask.

'You can keep your head, for now,' she said. 'Ride with me, and tell me more of Edana's plan.'

CHAPTER EIGHTY-ONE

CORBAN

Corban danced out of reach of Gar's sword but the Jehar warrior gave Corban no respite, stepping nimbly in, forcing Corban to block a savage combination of three, four, five blows that targeted his skull, eyes, throat and chest, a sweeping loop that would have taken his leg off below the knee and ended with a short, straight lunge to Corban's belly. Corban parried and countered, pushing Gar onto his back foot, striking high and low, steering him towards a twisted root poking from the ground. At the last moment Gar spun away, a half-circle that brought him round to Corban's left flank, Corban swaying and blocking a horizontal blow aimed at his waist. Corban rolled his wrist to stab at Gar's armpit, but he ducked somehow, and nodded his head at Corban, a recognition that Corban had never received from Gar before.

Forms swirled around them, men, women, giants sparring, training, but Corban's only focus was on Gar and his sword.

Then Gar was closing again, blows a maelstrom about Corban, chopping, stabbing, spinning, striking, feinting, lunging, but Corban blocked them all and slowly began to counter. As he came out of a combination attack he saw Gar hesitate for a heartbeat and punched a short lunging stab at Gar's gut. Gar swayed but the blow still caught him, the blunt wrapped tip of Corban's blade stabbing into Gar, just above his hip.

Corban was so stunned to have touched his blade to Gar that he just stopped, grinning foolishly.

'I think I just killed you,' Corban said.

'Perhaps,' Gar grunted. 'Or perhaps not, if you missed my intestines.' He looked down at the tip of Corban's sword, frozen where it had struck, then nodded. 'I think you would have missed them. Just.' He shrugged. 'You may have nicked them, in which case I'd likely have died in agony, screaming, a ten-night later.' He looked up at Corban and smiled humourlessly. 'You, however, are dead right now.'

'Wha—?'

Corban realized that Gar's sword was resting against his throat, a pressure over his artery.

'But, I killed you first,' Corban said.

'No. You gave me a wound which may or may not have killed me in some days' time.'

'You *let* me stab you, so that you could stab me back?'

'I did,' Gar said, smiling, which was disconcerting in itself. 'Sometimes you have to take a wound to give a wound.' He stood straight and brushed Corban's training sword away. 'A good blow. You have come so far, Corban. We have reached the point where to kill you I have to risk death myself.'

Corban let that sink in as Gar walked away. He followed, threading through the training warriors around him, on into their new camp. They'd moved south, closer to Nathair and Lorcan's encroaching warbands. The last moon had seen a myriad of skirmishes and assaults on their enemy, growing ever more desperate as Drassil loomed closer. Although many of Nathair and Lothar's warbands had fallen, and their progress slowed, they had not been stopped. They would reach Drassil soon.

And so we must attack them soon, an all-out assault, seek to finish them before they reach Calidus, whether Veradis' stratagem is ready or not.

Late last night Dath had returned to the camp, part of the constant rotation of warriors that were stalking the forest around Lothar and Nathair. He'd brought word of a plan that Coralen had devised. Corban shuddered as he thought of it, acknowledging its potential, but still . . .

He saw Brina and made his way over to her.

'Brina – I wanted to ask you about Coralen's idea.'

The sound of wings beating drifted down to them, and the raucous cawing of a crow high above. Corban and Brina both looked up and watched it spiral down through the trees, the bird squawking more and more excitedly.

'Is that . . . ?' Corban said.

'It can't be,' Brina breathed.

And then the crow was flapping its wings, slowing its descent, heading straight for them.

'*BRINA,*' it squawked, '*CORBAN.*'

'*Brina, Brina, Brina, Corban, Corban, Corban,*' Craf was crowing jubilantly as he landed on Brina's shoulder, hopping from foot to foot, cawing, flapping, running his beak through Brina's hair, rubbing his head against hers.

Corban was grinning as if it was his nameday, and Brina was blinking away tears.

'Where have you been, you stupid crow?' Brina asked Craf.

'*Edana,*' Craf squawked. '*Bossy,*' he muttered. '*Craf do this, Craf spy there, Craf find that, Craf fly here.*'

Corban and Brina stared at each other, incredulous.

'How did you find us, you marvellous bird?' Corban asked, scratching Craf's neck through his ruffled feathers.

'*Craf clever,*' the bird squawked indignantly. '*Craf search for Drassil. Find you.*'

A huge crowd had gathered around them now: Veradis and Balur, many others. Cywen appeared.

'Craf!' she said, 'Welcome back. Have you come from Edana?'

'*Ahh, message, message,*' Craf said.

'You've a message from Edana? Well, why didn't you say so, you fool crow!' Brina scolded. She was still smiling, though. Craf hopped from her shoulder to Corban's, giving Brina a sulky look.

'*Edana coming,*' he said.

'Edana? Coming here?'

'*That's what Craf said. Here. Warband. Two thousand men.*'

There was uproar for a while then as they all tried to get as much information out of Craf as possible.

In the end Corban was certain that Edana was coming to Drassil, after a great battle where she'd won Ardan's freedom. However, it sounded as if Rhin was bound for Drassil too.

'Edana must be guided in, shown the fastest way,' Veradis said. 'We could surely do with another two thousand swords.'

'Aye,' Corban agreed.

'Brikan would be the quickest way,' Veradis continued. 'It is a tower in the south-west of Forn,' he clarified in response to a blank look from Corban.

'*Craf knows it, flew over it,*' Craw squawked. '*By river. Stone bridge.*'

'That's the one,' Veradis said, pleased.

'Tell Edana to ride there, and we shall send a guide for her,' Corban said to Craf. 'There'll be a road after that, and then a tunnel.'

'*Tunnel,*' Craf shuddered, one of his feathers falling out.

'You don't need to go into the tunnel, just help Edana get to it. This is very important, Craf. All of our lives may depend on it,' Corban said.

CHAPTER EIGHTY-TWO

FIDELE

'Get out of the boat,' Lykos said to Fidele. He'd cut the rope that tied her to one of the benches, and also the rope binding her ankles – only her wrists were still bound. She rose and clambered ashore.

They were standing on a rocky beach, an island of grass, scrubby trees and dark rock rearing above her, behind her the lake, lapping at the shore. Fidele pulled a face at the thought of it. As the Vin Thalun had rowed across it she'd seen dead fish floating on the surface; the stink of death and rot wafted off the water along with the fog that curled lazily upon it. She looked back at the lakeshore now, beyond it saw endless rolling grass plains. They'd camped on the lakeshore last night; the grass taller than she'd expected, much of it as tall as a man. As she looked at it now she thought she saw a ripple within it, moving against the wind, then a splash in the lake. She stared, but there was nothing else.

'No point looking backwards,' Lykos said as he tied a longer strip of rope to the bonds at her wrist, then knotted it to his belt. 'Especially when our future is so bright.' He grinned, tugging on the knot to make sure it was good. 'Wouldn't want you to get lost on this island, now.'

As soon as he'd set foot on the island Lykos had sent out a scouting party. Now, while they waited for word, Lykos' other men were hauling the five boats further up the beach, roping them to wind-battered branches. The Kadoshim, led by the one perpetually surrounded by flies, were marching confidently further ahead, up to a strip of jagged rocks set like a natural barrier between the beach and the island proper. He turned and called impatiently to Lykos.

'Wait a while, some of my lads are scouting it out,' Lykos called back.

'I've waited long enough on those boats,' the Kadoshim growled, his voice strange, multiplied, as if there were an echo within his own throat. 'It's time to kill something.'

'His name's Legion,' Lykos whispered conspiratorially to Fidele as he strapped a leather and iron buckler to his left arm. 'Not the most patient creature. And angry, most of the time.'

'He ate Agost's face,' Fidele said, shuddering.

'Aye. He has issues. Handy in a scrap, though.'

Figures appeared from a treeline on the island: Vin Thalun moving fleet-footed as they reached the sharp rocks of the beach.

'News?' Lykos shouted.

'We found a cave, think it might be something,' one of the Vin Thalun called. 'Left some of the other lads to keep an eye out.'

'Right, time to go and find us some treasure,' Lykos smiled, pulling on Fidele's rope as he strode up the beach.

The sun was halfway to highsun, bright in a sheer sky, though there was little warmth in it. A wind blew off the lake, tugging and making tendrils of the mist, sending it rolling up the island's beach like the tide.

Lykos dragged Fidele up onto the jagged rocks at the beach's end, Fidele slipping and gashing a knee, Lykos just hauling her on. She yanked on the rope in frustration and he turned and strode back to her, backhanded her across the cheek, sending her reeling to her knees, receiving another gash on the rocks. Then he bent and half-lifted, half-carried her to more even ground.

'Do not do that again,' he snarled. She tasted blood trickling from her nose. Glared back at him.

'Ach, but there's a fire in you,' he said, suddenly grinning. 'Come on, don't want to miss the fun.' He hurried off after his disappearing men.

The ground sloped upwards; the island seemed to climb steadily towards dark-faced crags. They stepped beneath a copse of trees where the undergrowth grew thick, long thorns snagged at Fidele, ripping a hole in her breeches.

Lykos strode ahead, catching up with his men. As they climbed higher Fidele felt something change around them. She could not explain what it was, but abruptly her skin was prickling, the air feeling heavy, oppressive, and the men around her were walking slower, glancing at the shadows.

'Aegus, where's this cave?' Lykos called out.

'Just ahead,' a Vin Thalun said, a dark-haired man with a large part of his upper lip cut away, showing rotting teeth.

A shadow loomed out of the trees, Fidele jumped, but it was Legion, the Kadoshim.

'Anything?' Lykos asked.

'Something,' the Kadoshim muttered, sounding confused. It sniffed. 'Blood.'

Lykos drew his sword.

They emerged from the trees, bright sunlight making Fidele blink, a metallic stench hitting her nose.

The ground levelled before them into a grassy glade, one side of it overlooking a steep drop to the lake, punctuated by ledges with wind-blasted trees, jagged rocks at the bottom. The other way led to a sheer cliff face about fifty paces away. It rose high in staggered slabs, a cave mouth gaping wide at its base, but it was not the cave that Fidele was looking at.

Bodies were strewn everywhere, or parts of bodies – arms, legs, heads, piles of intestines heaped in great steaming mounds. One head sat upon a boulder staring at them with tongue lolling, a hole in its skull, brains oozing out. A wide bloody track lined the grass, disappearing into the darkness of the cave.

'Asroth's stones,' a Vin Thalun whispered.

Above the cave's mouth were ancient runes, dug deep into the rock.

'*Gach fir bás*,' Lykos read.

All men die.

Then *things* were leaping at them, bigger than men, on two legs but fur-covered. Fidele glimpsed long muzzles and curved, yellowing teeth. They howled as they came. One crashed into a Vin Thalun and he tumbled across the glade, a great rent in his belly, guts spilling.

Then all was blood and screams and madness.

Lykos sidestepped and slashed at a huge form, something clanging off of his buckler. He stumbled, ducked, an arm smashed into his shoulder, hurling him through the air, yanking Fidele off her feet, sending her rolling on the bloodstained grass. A heavy foot thudded by her head, shaggy-furred, and Fidele looked up at a huge figure towering over her. She caught a rushed image of teeth and claws before it surged at a Vin Thalun, lifting him from his feet and dropping him onto its bent leg, bending him like a twig. Fidele heard the Vin Thalun's spine crack like a frost-hard branch, the warrior screaming, sword dropping from his fingers, then his throat was a red gash, blood spurting, the beast hurling him tumbling across the ground, searching for its next victim.

The cord around Fidele's wrists pulled taut and she was dragged a short way, closer to the sword she'd just seen dropped. She snatched it up as the cord went slack, Lykos leaping back towards her, something huge bearing down upon him.

He threw himself to the ground, rolled, came up facing the creature that chased him, ducked inside a wild swing and punched his short sword up into its belly.

Fidele heard a grunt, saw Lykos hammer on the pommel of his blade, pushing it deep, to the hilt, then rip it free, an eruption of blood. The creature dropped to its knees and Lykos grabbed its fur-covered head and ripped.

A mouth full of bristling teeth opened wide, then tore loose.

It's a cloak of fur! An animal skin, a bear?

Lykos pulled it free, revealing a human face and shoulders, though its features and muscles were slab-like, small dark eyes in a flat, angular face.

Giants.

'They're GIANTS!' Lykos yelled.

The Vin Thalun rallied. Fidele realized that they outnumbered their attackers, and in a dozen heartbeats more of the fur-cloaked giants had fallen, the rest being pushed back towards the cave.

Fidele gripped the sword she'd taken and hacked down on the rope binding her to Lykos. He felt the jerk on his waist, turned and saw Fidele with the sword. She swung it at him as he rushed at her, but she could get no strength into the blow with her hands bound and he contemptuously slapped the blade away, punched her in the gut, doubling her over, then again on the temple. There was an explosion of white light in her head as her vision blurred, the world dimming, swaying, the ground rushing up to slam into her face.

She lay there, dazed, clinging on to consciousness, rolled over. Lykos shuffled forwards, dragging Fidele by the part-frayed rope. He darted in viper-fast to stab at a fur-cloaked giant, then leaped back. Legion slammed into the giant Lykos had just stabbed, grabbed it by throat and groin and hoisted it into the air, impossibly strong for his size, hurling it at a boulder. The giant tried to rise but Legion was upon it in a bound, grabbing its head, slamming the back of its skull into the boulder, again and again, laughing as he did it, flies swarming, buzzing, crawling around, over, into, the shattered skull.

A haunting sound echoed out of the cave mouth and the other giants retreated into the darkness.

Lykos shouted a command, halting his men from pursuing, then torches were dragged from packs, flints sparked and dried grass and rushes lit. A few torches were hurled into the cave, flaring bright, revealing no giants lurking to ambush them again.

'Up, you bitch,' Lykos snarled, dragging Fidele to her feet by her hair. 'Aegus, Hesp,' he shouted, and two Vin Thalun strode over, one of them the man with only half a lip. 'Watch this woman for me,' Lykos said as he sliced away the rope Fidele had frayed, re-bound her wrists with new rope and handed it to No-Lip.

Lykos twisted his fingers in Fidele's hair, dragged her close and kissed her hard on the lips; she squirmed but his grip was iron.

'I'll see you soon,' he said, part smile, part snarl.

'With me,' Lykos yelled as he strode into the cave's jaws, Legion and the Kadoshim prowling after him, the Vin Thalun following more cautiously.

Fidele looked between the two Vin Thalun. Aegus sneered at her; the other one, Hesp, young, fair-haired, with scars latticing his face and arms, was ignoring her, focused on cleaning blood from his short sword.

Shouts and screams echoed out from the cave, No-Lip and Hesp were instantly alert.

'They could all die in there,' Fidele said. 'Think on that.'

Aegus yanked on the rope, pulling it tight, burning Fidele's wrists and making her grunt with pain.

'Just a warning,' he said. 'No funny business.'

Fidele gave him a scornful glance and looked about the glade. It was littered with the dead, crows squawking above, a few of the braver ones already landing for their feast. She looked beyond them, amongst the shadowed trees, thought she saw a movement. Squinting, she strained her eyes. Definitely something moving far down the slope, deep within the trees. Shadows, many of them, though one was closer, far ahead of the others. It coalesced into a man, and he was running up the slope and her heart leaped.

Maquin.

CHAPTER EIGHTY-THREE

MAQUIN

Maquin ran, not really feeling the pain in his legs that he knew must be there, or the burning sensation in his lungs as they laboured for air, his body pushed to its limits. He did not feel the ache in his shoulders and back, arms and legs, from the swim from lakeshore to island, nor did he notice the weight of his dripping clothes.

All he knew was Fidele.

He could see her, bathed in sunlight, hands bound, one side of her face red and starting to bruise. As his eyes shifted to the two Vin Thalun with her he felt his lips curl in a snarl. They hadn't seen him yet. He pulled a knife from his belt, another from a sheath buckled across his ribs, then he was bursting from the trees into a scene of slaughter, the piled meat of the dead all about.

The Vin Thalun heard him now, both twisting and staring, a moment of disbelief. A strangled cry of fear.

'The Old Wolf!'

He leaped a body, had a frozen moment to see his enemies clearly, one fair-haired, one with a scarred face, then he was on them. Fair-Hair swung his sword, a short horizontal chop at Maquin's waist, a wise blow, unlikely to miss, except that it did because he was too slow, had not gauged Maquin's speed. He was running at full sprint, no slowing, no hesitation, and before Fair-Hair's blow was halfway to Maquin's waist there was a knife hilt buried in his groin, ripping up as Maquin crashed into him, rolled around him, spinning away.

'I'll kill her,' Scar-Face shouted, unable to hide the tremor in his voice, and lifted the rope attached to Fidele, only to find a severed end dangling in his hand. Maquin had slashed at it as he'd collided with Fair-Hair.

'Come on then,' Scar-Face snarled, did not wait for Maquin but lunged forwards, stabbing at Maquin's gut.

Maquin parried, sword grating as he swept Scar-Face's blade wide, Scar-Face's buckler punching at his face, Maquin ducking the blow as if it were all in slow motion, the blooded knife hooking behind his attacker's knee, stabbing deep, slicing up through muscle. The warrior was falling backwards, Maquin's knee dropping onto his enemy's chest, his other knife at the man's throat, slashing through flesh, cartilage, vertebrae.

He stood over his enemy, blood-spattered, nostrils flaring, chest heaving.

Then Fidele was in his arms, their bodies tightly pressed, moulding into each other, Maquin wiping hair from her face, Fidele whispering words in his ear, and they were fiercely kissing.

'You found her, then,' a deep voice said behind them. It was Alcyon, smiling, breathing hard.

Maquin saw his expression change as he looked around the glade and saw giants amongst the dead.

'What?' He crouched beside one, staring into his face.

'Are they your clan? Are they Kurgan?' Maquin asked him.

Alcyon shook his head. 'I do not know. I don't understand.'

Others were emerging from the trees, now – Teca, Javed and a handful of pit-fighters, Alben, Spyr and the men of Ripa – all staring around at the blood-soaked glade.

Maquin looked into Fidele's eyes, held her cheeks gently.

'Did he hurt you?'

'Nothing worse than this,' Fidele said, touching the side of her face that was swollen and bruised from Lykos' punch. She swayed, eyes fluttering and Maquin caught her, lowered her to the ground, crouching beside her.

'It's nothing,' Fidele said, trying to rise and failing, then leaning over and vomiting onto the grass.

'Some water,' Alben said, crouching beside Maquin. 'Hello, my lady.' He smiled as he helped her drink from a skin, looked into her eyes, asked her to track his finger. 'Rest a short while, you've had a blow to the head. It will pass.'

'Is this real?' Fidele said, touching Maquin's face, squeezing Alben's hand.

Shouts, screams, the din of battle echoed from the cave mouth.

'Lykos,' Maquin snarled.

'The starstone torc,' Alben said.

Maquin stood. 'Spyr, pick a few lads, guard Fidele. When she's able, get her down to the boats. We'll be taking them home. Lykos won't be needing them where he's going.'

Fidele grabbed Maquin's hand. 'Kill him,' she said fiercely.

'I intend to,' Maquin growled.

'And be careful,' she added. 'There are Kadoshim with him.'

Maquin sheathed his knives, drew his two short swords. 'You hear that?' he said to the small warband. 'Kadoshim. You have to take their heads.'

Alcyon drew his two axes, other men their swords, Teca looked at her bow. 'I'll settle for Vin Thalun,' she said.

Maquin bent and brushed his lips against Fidele's cheek. 'I'll see you after,' he said, and then he was stalking into the tunnel, Teca a half-step behind him, bow loosely nocked. Alcyon and Tain followed, Javed, Alben and their men spreading behind them.

Just beyond the entrance, torches were guttering on the ground, sending shadows dancing wildly as Maquin strode past them. He was on a wide path, sloping and spiralling downwards. After the first bend there were iron sconces hammered into the rock walls, flames flickering, shedding light on still forms scattered on the slope: Vin Thalun, two more giants in their bear-skins. The din of battle grew louder as the tunnel opened up into a great chamber below them. And in the chamber battle raged, flames in great bowls of oil illuminating the violence between men and giants.

At the far end of the chamber wide steps led up to a raised dais, and upon it was a stone chair, a giant sitting on it. Even at a glance, though, this did not look like an ordinary giant. He was tall, but had little of the bulk of the other giants in the room, his frame withered, skin hanging from his arms and cheeks in wrinkled folds, his scalp all but visible through wispy white hair. A thick torc of dark iron was draped about his neck, looking too heavy for the giant to bear. A handful of giants stood protectively in a half-circle about him, swinging at any approaching Vin Thalun.

Even as Maquin saw this, a Kadoshim charged the group around the throne, sword high, a flurry of blows clanging off a hammer-shaft, a giant reeling as a blow cut through his defence. At a glance it was clear to Maquin that Lykos and his Vin Thalun were going to win this fight.

Not while I'm still breathing.

He launched into a loping run, spiralling down into the mael-strom. Behind him he heard the thud of feet, the thrum of Teca's bow, saw a Vin Thalun drop with a feathered shaft in his neck.

A great roaring cry filled the room, echoing, filling Maquin's ears.

It was Alcyon. He had paused, twin axes raised over his head, and he was yelling, 'KURGAN!'

Many in the chamber stopped, stared up at him. Some of the giants called back to him in guttural voices. Alcyon grinned, a fierce thing, and then he leaped from the path, down into the chamber, scattering a dozen Vin Thalun that were hacking at a giant fallen to one knee. A Kadoshim rushed at Alcyon as he rose from the ground and Alcyon's axes swung, great looping circles, the Kadoshim's head soaring through the air in a welter of blood. Its body crashed to the ground, a gush of black vapour pouring from its neck, forming night-black wings, two red eyes, screaming hatred, then it was fading, smoke in the wind.

That's how you do it, Maquin thought, feeling the battle-joy rising up within him. He burst onto the chamber's floor, gutted one Vin Thalun, buried his blade deep into the armpit of the next, spun, ripping his blades free, chopped into another between neck and shoulder, dropping him.

'It's the Old Wolf,' a Vin Thalun shouted; the cry was taken up, rippling around the room. Then Javed was flying into the chamber, his Freedmen behind him, a swirling wave of muscle and iron flow-ing into the battle.

The world slowed for Maquin, reduced to the next face, the glint of iron, the spray of blood. He swayed and twisted his way past a dozen blades that were intent on opening his veins, eddying past each blow, Maquin striking back unerringly, opening throats and bellies, cutting hamstrings, stabbing groins, slicing tendons, men falling in a wake of the dead behind him, and all the time he was searching for one thing. One man.

Lykos.

Maquin paused, the calm at the centre of his own storm.

Then he saw him.

Lykos, on the steps to the dais, his buckler dented, short sword dripping blood, a snarl on his face. He had Vin Thalun about him, Kadoshim as well, and they were storming the few giants left upon the dais, protecting the ancient one.

'LYKOS,' Maquin bellowed, and the Vin Thalun turned and saw him.

Hatred and fear chased across his face.

Maquin ran at him, swung at a Vin Thalun in his way, cut deep into his thigh, kicked him to the ground, then a Kadoshim was running at him, a woman, curved sword high in a two-handed grip. Maquin spun as the blow descended, chopped a backswing at the Kadoshim's neck, bit deep, her head tilting at an unnatural angle. A manic grin twisted her face, black eyes boring into Maquin as she came at him again. Maquin swayed away, too slowly, a red line opening from shoulder to elbow, then hands were grasping the Kadoshim, across her forehead, yanking her head back, and a curved knife was sawing at her throat, the head falling away, demon-mist hissing from its neck, raging its malice for a moment before it was evaporating.

Javed kicked the headless body to the ground, grinned at Maquin, who nodded his thanks, then Javed disappeared into the carnage.

Maquin searched for Lykos, saw him and a Kadoshim on the top step, hacking one of the last giants to pieces.

A horn blast rang out in the hall, echoing, vibrating, growing louder. The ancient giant had risen from his chair and had a horn to his lips. Maquin shuddered to a halt, clasped his hands over his ears, saw all about him doing the same thing.

The horn sound faded, though still echoing in Maquin's ears, and he struggled to move, to do anything except keep his hands clasped to his ears. The ancient giant looked around at them all, a mixture of horror, grief, disgust upon his face.

'It was not supposed to be like this,' the giant said, his voice like parchment scraping together, yet carrying through the chamber. 'Has nothing changed in all the long years? Who are you all? Where is Ethlinn ap Balur?'

'What are you talking about, old man?' Lykos grated, hands still at his ears.

The giant regarded Lykos as Maquin would an annoying fly. 'I am talking of Ethlinn, child of Nemain, heir to the giant throne, who else? She should have claimed the spear, opened the door. Then come to me here. Where is she?'

'She is fighting these Kadoshim that hold Drassil,' Alcyon said, taking a step forwards.

'Kadoshim.' The giant looked at them all, stared at the one close to Lykos, the one with a swarm of flies swirling around him. 'Ach, when will it end?'

'Who are you?' Alcyon asked.

'I am Halvor, Voice of Skald,' the old giant said. 'Who are you?'

'I am Alcyon, last of the Kurgan.'

'Alcyon?' another voice said. One of the giants in bear-skins took a step forwards. 'Alcyon ben Dayir? Alcyon who ran?'

Alcyon stared, frowned, 'Cota?'

The Kadoshim surrounded by flies lurched forwards, staggered up the steps to the dais.

'You talk too much, old man,' he said, and rammed his sword into Halvor's belly, up to the hilt. With his other hand he grabbed the torc around Halvor's neck and ripped it off, holding it high.

CHAPTER EIGHTY-FOUR

LYKOS

Lykos ran for the slope leading from the chamber, calling Vin Thalun to him. He heard Legion laughing behind him and a quick glance over his shoulder showed the Kadoshim looking as if he was enjoying himself. He'd thrown Halvor to the ground, still alive by the look of his feebly moving limbs, and Legion was beating him to death with the iron torc.

They were surrounded by enemies. He glimpsed the Old Wolf, trying to head him off, saw men in black and silver, others clothed like pit-fighters, a handful of them leaping in front of him.

How the hell did they get here?

He kicked the rim of a fire-bowl as big as a shield, spilt oil and flame over a warrior charging towards him, saw him ignite like a torch. The man's screams were terrible as Lykos swerved around the flames, leaped at the rock wall of the chamber and started hauling himself up. Then hands were grabbing his ankle, pulling him back down. He felt a hot line slash across his belly, saw a face grinning viciously at him, knife in hand.

It was Javed.

'How does it feel to be in the pit with the rest of us?' Javed snarled, stabbing at him. Lykos rolled, threw his buckler at Javed's face, making him sway to avoid it, then Lykos was back on his feet, slashing at Javed.

The pit-fighter spun around his sword, somehow, and then he was inside Lykos' guard, punching him in the face, stabbing again, but Lykos managed to twist out of the knife's way, grip Javed's arm, tried to bring his sword round.

Pain exploded in his nose, an explosion of white light as Javed headbutted him. He staggered, saw Javed's knife pulling back, knew he could not stop it.

Then an arm snaked around Javed's neck. Legion's grinning face appeared, yanking Javed back, biting into his neck. Javed screamed as the Kadoshim ripped a chunk of flesh from Javed's body.

'Guess you lose,' Lykos said as he plunged his short sword into Javed's belly, twisted it, sawed it upwards.

Javed's scream rose in pitch, trailed off to a gurgle.

The chamber was heaving with battle again. Lykos ran back to the rock wall, leaping and scrambling for purchase. He dragged himself up onto the slope, hauled up the Vin Thalun behind him, and yelled for Legion, who had become distracted with killing again.

Legion finally saw him and hurled the torc to him. It spun through the chamber, flames glinting on it, and Lykos plucked it out of the air. It was cold to the touch and heavy, far heavier than it looked. He placed it around his neck, thought for a moment he heard the whisper of voices in his ear, then they were gone. Crouching, he pulled another of his men up the chamber wall onto the slope, felt air whistle over his head, heard a gurgled yell behind him, and one of his men was dropping with a knife in his throat.

He looked back into the chamber, saw Maquin pulling another knife from a sheath.

Time to go.

He turned and ran, a handful of survivors with him. They pounded up the slope, spiralling higher, then one of his lads stumbled and fell, an arrow sprouting from his chest. Up ahead a woman was pulling another arrow from a quiver, nocking it.

He gritted his teeth and ran at her, but she stayed calm, loosed, the arrow sending the man beside him spinning to the ground, rolling back down the slope. Before she had another arrow ready, Lykos was upon her, slashing with his sword, but she ducked, hit him in the side of the head with her bow, sending him stumbling. He kicked out, caught her hip and she staggered back, one foot slipping over the edge of the slope. For a moment she teetered there, as if suspended, arms windmilling, then with a cry she fell. Lykos wasn't sure how far the fall was, didn't care, as long as she was out of the way. He ran on, only three men with him now.

It's going to be a race for the boats. Could do with more than this to help me row all the way back to Drassil.

He paused, looking back down into the chaos below.

Fire had spread, engulfing almost half of the chamber, the other half filled with battling bodies. He couldn't see many of his men left; a handful were trying to get to the slope. Of the ten Kadoshim that had walked into the cave, Lykos could only see three – one of them Legion, who was still slaying with a joyous abandon. They seemed to be keeping the enemy more than busy.

They'll come if they can.

Lykos shrugged and continued up. Soon, seeing daylight ahead, he ran faster, wanting to be away from here, though there was one other treasure he wished to find before he left.

Fidele.

He burst into pale sunlight, blinked as his eyes adjusted, saw the backs of three men heading into the trees and smiled, because between them was a figure he'd recognize anywhere.

'Pick your man,' Lykos said to the men with him, focused on a grey-haired warrior to Fidele's right, and charged.

Lykos gave no battle-cry but the group heard him coming and spun to face him. He glimpsed Fidele's face, pale-skinned, eyes wide, then Grey-Hair was moving at him, striding out of the trees back into the glade, a spear held low, two-handed, levelling at Lykos' belly.

Lykos saw the warrior's muscles bunch, begin the thrust intended to skewer him. He twisted right, swung at the same time, felt a line of hot fire rake his ribs, hacked down at the spear shaft, splintering it, and slashed his sword deep into the warrior's neck.

Lykos kicked the body off his blade.

One of his men was down, two were circling around Fidele's remaining guard, but she was nowhere to be seen. Then Lykos heard footsteps behind him, leaped without thinking, saw a sword lunge into the space he'd just occupied, Fidele on the end of it.

He grinned at her.

'Thought you'd seen the last of me?' He swatted her sword away, and she back-stepped into the glade, holding the sword in front of her, its tip trembling. Lykos advanced, smiling, and she stabbed at his belly, but there was little strength in the thrust. He knocked it away and continued advancing as she shuffled further back, towards the glade's edge. She looked unsteady on her feet, her eyes unfocused.

Still feeling the punch I gave her?

She stopped at the edge of the cliff, stones rattling down to the lake far below.

'Nice view,' Lykos said conversationally, still moving closer. His sword slammed onto hers, a twist of his wrist and Fidele gasped, a cut appeared on her forearm, her sword dropping to the grass. Behind him Lykos heard the clash of blades, a man grunt in pain, a thud as his lads finished off Fidele's last guard.

'Enough of this,' Lykos said, holding his hand out to Fidele. She glanced behind her, down at the long drop to the rocks below.

'Don't be foolish,' Lykos said. 'Come with me, live. Who knows, you may escape again.'

Fidele threw herself at him, spitting and snarling and they reeled close to the edge, Fidele punching him in the head a dozen times and raking bloody grooves in his face with her nails before Lykos had caught her wrists. He slapped her across the cheek, hard, shook her, and her eyes spun, her colour draining.

She's still concussed. Good. Should make her more manageable.

'Stop this foolishness. You're coming with me,' he growled at her. He heard the thud of feet behind him.

'Let her go,' a voice snarled.

CHAPTER EIGHTY-FIVE

MAQUIN

Maquin froze for a moment as he emerged from the cave tunnel, eyes adjusting to the sunlight. He gripped his two short swords, both red to the hilt; he was splattered from head to toe in his own blood and the blood of his enemies.

He scanned the glade, filled only with the dead. Then he saw them.

Two figures at the rim of the glade.

Lykos, holding Fidele by one hand, dangling her over the cliff edge.

'Let her go,' Maquin snarled, stalking towards them.

'That's a poor choice of words,' Lykos observed. 'Are you sure?' He jerked a wrist, setting Fidele wobbling, only her toes on the cliff edge, back arching over into thin air.

'Pull her back,' Maquin said, closing the distance between them.

'Maybe I will, and maybe I won't,' Lykos said. 'But what is going to happen here is this. You're going to STOP!' He screamed the last word, spittle flying. Fidele swayed and Maquin froze.

'Good,' Lykos muttered. 'That is good. We need some rules here. The most important one is that I will be telling you what to do, not the other way around.'

'You are trapped,' Maquin said. 'Finished. If you stay there, more of my friends will be joining us, any moment now. If you let her fall, I will kill you.' He shrugged. 'Let her go.'

'That one's not going to work on me,' Lykos said, grinning and shaking his head. 'I've tasted something of her charms, know the effect she has on a man. Please don't insult me by pretending she doesn't matter to you.'

Shouts and screams echoed from the cave mouth, sounding close. Lykos glanced that way, then back to Maquin.

'I think I need to be going, so this is what's going to happen. You're going to take one of your many knives and cut your own wrist, right here, right now. I'm going to watch you bleed out and die, and then I'm going to leave, taking Fidele with me. If you don't do that, then I'm going to throw Fidele over this cliff and take my chances with you and whoever comes out of that cave mouth.'

'No,' Fidele gasped.

'One of you is going to die here. You get to choose, Old Wolf.'

Maquin stared at Fidele, a long, timeless moment.

The clamour of battle rang from the cave, closer again. Lykos' head snapped around.

'If I'm going to die, sure as Asroth lives, she's going to die too,' Lykos snarled. 'You think I won't?' His face twisted, a mask of rage. 'No. If I cannot have her, then no one will.' He shifted his weight, face set in determined, hate-filled lines.

'No,' Maquin cried. He dropped his swords, drew a knife from his belt, rested it against the vein in his wrist.

'Maquin, please, no,' Fidele said to him. She was crying. 'If you die, he wins, and I am worse than dead. You know what he will do to me . . .'

'I . . .' Maquin said, knife blade trembling at his wrist, a trickle of blood where it had broken the skin. The thought of her dying was unthinkable, unbearable.

'It is you that has to live,' Fidele said. 'You *have* to kill him.'

'Get on with it,' Lykos snarled, eyes flitting from Maquin to the cave mouth. 'She's getting heavy.'

As long as she lives, there is hope for her. Alben, Alcyon, they are coming . . .

'Maquin,' Fidele cried. Again, desperately. 'Maquin, look at me.'

He met her eyes. Tears ran down both their cheeks.

'If one of us lives, then so does something of the other,' Fidele said. 'I love you,' she whispered, and jerked her hand free of Lykos' grip.

For a long moment she seemed to hang suspended in the air, eyes locked fiercely with Maquin's. Then she was gone. Lykos lunged at her, but his hand clasped nothing but air.

Maquin opened his mouth to scream, but nothing came out. He felt as if a fist had clamped around his throat, a vice drawn tight about his chest. He stumbled forwards, arms outstretched, dropped to his knees, gave a great wracking sob, his vision blurred with his tears.

'Well, that was a waste,' Lykos said, staring over the ledge.

Maquin stood, blinking tears from his eyes. 'Now you die.'

Fear danced across Lykos' face, but it settled into anger. He stepped away from the edge and drew his own sword.

'We've all got to die sometime,' he growled.

Maquin heard the thud of feet, began to turn, but something slammed into his back, sending him flying through the air, crunching to the ground, swords gone as he rolled. His vision blurred, came back into focus and he saw a black-clothed warrior, maggot-white face, dark veins threading the skin, black eyes regarding him through a cloud of flies.

'Legion!' Lykos called. 'I have never been happier to see you!'

Other figures were emerging from the smoke-filled cave: more Kadoshim, a handful of Vin Thalun, then Javed's Freedmen, the black and silver of Ripa. A giant in bear-skins. Another giant ran from the cave, screaming, his body engulfed in flames. He stumbled and fell. Was silent.

Maquin pushed himself up, felt the world spinning, looked for Lykos.

Kill him. She asked me to kill him. Kill him. Kill Lykos.

His hand found the hilt of a sword, the other gripping a knife hilt at his belt.

'To the boats,' Lykos yelled at the creature he called Legion.

'Soon. After I've tasted the jelly of this one's eyes,' the Kadoshim called, striding after Maquin.

Lykos shrugged and ran as more men and giants spilt from the cave, a running battle.

Maquin launched himself at Legion and buried his knife hilt in the Kadoshim's jaw, punching up until the tip scraped against bone.

The Kadoshim grinned and grabbed Maquin by the jerkin, back-handed him, sending him spinning through the air, tumbling across the ground, losing the grip on his sword again. As he came to his feet he saw Legion grab the knife that was rammed up through his jaw and slowly pull it free. Maquin heard bone grating.

'It's always better when you put up a fight,' Legion said as he stalked after Maquin. Maquin danced backwards, knives hissing into each hand, one slashing at the outstretched fist, and severed fingers spun away.

'Come here,' Legion snarled, leaping at Maquin.

Maquin ducked, flies filling his vision, and pivoted away.

Stop fighting on instinct – that's a Kadoshim. I have to take his head, and knives aren't the tool for that job. And those flies aren't helping.

Maquin turned and ran, jumped over the flaming body of a dead giant, fist closing about an edge of cloak that wasn't on fire. He swung it about his head and hurled it at Legion like a flaming net. Flies buzzed as they were seared into charred ash.

'Better; I can see you now,' Maquin said, reaching down and plucking a sword from the grass. 'And I'll need to see you if I'm going to take your head.'

'That's the spirit,' Legion said, charging at Maquin, 'though I doubt you'll be so bold when I'm sucking the marrow from your bones.'

Maquin swung a savage overhead blow, the Kadoshim's left hand went spinning through the air.

'I'll take you down a piece at a time if I have to,' Maquin growled, bent and snatched up one of his short swords.

'You've made me angry, now,' Legion growled, and reached his remaining hand over his shoulder to draw his Jehar sword.

Their blades met, a harsh clash of sparks, a score of blows as Legion struck at Maquin, faster than eyes could track. Legion's onslaught forced Maquin back, the speed and savagery of it over-whelming, until Maquin had his back to a tree.

'I will feast on your flesh, rip your guts from your belly while you still breathe,' the Kadoshim grunted as he swung his sword. Maquin ducked low, Legion's sword thrumming deep into the tree as Maquin dived and rolled, saw a spear-blade in the grass, grabbed it and hurled it at Legion as the Kadoshim ripped his sword free and turned.

The spear pierced Legion's belly, punching through iron rings, leather and flesh and pinning him to the tree. The Kadoshim began

483

to pull himself bodily along its length, then Maquin was running at him, screaming a wordless battle-cry, swinging his sword two-handed, chopping into the Kadoshim's neck, slicing through flesh, cartilage and bone into bark, splinters spraying. Legion's head toppled to the ground, his body held upright by the spear.

A torrent of black mist poured from the Kadoshim's neck, swirling into the air above Maquin. It boiled above him, separating into a host of winged forms, spreading through the glade, blotting out the sun, myriad coal-red eyes glaring down at him. A multitude of wings beat their fury, a great pulse of air buffeting Maquin. As one, the winged demons shrieked, Maquin and all else in the glade clutching their ears, rocking as if they had been blasted with a great wind.

And then the black cloud was melting, a ragged, tattered banner pulled apart by a cold wind blowing up the cliffs from the lake below.

Maquin felt a hand on his shoulder, looked up to see Alcyon standing over him, Tain behind him, with another giant in bearskins. Maquin grabbed a fistful of Legion's hair and lifted the decapitated head, then staggered to the cliff edge and looked down. Upon jagged rocks lapped by water Maquin could see a body, limbs twisted at impossible angles. A spray of black hair spread across the rock, the bright splash of blood about it.

Maquin swayed, eyes fixed on Fidele, feeling a wave of grief so huge and raw that he thought his heart would surely stop beating. Wished it would. Time passed and he realized he was weeping, his body shaking, wracked with great sobs. He felt men gather behind him, Alcyon, Alben limping to his side, many others. All stood in silence and stared at the body broken on the rocks.

Beyond the rocks the lake spread, and upon it Maquin saw a single boat appear, pinprick figures in it rowing frantically, heading towards the river that flowed through grasslands and further, barely visible, into the green bulk of Forn.

'LYKOS,' Maquin screamed, his voice ringing out, and a body in the rowing-boat turned, looking up at them. Maquin took a step back, swung the decapitated head in his fist and hurled it arcing into the air. It spun high, dipped and fell, eventually hitting the lake far below with a tiny splash, only what looked like a few strides from the boat. Maquin could see the head, bobbing on gentle waves.

'I'm coming for you, Lykos,' Maquin bellowed through cupped hands, 'and neither demons from the Otherworld nor flesh and blood will stop me.'

CHAPTER EIGHTY-SIX

CAMLIN

Camlin rode out of the tunnel into a world of wonder. There were trees everywhere, which he had expected, but such trees! Wide-trunked, high-branched, and they climbed so high, the canopy above thinning with winter's onset, light trickling through splayed fingers, diffuse and distant. It was hard to tell, but Camlin guessed that it was somewhere between dawn and highsun. In the Darkwood he'd always loved that sense of space and yet of cover, both above and around him. Here that was magnified a thousandfold. He felt he'd come home.

He looked down at Meg, who was riding a pony behind him. He smiled at her now, but saw she was too wide-eyed at the forest to pay much attention to him.

The rest of them were all the same, even Edana, who rode beside him, following their two guides, men clothed in the black and silver of Tenebral. Camlin had almost put an arrow through one of them before Craf had squawked that the men were allies fighting against Nathair and not enemies.

Says a lot when you've come to trust a crow on matters of life and death.

They rode on a short way and six figures emerged out of the forest gloom before them. Edana lifted a hand and reined in, her warband spilling from the tunnel mouth, two thousand men spreading into the forest behind her.

A young warrior walked towards them, graceful and confident. He was clothed in forest leather and wool, dark-haired, serious-faced, a stubbly beard, broad at chest and shoulder, like a black-smith. A silver arm-ring curled around one of his biceps, catching

Camlin's eye, and he had two swords hanging from his belt, one long, one short.

A smile spread across Camlin's face.

A wolven emerged from the undergrowth, bounding out of the shadows and loping alongside the warrior as he stopped before them, looked up at Edana and Camlin and smiled at them.

'By Elyon, but it's good to see you, lad,' Camlin said.

His horse snorted and shied at the smell and presence of a wolven, but he whispered soothing words, stroked its neck and tugged on the reins and it settled.

'Welcome to Forn Forrest, my Queen,' Corban said, and then he dropped to one knee.

Edana slipped from her saddle and strode to him. 'Corban, there'll be no kneeling between us,' she said, 'and as you're the Bright Star of prophecy, perhaps I should be kneeling before you.'

'But, I swore an oath,' he said.

'I release you from it,' Edana said, waving her hand.

Corban started to say something but then the other figures came forwards.

'Do what you're told for once in your life,' a red-haired warrior said, hauling Corban to his feet. Camlin remembered her from Rath's crew in Domhain. Sullen and argumentative, she had been, and very handy in a scrap.

Camlin felt a swell of emotion as he recognized all of those who had fled Dun Carreg on a windswept night, crossing a sea, then travelling through Cambren and Domhain together. Gar with his curved sword across his back, Farrell beside him, still clutching a war-hammer in his ham-fists.

'Hello, Camlin,' a voice said, and Camlin looked down to see Dath staring up at him, clothed in brown and green wool, a leather jerkin, a cheeky grin splitting his face. He held an unstrung bow in one hand, a quiver of arrows hanging from his belt.

'Dath!' Camlin cried out as he jumped from his horse and embraced the young man, squeezing him tight. 'Dath, my lad!' And then they were all scrambling out of their saddles, greeting their friends and companions of old. Even Brogan had joined the reunion, lifting red-haired Coralen up off the ground and swinging her round.

Camlin noticed a small woman standing a little behind Dath, dark-haired and with a curved sword like Gar's across her back. Dath reached out and took her hand.

'Camlin,' Dath said, 'I'd like you to meet my wife, Kulla ap Barin. She's a Jehar warrior.'

'Wife! Good grief, lad, what else have you been up to while I've been away? Any bairns?'

'We are working on that,' Kulla said matter-of-factly, Dath blushing like a ripe red apple. Camlin laughed.

'Talking of bairns, who's this?' Dath asked, and Camlin saw Meg peering around his leg at Kulla.

'Ah, this is just a small stray waif I can't seem t'get rid of. Her name's Meg,' Camlin said, still smiling.

'I've saved your life more times than I can count,' Meg said indignantly. 'The last time I threw stones at that Rafe, and before that, a giant! But fine! Save your own life next time.'

'Fierce little thing, aren't you?' Dath said. 'I'm very pleased to meet you.' He held his arm out in the warrior grip, which Meg seemed to like, because she took it.

'Throwing stones?' Kulla said. 'That's no good. Has anyone taught you how to use a sword?'

'She's nine summers old,' Camlin said.

'I had a sword in my hand from my third nameday,' Kulla snapped.

'That explains a lot,' Dath muttered.

'So, Meg, when we get back to our camp, I shall teach you how to use a sword.' Kulla looked Meg up and down. 'Maybe a small one, to start with.'

Meg grinned.

'Rafe?' Dath said, looking at Camlin.

'Aye,' Camlin replied, his mood changing. 'He's got a lot t'answer for, that lad. Last thing he did was murder Baird.'

'What!' a voice cried – Coralen. She strode over to them, Brogan following.

'Aye, lass,' Camlin said. 'He put a knife in Baird's belly. Then he ran off after Rhin, who's headed to Drassil herself. Brogan and me, we were coming after him alone for a dose of vengeance, before Edana joined the party.'

'Baird was one of the finest, meanest fighters I've ever seen,' Coralen said, looking as if she might have a tear in her eye, though she seemed angry enough to fight a bear, as well.

'That's a truth,' Brogan grunted.

'I don't doubt it,' Camlin said, 'but Rafe's . . . changed.' He looked at them all. 'He's drunk from the starstone cup. Apparently that does things to a body. Makes 'em stronger, faster. And gives you a longer life, as well.'

'We'll see what I can do about that,' Coralen growled.

'Seems that we're in the company of like-minded people,' Camlin said to Brogan, slapping his arm.

'Aye,' Brogan said. 'I owe him for a sore head as well as for Baird, but as long as he dies, there'll be no arguing from me.'

The camp was busy, everywhere Camlin looked, men, women and giants were industriously carrying out tasks, tending to weapons and a hundred other things. Edana and her warband were greeted warmly and with much enthusiasm.

Not that I'm surprised. An extra two thousand swords is never a bad thing.

Camlin heard the thrum of arrows leaving bows, the thud as they pierced wood.

A fine sound.

He looked to see a line of archers, over thirty strong, all aiming and firing together.

Dath tapped his arm.

'My idea, that,' Dath said with a grin. 'Thought of you and your ambushes, and the damage done by just you and me when we'd shoot together. Thought, what if thirty or forty were doing the same thing . . .'

'Well, there you are, great minds think alike,' Camlin said with a smile. 'The same thing has crossed my mind. I've got my own crew of over forty lads and lasses that can draw a bow. Did a fine job in the battle of the Baglun.'

'Maybe we should introduce our crews,' Dath said.

'Now that's a fine idea.'

'And I'll need to hear about this battle of the Baglun.'

'Aye, you will, lad.'

As Corban and others helped settle Edana's warband, a group of men and women approached them. Camlin recognized Brina and Cywen walking with them, and blinked at the sight of two giants striding amongst them. One a woman, one white-haired and ancient as a knotted oak, only one eye in his head.

Corban introduced the group to Edana as Camlin joined them, then they were being led through the camp, into a small glade where a fire-pit burned, with logs and tree stumps scattered around to sit upon. Corban sat, and Camlin noticed that wherever he went, Farrell and Gar were as shadows behind him.

'Well, lass, you've either the best timing in the world, or the worst, turning up the day before this fight,' Krelis said.

'Well, I'm here to help,' Edana said, smiling at the big man.

'I must tell you, Edana, the odds are not good,' Corban said.

'We are used to poor odds,' Edana said, and behind her Vonn snorted.

'We are choosing to fight on the morrow only because we have to,' Corban continued. 'Nathair leads a warband, some four or five thousand strong. If we do not stop them on the morrow they will reach Drassil and combine forces with the warband there.'

'Would have been best to pick them off in the forest,' Camlin said.

'We've been trying,' Coralen snapped.

'Two thousand eagle-guard have been defending the warband as it moves,' said Veradis, the brother of Krelis. 'There are fewer of them, now.'

'We have been nipping and biting at them through twenty leagues of forest,' Corban said, 'and I think it's fair to say that we've taught them to fear the night, and not to leave their camp less than a hundred at a time. But they are too large a force to have broken them.'

'So you have to fight them, before it's too late,' Edana said.

'Aye,' Corban said. 'So, we fight on the morrow. I cannot tell you how great an encouragement your arrival is to us.'

'The odds are steep, but we do have a trick or two up our sleeves,' another warrior said, a man draped in furs, long hair bound into thick warrior braids. A single-bladed axe hung at his belt, another was slung across his back.

Wulf, Camlin reminded himself.

'A well-planned trick can turn a battle,' Edana said, glancing at Camlin.

'So, a warband in the forest, and one in the fortress. And us in between?' Halion asked. He'd been quiet, as usual, listening rather than talking.

But he misses nothing.

'We are, of course, expecting a counter-attack from the fortress,' Veradis said.

'Calidus and his lot don't usually venture out of Drassil these days,' Wulf said. 'They've been stung too many times. But the noise we're going to make on the morrow would likely be too much to resist.'

'And how will you meet this counter-attack, if you're engaged with Nathair's warband in the forest?' Edana asked.

'That's a good question, there,' another of Corban's captains said – Tahir, a young warrior with long, thick-muscled arms. 'We haven't answered it to our satisfaction, yet.' He caught Camlin's eye and smiled.

'We have to break Nathair and Lothar swiftly,' Corban said. 'No more harrying their heels. We hit them hard, break them and scatter them in the forest, before they reach the plain, and before any relief force sent by Calidus can reach them.'

'A charge of horse on the plain of Drassil may help there,' Veradis said thoughtfully.

'We are here to help you, and in the helping, kill our enemies,' Edana said, her expression serious. 'I fear I have some grim news for you. Rhin, Queen of Cambren, is also in Drassil.'

'Scouts reported a force to the north,' Gar said. 'I've sent out more scouts, but heard nothing more.'

'It's Rhin,' Edana said. 'She travelled by a different road to us, heading north first, but she had over a ten-night's start on us. She has brought the starstone cup to Calidus.'

'The starstone cup,' Corban said. 'Then that only leaves the necklace and torc unaccounted for.' He shared a look with Brina.

'Not the necklace,' Edana said and gestured to Halion. He reached inside his cloak and pulled out a leather-wrapped package. Unbuckling it, he lifted out the starstone necklace. Its black stone leaked shadow.

Gasps rippled around their circle.

'We took it from Rhin,' Edana said.

'Bet she wasn't happy about that,' Dath whistled.

'So, all of the Seven Treasures are here, except for the torc,' Corban breathed, eyes fixed on Brina.

'And Maquin and Alben may well return with that at any time,' Veradis said.

Brina shared a meaningful look with Corban. He nodded.

'Craf,' Brina called, looking up at the branches above them.

'*Yes*,' a squawk drifted down.

'Go and have a look at Drassil, see if Rhin and her warband of miscreants are lurking in there somewhere.'

Ah, it's good to see you, Brina. See you haven't lost any of your bite.

'*Edana asks nicer*,' Craf cawed down at them, but a branch creaked and wings flapped.

'Rhin has a great warband about her: all of the west, including Conall and the swords of Domhain, as well as Uthas and the Benothi giants,' Camlin said.

'Uthas!' Balur One-Eye said, his voice sounding like hammered iron.

'Aye.'

'Ach, but the morrow is looking to be a bloody day,' One-Eye growled. And smiled.

'Best see if we can find a way for it to be our enemies' blood, and not ours,' Corban said.

'Four or five thousand in Forn and, now Rhin has arrived, at least that again in Drassil,' Krelis said. 'I'm all for slaughtering my enemies, but that's a lot of men to kill.'

A silence fell as they all thought about that.

'Well, you make the road by walking it, as my old mam used to say,' muttered Tahir.

And so they set to planning the greatest battle since the Scourging.

Camlin stood up and paced around the clearing. Everyone else was deep in the discussion of how their forces would be organized on the morrow. He was happy with the part he'd be playing, so he made his way around to Cywen and sat beside her.

'It's good to see you, lassie.'

'You, too, Camlin.' She smiled up at him, and he remembered a girl standing in the Darkwood, fierce and defiant as her death was ordered by Morcant.

'I thought you'd like t'know,' Camlin said quietly in her ear. 'Morcant is no longer in this land of the living.'

He saw a twitch of anger at Morcant's name, eyes widening as realization followed, the faraway look a rush of memory gives, then a tear or two.

'He slew my Ronan,' she whispered. 'Ah, but he was fine. We'd kissed for the first time, that day, you know.' She smiled, a fragile, vulnerable thing that twisted into something bitter. 'And Morcant stole all that could have been.' She looked down at her hands, and Camlin remembered her holding them to a warrior's throat, trying to stem the tide of life as he bled out in a dozen heartbeats.

Wings fluttered above them and Craf circled down, landing on Brina's knee.

'*Rhin there*,' the crow muttered glumly. '*Many new spears.*'

A silence settled over them.

'And on the morrow we'll kill the bastards,' Krelis said.

'Aye,' Corban said. 'We've done all that we could to stop Nathair and Lothar, and we've picked off a lot of their warriors, but they will still reach Drassil on the morrow. We cannot let that happen. So, Nathair and Lothar first . . .' Corban paused, looking around at them all. 'If we can break them quickly, if we can keep our enemies from uniting, and if we avoid Calidus and Rhin's warbands unless we can lure them into the forest and fight on our terms . . .'

'And if Maquin returns with the last of the Seven Treasures,' Brina whispered.

A lot of ifs there, thought Camlin.

'What does that mean?' Edana asked. 'If Maquin returns with the last of the Treasures?'

Corban and Brina shared a look.

'Brina has a plan,' Corban said. 'A way to end this war. Not just to defeat the warbands arrayed against us, but to defeat Asroth, the Kadoshim, all of them.'

'How?' Edana said.

Corban opened his mouth and began to speak.

When he had finished, a silence filled the glade. Eventually Edana stood.

'Well, I think it's about time I saw this fabled Drassil,' she said.

CHAPTER EIGHTY-SEVEN

RAFE

Rafe dug his heels into his mount's ribs, urging her to climb the slope towards the bright light. Scratcher barked as he loped beside him.

He's as happy as I am at the thought of getting out of here.

They were in a huge tunnel, had been for a ten-night, now, riding hard with Rhin and her five thousand-strong warband.

Rhin cantered up the slope ahead of him, Geraint and Conall with her, as well as Uthas and his shieldman, Salach. The other Benothi giants were further down the column, acting as rearguard.

Rafe's horse clattered out from the slope into a huge chamber, bigger than anything Rafe had ever seen before. He let go of the reins, just let the mare take him forwards as he gazed around, awe-struck. The chamber seemed circular, a great flagstoned floor curling around something that looked like the trunk of a tree, only it couldn't possibly be, because it was about a thousand times too big for that.

It can't be a tree. Must be something carved to look like a tree. Some giant magic.

The stone floor was bordered on his right by steps that followed the curve of the chamber, rising up to a set of huge doors that were wide open, light pouring through them.

I don't even know what time of day it is, after being in that tunnel so long.

It felt like highsun, though, and judging by the angle of the light coming in through the doorway he was about right.

Highsun on Midwinter's Eve. The day I arrived at Drassil.

Pale light also leaked into the room from velum-like windows

495

high above, as walls arched and curled overhead, stairwells carved into them. Just looking up at them made Rafe feel dizzy.

Rhin reined in her horse before an old man with patchy silver hair on a peeling head. He looked as if he'd seen better days. Rafe recognized him though, had seen something of his features before, although then they had been framed within the flayed skin of a dead man.

So that's Calidus. Doesn't look half as scary in real life.

Surrounding him were the pale-skinned Jehar warriors who had been their guides through Forn, maybe two hundred of them. Clothed in black chainmail, curved swords strapped across their backs, skin pale as death. But it was their eyes that bothered Rafe most of all, like dark wells that bored into your soul. They gave Rafe gooseflesh.

Behind them were more warriors, but these were normal men, clothed in a uniform that Rafe recognized: the black and silver of King Nathair. They were rowed in neat ranks, forming a protective square around a long table and dais that backed onto the trunk of the giant tree. On the dais was a huge black cauldron, behind it a big throne-like chair, a pile of heaped bones upon it. Either side of the throne a weapon stood. On one side there was a double-bladed battle-axe, the blades made of black iron, like the cauldron, and on the other side of the chair a long spear leaned. Its leaf-shaped blade was fashioned from dark iron, too.

Rhin dismounted and walked forwards, Uthas joining her, and together they dropped to one knee before Calidus.

'Well met,' Rafe heard Calidus say, gesturing for them to rise. 'Where are they?' he asked of Rhin, sounding impatient. Rhin turned her head, and Rafe slid from his horse, unbuckling a small wooden chest from his saddle and hurrying forwards.

Rafe dropped to one knee as Rhin had instructed him and held the chest up to Calidus.

'The starstone cup,' he said, opening the lid.

'And the necklace?' Calidus asked, a frown menacing his face. He looked to Rhin.

'Edana has it,' Rafe said.

Calidus' hand whipped out and fastened around Rafe's throat, squeezing, dragging him to his feet. Rafe spluttered, tried to talk, but Calidus was choking the life from him. Black spots appeared before his eyes.

'Edana is coming here, a warband at her back. She will have the necklace with her,' Rhin blurted.

The grip around Rafe's throat loosened. He was dropping, felt cold stone slam into his face. Gasping, he lay there and looked up at Calidus, saw the old man was smiling.

What a place, Rafe marvelled as he rode through the streets of Drassil, gazing up and all around, looking at the huge tree trunk rising out of the great hall, branches spreading wide over the fortress.

I am walking in the land of faery tales.

Stone buildings reared tall everywhere he looked, and amidst them, filling every street, was an endless host of warriors. The street Rafe was riding down was busy with Rhin's warband being directed to stables and paddocks, but all about them, bustling industriously through side streets and courtyards, were men from other warbands, some clothed in the black and silver of Tenebral, others in weathered leather vests and jerkins with bucklers on their arms, rings bound in oiled beards. And scattered amongst them the black-eyed Jehar prowled, only a few, but wherever they went, men parted for them.

Scratcher seemed to be taking it all in his stride, though, bounding around, sniffing as if it was all a new adventure.

Rafe settled his mount into its stable, cleaning his tack, rubbing the horse down, checking hooves, trimming them with a sharp knife. When he was done he walked along the stable-block, a long row of pens.

Something crashed into the stable door to his left and he threw himself away, slamming into the wall. A stallion's head was looking at him over a stable door, had reared and kicked out as Rafe passed by.

It was a fine-looking animal, skewbald, white and tan patches. Rafe reached into his pocket and pulled out half an old apple and held it out. The horse snorted, then sniffed, then nibbled.

'There y'a go, lad,' Rafe said, rubbing its forehead. He unlocked the door and stepped inside and had a good look at the animal. It was tall and powerfully built, all muscle and spirit.

'You're a warhorse, sure enough, built for battle,' he said, patting the stallion's flank. 'Not like the mare I've ridden half to death coming here.' There was something familiar about him . . .

'Nice animal,' a voice said from over the stable door. It was Geraint, Rhin's battlechief.

'Have him saddled as a second mount for me on the morrow,' Geraint said and strode off.

'I might just forget to do that,' Rafe whispered into the stallion's ear, making it twitch. 'Might be you end up as my horse, instead.'

Rafe walked out into the courtyard and climbed a stairwell to stand on the battlements above Drassil's great gates. He whistled to himself as he looked west over a wide plain that rolled up to a wall of trees. The trees encircled the fortress, climbing high, a menacing ocean that rolled into the horizon, the red ball of the sun sinking into them, relinquishing the world to night. Above him the branches of Drassil's great tree swayed, gusts of wind blew cold around him.

As he stared he saw movement in the treeline, shadowed figures, on the edge of dusk.

Behind him he heard footsteps, the slap of leather on stone, and a hand clapped him on the shoulder. It was Conall. Rafe pointed as the shadows from the treeline stepped into the light. There were a dozen figures, some mounted. Three giants. Two warriors on foot, one a woman with a shock of red hair that caught the sunlight. The other a man, standing beside a broad-chested wolven almost as big as a horse, its bone-white fur streaked with scars.

Rafe felt the breath catch in his chest, a rush of hatred.

Corban and Storm.

'Cora, Hal?' Conall whispered.

They both stared in silence.

Then Rafe's eyes took in the riders, saw a blonde-haired woman cloaked in grey.

'That's Edana,' Rafe said.

'I think it is,' Conall agreed.

'How'd they get here so fast?'

'Where there's a will, there's a way,' Conall muttered.

They stared a while longer.

'We're wanted,' Conall eventually said.

'Who?'

'Our masters, who else?' Conall said with a twist of his lips. 'For a council of war.'

Rafe sat in the great hall, stiff and uncomfortable in a straight-backed chair, the long table in front of the cauldron and Treasures stretching before him. It wasn't only the chair that made him feel uncomfortable. Calidus unsettled him. Not only his appearance, but something else. There was something terrifying about him, a sense that he could slit your throat at any moment, and smile while he was doing it.

It was dark now, night coming early on Midwinter's Eve, and torches had been lit, crackling in the cold draught that swirled around the chamber. Jehar warriors guarded them, over two score of them that Rafe could see prowling the torchlit room.

And probably more of them lurking in the shadows.

He shivered, shifting uncomfortably in his chair.

Why do they want me here? A huntsman from Ardan at this, a council for war concerning the future of the Banished Lands?

His eyes wandered the room, drawn to the Treasures. Cauldron, axe, spear and cup.

Four of them. Maybe that's why I'm here – because I found the cup, and have drunk from it.

'They will attack soon,' Calidus said, breaking the silence. 'On the morrow, or the day after.' He shrugged. 'Soon.'

Rafe found Calidus hard to look at: much of his scalp was hairless, looking more like a melted candle than a head, and his face was the same, parts of his lip and cheek charred, his beard only growing in scraggly silver tufts.

'Why would they attack us here?' Geraint asked. 'I've walked the walls – this fortress is strong. It would take many thousands to breach these walls, and then only if they were poorly defended. And between our swords and your warbands of eagle-guard and Vin Thalun we must be close to seven thousand strong. Only a fool would attack us.'

'The world's full of fools,' Conall observed. 'Perhaps a few of them are gathered out there.' He waved a hand.

'They're *not* fools,' Calidus said. 'Do not underestimate them. They will attack Nathair and Lothar soon, because the road they are building is only a few days from the plain of Drassil. They will not want Nathair and Lothar's warbands to unite with us.'

Geraint snorted. 'Has the world ever seen such a warband? We are undefeatable.'

'Once before, such a force was gathered,' Calidus mused, 'but it's been a while. Undefeatable? Maybe, when we are together. But separate?' He shrugged. 'They know they cannot allow those warbands to enter these gates, so they will seek to stop them, will attack them, on the morrow, or the next day.'

'And what would you have us do?' Rhin asked.

'It will be too good an opportunity to miss,' Calidus said. 'They cannot number more than fifteen hundred swords, so they will throw everything they have at Nathair.'

'Edana's with them already,' Conall said casually.

'What?' Rhin gasped.

'It's true,' Rafe said. 'We just saw her, at the edge of the plain, looking up at us.'

'The *bitch*,' Rhin spat. 'I still cannot comprehend how she dares to chase after *me*. I'll squash her, hang her from the highest branch, let the crows feast on—'

'Enough,' Calidus said. 'You're starting to sound like Legion. And besides, it is in your favour that she has followed you here, bringing the necklace with her. Otherwise you would not be sitting so comfortably . . .'

'But how did she get here so fast?' Geraint muttered as Rhin looked away.

'We are not the only ones that can ride hard, I'm guessing,' Conall said.

'It makes little difference,' Calidus said. 'Unless she has brought four or five thousand swords with her.' He looked questioningly at Rhin and the others.

'Not possible,' Rafe said. He thought about it a little. 'Maybe fifteen hundred, two thousand at most, definitely no more than that.'

'So, our enemy could number at worst three and a half thousand.' Calidus tugged at the wisps of beard on his chin. 'That could be a danger to Nathair and Lothar.'

'Surely not,' Geraint said.

'Our enemy are well practised in fighting in that forest. And they are no rabble. Do not underestimate them.' Calidus flicked some skin from his fingertips and frowned. 'Well, then, the plan must remain the same. When our enemy assaults Nathair and Lothar we shall ride out and attack their rear. We will crush them, Nathair the anvil, and us the hammer.'

'In the forest?' Rafe asked, not liking the thought of that. He remembered the last forest battle that he'd been involved in.

'No, not in the forest. When Nathair and Lothar push through to the plain around Drassil,' Calidus said.

If they get that far, Rafe thought.

'Will you lead the attack, Lord Calidus?' Geraint questioned.

'I will not be leaving Drassil,' Calidus said, 'and I will keep much of my warband around me. Around the Treasures.'

Geraint frowned. 'Would the best plan not be to lead out the full might gathered here and crush our enemy? A decisive strike that would be overwhelming and make victory inevitable.'

'And leave the Treasures unguarded?' Calidus hissed, staring at Geraint as if he had lost his wits.

'Not unguarded,' Geraint said, 'but surely the walls of Drassil and a few hundred swords would be enough to—'

'No,' Calidus snarled. 'The Treasures are all. They must be protected.'

'Let my warband lead the attack,' Rhin said eagerly.

'You have been a faithful ally, though you have failed me,' Calidus said, tapping a finger against his chin. 'And a charge of horse may be the best way to fall upon our enemies' backs.' He smiled at her. 'If you wish for that honour, then I will not deny you.'

'My thanks,' Rhin said. 'Conall, you shall lead my vanguard.'

Conall looked at her, then raised his cup. 'You do me a great honour, my Queen.'

What she meant to say, Rafe thought, *is that you will die first, Conall. You may win glory on the battlefield, but I imagine you'll also be dying on it. Rhin does not forget a betrayal.*

'Geraint, Conall, I thank you for your counsel and your service,' Calidus said. 'If you would go now and ready your men for battle.'

The two men looked at Calidus a moment, slowly realizing Calidus was dismissing them. They looked to Rhin.

Rhin nodded curtly at her two battlechiefs and they rose and left.

When she was sure they had gone Rhin leaned over to Rafe and whispered in his ear.

He listened intently, then nodded.

New tasks to complete, and a chance to redeem myself in Rhin's favours.

'So,' Calidus said, looking from Rhin to Uthas, 'you have both done well, have earned great rewards. We stand on the brink, now, so close.'

'It will be a great step, defeating the Bright Star and all those who oppose us in one decisive battle,' Rhin said.

'Aye,' Uthas agreed. 'Balur and Ethlinn, as well.'

'Yes,' Calidus said. 'But that is not all that will happen on the morrow.'

He leaned conspiratorially forwards, his face in darkness.

'Asroth will become flesh,' he whispered.

Rafe felt shivers dance down his spine.

'But we only have four of the Treasures,' Rhin said. 'What of the necklace, torc and the dagger?'

'Edana has the necklace, and she is out there. You have only to take it from her,' Calidus said, a threat in his voice. 'Redeem your past failures.'

'I will,' Rhin said. 'But that still leaves the torc and dagger . . .'

Calidus clapped his hands, and three figures appeared from the shadows – two Jehar, either side of an older man, black-haired with streaks of grey. He looked exhausted, eyes black hollows, and his clothes were sweat-stained and tattered; blood crusted on dozens of wounds, a short sword hung at his hip. Even so he walked towards them with a confidence and charisma that Rafe had seen in very few men, a controlled anger in his eyes and the hawk-like twitch of his head. A heavy oversized torc of black iron hung around his neck. It seemed to weigh him down.

'All of you, may I introduce my oldest ally in these Banished Lands: Lykos, Lord of the Vin Thalun.'

Lykos threw himself into a chair, poured himself a drink of something dark and leaned back, one boot up on the table. He drank deeply, wiped his mouth, and then took the torc from around his neck and threw it disdainfully onto the table. It rolled in a circle, all eyes upon it, thudded to a stop.

'You have *no* idea what I've been through to bring you this,' Lykos said, then poured himself another cup.

Calidus laughed, long and loud, a maniacal edge to it.

'And what of the starstone dagger?' Uthas asked. 'Do the Jotun not have it?'

'The Jotun? They did have the starstone dagger,' Calidus said, sipping from his own cup of wine. 'But no longer. Asroth is not idle in the Otherworld. He has captured a prisoner.' He smiled, a gloating, satisfied thing. 'Now Corban, the so-called Bright Star, has the starstone dagger, and on the morrow I shall take it from his mangled corpse.'

CHAPTER EIGHTY-EIGHT

CORBAN

Corban was in a grey world, standing in an empty corridor, some-how knowing that he was deep underground, with the weight of a mountain above his head. He looked both ways, saw no one, and for some reason felt compelled to walk down the corridor.

Doors were set along both walls, thick oak doors with iron-barred view holes. Corban peered through every door, seeing the small chambers within. They were all empty, until he came to the last one.

A figure, its back to him. Dark-haired, tall. Great wings of white feather furled across its back. It must have heard Corban because it turned, a tear-stained face stared at him, a thick cord of cloth tied around its mouth, gagging it.

It was Meical.

'How? Who has done this to you?' Corban asked.

Meical took a step towards him, but a thick chain rattled on the floor and Corban saw that a manacle was shackled to Meical's ankle, the chain bound to a great pin that was sunk into the stone floor.

Meical stared at him with grief-filled eyes.

Corban woke to the grey of dawn.

What was that? Meical, imprisoned? Has he been captured by Asroth and the Kadoshim? Shadows were all around, Coralen's body curled against him. He shifted and her eyes opened, a long sigh. Corban stroked her cheek. He remembered what today was.

I cannot do anything about Meical now.

'It's time,' he said.

In silence they rose, crouched by the stream they'd slept beside and washed in, banishing the last remnants of sleep. The day was cold, the water icy, making Corban gasp. They dressed for war, still in silence, helping each other, tightening buckles and straps. Corban tugged on his boots, then pulled his mail shirt on over a thick woollen undershirt. It was heavy but felt good, a fine fit. He shifted his shoulders, letting it settle. Coralen lifted a leather surcoat over his head, a four-pointed star on its chest.

Nothing to do with any false prophecies. I choose to stand against Asroth, against Calidus and Nathair. If that makes me the Bright Star, then so be it – I choose to be the Bright Star.

He helped Coralen put on her own mail shirt, taken from a dead eagle-guard that had no more need of it, and then cinched tight the straps and buckles of her leather jerkin. Sword-belts were buckled, two swords on Corban's, a sword and three knives on Coralen's. And their wolven claws, tied with a thong to their belts, for now. Coralen adjusted Corban's wolf's-head torc, and his arm-ring of silver.

Corban took Coralen's hand, looked into her eyes. He opened his mouth to speak, but she put two fingers upon his lips.

'No words can say what I feel,' she whispered.

'Only this, then,' Corban said. 'I love you.'

'I know.' She grinned, and kissed him.

Corban heard footsteps, the darkness was lifting now, everything a shade of grey. He knew the steps were Gar's before he saw him. His old friend was dressed for war, a shirt of dark mail, hair tied back tight to the nape of his head, sword hilt jutting over one shoulder, his father's axe at his belt. He just looked Corban up and down and nodded. Then the others began to arrive. Brina and Cywen together, then Farrell, grim-faced, hair and beard bound with warrior braids, war-hammer rearing over one shoulder, longsword at his hip. Finally Dath and Kulla.

'Where's Laith?' Dath asked Farrell.

'Still asleep. Snoring, truth be told, though don't tell her I said that,' Farrell said with a shrug. 'She's not one for mornings. She'll be along after.'

'Long as she doesn't miss all of the excitement.'

'Not likely,' Farrell said. 'I don't think this one will be over by highsun.'

That's for sure.

'You could have waited for her,' Corban said.

'Ban, I'm your shieldman. Of all days, she'll know where to find me today. By your side. Wherever you are, that's where I'll be. Guarding your back.'

Corban smiled at his old friend, went to say something but found there was a lump in his throat that wouldn't allow any words out.

A flapping of wings announced Craf's arrival. He alighted on Brina's shoulder.

'*News*,' he squawked.

'Go on, then,' Brina said, scratching the bird's neck.

'*Starstone torc in Drassil.*'

A flurry of questions, Brina cutting over them.

'You're sure?' she asked.

'*Yes, sure,*' Craf croaked. '*Saw it, with axe, spear, cup and cauldron.*'

A long silence followed as the weight of that knowledge settled into Corban and his companions.

'This is it, then,' Dath said. Corban could hear the tension in his voice, felt it in his own chest – a stirring of fear, excitement, anger, back to fear. Kulla squeezed Dath's hand.

'Aye,' Farrell agreed.

'It is,' Corban breathed out.

They stood in a circle, hands slipping into hands, and just looked at each other, smiles creasing faces, tears rolling down cheeks. It lasted a long, timeless moment.

'One way or another, now, this war will be over by tonight,' Corban said.

They all knew what that meant. Victorious and alive. Defeated and dead.

'I'm scared,' Corban said into the silence.

'I'm scared, too,' Gar said. Murmurs of agreement rippled amongst them.

'But all feel fear, both the coward and the hero, and all those in between,' Farrell said.

'Aye. It's what we do about it that counts,' Dath muttered.

'And what are we going to do about it?' Coralen asked, though Corban already knew the answer.

'We're going to fight,' he said.

A stillness as they squeezed each other's hands and found their courage in that silent place.

'We all ready, then?' Brina asked.

'Not quite,' Corban said. 'Storm,' he called, and the wolven emerged from the gloom. 'Time for you to get dressed.'

Corban made his way into their camp. His friends were lined behind him, Storm's mail coat rippling as she moved. It fitted her perfectly, leather-studded collar snug about her neck, buckles and straps under her chest and belly pulled tight so that the mail coat looked like another skin, flowing and undulating with each muscular contraction and extension. Corban had given Storm an opportunity to become accustomed to it during raids on Nathair and Lothar's warband. She'd scratched at it at first, but Corban had adapted it with an under-rug of wool so that it did not rub, and now she looked like a sleek statue carved from iron, fluid and molten metal. Corban could feel the weight of her steps beside him shivering up the soles of his boots.

'You're making everyone stare,' Corban told her, and she was.

Brina walked beside him.

They had met with Corban's captains, told them Craf's news. All of them knew now how that would change the plan of battle. The strike against Nathair and Lothar would remain the same, but now, instead of avoiding Calidus, they wanted to keep his eyes fixed on the plain, and if possible draw him and his thousands from Drassil. Much could go wrong.

'We could go now,' Brina said to Corban.

'No. I must be seen on the battlefield.'

Brina grunted, but gave up as they'd discussed this already.

'When we go, we will need to move fast,' she said to him.

'Aye,' Corban replied. 'We need to stay close to each other.'

'Yes. So don't go getting carried away and running off to stab people.'

'This is a day for stabbing people.'

'I know that,' she said. 'But just be selective.' He felt her hand slip into his. 'And stay safe, Ban. There are very few people on this earth that I care about, but you're one of them.'

'Love you, too, Brina.'

He squeezed her hand and she humphed at him but there was a smile tugging the corner of her mouth.

Corban stopped at the crest of a shallow hill at the southern end of the camp. He stood there a few moments, eyes closed, the enormity of this day filling his head, falling upon him like an avalanche. It almost took his breath away.

He opened his eyes.

The warband was massed before him. Amongst the crowd he saw Jehar, giants, men and women from so many realms: Ardan, Narvon, Domhain, Isiltir, Tenebral. Everywhere he looked he saw the emblem of the Bright Star, upon banners, shields, surcoats, cuirasses, the sigil uniting such a diverse gathering, the symbol of what bound them all together. Three and a half thousand swords, all looking to him.

He took a deep breath.

'Today we fight,' he said, the crowd before him still as a windless lake.

'We've suffered, lost much, had much taken from us. But today is the day we say, NO MORE.' He saw nods and grunts ripple around the warband. His eyes flickering across so many, giants, men and women, Haelan looking at him with shining eyes, Camlin, a wry smile upon his face, Vonn and Halion, many others, finally Gar.

'I am proud to stand beside you. I know that none of you fights for riches, nor for glory or for fame. We fight for something simpler and more powerful.' He tapped his chest. 'We fight for those we love.' He felt a lump in his throat, his mam and da filling his mind, saw many about him with silvered eyes.

'And that truth shall give us the courage we need,' he cried out. 'On this day we will march out to meet our enemies, those that have slain our kin, stolen our homes and would take our lives, and we shall show them what drives us. TRUTH AND COURAGE.'

Voices shouted out then, a wall of sound, echoing his cry of *TRUTH AND COURAGE.* He felt a surge of passion as he looked about at them all, pride in them, a fierce bond of love and brotherhood for this warband, full of so many who were just like him, scared, angry, pushed too far, ready to stand against evil in defence of their kin and loved ones.

'This day,' he cried, shouting now, 'we will live or die, but whatever the outcome, this will still be the day we avenge ourselves for those we've lost, the day we right the wrongs done to us, or die in the trying. It will be a dark day, a bloody day, a proud day, for this is the day of our wrath.'

'WRATH,' the cry went up, ringing and echoing through the branches.

'WRATH.'

The roar was deafening, all yelling with a fierce passion, banging weapons on shields, stamping feet, echoing on and on.

'Well, if Laith's not awake now, she must be deaf,' Dath whispered to Farrell.

'Are they ready?' Corban asked Veradis. They both looked across the camp, heard the clang of iron, Balur swearing loud enough to scare birds from trees.

'They'll have to be,' Veradis said.

'Veradis,' Corban said, gripping the warrior's arm as he turned away. 'You asked me a question once, about forgiveness . . .'

'Aye,' Veradis said, still as stone now.

'My answer is, yes,' Corban said.

Veradis exhaled.

'My thanks,' he said.

Beside him Corban saw Halion talking to Craf, who was perched on Brina's shoulder. The warrior leaned close to the bird's head and spoke quickly and quietly. When he was done, Craf squawked a complaint, but bobbed his head. Halion walked away.

'Keep an eye over us, make sure there are no nasty surprises out there,' Corban heard Brina say.

'*Win and live, or Craf be lonely and sad,*' the crow said, riffling its beak through Brina's hair, then flapping into the sky.

'And you fly safe, you scruffy old crow,' Brina muttered.

Corban felt a wave of fear wash over him as he looked at Brina and the others.

I have tried, planned for every eventuality and outcome, but now we are on the brink. March into this battle and we could be marching to our deaths. Coralen, Cywen, Gar, Brina, Dath, Farrell . . .

The thought of them dying – it threatened to take his very breath away.

And yet, it must be done. Calidus must be fought, and who else is there but us?

He untied his wolven claws from his belt and strapped them onto his left fist, pulling the buckles with his teeth to cinch them tight, then he strode from the hill, his captains falling in behind him, horses neighing and stamping as riders mounted up. Like a great beast waking from sleep the warband lurched into motion and moved into the forest, and behind them Storm lifted her head to the sky and howled.

CHAPTER EIGHTY-NINE

NATHAIR

Nathair heard a wolven howl, loud and long, the sound of it echoing through the forest, setting birds to flight. It chilled his blood, a note within it that resonated with spine-tingling malice, and he knew that it was not only he who felt it. All about him his eagle-guard paused, a ripple passing through them. Even his draig sensed it, head cocking to one side, its lumbering gait stuttering for a moment before it carried on.

It is Corban's wolven, Storm. I know it.

The beast had been seen enough times over the last few moons, flitting through the shadows of Forn, stalking them, picking off any who strayed too far into the forest. Nathair had heard men talking about the wolven at night while sitting around their fires, how it was not mortal, that it was deathless.

I'll show them how deathless it is, if only my draig could get a hold of it.

Nathair was situated at the head of the column, before him a few hundred eagle-guard in loose formation, their wall eight rows deep, spreading back around him, narrowing into a three-row column that carried on back along either side of the road and workforce that was labouring frenziedly to get this road built and onto the plain of Drassil for wains, horses, auroch and four thousand feet to tramp across.

When I found Gundul we had six thousand swords between us. Now Lothar has three thousand left, and my eagle-guard number little more than a thousand. But after three moons of constant raids and attacks you have to expect to lose a few men. Two thousand, to be exact, though over a

*hundred were men caught trying to desert. Lothar made quite the example
of them. A ruthless man. I admire him, even though he isn't so easy to
manipulate as Gundul.*

As he looked back he saw Lothar riding up the line towards him,
his warband a crush of men beyond the few hundred labourers
working on the road. He had ordered his warband into their best
gear today, as they expected either to reach Drassil or to be given
battle.

*Probably both. Corban and his rabble cannot hope to stop us, but surely
they will not allow us to reach Drassil uncontested.*

The sound of hooves drumming. Lothar did look impressive as he
cantered up on his black stallion, mail shirt gleaming and freshly
scrubbed with sand, white cuirass polished, the black hammer of
Helveth embossed upon it, a cloak of white wool with ermine trim
about his shoulders and a silver torc around his neck, warrior braid
bound with silver wire. Ten Kadoshim ran alongside him, falling in
around Lothar and Nathair to walk with them.

Lothar nodded to Nathair curtly, as an equal, which never failed
to annoy Nathair, and then spent a few moments controlling his
mount as it shied away from Nathair's draig, which secretly pleased
Nathair.

'How long?' Lothar asked, peering into the gloom of the forest
ahead. Only tree and shadow filled their horizon.

'If we rode hard we'd see Drassil before the sun was halfway to
highsun,' Nathair said. 'But at this pace –' he shrugged – 'sunset.'

'And the enemy?' Lothar muttered, eyes scanning the gloom to
left and right.

'No sign, yet,' Nathair replied.

'I heard that beast howling. Everyone did. They're out there.
They will attack.'

I know. I would if I were them.

'They are a rag-tag warband, made up of a dozen different factions,
all with different leaders,' Nathair said. He paused, catching a
scent on the air, off to the north.

'Do you smell that?' Nathair asked Lothar.

'A fire? Perhaps we are close to their camp?'

Then it was gone.

'This Corban is supposed to lead them,' Nathair continued, 'but who really knows? And with the size of our warband, Corban and his rabble may not even have the stomach for a contest with us. The outcome would be inevitable.'

And then, as if naming called, there were figures solidifying out of the shadows on the path ahead.

Nathair felt a jolt of surprise, and then fear, because they were dressed in the black and silver of Tenebral, a line of thirty men blocking the path, trees thick on their flanks. Their shields formed a loose wall, and from Nathair's height on his drag he could see they were at least six rows deep. The only difference in their appearance from his own warriors was a white star upon their shields. That made him angry.

The warband of Ripa. Krelis' men. They are no match for my Draig's Teeth.

To prove his contempt, Nathair allowed his eagle-guard to march another few score paces. His eagle-guard stopped with well-oiled practice, shields coming together in a loud crack, the flanks rippling together to face outwards along both sides of Lothar's workforce.

A figure stepped out from the enemy warband, not Krelis, as Nathair was expecting, but someone even more familiar.

It was Veradis.

For a moment Nathair felt a smile tugging at his mouth and had to stop himself from leaping from his draig and embracing his old friend.

Veradis was looking straight at him, and Nathair saw that he was stroking the palm of his hand, the scar from that night when they had sworn an oath to each other, become blood-brothers.

'Well met, Nathair,' Veradis called out.

'My friend,' Nathair said. 'Why are you stood against me?'

Veradis took a few steps forwards, stopped only a dozen paces from Nathair's shield wall.

'Because you are wrong,' his friend said simply.

And in that sentence, just for a moment, Nathair felt all of his arguments, his politics, strategies and oh-so-rational excuses fade away, and he knew Veradis was right. He bowed his head and squeezed his eyes shut tight.

How have I ended up in this place. A pawn of Asroth?

He already knew the answer.

Ambition. Greed. Power. And cowardice. I am a coward. I chose to live and swear an allegiance to my enemy, rather than die with my head held high and my conscience clear.

At that moment, pure as white-hot flame, he despised himself.

He realized there was a great silence around him, looked up and saw Veradis staring at him, eyes pleading with him to do the right thing.

I could turn, even now. Join Veradis, destroy Lothar's warband. It would make such a difference to their campaign that I would be forgiven my past mistakes, and with Veradis I could lead them to victory.

A blur of motion drew his eye: on the right flank, amongst the trees, bone-white, moving fast, in and out of view. A wolven leaped out of the trees and stalked along their line, head low, amber eyes seeming to glow as it eyed the rows of eagle-guard. It looked up, at Nathair's draig, and Nathair heard it growl, its coat shimmering and rippling like molten silver in the twilight, long curved teeth in slavering jaws.

So this is Storm.

Nathair felt a rumble in his draig's belly, an answer to the wolven's challenge.

Storm prowled onto the path close to Veradis, and another figure stepped out of the shadows, the wolven padding to him. A young man, black-haired, broad-chested, dressed simply in chainmail shirt and leather surcoat. A four-pointed star emblazoned his chest.

'You are Corban?' Nathair asked him.

'We have met before,' the young warrior said. 'Do you not remember?'

'I do,' Nathair said. He remembered a young lad, more a boy, staring up at him from a blood-soaked floor, crouched over a dead man, telling Nathair that he would kill him.

'You swore you would kill me.'

'I did,' Corban said.

'You may try, if you are brave enough.'

A look of pure hatred flickered across Corban's face, slowly marshalled, smoothed away.

He has some self-control.

Corban took a long, frayed breath and looked at Veradis. Finally he turned his gaze back to Nathair. 'And you may join us, if you are brave enough.'

'Wha—?'

'You could join us,' Corban repeated. 'Calidus is our enemy here, the enemy of all mankind. He has lied, murdered and manipulated his way to Drassil. He has used you, but you can end that now.'

'Join us, Nathair,' Veradis urged him. 'Corban is offering you a chance. Turn away from the path you've chosen, remember who you are, remember our dream. Our oaths. Our friendship.'

Nathair stared at Veradis, felt a moment of longing for the simplicity of those times.

'And Corban?' Nathair asked.

'He will forgive you. He is the Bright Star. We should have followed him from the beginning.'

A new emotion reared up in Nathair, then. Jealousy.

Forgive me! The Bright Star! I bore that title for so long, and now you are so quick to give it to another. Do you think him a better man than me?

Nathair felt something cold slam shut within him and drew himself up straight in his saddle.

'I offer you the same choice, Veradis. Join me. I will forgive you, and your men. Come, be my first-sword, my battlechief again, be the man you were supposed to be. You swore an oath to me, and you are not an oathbreaker. Or are you?'

Veradis stared up at him, mouth twisting.

'It was all a lie,' Veradis whispered.

'Join me,' Nathair commanded. Then quieter, 'I can make this right.'

'No,' Veradis shook his head. 'You can't. You don't even know what right is any more.' Silent tears streaked his cheeks.

'Are you going to listen to these fools much longer?' Lothar asked him.

No.

He smelt smoke again, but ignored it, eyes fixed on Veradis and Corban.

'Sound the advance,' Nathair said to the horn-man beside him. 'Caesus, wipe this mob from our path,' he called out, horn blasts ringing.

515

'So be it,' Veradis said sadly, the whipcrack of eagle-guard slamming shields together and advancing drowning out his words.

Corban and Storm melted back into the darkness and Veradis marched back towards his shield wall, yelling as he went. To Nathair's great surprise they started to retreat. It was organized, even quite impressive, not turning their backs on Nathair and his advancing shield wall, but nevertheless, they were retreating.

This is going to be easier than I thought.

CHAPTER NINETY

VERADIS

Veradis bellowed his orders, felt a rush of pride at the way his men were retreating in disciplined ranks, ten paces, twenty paces. Thirty, more. He followed after them, moving to the side of the trampled path, in amongst the trees.

Nearly there.

There was a pain in his chest, a physical manifestation of how he felt at Nathair's rejection of peace.

Of redemption.

So much could have been saved, so many lives. And our friendship.

He stepped over a shallow ditch that cut across the trampled track, strode another score of paces and sucked in a deep breath.

He's made his choice, and I have made mine. Nothing else to be done but see it through.

'BALUR,' he yelled.

Immense shapes emerged from either side of the path that the shield wall had just vacated: giants, lumbering under a great weight. Veradis saw Balur first, a thick plate of iron strapped across his torso, hammered and shaped to cover the giant from neck to hips, like a leather cuirass; more moulded plates were strapped and buckled about his shoulders and arms, iron bracers wrapping tight about his wrists and forearms, and the same with his legs, iron greaves enfolding ankles and legs. Upon his head he even wore a helmet of iron, a nose-piece and cheekplates making his face a shadowed thing. He looked like a walking forge. In his arms he held a wooden shaft longer than a spear, banded and butted with iron, at its head a single, wicked-looking axe-blade with a long curved point tapering like a beard. Another nine giants emerged from the shadows clad like

Balur in plates of iron and gripping the spear-long axes, and then another score clothed in their leather and fur, all wielding their traditional weapons of hammer and double-bladed axe.

Balur strode towards the oncoming shield wall, those armoured like him falling in either side, forming a wall across the path, flanked by the other giants.

Veradis saw Lothar cantering back down the line to his massing warband, the Kadoshim that had accompanied Lothar staying with Nathair. At the sight of Balur and his giants Nathair frowned from his vantage point upon his draig, but he allowed his shield wall of eagle-guard to proceed. Veradis shifted his gaze to them, thought he saw Caesus at the centre of the front row.

My position, where I would stand amidst my Draig's Teeth. And now I would call the halt before these giants, lock shields, brace my feet, and allow my enemy to throw themselves to their deaths.

He blew out a long breath as the shield wall rippled to a halt, muffled orders shouted, shields locking high.

'Giants will not save you,' Nathair called from behind the shield wall, 'we have faced them before and triumphed.'

Not these giants, you haven't, Veradis thought.

'SHIELD-BREAKERS, FORWARDS,' Veradis bellowed, and Balur and his comrades lumbered forwards, slowly, each step a ponderous thundering drumbeat. Before them the shield wall stood, silent and implacable.

They will be waiting for the roar of warriors, the thunder of their charge, the first avalanche-like impact. Veradis' fingers twitched to the hilt of his short sword, feeling almost as if he was there, alongside them, his one-time sword-brothers. Now his enemy.

'NOW,' Veradis yelled, Balur and his Shield-Breakers rippling to a halt, well out of range of the shield wall and its short stabbing swords.

They need the crush of flesh upon their shields to reap their harvest of blood.

As one, the giants' axe-shafts shot out, arcing high, slammed down onto the heads of the first row of eagle-guard and were explosively yanked back, the tapering points of the axes hooking behind shield rims, dragging them and the warriors gripping them tumbling into the space between giant and eagle-guard, some sprawling on the ground, others stumbling on unsteady feet. The axes rose and fell, hacking down into iron helms and leather-covered shoulders and backs.

Eagle-guard screamed and died, an explosion of blood as half of the first row were dragged to their deaths, huge gaps suddenly appearing in the shield wall. Veradis heard Caesus yelling orders, men shuffling forwards to fill the gaps.

Giants from the flanks of Balur's row ran forwards and finished any eagle-guard still breathing in the killing ground, crushing or splitting skulls with hammer and axe, then leaped back to the flanks as Balur's axe-men raised and slammed their weapons down into the shield wall a second time, repeating their grisly attack, men screaming, shields splintering, blood spraying as more men were dragged tumbling to their deaths. The Shield-Breakers ripped another half-score of men from their formation, and Veradis saw men in the wall hesitate, slow in their movement forwards where before they had moved like a machine, thoughtless habit and instinct guiding them.

Fear is swaying them now.

The gaps closed, though, the line reforming, shields crunching together.

Footsteps behind him and Krelis appeared. He was holding a flaming torch.

'How goes it, little brother?' he said, watching as Balur and his kin continued their bloody work dragging more men screaming to their deaths. Krelis whistled. 'I'm glad we're on the same side,' he muttered.

'All's ready,' Veradis told him. 'We just need to hold them here a little longer.'

'Shall I?' Krelis said, waving his torch at the shallow, narrow ditch before Veradis' feet that cut across the path. It glistened with fluid – tree sap and other combustibles that Brina had helped them gather.

Must hold them here, let the whole of Lothar's warband gather behind them into one large maul.

'Wait till we see the flames, that's what Corban said. Else we'll give them warning. Patience, brother.'

'Not my best quality,' Krelis growled.

The killing ground was piled with the dead, the earth blood-soaked, and still the giants continued to hook, drag and kill, the shield wall as yet having no answer for this deadly stratagem.

I would move, march forwards, try and close with them, rather than stand and wait for my death to descend upon me. That is the weakness in this attack. A sudden charge and the giants would be vulnerable. They may be wrapped in iron, but there are still gaps, knee and hip joints, gut and elbow. But it is hard for a battlechief to see that in the heat of the moment, when his men are dying to left and right, when his own death looms large, as close as a breath upon the neck.

And even as Veradis thought it, he heard Nathair's horn-man blowing the signal for a fast advance, shouted commands echoing from the front line of the shield wall.

So Nathair still has something of his tactical skill, then. I must not forget that it was his plan that gave us victory over the draig-riding Shekam.

The shield wall lurched into motion, not as fluid as Veradis would have expected, but it kept the shields tight, the wall solid, rows behind packed close and firm. Even when they marched over the bodies of their fallen sword-brothers the line did not break. Veradis grunted approvingly. He pulled a horn to his lips and blew on it, one long note. Balur's head tilted his way, and then the giant's voice was booming and he and his Shield-Breakers were retreating, moving back and towards the forest, sinking into the trees and shadows, revealing behind them on the track the shield wall of Veradis' men, silent and still.

'Remember, big brother, wait until you see the flames,' Veradis said, and then he was running, back towards his men, tugging on his helm, taking the shield offered him and slipping it onto his arm. He fell in at the centre of the first row, looked at the men either side of him and gave them a fierce grin.

'SHIELD WALL,' he yelled, and their shields slammed together with a concussive thud.

Veradis willed his men to hold.

CHAPTER NINETY-ONE

NATHAIR

Nathair sat and stared at the mangled carnage that had been the front rows of his shield wall. Shock had frozen him for too long as the deadly genius of Veradis' Shield-Breakers had unleashed their fury upon his Draig's Teeth.

Now, though, he was back in control of his wits.

Over a hundred men dead, in less time than it would take to count them, but I have a thousand of my eagle-guard about me still, give or take. This is not defeat, Veradis, merely a blooded lip.

'Let us deal with them,' one of the Kadoshim close by said to Nathair.

'Soon,' Nathair replied.

He held his draig back as the shield wall marched forwards, allowing more men from the surrounding flanks that stretched all the way back to encompass Lothar's warriors to hurry forwards and fill the gaps of the fallen, thickening the wall upon the track until it was fifteen, twenty rows deep, and more joining it all the time.

The iron-covered giants with their axes had fallen back, disappearing into the gloom of the forest, and now blocking the way on the path ahead was the original shield wall that had stood behind Veradis.

He felt a rush of anger, that his old friend would betray him like this. Would stand against him.

He has chosen his death. They are men, and they are not my Draig's Teeth.

Even as Nathair watched, the front row of his shield wall slammed into Veradis' line. There was a concussive crash that seemed to ripple outwards, shaking leaves from branches, and Veradis' shield wall bent at the edges, like a pulled bow. Nathair held his breath, thinking with every heartbeat to see the enemy line shatter and break apart. A cloud of smoke rolled across the path, for a few moments obscuring the locked shield walls. Nathair heard the screams of men, heard the dull thud of iron on wood, the pushing and heaving of hundreds of men.

Veradis' line held but the sheer weight of Nathair's eagle-guard began to tell. It was twice as many rows deep, and more men were joining it, at least four or five hundred men packed into the track before Nathair. Then men from the flanks began to scream.

They were being dragged from the wall, the giants in the forest had returned to strike from the shadows, tugging men out of formation and hacking them to pieces.

I need to scour those giants from the trees, else my men on the track will be like rats in a barrel to them. Perhaps that is a task best suited to the Kadoshim.

Another billow of smoke rolled across his vision.

That is not from campfires.

Nathair looked to his left, and for a moment did not believe what he was seeing.

The forest gloom was thicker all along their western flank, a wall of roiling darkness. But within it flickered orange light, blooming and spreading.

Fire and smoke.

Even as he saw it, there were shouts along the flank, and then from the front a wall of flame suddenly arose, searing across the track and carrying on into the forest, carving a line through his eagle-guard, cutting the track in two, separating his shield wall from the main body of Lothar's warband and the remaining eagle-guard that were protecting it. Hundreds were on the far side, fighting on against Veradis' wall, oblivious to the flames.

That will not stop us. A brave man may jump those flames, if he has room. I remember a young eagle-guard doing just that in defence of his prince.

More shouts of warning rose up from the left flank as clouds of smoke began to billow over them, the flames behind the rolling smoke growing clearer, the whole forest to the west seeming awash with them.

Do they hope to trap us here against Veradis' bottle-neck and burn the rest of us to death?

Then Nathair heard something else, a scuttling sound that grew louder, and as he looked the very forest floor appeared to . . . move.

He peered harder, trying to pierce the gloom of the forest, saw undergrowth swaying, collapsing under the weight of some invisible force, a wave like a great slick of oil spreading over the forest, black and scuttling. Getting closer and closer.

Nathair felt a fist of fear clench around his heart. He did not know what it was, but instinctively he knew that it wasn't anything good. Beneath him his draig rumbled uneasily, shifting from foot to foot.

And then the first row of his eagle-guard that edged the western flank just . . . disappeared.

They collapsed beneath a black tide that surged towards the main bulk of Lothar's warband, engulfing hundreds of men in a few heart-beats, arms flailing, feet kicking as they fell to the floor, screams rising and cutting off, wails, bodies twitching. The next row behind them turned and ran, back into the row behind them, and then the whole western perimeter of Nathair's defensive line was gone, either swallowed by the black tide or running frantically from it, up the embankment and into Lothar's massed warband.

The eagle-guard fighting Veradis were oblivious, cut off from this new threat by the wall of flames that dissected the road.

'What the hell?' Nathair cursed, and the Kadoshim about him drew their swords, three of them stalking through the crowd that was pressing towards them. Blood spurted as one of them hacked at men, and then a space was parting before them and they were stand-ing alone at the base of the embankment, the black tide swirling towards them.

The first Kadoshim slashed at it with his sword, then the darkness was at his boots. It spread over his feet, up the boots, onto his breeches, the Kadoshim swatting at his legs, knocking clumps of whatever it was off of him, but the darkness continued climbing, and then Nathair saw shreds appearing in the Kadoshim's clothing, blood welling from its legs.

Then Nathair realized what it was he was seeing.

Ants. Like the ones near Jerolin, all those years ago. They were un-stoppable, and shredded the flesh from anything that got in their way. They were my inspiration for the shield wall.

For a few terrifying moments he just sat in his saddle and stared, frozen with fear.

The first Kadoshim turned, took a few staggering steps up the embankment, then dropped to its knees, looking confused as to why its body was not working properly. It reached out to the two behind it, who were already stamping on the never-ending wave of insects, one of them dark to the knees. The first one fell face-first to the ground, rolling and thrashing as the ants swarmed over its torso, up its neck, filling its mouth, crawling out of its nose, shredding and ripping its flesh, its body spasming for a few moments, before it shuddered and was still, black vapour gushing from a score of wounds, forming into a mist-wraith in the air, screeching its rage before it evaporated into the gloom.

So taking their heads is not the only way to kill them.

Then the ants were sweeping up the embankment, a tide of them as far along the road as Nathair could see, smoke and flame behind them, engulfing eagle-guard, labourers and warriors from Lothar's warband, everyone scrambling away from them in a panicked frenzy, bodies crushed, pushed flying, trampled as close to four thousand men tried to run south, down the road's embankment and into the forest.

The first ants reached his draig's feet and it lifted one foot, squashing many with a crackling splat, but hundreds more were already there, swirling up the draig's talons and onto its foot, mandibles ripping at the flesh beyond the curved claws.

The draig bellowed.

Nathair yanked on his reins, shouting in the draig's ear, the command to turn, to run, and it was happy to obey, lumbering into a shambling gait, turning right, down the embankment, crushing any eagle-guard before it as it headed eastwards into the forest.

'With me,' Nathair cried. 'With me.' He tried to gather eagle-guard behind him, desperate to lead as many as he could through the forest and to safety. Warriors fell in behind the draig, following the path it made through the undergrowth, and soon they had outdistanced the flow of ants, though behind him Nathair still heard the screams of men being eaten alive.

Glancing back, he saw at least a few hundred of his men running in his wake, some of Lothar's warriors in their white cloaks amongst them, more gathering to him as his draig ploughed into the forest.

I'm going to need every last man, because even if we make it to the plain before Drassil, I'm betting there will still be a fight ahead of us to make it to the gates.

He cursed Corban and Veradis, and guided his draig looping east and then north into the forest.

CHAPTER NINETY-TWO

CAMLIN

Camlin heard screams drifting through the forest, along with the stench of woodsmoke.

Sounds as if they're being flayed with a hot knife, and not just a few of them, either. 'Think someone's having a bad day,' he muttered to Dath, who was crouched only a few paces away.

'Should find out who soon enough,' Dath replied, running the flat of his palm over the score of arrows that he'd stabbed into the cold black earth of the forest.

Men and women were spread in a long line either side of them, almost eighty archers in total, all of them with bows strung and quivers full. Behind them stood a hundred or so Jehar warriors, Kulla, Dath's wife, one of them. They were led by a man named Akar, grim-faced and dour.

'Here they come,' Dath said.

Camlin stared into the forest, saw clouds of smoke billowing amongst the trees, and heard a low rumbling thunder, growing closer, and behind it those piercing, continuous screams.

'Be ready,' Camlin called out, standing and rolling his shoulders. 'And remember, first arrow together, then in your own time, fast as you can.'

He plucked an arrow poking from the soil in front of him and loosely nocked it, waiting.

He didn't have to wait long.

The shouting and screaming grew, louder and louder, and then shadows were moving through the trees. Individual forms began to solidify within the stampeding mass, a horde of men running in Camlin's direction, more than Camlin could begin to count, many in the black and silver of Tenebral, more clad in Helveth's white cloaks.

'Tell us when,' Camlin muttered to Dath.

The enemy were within range, now, but Dath waited.

Good lad. They need t'be close enough for an arrowhead to punch through leather and mail.

Another twenty paces, covered in four or five heartbeats.

'READY,' Dath yelled, and eighty archers drew their arrows, sighting a target within the onrushing wave of men.

'LOOSE,' Dath cried and Camlin's arrow was thrumming from his bow, sinking into an eagle-guard's throat, sending him crashing to the ground, a handful of men behind him snared by his fall, tumbling with him.

All along the front of this wave of flesh and blood men fell, legs crumpling beneath them, but the wave kept coming.

Before the first man had stopped rolling, Camlin's second arrow was on the string, drawn and loosed, another man spinning and falling; again, another down; another, every time a knot of men going down as one, so tightly were they running together. And beside him Camlin heard Dath's bowstring thrumming, a constant rhythm.

The plan wasn't just to kill indiscriminately, though of course taking down the numbers of the enemy was vital.

Especially when they outnumber us so heavily.

The plan was also to keep the survivors of this warband running blindly into the forest, and, if possible, to steer them east or south, away from Drassil. Because, once the panic was over, there would still be a lot of men wandering around Forn Forest with allegiances to their enemy, so the more that were lost and unable to find their way to Drassil, the better.

Of course, the more that's dead, the better.

To his left Camlin glimpsed a man mounted on a white stallion, other riders about him, galloping hard past the line of archers. Shadowy shapes were running alongside them, dark blurs, and it took a moment for Camlin to realize they were Kadoshim.

Lothar and his shieldmen, with a Kadoshim bodyguard.

He thought about trying to put an arrow into Lothar, but the horses were past him before he'd had a chance for the thought to reach his fingertips. He shrugged and carried on.

Another arrow nocked and loosed, the enemy close enough now that Camlin was confident his arrows would pierce a cuirass and mail beneath, no longer taking his time, just nocking and loosing as fast as he could.

When he could see the whites of men's eyes he realized that they weren't going to swerve away.

Another arrow loosed and he was thinking about moving, even though the plan had been to stand their ground; being trampled to death by a horde of terror-stricken men didn't feel like the best end to the day.

'Dath,' he shouted over the din.

'Trust the Jehar,' Dath shouted back.

You'd have to say that, you're wed to one.

One more arrow plucked from the soil, nocked and loosed, a man falling only forty or fifty paces away, and Camlin was reaching into his quiver for his next arrow.

Though I might be flat on my back with someone's boot on my face before I've loosed this one.

Then behind him Camlin heard the hiss of swords drawn, the drum of feet, and over a hundred Jehar were running through the gaps between the archers' line, swords held high in two-fisted grips, all screaming the same battle-cry.

'TRUTH AND COURAGE.' The shout echoed off the wall of warriors running at them, and then the Jehar were carving into the enemy, blood spraying in a hundred arcs, heads and limbs flying, men falling before them like scythed wheat.

The archers drew in tighter formation and began loosing higher, arrows arcing over the Jehar's heads before they descended into the bulk of the enemy warband. It was tricky shooting, avoiding low branches while still getting enough height to drop down upon the enemy.

Then came a pounding vibration through the ground and a roar that made Camlin pause and stare in disbelief at the massive shape punching through the fleeing warband. A creature with long teeth and scythe-like claws, bellowing its fury, a man clad in silver and black sitting upon its back, striking about him with a long sword.

Camlin stood frozen for a dozen heartbeats as this beast smashed a way through all before it like a battering ram, then powered on into open space, straight at Camlin.

Suddenly Dath was leaping, crashing into him, throwing him out of the way of the onrushing creature and its rider and they were both tumbling across forest litter, other men and women jumping and scrambling out of the way, some too late, hurled through the air with bone-crunching force.

The beast hurtled past them and disappeared into the forest, hundreds of surviving warriors following in its wake, most dressed in the black and silver of Tenebral, but with a scattering of white-cloaks amongst them.

'What the hell was that?' Camlin said as he climbed to his feet.

'That was Nathair and his draig,' Dath said, spitting leaves from his mouth.

The surviving Jehar were coming back to them now, most of the remnants of the enemy warband gone. Kulla found Dath; she had a long scratch over one of her eyes.

Akar joined them, looking as if he hadn't been touched in the battle. He was gazing after the bulk of men who were fleeing raggedly into the forest, far fewer of them than there had been running at them not so long ago. It was hard to tell in the gloom and trees, but Camlin was certain that there were a lot less than four thousand men left in that warband.

Smoke rolled over them, the crackle of flames in the distance, and then Camlin saw the ants sweeping towards them, a black scuttling carpet of mandibles and legs, a good few hundred paces away. They clustered on the dead that had fallen to the Jehar or lay with arrows protruding from their bodies.

I was planning on cutting a few of those arrows out and taking them back, but I don't think I will now.

The ants were slowing, feasting on the recently dead, but they were still too close for Camlin's liking.

'We need to go,' he said.

'Which way?' Akar said, looking between the fleeing warbands. The larger one, led by Lothar, was still running wildly into the forest, the smaller one was following the draig.

Camlin and Dath looked at each other, then at the carnage the draig's passage had caused.

'Best get after Nathair and his beast,' Camlin said.

'Aye,' Dath agreed.

Because they both knew that it was heading straight for Drassil.

CHAPTER NINETY-THREE

VERADIS

Veradis leaned into his shield, felt the scrape of short swords against it. A low blow glanced off the iron strips on his boot and he stamped on the blade, chopped down to hear a muffled scream.

The man beside Veradis fell, a short sword slicing high over the top rim of his shield, into the man's mouth. He was the third warrior to die that side of Veradis; another quickly filled the void.

Hardest shield wall battle I've ever fought. It was easier against giants.

He'd put three men down that he was sure of, and hobbled another, severing tendons in his enemy's ankle, but beyond that he did not know how the battle was going, only that a ripple of flame had washed over him some time ago, signalling the coming of the ants. And he'd thought he'd heard screaming, further away, but he couldn't be sure, the din of battle a fog about him.

The only other thing he knew, and the most important, was that he hadn't moved, and nor had his men about him.

We've held them. Held the Draig's Teeth. Feels like we've been here for three days, but we've held them.

Veradis glanced over his own shield, saw a face he recognized wielding the sword that had just put the man on his left down, his face bloodied and pale behind the linden and iron.

Caesus.

Veradis snarled at him and slammed shields with the young warrior, stabbed below the rim of his shield, seeking to slice through leather and tendon, but felt his blade grate on iron-stitched boots like his own. He pulled back just as a sword stabbed at his hand, and instead went quickly over the top of his own shield, stabbing at Caesus' eye, catching his cheek instead, leaving a red weal of blood.

There were screams, growing louder, a ripple through the shield wall, and abruptly he was stumbling forwards. He fell to one knee, saw that Caesus was falling away, running, the wall about him disintegrating. Veradis glimpsed Balur to one side, other iron-wrapped giants with their long axes hacking into the flanks of the eagle-guard, and behind them a wall of flame.

The Draig's Teeth have broken. Held at the front, giants on their flanks, flames at their backs.

Hard men. But still only men.

He glimpsed eagle-guard fleeing through the trees to both sides, saw Storm leap on one, rolling, blood spraying as she came to a halt and stood upon her prey. Corban emerged from the treeline, his sword bloody, Farrell with him, his war-hammer matted with bone and hair. Corban offered Veradis his hand and pulled him back to his feet.

'Nathair?' Veradis asked.

'He fled east, on his draig.'

'It worked, then? The fire, the ants?'

'Aye,' Krelis said, emerging from the trees, dragging an eagle-guard by the scruff of his mail shirt and throwing him at Veradis' feet.

It was Caesus.

'You ready to fight for us, lad?' Krelis asked him.

'I serve only Nathair,' Caesus said, glaring up at Veradis.

'Say one thing for Nathair,' Krelis said, 'he does inspire some loyalty in his lads.' He gave Veradis a knowing look. 'Got more than a few like him running around in the woods,' Krelis continued, looking back to Caesus. 'Doesn't feel right putting a sword in them when they're not fighting back; they're men of Tenebral, after all, but we can't have them wandering around behind us, and we can't spare the men to watch them.'

'Break some bones,' Corban said. 'A good man gave me that advice once. Break the bones in their sword hand. They'll not take the field against us again today.'

'Good idea,' Krelis said, nodding. 'I like it.' He looked down at Caesus and grinned.

Coralen emerged from the trees, three eagle-guard walking before her sword-point, and she deposited them alongside Caesus.

Wulf stepped from the gloom, and his men about him. It had been they who had lit the fires behind the ant colonies and guided them east into Nathair and Lothar.

'Worked a treat,' Krelis said to them, grinning broadly. 'But that was the easy part.'

'Aye,' Corban agreed. 'Now for Drassil, for Rhin and for Calidus.'

CHAPTER NINETY-FOUR

UTHAS

Uthas stood upon the battlements of Drassil. Up above him the leafless branches of the great tree clawed at the sky, and above them heavy clouds shrouded the world, slate-dark and oppressive. The gates of Drassil faced west onto the wide plain, beyond it the trees of Forn a wall of shadow. A cold wind tugged at his cloak and warrior braid, sending a shiver through him.

Salach stood to one side of him, battle-axe sharp and ready, his face as sullen as the sky.

To Uthas' other side stood Rhin, regal in her black and gold, a thick sable cloak about her, silver hair gleaming. And beside her Calidus and Lykos, both clad in shirts of mail, leather-bound, grim-faced. Stretching either side of them all were a line of black-eyed Kadoshim, and beyond them, lining the walls of Drassil, were his Benothi kin: a grim line of giants, their thick-muscled torsos swathed in leather and chainmail, tattoos of thorn and vine swirling up from their wrists, each one their own *sgeul*, the Telling, testament to the lives they'd sent across the bridge of swords.

They are an impressive sight, and their sgeuls *will grow this day*, Uthas thought with pride.

All of them stared southwards in silence, at the plain of Drassil and dour Forn beyond.

Where are they?

It was halfway to highsun now, a pale gleam marking the sun's journey, and for some time a mixture of sounds had been drifting out from the murky green of the forest. Screams, and more recently clouds of smoke filtering up through the canopy to be frayed by the cold wind. Uthas saw a blush of orange and red as flames bloomed, deep within Forn, at least a league away, maybe further.

And the screams were spreading, expanding through the forest.

Not a good sign. They should be getting closer, moving along the line of the road. That is what we expected, for Nathair and Lothar to push Corban and his rabble back.

Uthas looked back at the courtyard, which was full to overflowing with Conall and his warband, close to fifteen hundred men, horses and riders, most of them standing with their mounts. Rammed into the streets behind them was Geraint and his warband of four thousand men. All waiting.

They should have ridden out long ago. All is clearly not going well for Nathair and Lothar; they need our help.

But when Uthas had suggested this to Calidus he had snarled a refusal: *And send more men into ambush and death within those trees. No. We will wait until we can see our enemy.*

'Any sign?' A voice shouted up to them – Conall, close to the gates of Drassil, stamping his feet and blowing into his hands.

'No,' Rhin called down to him.

'We could ride out onto the field, prepare a line.'

'You cannot ride out to fight a foe that isn't there,' Rhin snapped. 'Wait.'

'I hate waiting,' Conall muttered, though he said no more, just went back to blowing into his cupped hands. Uthas noticed that Rafe the huntsman was standing near him, holding the reins of a horse.

A hiss from Rhin drew his attention back to the horizon.

Shadows were shifting in the treeline to the west, directly before Drassil's gates, and then figures were emerging. First came a lone warrior and a wolven, big as a horse, padding at his side. Its coat rippled and shimmered like molten silver. Then more came: a handful of men, a trio mounted on horseback, more and more spilling from the forest, an array of warriors. Uthas saw many in the black and silver of Ripa, but there were many others, red-cloaks of Isiltir, a knotted clump of men wrapped in leather and fur, clothed like miniature giants, and then behind them real giants, forty, fifty, still more coming.

Most of the rabble halted a dozen or so paces from the forest, clinging to the treeline.

'Where is Nathair?' Uthas heard Calidus mutter. 'Where is Lothar?'

A handful of the new arrivals carried on, approaching the gates of Drassil.

The warrior and wolven walked at their head. Uthas remembered them from Murias, though he had had only scattered glimpses. He had been fighting for his life, after all. They had both grown, that was clear enough, Corban – for that was who it must be – though young, strode with a warrior's grace and confidence. He was dressed simply, in mail shirt and leather surcoat, a four-pointed star on his chest. The wolven beside him was huge, even for its species, and its coat rippled like liquid. Uthas looked closer and saw it was wrapped in chainmail. As he stared at it, the beast looked up at him and he saw its lip curl back in a snarl, amber eyes and dripping fangs full of malice. He had to stop himself from taking a step back.

Behind them he saw a diverse collection. A man clothed in the black and silver of Tenebral, a bright eagle on his cuirass. A Jehar warrior, sword hilt jutting over his back; beside him a warrior as broad as a bull, hefting a war-hammer as if he were a young giant; one rider upon a horse – Edana, wrapped in mail and a grey cloak, her fair hair braided into a thick warrior braid, a circlet of gold entwined about her head.

A crown! Rhin won't like that. She won't like that at all.

And three giants. His breath caught for a moment as he focused on them, and he felt Salach stiffen beside him.

Ethlinn walked at their head, and no longer did she look like the frail dreamer that he remembered. She was straight-backed, dressed for war in leather, fur and iron, a spear in her hands. Behind her strode another giantess, muscular and strong. She was not Benothi, the sides of her skull were shaved clean, a thick mass of dark hair limed and braided down the centre of her hair.

'Kurgan?' Uthas murmured, a memory from the lore stirring in his mind. Beside her walked Balur One-Eye, wrapped in thick iron. His white hair spilt from beneath his helm, the lattice of his scarred empty eye socket staring straight up at Uthas.

Fear and rage coursed through Uthas' veins. He had drunk from the cup and felt young, strong. How dare this ancient old fool stand against him?

Today you die, old man.

Corban and his wolven padded to within fifty paces of the gates, then stopped, his unlikely band of allies arrayed behind them.

'If you are here to surrender, we accept,' Lykos shouted down to them. 'Lay down your arms, muzzle your pet, and we'll open the gates for you.'

Corban and the others just stared up at them.

'No?'

Another silent response.

Lykos leaned over to Calidus and whispered loudly. 'Foreigners, eh! No sense of humour.'

Even Salach chuckled, shoulders rippling.

Corban cupped his hands to his mouth and called up to them.

'No surrender. No bargaining, no offer of peace or treaty. I came to tell you one thing, Calidus.'

'And what is that, you arrogant cub?' Calidus yelled down to him.

'Your death is coming.'

Corban turned and walked away, the wolven stalking beside him.

'Rhin?' Edana shouted from horseback.

'I see you, you thieving bitch,' Rhin called down, 'and before this day is done I shall rip that trinket of gold from your cold, dead skull.'

I thought the crown would anger her.

'You will never return to the west,' Edana shouted up to her. 'You have run, and now you have nowhere left to hide.' Before Rhin could answer, Edana turned her horse and cantered after the others.

Rhin turned a darker shade of scarlet, a string of curses flowing from her mouth.

I would not wish to be Edana if Rhin gets her hands on her today.

'UTHAS,' Balur One-Eye cried out, 'Betrayer, murderer of Nemain; today justice will find you.'

Uthas felt his own rage bubble up, barely contained. 'Fine words,' he bellowed, 'from one who slew his own king.'

Ethlinn rested a hand on Balur's arm and stepped forwards.

'Warriors of the Benothi,' she cried. 'Today I claim my birthright. I am Ethlinn ap Balur, and I am Queen of the Clans.'

What?

Uthas had expected her to stake her claim as the Benothi's rightful leader – but all of the Giant clans?

That is my place!

'Behind me stand Benothi and Kurgan,' Ethlinn cried. 'It is time to become one clan again. Uthas has led you wrong, but I will forgive you and welcome you, if you leave him now. Spill the blood of your kin no more.'

And then she was turning, striding after Corban, the other giants with her.

Uthas' lips quivered with rage, his moustache twitching.

It is I who will be Lord of the Clans after this day.

'Salach, take her head,' he hissed.

'I swear it,' his shieldman growled.

Where are Nathair and Lothar? Even without them we are unbeatable within these walls, but there were over six thousand swords in Forn. Surely they cannot have been defeated?

Deep within Forn smoke roiled above the canopy, flickers and flashes of flame now, spreading wider.

A great fire must be blazing within the forest. Have Nathair and Lothar been trapped and burned?

Uthas glanced at Calidus, saw doubt gnawing at him.

Then there was a crashing and roaring to Uthas' left, to the south of the plain.

A shape emerged from the southern treeline, a beast upon four legs, low to the ground, wide-chested and muscular, razor-sharp talons on its bowed legs. A draig. And a man sat in a saddle upon its back.

Nathair.

The draig lumbered forwards and then paused, gave a booming roar, and behind it warriors spilt from the forest, hundreds of them, both eagle-guard in their black and silver, and Lothar's white-cloaks.

The eagle-guard were moving into formation, forming a shield wall in orderly, disciplined lines. Nathair was yelling and gesturing to the white-cloaks, and Uthas saw them gathering into two groups, massing about the shield wall's flanks like white wings.

Corban and his companions were running now, veering towards Nathair, their warriors along the western treeline moving with them, making to bar Nathair's path to the gates of Drassil.

Then more figures were pouring onto the southern plain, spread in a scattered line behind Nathair and his troops. These newcomers were mounted on horseback, a dozen, more, their riders trailing white cloaks. Black figures on foot followed not far behind them.

'Lothar and his Kadoshim,' Calidus said.

The King of Helveth galloped to Nathair, his mounted honour guard about him, all the while more warriors on foot emerging from the forest, staggering and disordered, but soon massing together.

There must be a thousand of them, at least, and more are still coming.

So Corban attacked them, routed them from the road, but the survivors have managed to make it through the forest.

Corban and his warband were sweeping south across the plain towards Nathair and Lothar, the numbers appearing to be roughly even, though with every heartbeat more eagle-guard and white-cloaks were stumbling out from the forest.

'They will need our help,' Uthas said.

Rhin looked to Calidus, who nodded, and she turned to look down into the courtyard and shouted.

'Conall, your waiting is over.'

CHAPTER NINETY-FIVE

CORBAN

Corban ran across the plain, men shouting battle-cries, bellowed orders swirling behind him, the thunder of thousands of feet, Balur's voice rising above all else, but all Corban could focus on was Nathair, sitting on his draig, a longsword in his hand, twisting in his saddle and yelling orders to his warriors. The eagle-guard behind him were locking into a shield wall, already wide and deep, many of Lothar's white-cloaks forming up on his flanks. But Nathair was out in front of them, vulnerable.

Well, not exactly vulnerable – he has a draig.

An image flashed through his mind, of his da, fallen to his knees in the feast-hall of Dun Carreg, Nathair standing before him, plunging a sword into his chest.

He grabbed hold of Storm's collar and urged her on.

Storm opened her gait, moving from lope to run. Corban was pulled from his feet, one fist gripping the leather collar around Storm's neck. He swung his legs and ended up on Storm's back, felt the wind whipping his hair, dragging tears from his eyes. Behind him the sound of his followers lessened, Storm opening a gap between them as she flew towards Nathair. They were two hundred paces away, a hundred and fifty, Storm almost flying.

Then white-cloaked riders suddenly filled his vision. They had broken away from the black-clothed Kadoshim that were following them, all of them coming between him and Nathair. A man with black hair and a golden circlet in his hair was riding straight at him.

Lothar, King of Helveth.

Corban snarled in frustration.

Come between me and my vengeance.

Storm crunched into Lothar's stallion, her jaws fastening about its muscular neck and her body swinging to crash side-on into the horse's flank. Corban used Storm's momentum to throw himself into Lothar, ripping the man from his saddle before they both slammed into the ground, rolling and tumbling in a spray of turf.

Corban rolled away from Lothar, rising to his feet and dragging his sword free, and ran at the King of Helveth, who was desperately trying to draw his own weapon.

A horse and rider rode between them, the warrior stabbing a spear at Corban. He swayed away, caught the shaft in his wolven claws, with a twist of his wrist locked it and dragged the warrior forwards, stabbed his sword up into the man's armpit, raked his claws along the horse's flank, sending it leaping forwards, the rider toppling backwards from his saddle.

Lothar was still standing the other side, one of his shieldmen dismounting to give his King his horse.

Corban surged forwards, ducked the shieldman's sword swing and slashed at the man's face with his wolven claws, sending him stumbling to one knee. Corban stabbed him in the throat, then grabbed Lothar's belt as he tried to swing into the saddle. Lothar snarled and attacked him.

He was good, his attacks solid, economical, well balanced, but Corban was better, and a cold rage fuelled him. Corban harnessed it, letting it fill him, not control him. He blocked four blows from Lothar, deflected the fifth wide and back-swung his blade across Lothar's chest, making him stagger. Corban strode after him, stepped inside a desperate lunge at his head, punched Lothar in the face with his hilt, sending him crashing to the ground, and stabbed him two-handed through the chest, his blade bursting out through Lothar's back and into the earth behind him.

A yell of fury made him spin and he saw one of Lothar's mounted shieldmen bearing down on him, sword raised, only to see him sent flying from his saddle, a hammer-blow slamming into his chest.

'You've got to stop running off like that,' Farrell grunted at him, breathing hard, then Gar swirled past them, iron clashing as he grabbed a warrior's reins and chopped at the man's head. Another white-cloak fell to the ground before Corban, one of Laith's daggers sticking from his belly.

Corban grabbed Lothar's circlet from his brow and mounted the nearest riderless horse. It danced on the spot a moment but Corban leaned low, patting its neck and whispering in its ear, and it calmed.

Most of Lothar's shieldmen were down, Gar, Farrell and Coralen making short work of the few still alive. Nathair was still rallying his warband, waiting to gather as many stragglers from the forest to him as possible. They had grown formidably, eagle-guard and white-cloaks combined together numbering perhaps over a thousand strong already.

He could see Veradis bellowing at his warband, his men gathering into a shield wall of their own, Balur and his iron giants with their long axes looming to either flank. On this side of Veradis' shield wall Krelis was breaking into a loping run, with his warband of black and silver a mass behind him, and behind them were Tahir's men of Isiltir. They were running at the Kadoshim that had arrived with Lothar, at least three score of the black-eyed warriors hurling themselves towards Krelis and his men.

Men and women burst from the treeline, a hundred or so in dark chainmail, swords drawn, raised high over their heads, running into the plain. For a heart-stopping moment Corban thought it was more Kadoshim running straight at him, but then he recognized Akar, Kulla behind him, and saw that they were angling across the field to engage with the Kadoshim.

Corban kicked his mount into a canter, pounding the turf between the two massing warbands.

'Your King is dead,' he yelled, kicking his horse into a gallop to surge past Nathair's draig and the shield wall, showing them the blood-splattered circlet, repeating his proclamation, yelling it at the top of his voice, then hurling the crown into their massed ranks.

Arrows whistled and flitted from the treeline, and white-cloaks started to fall.

Corban was about to turn and ride back to Krelis' flank and lend his sword to the battle against the Kadoshim when a hand closed on Corban's arm. It was Gar, sitting on a dun mare.

'It's time,' the warrior said. 'The plan has worked.'

Corban looked at the battle spreading upon the field, saw faces that had followed him, felt a weight of responsibility for them, and a surging desire to fight, to kill his enemy and lose himself in the simplicity of battle. His eyes fixed on Nathair, and an overwhelming urge to kill him flared bright in his belly.

'Look, the plan's worked,' Gar repeated, pointing at the gates of Drassil, which were swinging ponderously open, riders pouring out from the fortress in a flood.

Calidus has taken the bait!

'Come,' Gar said. 'We can end this, but we have to go. Now.'

Corban's eyes found Nathair.

He is not the real enemy, just another pawn in this game of angels and demons. Calidus is the one that needs to die.

'Ban,' Gar said, tugging his arm.

'You're right,' Corban said, and together they rode from the field.

Corban met Brina in the forest north of Drassil's gates, at a makeshift hospice she had built. Many were there, ready to tend the wounded; injured warriors were already filtering in. Brina was standing with a handful of men, three of them giants. Corban recognized Alcyon and his son Tain, but there was a new one, bigger and bulkier than Alcyon, his head shaved in the same way as Alcyon and Tain, a thick strip of hair running down the centre of his head.

Brina was tending a man, her fingers resting on his throat. It was Maquin, standing with a few of Javed's Freedmen. All of them looked exhausted, sweat-stained and close to collapse, but Maquin was worse. His eyes were dark hollows, his mouth twisted in a bitter snarl, as if he mocked and hated death, but yearned for it at the same time.

'Fidele's dead,' Brina said quietly as Corban and Gar reached her.

'Let me go,' Maquin said. 'I am going after Lykos.'

Corban looked at Maquin. His voice was a monotone, and there was a tremor in his hand. He swayed slightly, as if the effort of remaining still and upright were too much.

Fatigue.

'I suspect if you wait a little while he might come out onto the plain and fight,' Brina said. 'If the battle goes as we hope. Might be easier than trying to get through those gates. Perhaps use the time to eat and drink. You don't want to find him and then fall flat on your face.'

'That won't happen,' Maquin mumbled, 'but some water would be good.'

Brina nodded to Alcyon, and the giant led Maquin to a log, sat him down and went in search of water and food.

'So,' Brina said, looking at Corban. 'We need to go.'

'Aye,' Corban replied.

Footsteps drummed and Coralen came running into the glade. Dath was with her, Kulla as well, then Farrell and Laith a dozen paces behind.

'Corban, this . . . really is . . . getting . . . ridiculous,' Farrell panted, leaning against a tree. 'It's making me angry. Can't you just stay in one damned place and fight?'

'It's a busy day,' Corban said with a shrug.

'Is this it, then?' Dath asked. 'The plan?'

'Aye,' Corban said. He looked at them all, a still moment in the midst of carnage and blood and fear. 'You don't have to come with me.'

'Oh, shut up, Ban,' Dath breathed.

'Aye,' Farrell grunted. 'As if we would do anything other.'

'But—'

'Listen to your friends,' Coralen said. 'And shut up. We're coming.'

Corban nodded. 'All right, best be doing it, then, before the battle's over.'

'Is it far to go?' Farrell asked.

'A little short of half a day on foot,' Coralen said.

Farrell looked miserable, even about to cry.

'Which is why I've borrowed some horses from Edana,' Brina said. 'Now let's be off.'

Farrell's relief was palpable.

'Small mercies,' he whispered.

'Do your good work,' Brina said to Craf, who had been watching the exchange silently from a log beside them. Brina scratched his neck and threw him something slimy. He caught it and gulped it down. 'And we'll see you at the meeting point.'

'*On the old oak tree,*' Craf squawked as he took to flight.

CHAPTER NINETY-SIX

RAFE

The gates of Drassil opened and Rafe followed Conall and a hundred other warriors that rode before him, along with close to fourteen hundred others. He glanced back once at the stables where he'd left Scratcher tied up. Didn't want his hound caught up in this. He had enough to worry about.

The din of battle was faint, a swirling eddy drowned out by horses' hooves as they clattered into the tunnel that led through the gates and out into the open of Drassil's plain.

Conall rode a way ahead, then reined in and looked back up at the walls, at Rhin, no doubt, as riders spread to either side of him, gathering into a line over a hundred horses wide. Rafe guided his mount into line a few rows almost directly behind Conall. He patted his horse's neck as they waited for the full strength of the warband to pour out through Drassil's gates and gather behind Conall.

'You're a beauty,' Rafe whispered in his new horse's ear, leaning forwards. 'Too good for Geraint. Glad I found you, and I'll make you a deal. I'll try and keep you alive as long as you return the favour.'

The skewbald stallion arched his neck and stamped the ground.

Can probably smell blood and battle. Doesn't look as if he's scared of it, though. Looks more as if he wants to get stuck in.

Rafe sat up straight and tried to see what was happening.

Battle was raging, that was clear, a mighty din rippling up from the south of the plains. He could see giants, and hear the roar of Nathair's draig every now and then, which set his stallion to snorting and its ears flicking back tight to its head, but if anyone was close to victory or had the upper hand, he could not tell.

We should change that soon enough, though, Rafe thought. *Fifteen hundred of us charging onto their rear should set them to running quickly enough.* He looked up at the sky, saw the pale gleam of sun through thick cloud. *Battle'll be over by highsun.*

Horns blew then and Conall drew his sword, saluted to Rhin on the battlements and kicked his horse on, into a trot, turning at an angle to head south.

The host moved after Conall, there was a lurching moment when Rafe was jostled by mounts either side of him. Dry-throated fear reared in him and he wished he'd had a last drink from the water skin hanging on his saddle.

Too late now, Rafe thought as they moved across the plain, aimed straight at the rear of the enemy warband, the drum of hooves a constant thunder, the creak and rattle of harness and mail combining into an all-consuming fog of sound. Rafe thought of Rhin's words to him, last night during the council of war.

A chance to redeem myself, after failing Rhin over the necklace.

He jostled with riders either side of him, kept his eyes on Conall's back.

Then horns sounded from behind, from Drassil's battlements, a discordant sound, a clamour of warning.

The advance stuttered, Conall and fifteen hundred other men craning their necks to see what was wrong. Figures on Drassil's battlements were pointing, towards the treeline directly west of Drassil's gates. Rafe stared that way and saw a long line of riders emerge from the forest, a hundred horses long, at least, warriors in the grey of Ardan, Edana at their head, looking like a warrior-queen from the old tales, mail shirt gleaming, a naked sword in her hand. On one side of her rode Vonn, on the other, Halion. And behind them, more and more riders spilling from the gloom, spears and swords glinting in the pale light, hundreds of them, easily a thousand, with still more appearing.

A long silence settled as the two warbands considered each other, misted breath from horses' nostrils rose in the cold air, a hoof stamping, a whinny, and then Edana was shouting a command, pointing her sword and kicking her mount into a canter, the host of riders behind her spurring into motion, a great wave.

Conall was shouting, urging his horse on, dragging on his reins to turn towards them, Rafe and the whole warband doing the same, stuttering into a canter towards Edana, who was gaining speed, her mount leaping into a gallop, and behind her a great roar went up from her warband as they joined her, the thunder of it filling Rafe's ears, and Rafe felt his stomach clench in fear, suddenly not wanting to be here.

Charging an enemy that were on foot and from behind was one thing, certain victory virtually guaranteed, but this – this was something else entirely, this was much more like actual *battle*.

Rafe felt his horse's muscles bunching and flexing, felt his need to run, excitement quivering through the animal.

He's a warhorse, all right, he actually likes this.

Conall was pulling ahead, outpacing his fastest warriors, bent low over his saddle, sword drawn, hurtling towards Edana and Halion, who likewise were pounding ahead of their own warband, a gap widening. Conall screamed wordlessly, laughing, and Rafe understood, for a moment, what men called the joy of battle as a great jolt of exhilaration flooded through him and he yelled in sheer exultation.

And then, inexplicably, Conall was leaning back into his saddle, sheathing his sword, dragging at his reins, blowing on a horn at his belt, yelling for his riders behind him to pull up. His mount was skidding, slowing, behind him hundreds doing the same, Rafe yanked on his reins in horror, desperately trying to avoid going down in a tumbling heap, because that would surely mean a trampled death. All about him riders pulled their mounts back under control, slowing from the gallop, horses neighing wildly. Ahead of him Rafe saw Conall leaping from his saddle, even while his horse was still moving, turf spraying. The regent of Domhain was striding forwards. Rafe saw Edana and Halion slow, the warband behind rippling, and Halion was jumping from his saddle, too, marching towards Conall, and then they were slamming into each other, embracing, laughing, hugging, the two warbands coming to a halt only a handful of strides apart. Rafe saw Edana smiling.

Halion and Conall parted. Rafe spied tears on the two brothers' cheeks.

Edana spurred her horse forwards.

'Conall ben Eremon, is this your way of surrendering?' she asked Conall, voice loud and crisp, spreading over the battlefield.

'Let's call it a last-minute alliance,' Conall said, waving an arm in the air. 'We can sort out the details later.' He hugged Halion again, slapping his back and kissing his cheek. 'Ach, but it's good t'be friends again. I've missed you and your serious face.'

'And I've missed your madness, you lunatic,' Halion laughed.

Conall looked back up at the walls of Drassil.

'As if I'm going to be riding my own brother down! She never had the measure of me.' And with that he was ripping his cloak of black and gold from his shoulders, waving it around his head and hurling it aside. All around Rafe men were doing the same. He looked at them aghast, then realized he had better follow suit.

Looking at the faces of the warriors about him, all men of Domhain, he saw no shock or surprise in their eyes. A glance at Edana's warriors showed the same expressions, satisfaction and joy in a plan well executed.

Of course they knew. Rhin, it looks as if you've been out-betrayed! That is not going to go down well with her, not at all. Though she does have one last die to roll. Me.

Rafe ducked his head down, suddenly finding himself in the middle of his enemy's warband. The last thing he wanted was for Edana or Halion or Vonn to see him.

Conall was looking up at the walls of Drassil, and Rafe turned and stared. He could clearly see Rhin standing beside Calidus and Uthas, could just about feel the rage that was contorting her features.

'Do you think Rhin's got the message?' Conall said to Halion and Edana.

'I would imagine so,' Edana said.

'Just to make sure,' Conall said, and he cupped his hands to his mouth.

'Rhin, you're Queen of Domhain NO MORE,' he cried. 'So you can KISS MY ARSE.' He dropped his breeches and bared his backside to Drassil's wall, waved it around a little, whooping and laughing, more guffaws rippling through both warbands. Even Rafe chuckled.

'Do you think she understands now?' Conall asked, still waving his backside in the general direction of Drassil.

A high-pitched, rage-filled screech rang out from the walls, drifting across the plain to them.

'I suspect she does,' Edana said with a grin.

Then horn blasts were ringing out from the fortress, riders spilling out from the gates, forming up on the plain before the walls.

'Geraint,' Conall said. 'He's a good man. I like him. And a good battlechief. Loyal. It'll be a hard fight.'

They watched as more and more riders poured through the gates, as many as Conall's warband, then more, many more, and still more flooding from the gates.

Conall pulled up his breeches and climbed back into his horse's saddle.

'Time to spill some blood,' he snarled.

CHAPTER NINETY-SEVEN

CORALEN

Coralen rode beneath high-branched trees up the slope of a gentle hill, threading through the fringes of Forn; Corban and the others were behind her, Storm a shadow ahead of her. The noise of fighting swirled up to them from the battlefield. Riding away from it was one of the hardest things she'd ever had to do, and she knew she was not the only one feeling its pull. At the crest of the hill her horse's hooves cracked on ancient flagstones, remnants of the giants' road that Jael of Isiltir had discovered and rebuilt.

Coralen reined in and waited for the others to catch up with her. Corban and Gar, Farrell, Laith, Dath, Kulla, Cywen and Brina. They joined her on the road and for a moment they all hesitated, looking back onto Drassil and the battlefield.

To the south Nathair's and Veradis' shield walls were locked together, like two competing bulls, and they seemed to form the core about which other warbands swirled and fought, Coralen glimpsing giants, a draig, red-cloaks and white. Closer still were a host of mounted warriors arrayed along the treeline of Forn, thousands strong, a blonde-haired figure riding along its line, shaking her sword in the air.

Edana. Not the princess I remember, struggling to be heard in Eremon's court.

Coralen's breath caught in her chest as her eyes found Halion, and beside him, Conall. Her brothers.

Halion was right, then. Conall has joined them.

She grinned.

Edana's combined warband was facing another host of horsemen, drawn up before the walls of Drassil, a sea of black and gold. From

Coralen's vantage point she could see that, even with Conall's warband swelling Edana's ranks, they were still outnumbered by the enemy massing before them.

Yet it was the host in grey that charged first.

It reached them as a distant rumble; the warband moved forwards slowly, gaining speed and bursting into a gallop, a huge roar of battle-cries ringing out over the plain, and then Rhin's warband of black and gold was moving too, slower to the gallop, but gaining momentum eventually, and their line was wider and thicker.

The two charging warbands came together, a percussive thunderclap of sound booming outwards, rippling up to them on the slope as six or seven thousand men and mounts slammed into each other. The flanks of the larger host curled around the edges of Edana's warband.

They sat on their mounts a long moment, on the brink of riding back down, watching the battle unfold. Watching friends and comrades fighting for the future of the Banished Lands, fighting for their lives, and maybe dying, right before their eyes.

'We can't help them,' Brina snapped. 'If we stay, all will die. We have to go. Now.'

'Let's go,' Corban snarled. 'Let's end this.'

And he yanked on his reins, kicked his horse on, and then they were all riding hard down the giants' road, into Forn and away from the battlefield.

CHAPTER NINETY-EIGHT

UTHAS

Uthas stared out onto the battlefield, his knuckles white around his spear shaft. The cries and screams of battle were close and immediate now, before the gates of Drassil was a great heaving maelstrom of bloodshed. The charge of Edana's cavalry had carved deep into Geraint's larger force, carrying many grey-cloaked warriors close to the fortress' walls. The field before Uthas was a bucking, heaving mass of warriors, horses screaming, rearing, kicking, men slashing and stabbing and dying.

This is no simple victory, the sweeping away of a desperate rabble forced to fight. Numbers are still in our favour, and we have reserves behind us that our enemy cannot counter, but this will be no easy triumph. If we win at all it will be a close and hard-fought affair. Now is the time to send us out, to strike and crush our enemy while they are engaged and pinned down.

Uthas shared a look with Salach, knew that he was thinking the same thoughts. They both looked to Calidus.

The Kadoshim was staring out at the battlefield with an expression that shifted between fury, concern and disgust. Beside him Rhin was caught up in some bout of twisted rage, her fingers curling, lips twisting as half-whispered curses bubbled from her mouth.

Conall's betrayal has hit her hard.

Calidus took a long, shuddering breath, barely controlling his rage, then he turned and called down into the courtyard, ordering the remaining eagle-guard within the fortress to prepare for battle. Men ran from the courtyard, yelling orders.

*

'Lykos, gather your men,' Calidus said, turning to the Lord of the Vin Thalun. 'Every last Vin Thalun warrior except those guarding the Treasures – take them now and turn this battle.'

'Aye,' Lykos grunted. He turned and stalked down the stairwell, bellowing to his men.

Good, with the Vin Thalun and the eagle-guard that will be another three thousand men into the field. If nothing else, we will overwhelm our foe.

'And you, Uthas. Take your people and crush your enemies. Stain the ground red with Ethlinn's and Balur's blood.'

Uthas felt a ripple of excitement, part fear, part longing. His dream was so close to fruition, a spear-thrust away.

'Drassil shall be emptied and our warband will roll over my enemy like a great flood,' Calidus growled.

Good. As we should have done earlier. Calidus' anxiety to protect the Treasures has overwhelmed his judgement, and he has underestimated this Corban's abilities as a strategist.

'What of the Treasures?' Rhin asked, seeming to have mastered her rage. There was worry in her voice.

'Indeed,' Calidus snarled. 'Now they will only be guarded by me and my Kadoshim, thanks to your man's betrayal. You have much to atone for.' Calidus gave her a humourless smile. 'You will stay at my side and pray that the Treasures remain safe.'

'Salach,' Uthas said – his shieldman grunted a response – then louder, 'Benothi, with me.'

And Uthas strode from the battlements, the footfall of his clans-people drumming on stone behind him.

Uthas was the first through Drassil's gates, Salach and Eisa behind him like wings, the Benothi stomping out onto the battlefield in their iron-shod boots, war-hammers and battle-axes unslung from backs, gripped by grim-faced warriors.

It was very different down here from watching the battle unfurl from Drassil's high walls. The stench of blood and faeces hit Uthas first, then screams, battle-cries, iron on iron, the thud of flesh slamming against flesh, shield against shield, all mixing into one deafening din, swirling and eddying, rising and falling as Uthas strode through the carnage.

He led his clan, skirting the struggle between Geraint's and Edana's mounted warbands, aiming at the battle-storm that was raging between the two shield walls, for it was there that he saw giants. He glanced back one more time, reassured himself that he was not alone, and glimpsed Lykos leading his Vin Thalun, running out through Drassil's gates. There were no organized ranks amongst them like the eagle-guard – more like a tempestuous flood, and they swirled south, following Uthas.

Lykos thinks the same as me, better pickings amongst the enemy on foot.

Uthas set his eyes on a giant to the south, surrounded by white-cloaked enemies, sheathed in iron. He started to run, great loping strides.

CHAPTER NINETY-NINE

CYWEN

Cywen suppressed a shiver of fear as they rode past a huge carcass, its flesh mostly gone, picked clean by the forest's myriad predators. As she looked at it she could still see its flat-muzzled skull and long teeth bearing down on her, scythed claws raking the earth.

For an instant she wished that Buddai were with her, but he was still limping from his last encounter with a draig. So she'd left him tied up at their camp hospice, with Sif and Swain keeping an eye on him. Buddai had not been happy about it, but the bone of a large boar had helped to soften the blow.

Haelan was sitting in front of her, her arms around him holding the reins. He'd followed them into the forest, Pots and Shadow with him, and the trio had quickly been discovered by Coralen and Storm. Brina had interrogated him and to Cywen's surprise Haelan had stood his ground. He'd guessed where they were headed and was adamant that he could help. So Brina had let him stay.

And then the smell hit her.

Draig dung.

The horses started to whinny and snort, ears twitching fearfully.

'We'll have to walk from here,' Coralen said. Cywen and Coralen led the way.

The smell became progressively worse, and then Cywen saw the dung hills. The group crept forwards until they saw the rim of the slope that went down to the draig mound and the tunnel that led to their lair. All of them fell to their bellies and crawled the final part of the way until they lay in a row along the slope's rim, peering over.

'Well, I'd best get on with it, then,' Kulla said matter-of-factly.

Dath caught hold of her hand.

'I don't want you to do this,' he said.

'I know, but this is one of those things that has to be done, and I'm the best one for it.'

'I can run fast,' Dath said.

'Aye, but not as fast as me.'

Dath stood and stared at her, face twisting and knotting with worry.

Kulla stroked his face and smiled.

'I love you, my Dath,' she said, then wrapped a strip of cloth around her mouth and one around her eyes. She reached out, hand touching one of the dung mounds, and then she threw herself into it.

The stench was overwhelming, an explosion that assaulted Cywen's senses, even from where she was lying on the slope's rim. She saw Dath sway as the smell hit him.

Kulla rose from the ground smothered from head to toe in draig dung. She pulled the two strips of cloth off, blinked at Dath and then strode down the slope to the draig lair. She looked back once, at the cave-like entrance, and then she was gone.

Dath came and lay down beside the rest of them, looking about as miserable as it was humanly possible. Corban reached out and squeezed his arm.

They all lay there and waited, then Cywen heard a noise. A rumbling roar, deep underground, echoing out through the tunnel entrance. More roaring, louder, overlapping, and then Kulla exploded from the passage entrance, a draig egg tucked under one arm, speeding straight up the slope and onto the flat forest floor, still running as fast as she could in the opposite direction from her companions.

Then the draigs were coming: one, two, three of them bursting from the passage that led into their lair. The three of them fanned into a line on the slope, pausing to flicker and taste the air with their tongues, then their huge-taloned claws were hurling them up the slope and into the forest after Kulla, even though she had run so fast that Cywen could see no sign of her.

They can smell their eggs better than they can see.

And that was entirely the point.

Corban and Brina had gone over the plan with the others a thousand times. The fastest runner, covered in dung, snatched an egg and then ran, leading the draigs out and away from their lair for as long as the runner could manage. Meanwhile, the others would take advantage of the draigs' absence and head into the tunnels. When Kulla was at her limit the plan was for her to hurl the egg away and freeze. Cywen was certain that being covered with draig dung and remaining motionless would make anyone undetectable to the draigs. It had worked for her.

'Come on,' Corban hissed, and then all of them were running down the slope, hurrying into the darkness of the tunnel. Storm, Shadow and Pots followed last.

Cywen ran behind Corban and Coralen. Haelan sped ahead of them, his torch leading them through a long passage. It opened up into the chamber that contained the nest. Haelan slowed to look at the eggs, piled in the middle like charcoal-stones in a forge. He ran on, taking an exit almost directly opposite the one they'd entered the chamber by, leading them on, deeper and deeper into the labyrinth.

At the next turning Corban called for a stop and Haelan paused. Corban counted, making sure they were all still together, Storm and Shadow's eyes glowed in the torchlight.

Cywen looked at the fork in the tunnel before them, and for the life of her could not remember which way led to the roots and crack in the roof that burrowed into Drassil.

'Haelan,' she hissed, 'do you know which way to go?'

'Of course,' Haelan said, holding his torch high. 'It's that way,' and he pointed to the right-hand fork.

'How do you know?' Cywen asked.

Haelan waved the torch lower to the ground. Cywen saw something on the ground flash white. Then she remembered.

'Sif's stones,' Haelan said with a grin.

CHAPTER ONE HUNDRED

CAMLIN

Camlin stood in the treeline and tracked a white-cloaked warrior who was behind Wulf with his sword raised high. Camlin loosed, his arrow punching through the warrior's throat; the man's legs buckled and he tumbled into Wulf.

Wulf spun around, axe pulled back to strike, face twisted in a snarl, and then he saw the arrow, realized his enemy was dead. He shoved the corpse away, looked to the trees and saw Camlin grinning at him, dipped his head in thanks and then returned to the fray, smashing a white-cloak in the face with the boss of his shield, swinging at his head with his axe.

Camlin searched for another target.

At first he had loosed arrow after arrow at the white-cloaked warriors massed on the left flank of Nathair's shield wall. It had been too good an opportunity to miss and the combined forces of his and Dath's archers had inflicted vicious damage upon the survivors of Lothar's warband.

It was harder to get a clean shot now, as the hand-to-hand fighting was a furious whirlwind, white-cloaks were interspersed with Wulf and his crew, Kadoshim and Jehar, as well as a handful of giants. Balur One-Eye was hacking at white-cloaks and Kadoshim alike with terrifying fury, sending heads and limbs flying, mist-wraiths forming in the air all about him as he tried to carve a way to Nathair's shield wall, which was wider and deeper than Veradis' and looked to be hammering ten hells out of the smaller wall of shields.

A cloud of smoke engulfed Camlin and his crew, rolling out onto the plain, and a wave of heat warmed Camlin's back, the sound of crackling and wood splitting too close for his liking. He glanced back, saw smoke and flame hungrily spreading through the forest.

Time to join the party, he thought and shouldered his bow.

'Enough tickling them,' Camlin shouted, drawing his sword. 'Time to show them we're more than elm and feathers.' With that he was running out from the treeline and shouting, 'FOR ARDAN AND EDANA,' as his battle-cry, which took him by surprise.

He slammed into a white-cloak, hacking down between shoulder and neck. The man's chainmail held, but Camlin felt the warrior's collarbone snap, kicked his legs from under him and stabbed down into his throat as his momentum carried him on, swinging two-handed at the next warrior in front of him, sword taking the enemy high in the head. Camlin kicked him to the ground and looked for someone else to kill.

But what was left of the white-cloaks on this flank were gone, either dead, dying or swallowed into the ranks of Nathair's shield wall.

That still left a handful of Kadoshim, but Akar and his Jehar were amongst this flank in all their righteous fury, teamed with Wulf's axe-wielders and Balur and a dozen other giants. Mist-wraiths were forming in the sky with great swiftness.

Then it was just Nathair's shield wall that was facing them.

Camlin stood and stared at it as he gathered his breath and watched Balur lay into it with his long axe.

That wall's an amazing beast, put together like a chainmail shirt, weapons bouncing off it.

Camlin watched in horror as he saw a handful of Wulf's men attack it, their axes bouncing off the interlocked shields, short swords stabbing out as the axe-wielders moved too close, falling away with stab wounds in bellies, legs, throats. Camlin saw five men fall in as many heartbeats.

Don't want to get too close to that, the beast has got a bite on it.

Balur and his kin were doing a fine job, though, slamming axes into the flank-men of the wall, hooking and skewering shields, dragging men out of formation and into the open, hacking them to death in a matter of moments.

Don't think I'm much use against that – can't see too many arrows getting through all that wood and iron. Think I'll see if I'm needed else-where.

He scanned the battlefield, but nothing was clear apart from a lot of death and dying, with smoke starting to roll thick across it from out of the forest. For a moment the enormity of it struck him, a scene like nothing he'd ever witnessed before, so many disparate peoples from across the Banished Lands, all trying to end each other.

He glimpsed a knot of Ardan's grey, to the north, mounted, battling against men in black and gold.

Edana's where I should be, and killing Rhin's men seems like a good idea to me, he thought, and set off at a loping run, the crew of archers following him.

UTHAS

'ONE-EYE,' Uthas heard Salach bellow, as he rammed his spear into a warrior clothed in black and silver.

My sgeul is growing this day.

Uthas had led his Benothi into the flank of a mass of warriors, most of them clothed in black and silver, some red-cloaks amongst them. But he was not interested in fighting them. He was trying to reach a handful of giants beyond this swirling mass of black and silver, giants of his clan, the Benothi, some of them clothed strangely in great plates of iron, and wielding single-bladed axes on shafts as long as saplings. Amongst them other giants ranged.

They are my people. I do not wish to slay them. Only Balur and Ethlinn; then the rest will bow to me. I'll let Salach have One-Eye, it's Ethlinn I will see bleeding into the cold earth.

And then he saw her, stabbing her spear at a white-cloaked warrior, defending the back of one of the iron-wreathed giants.

One-Eye fears you, Uthas had said to his shieldman earlier, and perhaps he did, for Salach was a great and renowned warrior amongst the Benothi, a hundred raids to his name, his *sgeul* many-thorned, and he had slain Sreng, Nemain's shield-maiden, accounted the greatest blade amongst the Benothi, apart from Balur. But One-Eye's reputation was a thousand years old, and he was ancient now. Old and slow.

Still, I doubt that One-Eye fears anyone. And I would rather face Nemain's get than Balur.

Uthas waded through the black and silver towards Ethlinn, his spear jabbing, smashing the butt-spike into a face, spinning the weapon and stabbing through a chest, lifting the warrior bodily from the ground and hurling him through the air, onto the next man in his way. His Benothi followed behind him, carving a way through their enemy, Salach screaming Balur's name with every blow, the battle-rage coming upon him.

Then Ethlinn saw him.

She was frozen, staring at him, and then was striding towards him, smiting white-cloaks out of her path to get at him, and he doing the same to those in black and silver foolish enough not to run from his wrath.

And then space was opening between them, warriors scrambling away from him, and Ethlinn was so close. Behind her he saw a horde of men appear, running along the flank of Nathair's shield wall, axe-wielding warriors clothed in leather and fur, and the dark-clothed Jehar, swords raised high.

The few that escaped Murias and the cauldron's touch.

Jehar and axe-wielders alike were hurling themselves at the white-cloaks.

But other figures were appearing behind them. Giants, some wrapped in iron, others clothed as giants in fur and leather. They were all running towards him and his Benothi, and Balur was at their head.

Uthas felt a jolt of fear, a snake uncoiling in his belly.

I have drunk from the cup, I am stronger, faster than I have been for five hundred years.

Aye, but is that strong and fast enough to defeat Balur One-Eye?

'Salach,' Uthas yelled, 'your foe comes. Seize your glory, make your name, become the legend who slew Balur One-Eye.'

He saw Salach running past him, snarling, his battle-axe raised high, and Uthas charged at Ethlinn.

They will both die now, then the clans are mine.

He screamed a wordless battle-cry and stabbed his spear at Ethlinn, a two-handed lunge, low to high that would have punched into her gut and taken her from her feet, but she rolled her shoulders and her spear tapped his spearhead wide, slid down the shaft and raked his knuckles, she made her own lunge, which he swayed away from, and instead of piercing his eye it slashed his cheek, blood sluicing into his beard.

To his left he saw Salach attack Balur, the black-haired giant hacking at Balur's longer-reaching axe, splintering the shaft and charging in close.

Balur's finished.

He backed away from Ethlinn, swaying left and right as she made short stabs at his chest and throat, knocked her spearhead high and slammed the butt of his shaft into her gut, making her grunt. There was a percussive whirl of slaps and sparks as their spears clattered and chimed together, and then Ethlinn was stepping out of range and they began circling one another, the grating clang of iron connecting with iron as Salach chopped at Balur's chest, sparks exploding from the iron plate that One-Eye wore, sending him stumbling backwards.

Giants were forming a ring around them, his Benothi, Ethlinn's followers – Benothi and Kurgan – all grim and silent as they watched Salach and Balur, Ethlinn and him.

Good. They can watch them both die.

Uthas feinted a lunge at Ethlinn's belly, jabbed lower, at a thigh, but she danced around it, stepped in close, holding her spear like a staff and slammed it onto his foot, slashed the blade horizontally at his belly but he jumped back, her spear-tip sparking as it raked his chainmail, tearing a line of links.

Ethlinn was smiling.

Uthas felt his neck flush with anger. How dare the frail dreamer mock him? Sweat dripped into the cut on his cheek, stinging. He snarled and stabbed, stepping around Ethlinn's block and counter, gripped her spear shaft and pulled her off balance, towards him and his spear point, angled at her throat. Somehow she rolled around it and then her fist was slamming into his cheek, rattling his skull, staggering him, and he tasted blood. He stumbled back, swinging his spear wildly to keep her away, but she was just standing a few paces out of reach, watching him.

'Thought me an easy victory?' she sneered at him. 'You forget whose blood runs in my veins.'

They both glanced at Balur and Salach, saw that with one fist Balur had gripped Salach's axe-haft, stopping it mid-blow, and with his other hand Balur had torn his iron helm from his head and was bludgeoning Salach with it. Uthas saw a spray of blood and teeth.

Uthas felt a flicker of panic.

'*Lasair*,' he commanded, and flame burst up from the ground around Ethlinn's feet, Uthas lunging forwards at the same time.

'*Sioc*,' Ethlinn said contemptuously and the flames crackled into glittering frost. She spun away from Uthas' lunge, her spear whipping around, the butt cracking Uthas in the back of the head. He staggered forwards, turned, desperately fending off the blows as Ethlinn attacked in a constant assault.

There was a hot pain in his hand, a strange numbness, and he looked down to see his fingers scattered upon the grass. His spear fell from his grasp just as Ethlinn's spear-butt crunched into his jaw, sending him stumbling backwards. He felt hands hoisting him up, saw that it was Eisa behind him.

'Help me,' he croaked, but she only stared at him in stony silence. She shook her head. 'You murdered Nemain.'

Then hands were pushing him back into the circle to drop on his knees before Ethlinn.

Something thudded onto the ground beside him. Salach's head, dark hair matted with blood, one side of its face a bloody pulp.

Balur came to stand at Ethlinn's shoulder.

How can it come to this? It cannot be ending like this. I have drunk from the cup.

'Mercy,' he cried.

Ethlinn's eyes narrowed. 'You don't deserve it.'

Then her spear-blade lunged forwards, and he saw it sink deep, dark heart's-blood welling. He took a rattling breath that didn't seem to work, and then the world was growing dim, narrowing to a tunnel of light, Ethlinn's grim face at the end of it, and he was falling . . .

CORBAN

Corban looked up at the hole in the tunnel's roof. A thick root had bored through, earth falling away to form a ledge and, from there, a twisting passage to Drassil.

They were gathered in a huddle, drinking from a water skin, gasping and sweating from the long run through the stifling tunnels. Haelan had led them unerringly through the maze of passages, though Corban had lost all track of time.

'Well, that was quicker than before,' Cywen said.

'We didn't get lost this time,' Haelan said. 'Just had to follow the stones, and stay away from the tunnels with two stones before them. And we ran all the way instead of creeping.'

Farrell grunted in disgust.

'Are we waiting here for a reason?' Brina snapped. 'Hoping some draigs might join us, perhaps?'

And with that they were climbing up into the hole. Coralen clambered up first, helping to lift Haelan and Pots and Shadow, the rest of them hauling themselves up, climbing towards the grey light that glowed above. Storm was the last one up, her bulk squeezing through the hole, dislodging a cascade of dirt.

'This is it,' Cywen said, pointing as they joined her. 'That light leads to the courtyard.'

'Haelan, you wait for us here with Pots and Shadow,' Corban said. He held Haelan's gaze. 'No following, on your oath.'

Haelan frowned. 'My oath,' he grudgingly said.

'Right then,' Brina said. 'Let's do this.'

Cywen thought the healer looked scared, just for a moment.

Cywen climbed from the hole into the courtyard first, Corban after her. It was still daylight, and the sun beginning its twilight descent. The courtyard was deserted, the sounds of battle a distant boom and thunder, like the sea battering upon the cliffs of Dun Carreg. Quietly the others emerged into the still courtyard. Haelan's pale face stared out at them from the hole beneath the oak tree, Pots and Shadow with him.

'Thank you,' Corban said to him, crouching down. 'We are here so quickly because of you.'

Haelan grinned.

'One of us will come and get you when we're done,' Corban said and rose.

If any of us can.

There was a flutter of wings from above.

'*All Treasures in big room with tree,*' Craf squawked, flapping down to them.

'Even the starstone torc?' Corban asked.

'*Yes, torc there,*' Craf confirmed. '*And cauldron, spear, axe and cup.*'

Corban touched the dagger sheathed at his waist and the necklace in his pocket.

They shared a grim, silent look, and then moved swiftly and silently through a deserted Drassil.

LYKOS

Lykos jogged across the battlefield towards the two shield walls, short sword in his fist, buckler strapped to his forearm, the remnants of his Vin Thalun spread behind him like a tattered cloak.

Fifteen hundred men left from over four thousand. So many have fallen. That made him angry.

His first kill was a man of Ripa.

My ancient foe.

Lykos ran on, a blood-splattered grin upon his face.

His Vin Thalun hit the battle like a plague-filled wind, spreading death, taking near a hundred lives before the enemy even knew they were there. Eventually, their progress slowed, especially when a score of Jehar decided to engage them with their curved swords. Lykos swerved away from them, looking for easier blood, leaving the screams of his Vin Thalun behind him.

Rowing two hundred leagues in less than two moons and fighting a battle in between has left me a little tired. Even my bones are aching. I'll take the easier fight if I can.

The pain of that long row home was fading now, though, and it had been worth it to put some distance between him and damn Maquin. Seeing him standing on that cliff top, swearing vengeance and hurling Kadoshim heads at him – well, it had chilled even his blood for a few moments.

He blinked as an axe came hissing towards his head, swayed out of its way by a hair's breadth, punched the fur-wrapped axe-man in the face with his buckler and stabbed deep into the man's thigh with his short sword.

The axe-man dropped to his knees, face ashen-pale as his life-blood gushed like a river down his thigh. Lykos stabbed him in the throat, just for the joy of it, then kicked him off his blade.

He let out a great battle-cry and saw Nathair upon his draig, the beast stamping on a red-cloaked warrior, its jaws lunging down to tear the man's head from his shoulders. Then Lykos spotted another familiar man, dressed in the black and silver of Ripa, big as a bull with a great black beard. He was beating a white-cloak to the ground, hammering a longsword into the man's upraised shield.

Krelis of Ripa. How many times have you chased my war-galleys? Thwarted my raids? Killed my men? Spoilt my fun?

He grinned and ran at him, knew that at least some of his men were not far behind.

Angling through the crowd of warriors, Lykos approached Krelis from behind, pulled his sword back to hamstring the big man, but Krelis spun around, shield tight to his body, longsword hissing in a horizontal arc, nearly gutting Lykos. He skidded to a halt, leaped in after the blow had swung wide, but Krelis' big round shield slammed into him before he had a chance to dart in and stab somewhere unprotected.

'Slippery little snake,' Krelis said, then his eyes narrowed as he recognized Lykos. 'Ah, travelling three hundred leagues from home is about to become so very worthwhile,' he growled and strode at Lykos.

Krelis was a skilled warrior. He assaulted Lykos with sword and shield, never over-extending, keeping his defence tight, his sword sweeping, looping, stabbing, and Lykos steadily retreated, searching for a weakness, hoping to counter-strike, but all he did was notch his sword and buckler and retreat over two score paces.

That had been part of his plan, though, and suddenly Krelis found himself amidst a sea of Vin Thalun, few of his own men about him.

'TO ME,' Krelis cried in his booming voice, and Lykos saw a surge of black and silver coming his way.

Need to finish him now.

He saw his Vin Thalun closing on Krelis, closer than the black and silver.

Then Krelis surged forwards, taking Lykos by surprise, his shield slamming him backwards, sword looping low. Lykos took the blow on his buckler, the iron twisting, his arm going numb from wrist to shoulder.

'LADS,' Lykos bellowed as he tripped over a dead man, rolled behind him, lifted the corpse to catch Krelis' sword in its belly.

The Vin Thalun closed with Krelis' men, a score forming a barrier between Krelis and his warriors, a trio of Vin Thalun turning on Krelis, chopping at him from behind, sending him crashing to his knees, Lykos gripping his wrist, holding Krelis' blade snared in the corpse's body as his lads hacked at Krelis' back, blood spraying in gouts now.

The men of Ripa let out a great howl, hammered ferociously at the Vin Thalun.

Lykos let go of Krelis' hand, stabbed his short sword into his armpit, pulled it out slowly, smiling at the Lord of Ripa. Krelis, still on his knees, swayed and toppled backwards, staring up at Lykos.

'No honour, in that,' Krelis whispered, blood gurgling over his lips.

'Honour is overrated,' Lykos sneered at him and smiled as he died.

CORBAN

Corban saw the great hall of Drassil before him.

They had taken a deep looping route through the fortress, avoiding the area where Cywen had told them most of the warbands barracked, always clinging to the shadowed ways, Craf scouting above, warning them when to hide. For most of the desperate, heart-in-his mouth run through the streets it had felt as if they were in a deserted place and now here they were, in the courtyard before the great hall.

The huge gates were open, as they had always been when Corban was a resident of Drassil. A dozen Vin Thalun guards lounged on the steps leading up to the gates, gathered in a half-circle, bone dice rattling on a throw-board between them.

Do they not realize the battle for the future of the Banished Lands is taking place beyond those walls?

He took a deep breath, looked at his friends, saw grim, determined faces staring back at him. Then Gar was marching across the courtyard, straight towards the open gateway and the Vin Thalun guards. At the same time Corban and the others slipped around the shadowed alcoves of the courtyard.

A few of the Vin Thalun looked up at Gar, seeing nothing more than a Kadoshim walking towards them, a sight they were no doubt used to. A closer inspection would show a lack of black eyes and veins threading Gar's body, but for the moment they were relying on the laxity in the guards.

It worked to a point.

'Oi,' one of the Vin Thalun said as Gar reached the first step to the gates, and then Gar's sword was in his hands, two Vin Thalun collapsed on the steps, choking on their own blood. The rest of them were scrambling backwards, drawing swords, spreading into a half-circle around Gar, though another man had already fallen before the first Vin Thalun struck at Gar.

Two others crashed to the ground and rolled down the steps, one with an arrow through his neck, the other with a long dagger lodged between his shoulder blades. Then Storm was amongst them, men screaming, blood spraying.

It was almost over before it had begun.

'No point in tiptoeing now; I'd imagine we've announced ourselves,' Farrell said, as they ran through the gates.

Corban paused, looking down into the great hall; the trunk of the great tree where the chair of Skald was situated filling the hall's core. About it the Starstone Treasures were arranged: cauldron, axe, spear, torc and cup, all in a circle, two spaces left empty. Strange designs and runes had been etched upon the ground around and between the Treasures.

And before them were ten Kadoshim, staring at Corban and his companions with their dead black eyes.

Farrell slung his war-hammer across his back and drew a longsword.

Corban charged into the hall, leather boots slapping on stone, raising his sword high, a mirror image of Gar, who ran beside him, the thud of feet behind them.

The Kadoshim sprinted to meet them, curved swords hissing into their hands, their pale faces twisted with hatred.

One grunted with an arrow through the eye, took a faltering step and ran on, another one staggered and halted for a moment as one of Laith's daggers slammed into its chest.

The two groups met upon the lowest steps, iron and flesh meeting, Storm leaping to crash and roll with a Kadoshim between her claws. Her jaws clamped about its head, teeth sinking deep into its neck, ripping, shaking, sawing until the head was torn free; the first mist-wraith formed in the air above them, screeching even as it was fading.

Farrell took the head of the Kadoshim that had Laith's dagger in its chest, and Gar took another a few heartbeats later: two more mist-wraiths hissed into the air. Corban exchanged a flurry of blows with what was once a female Jehar, locked her blade wide with his wolven claws and sent her head spinning before turning to help Coralen.

The Kadoshim attacking her was gashed from Coralen's attack, across shoulder and thigh, throat ragged, but it came on at her regardless. Corban ran at it, staggering it for a moment, and then Coralen's sword whistled through flesh, cartilage and vertebrae, the head bouncing down the stairs.

A brief shared look and then they were back to fighting for their lives.

Corban heard giantish shouting, and turned to see Brina and Cywen hurl vials at one of the Kadoshim. There was a *whumph* of air as the Kadoshim was engulfed in smoke and flame, wreathing it like a human torch; it dropped to one knee, where Laith decapitated it with one of her daggers.

Corban saw Gar fighting two Kadoshim, one of them circling him viper-fast, a blow catching him on the hip, sending him stumbling, his guard too low for a moment.

NO, Corban screamed wordlessly, running, but Storm was there before him, slamming into both Kadoshim, sending one hurtling through the air, jaws clamping around the other's arm, shaking it. The Kadoshim struck at Storm with its curved sword, a slash that crunched into Storm's shoulder, would have carved through flesh and ribs, but her coat of mail deflected the blow, and then Gar had taken the Kadoshim's head.

Two more Kadoshim fell and then Corban saw the last survivor, chasing after Dath as he put arrow after arrow into it. Dath dropped his bow, drew his sword, parried the first rush of blows, stumbled as he retreated, and the Kadoshim was standing over him, sword raised. Then Coralen was there, Corban two spaces behind and the Kado-shim was being slashed and battered, reeling from a dozen blows before its head was sent flying through the air.

'Where's Kulla when you need her?' Dath breathed. Then, 'Don't tell her I said that.'

'I promised her I'd look after you,' Coralen said, helping Dath up.

'Well, that's embarrassing,' he muttered.

'We all have different strengths,' Coralen smiled, passing him his discarded bow.

'Corban!' Brina hissed, standing before the Starstone Cauldron. 'The Treasures.'

He hurried over to her and handed the starstone dagger and necklace to her.

'Now, be ready,' Brina said, 'each of you. Cywen and I will perform the incantation, and then all of the Treasures will be hurled inside the cauldron; only together can they be destroyed.'

'Get it done,' Gar growled, turning to face the stairs and open doors, sword drawn. The room was scattered with the headless corpses of Kadoshim. Corban and the others formed a half-circle around Brina and Cywen, the trunk of the great tree protecting their rear. Brina stepped inside the circle of Treasures and approached the cauldron.

There was a pause and then Corban heard Brina's and Cywen's voices ringing out.

'*Seoda cloch réalta, ó deannaigh tháinig tú, agus deannaigh beidh tú ar ais . . .*'

Corban, a familiar voice whispered in his head and he looked around. No one was there. *Corban*, the voice said again, and this time Corban knew it.

Meical.

He felt strange. Suddenly the world was dimming about him and he blinked, heard Meical's voice again, felt a tugging sensation, deep within.

He is calling me to the Otherworld, summoning me.

No. I am your puppet no more.

Corban fought the sensation, gritting his teeth, setting his will to staying, focusing on his surroundings. Meical's voice faded and disappeared.

Corban shook his head and looked at a Kadoshim corpse close by, anything to keep him anchored here, in this chamber. The colour of the Kadoshim's arm had changed from the pale, black-veined appearance to something resembling normal.

Now that the demon has been evicted from his flesh. He looked at other corpses, saw it was true for them, too. A thought nagged at him.

Only ten Kadoshim, left here to guard the Seven Treasures . . .

Brina and Cywen's voices were echoing behind him, something soothing and hypnotic about their words, even though Corban did not understand them. He looked at the empty spaces in the circle, now filled with the starstone dagger and necklace. That he had brought here.

Ice trickled down his spine.

'They know,' he whispered. Then, louder, 'It's a trap.'

'What?' Gar snapped at him, then the trapdoor to the tunnel was opening, Kadoshim pouring out, two score, three score, more figures appearing through the great doors, marching down the stone steps, Calidus and Rhin, a score of her shieldmen about her, more Kadoshim at their backs, a hundred at least.

Calidus was smiling at Corban.

MAQUIN

Maquin prowled through the battlefield, skirting the mounted warriors still clashing at the northern half of the field, working his way along to the south, where the fighting seemed to revolve around two shield walls, a storm of men of various allegiances swirling about their flanks, giants striding amongst them. The bulk of these men were Vin Thalun and the men of Ripa, engaged in battle with a savage ferocity that made Maquin snarl with respect.

Only a short while ago he had felt close to collapse, had sat in the hospice with his hands trembling, but then he had heard the din of battle, and he had thought of Lykos. And now he held a sword in his right fist, a knife in his left, and both were already bloody to their hilts.

A handful of Vin Thalun appeared before him, bearing down upon two men of Ripa who were shoulder to shoulder, frantically defending themselves. Maquin strode into their midst, his sword opening a Vin Thalun throat, knife slicing a hamstring, sword stabbing down, kicking an ankle out, feeling bone break, parried a wild blow, ducked under it and slammed his knife into a belly.

One of the Vin Thalun ran, staring at Maquin's face, screaming 'OLD WOLF,' over and over. The two men of Ripa nodded their thanks and fell in behind Maquin, picking up the chant and following the Old Wolf as he waded into the battle.

Maquin grinned as he killed, the battle-joy rushing through his veins, all who came against him seeming slow, as if wading through water, and Maquin slew them all. He knew what was different now, what had changed. For a while he had noticed that a new hesitancy had crept into him, into the way he fought, allowing on occasion some men to escape his blades.

That was gone now.

It had been Fidele, it had been the desire to live, to taste life with her. But now she was gone, and he did not care, and that made all the difference. All whom he fought, no matter how strong, how skilled, how fast, all of them had that desire at their core. To survive. To live.

He did not. And so he fought as one that did not fear death, he embraced its coming, knew it was close, and welcomed it.

Men fell before him, a wedge of men from Ripa gathered behind him. Maquin glanced back once and saw that the Freedmen, Alcyon, Tain and Cota were with him too, striding at his flanks, slaying, blood-drenched and battle-grim.

And on he marched, into the storm of iron, killing, searching, the cry of *OLD WOLF* circling around him like a murder of crows, his banner a battle-cry that spread dread as men heard it.

And then Maquin saw him, a few score men between them.

A Vin Thalun, a half-crushed buckler upon one arm, short sword bloody and notched, a savage glee upon his ring-bearded face as he hacked a man of Ripa to death.

Lykos. Your death is here.

CORBAN

'Hurry,' Corban barked at Brina, hefting his sword.

We are going to die here. He knew it as fact, a cold fist around his heart.

There are too many: Calidus, Rhin, near two hundred Kadoshim. He felt a wave of fear, debilitating, draining his strength.

No. Fear is the enemy. Control it, use it. He thought of Gar on a spring meadow beside the sea, the call of gulls in the background, so long ago, and Gar offering to teach him, to train him, to help him control his fear.

And Corban did. Perhaps it was his greatest act of valour this day. He set his will to mastering the uncoiling wyrm that slithered through his belly, spreading into his veins, trying to steal his strength and resolve, to make him *less*. He breathed deep, focused his thoughts on why he was here, why it mattered, what he could still do. On his loved ones. He mastered his fear.

I can give Brina a little more time, even if it is only heartbeats, to let her finish whatever it is she's doing. Let her destroy these Treasures, and with them any chance of Asroth crossing over to this world of flesh.

That's worth dying for.

Calidus and Rhin were at the foot of the stairs now, crossing the flagstoned floor to them, Rhin stepping over the corpse of a headless Kadoshim. Their living brethren trailed behind Calidus and Rhin like a shadowed cloak, and more Kadoshim from the trapdoor spread around them.

Storm growled.

Brina and Cywen's voices still rang on.

Laith was the first to move, hurling one of her daggers at a

Kadoshim that stepped menacingly towards Farrell, and then all was motion: Farrell hacking off the Kadoshim's head, Storm leaping, Corban, Coralen and Gar stepping forwards together.

Mist-wraiths formed in the air, a hissing, screeching audience that pulsed with the rhythm of battle, more appearing as the first ones faded.

Corban heard Storm snarl and then whine, his sword arm taking on a new frenzy as he tried to cut his way to her, and beside him Gar fought, swirling around the Kadoshim in a dance of death that left heads and limbs spinning in its wake.

'ENOUGH,' Calidus cried out, a ripple through the fight as the Kadoshim backed away, leaving Corban and his companions breathless, bloody. Dath was on his back, sword raised in defence against a Kadoshim that stood over him, but the black-eyed creature stepped away.

A howl echoed through the chamber, human, filled with grief and pain, transforming to rage.

Farrell.

He was standing over Laith. Her body was twisted, a great pool of blood spreading about her, lifeless eyes staring. Farrell was bleeding from a dozen wounds, weeping, one side of his face slick with blood, his longsword dripping black clots of Kadoshim gore, their bodies heaped about him, and at his side crouched Storm.

She growled at Calidus, made to leap again.

'I said, *enough*,' Calidus snapped, and as he spoke a black cloud of smoke swirled from his mouth, a great poisonous breath that split into many tendrils, swirling across the stone floor, spreading out, seeking. One wrapped around Storm, coiling about her legs, threading around her body like a fast-growing vine, and she growled, ears flat to her head. The black smoke pulled tight and Storm was yanked from her feet, paws held in an unbreakable grip. Corban made to move but a tendril of the smoke was already coiling about his ankles, pulling tight, rising higher, wrapping him in a cold embrace, the smell of rancid breath washing over him as it pinned his arms and caressed his neck.

Within moments all of them were trussed and writhing on the ground.

'You see,' Calidus said conversationally to Rhin, 'my power grows now that the Treasures are together, their bond to the Otherworld so much stronger.'

Brina and Cywen's voices still continued, and Corban felt a pulse of power ripple between the cauldron and Treasures, a ringing in his ears.

'Stop that,' Calidus snarled. More of the black vapour billowed from his mouth, surging towards Brina and Cywen, dragging them away from the cauldron and throwing them to the ground.

Calidus picked his way through the dead, past Corban and his companions, and stood over Brina.

'So, you're the witch that would have ruined my grand designs, foiled the plans and schemes of Asroth that have taken eons to come to fruition.'

'Sounds about right,' Brina said, glaring up at Calidus.

'Oh, some spirit. Good. It will make your screams all the more beautiful.'

'Oh, please, spare me your melodramatic threats,' Brina snorted. 'You don't scare me. You're nothing but a lot of hatred, hot wind and bitterness tied up in a bag of over-cooked flesh.'

'On second thoughts, I don't think I'll wait for the screaming,' Calidus said. 'I can't see you begging, which would spoil much of the fun.' He drew his sword and stabbed it into Brina's chest, a sharp gasp of pain escaping her lips as Calidus leaned into the blow, forcing it ever deeper, until its tip grated on stone.

NO!

A silent scream inside Corban's head, hot tears flooding his eyes. He kicked and bucked, but the tendrils of smoke held him tight. He stared at Brina, saw her gasp and writhe as Calidus stood over her, a smile upon his lips.

'Brina,' Corban grunted through his straining, and her head turned towards him. Their eyes locked, just for a moment, a whisper escaping her lips, and then she was still. Blood spread in a slow pool beneath her, running into the flagstone grooves.

Corban let out a scream of rage, pure and primal, his eyes bulging in his face, veins in his head and neck looking as if they would burst as he tried to break his bonds, grief and fury filling him, fuelled by his helplessness.

How many loved ones must I watch as they are murdered?

579

Tears blurred his eyes and he turned his gaze upon Calidus. He heard the squawking of a crow, far above.

Please, Craf, stay away. Please.

Calidus came to stand over Corban, peering down at him as if he was an insect he was considering squashing.

'You may be wondering why you're all still alive,' Calidus said. 'You are the sum of my foe in this world, and a sorry, pathetic lot you are, but still, my Lord Asroth will find it entertaining to be presented with you. A gift for him to destroy at his leisure.'

'I am going . . . to . . . kill you,' Corban grunted, muscles bulging as he strained against his bonds, eventually collapsing with the effort. Calidus just studied him.

'How pathetic you humans are. So much emotion wrapped up in weakness, leading you to attempt the impossible, lying to yourself, time and time again. *Hope*, I think you call it. And yet always you fail. Your whole experience has been death and misery, failure and yet more death, and still you refuse to face the truth. A breed with such a talent for blind delusion and denial deserves to be exterminated.' He shook his head, then smiled, crouching down beside Corban and reaching out a long-nailed finger to trace Corban's cheek.

'It is just all too easy,' Calidus nodded to himself, smiling. 'Well, as much as I'm enjoying this, I do have work to do.'

He strode into the circle of Treasures.

'Rhin,' Calidus said, 'with me now.' They approached the cauldron, Calidus muttering under his breath, a whisper of words that spread through the chamber like a breeze.

The cauldron pulsed.

'*Dark doras, idir saol na fola agus cnámh, agus saol na spiorad, beidh tú ag oscailt anois*,' Calidus chanted, Rhin adding her voice to his. Calidus bent over Brina's corpse, the endless words pouring from his mouth as he snatched up Brina's body and heaved her into the cauldron. It swelled, a rippling of iron, seemed to expand as dark tendrils of light leaked from it and glided across the floor like mist, each one touching one of the other Treasures, and each of the Treasures twitched, seemed to grow darker, night-black, sucking light into itself. The shadows in the room deepened, the mist-like tendrils growing thicker, more solid, pulsing like an artery, rippling back towards the cauldron.

'More flesh,' Calidus said, 'it needs more.' He strode to Laith's body, Farrell screaming curses as Calidus heaved her up into his arms and half dragged the giant's corpse to the cauldron; Kadoshim moved to help him throw her body into the dark open maw.

And then there was an explosion of darkness, a great cloud of night boiling out of the cauldron, flooding the chamber, a crack that set Corban's ears ringing.

And then another sound.

The beating of wings. A host of them, the noise of them filling the chamber, the whole world, a great cry of victory following it, drowning all else out.

Then the darkness was retreating, as if it were being sucked back into the cauldron. And figures were exploding from the cauldron's mouth: the Kadoshim in their true forms, leather-winged, pale as milk, wrapped in mail and carrying shield, sword and spear. An endless fountain of them pouring out from the cauldron, up into the chamber's highest reaches, spreading, some touching down on the stone floor, gazing at their flesh-wreathed bodies, some laughing, braying with delight, others snarling, hatred made flesh.

One figure floated down to Calidus, dark wings slowing his descent, stirring up a cloud of dust, appearing as if he glided to the earth. The ground steamed and hissed when his booted feet touched the stone. His skin was pale as death, black-veined like a rotting leaf, though his face was handsome, chiselled in sharp lines, blue-black lips smiling, silver hair bound in a warrior braid that coiled about his shoulders. He held a naked sword in his fist.

Asroth.

He raised a fist before his eyes and slowly clenched it, a look of pleasure upon his face, as if he savoured the sensation of knuckle and bone, of flesh and skin stretching and contracting, of blood pulsing in his veins.

'Ah, Calidus, my beloved captain,' he said, reaching out the same hand to cup Calidus' cheek. 'You have served me well, will be rewarded beyond all others for this great deed.'

'All is for you and your glory, my King,' Calidus said, and sank to one knee before Asroth, Rhin knelt too.

Asroth looked about him, at the great hall, at Calidus and those prostrating themselves before him, up at his dread legions spread above him like a dark halo, more of them still flowing from the cauldron in an endless outpouring, and finally at Corban and the others shackled in bonds of smoke at his feet.

'My gift to you,' Calidus said, rising from the ground. 'Your enemy the Bright Star and his captains.'

Asroth's lips stretched, an oil-black smile.

'Is the battle over before we have arrived?' he asked.

'No, my King,' Calidus said. 'The fields of Drassil are thick with those that fight against you, ready to be slain. I thought that these here before you would be best saved for your victory celebration, when the battle is done, where you could savour their screams and torment.'

Asroth's smile grew broader.

'A fine plan,' he said, crouching down and leaning close to Corban.

'And I *will* savour every scream,' Asroth said, breath washing over Corban, damp and cold, 'you who have stood against me, raised a warband against *me*.' A glimmer of rage twisted Asroth's features, his black eyes endless pits of cruelty and malice, and Corban felt the blood in his veins turn to ice.

'Later,' Asroth growled as he stood, then turned his eyes to his Kadoshim.

'We shall celebrate this moment later,' he cried out, 'but first, let us accomplish what we have come here to do. Let us take our revenge upon Elyon the Great Deceiver. Let us go forth and slay.'

A great roar filled the chamber, Kadoshim screaming their agreement, and with that the muscles in Asroth's legs bunched and he leaped into the air, great wings beating and taking him effortlessly higher, gaining speed, ever faster as he climbed, towards one of the great windows in the high roof.

Asroth burst through the window's thin fabric. Light blazed in, then was just as quickly blocked out as his demon horde followed him, smashing the hole ever wider, crumbling stone and shattered wood crashing to the ground as countless wings took the Kadoshim-made flesh out into the skies of the Banished Lands.

CAMLIN

Camlin stood beneath the fringes of the forest, his archers about him, and loosed another arrow at a black and gold-cloaked rider, saw the warrior topple backwards in a spray of blood.

Behind him, through the trees, he could see the healers and wounded gathered in a makeshift hospice. He had decided that he and his crew were best placed in front of them, a last line of defence to try and keep the battle from engulfing them, and at the same time he was close enough to Edana and her warband to thin the ranks of Rhin and Geraint's horde of black and gold.

Though that's not so easy, with the whole mass of 'em in constant motion.

Everywhere was madness, the plain flooded with corpses. Half of the battlefield surged with mounted warriors, the men of Ardan and Domhain fighting valiantly, but it was clear to Camlin that they were losing, as Geraint's warband steadily gained ground.

To the south it looked much the same, a tale of steady attrition grinding slowly towards defeat, though from Camlin's position it was impossible to be sure.

Directly ahead and between Camlin and the gates of Drassil were a host of eagle-guard in their disciplined rows, a sea of black and silver with their big shields held in front of them.

A thousand at least – more, most likely.

He felt his heart sink, for the first time the possibility of defeat seeping through him. So far it had been tactics, tricks and a whole lot of heart that had seemed to keep the enemy reeling, regardless of their huge advantage of numbers. But now, it was just sword against sword, man against man, out on a flat plain, no more strategies or tricks left to play.

Must admit, it doesn't look good.

He sucked in a deep breath, for a moment considered grabbing Meg and getting the hell out of there. She was close by, helping in the hospice, and under strict orders from Camlin to stay there. The only reason he thought she might listen was that she'd grown attached to Cywen's hound, Buddai, and his vicious-looking brood of pups.

I could leave. No point dying for a lost cause.

Then he caught a glimpse of Edana, blood-spattered, sword held high, meeting a hard-swung blade. Even as his hand reached for another arrow, Camlin thought of Edana's faith in him, the words she had said back in Ardan.

I'd die for you, for all of you. It looked as if she was living up to that promise, out there on her horse, swinging a sword at her enemy, at warriors trained for battle.

Takes some stones to do that.

And you told her you'd die for her, too . . .

His arrow punched into Edana's opponent, deep into his armpit. Camlin heard the man's scream over the din of battle, then Edana's sword crunched into his helm and he was toppling from his saddle.

Camlin felt in his quiver for another arrow, painfully aware that he was running low.

Pick your targets, make every one count.

A sound rippled across the battlefield. It began as a distant roar and Camlin froze with his arrow half out of its quiver, staring at Drassil.

A great spiralling plume of what looked like smoke was rising from deep within the fortress, heading towards the battlefield. As Camlin watched, it spread into the sky like an expanding cloud, swirling towards the battlefield.

That's no fire smoke.

As the cloud grew closer Camlin could make out shapes, becoming clear. Great wings beating, the glint of iron, sunlight on sword and spear and mail. A shiver of fear ran through him, his blood freezing in his veins.

Demons of the Otherworld. So it's true, then, what Craf said we've been fighting against. Didn't really believe it until this very moment.

Even as he watched, Camlin saw the cloud swooping lower, spreading over the battlefield, blotting out the sun, and then he heard them, screeching hideous battle-cries as they swooped down, flying low over Edana's warband, striking out with their weapons, hauling riders from saddles, lifting them high and hurling them spinning to their deaths. At their head a silver-haired figure led them, a mighty, glorious figure, longsword slashing, cutting a rider in two as he swept low over Edana's warband.

Is that Asroth, himself?

Camlin fought the urge to turn and run.

One winged creature slammed into a rider close to Edana and beat its wings harder, dragging the warrior flailing from his saddle and up into the air. With more instinct than thought, Camlin had his arrow nocked and was drawing, aiming, accounting automatically for wind, speed, angle and he was loosing.

It pierced the Kadoshim through its side, angling upwards, through ribs and deeper. The Kadoshim let out a strangled cry as it dropped the warrior in its arms, its wings faltering, and for a timeless moment it hovered in the air, then it began to fall, picking up speed until it was plummeting to the earth.

The Kadoshim crashed to the ground before Camlin, an explosion of turf as it rolled and skidded, a snarl of twisted limbs and wings, turning until finally it came to a halt. As it tried to rise, Camlin stepped from the trees, kicked it, then drew his sword and stabbed it through the throat.

Don't want that thing getting up.

Other archers emerged from the treeline, staring at this creature from another world.

'Ugly-looking thing, but flesh and blood, like the rest of us,' Camlin muttered. He looked up at the warriors around him.

'If they bleed, we can kill them.'

He stood and stared at the battlefield, the winged Kadoshim scattered over the whole field, spreading fear and mayhem as they went.

'What shall we do?' one of the archers asked.

'Get back into some cover and keep shooting those bastards out of the sky.'

Back in the trees Camlin stopped and stared into the mass of horseflesh that was jostling around Edana's banner, ready to pick off any more of the enemy that fancied itself as a queen-killer, as well as demons swooping down from above. And then he saw a face he recognized.

That can't be right.

He narrowed his eyes, took a few paces closer, out of the forest, and focused on the few riders to the right of Edana. He saw Halion, Vonn and Conall close by, Conall laying about him with his sword, obviously enjoying himself. And, there, a rider behind them, on a magnificent skewbald stallion that looked as if it was enjoying the fight as much as Conall, biting at horses in front of it, hooves lashing out at the enemy. Upon it, a figure he'd know anywhere.

Rafe! That bastard.

Camlin saw Rafe kick at his horse, guiding it closer to Conall, who glanced back at Rafe and flashed him a smile.

Rafe grinned back, and then Conall's attention was back on the warrior in front of him. Rafe drew closer still, their horses pressed tight together, and then he pulled his sword back and with all his strength stabbed Conall in the back.

'NO!' Camlin screamed, but no one heard him over the clash of arms.

Rafe's sword-tip pierced low, through leather and mail, angled upwards, went deep and Conall stiffened, arching backwards, crying out.

Camlin's arrow was drawn and loosed, grazing Rafe's shoulder as he ripped his blade free. He glanced at his wound, then twisted in his saddle and saw Camlin.

Stay still, just a moment.

Rafe frantically kicked his horse in the ribs, urging it deeper into the mass of combat.

Towards Edana.

Conall swayed in his saddle and began to topple.

Camlin ran out from the cover of the trees, weaving through the combat, ducking a sword swing, punching his bow into a face. He saw Conall slip from his saddle, falling, down into the mud and blood, Halion yelling, leaping from his horse after his brother. They disappeared from view. A glimpse of Rafe plunging and rearing through the crush, ever closer to the unsuspecting Edana.

Camlin grabbed the reins of a riderless horse and dragged himself into the saddle, shouting and yelling, spurring it into motion. He ducked low as a Kadoshim swept close overhead, grabbing a man of Ardan and ripping him from his saddle, hauling him high into the air.

Camlin glimpsed Halion standing over Conall's body, wielding his blade two-handed as horses reared around him, swords and spears stabbing down at him.

Rafe was right behind Edana now, a wicked grin upon his face as he drew his sword arm back.

Camlin closed fingers around his last arrow, cursed at his horse to stay still, drew his bow, took a deep breath, and loosed.

The arrow slammed into Rafe's back, high, into his right shoulder-blade. Rafe cried out, swaying, falling low over his horse's neck. He looked back, eyes fixing on Camlin.

Vonn turned in his saddle and saw Rafe behind Edana, shouted a curse at the traitor, a warning to Edana. Rafe pulled on his reins, his mount taking him out of range as Camlin rode towards them, shouldering his bow and drawing his sword, burning with the desire to kill Rafe. Then he saw Halion, still standing over Conall, blood-matted, sword raised against a storm of blades. Camlin's horse veered towards him, crashing through friend and foe, and then Camlin was chopping into a back, hacking at a wrist, calling for Halion to reach out.

'I'll not leave him,' Halion shouted back, stabbing at a rider as Camlin desperately tried to carve a way through to him.

And then a spear stabbed down into Halion's back and there was blood on his lips, a cough, more blood matting into his beard. He looked up at Camlin, swayed and fell onto his brother.

Camlin screamed a wordless battle-cry, hacked frenziedly at the enemy before him, but he could not reach Halion and slowly he was swept away. Eventually, exhausted and grief-stricken, he broke out of the press and sat upon his horse, breathing hard.

One person filled his mind and he scanned the battlefield, then spurred his horse on, towards the walls of Drassil.

Got me some hunting to do.

LYKOS

Lykos stared into the skies, his guts turning to water for a moment as he saw the Kadoshim descending from above on wings of death.

So Calidus has done it, then.

Lykos briefly wondered about the wisdom of opening a doorway to the Otherworld.

Little too late for that. You've rolled your knuckle-bones. Just have to hope the Kadoshim are happy to share the world.

One of the Kadoshim flew perilously close, swooping overhead, the wind of its passing staggering him. Lykos ducked, raising his arms to protect himself, but it passed over him, screeching, and grabbed a red-cloaked warrior of Isiltir, hauling him screaming into the air. Its wings beat powerfully, higher and higher, until with a maniacal screech it let the man go. Its victim spun to earth, tumbling and thrashing through the air, then smashed to the ground, abruptly still, his body twisted and broken.

Do they know I am their ally? Or was that just luck?

With the coming of the Kadoshim the battleground had become a place of total chaos: fear, slaughter, panic, death and pandemonium from both enemy and ally alike.

He winced as another of them swooped overhead, skewering one of Ripa's warriors with its spear. As it began to rise, a white-haired giant ran through the crowd and jumped, swinging a double-bladed battle-axe. It caught the Kadoshim in the chest, cleaving it almost in two. A spray of blood fountained over those below as it plummeted to the ground. A roar went up amongst the surrounding warriors.

So they can be killed more easily than the possessed Jehar. Becoming flesh is a double-edged sword: it brings all the pleasures, but also the dangers. Maybe it's time I made a tactical withdrawal.

With the coming of the Kadoshim the battle was obviously won, and Lykos was feeling weary to the bone. After he'd slain Krelis the men of Ripa had gone berserk. They'd attacked him and his Vin Thalun with a savagery he'd only seen in the fighting-pits. It had been hard, grim work, and for every man of Ripa that fell, Lykos suspected he'd lost two, maybe three of his own men.

Might be time to save the lads I have left, and go find something tasty for the victory drink that's surely coming.

Then he heard a chant, words drifting on the wind that chilled his blood more than any Otherworld-spawned demon ever had.

Old Wolf. Old Wolf.

Lykos looked in the direction it was coming from, watching a wedge of men heading his way, a few giants amongst them, cutting his Vin Thalun down at an alarming rate. He saw Maquin, only a dozen paces away, running straight for him. His eyes were fixed on Lykos and they were blazing, with madness, with bloodlust-joy. Lykos took an involuntary step back.

I should have let Jael kill him, never taken him as my slave, never thrown him into the pits. I've created a monster.

He saw a Vin Thalun fall away in a spray of blood, throat spurting, another man fold over, a sword through the gut, the next one spinning with his skull crushed by Maquin's sword-pommel. Then the Old Wolf was four or five paces away, just one more man between them.

Lykos sighed, looked at his twisted buckler, hefted his notched and bloody short sword and snarled.

The Old Wolf needs putting down, and if you want a job done properly . . .

He set his feet as Maquin slammed into the Vin Thalun between them. Lykos didn't wait, but ran in, kicked his man in the back, sending Maquin staggering, and swung his short sword. It clipped Maquin's shoulder, but the Old Wolf had somehow guessed where Lykos would strike and had placed his Vin Thalun attacker between them; Lykos' blow killed his own man.

Maquin shoved the body back at Lykos, causing him to stumble back just as Maquin's sword came at him. He threw himself under the sword blow, knocking Maquin's knife away with his buckler, smashing his sword hilt into Maquin's face, sending the Old Wolf staggering, blood running from his nose.

'So you bleed, too,' Lykos growled.

Maquin cuffed the blood, gave a feral grin and came at him again.

A flurry of blows, sword and knife, stabbing, chopping, coming fast and furious, from every angle possible, Lykos shuffling backwards, frantically blocking and always steadily retreating before the unrelenting fury of Maquin's assault.

He looked desperately for support from his men but saw three giants, all with their heads shaved apart from a thick strip down the middle, finishing off the last of his guard.

I hate it when a plan goes wrong.

Maquin stalked towards him, sword and knife twitching.

'To be fair, I didn't push her over the cliff. She just . . . let go,' Lykos said.

'Don't mention her,' Maquin growled, a vein pulsing in his temple.

'She wasn't as pure as you might think,' Lykos smiled, and Maquin leaped at him. He was expecting it, but still it came almost too fast for him to see or react to. A pain lanced along his hip, Maquin's knife slicing a red line, and then his left arm with the buckler was in a lock, somehow, Maquin's arm over it. The Old Wolf shifted his weight, a sudden movement and Lykos was screaming, an explosion of pain in his now dislocated shoulder, his buckler ripping free as he fell as if he were a puppet with his strings cut.

He lay on his back, saw Maquin's face twist, smile or snarl, and his arm pull back for the death blow.

Then Maquin was hoisted into the sky, a Kadoshim's wings framing him, a serpent-like face laughing.

Good riddance. I can even live with not killing you as long as this time you stay dead.

Lykos staggered to his feet, swayed with nausea as pain jolted through his shoulder and curled his arm protectively into his chest. He began to stagger towards the safety of Drassil, felt blood trickling down his hip, a burning pain, and his shoulder throbbed rhythmically with every step.

Bastard almost had me. Guess the Kadoshim do have their uses.

He heard a furious screech from somewhere above. Stumbling to a halt, he looked up to see that Maquin had twisted in his captor's grip and was furiously knifing the beast's belly, opening its guts. Then the Kadoshim was falling, dead in the air, Maquin holding it tight.

The fall must kill him. They are too high. Please, the fall must kill him. Asroth below, I have sold you my soul, conquered half the Banished Lands for you. Do this one thing for me. Kill that lunatic.

Lykos watched horror-struck as he saw Maquin climb around the Kadoshim's body, even as they were plummeting, somehow dragging himself up onto its back, wrapping one flapping leathery wing around himself.

They slammed into the ground, a few hundred paces away, earth and grass exploding around the body, a cloud of dust, slowly settling.

Lykos breathed out a long sigh of relief.

Then a wing twitched, was thrown off, and Maquin rose from the Kadoshim's ruin, a long cut across his forehead, a limp in his left leg, but other than that he appeared to be infuriatingly healthy.

'Elyon above and Asroth below,' Lykos whispered, feeling a cold breath upon his neck.

'LYKOS,' he heard Maquin scream.

Lykos began to run.

CORBAN

Corban lay upon the cold stone floor, wrapped in coils of unbreakable smoke, and watched as the torrent of Kadoshim continued to pour from the cauldron. His friends lay about him, just as helpless.

I've led us to this. Brina dead. Laith dead. All for nothing.

He felt as if his heart was stopping in his chest at the thought of Brina. He remembered that first night when he'd crept into her cottage and tried to steal something to prove his courage to Rafe, Edana and the others; Brina had caught him, scolded him, but even then been kind to him, allowed him to take a bone comb of hers to show the others that he was no coward. From that night on she had become a part of his life. Terrifying, abrasive, downright rude most of the time, but he had come to love her like kin.

And now she's dead. Thrown into the cauldron like a piece of meat.

How did Calidus know I was coming here? Bringing the last two Treasures?

He remembered the voice in his head, just before the trap had been sprung, calling him to the Otherworld.

Meical.

Corban closed his eyes and thought of the Otherworld, focusing on the fortress he had been taken to, where Meical had been, the throne room carved into high mountains amongst the clouds, and then he felt himself spinning, faster and faster, falling into darkness.

He opened his eyes to find he was standing at the top of a stairwell, the world around him made up of shades of grey. He reached for his sword and was reassured to feel it sheathed at his hip. Great arched windows opened onto a clouded world, mountain cliffs rearing high. A sound grew, louder with each passing moment, like approaching thunder. Corban stared out of the windows and saw a vast host appear, wings beating in steady unison, propelling warriors through the sky, sweeping through the clouds and mountain heights like a great white-winged avalanche; they were not Kadoshim, but the Ben-Elim, hundreds, no, thousands of them, winging through the air in gleaming shirts of scale-mail, bright spears and swords in their fists, eyes blazing with fury.

Like a hurricane the host swept past him, hurtling like a cast spear, and then they were fading into the distance.

Corban looked back to the staircase and strode down it, hesitantly at first, then faster, until he was running into darkness and torch-light. He paused at the bottom, recognizing the corridor before him, and then strode on, not stopping until he was standing before the chamber that held Meical. This time he kicked the door open, shattering the lock, and strode in. Meical was still there, chained and shackled, mouth gagged. Corban tore the cloth from the Ben-Elim's mouth and drew his sword.

'How did Calidus know I was going to try and destroy the Treasures?'

Meical could not meet his gaze.

'Did you betray me?' Corban snarled. 'Again.'

'Not I,' Meical whispered.

'It could only have been you.'

'Not I, but my kin,' Meical said. 'Why do you think I am here, condemned by my own people.'

Meical raised his eyes and met Corban's gaze.

'I stood for you,' the Ben-Elim said, 'I refused to betray you again, but they do not understand, would not listen.'

'What did they do?'

'One of my kin allowed himself to be captured, knew he would be tortured, and told Asroth of your plan during that torture.'

'I . . . don't understand,' Corban said. 'Why would they do that? Don't they want me to defeat Asroth?'

'What they want, Corban, is the portal opened, a pathway to your world of flesh.'

'What!'

'That has been the plan, always, thousands of years in the making.

For the Ben-Elim to become flesh, to enter your world, to protect Elyon's creation. To become your guardians.'

Corban staggered back a step, his sword-point wavering.

'So that is where the Ben-Elim host was going?' he said. 'How can I stop this?'

'You cannot stop it, now. But maybe the cauldron and Treasures could still be destroyed, keeping all from crossing over.'

'And what of those left in my world?'

'They will be trapped there. Unless they are slain.'

'Will that send their spirits back here, like the Jehar? Like you?'

'No, Corban. Once my kind and the Kadoshim become flesh, truly, not just their spirits invading and controlling another's body, like a puppet, then they can die. Not of age or sickness – to that we are immune – but we will be vulnerable to sharp iron. Dead is dead. They will cross the bridge of swords, just as your kind do.'

'Then why come? Why do this, risking death.'

'Sometimes the prize is worth the risk. Asroth and his Kadoshim seek to annihilate all humankind, to wipe your memory from the earth. The joy of slaughter and the victory over Elyon, those are what drive Asroth and the Kadoshim. As for the Ben-Elim –' Meical shrugged – 'duty drives us. We have seen this path as the greatest service to our King, the greatest way to prove our devotion to him.'

A silence settled between them.

'So Asroth can be slain?' Corban said.

'Aye,' Meical smiled. There was no humour in it.

'I must go back and break my bonds,' Corban muttered.

'Where is your body of flesh?' Meical asked him.

'In Drassil's great chamber, bound with bonds of smoke by Calidus,' Corban answered.

'Set me free, that I may help you,' Meical said.

'You? I have tasted your help,' Corban said bitterly.

'I swear to you, with all that I am, I will never betray you again.' He held his shackled wrists out. 'Set me free.'

Corban raised his sword.

Corban opened his eyes, his cheek was pressed against cold flagstones, and he lifted his head. Calidus was standing close to the cauldron, Kadoshim still pouring from it.

Then a new sound drifted out of the swirling vortex that was the cauldron, not just the beating of wings and the joy of the Kadoshim horde. Now there were distant shouts, screams, faint as a fading dream, but growing. Then the clash of weapons.

Calidus froze, head cocked to one side.

Corban smiled.

White wings suddenly began to pour out through the cauldron, coats of gleaming mail and bright blades, Ben-Elim locked in combat with Kadoshim, swirling up high, swooping around the chamber, weapons clashing, voices shouting out battle-cries, bodies crashing into the curved walls or slamming to the floor in death and ruin, others tangled together, still fighting, stabbing, snarling, biting. More and more Ben-Elim appeared as Corban stared at the cauldron, the balance between Kadoshim and Ben-Elim changing in heart-beats, and soon more white-feathered wings than Kadoshim were pouring out through the cauldron as Calidus looked on in growing horror.

It's a gateway, Calidus, and it's not just the Kadoshim you've let through. Anything from the Otherworld can enter now, and that means the Ben-Elim too.

The wingless Kadoshim that had once been Jehar also leaped to the attack, their swords slicing at the angelic-looking warriors, severing wings, blood spraying, but still the Ben-Elim swooped down on them from above in greater and greater numbers, and soon wraiths of vapour were filling the chamber as the Jehar-possessed screamed futilely and perished.

'What's going on?' Cywen called to Corban.

The turning of the tide, thought Corban. *If Meical keeps his word.*

For what felt like days Corban lay and stared at the host of winged warriors emerging from the cauldron, swamped by the almost deaf-ening din of battle in the chamber, hoping against hope to see Meical appear.

Calidus and the remnants of his Jehar Kadoshim were swept away in the battle. Rhin retreated into the shadows, her shieldmen draw-ing tight about her, staring in awestruck horror at the fury of the combat around them, at the Kadoshim and Ben-Elim slaying one another with feral rage.

And then Meical was there, exploding from the cauldron, a different being from the shackled, broken figure Corban had seen only recently. Now he was glorious in his war gear, black hair tied back tight to his nape, bright scale-mail rippling like another skin, his eyes ablaze with fury. He hurtled from the cauldron and shot up high into the chamber, hovered a moment, great wings beating as he exchanged a flurry of blows with a hissing Kadoshim. Corban saw him slice through one of the demon's wings, sent it spinning back down to the ground, crashing to the stone floor a few paces away from Corban.

Meical fell upon it, booted foot upon the Kadoshim's chest, his sword crunching into its skull, shattering it, an explosion of bone and brains. He hissed at the dead Kadoshim, a primal thing, and then looked about the chamber, seeing his ancient enemy all about him. His white wings beat, lifting him from the ground, hovering in place as he appeared to be choosing his next foe.

He's going to leave us here. Break his oath to me and return to his kin.

Then Meical's eyes fell upon Corban, taking in his friends and Storm. He hovered for a few heartbeats, eyes flickering across the many Kadoshim about the chamber, then he touched his feet back to the floor, wings folding behind him, the fire in his eyes dimming. Muttering, he waved his hand, and the smoke binding Corban and his friends evaporated, like mist in the sun.

Meical held his arm out to Corban, who lay on the ground, staring up at the Ben-Elim. Corban took his hand.

The room was a maelstrom of battle around Corban as he climbed unsteadily to his feet and ran to his friends, helping Coralen stand, the others gathering around: Gar, Dath and Cywen, Storm limping, Farrell with his red-rimmed eyes. The Ben-Elim were still flooding from the cauldron and many were now soaring out through the huge rent in the chamber's roof to engage their ancient foe in the skies above Drassil. Corban saw one Ben-Elim stare at Meical for a moment before it flew out of the chamber.

'What's going on?' Dath asked.

'And what do we do now?' Coralen asked, looking at Corban.

'We kill Kadoshim,' Farrell growled.

Corban looked at Meical.

'We finish what we set out to do,' Corban said, holding Meical's gaze. The Ben-Elim nodded.

'Cywen, can you perform Brina's ritual, and destroy the Treasures?' Corban asked her.

With a beat of his wings Meical swirled away from them, chopped two-handed at a Kadoshim that flew screeching at them from above. It crashed to the ground.

'I . . . yes . . . I think I can,' Cywen said, looking at the cauldron – there was still a steady flow of Ben-Elim rushing through it.

Meical alighted back beside them.

'Don't you need to go and fight Asroth?' Dath asked him.

'I will not need to go in search of Asroth. He will soon hear that we Ben-Elim have control of the gateway. He cannot allow that. He will return here.'

Dath looked around at the others and gulped.

'We'd best get a move on, then,' Farrell said.

CHAPTER ONE HUNDRED AND TEN

MAQUIN

Maquin saw Lykos.

Trying to escape, again. Not this time, thought Maquin.

He followed his prey.

His whole body hurt, a gash from his fall leaking blood into one eye, his knee pulsing with pain, but he could run well enough.

Time for pain later.

He picked up speed, veering around men fighting for their lives, one eye checking the skies above him as Kadoshim swept low, slashing and stabbing, grabbing to drag people screaming into the air. Maquin swung at enemies as he passed them, even if it was just a shove that knocked them off balance and gave their opponent an opening. Once he turned and struck at a swooping Kadoshim, hacked off a grasping hand and scoured a line through a leathery wing, then turned and ran on, his eyes fixed on the Vin Thalun Lord limping ahead.

The gap closed.

Maquin could see the forest looming now, smoke billowing from it, the crackle of fire that had been a distant thing now bright, animals and birds taking flight from it.

Lykos had paused and was staring towards Drassil. As Maquin followed his gaze he saw white-feathered men in gleaming mail soaring from the fortress and spreading over the whole battlefield. Wielding sword and spear, they attacked the Kadoshim with a fury Maquin had never witnessed before, not even in the fighting-pits, where men were reduced to tooth, nail and animal instinct. As Maquin watched he saw two forms locked together spin low over the battlefield, crashing and skidding only a few score paces ahead of him, warriors smashed out of their way or leaping, earth spraying in a fountain-like wake behind them.

They rolled to a halt, wings still beating, limbs moving, the white-feathered Ben-Elim rising, only to plunge its sword into the Kadoshim's chest, punching through, pinning it to the earth.

The Kadoshim shrieked, twitched and was still. The Ben-Elim leaned upon its sword for a moment, breathing heavily, then ripped its blade free, bellowing a victory cry and leaping back into the air, wide wings powering it back into the airborne melee.

Maquin saw Lykos glance his way, his eyes widen, a flash of fear, and then the Vin Thalun was running again, turning west, towards the forest.

Angels. Demons. I care not. It's time for you to die, Lykos.

Trees closed around Maquin as he stepped into a world of instant twilight, shadows shifting around him, the murky gloom an ideal place for hiding. Maquin bent to one knee, listening, fingers touching the forest litter. When he lifted them, his fingertips were tinged red, before him a broken twig showed more blood, fresh and glistening.

He ran on, deeper into the forest, and then he heard him. Maquin smiled mirthlessly to hear panic in his prey's passage, an attempt at stealth overruled by the breath of death upon his neck. Maquin moved into a small glade, the trees opening up a little, changing from dense scrub to high-branched oaks, the forest litter thick and flat. Maquin paused, heard only the crackle of the forest fire growing ever closer. A cloud of smoke rolled across the glade.

Maquin walked on, heard the rustle of leaves on the ground, spun round to see Lykos leaping at him, sword stabbing up at him, aimed at his gut. With a contemptuous snarl, Maquin slapped the sword away, sidestepped, slashed his knife at Lykos as he stumbled past, opening a red line above the back of the Vin Thalun's knee. Lykos staggered on a few steps, fell to one knee, stabbing his sword into the ground, leaning on it to stop himself from falling.

Maquin circled him, keeping wide, a wolf circling a dying snake, until he was standing directly in front of Lykos.

There may still be poison in his fangs.

One side of Lykos' breeches was blood-soaked to his boots, from the cut on his hip. His left arm was held tight to his body as if he cradled a child. And his face dripped sweat and grime, eyes wide with fear and anger, chest sucking in deep, ragged breaths.

'Get up,' Maquin snarled.

Lykos raised an eyebrow, but he pulled himself upright, leaning heavily on his sword, then stood there, swaying.

'No more running,' Maquin said.

Lykos looked down at his leg. 'I think you've made sure of that.'

Maquin sheathed his sword over his back and drew a knife instead.

'How many knives do you possess?' Lykos asked, annoyed.

'Better too many than too few,' Maquin growled.

Lykos nodded.

'Well, I think it's only fair to say; you win.' Lykos started to chuckle.

'What's funny?' Maquin asked.

'You. I think you take life too seriously. You should laugh more.' He coughed, grimaced.

'You stole that from me,' Maquin said, 'stole everything: laughter, friends, honour, humanity.' He bowed his head. 'Fidele . . .'

The memory of her face filled his mind for a moment.

He strode forwards, caught Lykos' feeble attempt at defence on his knife blade, twisted his wrist and sent Lykos' sword spinning away. Then Maquin was in close, punched his other knife hilt onto Lykos' injured shoulder, heard him scream, headbutted him on the bridge of his nose, blood exploding. Lykos stumbled back a few paces, wobbled and fell on his backside against a tree. Maquin followed, hauling Lykos up, holding his arm high, against the tree, and stabbed a knife through the Vin Thalun's palm, deep into the wood behind. He drew another knife and slammed it in a little lower, into Lykos' forearm, the blade grating between bone, pinning Lykos to the tree.

Fresh screams, loud and raucous. Slowly they faded to bubbling groans and whimpers.

'Please,' Lykos begged. 'Please.'

Fire crackled behind Lykos, more smoke billowing through the glade, and Maquin saw a shifting in the undergrowth – ants like black liquid were spilling out around Lykos' feet, fleeing the fire.

Maquin backed away to a safe distance and watched Lykos look down at the ants that were pooling around his boots, a few of them scuttling up, over the leather and onto the soft wool of his breeches. He saw the Vin Thalun's eyes widen at the first bite of their mandibles, then more of them, climbing, biting.

'No, no, please, no,' Lykos blurted, jumping and twitching as mandibles tore through his breeches and snipped at his flesh. 'Just kill me, please, please kill me,' Lykos begged. More and more ants were flooding up his leg now, some gathering around his other foot, even as he tried to stamp on them, jerking and jumping as if he was performing some insane dance.

Maquin took a few more paces back, arms folded, making sure the ants didn't decide to come his way. For now there were not enough of them, and the ones that were there seemed content with Vin Thalun flesh.

Ants reached Lykos' groin.

He sucked in a deep breath and screamed. Such a scream as Maquin had never heard before, not even in the pits. Lykos' eyes bulged, his face bursting red. And Maquin watched him.

Lykos' screams rose and fell as the Vin Thalun passed in and out of consciousness. Maquin sat down and reached to his boot and drew another knife, its edge wickedly sharp.

Lykos bubbled out a hoarse string of semi-coherent words, begging, pleading with Maquin for the release of death.

Maquin looked at the blade in his hand, twisted it, then he put it against his own wrist.

It's over now. Jael is dead, Kastell avenged. And I am avenged against Lykos.

The ants were swirling around Lykos' belly. He was hanging limp, suspended by the two knives in hand and arm, snot bubbling from his nose, dribble hanging from his mouth, driven near-mad and insensible with the pain.

Maquin pressed the knife edge against his wrist, saw it hover over the dark vein. A bead of blood appeared.

The din of battle echoed through the clearing, rising over the forest fire and Lykos' death rattle. It stirred something in him, the clash of arms, battle-cries, and somewhere deep within him his spirit rose, as if answering a call.

Battle.

He looked at the knife, at the blood welling on his wrist. Then he stood, gave Lykos' corpse a last look and stalked from the glade.

Towards the sound of battle.

CORBAN

Corban stood with his back guarding the cauldron and Treasures, his friends spread in a loose circle around them too, with Meical hovering, swinging his sword with savage joy at any Kadoshim that came too close. Cywen was standing close to the cauldron.

She started to chant. '*Seoda cloch réalta, ó deannaigh tháinig tú, agus deannaigh beidh tú ar ais . . .*'

At first no one in the room heard, as it was still seething with battle; Kadoshim and Ben-Elim were more interested in cutting, stabbing, hacking and tearing each other to pieces. Corban took a moment to check Storm over, heard her whine when he ran a hand over her shoulder, and found a deep gash in her left paw that carried on up into her leg. He ripped a strip of cloth from his linen under-shirt and bound it tight for the moment, thinking he would have to tell Brina about it soon.

But I can't. She's dead, gone.

Grief and rage were circling through his body, punctuated with waves of weariness and fear. He wondered how the battle outside was faring and felt a fresh wave of worry for his friends and warband beyond Drassil's walls, made worse by the knowledge that Asroth and his demon horde were loose in the skies above them.

I should be there, fighting alongside them.

Cywen's voice drifted in and out, and Corban felt a pulse of power ripple through his body.

No, this must be done, is the only hope of victory, of saving any of us. See it through. And I left Akar in charge – he knows what must be done.

Meical stood between Corban and Gar, eyes flitting through the Kadoshim above. Corban could see that he was eager to fight but was resisting the urge so that he could fulfil his oath to Corban and the others.

Abruptly, there was an enormous booming crash, part of the chamber's roof imploding, stone and wood crashing down to the floor, an explosion of dust. Kadoshim were rushing into the chamber, Asroth at their head, demons spread behind him, hovering a moment and then launching into the overwhelming numbers of Ben-Elim that had been slowly filling the room.

Beside Corban Meical tensed, his wings pulsing, lifting him up into the air, but he only hovered over Cywen, sword held protectively ready. A Kadoshim flew near to him and his sword sang, the Kadoshim's head flew in a different direction to its body, which careened on to crash into the great tree.

Dath tracked targets, sent Kadoshim tumbling through the air with his arrows.

Figures emerged from the shadows of the chamber. Calidus and a handful of his Jehar were striding towards Corban, behind them Rhin and her shieldmen.

Corban felt a wave of hatred flood through him, stealing all else from him for a moment as he saw the man who murdered his mam, murdered Brina, who had orchestrated so much death and destruction. All he wanted to do was bury his sword into Calidus' heart.

He took a step forwards, away from Cywen, then felt a hand on his arm.

Gar.

They shared a look.

Anger is the enemy.

Corban took a deep breath and mastered himself.

Meical saw Calidus and smiled.

'The last time I saw you was in this chamber,' Meical said, wings twitching. 'You cut off my head. I am thinking it is time I returned the favour.'

Meical strode at Asroth's commander, wings lifting him a little, eyes blazing his fury. Corban could see the aeons-old hatred between the two races encapsulated in that gaze.

'Rhin,' Calidus called out, 'get that bitch away from the cauldron.' He took a step towards Meical. 'Time I finished the job,' he snarled and leaped at Meical, their blades clashing, Jehar-Kadoshim swarming around the Ben-Elim.

Corban ran to help Meical, and then a handful of Kadoshim were swooping down, feet hitting the ground between Corban and Meical, charging at him and the others.

One thrust a spear at Corban, but he knocked it away with his wolven claws and stepped in, chopping overhead at the Kadoshim. It swayed, Corban's blow glancing off of its mail-covered shoulder, but his wolven claws slashed across its throat, opening up three deep gashes, and it fell away.

Another Kadoshim filled its place, this one striking at him high with a longsword, Corban retreating before a barrage of powerful blows that shivered through his wrist and into his shoulder, then something was grabbing him from behind, arms wrapping under his arms, and he was leaving the ground, a sense of weightlessness as he was hoisted skywards. He twisted, saw a Kadoshim's manic grin and blue-black lips as it lifted him higher. He tried to swing his sword at it but could get no strength in the blow.

Coralen appeared out of nowhere. She jumped onto the Kadoshim Corban had just been fighting on the ground, ran up his back, pulling on a wing to help, and then launching herself from its shoulders. She all but flew through the air, crashed into the Kadoshim that was lifting Corban, wrapped her legs around it and, before it had a chance to react, she was punching her wolven claws into its side. The mail links of its armour shattered, then blood was gushing, the creature screeching its pain, swirling in the air, and the three of them were falling, crunching to the ground, Corban hitting stone, the Kadoshim falling on him, flattening him to the ground. Coralen hauled the corpse off Corban and gave him her hand.

He nodded his thanks to her.

And then another Kadoshim slammed to the floor in front of him, feet spread wide, ground smoking, a silver warrior braid coiled over one shoulder like a thick-bodied serpent.

Asroth.

His black eyes regarded Corban.

'Bright Star, it is time I heard you scream.'

HAELAN

Haelan ran, faster than he had ever run before.

He was back inside the draig tunnels, sprinting down a long passage. Behind him he heard the roar and rumbling thunder of draigs.

They were chasing him.

Because under his arm a draig's egg was tucked tight to his body.

It seemed like a good idea at the time.

Not so much, now, though.

His lungs were burning, each ragged breath a desperate clawing for oxygen.

He'd tied Shadow and Pots in the tunnel, didn't need them with him. The thought of one of them taking the wrong turn and getting eaten by a draig was too much for him to bear. Then he'd climbed back down the root-hole into the draig tunnels. When he reached the chamber with dung mounds in it he'd thrown himself into one, gagging and retching as he carried on to the egg chamber.

He'd crept in, grabbed an egg from the pile, turned and run. Not many heartbeats later he'd heard draig claws tearing up the earth behind him. He could hear the rip and tear of long talons, the grunting, rasping breath, and knew that he was almost finished.

Turning a corner, he saw the root of the oak tree and felt a rush of hope. Another dozen paces and he was hurling the torch over his shoulder, swinging and climbing, hauling himself up onto the ledge. As he scrambled higher through the crumbling tunnel he felt the root beside him shake; the draig below was ripping and tearing at it, jumping and shoving its jaws into the hole.

Then it roared.

He almost fell back down to the red maw of its open jaws, almost dropped the egg, wanted to cover his ears, but he climbed on, reaching the passage where he'd tied Pots and Shadow. They were crouched together, ears back; Shadow was growling. Haelan slashed the rope he'd used to tie them and carried on running, Pots and Shadow following.

A great thumping boom shook the tunnel, rippling up from below, staggering him into a wall as earth was shaken loose about him. He righted himself, heard a ripping sound, the terrible tearing sound of draig claws, and then earth was collapsing in the tunnel. He looked back and saw a draig appearing out of the root tunnel.

It's literally digging its way after me.

As I hoped.

He turned and ran, down the passage, into a beam of daylight, up the slope and burst out of the hole into the courtyard.

It was empty, the sound of battle distant and eerie.

Haelan ran, Shadow and Pots speeding along beside him, Pots with his tongue hanging out, looking like the happiest dog in the world. There was a muted crash behind Haelan, then a rumbling thunder. The ground rippled under his feet. He ran on, desperation fuelling him.

The ground shook, a wave began beneath the oak tree at the centre of the courtyard, throwing him from his feet. He clung desperately to the egg under his arm as he rolled and sat up, looking back into the courtyard.

Flagstones were exploding outwards, a fountain of earth and stone and root.

And then the first draig appeared, shoving and clawing up from the bowels of the earth. It hauled itself onto even ground and shook, a great cloud of dust billowing out from it. Then another draig was rising from the ground, followed immediately by a third.

The three of them stood there, tongues flickering, heads turning on thick necks, tails swishing. Then they scented their egg, and claws were scrambling on stone, bowed legs pumping, and they were after him.

Haelan jumped to his feet and ran.

The streets of Drassil were deserted. Haelan hurtled down the centre of streets, heedless of anyone or anything, his legs pumping faster than he'd ever run before. Past Cywen's old gaol and hospice, through the alleys, closer and closer to the courtyard and main gates. Battle roared louder and Haelan glimpsed strange shapes in the air, but he didn't dare spare a moment to study them. The thunder of the draigs behind him was growing louder.

Too close. They're going to eat me.

And then he was at the courtyard. Even this was mostly deserted, the great gates open, no one manning them now. Drassil had been emptied.

He ran on, past rows of stables, Pots barking excitedly, Shadow loping as silent as her name.

The draigs charged into the courtyard behind him.

Haelan burst out through the archway and onto the battlefield, saw a chaotic confusion of battle and skidded to a halt, feeling his stomach turn to water as he realized the shapes he'd seen in the sky were winged warriors, seemingly on opposing sides, dark wings and light wings, looping in a swirling dance of aerial combat. It was hypnotic to watch them in their beautiful flight of death.

Get a grip on yourself. You're about to be trampled to death by three wild draigs.

To his horror he saw that the draig dung was peeling off of him, falling away in chunks, leaving great patches of his skin exposed.

The draigs will be able to smell my scent!

I need to get rid of this egg.

He sucked air into his burning lungs and looked at the battlefield.

To his right, the north of the battlefield, all he could see was warriors on horseback, a sea of black and gold, though as he stared he saw Edana's grey as well, herded back towards the western fringes of Forn.

To the south-west stood a great block of eagle-guard, inching their way ever deeper into a melee of battle, killing as they went. Haelan saw Vin Thalun that way, a few giants standing tall in the crowd. And Nathair, sitting astride his draig.

That sealed it for Haelan.

That way, then.

And he was off and running again.

The draigs burst through the archway behind him and out onto the field. They, too, paused for a moment, their flickering tongues tasting the air, and within heartbeats their flat-muzzled heads were fixing upon their egg, and then they were breaking into a lumbering charge.

Haelan could see the rearguard of the eagle-guard ahead of him now, a line of black leather and chainmail, iron-shod boots drumming on the ground as they marched in close-packed discipline. Haelan was a hundred paces behind them, and he could hear the thunder of the draigs behind him.

Faster, run faster.

Seventy paces behind the soldiers, the pounding of the draigs filled Haelan's whole world.

Forty paces and he thought about doing it now, but he knew it was too far.

Just a few heartbeats more.

A draig roared behind him, jaws snapping, a cloud of foetid breath.

Ten paces, and faces turned to look back, saw the draigs.

Haelan hurled the egg, high and arcing, over the back ranks of the eagle-guard, the egg spinning, dipping, falling now, disappearing into the eagle-guard, fifteen or twenty rows deep. Haelan swerved left, skidding, one last burst of speed, and he was veering away from the eagle-guard, Pots and Shadow with him, running into open space, diving, rolling.

And behind him, a concussive slap as three draigs slammed into the marching eagle-guard.

NATHAIR

Nathair sat upon his draig, swinging his sword at another red-cloaked spearman.

His blow clanged off the man's helm, denting it, sending the warrior toppling to the ground, unconscious or dead with a cracked skull.

It was late in the day, the sun a pale glow sinking into the green of Forn, and the sky was dark with Kadoshim and Ben-Elim.

Kadoshim I am pleased to see, but Ben-Elim! How did that happen?

So far the angels and demons had not ventured in large numbers to this southern fringe of the battle, which Nathair was grateful for, though he was frustrated as well.

Half the day my shield wall has been battering at Veradis' smaller force, and yet they still haven't broken.

Countless times Nathair had attempted to assault Veradis' flank with his draig and a few score of his own shieldmen, but giants in their armour and armed with long spears and axes, combined with a few score red-cloaked warriors wielding thick-shafted spears, had formed a prickly hedge of sharp iron that had kept them from reaching Veradis' flank.

Nathair took a moment to wipe sweat from his eyes and survey the field.

And then he smiled, for he saw a great square of his eagle-guard, over a thousand men.

Calidus must have sent them to my aid.

They were in the thick of the battle, wading through a sea of the enemy towards him.

'Victory,' Nathair breathed, for he knew that this would mean the breaking of Veradis' shield wall.

And the annihilation of all our enemy south of Geraint. He could almost taste the glory of that victory.

And then Nathair saw a sight which at first he did not understand.

A small figure was running after his eagle-guard, hurling something small into the air, almost into the heart of his marching warriors. And behind that small figure were three enormous shapes, surging across the field, heading straight towards his eagle-guard.

They were draigs.

What?

Even as Nathair bellowed orders to his horns-man the three draigs crashed into his eagle-guard. Men flew through the air like twigs, spinning, limbs flailing, the three draigs driving deep into the eagle-guard formation, their heads low, thick necks flicking men into the air, legs and razored talons crushing and ripping warriors to shreds, leaving behind a trampled, tattered red ruin of flesh, blood and bone. Moments before, it had been Nathair's pride, his salvation and the likely turning-point of the battle. In a dozen heartbeats it was shattered.

Nathair snarled in frustration and despair, shouted orders at the shieldmen around him and screamed into his draig's ear, jabbing his heels into it and yanking on the reins. It gave out a loud roar and lurched forwards.

Enemy spearmen jabbed at it, but Nathair urged it on regardless, his shieldmen rushing to batter them out of the way and create a space for the draig to break through to Veradis' shield wall. Gashes opened up along the draig's shoulders and flanks, deep wounds in its flesh. Nathair leaned low, chopping at spears, splintering them, severing a hand, but still the spears stabbed, his draig bellowing in pain, Nathair kicking at it, yelling it on in a wild-eyed frenzy.

There was a blood-chilling cry from above and Nathair glanced up to see a handful of Kadoshim swooping from above, diving and stabbing at the men massed before Nathair's draig, one of them hoisting a red-cloaked warrior into the air and hurling him away. Men scattered, ducking, running from the Kadoshim; more were swooping upon Veradis' shield wall, and then Nathair's draig was bursting through the gauntlet of spears, Veradis' shield wall was straight ahead, Nathair's own wall to his left. Another screamed order from Nathair and his draig was rearing up onto its hind legs, then slamming down again, onto the massed ranks of the wall in front of it, shields splintered to kindling, bodies beneath them crushed and mashed to pulp.

What if Veradis is down there?

Nathair searched the faces of the dead, peering at the shieldmen who were staggering back from his draig's onslaught, but he saw Veradis nowhere.

He could be amongst those at my feet, mangled beyond all recognition.

Nathair knew that Veradis always chose to be front and centre of his shield wall, the most hard-fought spot, and Nathair had always respected him for that. Then he remembered Veradis' words to him earlier.

He has rejected me. Chosen another lord. Another Bright Star. And he told me that Corban would forgive me!

That galled him in so many ways he could hardly bear to think it through.

Veradis has made his choice. And if it has put him on the defeated side, and in front of my draig, then so be it.

'ON,' Nathair screamed, urging his draig deeper into the warband, its jaws snapping, crunching, talons raking warriors as it thrust itself further into Veradis' shield wall, and behind him his own shieldmen came, a wedge into the gap his draig had smashed, and even as Nathair looked down from the vantage of his high saddle he saw Veradis' shield wall splinter and break apart.

CYWEN

Cywen felt power pulsing through her body as she chanted the spell of Unmaking, desperately trying to keep her focus on the cauldron, though she was aware that Asroth had returned to the chamber and was standing before Corban. She heard their blades clash, Storm snarling, Meical shouting. A snatched glance and she saw them, and beyond was Gar, locked in a whirlwind of blows with Calidus and his Jehar Kadoshim.

I must help them.

No, the reason they fight is to buy me time, else it is all for nothing.

'*Cré agus aer, tine agus uisce, ordaímse duit anois, iarann dorcha a chur ar ceal,*' she continued, then something slammed into her body, sending her crashing to the floor. She looked up, saw Rhin striding towards her, shieldmen about her; the one that had struck her was close by.

'Kill the little bitch,' Rhin ordered with a flourish of her hand.

Cywen stood shakily and reached a hand inside her cloak as the closest warrior approached her, a handful of Rhin's shieldmen rushing in behind him.

'*Tine agus lasair,*' Cywen cried as she threw vials at the first warrior. They smashed on his leather harness, and then flame was engulfing him, the man screaming, staggering into the closest warrior; flames danced across to him as well, the stench of burning flesh abruptly redolent in the air. Both men stumbled forwards, arms slapping futilely at the flames, dropping to their knees, crashing to the ground. Other warriors surged past them, giving them a wide berth. Cywen backed away, one hand reaching for a knife hilt.

The warrior nearest to Cywen collapsed with an arrow through his eye, then a form was stepping in front of her, huge, a war-hammer in his hand.

Farrell.

He swung his hammer and caved in the skull of the first warrior, swung again at the next warrior, shattering both the shield and the arm it was strapped to. Farrell kicked him to the floor. Another man staggered backwards and collapsed, an arrow sprouting from his chest. Farrell spun in a circle, slammed his hammer into another man's chest, lifting him from the ground and hurling him through the air.

And then the rest were hesitating, spreading wider around Farrell. Rhin appeared from behind the pillar of flames that still crackled greedily. A dozen men surrounded her, more than Cywen wanted to see. Without hesitation, Farrell strode towards them. Cywen followed, a throwing knife in each hand. Her first one sank into a warrior's throat.

Rhin barked a command and the warriors around her were spreading into a line, moving on Farrell, curling around him. Swords flashed, Farrell blocking with his hammer-shaft, swinging great looping strokes to give himself space, but there were too many men. A blow landed on his shoulder, another on his hip, blood welling, and he dropped to one knee. Cywen hurled another knife but a warrior caught it on his shield. An arrow sank into a thigh, staggering a man, but more closed on Farrell. Then Coralen was there, swirling through Rhin's warriors like a violent storm, sword and wolven claws leaving trails of blood in her wake, men falling, dead before they realized it. The survivors broke and ran. Cywen hurried to Farrell, helped him stand with a grimace, and then all three of them were moving on Rhin.

Rhin backed away, pulled a knife from her belt and slashed her hand, with a flick of her wrist sent droplets of blood spattering over them.

'*Sruthán*,' Rhin snarled and the blood on Cywen's cloak and vest began to hiss and smoke, burning through wool, leather and flesh. She heard Farrell grunt with pain, even as pain bloomed on her own arm, skin sizzling.

'*Uisce*,' Cywen cried, slicing the palm of her own hand with a knife and spraying droplets of blood over herself and her companions. The burning on her arm ceased.

'After her,' Cywen cried as Rhin backed away, threading through the combat of the chamber. They followed, Cywen glimpsing Corban trading blows with Asroth, a flash of fur as Storm rolled entwined with a Kadoshim, then she saw Rhin, close to the trunk of the great tree. Cywen, Coralen and Farrell spread around her, a half-circle, Rhin pressing her back to the bark.

'Nowhere left to run,' Cywen said to her.

'You are young,' Rhin said. 'And naive. Much can change in a few moments.'

She started to chant, '*Cloch a bheith bog, fiachmhúchta bás.*'

Cywen took a step towards Rhin and found she couldn't – her feet were sinking into the stone. A rush of panic and she jerked a foot away, but the stone clung to it like honey, sticking, holding, and with her sudden shift of weight her other foot sank deeper, up to the ankle. She looked about wildly, saw the same was happening to Farrell and Coralen.

'You see,' Rhin said with a smile, 'the ground can shift under your feet very quickly if you're unprepared. And I'm *always* prepared.'

She raised her hand, mouth opening for another spell. There was the whistle of air, a *thunk*, and then Rhin was staggering back, a knife hilt protruding from her chest.

'You power-mad bitch,' Cywen said coldly. 'So much death in Ardan because of your ambition. The assassination of Uthan, Prince of Narvon, the ambush in the Darkwood, where my Ronan fell. Setting Morcant loose like a feral dog.'

Rhin swayed, leaned against the wall. Blood seeped around the knife hilt. Her hand reached up and grabbed it, a grimace of pain, and then she pulled it free, stood straight and smiled calmly.

Cywen threw another knife, but Rhin moved like a snake so it slammed into her arm instead of her chest. She staggered a step then ripped the knife free and hurled it back at Cywen.

'I'm harder to kill than I look, little girl,' she said with a sneer.

Rhin started to mutter, the air about Cywen rippling. Abruptly, Rhin stopped, staggered and fell back, a look of surprise on her face as she looked down and saw one of Dath's white-fletched arrows protruding from her belly. She plucked at it.

Another knife slammed into her chest, high, then another arrow was sprouting from her chest, throwing her back against the tree, another knife into her gut. An arrow through her throat, blood welling from all the wounds, seeping into her clothes. With a sigh she slipped slowly down the great tree, leaving a trail of blood.

The ground around Cywen's feet solidified. She stepped free of it and stood for a moment over Rhin's corpse.

'For Ronan,' she whispered.

'The spell,' Coralen said, and Cywen ran back to the cauldron, words of power forming on her lips.

VERADIS

Veradis felt the shield wall breaking before it actually happened.

He was standing a dozen rows back, had rotated his position for the first time since the shields had first locked on the field, and that was only because he could barely keep his fist clamped around his sword hilt because of a numbing cramp in the muscles of his hand. But he was worried that the shield wall would not hold without him there, in the heart of the front row, where the storm of iron was fiercest. A shield wall was made of many men, but, this day, he also knew that he had been the glue that had stopped it from collapsing a hundred times. That was no boast, and it was impossible to hold a whole line, to be at every point where a crack or fissure was forming between shields or within men's minds, but what he had done was give his men heart. He had shouted himself hoarse, praised men for every effort he witnessed, and a hundred others he'd imagined. He had mocked and taunted the enemy and bellowed encouragement to his own sword-brothers whenever he'd had breath, and he'd slain more of his enemy than he could remember.

And so they had held, for over half a day against overwhelming numbers.

But now his shield wall was dying.

He felt it like a stuttered sigh that rippled through the ranks, a death rattle before that last breath. It had followed a crash that rocked men on their feet even as far back as Veradis' twelfth row.

Veradis heard the roar of Nathair's draig, saw Nathair's outline rearing above the rim of his shield.

His draig is amongst us.

A scream from above drew his attention to the skies. A swarm of winged beings were fighting, some in dark mail with great bat-like wings, against white-winged warriors. They were twisting and turning through the air in the way that Veradis had once seen two falcons fighting over the same prey, a plump pigeon that had taken the opportunity and fled.

I hope that is not what we are to both of those sky-borne warbands. Prey.

Even as he stared at them, Veradis saw figures sweep down from above, dark-winged demons wielding sword and spear, stabbing and hacking at Veradis' men, screeching war-cries and death that chilled the blood. Veradis felt his own courage waver, and in that moment he knew his shield wall was broken.

Nathair's draig was rampaging through the remnants of Veradis' ranks, some men still holding, frozen out of fear more than anything else, the draig bellowing. Veradis saw deep wounds along its side and realized it was badly injured.

Nathair's eagle-guard were advancing, trampling over Veradis' fallen men, swords stabbing down to finish off the wounded.

'TO ME,' Veradis cried, rallying his scattered men.

Deeper in the battlefield Veradis saw groups of Vin Thalun, Jehar, white-cloaks and red-cloaks engaged in battle, beyond them great beasts rampaging across the field.

Draigs? Where did they come from? They were trampling all about them indiscriminately; as Veradis stared dumbfounded he saw one bend its neck and pick something up from the ground, then turn and lumber back towards the gates of Drassil. One followed it, one remaining. Closer, Veradis saw a large knot of giants that were pushing towards him, but here Veradis was surrounded by only the fallen or the fleeing.

Then roaring rang across the battlefield again and Veradis' head snapped back to Nathair. In horror he watched as the draig snatched a man of Ripa, its jaws clamping around the warrior's head and shoulder, lifting him from the ground, shaking him like a hound with a rat, then flinging the dying man through the air.

A hot anger filled Veradis then, and he sprinted towards Nathair, picking up speed with each step, stooping to grab a spear from a fallen red-cloak and skidding to a halt a few score paces from Nathair.

'NATHAIR!' Veradis bellowed, brandishing his spear at his former King.

Nathair's face twisted as he spotted Veradis yelling his challenge. He regarded Veradis a long, drawn-out moment, and then he bent forwards in his saddle, whispered in the draig's ear, and it was charging him.

The ground thundered, taloned feet tearing up the ground, the draig opening its huge jaws to roar, teeth like daggers, saliva dripping. Nathair leaned low in his saddle, sword arm rising. Veradis saw it all as if in slow motion, set his feet and stood his ground as the draig closed the distance at a terrifying speed – forty paces away, thirty, twenty, a deafening roar echoing from its jaws.

Veradis hefted the spear in his hands, found the balance and hurled it, straight into the draig's open maw.

The draig screamed, blood exploding from its mouth in a great gout. It thundered on towards Veradis, a spasm rippling through its body, legs failing, its momentum carrying it. Veradis leaped to the side, too late; the draig slammed into his leg, spinning him like a twig, talons raking his torso, and Veradis was flying through the air, hot pain igniting in his chest, his knee, and then the ground was slamming into him, driving the breath from his body. He tried to focus, saw the draig collapsing, ploughing into the earth, an avalanche of muscle and bone, Nathair hurled from the saddle, disappearing in the dust cloud that rose up and engulfed the draig.

CAMLIN

Camlin rode up a slope and into the trees, pausing for a moment to look back.

The battlefield was chaos, the skies filled with aerial combat, Kadoshim and Ben-Elim looping and diving, Edana and her cavalry still holding against Geraint, and further south it looked as if the shield walls had disintegrated, the field turned to a chaotic blood-soaked melee.

Are those draigs?

For a moment he thought of riding back, doing what he could to help, but then a face filled his mind.

Rafe.

Camlin had tracked him through the battlefield, lost him and found him a dozen times, always too far away to risk one of the half-dozen arrows he'd managed to snatch from corpses, and then he had seen Rafe break away from the combat, riding up the slope that marked the northern edge of the battlefield towards a wall of trees. A grey hound had been padding along beside him. Rafe had disappeared into the forest, and Camlin knew that he was fleeing.

Can't let him get away this time. If by some miracle we win this battle Edana'll never be safe, with him lurking in the shadows. And besides, he killed Baird and is responsible for Halion . . .

At the thought of his friends, Camlin felt the weight of grief shift in his belly and gritted his teeth. With a click to his horse he rode into the trees. The world turned to twilight, shades of grey dappled by the shift of leafless branches high above. He came upon an ancient road of stone slabs, moss-covered and crumbling. Fresh hoof-marks were easy to spot, and Camlin picked up his pace, his bow and reins in one hand, his other resting gently on the fletching of an arrow in his belt-quiver.

He reined in, cocking his head to one side, straining his hearing.

What's that?

A resonance on the edge of sound, a shift in the forest. His horse whinnied, ears back.

Something's not right.

Camlin swung down from his saddle and crouched on the old road, one palm flat against cold lichen and granite.

A vibration trembled into his fingertips, faint as a whisper. Stones skittered down the embankment of the road.

And then Rafe was bursting from thick foliage, his magnificent stallion powering him onto the road and straight at Camlin, sword raised high, only a dozen paces away. Somehow Camlin managed to nock and draw an arrow, still crouching, Rafe's horse almost upon him. He loosed; Rafe yanked on his reins and swayed, the arrow hissing past his head, nicking his ear, then Camlin was drawing his sword, rushing in close to the skewbald stallion, stabbing at Rafe.

Swords clashed, Rafe sweeping Camlin's strike away, a flurry of blows as Rafe tried to cave in Camlin's skull, the strength in each blow beating Camlin down, sending him staggering. He tried to get in close again, but Rafe's stallion's teeth were snapping at him, and then he was jumping away, realized he was close to his own horse and leaped at it, grabbing the saddle, trying to heave himself up.

Rafe's stallion reared, hooves lashing out, and Camlin's horse was screaming, bolting from the road, dragging Camlin a few score paces before he lost his grip and fell with a thud to the ground, cold stone slamming into his face, then he was rolling, slowly coming to a halt. He pushed himself up onto one knee, shook his head, reached for his bow but couldn't find it.

''Bout done with you putting arrows in me, old man,' Rafe said. He'd reined his horse in, was smiling at Camlin. He rolled his shoulder, grimaced at the pain of Camlin's last arrow.

How does he keep recovering from my arrows? I need to have me a drink from that starstone cup.

'Thought I didn't know you were sniffing after me,' Rafe sneered. 'I saw you. Don't think you're the huntsman you like to think you are.'

Damned if I'm going to let this snot-nosed runt be the end of me.
Camlin tried to stand but felt an explosion of pain in his knee and
his leg buckled. He heard Rafe laugh, then spur his horse on, hooves
thundering towards him.

RAFE

Rafe felt the joy of victory flood through him. Camlin lay a crumpled heap on the road ahead of him, no way of escaping his stallion's charge.

I've been looking forward to this moment a long time. And I'm about done being shot by him. Knew I had to do something about him, that I'd never get a chance at skewering Edana with him sniffing after me. Looks like my trick worked, luring him into the forest, setting an ambush.

Then figures were bursting from the trees, running up the slope to Camlin, one small, one large. The small one was a girl; he recognized her from Ardan, red hair, an oversized helm strapped to her head. The large figure was a hound, brindle-coated and broad muzzled. He knew him as well: Buddai, Thannon's old hound.

The girl grabbed hold of Camlin's arm and tugged at him, but it had little effect. Buddai set his feet protectively before the girl and Camlin and snarled at Rafe and his horse, hackles rising.

Good, I'll trample all three of them, then.

Rafe bent lower in his saddle and urged his horse faster.

'You're a rare find,' he whispered to his mount, 'more vicious than a sack of snakes.' He grinned.

Movement flitted in his peripheral vision, shadows within the trees, but he ignored them, everything about him focused on the trio in the road before him, the thought of Camlin trampled to pulp filling him with a wild bloodlust.

He saw Buddai crouch, muscles bunching, lips drawing back in a snarl, only a dozen paces separating them; the crack of his mount's hooves on stone filled Rafe's ears.

And then his stallion just . . . stopped. A straight-legged, stone-grating, skidding stop, and Rafe was suddenly airborne, flying weightless through the air, spinning over Camlin's head and crashing down to the earth with a bone-jarring thud.

For a moment he just lay on his back, looking up at patches of sky through winter-shorn branches. He heard the drum of paws and felt a surge of fear as he thought that Buddai was coming to rip his throat out, but then a rough wet tongue was licking his face and Scratcher's grey-haired muzzle was looking down at him. The rope he'd tied the hound with back in the stables was ragged and frayed. Scratcher had chewed through it and found Rafe as he left the battlefield.

The only thing that's loyal to me.

He sat up, felt fresh blood trickling from the wound on his back where he'd recently removed Camlin's last arrow. A dozen paces away his horse was standing with head dipped to Buddai, who was acting like a pup, barking and jumping up to lick the stallion's mouth, tail wagging.

You'd think they were best friends!

And then he remembered: a paddock back in Ardan, on the meadows below Dun Carreg, Gar's stallion and Thannon's mare.

That's Corban's stallion!

No matter, I'll finish them myself. An old man and a bairn, and Camlin can hardly stand.

Rafe rose and drew his sword.

And I've drunk from the starstone cup.

He strode towards Camlin, who was desperately trying to stand. The girl ran to fetch Camlin's blade. She hefted it from the road and hurled it to Camlin, who caught it and used it to lever himself upright.

'Time for you two to die,' Rafe said as the girl sped back to stand beside Camlin.

'Get out of here, Meg,' Camlin said.

The girl reached inside a pouch on her belt and hurled a stone at Rafe. He swayed, heard it whistle past his ear.

'Think I'll kill you first,' Rafe said to her, raising his sword and lunging forwards.

But then Buddai was between him and Camlin again, snarling, making Rafe stagger backwards.

'Scratcher,' Rafe commanded, his hound loping forwards, baring his teeth at Buddai. The two dogs snapped and growled at one another, and then shapes were bursting from the foliage next to the road – wolven, lots of them, padding up the embankment, circling Scratcher, snarling at him. They weren't fully grown, Rafe saw at a glance, all of them adolescents, but they were knotted with muscle and their teeth looked long and sharp. Then Buddai jumped, slamming into Scratcher, rolling with him across the road and down the embankment, the wolven following him in a mass of snapping fur and muscle.

Camlin and Meg stared after the hounds and wolven; never one to miss an opportunity, Rafe leaped at them.

Meg scurried out of his way, Camlin swinging his sword to block Rafe's swing, iron sparking, Camlin staggering back, swaying on his injured knee. Rafe followed with a succession of blows, Camlin parrying desperately, swinging back at Rafe, but the blow was feeble and Rafe slapped it away, stepped inside Camlin's guard and kicked him in the knee.

Camlin dropped to the ground, howling, and Rafe stood over him, raised his sword.

A crunch in the back of his head and Rafe stumbled forwards, stars and darkness exploding before his eyes. He twisted to see the girl reaching for another stone in her pouch.

Camlin first.

He raised his sword again, then pain ignited in his foot. He looked down to see that Camlin, still on the ground, had stabbed him with one of his arrows.

He screamed, kicked Camlin in the gut with his injured foot, not sure whom it hurt more. Camlin rolled away, coughing blood.

'Get away from him,' he heard Meg screeching, running at him with a dagger in her hand.

The creak of wood from the other direction: Camlin had found his bow on the road, was nocking and drawing an arrow. Rafe twisted away, reigniting the pain in his foot, slipped around Meg's clumsy blow and grabbed her by the throat, lifting her in front of him, grabbing her dagger and putting it to the artery that pulsed in her neck.

He was just in time, as Camlin was kneeling in the road, a drawn arrow aimed straight at Rafe.

'Let her go,' Camlin growled.

'I'll cut her throat,' Rafe said, taking a step towards Camlin.

Get close enough, use the little bitch as a shield. Kill him, kill her. Good plan.

'You shouldn't have come after me, old man,' Rafe said, taking another step.

'You killed Baird, and Halion,' Camlin grunted, spitting blood.

'Halion? I saw him jump after Conall. Good.'

The truth was that he'd not enjoyed killing Conall, but Rhin had set him that task. Conall and Edana.

Slay them both and you'll be forgiven your past failings, Rhin had whispered in his ear during their council of war the previous evening, and he knew what failing again would mean.

He took another step towards Camlin, only a few paces between them now.

Then there was the scuff of paws. Buddai and the wolven appeared, circling Rafe, hackles bristling. There was blood on their jaws, dripping from their teeth.

Rafe felt a whisper of fear, and sadness as well. Scratcher had saved him more than once, and he'd hoped for a little more help now.

And I'll miss the hound. Only friend I've got.

'Call them off,' he snapped.

'Let her go,' Camlin said.

'I'll trade you – her life for mine,' Rafe said. 'Call those blood-thirsty beasts off and I'll let her go.'

Meg slammed the back of her head into his face. He heard his nose break and staggered a step, his grip around her throat loosening a fraction and then she was twisting like an eel in his hand, slipping, jumping away from him.

Rafe stood there a moment, staring at Camlin, along the length of his arrow.

'Mercy,' Rafe whispered.

'Mercy?' Camlin said, pulling a face. 'Bollocks to that,' and he released his arrow.

Rafe opened his mouth to scream, but then the arrow punched into his chest, a short sharp pain and then something slammed into his cheek. The ground. He blinked, or at least he thought he blinked. He couldn't feel much. Nothing, in fact. He could still see, though, see Camlin's boots approaching, but even they were fading, everything fading . . .

CHAPTER ONE HUNDRED AND EIGHTEEN

CORBAN

Corban reeled and staggered. Asroth was bearing down on him like a mountain, sword trailing black smoke. Drassil's great hall was a heaving arena of war, a fight for life or death filling every part of it. Dimly Corban glimpsed Gar on the steps, crossing blades with Calidus and a handful of Jehar, above him Meical beset by Kadoshim, and beneath it all the hypnotic intonation of Cywen as she chanted Brina's spell of Unmaking. When last he'd looked, Corban had seen Coralen and Farrell desperately defending his sister from Kadoshim, though he didn't know how long ago that had been. Time seemed to change as he fought Asroth; he felt as if he'd been trading blows with the Lord of the Kadoshim for days, but it might also have been only a handful of heartbeats. Blood and sweat were stinging his eyes, countless cuts and grazes about his body where Asroth was proving faster and stronger than him, and the gap felt to be widening, each blow containing more power than Corban had ever encountered before.

Can't go on like this much longer, it's like fighting Balur One-Eye with wings.

When Asroth had first attacked him, Farrell had been at his side, and together they had held Asroth at bay, but then Kadoshim had swooped upon Cywen. Corban had yelled for Farrell to protect her, and that's where his friend was now, standing before her, hammering Kadoshim from the sky.

Corban gritted his teeth and charged at Asroth, swinging his sword, the demon leaping back, replying with an overhead strike. Corban, meeting it, shifting his weight to deflect it wide, saw it hack into flagstone, spraying chips of rock. Now Corban was spinning to chop into Asroth's waist, but a beat of his wings and he was gone, sweeping over Corban, landing behind him, slicing down at Corban's head, Corban rolling his wrist, turning Asroth's blade, falling back, off balance. Asroth's wings pulsed, air blasted Corban, rocking him backwards, and Asroth was surging forwards, swinging and hacking, chopping and stabbing, Corban beating the attack away, each blow shivering through his arms and shoulders. An arrow punched into Asroth's arm, the Kadoshim looked at it, snarling and then ripping it out. Corban took the opportunity to lunge in, cutting at Asroth's knee, raking at his wings with his wolven claws, Asroth leaping away, so that the wolven claws slashed only air, the tip of Corban's sword slicing through demon-skin and flesh, droplets of blood splattering. It was only a shallow cut, but Asroth scowled at it.

'That's the trouble with becoming flesh,' Corban said. 'Means you can bleed and die like the rest of us.'

Rage twisted Asroth's face and he came at Corban like a storm; as he did so, two more Kadoshim were swooping in, one either side of him. Corban backed away, felt the steps behind him. He breathed deep, calmed his fear, set his feet, raised his sword into stooping falcon.

'Come on, then,' Corban snarled at the Lord of the Fallen.

Corban sidestepped a spear lunge from one of the Kadoshim, a chop from his sword splintering the shaft. He saw the Kadoshim drop from the sky, one wing crumpling, an arrow through its shoulder.

Dath, you are worth your weight in gold.

Coralen ran in, hacking and slashing at the wounded Kadoshim.

A Ben-Elim swooped low, spear jabbing at Asroth, but he swayed aside, grabbed the spear shaft, dragging the Ben-Elim close and stabbing deep into the angel-warrior's neck, blood spurting, Asroth flinging the body away.

Corban lunged, deflected a blow from Asroth, spun in close and punched his wolven claws into Asroth's thigh. A bellow of pain filled the room. Corban tried to pull his claws free, but Asroth reached down and clamped a huge hand about Corban's wrist, beside him the other Kadoshim was raising his sword.

Then that Kadoshim was gone. Farrell stood in his place, his war-hammer matted with blood and bone.

Coralen turned from the fallen Kadoshim and ran at Asroth. He beat his wings, making her stumble, and backhanded her across the jaw, lifting her bodily from the ground and hurling her through the air, to crunch into the stone stairs. She didn't get back up.

'NO!' Corban screamed, tugging and wrenching against Asroth's grip, but the Kadoshim Lord beat his wings, rising from the ground. Still holding tight to Corban's wrist, he lifted him into the air, Asroth swinging his sword at Corban's head, Corban blocking, numbing pain shuddering through his wrist and up his arm, Asroth's wings pumping, carrying Corban higher.

There was a snarling growl and Corban glanced down, saw a glimpse of fur and flashing teeth: Storm running and leaping from the stairs, arcing high into the air, jaws opening wide, slamming into Asroth.

A bone-jarring crunch, and the three of them were spinning in the air, the sound of Storm snarling and slavering as her claws scrabbled for purchase, jaws locking onto Asroth's arm, tearing flesh. Another bellowed scream, Asroth releasing his grip on Corban, and suddenly Corban was falling, careening back to the ground, weightless for a few heartbeats before he slammed into the stone floor, rolling, sword skittering away. He climbed to his feet, ran and snatched his sword back up, saw Asroth plummeting to the ground, battering at Storm. The wolven's teeth tore free of Asroth's arm and she was falling, Asroth winging back up high, disappearing momentarily amidst the frenetic blur of battling Ben-Elim and Kadoshim.

Storm crunched to the ground with a whine, but leaped to her feet and searched the sky for Asroth. Corban whistled for her as he ran to Coralen's side, fear churning in his gut. She was so still.

He crouched beside her, saw that she was still breathing, her jaw bruising blue-black, a trickle of blood running down the back of her head and onto her neck. Storm reached them, sniffed Coralen and whined. She was bloody and battered, her chainmail coat slick with blood, rent and tattered in places.

The beating of wings behind him.

'Storm, guard,' Corban commanded, standing and stepping away from Coralen, looking up. Asroth was returning, a swarm of Kadoshim swirling about him, Ben-Elim sweeping in with looping attacks. Storm growled and took a pace after Corban.

'No,' Corban said, holding a palm out. 'GUARD.' Storm turned in a circle, then stood over Coralen, snarling and snapping at any who came near.

Come on, Cywen, finish your spell.

He saw her standing before the cauldron, still chanting, straining as if carrying a great weight. Dath stood one side of her, loosing arrows at any Kadoshim that flew near, and Farrell guarding her other side, bloody and battle-grim, swinging his war-hammer with savage fury. To Corban's left a mist-wraith formed in the air, screeching its wrath, beneath it Gar was still fighting Calidus, only one of his Jehar left beside him now.

You slew my mam, Calidus. Gar will not stop until you are dead or he is.

And then Asroth was hovering before him. One arm was torn and ripped bloody, and he limped as he walked, blood leaking from the wound Corban's wolven claws had made.

'The Banished Lands are not for you,' Corban yelled up at him. Kadoshim hissed back.

Meical came swooping down from above. Brandishing his sword, he sheared a wing from one Kadoshim and crashed into another, the two of them spiralling into a dive, skimming the ground and then looping high.

'You're more trouble than I thought, Bright Star,' Asroth growled, alighting a score of paces before Corban, 'but now you'll die, all the same.'

Corban didn't bother replying, just ran at him.

Kadoshim flew at him and he ducked one's sword swing, spun around another's spear, slicing into its neck, stabbed up at another, piercing its belly, blood spraying, raining down on him. More rushed to bar his way to Asroth, but he was unstoppable, felt time slow around him as he felt the battle-joy come upon him. Dimly he was aware of Ben-Elim swooping on Asroth's guard from all angles, saw Meical swirl in front of his vision, decapitating one Kadoshim in Corban's path, dragging another into the air, and then Asroth was before Corban.

Their swords clashed, an explosion of sparks and smoke, Corban swirling around him, moving from one attack to the next, a combination of blows that struck at Asroth from all angles, stabbing, chopping, lunging, blood welling as Corban scored red lines across the pale landscape of Asroth's flesh.

Asroth retaliated with a ferocity born of pride that only a king can muster, striking at Corban with blows that chipped stone and smashed rock, and slowly Corban began to tire. Asroth beat him back until his heels touched the hall's steps again, then slowly he began to retreat up them. Sweat and blood blurred Corban's vision, his arm a leaden weight. A red line opened up across his thigh, another down his forearm, and Asroth grinned at him, blue-black lips stretching.

Halfway towards the chamber's open doorway Corban stopped, setting his feet on a wide step, and for long moments they traded blows there, then Asroth gave a great beat of his wings, rocking Corban backwards. The Lord of the Kadoshim was suddenly airborne, slicing down at Corban as he swept over him. Corban, too slow in his counter, saved his head but took a wound to his shoulder, feeling as if a line of fire had ignited in his muscle.

Asroth landed on the steps above Corban, his sword crashing into Corban's, sweeping it wide, and he kicked Corban in the chest, hurling him down the stairs, Asroth gliding after him.

Corban rolled down a dozen steps and finally came to a halt. He heard someone cry his name, reached blindly for his sword but he couldn't find it, then a weight was stamping onto his wrist, crushing it. Asroth's boot.

'Time to cross the bridge of swords,' Asroth said, raising his sword.

Corban tugged and heaved at his trapped arm, but he was held fast.

Asroth's sword sped towards him.

Then a figure was there, iron flashing, sparks incandescent. A man was standing over Corban, taking the full weight of Asroth's blow and holding it.

Gar.

He rolled his wrists, sending Asroth's blade slicing into thin air, and twisted his hips, sword flashing, a horizontal cut that sent Asroth reeling, a red line pouring blood across his forehead. Asroth cried out, staggered backwards, and then something crashed into him, an explosion of white feathers – Meical was sweeping in, the two of them rolling, tumbling, snarling, rising into the air, still twisting and turning.

'Give me your hand, Ban,' Gar said, reaching an arm down to Corban.

'Gladly,' Corban muttered, wincing from what felt like a thousand wounds as he struggled to rise.

Then a sword-point burst through Gar's chest, his blood exploding over Corban. Corban staggered to one knee, saw the sword ripped back and out of Gar's torso as Calidus appeared behind him. Gar's sword dropped from his hands and he stood there a moment, swaying, staring at Corban. Blood welled from his mouth and he sighed, falling forwards, into Corban's arms.

MAQUIN

Maquin wiped blood and sweat from his face, pausing to look around. The dead were heaped about him, a trail behind, a Kadoshim demon croaking a death rattle on the ground at his feet. With Lykos' death accomplished, he had returned to the battle feeling reborn, all of life's cares and demands stripped away. He felt *pure*. A white flame burned within him, fed by and yearning for the death of his enemies. And so he had walked through the battlefield like an angel of death, men falling before him as wheat before the reaper.

He paused now to look around, not even knowing where exactly on the battlefield he was, and as he looked, the enormity and tragedy of it all sank into him. He was standing roughly in the centre of the field, and the dead were everywhere. Piles of them heaped together or spread about like scattered seed: men, women, horses, giants, so many of them, and all just meat and bones now. To the south Maquin saw a sea of warriors, mostly on foot, with islands of open plain amongst them; the south-western fringe right up to the treeline was more densely packed with combat. Black and silver dominated the southern half of the field, though no longer in the shield wall formations that Maquin had seen earlier: men were scattered, fighting, some fleeing. Vin Thalun were thick on the field as well, but there were others, a solid knot of giants further away, the flash of red-cloaks, some white-cloaks, still. A draig.

Nathair's draig? It can't be, no saddle or harness, and no Nathair.

And then he saw two other draigs, their backs to him, lumbering through the gates of Drassil and disappearing within the fortress.

On Maquin's left and filling most of the northern field were a thick press of horses, where mounted combat was furious and savage between grey-cloaked warriors and those in black and gold. Edana's warband looked to be encircled and pushed back towards the western fringe of the battleground, their backs to the treeline.

Maquin looked between the shield wall of eagle-guard and Rhin's warband and saw that Edana was beaten, no matter how valiantly she and her men fought, and it didn't look as if there would be any help from the south, which told a tale of the enemy in greater numbers, though at a glance battle seemed more evenly balanced amongst them.

Maquin looked up to the skies and saw a sight that on any other day would have taken his breath away.

It was thick with Kadoshim and Ben-Elim, another battlefield in the sky.

Hordes of dark- and white-winged warriors fought and died in the air, bodies crashing from above to wreak ruin upon the battlefield, blood raining down, limbs, feathers, as Ben-Elim and Kadoshim swirled and swooped and stabbed and hacked at one another.

We are beaten. There is no victory against this host. But there is still a song to be made.

The need to kill was heavy upon him, knife and sword twitching in his fists, but he took a moment to decide where. His eyes touched upon a knot of red-cloaks to the south, beset by Vin Thalun and eagle-guard.

'Tahir,' he breathed.

My Gadrai sword-brother, one of the few people who still draws breath in these Banished Lands whom I would call friend. If he still stands.

He walked south.

The battleground was fluid here, unlike in the crush to the north. Battle ebbed and flowed, warriors fighting, fleeing, dying. Maquin stepped over a decapitated giant, past a Ben-Elim and Kadoshim that fought upon the ground, both of their wings tattered ruins.

Maquin found Tahir alone atop a small mound, half a dozen Vin Thalun surrounding him. Before they knew Maquin was there, two of them were down, lifeblood soaking into the mud. Another struck at Maquin, but his blow was swept wide and he died on Maquin's sword. Tahir grinned at Maquin and hacked a hand from one as Maquin hamstrung another, stamping on his throat and crushing his windpipe as he fell. The last Vin Thalun stumbled back, realizing who Maquin was, then turned and fled, screaming 'OLD WOLF,' as he ran.

'Well met, my brother,' Maquin said to Tahir as they embraced, both slick with blood.

'It's good to see you,' Tahir grinned, 'even if the sight of you may well give me nightmares for the rest of my life.'

Maquin smiled, a strange feeling.

'The battle is most likely lost,' Maquin said flatly. 'You should find Haelan and leave.'

Tahir didn't reply, but instead was staring towards the southern part of the field.

A draig was lumbering across the battleground, focused on something in front of it, crushing and hurling and trampling anyone who stood in its way.

'What's it after?' Maquin said, but then he saw it too. A small figure, sprinting and weaving through the combat, a high-pitched shriek coming from him.

'Haelan,' Tahir said. 'That draig's after Haelan.' Then he was off and running, shouldering men out of his way, hurtling across the battlefield. Maquin followed, had seen on Tahir's face an emotion he knew all too well: the need to fulfil your oath, the fear of failing it.

Tahir ran fast, angled to head off Haelan, but Maquin could see he was not going to reach the boy before the draig did. He picked up his pace and changed his angle, sheathing his short sword as he ran and drawing another knife.

A Vin Thalun appeared in front of him, disappeared just as quickly, blood spurting from his throat. Maquin charged on, Vin Thalun scrambling to get out of his way now, and then he was twenty paces from the onrushing draig, ten, five, and he was leaping, flying through the air, crashing into the draig's side, punching his knives into it, through leathery scale and into the flesh below. He swung there a moment, legs dangling, the draig roaring, slowing, head twisting upon its thick neck, teeth snapping at him, but it couldn't reach him. He caught a glimpse of Tahir bending low to sweep Haelan into his arms heartbeats before the draig thundered by, and then Maquin was climbing up the draig, using his knives as a climber uses hand-holds, pulling one out and stabbing higher, then the same with the other knife, on and upwards, leaving a trail of leaking wounds until he was sitting on the draig's back, legs clamped around its neck and shoulders, stabbing a bloody frenzy. The draig skidded to a halt, turf exploding in fountains about its taloned claws, and then it was spinning and rearing as it attempted to dislodge, rip and tear Maquin.

Maquin stabbed and stabbed and stabbed, saw a glint of bone, and then the draig was rearing up onto its hind legs, crashing backwards. Maquin pushed away, leaped into the air, but something clamped around his leg, the draig's jaws snatching him back, dragging him to the ground with bone-slamming force.

The pressure on his leg disappeared, waves of pain pulsing up it as he lay on his back, gasping for breath, staring up at grey clouds and the silhouettes of winged creatures. Dimly he heard the draig roar, glimpsed it flailing on the ground as it slowly righted itself.

Get up and kill it.

He tried to stand, his leg numb. With a grunt, he managed to turn over and push himself onto one knee. Hot shafts of pain lanced up his leg, taking his breath away.

Numb is better.

He looked down at his damaged leg, saw it was a mass of puncture wounds, flesh torn, shattered bone sticking out above his knee. His vision swam and he fought the urge to vomit.

The draig approached him, head swaying, lopsided, blood running down the creases of its neck, pooling on the ground.

Think my knives have done some damage.

It opened its mouth and roared, blood and spittle spraying Maquin, then the draig stumbled forwards.

Maquin tried to move, pushing off the ground with one hand and one leg, his other hand finding a knife hilt, then the draig's jaws were clamping about his torso, teeth like daggers piercing him. It lifted him into the air and shook him like a hound with a rat, the world fading around him. Maquin heard the crackle of bones breaking, felt things inside tearing, his energy draining.

The sound of shouting filtered through the ringing in Maquin's ears and he saw blurred images of men stabbing at the draig with spears. Then the world came back into focus. He was still in the draig's jaws, the beast swaying, men all around.

Maquin tried to move, coughed blood and realized he couldn't feel his legs. But he could feel his fist, and the knife hilt within it. He looked along the muzzle of the draig, straight into its soulless eye, and then, with the last strength in his body, he lifted his knife and buried it in the draig's eye, stabbing through the soft jelly, deep into its brain, right to the hilt.

The draig spasmed, a ripple of jerks triggering along its torso and limbs, and then its legs were folding and it crashed to the ground, tail twitching, Maquin rolling from its lifeless jaws.

He heard more than he saw, though even sounds were distant, as if through water. And he felt cold, an icy numbness working its way inwards, through his limbs and into his torso, his chest, behind his eyes.

Hands gripped him and he realized he was being turned, faces appearing over him: Tahir, a young lad beside him, red-haired and freckle-faced.

Kastell? Is that Kastell? No, it's Haelan, but he looks so like Kastell.

Tahir was saying something, his mouth moving, and tears were falling from his eyes. Maquin tried to smile, to tell him it was all right. That he was happy to die. To let go. To find peace. He opened his mouth, felt his lips moving; Tahir was bending low, then the darkness was filling his vision, Tahir's face fading, fading . . .

Maquin was standing before a bridge of stone. About and behind him, the world was slate grey, but on the far side of the bridge a mist rolled, golden and hazy, like summer memories.

He took a step onto the bridge, realized he had a sword in his hand and, looking down, he saw countless blades set within the stone, some still keen-edged, others notched and rusted. He walked on, eyes fixed upon the golden mist.

At the centre of the bridge a man stood. No, not a man, a Ben-Elim, white-feathered wings spanning the bridge. As Maquin drew nearer the Ben-Elim furled his wings and stepped out of Maquin's way, giving him a single nod of respect.

Maquin walked past him, carried on towards the mist, saw shadows within it, figures. One stepped out: a woman, dark-haired, beautiful. She was smiling at him.

He felt his mouth stretch in a smile and with a clatter let his sword drop from his hand. It sank into the bridge, became a part of it. Maquin didn't notice; he was too busy running.

CORBAN

Corban held Gar in his arms. Blood was pulsing from the wound in Gar's torso, soaking through his shirt and mail, breath a stuttering, blood-speckled whisper on his lips. Slowly Gar's legs gave way and he slumped to the ground, Corban lowering him gently. Tears blurred Corban's eyes as he crouched with his mentor and greatest friend. He knew there was no coming back from a wound like that.

'Hold on,' Corban whispered, his voice cracking. Gar's head came up, trying to say something, Corban lowered his ear.

'Calidus,' Gar breathed.

Corban looked up, saw the Kadoshim coming at him and threw himself backwards to avoid a swing that would have taken his head, feeling pain exploding in his shoulder from Asroth's blow, and a hundred other places. Corban rolled to his feet, saw Calidus stepping over Gar's body.

He saw his sword on the ground, snatched it up and raised it, trying to control the grief and hatred that was boiling within him.

A Ben-Elim swept down from above, sword slashing at Calidus. The Kadoshim ducked, swinging his own sword, missing, the Ben-Elim reaching out and grabbing a fistful of Calidus' mail shirt, heaving him into the air with powerful beats of his wings, Calidus was twisting in his grip, trying to bring his sword to bear. Higher and higher.

Corban ran after them, tracking Calidus as he was carried higher, weaving amongst Ben-Elim and Kadoshim.

'CORBAN,' voices shouted, and Corban turned, saw Cywen, Farrell and Dath yelling, beckoning to him. He gave a last look to Calidus' disappearing figure.

'Kill him,' he whispered to the Ben-Elim, then turned and ran back, stooping to check Gar, who was ashen pale, the shallowest of breaths within his chest. With a grimace, Corban hurried to Cywen, not wanting to leave Gar, but knowing the destruction of the Treasures was what they had all risked their lives for this day. He would not betray Gar by abandoning that quest now. Cywen was standing before the cauldron. When she saw him coming, she threw a vial into its belly, saw it flickering with dark light. Sweat was pouring from her head, her body stooped.

'I need more,' Cywen said.

'More what?' Corban asked.

'The blood of an enemy,' she gasped.

Corban remembered Calidus heaving Brina and Laith into the cauldron. He signalled to Farrell, and together they grabbed a Kadoshim corpse from the ground and heaved it up and into the cauldron, its body slipping between the Ben-Elim that still poured through.

'*Fuil ar mo namhaid, cumhacht chun mo focail, seoda ó deannaigh ar ais go dtí anois deannaigh,*' Cywen cried, raising her arms, and behind them the other Treasures hummed with power.

'Now,' Cywen shouted, 'throw the Treasures in.'

Corban turned and ran, swerving across the dais, the dozen paces to the spear seeming far greater, Kadoshim and Ben-Elim everywhere, Dath and Farrell either side of him. A Kadoshim swooped down at him, blade raised, and their swords rang out, Corban ducking as he slashed high, cut through chainmail. Blood gushed down onto him, the Kadoshim crashed to the stone.

Then he was standing before the spear and snatched it up, the necklace, too, saw Dath grab the torc and cup and Farrell hefting the axe and running for the dagger, then Corban was sprinting back to Cywen.

A burst of wings slammed down before him: Meical and Asroth, still fighting, one side of Asroth's face slick and matted with blood, one of Meical's wings hanging limp. They rolled on the ground, snarling, spitting, cursing one another, blades clashing.

Corban swerved around them, heard Cywen screaming at him, yelling for him to bring her the spear and necklace. Dath and Farrell were already throwing their Treasures into the cauldron's maw.

Corban ran as Asroth rolled on top of Meical, raked his face with his taloned fingers and clamped his fist around Meical's throat; Meical was trying to rise.

Corban reached Cywen.

'Throw them in throw them in throw them in,' she cried, muttering her chant. A tear of blood leaked from one of her eyes.

Corban hurled the spear and necklace into the cauldron.

The cauldron swelled, rippling, expanding, in and out as if it were breathing, but with each breath it grew larger, and it began to glow, heat rippling out in waves, bubbles appearing in the iron.

'RUN,' Cywen yelled, and they all did, hurling themselves away from the cauldron, past Asroth and Meical, who were still struggling together, Asroth beating his wings, trying to fly away, Meical hauling him back down, hands reaching for the Kadoshim's throat. Dath was first off the dais. A Kadoshim was flying overhead, and Corban yelled a warning as the Kadoshim stabbed down with his spear. Dath twisted and the spear pierced his back instead of his neck. Corban surged forwards and grabbed Dath, lifting him, Dath groaning, lolling in his arms as Corban ran on. He glanced back, saw Cywen stumble and Farrell swept her up and threw her over his shoulder. Behind them the cauldron was swelling impossibly huge, bloated, and then there was a booming crack, all light was sucked into the cauldron, and for a pulsing heartbeat the chamber was drenched in utter darkness, then a burst of white light, blinding, a concussive explosion of air that hurled Corban from his feet, and molten liquid was fountaining out from the cauldron, glowing hot, incandescent, raining down upon the dais, upon Asroth and Meical, screams, a great hiss and a cloud of expanding steam engulfing the room. Corban climbed to his feet, lifted Dath, who seemed to be unconscious now, and tried to find Gar in the murk. He heard Storm growling and snapping and made his way to her. He found her with a pile of Kadoshim corpses heaped about her which she had slain while standing over Coralen.

He lay Dath down, felt his pulse, ripping cloth to bind the wound, then checked Coralen. She was still unconscious, but groaned a little when he moved her.

And then the cloud of steam was melting away. Corban saw Farrell and Cywen lying on the ground, knocked flat by the blast. Upon the dais the cauldron was gone, the other Treasures vanished with it. The Gateway to the Otherworld was closed; no longer was a flood of Ben-Elim or Kadoshim pouring into the room. And upon the dais still were Asroth and Meical, Asroth standing with wings unfurled, spread wide, Meical gripping him, pulling him back, the two of them locked together in snarling combat, frozen, captured forever within a cooling skin of iron.

VERADIS

Veradis staggered to his feet, grimacing with pain. His leather cuirass was a tattered ruin, great rents in it from the talons of Nathair's draig, and pain pulsed up his left leg. He put his hand to his chest, fingers coming away sticky with blood.

I still live.

He rolled his shoulders and drew his short sword.

I can still fight. That's all I need to know right now.

He limped towards the carcass of Nathair's draig. The beast looked smaller in death, a stain of dark blood pooled about its head. The dust cloud of its ruin had settled, and he searched for Nathair. About him knots of warriors fought, eagle-guard against his men of Ripa, Jehar against Vin Thalun and Kadoshim, angels and demons in the skies above, but Veradis ignored them all.

Must find Nathair.

He remembered Nathair being hurled from his saddle, thrown through the air, and he searched the ground.

He's not here.

A scuffle of earth behind Veradis and he was turning, raising his sword in an automatic block, and Nathair was there, swinging his longsword at Veradis' head. Iron sparked as Veradis swept the blow wide, Nathair surging forwards, his eyes wild, a flurry of blows. Veradis' leg slowed him and Nathair was striking his shoulder, staggering him, sending Veradis stumbling backwards, tripping over a dead warrior.

Nathair stood over him, nostrils flaring, sword rising, and Veradis kicked out, caught Nathair's leg, sent him tumbling to the ground.

They both rose unsteadily.

'You made the wrong choice,' Nathair snarled. 'This battle's won.'

'My choice had nothing to do with victory or defeat,' Veradis said. 'But right and wrong.'

Nathair lunged at him, Veradis stepping in to meet the blow. Instinct took over then, Veradis' body moving before he had time for conscious thought, and slowly, inexorably, he pushed Nathair back, across the battlefield, Nathair's defence becoming ever more ragged. A barrage of blows sent Nathair reeling, a cut to his forearm and his sword fell to the ground. Veradis drew his arm back for the finishing blow, sword-tip ready to stab through Nathair's throat, and Veradis . . . stopped.

The two of them stood there with battle raging about them, Nathair gasping for breath, eyes blazing at Veradis with a mixture of rage and fear, Veradis standing with feet set, sword-tip hovering, the muscles in his arm tense, trembling, as if caught and straining against some invisible grip.

I can't do it. No matter what he's done, who he's become, he was my friend once, and my King. I swore an oath to him.

Nathair burst into motion, knocking Veradis' sword wide, stepping in and headbutting him in the face, stars bursting in Veradis' vision.

'TO ME,' Nathair was yelling. Veradis shook his head, but figures were appearing about him: eagle-guard, four, five of them, more. Veradis slashed one across the throat, blooded another's arm, but blows were raining from all directions.

'Don't kill him,' Nathair shouted as a blow struck Veradis' shoulders, clubbing him to his knees, and then hands were grabbing him, holding him, and Nathair was standing before him, glaring down at him.

'You have betrayed me,' Nathair said, his expression shifting from anger to something more akin to grief. 'How did it ever come to this? We were blood-brothers. We were going to save the world.'

'You deceived me, deceived us all,' Veradis said.

'It was . . . for the greater good,' Nathair whispered.

'No,' Veradis said. 'I think you may mean, for *your* greater good.'

'You are right,' Nathair said, 'we have wronged each other. But of our two betrayals, yours is the greater.' Nathair stared around the battlefield, expression changing again, becoming cold, angry. 'You chose this rabble over me! I am King of Tenebral, High King of the Banished Lands, and you think a blacksmith's son more worthy than me!' He looked almost apoplectic with rage, eyes bulging. 'I would have made things right, given time,' Nathair ranted. 'Calidus, Lykos, Rhin, when the victory was won and I was emperor—'

'You were never going to be emperor,' Veradis said. 'Surely you realize that. Calidus was using you. Once this battle was won, he would have cast you aside.'

'NO,' Nathair cried. 'I was going to . . . deal with him.'

'Yet more betrayal?'

'Veradis, you once said you would leave the politicking to me. You win battles. I win thrones. Some things are hard to understand when you are too close, but afterwards, you would have seen that I was right.'

'You killed your father,' Veradis whispered.

Nathair stared at him, mouth open, about to say something but the words were gone or frozen in his throat.

'Keep your twisted vindications to yourself,' Veradis said. 'You killed your father. You opened his throat with your own knife, then stabbed yourself with the same blade to avoid implication. You are not the Bright Star. Maybe you could have been, once, if you'd chosen differently, but from that moment on you were the Black Sun.'

Nathair's face twisted, emotions flitting across it. Shame, grief, pride, rage. With a snarl he drew his sword back.

Behind Veradis there was a thud, a scream. Blood sprayed one side of Veradis' face, and a severed arm fell to the ground. Then all was chaos, Veradis throwing himself forwards, rolling away from Nathair, grabbing his short sword as he rose on unsteady legs.

Alcyon was standing close by, with eagle-guard attacking him – what was left of them. Even as Veradis stared, Alcyon's whirling axes took a head from its shoulders, blood fountaining, and then Veradis was rushing to his aid, stabbing an eagle-guard in the throat, trading blows with another, while Nathair circled Alcyon.

The last eagle-guard fell. Alcyon turned on Nathair, axes rising, Nathair cowering before the giant.

'NO!' Veradis cried.

Alcyon's twin axes hovered in the air.

And then something was happening around them. Veradis saw men, women, giants staring to the north.

Veradis looked too; even Alcyon turned to stare, Nathair frozen. All were gazing beyond the northern fringe of the battlefield, where the ground sloped up to the forest.

The trees were shaking.

And the ground was trembling, a vibration that Veradis felt rumbling up through the soles of his boots.

Shadows within the trees were moving, a shifting in the gloom all along the ridge of the slope. Figures emerged from the murk. Huge figures, of muscle and fur, of tooth and claw, of amber eyes and red jaws. Huge mail-clad bears. And upon their backs, giants, wrapped in leather, iron and fur, hair braided for war, battle-axes and war-hammers glinting in the fading sun. Hundreds of giants, stretching in a long line across the ridge, more shapes shifting behind them.

The might of the Jotun, and they had come for battle and blood and war.

A hush rippled across the battlefield as more and more stopped in the midst of their combat and stared, and there was a moment, one solitary, perfect moment, Veradis was sure, when all were silent upon the battlefield of Drassil, both above and below.

Veradis saw a giant at the centre of the line, war-hammer in his fists, blond hair a thick braid curling down one shoulder, moustache braided too. Beside him was a giantess, a longsword in her hand. Veradis recognized her.

The giant that gave Corban Storm's chainmail. Sig, Corban called her.

As Veradis watched, the blond giant's bear shambled forwards a few paces, and the giant surveyed the field.

He gave a shouted command as his bear lumbered onwards, Sig lifting a horn to her lips and blowing, echoed by other giants all along the ridge, and then hundreds of bears were lurching after him, a long line flowing out of the forest, over the ridge and onto the slope. They picked up speed, the bears breaking into a thunderous charge, and now Veradis was sure the earth was trembling.

'The Jotun have come,' Alcyon breathed.

The bears charging down the slope were bellowing and roaring as they came, a great wave of muscle and fur and fang surging towards the battlefield, the ground quaking beneath them, and then they were slamming into Rhin's warband of black and gold, men and horses heaved into the air at the first impact, others, crushed, cut and hammered down by axe and hammer, bitten and torn and trampled beneath a tide of the Jotun and their great bears, the line carving deeper and deeper into the battlefield, men and horses screaming and scrambling in their desperation to get away.

The giants' charge began to slow and Veradis saw the line bowing, bending back at either end, slowed at first by the crush of bodies as much as by any resistance, though resistance did start to build, for Veradis knew that Geraint, battlechief of Rhin, was no coward; nor was he a stranger to battle and war. Geraint sounded his horns, brandished his banners, rallied his men and led them against the Jotun.

Like a man waking from sleep, battle broke out across the field again, a stuttering ripple as all about Veradis warriors blinked, stared at their opponents and lifted their weapons. The roar of battle surged all around Veradis, the coming of the Jotun sparking new levels of ferocity.

Veradis looked to Alcyon, saw him still gazing at the Jotun, a look of awe upon his face. Nathair moved, slipping behind Alcyon. Veradis saw it as if in slow motion, Nathair's muscles bunching in his legs and arm as he drew back his sword and then stabbed forwards. Veradis leaped into motion, a yell of warning forming on his lips, but Nathair's sword was plunging into Alcyon's back, slicing through fur and leather, deep into his flesh, Alcyon crying out, arms flailing, and then the giant's legs were buckling and he was collapsing, Nathair ripping his sword free, a twisted smile upon his face, turning to meet Veradis, swinging his sword high, chopping down at Veradis' head.

Veradis caught Nathair's sword arm by the wrist, a grip of iron holding it above their heads, and he stabbed Nathair, sword-point punching through leather and chainmail beneath, into Nathair's belly, deeper.

Nathair grunted, looked into Veradis' eyes a long, shocked moment and slowly slumped forwards, his head falling upon Veradis' shoulder as if in an embrace. Then with a gasp his legs gave way and he was falling, slipping off Veradis' blade and slumping to the ground. Veradis stood and stared, blood dripping from his sword, vision blurred by his tears.

CORBAN

Corban stared at Meical and Asroth, both of them sealed in a case of black iron, or whatever it was that had spewed out from the cauldron as a result of the Seven Treasures' destruction. They looked like two magnificent statues created by a master smith, every detail and proportion exquisite in its perfection. And the iron still steamed, beneath its darkening rime a glow of molten metal.

Corban's ears were still ringing from the blast, though part of him was aware that it was deathly silent in the great chamber, Kadoshim and Ben-Elim staring in stupefied shock. Some of them moved; a Ben-Elim flew over the flood of molten iron that had slicked the floor and stairs of the dais, hovering close, tentatively reaching out a hand. Fingertips sizzled and hissed as he touched Asroth's wing, a gasp of pain.

Then a screech from a Kadoshim high in the chamber, a pulse of wings as one of the dark-winged demons flew at the figures, fast as an arrow, straight at Asroth. It smashed into the Lord of the Fallen and was hurled away in an explosion of sparks, its wings igniting, hissing as flame licked at them, eating away a portion of leathery skin before the Kadoshim's crash and tumble across the flagstones put out the flames. The Kadoshim rose, one wing half-burned, the skin on its shoulder and arm bubbling from where it had been scorched.

Asroth was unmarked.

He is imprisoned, if he still lives.

The other Kadoshim in the room, hundreds of them, must have thought the same thing, for all of a sudden they burst into motion, realization dawning, fear spreading.

Their King had fallen.

Kadoshim fled the chamber like a swarming nest of hornets, swirling upwards, seething through the two great holes in the roof, others beating their wings and flying through the main doors, and everywhere they went, the Ben-Elim went too, hacking and stabbing and slicing at them, sending Kadoshim tumbling through the air to crash around Corban and Storm. One Kadoshim tried to rise but Storm pounced upon it and shook it as if it were a rat.

Corban ran to Cywen and Farrell, both of them were unmoving. He lifted Cywen gently and she stirred and opened her eyes. Dark tears of blood had stained her cheeks, deep into the skin.

'You did it,' Corban said, stroking her cheek.

'Did I?' She blinked. 'Well, there's a surprise.' She smiled.

Corban carried her to where Storm stood over Coralen and Dath, ignoring the few Kadoshim and Ben-Elim that still fought in the chamber, and set her gently down, then he ran back to Farrell, the big man groaning, swaying as Corban helped him stand; he had blood seeping from a wound on his head, his eyes unfocused.

A Kadoshim swooped close to them, Corban and Storm stood ready, but it flew past, hurled itself into a Ben-Elim.

'Gar?' Cywen whispered, taking Corban's hand.

Corban bowed his head, felt the grief rising, a physical pain in his chest like a fist clenching around his heart. He tried to speak, but words wouldn't come.

'Where?' Cywen asked him.

Corban turned to point, not trusting his voice, and froze. He saw Gar's body upon the steps that rose in wide tiers towards the chamber's open doorway, but it was the figures beyond Gar that he was staring at. A Ben-Elim, wings tattered and useless, fighting another man, tall, slim, his face and head burned and puckered.

'Calidus,' Cywen whispered.

Calidus.

Corban drew his sword, felt a twinge from the wound in his shoulder and took a step forwards. Cywen grabbed his hand, tried to rise.

'No,' Corban said. 'Tend our friends. He's mine.'

'Take Storm,' Cywen said.

'She must stay and protect you all,' he said, looking at the prostrate forms of his loved ones, ordering Storm to maintain her guard.

He gritted his teeth and turned away, felt his hatred of Calidus giving him new energy as it bubbled through his veins.

'For Mam,' Cywen said behind him.

'Aye. For Mam. For Gar. For Brina. For Laith,' Corban whispered.

For all those that Calidus put on spikes in Drassil's courtyard. From the beginning he has been the puppet-master behind all of this. Behind Nathair. He is responsible for Da's death too, and so many more.

'For everyone,' he said.

'Bring me his head,' Cywen snarled as he stalked away.

He felt a fire ignite within him then. A cold flame, wrath and vengeance mixed, and he began to run.

Calidus fought back and forth across the steps, with a savage twist of his wrist, he sent the Ben-Elim's sword spinning through the air, then lunged, skewering him through the heart. He kicked the Ben-Elim to the ground, then turned and stared at Asroth, his frozen King.

Then he saw Corban.

Indecision flickered across the Kadoshim's face. He glanced over his shoulder towards the fading light that poured through the chamber's open doorway, looked as if he was thinking about running. He must have decided against it, for he turned to face Corban, set his feet and raised his sword.

Corban's hatred of this man, this *creature*, boiled up within him, overflowing in a wordless battle-cry that burst from his lips. He vaulted up the steps, leaping over Gar, still screaming, sword held high, gripped two-handed, smashing at Calidus. The Kadoshim blocked, staggering under the power of the blow, retreating as Corban struck again and again and again, wolven claws raking across Calidus' face, sword shattering a line through chainmail links. A thousand thousand hours of sword dance and sparring, of muscles stretched and pushed and fibres ingrained with forms and combinations and lunges and parries, of sweat and pain, determination and discipline, all were coming out in a few dozen heartbeats as Corban hammered at this creature before him, man, demon, the author of so much evil. Wrapped around all, screaming into his mind, was Gar – a man who had been his friend, his teacher, both brother and father to him . . .

Rage coursed through Corban, putting greater strength into his blows, more speed, and Calidus struggled; every other blow of Corban's was landing, Calidus was battered, cut, retreating, Corban powering after him, the rage growing, building, an incandescent fury surging through his veins and limbs until he felt he must glow with the purity of it. Until he felt he did not control his own body.

And he saw something in Calidus' eyes, a hint of gloating pride.

No. He is luring me, ensnaring me in my rage.

And he remembered Gar's first lesson to him.

Control your anger, for if it controls you it will surely see you slain.

And slowly Corban reined his anger in, like a runaway stallion, harnessing the power, giving it coalescing focus, directing it all at the death of this thing before him, Calidus. He saw something flash across the Kadoshim's face: frustration, a frown of disappointment?

'Your death is coming,' Corban snarled at him.

And then the real sword dance between them began.

Back and forth they fought, across the steps, the clash of their blades echoing, Corban drawing on all that he had learned, from Gar, from Halion, from Coralen, from both giants and men, entering that place where his body led him, reacting before conscious thought could have moved him, striking or lunging as opportunities flashed into existence, and Calidus blocked and parried everything, counter-striking, launching into blistering combinations, short lunges, sweeps and chops, drawing upon forms that Corban knew like his own skin, and others he'd never seen before. He had crossed blades with Calidus before, in the giant fortress of Murias. That time Calidus had beaten him and slain his mam, Corban had only been saved by Meical.

But I am a different man now.

He is good. A master, but he has been here a long time, a hundred years, Meical told me, planning and plotting, and learning sword-craft as well, it would seem.

It will not save him.

Corban struck Calidus half a dozen times, blows that would have turned a fight against a normal man, blows that would have let blood flow, brought pain and weakness, but against Calidus they had little impact, no telling effect.

Veradis had told Corban how he'd put a knife in Calidus' belly, thrown him into a fire, and Alcyon had hit him so hard with a war-hammer that his body had smashed stone, and yet he'd walked out of the flames, pulled the knife from his belly and brushed the splintered rock from his clothes.

He is not like these new Kadoshim, his true self become flesh. He lives in a host body, like the possessed Jehar.

I have to take his head.

And he remembered how Gar had spoken of fatigue coming upon him as he fought Ildaer, Warlord of the Jotun, a warrior whose stamina could last for a moon, and how the onset of that fatigue had nearly defeated Gar.

And I have to take it soon.

But as he fought Calidus he saw no opening, no weakness, no tell or repeating pattern of blows or combinations that might give him the edge he needed.

'*Deatach a chónaisceann,*' Calidus muttered, and opened his mouth wide, the same black smoke that had bound Corban and his companions issuing from his throat. Corban felt a rush of fear, but it was different this time: a breeze was tugging at it, fraying it even as it tried to wrap around Corban. It had no more effect than morning mist.

The Treasures, Corban realized. *He told Rhin they were making him stronger, so if they are gone, destroyed, then perhaps his powers are weaker now.*

Calidus didn't look happy about the fact.

'Your death is coming,' Corban whispered again.

There was a sudden flapping sound and wings and feathers fell upon them; Craf was descending on Calidus, scratching and pecking, ripping at his face. Calidus reeled back, lashing out. He caught Craf a solid blow with his hand, sending Craf spinning and squawking through the air. He crunched into a step and fell, flapped feebly and then was still. At the same time Corban swung with all his might, but Calidus swayed back, Corban's sword-point scoring half-a-thumb deep into Calidus' throat. Blood welled and dripped, but his head stayed firmly upon his shoulders.

'You'll have to do better than that,' Calidus said, his voice different, a ragged croak now.

Corban answered with a combination that sent Calidus reeling, tripping over a step, staggering and leaping out of range. His hand reached inside his cloak, pulled out a fold of fabric. He retreated a few more steps, Corban following. Calidus opened the fabric with deft fingers, revealing . . .

A flower.

A purple thistle.

And Corban knew it, felt something snatch in his gut, as if a fish-hook were in his belly.

The flower I left upon Mam's cairn.

Calidus smiled at him, seeing the recognition dawning in Corban's face.

'A lovely gesture,' Calidus said. 'I have her head somewhere.'

Corban flew at Calidus, an explosion – beating, hammering at his enemy. He saw the Kadoshim stumbling, bowed, barely able to meet Corban's blistering speed and strength. A sound filled Corban's ears, swamping his whole world. He slowly realized it was his own screaming, and then a quiet voice within his head, a whisper.

Gar's voice.

Anger is the enemy.

And then he heard Gar whisper something else to him.

Corban saw a smile twitch Calidus' lips as he flourished the purple flower at him, knew what the Kadoshim was doing, but it felt impossible to control his rage, to do anything other than unleash his wrath and fury. He feinted a blow at Calidus' belly, knew instantly that it was rushed, then slashed high, but his timing was a fraction out and the twist of his feet left his right side open a moment. He realized his error, began to shift his feet, and then something slammed into him, like a punch, a red-hot pain, lancing into him, through leather and chainmail, into flesh, above his hip. Calidus' sword was stabbing deeper, Calidus snarling a feral smile as he rammed his blade harder, punching in through Corban's belly and out through his lower back.

Distantly Corban heard someone screaming.

Corban and Calidus stood like that for a long, frozen moment, Corban staring down incredulously at the sword that had run him through, blood seeping into his mail shirt, a widening stain, then he looked up to Calidus' arrogant smile.

And then Corban reached out and wrapped his wolven-clawed fist around Calidus' hand.

'Sometimes,' Corban grunted, pulling himself up towards Calidus, along the length of the Kadoshim's sword, grimacing with both pain and rage, 'you have to take a wound to give a wound.'

And with all his might, a world of pain exploding in his gut, Corban swung his sword and cut Calidus' head from his shoulders.

CORALEN

Coralen opened her eyes.

She found she was lying on her back, a thumping pain at the base of her skull, another in her jaw, staring up at the domed roof of Drassil's great hall. Kadoshim and Ben-Elim wheeled and circled, though the Kadoshim were few.

'It's all right,' a voice was saying. 'Just lie still a while.'

She shifted her head and saw Cywen looking at her with an expression of great concern, and standing with one leg over her was Storm, her chainmail coat hanging in tatters, her belly vibrating with a deep rumbling growl as she tracked Kadoshim in the air above them. The wolven looked down at Coralen, her muzzle thick with crusted blood. She bent her neck and licked Coralen's face, then went back to growling at the sky.

Coralen looked from side to side, saw Cywen kneeling above her, Dath one side of her, unconscious, Farrell the other, groaning and trying to sit up. Cywen pushed none too gently on his chest.

'Slowly,' Cywen said.

'Where's Ban?' Coralen asked as she pushed herself upright so that she was sitting. The world spun, and she fought the urge to vomit. She put a hand tentatively to the back of her head and found a lump the size of an egg.

Storm looked towards the chamber's doors and started whining. Coralen looked, too, and saw high up on the tiered steps two figures silhouetted by the pale light of the open doorway. They were fighting, the most ferocious sword-crossing Coralen had ever seen.

She felt her breath catch in her chest.

657

One of them was Ban, she knew without doubt by the way he moved, elegance and strength merged.

Who is he fighting?

Then Storm was leaping away, a growl rippling from her belly.

Coralen pushed herself to her feet, felt a wave of dizziness, let it pass and stumbled after Storm. Behind her she heard Farrell grunting as he tried to rise again, Cywen swearing at him.

Coralen stumbled up the first steps that led to the doorway, swayed and nearly fell, had to pause and close her eyes.

Behind her she heard Cywen scream and her eyes snapped open, vision blurred, squinting, trying to focus on Corban.

For a moment what she saw made no sense. The two men, warriors in leather and mail, were standing close together. One was Corban, she knew, and the other one had no head.

Black mist poured from the headless man's neck, forming into the now-familiar wings and red eyes of a Kadoshim.

Calidus. It must be him. And Ban's killed him.

She felt a fierce pride in Corban, respect and love mingled.

But Cywen was still screaming, and she heard Farrell rise and call out, heard him come staggering behind her.

Why is Cywen screaming?

And where's Gar?

She started to move, a stumbling walk, breaking into a stumbling run.

The cloud of the mist-wraith was shredding now, disappearing, and the two figures fell to the ground.

Fear snatched at Coralen's heart.

No, not Ban, no, no, no.

Storm reached the two fallen figures. She started nudging Corban with her muzzle, whining, nudged him again, licking his face and hands.

Then she stood, raised her head to the heavens and howled.

Coralen ran to Corban, saw that a figure splayed a few steps below him was Gar. He lay in a pool of dark blood, face pale as milk, blood crusting on his lips and chin. His eyes tracked her, though.

Corban was sprawled upon a wide step, Calidus' headless corpse beside him, and a sword was sticking from Corban's body, low, between his ribcage and right hip.

Coralen threw herself down to him. His eyes were closed. Desperately she felt for a pulse, two fingers at his neck.

Nothing.

No.

His wrist.

Please, dear Elyon, let him live, let him live, let him live.

Nothing. No pulse. No breath from his mouth or nose.

Please.

She lifted his head, stroking him, willing breath into his body, hoping, praying, begging that his chest would rise and fall, but nothing happened.

He's gone.

She lay across his body and wept, behind her the sound of Storm's howl filling the chamber.

There was a thud close by, Farrell dropping to his knees beside her. He was weeping, too.

'I'm your shieldman, supposed to guard your back, supposed to keep you safe . . .' He was sobbing, his whole body shaking.

Coralen sat up, cuffed her tears and crawled to Gar, only a few paces away.

Gar tried to lift his head. He had a wound high in his chest, Coralen suspected a blade had pierced him through, as blood was pooling out from beneath his back. His mouth moved, bubbles of blood on his lips, and she knew that was never a good sign.

'Ban?' he said, his voice a wet croak.

Coralen sat beside him, wiped the blood and grime from his face and lips. She shook her head.

Gar groaned, squeezed his eyes shut, tears leaking from them. He flopped over, managed to get one elbow under him, attempting to drag himself to Corban. Coralen tried to help him. Farrell came and between them they lifted Gar and carried him to Corban's side.

'Ah, my Ban,' Gar breathed, lying beside Corban, looking at him. He took Corban's hand, and Coralen put her hand upon both of theirs. She could hardly see them for her tears.

She sat there a while, stroking Corban's face.

His beautiful, beautiful face.

She looked up, not knowing how much time had passed, but it couldn't have been long, for the sun still filtered through the open doorway behind her. Storm was lying beside Corban, her muzzle pressed in tight to his head. She was whining quietly.

She thought Gar was dead, he was so still and pale, but when she lifted her head his eyes fluttered open. More blood was upon his lips.

Coralen saw Cywen and Dath climbing the steps to them, Dath with an arm around Cywen's shoulder.

Behind her there was a squawk, a frail flapping.

'*Help Craf,*' the crow cawed.

Farrell did, hurrying to find Craf on the stairs. He brought the crow back to them, one of the bird's wings was hanging at the wrong angle. He broke out into mournful squawking when he saw Corban and Gar, and demanded to be placed upon Corban's chest, where he immediately lay down and started cawing softly.

Coralen looked about the chamber, saw Asroth frozen in black iron, many Ben-Elim still within the chamber, but only dead Kadoshim.

The battle's won, Coralen realized. *In here, at least. Asroth defeated, Rhin and Calidus slain, vengeance had. But I'd trade it all to have Ban back. Why did we not run, after Gramm's hold? Just leave, as Ban suggested, and make a new home, a new life?* She looked for Cywen and Dath, knew they must be close, now, but she couldn't see them for the tears in her eyes.

CORBAN

Corban kicked Calidus in the belly, doubling the Kadoshim up, punched him on the temple, dropping him to one knee, then kicked him in the head, sending him arching back into the air, high, to slam to the grey-cloaked ground. Calidus lay there, his breath ragged, a groan escaping his lips. He flapped his leather-dark wings, but to no obvious effect.

They were in the Otherworld, and Corban was finishing what he'd started in the world of flesh. They were in a valley with steep-sided cliffs, a flowing river of deep blue beside them, the grass growing green.

This is where I first came. When I saw Meical speak to the Ben-Elim. This river leads to a lake.

He shuddered as he remembered his last visit here, and his encounter with the creature that lived within the waters there.

'Get up,' he said to the Kadoshim now, striding over and kicking him in the ribs, lifting Calidus off the ground. Corban felt a pain in his belly, low, above his hip, but it was a dull, muted pain, one that he could ignore.

'No, stop,' Calidus spluttered as Corban followed him and kicked him again. Corban didn't stop. He dragged Calidus to his feet and punched him in the gut, hauled him back up by his braid-bound hair, silver even in this eternal world, though his features were more reptilian here, a scaly quality to his skin. And he had wings.

'What are you doing here?' Calidus said, a line of spittle dripping from his mouth as he pulled away, stumbling back.

Corban strode after him, drawing the sword at his hip. He looked at it a moment, saw that it was still the sword his da had made him, wolven-pommelled, though it was different here, burning with a cold fire. Calidus held a hand out.

'I'm going to finish what I began on Drassil's steps,' Corban said. 'I'm going to kill you.'

Calidus choked back a laugh. 'You can't,' he hissed.

'Watch me,' Corban snarled and chopped at Calidus two-handed. His sword sheared through Calidus, from collarbone to hip, but as Corban's sword passed through his body the wound healed up, became a raw, inflamed scar, like the wound upon Calidus' neck.

Calidus screamed and collapsed writhing upon the ground, but still smiled up at Corban with bloody teeth.

'What I mean,' Calidus said, gasping, 'is that it is virtually impossible to destroy a soul. Wounds that would cause death in your world do not have the same effect here . . . We could do this for an eternity.' He looked up at Corban. 'You've won. Asroth is imprisoned. Our plans lie in ruins, our hosts vanquished. Is that not enough for you?'

'No, it's not,' Corban growled and raised his sword again, but it hovered at its apex. As much as Calidus deserved an eternity of pain, Corban was not one for torture. A painful death, yes. But torture . . . ?

Then he had a thought.

He reached down and grabbed Calidus by a leathery wing and began to drag him across the grass until they reached the lake with the red-leaved tree beside it.

'What are we doing here?' Calidus said, a new edge of fear creeping into his voice.

Corban put a hand to his mouth and shouted.

'VIATHUN,' he yelled, and waited.

'What?' Calidus said, the fear in his voice rising a level. 'What are you doing? Not hi—'

Corban punched Calidus in the gut again, dropping him to his knees.

The waters of the lake bubbled and boiled, and a figure appeared: a man, wrapped in a black flowing cloak. He rose out of the lake, visible to the waist, and began to speed towards them, as if the water were carrying him on a great wave. He stepped onto the lakeshore and approached them, oil-dark hair, his skin grey-mottled and dark-veined, cloak swirling around him like a living thing.

Corban remembered it well, and hoped that he wasn't making a mistake.

Viathun stopped a score of paces before them and looked first at Calidus, upon his knees, and then up at Corban.

'Welcome back,' Viathun said. 'A surprise.'

'Aye. For me, too,' Corban said. 'I am hoping that this visit will be more mutually beneficial than the last one.'

'Well, the Ben-Elim tried to poke me full of holes last time, so that shouldn't be hard.'

'Aye, and you tried to eat my soul,' Corban said.

'We all have our appetites.' Viathun shrugged.

'Are you hungry now?' Corban asked.

Calidus whimpered, tried to flap away, but Corban held his wings tight.

'Always,' Viathun grinned, revealing the tips of very sharp teeth.

'Well, here you are, then,' Corban said, hurling Calidus forwards, 'though I don't imagine he tastes very nice.'

'Oh, you'd be surprised,' Viathun replied.

Calidus tried to run, but he was weak and feeble, and Viathun's cloak was viper-fast, oily tendrils whipping out and wrapping around Calidus' ankles and wrists, around his throat, coiling and flexing tight.

'What do you want in return?' Viathun asked.

'I want to go home,' Corban said. 'Back to my body in the world of flesh.'

'That's a trifle,' Viathun said, 'not a fair trade, really.'

'Well, then let's say you owe me.'

Viathun grinned then, his mouth suddenly too big for his face, teeth long and sharp and glistening.

'We have a pact,' Viathun said.

'You can still stop this,' Calidus said. 'Please, I can help you. You and I, we could achieve great things together, Corban, PLEASE.' The last word was screamed, as Viathun's cloak began to drag Calidus down the lakeshore.

'This is called justice,' Corban said to him, face hard as stone. He turned and began walking away.

'You pathetic excuse for a man, you have not won here, you can never win,' Calidus spat after him. 'Your mother screamed when I killed her, do you remember the blood on her lips?'

'I do,' Corban whispered, and carried on walking. He heard Viathun whispering words as he dragged Calidus into the lake, Calidus' screaming rising in pitch, the sound of water splashing, cascading, Calidus' yells becoming a choking splutter as the Otherworld faded around Corban.

Corban took a great, shuddering breath, feeling as if his lungs had been emptied of all air. Pain throbbed in his torso, above his hip, an explosion with every breath. And people were all around him.

I was stabbed in the belly.

There was a weight upon his chest, but as he sucked in lungfuls of air, gasping as if he'd just sprinted a league, he felt the weight move, a fluttering of feathers in his face, and Craf was squawking joyfully. And a rough tongue was licking his ear, his cheek, Storm making snuffling noises. She bounded away, spun in a circle, making people jump and shout, and leaped back, resumed licking his face. Corban tried to sit up.

The first face he saw was Coralen's. She was smiling at him, such a beautiful smile, it made his heart feel it had melted to mist.

There were tears on her cheeks.

'You're crying,' he said, though it came out a croaked whisper.

'Well, you were dead,' she answered, and started kissing him.

Voices rang out, other faces drifting into focus, all standing around him in a great circle. He glimpsed Balur One-Eye, Edana, a Ben-Elim with its white-feathered wings furled. Again he tried to move but pain stopped him. He felt pressures upon him, one of them around his wound, knew that Calidus had put a sword through him, which couldn't be good. He was surprised to see the sword was still there, though, hilt and some of the blade standing proud of his torso. Cywen was there, crouching beside him, her cheeks still bloodstained, though there seemed to be more tears now. She'd cut away his clothes around the wound and she was looking at him with an expression somewhere between incredulity and joy. She reached out a hand and stroked his cheek.

'I'm glad you're back,' she said, 'I don't think I could have managed without you.'

Corban put a hand over hers, smiled weakly at her. Then he tried to grab Calidus' sword and take it out. He didn't like seeing it there, sticking out of his body.

'No,' Cywen said, 'leave it there until I get you to the hospice. You'll lose too much blood.'

There was a gasping noise and Corban saw Farrell kneeling beside him. One side of Farrell's face was covered with blood, and he was weeping uncontrollably. He was saying things, but Corban wasn't sure if they were words as they were coming out in a spluttering torrent, and behind Farrell Corban saw Dath, leaning on Kulla. His old friend was smiling at him – no, grinning, wide enough to split his face, tears streaming down his cheek.

'Knew you wouldn't leave us like that,' Dath said.

And then Corban remembered it all.

'Gar?' he wheezed.

'He's here,' Coralen said, and Corban realized what the other pressure on his body was.

Gar was lying beside him, his head propped against Corban. And he was so very pale, looking at Corban with dark eyes. For a moment Corban thought he was dead, but then Gar blinked, and Corban saw the movement of his chest, shallow, breaths far apart.

'I've been . . . waiting for you,' Gar said, a whisper.

Corban made to move his hand, realized that Gar was already holding it. Corban squeezed it.

'I saw you,' Gar said quietly, 'take a wound, to give one.' His lips moved, and Corban saw he was smiling, no, laughing. A wet cough, and blood sprinkled his lips.

'I had a good teacher,' Corban said, smiling too.

'Things to say,' Gar whispered, 'need to say.'

Corban felt a knot of fear and anguish draw tight in his belly.

'Say them later, when we're both . . . healed,' Corban rasped.

Gar just looked at him, into his eyes.

'I love you, Ban,' Gar said, the words coming out a wet whisper, but there was strength in his grip as he squeezed Corban's hand. 'You are the son I never had, and no son could have made me prouder.'

Tears filled Corban's eyes. 'I love you, Gar, as my da, my brother, my greatest friend,' Corban whispered.

Gar's grip on his hand tightened, then slackened.

'Don't go,' Corban whispered, Gar's face a blur through his tears. 'Please, Gar, don't go.'

But he already had.

VERADIS

Veradis stood on the plain of Drassil, looking at two cairns, side by side. The field was full of them.

Three nights had passed since the battle of Drassil.

The greatest battle of our lifetime, and an end to war, I hope, Veradis thought.

Nathair was buried beneath one of the cairns, Krelis beneath the other. When Veradis had heard that Krelis had fallen in battle he had collapsed to his knees and wept. Of all people, his eldest brother had seemed indestructible to him, always larger than life, the natural leader that drew men to him with his smile, his common sense, his goodness and justice.

And now he's gone.

'This world will be an emptier place without you, my brother,' Veradis said, a tear running down his cheek. He kissed his fingertips and brushed them across the cold stone of Krelis' cairn. Then he turned to the other.

Nathair. He stood and thought about him a while, remembered their first meeting, during the interrogation of a Vin Thalun prisoner in Jerolin's dungeons.

Even from that moment Calidus was manipulating us.

Veradis drew his short sword at his side, ran a finger over the worn, sweat-stained leather of its hilt, finding a familiar lump, smooth, a curved shape set into the hilt.

A draig's tooth.

Nathair had given them out to all those who had stood in the shield wall against a charge of giants and draigs, or those who had ridden out with him against them.

You are my Draig's Teeth, Nathair had said.

And we had been proud to bear that name. So long ago.

A silent shadow passed over him, of great wings, the outline of a Ben-Elim as it flew silently across the sun.

The world is a different place, now.

He looked down at his short sword, the blade that had seen him through so many battles, taken the lives of so many. Giants, men, kings.

Nathair.

The memory of plunging his blade into Nathair's belly haunted him, that long moment as Nathair had looked into his eyes, disbelieving.

He stabbed Alcyon. And Veradis' reaction had been automatic, unthinking. His face twisted in a grimace and he sighed, raised the sword and slammed it into the earth before Nathair's cairn, making the wounds across his chest throb, the stitches pulling tight. He left his sword quivering in the ground, turned and walked away, a dozen black-and-silver-clad warriors falling in behind him.

He felt melancholy. He was used to the highs and lows that often followed battle – euphoria followed by a dark mood – but never like this. Perhaps because this time there was a void in his life. Before, he had always been moving on to the next task, the next engagement or battle. But now there were no more battles to be fought.

Because we've won. And I am feeling bleak, more so than ever before.

What am I going to do now?

I need to speak to Alben.

They marched back to Drassil, past a great bonfire of corpses, the Kadoshim piled high, now nothing more than a stinking pile of ash and charred bone. Smoke still rose from it in a breeze-torn column. Further off, Veradis glimpsed the carcass of Nathair's draig, crows thick upon it, picking it clean. And all over the plain there were rows of cairns, the battlefield of a few days ago now a field of the dead, so still compared to the storm of violence that had been unleashed upon it. A few men, women and bairns wandered the field, standing at cairns as he had just done, leaving a sprig of flowers, grieving the loss of loved ones. He saw Alben standing before one and thought to go and join him, then he realized whose cairn he stood before.

Maquin and Fidele's.

Alben had returned after the battle had ended, upon a boat with Fidele's body wrapped in linen. Veradis had heard how Maquin died, saving the young King of Isiltir and slaying a draig. Another friend that his heart grieved for.

Alben was standing with his head bowed, lost in thought; Veradis chose not to disturb him.

There is someone else I need to see.

Veradis strode through Drassil's gates. As he passed through the wide streets he saw such an array of disparate peoples as to make him smile at the strangeness of it. Giants. Jehar. Men of Ardan and Domhain, men of Isiltir and Helveth, of Carnutan and even the eagle-guard of Tenebral. And Ben-Elim, who were everywhere, their shadows flitting across the ground as they patrolled the skies, or walking through Drassil's streets, their wings furled.

That's a sight it will take me a while to get used to.

The day after the battle the prisoners had been gathered up – the ones that were left, or could still stand and talk – and brought before the leaders of this strange alliance, and a representative of the Ben-Elim had come as well, for they were allies too.

The prisoners had been given their freedom, and a choice.

Freedom to leave, to go back to their lands, their homes and families, or freedom to stay. To continue to serve. The vast majority of them were warriors, men and women following the orders of their lords, and they had become caught up in a war beyond their understanding.

Most had chosen to stay. Some had left the following day, using the roads built by Jael or Lothar to take them home, and Veradis understood that. But many, most, had just resumed their positions within the warbands of their realm, which was why there were eagle-guard mixed into Veradis' honour guard, marching alongside the men of Ripa. Even Caesus was there, his broken hand splinted.

The only people who weren't offered the option of freedom, who had been gathered up together, bound at the wrists and taken to a place of holding were the Vin Thalun. Reapers and reavers, they had done too much in this war of sorrows, committed too many atrocities. So they would be escorted back to Tenebral, put aboard ships and commanded never to return to the continent of the Banished Lands again.

Now Veradis saw the building he was marching to, the one he had first seen on a dark night, a bonfire blazing in the courtyard as Vin Thalun had begun to burn a witch.

It was a different place now; people mingled in the courtyard, giants laughing with men, the entrance doors thrown wide. A great brindle hound lay along the borders of a herb garden, a wolven cub tugging at its ears, and other cubs lazed around or played in the winter's sun. The hospice was heaving with activity: rows of beds full, men, women and giants in various states of injury, from amputated limbs to stitches to fevers, as well as those for whom nothing could be done, who were just waiting for death's final breath upon their neck, and people sat with them, trying to ease their passing with seed of the poppy, a mopped brow, a squeezed hand, a gentle word.

A small section of the hospice seemed to be dedicated to just one bed, with what looked to be a host of people around it. And animals.

Storm was sitting at the bottom of the bed, Craf the crow upon the bedpost, and Veradis saw Coralen, Farrell, Dath, Kulla, Akar, Balur One-Eye and Varan, Lord of the Jotun, even Haelan, the young King of Isiltir.

Now there's a brave lad. A little foolhardy, perhaps, luring three wild draigs from their lair, but his plan worked. Without those beasts trampling the eagle-guard reinforcements the battle could have turned out very differently. Isiltir's in good hands with him as King. He may be young to become King of Isiltir, but he'll have Tahir at his side.

Cywen was there, too, hovering over her brother.

Corban had been grievously injured, if half of what Veradis had been told was true, but from here Corban looked to be recovering well, sitting up in his cot and smiling. As Veradis looked at the small warband gathered around Corban's bed a thought struck him, simple in its clarity.

There it is, the difference between the Bright Star and the Black Sun, right there. Who stands at Nathair's cairn and mourns? And yet Corban is surrounded, not by those who serve or fear him, but by those who love him. Even a scruffy old crow. That tells a tale far clearer than a prophecy scrawled upon parchment. I am glad that I met him, that I discovered the truth before it was too late.

As he stood there, looking over at Corban and his companions,

Cywen turned away from the bed and saw him. There were red streaks down her face, but she did not look the worse for it. She stood there a moment, returning his gaze, and he felt something shift inside, as if something fluttered within his belly. It was not unlike fear, though pleasanter. And then she was shooing people away from Corban's bed, and he was looking elsewhere, feeling a flush of heat around his neck.

He made his way through the hospice and found who he was looking for. He stood over a large cot, and looked down on Alcyon. The giant was looking remarkably well, considering he'd been stabbed in the back only three days gone, and Nathair's blade had cut deep.

Alcyon smiled at Veradis and sat up, gesturing to a chair that sat empty.

'Raina and Tain?' Veradis asked.

'They are off finding food to bring me,' Alcyon said, 'I have a rare hunger upon me.'

'I am pleased to see you looking so well, and feeling so hungry,' Veradis said.

'Aye, well, I think the Ben-Elim are to be thanked for that,' Alcyon said. 'They are skilled healers as well as schemers and death-dealers, it seems. Corban was on the brink of death two days ago, and today he is sitting up and laughing.'

'As are you,' Veradis said.

'I feel as strong as a draig! And hungry as one,' Alcyon grinned.

'You are altogether a different person,' Veradis observed, thinking of the grim-faced silent sentinel that Alcyon had once been.

'Well, life is good, little man. Many good things have happened. Although many bad, too. I am sorry about your brother,' he said. 'I liked him.'

Veradis grunted, not trusting his voice to words, the grief too raw.

Alcyon studied Veradis and his expression turned sombre.

'He forced your hand,' Alcyon said. 'You had no choice.'

Veradis looked down at his hands. At the scar on his palm. The hands that had killed his King. Guilt whispered in his ear.

'There is always a choice,' Veradis whispered, words that he had spoken to Nathair, not so long ago.

'Aye. You could have let Nathair kill me,' Alcyon shrugged. 'I am glad you did not. Although this puts me in your debt twice over.'

Veradis snorted a laugh. 'I know you are right,' he said, 'but sometimes . . .'

'Let it go,' Alcyon said. 'Nathair was your curse, and now you are free of him.'

'Am I?' Veradis said. 'I see it in my dreams. My sword stabbing into him, the expression in his eyes . . .'

'Patience, True-Heart,' Alcyon said. 'Time is a healer.'

'Why do you call me that?' Veradis asked him.

'Because it is who you are.'

'I was not true to Nathair,' Veradis said, a murmur. 'I abandoned him, left him with Calidus. And now he is dead.'

'Your heart is true, Veradis. That is what I mean. You did remain true. True to yourself. Nathair was ever desperate for power and glory, and he tried to turn you onto his path, to drag you along it with him. A dark path, but you did not follow him. That took strength, here and here.' Alcyon poked Veradis in the head and the chest, and none too gently.

Veradis found it hard to listen to such kind words, as his opinion of himself was not so high, but he looked at Alcyon and saw genuine concern in the giant's eyes.

'Thank you,' he said.

'For what?' Alcyon frowned.

'For being a friend. I have learned that good ones are few and far between, and your friendship is something I value.'

'You are welcome, Veradis, and I, too, value your friendship,' Alcyon said solemnly. 'We will be friends for life. I know this.' He smiled, something Veradis was finally becoming accustomed to.

'Now, something else troubles you,' Alcyon said.

Veradis thought about denying it, shrugging it off, but this was Alcyon, and they had been through too much together for Veradis to lie to him.

'Aye,' he grunted. 'I feel lost, Alcyon. The battle is done, the *war* is done, and now I do not know what to do.' He paused a moment, emotion threatening to engulf him.

'You have lost much, my friend. Your kin, your King, your friends. The past threatens to overwhelm you. But life goes on.' Alcyon shrugged. 'And there is much to do. We must rebuild, try and make the future better than the past.'

'Aye,' Veradis smiled ruefully. 'I am just tired.'

'Try running all the way to Arcona, and rowing all the way back,' Alcyon grumbled, 'then I will allow you to talk to me of tired.'

Veradis laughed at that, the first real laugh for as long as he could remember.

'And I have heard a rumour about you,' Alcyon said, whispering now. 'That you are to be King of Tenebral.'

'What!' Veradis spluttered. 'Who said such a thing?'

'Alben,' Alcyon said with a shrug. 'It is not such a bad idea. I think you would make a fine king. But only if you want to be. There is always a choice.'

Veradis looked at Alcyon, shaking his head as the giant laughed.

CAMLIN

Camlin shivered and pulled his cloak tighter as he walked through the streets of Drassil. Meg strutted beside him, still wearing her too-big helmet. She also had a long dagger hanging from a belt at her waist, which looked about the size and scale of a sword upon her.

'Not sure you need that, now,' Camlin said, nodding at the dagger.

'Course I do!' Meg said. 'Kulla says there's Kadoshim about, still roaming the land. Can't just be good with a bow or a sling, you know.' She patted a bag of stones and a leather sling hanging from her belt. 'Kulla says most people end up needing to use a sword at least once in their lives. It's the ones that actually know *how* to use a sword that live to tell the tale.'

Kulla said this, Kulla said that.

Mind you, to be honest, the lass is probably right. But Meg's only nine summers old.

Camlin was walking with one arm curled up to his waist, and upon it a big black crow was perched, leaning into the fur of his cloak.

'*Craf cold*,' the crow muttered and, without thinking, Camlin tucked his cloak over the bird's splinted wing.

What am I doing!

'How did I even get roped into this?' he muttered to himself. 'Taking a crow for a walk.'

'*Camlin kind*,' Craf cawed.

He shook his head.

I'm a fool, nursemaiding a crow. Two days I've been doing this. If the lads from the Darkwood saw me now.

He realized he was stroking Craf's head as he thought that.

'I've been thinking,' Meg said as they strolled into a courtyard with a huge half-fallen oak tree at its centre, its roots torn from the ground and dangling in the air like great hanging vines.

'Uh-oh,' Camlin replied. 'Thought I smelt something burning.'

Meg kicked him in the shin, good-naturedly.

'Let's sit,' Meg said and they walked to the shattered tree, Camlin eyeing the outline of a filled hole. Balur and a handful of giants had shovelled earth and rock into it, but Camlin was still suspicious of it.

This is where Haelan led the draigs into Drassil, and where two of them left with their egg.

They sat on the stump, Meg's feet dangling, and Camlin set Craf down carefully on the trunk of the tree.

'When are we going home?' Meg asked him once they were settled.

'Ahh, now there's a question, and a good one it is, too. I'm waiting on Edana for that one. She's a queen, and a good, strong one at that, and she's got work to do here before she goes.'

'What work, though? I don't understand. I thought we'd won and could just go home, but the battle is near a ten-night gone, now. What's she waiting for?'

'She has to make sure that all that fighting, and all the lives given – well, that they weren't given in vain. She's doing what she can to make sure that the peace we've fought for lasts.'

Meg nodded at that, thoughtful.

'That's what I thought,' she said eventually.

She was quiet a while longer. Camlin watched Craf sharpen his talons on bark and groom his feathers with his beak. One of his wings was bound with a splint and bandage.

Poor thing, Camlin thought. *And he's been down about Brina and Corban.*

Camlin saw a worm wriggling in the earth and pulled it out, tossing it in the air to Craf, who swallowed it with a snap of his beak.

'*Thank you,*' the bird muttered.

'And when we get home,' Meg continued, 'what happens then?'

Camlin rubbed his chin. He'd been thinking a lot about that one, himself.

The honest answer was that he didn't really know.

Not sure what use an old brigand like me would be, now.

He looked down at Meg, saw a little wrinkle of worry in her brow.

'Whatever happens, I've been thinking I'm going to need me an apprentice. Someone that can track, that's good with a bow, a spear, a sword . . .'

Meg started to smile, a mischievous twist of her lips.

'So I'm thinking of putting the word out, seeing if anyone wants a trial . . . Ouch,' he said, as Meg kicked him in the shin again, with a lot more conviction this time.

'You want the job, then?' Camlin said, laughing and rubbing his leg.

'I do,' Meg replied. 'Think I'm just the one for it. The *only* one.'

'Well, I'll give you a trial run, then.'

She pulled a face at him.

Footsteps sounded and Camlin looked up to see Edana striding towards him, wrapped in a grey cloak, fur-trimmed in ermine. She still wore her shirt of mail, but it had been cleaned of blood and grime and polished with sand. It gleamed as she walked. Brogan No-Neck walked one side of her, Vonn the other, though he was pale, still, a pinched look to his face.

Pain will do that, and he has lost a hand.

Bandages were wrapped around the stump of Vonn's wrist. His hand had been mangled during the battle, fingers lost, bones shattered, an irreparable wound. Cywen and the others at the hospice had tried to save the hand but rot had set in and the only way to save his arm, and maybe his life, was to take his hand.

'There you are,' Edana said to Camlin. 'I've been looking all over for you.'

Camlin felt a knife-twist of grief in his gut as they approached. It still seemed strange to see Edana without Halion at her side – her first-sword, a constant guardian.

Most likely won't ever get used to it.

Conall, on the other hand, had survived. Rafe's blow had wounded but not killed, and Halion's sacrifice had saved Conall's life. He had spent most of the last ten-night in the hospice, but had shuffled out yesterday. Camlin had seen him only briefly, but he looked like a different man, broken-hearted.

Camlin rose and bowed as Edana drew near. Not a perfect bow, but for a Darkwood brigand Camlin thought it wasn't too bad.

'Two things,' Edana said. 'Firstly, I have a message for you, Craf. Cywen says that she wants to see you at the hospice. Apparently she has been telling you for the last two days that your wing should be good for you to fly, now, and so she needs to take off your splint.'

'What?' Camlin blurted.

Craf looked about as guilty as it was possible for a crow to look.

'So I've been carrying you around for two days when you could have been flying,' Camlin said.

Craf looked the other way, as if he'd heard something more interesting elsewhere.

'Why, Craf?' Camlin asked him sternly. 'Why have you done this to me?'

'*Because then it will be, Craf fly here, Craf fly there. Craf tired.*'

'You are more cunning than a weasel,' Camlin said, shaking his head.

'*Sorry,*' Craf muttered, though he didn't look sorry.

Camlin looked up to see everyone laughing, even Vonn.

'If any one of you ever tells another soul about this . . .'

More laughter. Even Craf started laughing, a croaking stutter.

I'm never going to live this down.

'You said two things, my Queen?' Camlin said to Edana, trying to change the subject.

'Yes. I almost forgot. I need you with me. We've a meeting to attend, and I'm almost late.'

'And you want me to come with you?'

'Well, of course. Since when does a queen not attend a council with her counsellor?'

'Counsellor? Me? Sure you'd not be better off with Craf in that role?'

'He's got a point,' Vonn and No-Neck said together. More laughter.

'Craf is more than welcome to come, but, yes, I am quite content that you are my counsellor, though you are much more than that.' Edana laughed at the face he pulled. Not embarrassed this time, just surprised.

Counsellor. Well, there's a turn-up.

'Well, I don't really know what to think of that, my Queen.'

Edana frowned a little, then, staring harder at him. 'You're not thinking of leaving me, are you, Camlin?'

Camlin opened his mouth to answer, but wasn't quite sure what to say.

'He thought you didn't need him no more,' Meg said. 'Didn't think you'd have much use for the likes of him.'

Camlin scowled at Meg.

Thanks, you little traitor, you.

'Camlin, are you mad?' Edana gasped. 'I will *always* have need of you. You're not just a talented bowman, Camlin. You've guided me across realms, through mountain and forest, hill and vale, saved my life more times than I can remember.'

'Aye, but you're not on the run any more, and I doubt you ever will be again.'

'Well, I hope not, but who knows what the future holds? Regardless, I will always want you by my side, or close enough to call, at least. Your talents are many. You are a gem, Camlin.' She smiled at him. 'Just in need of a little polishing, that is all. And above and beyond all that, you are my friend, whom I trust, and that is rarer than gold.'

Never in all my long life has anyone said such a thing to me. Just goes to show — sometimes it takes someone else to bring out the best in a man.

'So will you accompany me to the great chamber, to discuss the future of the Banished Lands with Ben-Elim, giants, other kings, queens, lords and ladies?'

'I will,' Camlin said, a broad smile upon his face. 'My Queen.'

CORBAN

Corban stood before a cairn, alone amidst an ocean of similar slate-grey islands. Even Storm kept her distance, a prowling guardian, somehow knowing that he was doing a solitary thing. The clouds were bloated, a light rain falling, and wind tugged at Corban's bearskin cloak. He was dressed in his war gear, his shirt of mail, the links shattered by Calidus' sword thrust repaired, his wolven-head torc around his neck, arm-ring tight about his bicep, and Coralen had rewoven his warrior braid, thick, as the giants wore them.

'I miss you, Gar,' he said to the cairn. 'So very much. I see you, every day, in the corner of my eye, just for a moment, calling me to the sword dance, teaching me, watching over me, guarding my back, as you did all my life. All my life. And I hear your voice, a whisper in my ear. Your last words to me in Drassil's hall. And I can still feel your hand in mine, squeezing.' He was crying now, the tears flowing freely. 'I will earn your sacrifice, I swear it, friend of friends. Every day. And I shall never forget you. I am going to build a legacy that you and Brina would be proud of. Your skill of arms. Brina's healing art. Of your love, friendship, courage and loyalty. The gifts you've given me will never be forgotten.'

He took out a slip of linen from his cloak then, and unfolded it. Lifted a purple flower to his lips, kissed it, and then placed the flower upon Gar's cairn.

One more lingering moment as he turned, looking at the field of the dead. Faces swam before his face: Halion, Krelis, Wulf, Javed, Maquin, so many, many more.

'You will all be remembered, your courage and sacrifice. I will never forget.'

And then he strode away, his cloak billowing and snapping in the wind. Storm padded close to him then.

He walked through the gates of Drassil into a place seething with activity. Horses saddled, wains packed and harnessed. Cywen sat a horse at the head of the wains, guarding over her herbs. He saw Coralen checking her saddle girth, Dath and Kulla already mounted, Farrell standing with the reins of his own mount and also of Shield's in his hand, the clatter of hooves as more riders trotted down flag-stoned streets from the paddocks. Amongst them there were Jehar, Freedmen, the remnant of Wulf's axe-throwers and their kin, including Hild and Swain and Sif, though Wulf was no longer with them – another brave man who had fallen during the battle.

Corban paused and stood in the shadow of the gate-arch a moment, unseen, watching. His eyes drifted up and beyond the courtyard, to the trunk of Drassil's great tree, rising high above them all, towering over the great hall. He could see the domed curve of the hall's walls, massive holes punched in it where Asroth and his host had burst forth into the Banished Lands.

And now he is entombed within there forever. Alive or dead? We know not. And Meical alongside him.

He sighed as he thought of the Ben-Elim, remembered the pain he had felt at Meical's betrayal.

But you came back to us, in the end. Were a true friend and stood for us, even against your own kin, for which I thank you. I wish that we could have spoken, and that we could have parted as friends.

Corban strode to Farrell and the others, more familiar faces standing with them: Edana, Camlin, Vonn and Conall, the King of Domhain. Giants loomed behind them – Ethlinn, Balur One-Eye and Varan.

'Well met, Bright Star,' Ethlinn said, bowing her head to him.

'There really is no need to call me that,' Corban said.

'The council meeting has just finished,' Ethlinn said. 'You did not come. The Ben-Elim are asking for you.'

Corban shrugged. 'Are you happy with the outcome?'

Ethlinn nodded slowly. 'We have reached an agreement,' she said. 'Made a pact. Drassil we will share. It is our ancient home, and we giants will return here, but the Ben-Elim wish to dwell here, also. Because of Asroth and Meical.'

'That is logical,' Corban said.

'I agree. We are not unreasonable, so we will share Drassil with the Ben-Elim. And together we shall fight the Kadoshim. Hunt the survivors down and destroy them.'

'The Ben-Elim,' Varan said. 'They have plans for you, Bright Star.'

Corban raised an eyebrow.

'The title *battlechief* has been mentioned.'

'I will hunt Kadoshim,' Corban said. 'But not for them, not on their terms.'

Balur One-Eye smiled at him.

'Whatever the future holds,' Ethlinn said, 'there will always be friendship between us. Between you and I, between your kin and mine.' She offered her arm to Corban then, and he took it in the warrior grip.

'You will be a fine queen, Ethlinn: beautiful, fierce and wise.'

Balur rumbled approvingly and Ethlinn smiled. 'Ah, but you have a honeyed tongue, Bright Star.'

'The truth is easy to say,' Corban smiled. 'Wherever I go, I will carry you in my heart, my giant friends. And if you have need, I will be there.'

'And we for you, Bright Star,' Balur rumbled. 'It was you that sowed the seed of reconciliation amongst us. You that united so many that in other times would have been enemies. If you need us, you have only to say the word.'

Edana stepped forwards.

'I got your message,' she said. 'You're really doing it, then?'

'Aye. I will build a new home from the ashes of Gramm's hold. A place of learning. Skill at arms, and the healer's art,' Corban said, feeling a thrill of excitement course through him at the thought of it. He'd looked around at the disparate peoples that had gathered into a warband to face Calidus and the Kadoshim, and he'd thought what a tragedy it would be for so much skill, and so many unique styles of fighting, to just fragment and disappear. But most of all it was for Gar and Brina. A way of remembering them. Of honouring them.

'It feels right,' Corban shrugged.

'You've always had good judgement,' Edana said.

'And you? You are confident in what has been agreed here?'

'I am,' Edana said. 'It is a time of change, but I believe it is for the better. And there are Kadoshim still roaming free in our world, of course, so I am happy to be a part of the hunt for them.'

'As am I,' Conall said. 'Don't like the thought of those leathery-winged bastards out there.' He shivered.

'Neither do I,' Corban said.

'Not so sure about the white-winged ones, either,' Conall said. 'They've good faces for a game of knuckle-bones; you'd never know if they were bluffing.'

Corban couldn't keep a smile from his face at that.

'But I must go home first,' Edana continued, 'and rebuild the west. Ardan and Domhain's rulers have been absent too long, and Narvon and Cambren are without leadership altogether.'

'What will you do?'

'I've suggested a solution,' Conall said, 'which I think makes sense on more than one level. Edana should marry me. Then we don't need to argue and haggle and squawk over Cambren and Narvon. We'll just have the lot and be done with it. And she's got a fine and kissable pair of lips, I have to confess to noticing.' He grinned at the shocked faces around him, especially Corban, Dath and Farrell's.

Vonn pulled a face and Edana just raised her eyebrows.

She stepped forwards and kissed Corban on the cheek, and suddenly Corban was acutely aware of Coralen's eyes watching him.

'You've come a long way since you sneaked into Brina's cottage,' Edana whispered in his ear. 'Safe journey,' she said as she stepped away. 'And I think Craf should come with you. He will be an excellent way for us to keep in touch.'

They both looked at the old crow, who was perched upon Camlin's shoulder. If it was possible for a crow to roll its eyes then Craf did it.

'You have to keep a firm hand with that crow,' Camlin said as Craf fluttered over to perch by Cywen, 'or he'll take advantage.'

'I know,' Corban replied. 'And rest assured, I won't be carrying him on my arm around the Banished Lands.' He grinned at Camlin, who swore back at him.

And then Corban was climbing into Shield's saddle, lifting his fist into the air and leading his followers out of Drassil. There was a clatter of hooves and crunch of iron wheels as the wains rolled, through the gate tunnel and then right, skirting the plain of Drassil, up the slope and towards Jael's road. Corban stopped at the crest of the slope and looked back, Coralen reining in beside him, Storm, Buddai and their cubs lurking in the shadows of Forn. Sig of the Jotun on her lumbering bear led the convoy. Corban had asked Ethlinn for the loan of her to become a weaponsmaster at his new school, so that all the peoples of the Bright Star's warband would be represented in this new endeavour. Sig seemed happy enough to be joining them, claiming she was looking forward to giving out bruises on a daily basis.

Corban didn't think she was joking.

As the convoy rode past him, Akar and his Jehar, the remnants of Hild's people, Teca the huntress and Javed's Freedmen, some riders filed out of the convoy and reined in beside him: Farrell, Dath and Kulla, then Cywen.

They sat their horses in a line and looked back at Drassil. A handful of winged figures rose into the sky, their flight straight towards Corban full of grace and power, a beat of the wings, then gliding. Within heartbeats the Ben-Elim were alighting in front of Corban, the wind of their landing sending leaves swirling. There were five of them, led by one called Israfil, who was the Ben-Elim's new high captain.

'What are you doing?' Israfil asked Corban.

'Leaving,' Corban said.

'But, you can't,' Israfil frowned, the expression strange upon his impassive face.

'I think I can,' Corban said. 'Why would you say that I cannot?'

'Because you fight for us, from Drassil. You will lead a warband to flush the Kadoshim out from their holes.'

'Meical told me that you are here to protect, not to command,' Corban said. 'That is why you came to the Banished Lands, why you schemed to become flesh. So that you could protect Elyon's creation. Us.'

Israfil and the other Ben-Elim regarded Corban with their usual emotionless faces; Corban was unable to tell if his words had any effect.

'That is right,' Israfil said. 'And Elyon created you free, so you may do as you please, but it would be best, for the greater good, if you remained in Drassil and fought from here. Together our success would be more thorough, the Kadoshim routed out the quicker.'

Farrell sighed. 'I don't think they're understanding you, Corban.'

'Then let me make it clearer,' Corban said. 'I am your puppet no longer. You hunt the Kadoshim your way, and I shall hunt them my way.'

Israfil's face twitched, glancing at the other Ben-Elim, and then he shrugged, a dismissal. He bunched his wings and burst into the air, spiralling upwards. The other Ben-Elim regarded Corban a few moments longer and then followed Israfil. Corban and his friends watched them fly back to the fortress as wains and riders filed past them into Forn. Corban was about to turn Shield and follow the convoy when he saw a lone rider galloping hard from Drassil's gates towards them.

Corban and the others waited.

It was Veradis, dressed in simple travelling leathers, though Corban saw his war gear harnessed to his saddle.

'I take it this is a yes, then,' Corban said with a smile.

'Aye,' Veradis said with a grin. 'I'll leave Tenebral to Alben. He'll make a much better king than I ever would.'

'Alben would make an excellent king,' Corban agreed. 'He has the patience for it.'

'All right then,' Veradis said, and guided his mount to join their line, jostling in so that he was next to Cywen.

'Hello,' Veradis said to Cywen. She just nodded a response, but Corban noticed that she looked happier.

'He and Cywen clearly like each other,' Corban leaned closer to Coralen and whispered. 'One of them should just come out and say it.'

He saw Coralen staring at him with a look of incredulity.

'What?' Corban said.

They all sat in a line then, looking at Drassil, at the field of cairns, at the great tree spreading its branches high and wide over the fortress. Corban thought of the victories and losses, the friendships and tragedies, all etched upon his heart in a tapestry of faces, and he knew the others were thinking the same. And as he looked and thought, he felt a weight leaving him, and an excitement building as he thought of the future.

New life, moving on. He felt a twinge of guilt, but moving on did not mean forgetting.

Never forgetting.

'We will never forget you,' he said quietly, though they all heard him say it, and they echoed him.

'We will never forget.'

Behind them Storm padded from the shadows and howled, her cubs lifting their heads and joining her, a mournful, wordless lament of love and loss ringing out across the field of cairns.

'Well, let's see what we can do with this freedom we've fought so long and hard for, then,' Corban said, and together they turned their mounts and cantered away from Drassil.